BOYFRIEND OF THE HOUR

NICOLE FRENCH

raglan

This is a work of fiction. Names, characters, organizations, places, events, and incidents are either products of the author's imagination or rendered fictitiously. Any resemblance to real people or events is purely coincidental.

ISBN: 978-1-950663-52-1

Cover Design: Raglan Publishing

To all my fellow neurospicies and their beautiful kaleidoscope brains.

WAYS TO EMBARRASS YOURSELF AT THE PLASTIC SURGEON'S
PROLOGUE

#13: Wear Wonder Woman Underwear insted of the pritty lace stuff

W ord of advice: don't ever turn twenty-four.
Twenty-three is great.
Twenty-three is *heaven*.
See, no one cares that you're a screw-up at twenty-three.

Here are the Ways I Know That:

1. They don't care that you barely passed high school and flunked out of college. Twice.
2. They don't blink if you earn minimum wage as a shot girl between gigs.
3. They don't say a word when you still live in your grandmother's house like a teenager.

No one cares, because at twenty-three, you're still just a kid figuring shit out.

Then twenty-four rolls around. Adulthood slaps you straight across both cheeks. And man, does it sting.

Within the space of a month of my birthday, I screwed up my knee, lost a part in a Broadway show, and was told I had to leave my childhood home so my grandmother could gallivant around Italy like a seventy-eight-year-old rom-com heroine.

I mean, good for her and all. After spending her golden years raising six grandkids, Nonna deserved a little fun. But honestly. No one ever mentioned that her third act came with a Greek chorus singing, "Time to grow up, Joni Zola."

Four months later, Nonna was about to leave. Reality had returned to kick my ass to the curb. And that, my friends, was essentially how I found myself perched in a paper gown on the exam table at the Manhattan Surgery Associates, waiting for a boob job consultation that would overdraw my checking account by at least sixty dollars and making lists in my head to pass the time.

Because that was the kind of decision-making I did at twenty-four. Work at a bar and need money for a new place to live?

Bigger tits were probably the ticket.

So much for growing up.

"Bet you don't get a lot of girls my age in here, huh?" I joked as the nurse, who was named Candy and who couldn't have been more than three or four years older than me, puttered around the exam room, gathering bits of equipment to take my vitals.

Candy gave me a wry look as she wrapped a blood pressure cuff around my arm. "Oh, we get all types here."

I pulled at one of the black curls at the nape of my neck that had escaped my messy bun. "Not just middle-aged women looking for tummy tucks and breast lifts? That's a relief."

Zero smile. Not even a chuckle while she took my blood pressure, removed the cuff, and typed the measurement into the computer in the corner.

Okay, so I tended to make dumb jokes when I was nervous. And yes, I was nervous. You would be nervous too if you had convinced yourself that the only way to achieve a better life was to have silicone balloons shoved under your nipples for a bargain deal of fourteen grand plus interest.

Did I have fourteen grand?

Helllllll no.

But they had financing options, so said my cousin. I had a cute face. I'd cross that bridge when I got to it. Right now I was just trying things on.

"Dr. Hunt is a genius," Candy said when she turned back with a device that looked like a bag clip. "You were really lucky to get this appointment—usually, his wait list is eighteen months. Extend your index finger, please."

I rolled my eyes. Could she be more of a cliché, the nurse half in love with the doctor? He probably looked like a Ken doll, with his skin pulled tight like Saran wrap over his bones and giant white veneers that looked like light bulbs instead of real teeth. I bet he had plugs, too. Honest-to-God doll hair.

No, thank you.

But I'd take his services if he was the best, and according to my cousin, he was. Was it my life's dream to have my tits done? Not particularly. Prima ballerinas and Broadway soloists weren't exactly known for having bowling balls floating off their chests. That was more the specialty of Eighth Avenue. And maybe lowly bartenders.

But what was a girl to do in my situation? All my life, I'd been good at exactly two things: dancing and flirting. Thanks to a ruined knee, the former was no longer an option. And since I had no other skills and no education, I had to maximize the latter.

Men loved a pair of good-sized cans on the lady mixing their high balls, right?

God, I hoped so.

"I wasn't *planning* to do something like this, but things happen," I said after Candy was done taking my blood oxygen.

When she didn't answer, I just kept talking.

"Most dancers don't want to have big boobs, but exotic ones do, right? My cousin Rochelle makes more than a grand *a night* working at Diamonds, that club in Hell's Kitchen. Do you know it?"

Candy shook her head. Of course, she didn't know it. Why would a nice girl like her know the strip clubs of New York?

"Are you an exotic dancer too?" she wondered, almost like she couldn't help herself.

I grinned. I knew I'd catch her interest somehow. I didn't have the sense in my head God gave me, according to Nonna and all five of my siblings, but I was the best in a family of charmers. *La civetta*, as my grandparents used to call me. Officially, that translated to "owl," but in Italy, it also meant a flirt.

"Nah," I said. "But since it's looking more and more like serving drinks is all I have going for me, I figured I might as well get the best tips I can. Nice girl like me should be able to find a sugar daddy in at least a week or two, am I right?"

Again, Candy didn't answer as she entered some other things into the computer.

Man, this crowd was dead.

I tried not to pout. I was just trying to be nice—make a little conversation. It made me feel awkward when people didn't talk back, and usually, I was very good at getting people to talk back.

Candy stood up from the computer and offered me another tight smile. "Dr. Hunt will be right with you."

The door closed behind her. Kicking my legs back and forth, I started scrolling through my phone when it buzzed with a call from my oldest sister. I rolled my eyes. As the de facto mother hen of the six Zola kids, Lea was nothing if not persistent. She would press redial for hours until I picked up.

Vaguely, I wondered if I should tell her where I was just to hear her squawk.

"Hey, I can't really talk now—"

"Where are you?" Lea demanded. "You were supposed to be at the house an hour ago. Kate and I got the dining room boxed up, and we have the truck here to bring everything to the storage center, but only for the next few hours."

I smacked a hand to my forehead as my stomach turned with guilt. "Shit. I forgot. I'm sorry."

"You *forgot?*" Lea's voice ricocheted through my phone's tinny speakers and off the exam room's hard, disinfected surfaces. "Joni, what the hell? Nonna needs to get all of her things out of the house this weekend, and then we have to clean and get everything ready for the new renters on Monday. We literally cannot do this without everyone pitching in. Even Matthew came down from Boston to help."

I winced, as if just hearing the schedule physically hurt.

And maybe it did. At least the reasons for it certainly stung a whole lot.

When my grandmother had originally announced she was moving back to Rome to spend her golden years with her sisters, everyone was overjoyed for her. After all, Nonna spent most of her life raising the six of us after we lost our dad. Now that we were grown, she deserved an adventure of her own.

It made sense for *them* to be happy. My siblings had all graduated out of the little brown house on Hughes Street.

Lea had her brood in Belmont, the first of us to step out.

Matthew had a life in Boston, complete with a new wife, step-daughter, and the little girl they were about to have.

Kate had her vintage clothing shop in Riverdale and too many new celebrity clients to count.

Frankie was raising her family in London with Xavier, the actual *duke* she had married last year.

And Marie, only ten months older than me, was currently attending culinary school in Paris.

Which left me, the family fuckup who still lived at home, with little more than a bright smile and a tight ass, to find her way into the world.

If I were a baby bird, I wouldn't just be kicked out of the nest. I'd be hurled.

"I wish I could say I'm surprised." Lea's voice took on that almost metallic ting of her particular brand of scolding, like a triangle that never stopped ringing. "But you knew this was coming. Nonna booked her ticket a month ago, and the new tenants signed a lease. Don't you have a calendar on that phone of yours? At least some way to keep track of things? Honestly, Jo, when are you finally going to grow up?"

The question pierced, just like every time she asked it.

"I don't know. When are you going to stop being such a freaking nag?" I retorted. "I'm at a doctor's appointment, and it slipped my mind. Shit happens. Besides, it's not like I can lift heavy boxes with this garbage knee."

I swung the knee on the exam table as if she could see it, making the paper under my leg crinkle like laughter.

"No, but you could at least do the bare minimum. Watch the kids while the rest of us move boxes, maybe. I can't exactly do much right now with these four running around me."

"No one told her and Mike to procreate like rabbits," I mumble to the smiling woman in a poster for vaginal rejuvenation surgery on the other wall.

"What was that?"

I sighed and tipped my face toward the light on the ceiling. I grinned. Finally, a place where boob lights made aesthetic sense.

"Joni! Are you even paying attention?"

Immediately, I sat up straight, yanked out of my daydream like I was still that kid in the fifth grade who couldn't pay attention from the back row. "Yes. Look. I'm...I'm sorry, but I really can't come today. Tom threw me an extra shift, which starts at five, and since, as you pointed out, I'm going to be homeless in three days, I need the money. I'll come up tomorrow, I promise."

There was another heavy sigh before something crashed in the background. "Dammit, Pete! Tommy, I told you to watch your brothers!"

I held the phone away from my ear while Lea finished berating her eldest. Better him than me, I supposed. Tommy was a sweet kid, but sometimes I thought she expected a little much of a ten-year-old. Then again, the same and more had always been expected of her—including taking care of me.

"Tomorrow," Lea repeated once she was back on the line. I could hear the warbling of Lupe, her youngest, in the background. She had maybe two minutes left on this call. "And for Mass."

I huffed. "On Saturday? Come on, I don't want to go to Mass two days in a row—"

"*Tomorrow*. And we are taking Nonna to Mass. She wants to go one last time with us, so we're doing it."

I huffed. "Fine, sure. I'll be there tomorrow."

"For Mass too."

"Oh my God, yes, I got it! Yes, for Mass too."

"And then you'll help clean *and* get your things. Your room's the last one, Jo. We need your stuff out."

With every task she threw at me, I felt like a sunflower at the end of fall, ready to wilt straight into the ground. I hated it when she did this—piled on the tasks. I wasn't going to remember all of them anyway, and they just made everything feel that much more undoable.

But Lea didn't hang up. She'd wait me out. She always did.

"Fine," I said as I flopped backward on the exam table. "I'll be there."

I waited for Lea to hang up, but she surprised me by asking another question.

"So, a doctor? Oh, are you finally getting a second opinion on your knee?"

"*No.*" I shut that one down quick. Whereas before I thought it might be funny to hear her reaction to me getting a boob job, I'd suddenly had enough of my sister's opinions. "I told you, that's done. The knee is finished, so I'm leaving that dream in the dumpster where it belongs."

There was an uncharacteristic silence on the other end of the line, filled instead with the "yummy noises" my niece made whenever she particularly enjoyed her Cheerios.

Oh, Baby Lupe, you have no idea how good you have it.

As if she heard me, the little one started to cry.

"Mama!" she howled. "Mo-mo-mo-mo-moooooooooooo!"

Saved by the baby, who sounded a whole lot like a bell. Or maybe a siren.

"We'll talk more tomorrow," Lea said, back to her more characteristically frazzled self. "I gotta go."

"Go," I repeated.

"*Tomorrow,*" Lea said again, clearly waiting for something in response.

I heaved a big sigh. Yeah, she was going to drag me up there herself if that's what it took.

"Tomorrow," I repeated yet again. "I promise."

The call ended, and I sat back on the table, toying with my escaping curls again and swinging my feet back and forth again. Weird how these tables positioned grown-ass adults so high up that they had to swing their feet like kids. I always liked this feeling, though, the way it made me feel weightless, even though I was still sitting on something. My feet looked so small from up here. At least I'd shaved my legs, but maybe I should have painted my toes before coming here—the hot pink was starting to chip. Then again, all my nail polish was in my room in Belmont, a room I had exactly two more days to vacate, and who knew where I was going to end up sleeping, and—

A knock at the door interrupted my wandering thoughts. I sat up quickly as the door opened.

"Giovanna?" a deep voice spoke from the other side of the door.

"Er, yeah," I replied.

The door opened fully, and a man dressed in a pair of gray slacks, polished brown shoes, a pressed gingham shirt, and a white lab coat entered, carrying a clipboard. I couldn't really see his face, since he was studying the papers on the board. The best view I got was of the rims of his glasses, shoulders that barely seemed to fit under his coat, and a mop of lush, curly brown hair that was the only even slightly disheveled thing about him.

And then there was the fact that the man was approximately the size of an large oak tree. Far too tall to be anything but a linebacker for the New York Jets. Maybe the Giants. Certainly not a surgeon.

"Giovanna Zola," the doctor read as he sat down on the stool and turned to the computer. "I'm Doctor Hunt. You're here for a consultation for a breast augmentation, correct?"

"Um, yes. That's right." It was kind of odd talking to the back of someone's head. "Gotta get some moneymakers. I can't rely on charm alone these days."

Not even a puff of laughter. The office was officially *the worst*. I couldn't have been the only patient to tell a titty joke or two.

The doctor continued to mutter through my chart, as if talking more to himself than to me. "Age, twenty-four. Height, five feet, six point two five inches. Weight, normal. Hmm, your blood pressure is a little low, so we might need to watch that. I'll make sure the anesiologist is aware."

"It's probably from all the dope I smoke in my free time," I joked, though I mentally kicked myself for saying it out loud.

Yes, I tended to say inappropriate things when I was uncomfortable. And something about this clinic, with all its sterile surfaces, competent and highly educated people, and the doctor who wouldn't even look me in the eye while he was speaking, made me *very* uncomfortable.

But at least I got a reaction. The doctor straightened immediately, shoulders spreading with the intent of a condor about to take flight.

"Do you actually use drugs?" he asked the computer. "Because if that's a joke, it's really not fun—Joni?"

The doctor finally turned around, and my jaw fell open as the list in my head wrote itself faster than I could make yet another insensitive crack.

<u>Unbelievably True Things about My Plastic Surgeon</u>

1. He can totally pass as Clark Kent.
2. He has the velvety-est brown bedroom eyes in existence.
3. I actually…know him.

ONE

THINGS TO REMEMBER AT YOUR NEW JOB

#4 a slice isnt the Same as a twist

Four months earlier

"Tell me it's over this time."

Rochelle Ortiz twirled her straw in the Long Island iced tea, then took a long sip as she peered up at me.

About to start her shift at Diamonds, a strip club a few blocks away, my cousin had stopped into Opal for a free drink and to celebrate the fact that I'd just been promoted from shot girl/go-go dancer to bartender two nights a week. After recovering enough from ACL surgery to walk around, tonight was my first shift, which had mostly consisted of Tom, the middle-aged owner, teaching me the ropes. Sure, it took me three times to get Rochelle's drink right. But I figured that wasn't too bad for day one.

I shrugged as I wiped down the bar, trying to remember if I'd already cleaned this part again after spilling a bottle of bitters earlier. Opal was an odd blend of new and old, with the battered walnut bar top and exposed brick blending with velvet chaise couches and the sleek platforms built into the big violet wall at the far end of the lounge. Tuesdays and Thursdays were slow nights, and I was supposed to be helping to get things ready for the weekend rush.

So it wasn't my best first day on the job. But I was trying.

"I *think* it's over," I said. "I mean, he kind of broke up with me too, don't you think?"

"No, Shawn did that thing he always does." Rochelle tapped her long nails on the bar. This week, they were pink with blue stripes that reminded me of a Barbie-themed racecar. "He loses interest, tells you he wants a space. Then he comes back a few months later looking to get laid. This time, you busted your knee, so he can't brag anymore that he's banging someone on Broadway. I could have put money on him asking for another 'break.'"

I sighed. I couldn't argue. Shawn was just one of many cycles I had seemed to slip back into lately.

"Well, this time, *I'm* done," I said firmly. "And I told him that, too."

"You did?"

I knew why Rochelle was surprised. Saying no to Shawn Vamos had never been something I was good at.

I chewed my lip. "It's going to sound weird, but it was the music."

My cousin gawked, making her thick, curly hair shake around her shoulders. "The music?"

"Yeah. We were driving back from Long Island, and he put on that shitty EDM he thinks is so hot. And I'm sitting there, and he *knows* I don't like Dead Mouse Seven or whatever the guy's name is, and he doesn't turn it off or even ask me what I'd like to hear." I screwed up my face, like I'd tasted something bad. "It's small, but I realized that in all the car rides I've taken with him, Shawn has never once checked what kind of music I like. Just put on whatever he wanted, and that was that. So I was done."

I shrugged. It really was that simple.

I hoped.

Rochelle took another long sip through her straw. "I mean, normally, I'd say that's small potatoes, but I'm actually proud of you, *mami*. Fuck Shawn. He's an asshole, and I'm glad you're done with that loser." She finished the drink with a noisy slurp and set it on the bar in front of me. "All right, I'm out. Gotta get over to the club. Sure you don't want to audition?"

I tipped my head from side to side. Rochelle, a former dancer like myself, had been lobbying for me to join her at Diamonds since I got my brace off. The money was good, she said, especially for someone like me—a born flirt.

But I wasn't sold. I blamed it on the six more weeks of PT I was supposed to do, but really, I just wasn't ready to graduate from performance art to full-on exhibitionism. Not yet.

I traded kisses with my cousin. "Call me this weekend. We'll go out."

"Bet."

Then she was gone, leaving me to continue serving drinks and daydream about the career that, up until two months ago, I thought I was going to have. The shiny wood reminded me of a stage I'd once danced on, and my fingernails were bright pink, just like the shoes I wore in that show. A community theater production of *The Wizard of Oz*. I was twelve, I think. I played a munchkin.

It's funny. I barely managed to pass the sixth grade that year (still didn't understand what the hell a square root was), but I remembered that choreo like it was yesterday.

"Joni, it's last call."

Step, one, pas de bourrée. Step, kick, plié, shuffle step. Turn, three, shuffle step, leap. I popped up onto my toes, my muscles silently begging to follow along with my fingers.

God, I missed dancing.

"Joni!" The husky voice of Tom, the owner of Opal Lounge, yanked me out of my inner grumbling.

"Who! What? Oh, shit!" The pint glass I was filling with club soda was overfilling onto the bar top. I jumped, barely avoided splashing myself with seltzer, then handed the wet glass to an annoyed-looking customer.

He didn't leave a tip.

I couldn't say I was surprised.

"You sure can zone out better than anyone I ever met, kiddo,"

Tom remarked as he pulled a roll of cling wrap out of a drawer. "But I told you, if you're gonna pour drinks, you gotta pay attention."

"I know, I'm sorry," I said for what was probably the thousandth time that night as I wiped up the mess. "I'm just kinda over-whelmed. First night and all. But I'm trying really hard, I promise."

I offered him the biggest, brightest smile I could muster, the one that usually got me free coffee or scooted me into auditions five minutes late.

Tom might have been a gruff old guy, but he was no more immune to that grin than most. His face reddened over the edges of his silver handlebar mustache. "Let them know it's last call, will you? I want to get out of here before four."

"No prob, Bob."

I turned to the mirror behind the liquor bottles, adjusted the girls in my favorite green crop top that matched my eyes, fluffed my dark hair around my shoulders, and retouched my pout with pink gloss. It was science: a little cleavage and lipstick increased my tips by a factor of…well, I don't know. I never was never that good with math. They got a little honey, I got a little money. Simple arithmetic, right?

Slowly, I worked my way through the last few customers. I managed rum and cokes for some college kids that didn't seem too horrible. I'm pretty sure I messed up that last round of cosmos for the ladies' night, but they were too gone to care.

"Last call," I told the patron sitting at the far end.

All I got was a view of silky brown curls while he stared down at a tumbler of something brown over half-melted ice.

"Hey, handsome," I tried again. "Can I getcha anything else?"

When he still didn't answer, I snapped my fingers under his gaze. The man jerked upright to stare at me with the biggest, deepest, chocolatiest brown eyes framed by thin wire-framed glasses. Looking into them was like falling into the coziest blanket on the planet…naked. Like staring at two steaming cups of hot fudge begging to be poured all over my…sundae.

Sure, that's what I was thinking of. A nice, wholesome, PG-flavored sundae.

Until I got a look at the rest of him, and my brain zoomed from PG to NC-17 in half a second.

His lightly tanned skin was smooth, dappled with tiny freckles across cheekbones that could slice through any glass in the bar and a jaw rough with only the slightest hint of stubble. A neck corded with lean muscle and tension was literally buttoned up in a pressed blue shirt, which also pulled dee-liciously across a broad chest, even broader shoulders, and the forearms that flexed as he turned his glass back and forth between large, capable-looking hands.

His face was rugged yet refined. Sharp lines tempered by a few almost gentle elements. Some innate brutality soothed by a pair of wire-rimmed glasses and a necktie.

It was like someone put a librarian's costume on a UFC fighter. The combination shouldn't work…but hot damn, did it ever.

Did I have a thing for sexy nerds? Maybe. Nothing was more fun than corrupting the dorks my grandmother hired to help me pass math and English. They never lasted more than a few weeks, since Nonna generally kicked them out once the tutoring lessons morphed into make-out sessions.

I always got an A in those.

The customer's velvety eyes blinked through his lenses, and I swear I got a distinct whiff of hot cocoa.

"Did you say it was last call?" he asked.

The chocolate scent grew stronger. His deep voice was *that* smooth. In the back of my mind, I heard the opening piano riff of Sinatra's version of "All the Way." Cheesy, I know. But you'd be a sucker for oldies too if you were raised by a couple of Italian immigrants who graduated high school in 1957.

"Hello?"

I refocused. "I'm sorry. What did you say?"

Those brown eyes watched me, deep and brooding. "I asked why you were staring at me."

"Oh, sorry." I tapped my fingers against my hip, feeling like I'd been caught shoplifting, not staring out into space. "Just zoned out there for a minute, you know?"

The customer frowned. "Not really. I never 'zone out.'"

I balked. "Never? Not even when you're staring at a drink you barely touched?"

He shook his head. "No."

I waited for him to answer my little dig about his drink, but he didn't. "Lucky for you, then. I do it, like, all the time. It's pretty inconvenient."

"Surely not *all* the time," the man repeated as he pushed his glasses up his nose, which would have been perfect if not for a charmingly crooked bridge, like he'd been in a fight once, and it had never healed correctly.

Interesting. Was Clark Kent a fighter? Or was that only when he turned into Superman?

"Yes, *all the time*," I parroted him right back, this time with a really bad English accent, even though he didn't have one.

I used the same voice when I teased my sister's English husband. But Xavier at least rolled his eyes and chuckled at my shitty imitation. This guy just looked at me, zero comprehension in those big, beautiful browns.

Some people really can't take a joke.

"Ah, never mind," I said. "So, yeah. It's last call."

"I gathered."

"Well, do you want anything else?"

He examined his still-full glass. "I don't think so. I didn't particularly care for this anyway."

"I can see that," I said. "What did you order?"

The man rotated his glass another half inch on its cardboard coaster. "I asked for something strong. That gentleman brought me this."

"Hard day?"

The man's jaw tightened. "Hard night. I got off at two."

Graveyard shift, I figured. Probably a train operator or maybe a custodian somewhere, even with the collared shirt and tie. Yeah, that'd be tough on anyone.

Without asking for permission, I picked up his glass and sniffed. "Oh, you poor man, that shit is toxic."

I laughed. He did not.

Tough room.

"FYI, hon, if you want something good, you have to ask for it," I told him. "Otherwise, you'll just get well crap. Hold on—I'll get you something that isn't gasoline."

The man reared, then calmed when he caught me watching him. "That was a joke, wasn't it?"

I snorted. "Um, yeah. We don't actually serve gasoline. So long as we're clear."

I dumped his glass out in the sink before getting a fresh one and moved to the other side of the bar in search of the few bottles of decent booze we carried.

Glenlivet or Macallan? When rich men were trying to impress young women, they tended to order the latter. At least, Shawn always did.

"I would *definitely* hit that."

I turned around, confronted with a posse of dudes who *really* wanted to be that kind of man. It was like they all ordered the same "Financial Douche" costume from Party City, complete with the striped shirts, loosened ties, and overpriced suits. One, two, three, four investment bankers looking to score.

Sure, fine, I'd gone home with a few of those in my day. The investment banker. The car salesman. The party promoter. And so on.

They were all the same at their core. Men who thought the world was made specifically for them to use as they saw fit, who swaggered around New York looking for their next buck and their next prize.

Why not be the prize myself, even for just one night? Or ten years, in Shawn's case.

I grimaced. No, I was *not* going to think about Shawn right now. Not after he'd broken my heart—or maybe just my pride—for the millionth and final time.

No, no, no.

Maybe this one wasn't an asshole. Maybe he was just gross, the way he was ogling my boobs. They weren't even that big.

Down the bar, my chocolate-eyed customer watched our interaction carefully. I winked at him as I pulled the Macallan off the shelf, but he didn't smile or anything. He didn't look away either.

"Look at that," said the Finance Bro Number One. "I haven't seen an ass that nice since we were in Vegas."

I tensed, then turned from the liquor bottles, Macallan in hand. "Can I help you?"

The speaker, who had short blond hair with at least a metric ton of gel, offered a white-capped smile. "Sure. Can I get a to-go box?"

"For what?"

We didn't sell food beyond stale peanuts, and he didn't have anything with him.

"I'd like to take you home with me, baby," he said, then glanced at his buddies, who obediently chuckled at the lame come-on.

I rolled my eyes. "Good one. But I'm actually helping someone right—"

"We're having a little after-party at my spot around the corner," Gel Head interrupted, leaning across the bar so he could drag a finger down my forearm. "Wanna come?"

"Why? Is your mom gonna be there?" I cut back, stepping out of reach. "Hands off, fun boy."

I glanced over to where Tom was, but my boss had disappeared to the back office, leaving me out front alone for the first time all night. Of course.

"Oh, we got a hot one tonight. Come on, baby. How often does a girl like you get to party in a penthouse? Where do you live, a basement in Queens?"

I scowled. As it happened, my grandma's spare room in the Bronx—but fuck him anyway. "On the corner of Tenth and none of your goddamn business. Now, if you'll excuse me."

I focused on pouring Mr. Chocolate Eyes's drink, trying to ignore the twist of something sour in my gut. Like that time I ate nothing but oranges for two weeks in order to drop five pounds before an audition. I didn't even get the part, and all that citrus gave me heartburn. Apparently, so did assholes.

Gel Head followed me down the bar, then touched my bare shoulder this time.

"Yo!" I slapped his hand away, tossing a plastic bowl of cut limes to the floor. "Looky, no touchy! This ain't for sale, asshole."

"Aw, I love a bit of spark. And you got plenty. Don't she, boys?"

"She said to leave her alone."

We all turned to find Mr. Chocolate Eyes standing right next to Gel Head, glaring at the man like he was gum on the bottom of his shoe. He was taller than I realized, probably at least three or four inches over six feet, easily towering over the rat-faced hacks next to him.

They shriveled like raisins. Every last one of them.

"You should go," he told them. "Unless you'd like them to stay."

When he turned to me, those gorgeous brown eyes met mine and were full of clear, honest concern.

No motives. No games.

"I would not," I confirmed with a smile.

My surprise savior turned back to the group of four. "Well?"

He set a palm flat on the bar in a way I didn't *think* he meant to be threatening, but it certainly came off that way. You know, the way things normally do when you're obviously stacked and able to kick the other guy's ass with one hand tied behind your back.

Gel Head swallowed. "Fine, yeah. On our way out, man."

Mr. Chocolate Eyes and I both watched the men fumble their way to the exit.

"Well, now the drink is on me," I said, handing him his Macallan. "Thanks for the rescue. They were harmless, though."

Maybe not totally harmless. That sour feeling had lessened some, but it wasn't completely gone.

My customer accepted the glass, put it on a new coaster, and sank onto another stool in front of me. "I didn't like how they were treating you."

"I've gotten a lot worse; I can promise you that."

His expression shone full of something like sympathy, but not quite. "Well, someone like you shouldn't."

Someone like me?

What did that mean?

What kind of girl did he think I was?

Someone worth saving, I realized. Someone worth protecting.

With a hot face, I picked up a clean glass that suddenly needed a lot of polishing. "I guess I owe you one, then."

"Owe me?"

That chocolate gaze melted over my body, then floated back up. Unlike the sleazebags he'd just dismissed, there was nothing cheap about it. He didn't hide what he was doing, but it wasn't lewd. Just appreciation, pure and simple.

And hot. Very, very hot.

When he was finished, his gaze met mine again. And didn't move at all. "What could you possibly owe me for doing the right thing?"

We blinked at each other across the bar top like a couple of stunned deer. I didn't need to look to know my nipples were basically conducting a staring contest of their own. Meanwhile, my brain had gone completely blank as I searched for something, *anything*, to say in return.

And there was…nada. For the first time that I could remember, my racing thoughts were perfectly still.

"I—um—er—" I cleared my throat, suddenly annoyed.

I'd had about enough of this. I was Joni freakin' Zola. Neighborhood flirt, voted "Most Likely to Marry for Money" in her senior yearbook, she who had charmed her way out of not one but *three* speeding tickets. I was *not* about to be tongue-tied because of a guy.

"Here's your payback." With a quick glance to make sure Tom was still in the back, I popped up onto my toes and across the bar to deliver a quick peck to Mr. Chocolate Eyes's cheek.

Or so I planned.

Instead of sitting still like a good boy, he turned, and our lips mashed together in a—well, I wouldn't call something that awkward a kiss. More like a collision of soft lips, five-o'clock shadow, and that chocolatey scent married with scotch, soap, and *man*.

It lasted less than a second. At which point I flew back to my side of the bar as if I'd been shocked and found my target standing up again, fingers to his mouth like he'd just been stung by a bee.

"I—" He took a step backward. "You—"

"Sorry," I blurted. "I was, um, going for your cheek. You know, like some men ask for a kiss on the cheek in repayment for things?"

"Some men..." Mr. Chocolate Eyes drifted off, clearly still stunned, though his shoulders relaxed a bit. "People pay back favors in kisses?"

"Sure," I said as I twirled a bit of hair around my finger. "My grandfather had me do it all the time when he was alive."

Now I was comparing my knight in shining blue button-down to a grandpa. Smooth.

Mr. Chocolate Eyes seemed to meditate on that for a moment. "Well, then, I suppose I owe you one now."

"A kiss?"

I'm not going to lie. At the idea of *kissing* him, every cell in my body basically jumped up and screamed, "Encore!"

"No. You bought me a drink. I helped you with those men. You gave me a...whatever that was. Now it's my turn to owe you, according to your calculations."

Math joke. I knew he was smart. A big, delicious, super-stacked nerd.

Eyes still glued to mine, he picked up the drink I'd just set in front of him and poured every bit of it directly down his throat.

"Jesus," I said. "Savor it, why don't you? That's an eighteen-year-old scotch."

When he set the glass back down, his eyes were watering, and his voice was hoarse as he spoke. "It is much better than the other one."

Fuck it, I thought. I had some bravado left in here somewhere. Might as well put it to good use.

"I get off in thirty minutes," I said quickly. "Do you, um, want to go somewhere? Get to know each other better?"

I traced a fingertip across the bar provocatively, then leaned over, giving him the good solid view down my shirt that the previous investment dicks had been hoping for earlier.

But those chocolate eyes didn't move an inch. Instead, he offered a shy, sweet not-quite-smile that suddenly made the dim lounge feel very, very bright.

"It's all right." He pushed his glasses up his nose and stood. "I'll pay you back another time."

I watched as he dropped a couple of bills next to his empty glass, then turned to leave.

Lord, he looked almost as good walking away as approaching. The man had an ass that wouldn't quit. Like two scoops of ice cream molded specifically for my hands to grab.

"Wait." The word jumped out of my throat.

Mr. Chocolate Eyes turned. "Yes?"

"What's your name?"

One brown brow lifted. "My name?"

I dug deep and unearthed the smile that I delivered to *any* man when I wanted something.

The stranger swallowed but seemed otherwise unmoved.

Damn.

"Yeah," I said. "Your name. I like to know the names of people who owe me something. I'm Joni."

I held out a hand. But instead of accepting it, he put two fingers on the crisp hundred-dollar bills on the bar and pushed them toward me—at least twice what was necessary for the one shitty drink he'd ordered and the much better one I'd bought him.

"My name is Nathan."

I swallowed as I picked up the cash. "And you'll be back... Nathan?"

That half-smile appeared again as he nodded. "I'll be back. I always pay my debts."

TWO

WHY THE PLASTIC SURGEON ISN'T ACTUALLY HOT AF

#2 how the curl on his forehaed flops over his left brow when he tilts his hed.

Present

The clipboard fell to the floor with a loud clatter of particleboard meeting vinyl. For a second, I wondered if I was imagining things. Because really, what were the odds that the nerdy yet gorgeous barfly who sat quietly at the end of my section of a second-rate lounge was actually a plastic surgeon who served the rich and, well, *really* rich of Manhattan.

But the second he looked up, I knew it was him.

Mr. Chocolatey Bedroom Eyes.

Sir Curls Galore.

He Whose Name I'd Completely Forgotten but who sat silently on the same stool at the end of the bar every Thursday night, ordered the same scotch that he barely drank it, and seemed completely immune to my charms.

Honestly, I'd just figured the guy liked more T than A. Apparently, I was right, if he was a freaking plastic surgeon. The man was probably up to his eyeballs in perfect breasts he had *made* himself.

"I'm Doctor Hunt," he said. "Nathan, you might remember."

"Nathan," I repeated numbly. "Man, small world, isn't it?"

He shivered when I said his name, then seemed to snap out of it and turn to the dropped clipboard. "I—sorry—give me a moment."

I watched as he picked up the clipboard, then shoved his glasses up his long nose while he read through my chart again.

I could easily imagine what it said. Or *should* say, in this scenario.

Name: Giovanna Zola

Age: 24

Sex: Female

Occupation: Washed-up dancer and absent-minded bartender

Address: Her grandmother's house for three more days

Status: Desperate AF and suddenly horny

"Oxygen, ninety-eight. BMI slightly low, but that's typical of an ectomorph. Blood pressure on the low side too, but normal." Dr. Hunt was muttering to himself again while he paged through the chart.

I hooked my ankles together as I swung my legs back and forth. "Means I'm perfect, right?"

His head snapped up. "What?"

I grinned. "My chart. It tells you all the reasons I'm absolutely perfect. Except for these things." I pointed at my chest. "But you already knew that. I wouldn't be here otherwise, would I? Hey, how come you didn't tell me you're a doctor?"

Dr. Hunt's full mouth opened and closed several times, a perfect imitation of my sister Marie's goldfish, Tangerine. He died when we were twelve, but I used to love staring at the little guy blowing kisses in the bowl on her desk.

I had a feeling I'd like this guy's kisses even more.

He looked back at the chart, then to me again, and frowned. "I thought your name was Joni. This says Giovanna."

"You find me sitting in your room, and *that's* what surprises you?" I had to laugh. "You know, I should have guessed you're a doctor. Now that I think about it, you said you worked at the hospital once. But I probably thought you were a custodian."

The frown turned into a delicious scowl that made his glasses ride up his long, almost-straight nose. "I look like a custodian?"

I shrugged. "I don't know. Do I look like a bartender?"

He stared at me for a long moment but didn't answer.

So much for jokes.

Of course, I already knew Dr. Hunt wasn't much of a joker. In all the weeks he'd come to Opal, he'd never once laughed at one of my punch lines. Not *one.*

Didn't stop me from coming up with others, though.

I sighed, making my big red hoops swing back and forth over my shoulders. "Joni is a nickname. Short for Giovanna. I, um, couldn't actually pronounce my own name until I was almost seven, so the version I *could* say was the one that stuck."

I honestly didn't know why I told him that embarrassing tidbit other than the fact that I generally had a hard time not saying the first thing to pop into my head anyway. This was why Nonna was forever telling me to think before I speak.

"It's all right," Dr. Hunt said almost absently. "I didn't speak at all until I was almost four."

I brightened. "Really?"

It seemed unlikely. Smart guy like this—I assumed he had to be smart if he was a freaking surgeon—and he didn't talk until he was four?

Huh.

"Nathaniel was difficult for me until my palate formed completely." He nodded but didn't meet my eye as he flipped through my chart. Looking for what? Inconsistencies? Credit Scores? My personal dating history in case he wanted to ask me out?

In my dreams. Guys like this didn't fall for girls like me. They took us home for a night and forgot our names the very next day.

"Nathaniel?" I tested the name on my tongue. It tasted like the deepest, darkest chocolate. My insides warmed. "I could see that being tough for a toddler too. But I like it."

Dr. Hunt looked up, his dark eyes softened a bit. I wondered if he might smile, but he didn't. "Thanks. I like Giovanna too. I like the way it feels on my tongue."

His gaze flickered to my mouth. We stared at each other like it was completely normal for a doctor and patient to pronounce each other's names like they were the dirtiest words in the dictionary. As if I wasn't sitting here in nothing but a paper sheet, imagining exactly how this physician might growl the name while doing something a whole lot dirtier than reading it off a chart.

What was wrong with me?

Oh, right.

Desperate, remember?

Dr. Hunt sat on his stool and turned toward the desk to finish reviewing my chart like I wasn't a quivering mess on his exam table. Obviously, he wasn't affected by this odd tension. Something was very, very wrong with me.

"I should have known Nathaniel Hunt was you when I came in here," I babbled on, because I honestly could not deal with silence. "Should have remembered it from your credit card. I mean, how many Nathaniel Hunts are there in New York? Twenty? I doubt even that. But it's not something I would ever pay attention to, which my family absolutely can't stand. They always say I'm a dumb blonde without the hair color. I don't even have more than two cents to rub together."

Dr. Hunt turned back with another frown. "I don't think you're dumb. There's no logical reason you would know what I do for a living, since I never told you."

I smiled at the joke. But when he didn't return my smile, I realized he wasn't actually making one. Just pointing out a fact.

"Well, thanks," I said. "Maybe it's a good thing that my plastic surgeon is also kind of my friend."

For some reason, the doctor stiffened when I mentioned his profession.

He cleared his throat roughly. "So, a breast augmentation? Why don't you tell me more about what you want?"

I nodded, then hooked my ankles together to keep them from

jiggling. I was having an even harder time keeping still than usual. "I —I think it will, um, suit me. Improve things, maybe."

Dr. Hunt remained as still as a statue while he listened. "I don't— all right. Let's talk about what you're looking for in terms of size and shape."

I swallowed hard. This was the weird part.

"So, don't judge, but my cousin works at a strip club, and she said her tips doubled after she got hers done. She's a patient here, by the way. Rochelle Ortiz. Did you do hers?"

Nathan shook his head numbly. "No."

"I didn't think so. They gave me this appointment because there was a cancellation. And, well, you probably already know I'm not the greatest bartender, but I was thinking if I got, I don't know, something more Pam Anderson and less Emma Watson, I'd start raking it in. But more natural, okay. Like out to here, not here. And I don't want them to feel like rocks."

I mimed where I wanted my boobs to turn out, which felt weirdly like the way frat guys tended to talk about girls they liked. By the time I was done, Dr. Hunt's gaze hadn't moved from mine, but I honestly wasn't sure if he was listening anymore. His eyes had sort of glazed over, and his mouth had folded into a tight line.

"Well?" I asked. "What do you think? Bump me up at least four or five sizes, since there isn't much to work with. Do you think I can handle a triple D?"

Dr. Hunt blinked rapidly. "Triple—what?"

"D," I repeated. Sheesh, I hope he wasn't this distracted in surgery. "I'm barely a B-cup now, and that's if we're being generous. I figure if we're going in there, might as well do it right, you know?"

He blinked again, and this time, his eyes sharpened as they traveled over my body. There was nothing lecherous about it. He wasn't undressing me with his eyes, like too many bar patrons did after a drink or five. But I couldn't help feeling, well, naked under that intense gaze anyway.

Lord, the man could look right through a girl.

"Dr. Hunt?" I asked when he still didn't speak.

That seemed to yank him out of his...whatever it was. Stupor wasn't the right word. He was too focused to be daydreaming. But he wasn't exactly paying attention to what was coming out of my mouth either.

He hadn't even answered my question.

"All right," he said abruptly, standing up from the stool. "First, I'll need to take a look and perform a quick exam. When you're ready, please remove the top half of the gown. You can let it settle around your waist."

He turned around to wash his hands, dry them, then put on some exam gloves. By the time he was done, I was sitting topless on the exam table, trying and failing to remind myself that this was no different than getting a basic breast exam from my family doctor.

Because he *was* a doctor, after all. A stupidly handsome, annoying, broody, Henry Cavill-lookalike doctor, sure. But also kind of an antisocial dick—and maybe that was a good thing. The only one having unprofessional thoughts here was me, clearly.

Dr. Hunt turned around and stumbled, but that scowl was still fixed on his face as he approached the exam table.

I sat straight and tall. I wasn't a dancer anymore, but the posture had been beaten into me since I was barely able to walk. You can take the girl out of the dance studio, but you can't take the studio out of the girl.

I hated how true it was.

Dr. Hunt stood to one side of the table and reached out as if to begin the examination. I looked up at the ceiling and waited for that cold, clinical touch. And waited.

And waited.

When I looked down, he was frozen, hands out.

"Eh, what's up, doc?" I said in my very best impression of Bugs Bunny.

The doctor started, as if he'd been snapped on the nose, yanking his hands back to his side and practically jumping away.

"Everything all right?" I wondered.

He cleared his throat for what had to be the fifth or sixth time since walking in the door.

"You aren't sick, are you?" I wondered as I stretched one arm over my head to touch the nape of my neck, just like my family doctor usually had me do when she did the same exam.

Dr. Hunt tugged at his collar and shook his head. "No, I would never come to work ill."

I smirked. "I know. I was just joking. It's kind of hot in here, don't you think?"

"Oh." He seemed to think about that for a moment. "I was actually wondering if you were cold."

I glanced down. Okay, my nipples *were* standing at attention, but he couldn't know that probably wasn't entirely because of the room temperature. Or maybe he did. I doubted this was the first time a patient had been hot for doctor.

Even so, my shameless cheeks heated. "I'm not cold."

He was standing right next to the table, unable to quite meet my eyes. Close enough, however, that his scent of fresh water, soap, and a hint of coffee floated around me like a warm cloak. It smelled unbearably good.

"You aren't wearing cologne," I blurted out before I could stop myself.

God. Had I really just said that? Yes, I was impulsive, but I hadn't word vomited in years. Not like I did when I was a kid.

The doctor's brown eyes finally met mine again, clearly confused. "I—no, I'm not."

"Why?" I wondered. Now that the question had occurred, I had to know. "All the men I know are freaking doused in the stuff. Every boy I knew in high school took a bath in body spray every morning before class."

Dr. Hunt blinked, but to his credit, he didn't look at me like I was speaking a foreign language. "A lot of patients are sensitive to fragrance, and I don't care for synthetic scents anyway."

"Me neither," I agreed. "They smell fake. I have this perfume that I love that's only made from the oil of—"

"Gardenias," he said as the tips of his ears turned pink. Then, in a huskier voice: "I can smell it. It's…nice."

We blinked at each other like owls, and only then did I remember that I was still topless in front of the gorgeous doctor, talking about how he smelled, and listening to him admit that he was smelling me too.

Dr. Hunt cleared his throat for what had to be the twentieth time. "So. The exam, just to make sure there isn't anything irregular. Then we can go over your options and what would be best for your frame."

I nodded quickly, trying not to notice how absurdly chiseled his jawline was, bearing just enough stubble to catch a reflection from the lights overhead. Or that his hair was brown, but it was about a thousand different shades.

Once again, I looked up, waiting.

Once again, absolutely nothing touched my breast.

I turned back. Dr. Hunt was staring at my breasts like he'd just seen a ghost.

Jesus, were they *that* bad?

"Um...Dr. Hunt?" I ventured. "Nathan?"

Again, my voice seemed to disturb his trance. But this time, he whirled around as if he couldn't bear to look at whatever monstrosity he'd observed, sat back on his stool with a thump, and scooted as far away from me as possible.

"Everything all right?" I asked.

Obviously, it wasn't. Something was very, very wrong. Once again, he was looking at literally anything else in the room but me.

"I apologize, but I don't think I'm the appropriate doctor for this consultation."

"What?"

I looked down, wondering what the hell he saw that scared him so much. Nothing that I could see. Still the same preteen-sized-in-a-push-up-bra-if-I-was-lucky, mosquito-bite breasts I'd had since age twelve. Still completely inadequate for a job where half my tips came from customers who needed to think I was attractive. But not horror shows or anything. They were perfectly normal.

Dr. Hunt's voice was gruff as he spoke. Curt, almost irritable. "I said, I don't think I'm the appropriate—"

"I know what you said." I cut in, suddenly irritated. "I'm surprised, not deaf."

What the fuck was this guy's problem? I'd paid good money to be here and was planning to spend a whole lot more. The least he could do was take a look.

Dr. Hunt's gaze finally met mine, thick with something that looked weirdly like pity but not. Regret, maybe. Or sorrow.

"I'm sorry," he repeated. "It's not going to work."

I looked down at my breasts again, then back up to him. "What's wrong with them?"

"Nothing," he said a little too quickly. "I just can't do it."

Obvious bullshit.

"No way," I said. "I paid my two hundred dollars for this appointment, and I can't afford another. Are you or are you not a plastic surgeon?"

"Of course I am." Now Dr. Hunt was the one who sounded impatient. "I just can't be yours. I realize this is inconvenient, but—"

"It's beyond *inconvenient*, Dr. Hunt," I snapped, though I'd already yanked the sides of the medical gown closed. No more freak show for him.

Even more infuriatingly, he seemed relieved.

Asshole.

"I want to see your manager," I said, then bit my lower lip to keep it from trembling as tears pricked at my eyes. Fuck, why did I care so much what this stuck-up doctor thought of me?

Because I was already at rock bottom, that's why.

Because everyone else in my life thought I was a fuckup, and my sitting here was basically the next step to scraping the bottom of the barrel, desperate for any validation, even if it had to come surgically.

Because even if I *was* as pathetic as everyone said, for some reason I couldn't even try to understand, I didn't want *him* to think so.

"I don't have a manager," the doctor was saying. "It's a group practice, so we manage ourselves. You can see one of the other doctors if you like. They might have appointments in another few months. Otherwise, I'll make sure you receive a full refund."

"Fuck that." The words cut my tongue even as my voice shook. Totally inappropriate for this bright office, and certainly too uncouth for this posh neighborhood. "I don't *have* a few months—I only got this because of a last-minute cancellation. And if I don't—"

I cut myself off then. No, he didn't deserve my story. Not that he even cared. I was nothing to him, just another service worker rich men like him could treat like garbage, someone whose meager savings he could afford to turn down just because he didn't like the look of me.

A hand landed on my knee, warm and solid. I looked down to see that Dr. Hunt had scooted across the room so that he was right next to me, tall enough that even seated several inches lower than the exam table, he was almost able to look at me eye to eye.

If I could stop staring at his hand, that is.

It was a completely inappropriate way to touch a patient. But I supposed I wasn't that to him. Not anymore. Now I was just an object of something worse than derision. His pity.

He removed it almost immediately, like my skin was hot to the touch. Apparently, the rest of me disgusted him as much as my breasts.

"Why are you doing this?" he asked quietly. "Honestly."

"I, um, don't think that's any of your business."

I hugged my arms around my body and twisted my ankles together. I was naked except for this paper gown and my Wonder Woman underwear. I wanted nothing more than to put on my familiar jeans and hot pink sweater and get as far away from this room and this hot, mean doctor as possible.

"You just said we're friends," Dr. Hunt said. "So I'm not going to give you my professional opinion unless you tell me what brought you here. You're very young to be considering breast augmentation."

And there it was. The judgment I knew was waiting for me.

"I'm twenty-four, not fourteen, *Doctor*," I said with every bit of sass I could muster. Which was a lot, if you asked my sisters. "You've never had a girl my age in here looking to have her tits done?"

"I have," he admitted. "But they're generally women married to much wealthier men, women recovering from the effects of childbirth and breastfeeding, or strippers—exotic dancers, I mean. You're not married, you haven't had children, and you're not…"

I looked up. Did I really have to say my plans out loud?

Especially when I hadn't exactly voiced them to myself?

I mean, when my cousin suggested I visit her plastic surgeon, it wasn't because she was making a killing serving drinks. And while I'd *told* him it was because I wanted to earn more as a bartender, in the back of my mind, I probably knew I was lying too. That, in the end, I always knew I'd be right where Rochelle and too many other has-been dancers in the tri-state area ended up.

But clearly, I didn't need to say a thing.

"Oh." So much realization in one little word. So much shock in those big brown eyes.

I wanted to melt into a puddle on the floor just to slip under the doorway, away from the abject horror I saw there.

"Can I ask why?" His voice was stern and gentle at the same time. "It's certainly your prerogative. But I've seen you at the bar, Joni. You don't like it when strangers hit on you or make comments about your body, and they do it a lot. Once, a customer offered to give you fifty dollars to shake your chest at him, and you sprayed him with water until the bouncer took him outside."

I peered at him. I'd honestly never thought he'd even noticed me beyond the drinks I poured. Every other time I'd seen this man at Opal, he'd always sat quietly at his corner, staring at his scotch instead of consuming it.

"That was different," I said. "That guy was just demeaning. He called me sugar tits."

"And you think men receiving lap dances will be different?"

I glared at him. Who the *fuck* did he think he was, judging me like this?

"Fuck," muttered the doctor.

I couldn't have agreed more.

Without an answer, I jumped off the table and sprang into immediate, if awkward, action, clutching the gown to my body with one hand while I grabbed my clothes off the other chair in the room with the other.

It was hard. A lot of stuff fell. More than once.

"Joni." Dr. Hunt stood up. "Joni, stop."

"Nah, I'm good." I managed to shove one leg into my jeans, then the other, hopping around like an idiot in the process. My underwear just went into my purse. "And you know what, Nathan? You're right. You should definitely not be my doctor. Now, I gotta go and get back to my demeaning job."

"At a bar, or…"

"Oh my God!" I screeched. Christ on a *cracker*, the man really couldn't stop himself, could he?

I threw my coat over the disposable gown, not even caring that I was going to walk out of here looking like I'd escaped from a looney bin. My T-shirt was somewhere on the floor. Right now I couldn't have cared where.

"Joni, please."

Just before I reached the door, Dr. Hunt managed to capture one of my wrists, pulling me back to face him. His fingers burned, but it wasn't unpleasant. In fact, it was nice.

Maybe too nice.

"I didn't want to—I didn't mean to—" he stumbled. "Look, I don't care where you work. If you want to strip or dance or mix drinks, neither I nor anyone else should have a say about it."

"Thanks for stating the fucking obvious," I gritted through my teeth. "Now let me go."

The hand around my wrist felt like a brand I'd never known I wanted. The idea was infuriating.

"Not before—fuck, I just want to know why you have to change anything when you're perfect just the way you are!"

Time stood still. For a moment, we stayed there, staring at each other, my wrist braceleted by his big hand while his brown eyes met my green without a trace of judgment, but with something that resembled…fear?

What did *he* have to be afraid of here?

Ever so lightly, his thumb brushed the inside of my wrist, over the thinnest, softest layer, tracing the pattern of my veins.

I shivered even as a tear fell down my cheek.

He wouldn't say that if he knew the truth.

"This body," I said with a voice that creaked, "is *definitely* not perfect. And neither am I."

Dr. Hunt sighed and shoved his other hand into the mess of silky curls atop his head. "No, of course not. No one is technically perfect, but—"

"This body used to be good at *one thing*," I continued, uninterested in his rationalizing. "And now that's gone. So now I might as well be good at something else while I can because that's pretty much all I have left."

Dr. Hunt looked up, curiosity flaring as an eleven-shaped mark appeared between his brows as his hand dropped my wrist. "What do you mean, that's all you have left? What were you good at? What's wrong?"

It was more questions than he'd ever asked me in four solid months.

Another tear fell. No, this asshole did not deserve my sob story.

"You know what?" I used my free hand to swipe at my face. "No. As you said, you are *not* my doctor, so you don't need to ask these questions anymore. And you can also keep your know-it-all, judgy-as-fuck, stupid handsome nose out of my business. I can make decisions about my own body without you, thank you very much."

And with that, I turned to the door, leaving the doctor standing in the room, frozen like a statue, while he watched me leave.

I looked over my shoulder with the last shred of dignity I could manage. "See you never, *Dr. Hunt.*"

THREE

SISTERS IN ORDER OF MOST TO LEAST ANNOYING (TODAY)

#1 Lea

"It's for the best. I'd be a shitty stripper anyway."

Sitting at Rochelle's battered kitchen table in the Bronx, I took a shot of the very worst tequila on the market as if to punctuate the story of Most Embarrassing Doctor's Appointment Ever.

The next afternoon, I'd headed straight uptown as I promised, intent on helping my family as promised. Unfortunately, the idea of all that was a little too much for me to handle, so I'd taken a four-block detour for some lunch and liquid courage at Rochelle's apartment.

Okay, so I was avoiding. Not the packing. That I could handle. But the disapproving faces of my siblings after I skipped Mass, definitely.

I coughed. Oh, that stuff burned. "Anyway, yeah. I won't be working at Diamonds anytime soon."

Rochelle sighed, almost as if she was more disappointed by the news than I was. "I don't know about that Dr. Hunt, but Dr. Palmer is really good. Maybe you should ask for him instead."

I shook my head. "No way I'm stepping foot in that place again.

It's a sign, Chelle. And I doubt I'd get approved for the financing option anyway. The pamphlet said it was for people with over six fifty credit scores. I'd be surprised if I have a number at all."

"Kyle might advance you the money. He did for me, and not every club owner is willing to help their dancers like that, you know. It's a good deal."

Undoubtedly, it was. Rochelle had taken up the Diamonds owner's offer last year and, according to her, had earned back the money three months after she returned to work.

But I just shook my head. And it had nothing to do with the way the asshole doctor had called me perfect right before insulting me. Nothing at all. "These titties just aren't ready for icon status yet. That's all you, baby."

My cousin grinned, then shook her head with regret as she painted another clear coat of polish onto her nails, which were green with neon pink flowers this week. "It would have finally gotten fun working over there."

Rochelle and I had come up together in the same little dance studio in Belmont. We were Mrs. Suarez's top pupils and the only ones who had tried to make a real go of it in the city. Rochelle was even better than me, good enough to get into LaGuardia High School, the famous performing arts school in Manhattan. She hadn't, however, had patience with the grind of auditions. She started working at Diamonds to pay her bills about two years ago and hadn't been quiet about wanting me to join her.

Last summer, I'd finally agreed to meet her boss. But the day before the audition, I got the part in *Chicago*.

That too had felt like a sign.

"I might as well just keep trying to convince Tom to give me more shifts while I look for something else," I said. "I am getting better, you know. Yesterday, I was finally able to make a Long Island iced tea without looking up the recipe."

Rochelle delivered her patented side-eye. "Did they actually drink it?"

I giggled. "No comment."

The customer had, in fact, sent it back. But still, I *had* made it.

Instead of shaming me for my difficulty remembering things like that, Rochelle just chuckled with me and went back to painting her nails. That was one of a thousand reasons why we were friends.

"I might know of something else," she said.

I perked. "What's that?"

Nothing would be better than going home with good news for once. My siblings already all thought I was an idiot and a loser. If I at least had a job, maybe they'd cancel the plans and let me keep Nonna's house instead of renting it out.

"Kyle runs a bunch of other sorts of private clubs around the city," Rochelle said. "I serve drinks there during weeknights when it's slow at Diamonds."

"What do you mean, private clubs?" I wondered. "Like men's clubs?"

She started painting her other hand. "No, more underground. Apartments or basement, maybe. Sometimes a boat or maybe a warehouse. Anyplace rich men can drink and gamble."

I recoiled a bit. "Why don't they just go to Atlantic City?"

Rochelle gave me a look. The one that told me not to be so damn naive. "They don't want all that noise. Just some pretty girls while they play their little games. It's all very old-school."

"You mean like *Goodfellas*?"

Growing up in Belmont, I'd heard plenty about those sorts. Nonna still recounted the days when she and my grandfather had to tithe to the church *and* the local bosses when they were first getting started. Matthew had loads of stories from his days breaking up gambling and trafficking rings as a prosecutor in Brooklyn. Even Michael, my brother-in-law, was briefly involved with the Albanian mob when he was younger.

At least shaking it at a strip joint was legal. Even if my boobs were too small.

Rochelle, however, just snorted. "This ain't *The Sopranos*. It's just a bunch of old guys wanting to get away from their wives for the night, play some games, and look at girls without crappy music pounding in their brains. Easiest money I've ever made, I'm telling you."

I frowned. "So, it's topless?"

"Sometimes," Rochelle admitted.

I just stared at her.

"Okay, most of the time. But it's look, don't touch. Not unless you want. You could give a lap dance or two, but always your choice. Mostly, you just serve drinks and flirt."

I hugged my arms around my chest, considering. It wasn't that I was shy. As a dancer, I'd spent most of my life on display. Once, I'd done a production where we wore nothing but thongs, white body paint, and pasties. A body was just a body. I'd never felt the urge to hide mine.

But I'd never performed explicitly to be looked at…that way.

I could see the appeal. Granted, I'd never given an *official* lap dance, but grinding on some dude in the club wasn't that different, and I was damn good at that, bad knee or not.

"And Carmine still doesn't care?" I prodded, wondering again about Rochelle's long-time boyfriend. "About you showing the goods to other men?"

"Well, considering he's the doorman at Diamonds, no. If anything, we're *both* making more money now that he helps Kyle find locations. Plus, other men can look, but he's the only one I go home with. He knows that. I make *sure* he knows that."

I tipped my head, considering. Honestly, I had just as many dudes drooling over me at Opal. One less piece of clothing was the main difference, and Rochelle's gig sounded a lot more lucrative than being a two-bit bartender. Maybe I should get real about my actual skill sets and put them to use.

Time, after all, was running out.

"Well, I always wanted to do *Gypsy*." I shrugged. Something felt wrong about it, but I couldn't say what. "I'll think about it."

"Just let me know."

"All right, babe," I said. "One more for the road."

Before Chelle could stop me, I poured another shot and tipped it down my throat, relishing the burn, then the tingling in my head and eventual relaxation that would make bearing my family's disapproval that much easier.

"Good luck with the move. And with Lea," Chelle called as I grabbed my purse and headed out.

———

OUTSIDE, a cold wind was blowing through Belmont. The remnants of last week's mostly melted snow flurries made icy puddles around the curbs. It was the dregs of winter—the weeks after the merriment of the holidays had worn off, and now people were just buttoned up against frigid breezes and somber skies.

The streets around Belmont were relatively empty for a Friday evening. As I approached the little brown house on Hughes Avenue, the familiar scents of tomato sauce and car exhaust cut through the deserted park across the street. Next to our house, Victor Manuel's voice crooned through Mrs. Hernandez's kitchen window while clashing Pavarotti wails floated from one of the nearby Italian restaurants on 187th.

It wasn't anything fancy, and maybe just a shadow of the community and warmth Belmont exuded during warmer months. But it was still home.

For one more night, anyway.

I crept up the crooked front stoop, and the front door swung open before I even took out my key.

"My God, what took you so long?" Lea demanded without even saying hello. "We've been here for *hours*. And you missed Mass." She sniffed. "Joni, are you drunk? You stink like tequila."

"I work at a bar, Lea. I always smell like liquor." It wasn't a lie. I just wasn't answering her question.

Unfortunately, Lea could always smell a rat. Fortunately, she was too stressed to trap it with her typical tongue-lashing.

"Come on," she said, then yanked me into the house and up the stairs, where I could hear the rest of my family working to clear out the rest of the house.

"Out of the way!"

Lea and I stepped aside while Matthew and Michael carried an old mahogany bureau out the door toward the moving truck parked at the curb. They were followed by Xavier holding a nightstand.

"Why couldn't Matthew or Frankie pay for movers again?" I wondered as I watched them pass. "They both own the world now. They couldn't have spared a little to help our grandmother?"

Within the last year, both my brother Matthew and my older sister Frankie had married very wealthy partners.

"Probably because they don't think they're too good for hard work like *some* people," Lea said as we continued up the creaky old stairs.

"I don't buy it. Frankie's not the crank in the family, Lea," I said.

She turned around as if to argue more, then seemed to decide this particular fight wasn't worth it and shrugged. "They tried, but Nonna said no. Honestly, I think she just wants us all here one last night. Come on, you and I are taking care of *your* room. And you're not getting out of it this time."

"TOSS OR KEEP?" Lea asked as we sat in my room—or what would be my room for exactly one more night—shoving things into boxes.

There wasn't much. For a good chunk of my life, I'd split my time between dance companies, a few half-hearted attempts at school, and splitting a room with my sister Marie. It didn't leave much time for hoarding.

That was good since, for the time being, it was all going to sit in Nonna's storage unit until I found a place of my own. The only things staying out for sure were a few changes of clothes, toiletries, my iPad, and my earring collection.

Can't forget the earrings.

I looked up to where Lea was holding up my copy of *Milady Standard Cosmetology* and made a face. "Toss."

Lea turned the textbook over to examine the front. "You sure? It was so expensive, and you were only a few credits short—"

"Toss it," I ordered again. Just the idea of going back to cosmetology school made me want to jump out the window. "I literally *burned* someone's hair in a final exam. The Leslie Beauty Academy does not, under any circumstances, want me to return to their program. Give it to the Salvation Army for some other sucker to enjoy."

Lea gave me her patented "Joni's being an ass" expression but put the book into the box designated for charity and went back to the other items scattered across the little desk in the corner.

"Can I ask you a question?" she asked a few minutes later, after packing all of my stage makeup into a big plastic kaboodle.

I looked up from sorting sweaters. It wasn't really Lea's style to ask my permission to speak. "Sure…"

"What's the plan for tomorrow? I keep asking if you have a place, but you won't answer my texts."

I turned away as my cheeks heated.

How could I explain this to the sister who always seemed to have everything figured out? A full twelve years older than me, Lea had pretty much raised me and my other sisters as much as Nonna did. To hear her tell it, she changed most of my diapers, taught me to walk and talk, and even took me to checkups and dentist appointments. As siblings, we should have been equals, but when she looked at me like that, it was obvious that her experience would always outweigh mine.

Out of all the Zola kids, Lea was the perfect one. Nonna's "good girl." The one whose life had most closely mirrored our grandparents, especially once she and Mike took on the auto shop after Nonno died. They created their own brood of four mini Zola-Scarrones, took Nonna to church, made ziti every Sunday, and did everything that was expected of them while the rest of us flew the coop.

It went without saying that she should be done with me by now. But here I was, just as immature as ever.

And just as desperate to make her think otherwise.

Behind me, Lea sighed. "You haven't found a place, have you?"

I turned back from my closet. "No, but I will, I promise. I'm working on it, really."

Lea emptied another desk drawer of mostly pencil stubs, used hair ties, and other random crap into a trash bag. "Jo, you've been saying that for months. You're out of time."

"I know that. Don't you think I know that? I just need another few days. I have a few leads on some jobs, and—"

"Leads?" Lea shook her head, looking blown away. "That's all you have after four months? Some more leads?"

"Hey, any more boxes need to go down?"

We both turned as Frankie and Kate walked into the room, Kate with free hands, Frankie carrying a plate of amaretti, freshly baked by the way their sweet, almondy scent drifted through the room. A delicious and totally premeditated ambush.

"We're almost done," Lea said stiffly as Frankie set the cookies on the desk and then lowered her five-month-pregnant self into my chair.

"When's your flight?" I wondered as I snagged a cookie and popped it in my mouth.

"Four tomorrow." Frankie looked between all of us. "And that's it for a while. I'm not supposed to travel after six months."

She and Lea traded knowing looks. There had been a rash of babies in the family lately. First, Lea had baby Lupe last year, and then Frankie got pregnant again within a month of Matthew's wife, Nina. Everyone was settled and/or nesting like freaking ducks in a pond. Everyone but me.

"So, what is this, the Spanish Inquisition greased with cookies?" I joked as I grabbed another amaretto, ignoring the fact that I was the only one taking advantage of them. "I think the Spanish had better outfits, you know."

My sisters exchanged guilty glances around the room.

"Don't do that." Frankie's gentle voice broke through the awkwardness. "Don't mask your nerves with insults, Jo."

"Since Marie's not here, someone has to take them," I shot back.

I'd never admit it to anyone, but I missed my mousy wallflower almost twin like crazy. Despite being born only ten months apart, we were complete opposites and fought like cats and dogs. But home wasn't really home without the person I'd shared a room with for most of my life.

"Where are the kids, anyway?" I asked Lea as I considered a third cookie. Were I still auditioning, I would have limited myself to one, but these days, did it really matter? "Usually, they sound like a herd of elephants by now."

"The boys took the kids back to my house," Lea said. "They knew we needed to talk. All of us."

"So you said. What is this, an intervention?" I joked. To hell with it, I was going to have that cookie.

Every woman around the room clasped their hands in identical prayer-like positions while they stared at me with identical expressions of frustration, pity, and…dread. No one laughed. No one even argued. The room grew quiet.

And my family was *never* quiet.

"Wait," I said, cookie halfway to my mouth. "This…*is*…an intervention? For friggin' what?"

As a dancer, I'd been freakishly intense about keeping my body clean. Even though that career had ended almost four months ago, I wasn't much different. I liked to go out with friends, sure. And the occasional random dude. Fine. But I hardly drank, almost never touched drugs beyond alcohol, and basically treated my body like a temple. Compared to other twenty-four-year-olds in this city, I was a saint.

What addiction were they intervening? Nonna's baking?

"Did you find a place?" Frankie wondered at last.

I didn't answer, but Lea did it for me.

"She doesn't have anywhere to go," she said. "Still."

"Joni, seriously?" Kate put in. "You told me last week you had some leads."

Had I told her that? I wondered. Sometimes, I could barely remember conversations from yesterday.

"Honestly," Lea continued. "How can you leave something as basic as where you sleep to the last minute? It's crazy!"

"You know what's really crazy?" I demanded. "That I have five siblings, two of them with rich-ass partners, and none of them can give me any help. Not even a couch to sleep on."

I glared around the room, full of accusation.

Frankie, whose husband was one of the "rich-ass" ones, shook her head in that quiet, sweet way while she set a hand atop her pregnant belly. "I'm sorry, babe, but you know the townhouse is under construction until after the baby is born. The whole place will be covered in dust and workers."

A glance at Kate told me she wasn't willing to put me up either. "My studio barely has room for my bed, let alone an extra mattress. I really wish it could be different."

I turned to Lea, who was already shaking her head. "Mike would kill me. Our house is too cramped as it is with four kids. He already spends half his nights on the couch when Lupe can't sleep."

I flopped back in my chair. This couldn't be happening. It was almost like they *planned* it this way.

"Look," Frankie offered as she pulled at her ponytail. "Xavier and I can totally give you a deposit—"

"It's fine. I don't need it."

"Don't be a stubborn donkey." Lea dumped my old high school notebooks into a trash bag. "But I don't think she would get approved for a lease anyway."

I stared at my feet. Hating that she was right. Who was going to give a lease to a part-time bartender barely scraping minimum wage?

Really, it was the questions no one was asking that bothered me most. Why couldn't I get my shit together? Why couldn't I manage something as basic as rent or a job that required more than a few nights a week? Responsibilities, bank accounts, all the things adults were supposed to handle?

I tried. I really did. But every time I approached the mountain of things I was supposed to do every day, every week, every month, they all seemed so impossible. The world felt heavy and exhausting and fucking unbearable.

So, I'd ignore them for another day in favor of scrolling on my phone or sending memes to my friends. And the mountain grew. And grew. And grew.

Fuck.

I grabbed another cookie. Right now, they were the only things that seemed to help.

Unfortunately, when I looked around the room again, my problems were still reflected in the expressions that said the same thing: poor, sad, stupid Joni.

Just like they had my entire life.

I swallowed the cookie and scowled. "I said I can take care of myself, and I will."

"Oh, please." Lea's sarcasm cut through the room. "When have you ever had to do anything for yourself? Every single one of us took turns making your lunches and tying your shoes until you were more than old enough to do all of it. You have *never* had to lift a finger. You have no clue what it's like to take care of anyone else, much less yourself, for once."

"Lea!" Frankie hissed. "That is *not* helping."

"Well, it's the truth. And she needs a reality check. That's why we're all here, isn't it?"

"Don't hate on me just because you chose a life of perpetual housekeeping and four snot-nosed brats," I snapped at her.

"Don't *you* be a brat just because your life is empty while the rest of us have gotten our shit together," Lea retorted. "Grow the hell up and learn to think of more than just yourself."

"Lea!" Frankie tried again, to absolutely no avail.

"Christ," Kate muttered.

"I think of things plenty," I bit out, if only to stop my voice from shaking. "Who brings Nonna boxes of her favorite nougat from Gino's on Mother's Day, huh? And who takes her to her doctor's appointments? Or does her nails and helps her do her hair in the mornings and watches old movies with her whenever she wants?"

"You do, *civetta*."

We all turned to find Nonna entering the room, her face lined with sadness.

My grandmother had been a beauty in her youth—a dead ringer for Sophia Loren. Now, there wasn't much of a difference beyond some fine lines, the fact that her black hair was now dyed that way, and the way age had rendered her a bit more petite. At seventy-eight, she still had a whole life to live. Starting tomorrow.

I would have been happy for her if it weren't costing me everything.

"It's true," she said as her Italian accent, normally softened by more than sixty years in New York, thickened with emotion. "You can be a very kind girl when you want. Joni isn't always the baby. Not anymore."

"Just sometimes, then?" Lea and I traded glares, though her tone was admittedly less, well, bitchy.

"Better than nothing," I cut back. "And unlike *you*, I have a job."

"Hey," Frankie said sharply. "Raising children is most definitely a job, Jo."

I swallowed. Okay, that was a low blow. Especially in this crowd. Frankie had raised her daughter alone for four whole years. And it was no secret that Lea had to give up her own career to take care of her brood. And then there was everything she, Matthew, and Nonna had done for the rest of us.

But that was different. I didn't know how, but it was.

"Well, I got a promotion at Opal, didn't I?" I rattled on. "Tom has been teaching me how to mix drinks. I'm a bartender now, not just a shot girl or on the platforms."

"But it's been months since then," Kate pointed out. "And you still only work two shifts a week. Tom can't give you any more?"

I pressed my mouth into a thin line. I wasn't going to tell them about how many times Tom had refused that particular request, claiming my skills were not up to the chaos that took over Opal on the weekends. Or how many other bars had refused to hire me, given my lack of experience. Or how many other interviews for hostessing or waiting tables I had just plain skipped because I couldn't bear being told I was inadequate one more time.

"What else do you do with your time?" Lea wondered. "'Physical therapy'? 'Working out'?" She mimed bunny ears with each phrase that made me want to smack her.

"I *have* been doing physical therapy," I protested, but even I knew that was B.S.

When my union benefits lapsed, I hadn't been able to see a physical therapist for more than a few weeks after my surgery this summer. So, on my days off, instead of coming home to help or finding another job like I knew I should, I'd go to my old dance studio to continue with the exercises in the hope that maybe, just maybe, things would heal on their own.

It was the same every time. I'd get through a warm-up. Do a few simple routines. Feel good, if a little out of practice. That was to be expected.

Then I'd try something harder, like a fouetté or a jump.

And land right on my ass, knee throbbing, gritting through the pain.

Anterior cruciate ligament tear. That's what the doctors called the event that killed my dream in exactly one and a half seconds.

"Okay, okay, okay," Frankie said. "No one's keeping track. But there's still just the harsh reality that you have to move out, Jo. Nonna leaves tomorrow, and the new renters are moving in on Monday. Time's up."

"What if I just stayed here?" I blurted out. "Can't we just call the renters and cancel? I'd take care of the place better than strangers anyway."

Literally, everyone around the room snorted in unison. It was like being surrounded by a bunch of snarky horses.

"What?" I pressed. "I would! It's all paid off, isn't it? Honestly, Nonna, why can't I just stay here and take care of the house for you?"

Nonna just walked through the room and patted my cheek like she might a delusional child's. "I'm sorry, baby. It's done."

"Besides," Lea said with another *Joni-is-an-idiot* sigh. "Nonna has to pay rent in Rome too. What, do you think our seventy-eight-year-old grandmother should get a job waiting tables instead of you?"

"I didn't say that," I said. "Just that—"

"Are you really so selfish that you would rather cost her good income so you can keep freeloading forever?" Lea's voice was harsh, but not completely unfair. She knew it, and I knew it.

And so did everyone else, which is why they didn't argue with her either.

I opened my mouth, then shut it, trying and failing to keep my face from flushing bright red.

No. I wasn't selfish.

And I wasn't a freeloader.

I was just...scared. Not that I would ever admit that to anyone, but it was the truth. There was only one thing I had ever been good at, but that wasn't an option anymore.

All I had had after that was my family. Was this place.

And now I wouldn't have that either.

I looked at the bed where I'd only sleep for one more night, at the scattered boxes filled with old dance costumes, jewelry, and random bits and bobs, at my sisters, all watching me with equal parts fear and pity. My eyes pricked with tears.

"But—who—what—" I swallowed. "Where am I supposed to go?"

There was another shared glance around the room. Clearly, they'd been prepared for this moment. The one where I broke like an egg.

Lea reached into her jeans pocket and pulled out a set of keys. "Mike and I talked. You can use the breakroom in the garage until you find a place to land. Frankie's giving you the first and last—but you need to make rent, Jo. No exceptions."

She handed me the keys, and I stared at them, dumbfounded. "You want me to live above the auto shop? It doesn't even have a shower!"

"It's better than a shelter, don't you think?" Kate offered.

I looked between them and the keys. "But that place smells like motor oil and bad coffee and cigarettes, and I'll be woken up every morning by the greasy dudes who know exactly five words, and—"

"And it's a free roof over your head," Lea cut in sharply. "You can shower at my house down the block. That's the best we got."

"Maybe she could come to London with us..." Frankie started, clearly feeling sorry for me.

"That's just coddling her," Lea argued back. "We discussed this."

"Yes," Nonna agreed, though she was looking at me. "Lea is right. We decided."

Even Nonna was in on this shitty little 'reality check'?

My mind raced as I tried to come up with another solution. Anything besides a grimy shop room drenched in grease and my family's pity.

Maybe I could stay with a friend? Except none of my friends had extra space—they were either dancers living four to a studio or kids from high school who already had husbands and babies too. Rochelle would give me her couch, but Carmine would kick me out within a day or two.

Sleep at the bar? Doubtful. Tom did that himself half the week, and the only accommodation in his packed office was a cot in the corner.

Fuck. *Fuck.*

I felt a hand land on mine and looked up at Nonna, peering at me with a mixture of sadness and resignation.

"Joni, I'm sorry. I wish I didn't have to do this, but it's time for you to grow up. Time for *la civetta* to leave the nest."

My chin trembled, eyes pricking with unshed tears.

"Fine," I said, trying to keep my voice steady as I pushed back from the table, causing the chair leg to screech loudly on the wood floor. "I'll just fly the coop, then."

"Joni, wait," Frankie called as I stormed out of the room. "We can help you look—"

"Don't bother," I called, already yanking on my jacket and throwing my purse over one shoulder. "You just made it clear that from this point forward, I'm on my own. I'll figure it out myself."

FOUR

STEPS TO SNEAKING OUT OF A ONE-NIGHT STAND

#7 put your shoes on AFTER u leeve the apt

I tried to show my sisters. I really did. I marched right out of that house, hopped on the train back to Manhattan, skipped into Opal, and charmingly demanded at least five shifts a week and an advance on my next paycheck.

Tom just laughed and went back to pouring a beer. He did, however, offer me free drinks while I soothed my wounded ego and tried to come up with another plan.

Free drinking led to flirting with the crowd that flocked to Opal on Saturday nights to leer at the go-go dancers (who used to include me) and make out with anything that moved.

Flirting led to kissing a man with a silver earring and shaggy blond hair.

Kissing led to…well, I couldn't really say exactly what. Waking up in a stranger's bed with a raging hangover and a ray of sunlight piercing through the blinds like a needle straight to the eyeball, I guess.

Ouch.

Well, I *had* solved my housing problem. At least for one night.

And that had all led to this moment of muttering "Fuck," then wincing in the light. My voice sounded like it had been chopped up with razors. How many drinks had I had last night?

Still remaining horizontal, I took in my surroundings and patched together exactly where I was and how I'd gotten here.

Last call.

Way too much tongue.

A stranger who complimented my favorite thrifted miniskirt.

And he was...the lump now snoring next to me, whose name was...

"Dammit," I whispered. I honestly could not remember.

And I thought last night had been rock bottom.

Beside me, the lump shifted and emitted a sound like an elephant's chuff. Then he rolled onto his back, and I was met with an utterly normal face with a half-grown beard, a soft chest that needed a few months at the beach, and...well, not the biggest boner in the world underneath his blanket. Probably not even a medium-sized boner. It wasn't exactly a family-size camper, but enough to pitch a tent. Or a beach pop-up.

Yeah, it had come across that way last night too. I rubbed my face as a few more memories came back. Some sloppy kisses around my neck and heavy petting on the living room couch. Stumbling into his bedroom, where he made a few sad attempts to treat my clit like a light switch. Heavy breathing and a couple of weak thrusts against my thigh before the guy had totally lost his hard-on. And then Darren had passed out—

Darren! That was his name!

Or...wait... Was it Aaron?

Baron?

No, that couldn't be right.

Dammit.

I waited to see if the lump-that-probably-rhymed-with-Karen would move again. "Snuggles" weren't exactly on the menu this morning—not with my raging headache and his morning breath from Mordor.

When the lump didn't move for a solid sixty seconds, I began the slow dance of extricating myself from a man's bed and locating my clothes without waking him. Careful not to disturb the sleeping walrus, I tiptoed around the room and managed to locate my jeans, my black sweater, my underwear, and one sock. My bra had gone missing, but since the mystery man over there had rolled over twice since I'd gotten up, he was getting a souvenir.

Bummer. I liked that bra a lot. It was green and matched my eyes.

I dressed in the hallway of what was plainly a very nice apartment. A classic six, by the looks of the second bedroom, the formal dining room, and the living room I stumbled past. The eat-in kitchen was massive by Manhattan standards. Apartments this big were all over the Bronx, but in Manhattan cost a mint.

Looks like What's-His-Name did all right for himself. Enough that I'd probably want to see him again if I were that kind of girl.

But I wasn't. Not yet, anyway.

I slid on my Vans, located my leather jacket on the thick gray couch in the living room, and then, for no reason at all, paused at the front door to take a last look.

It really was a nice place. Sleek wood floors that were made for pirouettes. Comfortable-looking furniture that was luxe without being too flashy. Warm white walls decorated with black and white photographs that were a bit more interesting than the average crap at Target.

It was the kind of apartment that, under normal circumstances, I might want to hang out in for a while. Kick back. Have a cocktail. Just get comfortable.

But no. It was back to Belmont for me, where I'd accept the key to the garage with my head hanging low and say goodbye to my childhood home once and for all.

"Bye," I whispered to the apartment as I quietly opened the door. "I'd say 'see you later,' but we both know that's never gonna happen."

Kate: Joni, are you okay?

> Lea: Where are you? Are you alive?

> Frankie: Please come home. We are worried about you.

I STEPPED out of the elevator while staring at three of the dozen or so messages my sisters had sent last night and through the morning to the group chat called Hellcats after I'd stormed out of the house.

It was nearly one in the afternoon, which meant I'd been AWOL for almost fifteen hours and had skipped Sunday Mass too. After which we were all supposed to be finishing up with the final clean-out of the house and taking Nonna to the airport.

Somehow, the idea felt worse than my hangover.

Sunday afternoons weren't for mopping floors and staring at empty rooms. They were for drinks on the porch, and Nonna's osso buco, and chatting with whatever neighbors, cousins, aunties, or uncles who wanted to stop in from the neighborhood.

All things that would never happen again.

I paused in the lobby to let them know I wasn't dead.

> Got stuck downtown. Stayed the night. Be there in about an hour.

Their replies were instantaneous.

> Lea: Are you KIDDING me? We need you here NOW! WTF have you even been doing??

> Kate: Do we really want the answer to that question?

> Lea: Gross. No.

> Frankie: Xavier and Mike are unloading everything at the storage unit now. Nonna took all the kids so we could clean for her. Please come ASAP.

> Kate: We have your stuff to take to the shop.

Frankie: I grabbed a change of clothes
for you.

Lea: And soap to disinfect your cooch.

"Oh my God, disinfect your own freaking cooch," I said a little too loudly, ignoring the suspicious-looking doorman and pausing in front of the exit to message them back that I really was on my way.

"Excuse me, miss—Joni?"

I jumped at the sound of a familiar voice. A deliciously deep, velvety smooth, come-hither voice a girl dreams about saying all manner of dirty things to her in the dark.

Please, God, no. Not this man. Not now. Not when I look like a squirrel who just got run over by a semi.

Unfortunately, my bad luck just seemed to keep flowing like the freaking Hudson River.

I swallowed and found myself looking up at a pair of glasses-framed eyes the color of the darkest espresso I would have sold my soul to sip on right now.

Right before I disappeared out of pure mortification.

First, the doctor's office.

And now, the walk of shame.

Apparently, the universe really wanted to teach me some humility when it came to Dr. Nathan Hunt.

Fuck my life. For real.

"You have *got* to be kidding me," I muttered.

It wouldn't have been so bad if he didn't look so...smart. So capable. And so very sexy in that way only men who don't know it can be.

Even now, wearing probably the most boring outfit possible, Hunt looked more edible than any so-called "bad boy" I'd ever met —and Belmont was full with them. Who needed tattoos, Jordans, and a cigarette addiction when you could have sleek jeans, a blue button-up, and a North Face jacket?

I stole a quick glance at the floor-to-ceiling mirrors lining the lobby. Okay, I didn't look *quite* the horror show I imagined. Braless and rumpled, sure, but my clothes—a pair of painted-on black jeans, a red T-shirt, black sweater, and my thrifted leather jacket—held up all right. I still had shadows of mascara smeared under my eyes, and my dark hair was tied up into a knot of glorious bedhead, but maybe I was pulling off a "devil-may-care" attitude. The beaded fringe earrings that almost touched my collarbone finished off the look.

Then I exhaled with morning breath that would probably put out the sun. Or set it on fire.

Jesus.

I snuck a stick of gum from my purse, then flipped back around with the bright smile that every man on the planet besides *this one* responded to. "Dr. Hunt—oh. Hello. Um, how are you?"

Hunt frowned, his gaze still taking in my presence from top to bottom like I was an elephant in a tutu. It was an understandable reaction, considering yesterday I'd basically told him where to shove it.

"I'm fine," he said slowly. "What are you doing here?"

Was it that obvious I didn't belong in this plush lobby?

Yes, I decided. Yes, it was. Well, I'd go with it.

"It's not what it looks like."

He didn't respond.

"Okay, it is," I admitted with what I hoped was a mischievous wink. "Um, I'm walking home after a very long night. What are you up to? Getting into some trouble?"

Another slow blink. Another joke that fell completely flat. That seemed to be my specialty with this dude.

"I go to the gym in the mornings, and I just had brunch with some colleagues," Nathan replied as his gaze dragged down my body with an unexpected heat and landed on my shoes.

"Oh, was it good?" I asked.

"The gym or the brunch?"

I shrugged. "Both, I suppose." It was like the guy had never heard of small talk.

Hunt sighed with a heaviness that didn't seem completely appropriate for Sunday brunch. "Both were adequate, I suppose. I don't particularly care for the eggs at Bergdorf's—do you wear those shoes a lot? They have terrible sole support."

Huh. The good doctor changed subjects even faster than I did.

I glanced down at my checkerboard Vans slip-ons. Maybe not the most glamorous things, and a far cry from Hunt's brightly colored Hokas. My brother had the same pair. They were called Speed Goats, and my sisters and I made barnyard sounds every time he went for a jog.

They were also expensive, which is probably why this asshole, yet again, thought it was appropriate to judge my life choices.

"What do you think would suit my next walk of shame?" I snarked. "Merrells? Maybe some hiking boots?"

Hunt just shook his head, unperturbed by my sarcasm. "I don't think hiking boots would be necessary in the city. Maybe Danskos. A lot of nurses wear them. It's really important to have proper arch support if you're on your feet for hours at a time. Otherwise, you might end up with plantar fasciitis, Achilles tendinitis, not to mention flat feet, which can later lead to—"

"You know what, thanks," I interrupted. "I'll take a look."

If I hadn't already known he thought I was an idiot, this right here would have told me. Poor, stupid, wannabe stripper girl embarrasses a full-on doctor out of his mind, so he needs to point out that she dresses like a hobo too.

Except he said you were perfect, a little voice reminded me.

Perfect. Had he really said that in his office, or had I just imagined it?

Maybe he was going to say something about it now. Maybe he was going to mention his outburst, the fact that he had actually turned down a whole lot of money, because apparently, I was *too perfect* to touch.

I waited, watching, trying to find any clue in that stoic face of the turmoil I was currently feeling.

But there was nothing.

Nada.

Like it hadn't even happened.

My phone buzzed again—no doubt with more sisterly texts wondering if I was at the subway yet. I ignored them, only then noticing I'd missed a button on my shirt.

God, I was a disaster.

"So, I guess you live here?" I asked. Brilliant question, I know. But give me a break. My brain was still foggy from all the Jaeger. Or was it Southern Comfort? I believe my exact order to Tom was, "Give me something to make this day disappear."

I should have run right then. I needed a shower more than life; my head felt like a hammer was slamming into it, and my family was waiting to scold me out of existence. But instead, I lingered, waiting for the brown-eyed doctor to respond.

Because somehow, I just had to. I was starting to suspect I was a masochist.

Hunt frowned, making a brown curl flop adorably over his forehead. "Yes, I—you didn't actually say why you are in my building. Your chart said you live in the Bronx, so why would you be here?"

The question came out stunted, like he'd only just remembered to say it. Or maybe he was finally demonstrating some appropriate embarrassment. Honestly, it was cute. Annoyingly so.

But also irritating because was he *really* going to make me spell out the fact that I was slutting around New York just so he could offer yet another bit of choice judgment?

"Well," I said, unsure of why my hands were suddenly fumbling under that direct gaze of his. It made me babble all over again. "I, ah, sort of went home with someone last night. You're catching me on my way out before he wakes up."

The words jumped out before I could stop them, the way they often did when I was nervous. I *hated* that this guy made me so nervous.

But there was no reaction. None. Those chocolatey eyes just blinked as they waited for me to continue.

"He was a nobody, really," I went on, unable to stop now that I'd started. "Just some guy at the bar, and I didn't really want to go home after my shift. My family has been kind of annoying lately. You know how that goes."

More blinks. I guess he didn't. Dr. Nathan Hunt probably only took home a carefully curated selection of supermodels and socialites who lined up in his office to get their faces tweaked and asses lifted.

I continued babbling and fumbling with my shirt. "My sisters are actually expecting me now, but yeah. Um. His name was—ugh, will you judge if I say I can't remember? He had a really nice gray couch, that's all I know. Soft-looking, kind of velvet, with all the buttons that make it look super classy. Alden? Aaron? I swear his name started with an A…"

"Aiden?"

My mouth dropped. "*Yes*, that's it! How did you know?"

For the first time, Hunt's face was curiously expressive. I couldn't exactly read it, but the emotions were definitely there. A bit of a frown, his brows furrowed together like he was trying too hard to focus on something, and those big brown eyes pinned squarely on me, full of something…deep.

I shivered.

His throat rippled as he swallowed. "The gray couch. I recognize the description. It's a one-of-a-kind."

Great. Not only did Dr. Chocolate Eyes know I was the type for a no-name one-night stand, but he was apparently friends with the bearded lump under the sheets. I could just imagine him and *Aiden* grabbing beers and swapping stories about me.

Time to make my escape.

"Well, anyway," I said. "I gotta go. My sisters are waiting for me in Belmont."

As if on cue, my phone buzzed again. This time, I pulled it out.

> Frankie: What's your ETA? Are you at least on the train from wherever you are?
>
> Lea: I'm leaving the bathroom for you. You are not getting out of helping!

I rolled my eyes. Harpies, all of them.

"Wait."

I whirled back, only to almost run into the doctor head-on. He steadied me at the waist, then immediately released me, only to take my shirt and fix the button I had somehow only managed to do up wrong again.

As his hands worked steadily up the front of my body, I watched like I was trapped in a spell, one cast by his slow, even breathing and the subtle scent of soap, sandalwood, and clean water.

I only just managed to stay upright until he was done. Then looked up to see my reflection in his glasses.

"You did that fast," I mumbled, half incoherent, when he stepped away. "Thank you."

That won me another slight smile. Not a whole one, but just enough that a shadow of a dimple appeared in his left cheek.

The world really was a cruel place.

"I'm a surgeon," he said plainly. "I guess that means I'm good with my hands."

Another shiver traveled down my back as I stared at his obviously dexterous fingers. Good with his hands. Yeah, I'd *bet* he was.

For a second, I considered making a move. I had a whole arsenal of smiles that worked on all sorts of men—there had to be one that would work on him. I just hadn't found it yet. Then I could trade riding the train to Belmont for riding Nathan Hunt, make him forget I was an idiot, and pretend this shitty day wasn't going to happen.

But then I remembered the look on his face when I was sitting in front of him topless. The sheer horror in his eyes when he thought about touching me.

"Did you use protection?" he asked.

And just like that, any fantasy disappeared into a cloud of smoke with his *third* jab at my personal life.

"It can be difficult to remember if you are having sexual relations with someone under the influence of alcohol. You might want to get yourself tested soon, and then again in a few months if you think it's necessary…"

I flared as he went on about safe sex procedures in that irritatingly *non*judgmental voice that somehow sounded more judgmental than anyone I had ever met.

"You know what? Screw you, man," I cut in.

Hunt's mouth shut in a firm line, and he didn't respond, just remained frozen as I spun around and shoved my way out of his gorgeous building.

Outside, the clouds had been replaced by mockingly bright sunshine. People were smiling, birds were chirping, and I wanted to escape them all.

Unfortunately, I hadn't gone more than a few steps down the busy sidewalk when I heard him call my name.

"Joni!"

I turned, annoyed already by the way my skin prickled with excitement. Why did just the sound of my name from this condescending fucker excite me more than the quarter of an orgasm I'd accomplished last night, even after I'd just told him off?

Hard to get?

Had to be.

"Forget something, asshole?" I called as he approached, still holding his shoulder bag. "Another choice bit of advice, perhaps? Would you like to comment on how well I floss? Or maybe remind me to wear sunscreen?"

Hunt shook his head, and the curls on top swayed back and forth. "No, I didn't forget something. But you...I just wanted to say..."

He drifted off, and I waited for him to state the obvious. Tell me to be safer, make better choices, or avoid risky behavior like one-night stands and getting blackout drunk. Basically, change my whole life in the ways I knew I should, but couldn't quite manage.

Nathan looked down at my Vans. "Don't forget to buy a better pair of shoes. The Bronx is a long way to walk."

He waited for my response.

And waited.

And waited.

It took a while to sink in. But was it—had he—had Nathan Hunt, impassive doctor and unsmiling know-it-all, cracked a *joke* at my fucking expense? After all of that?

"Either you're an egomaniac or completely oblivious," I told him. "But either way, you're not fucking funny."

He frowned, then shoved a hand through his curls, making them stand up a little on one side. As if he realized what he was doing, he snatched his hand away. "I—what?"

"To be perfectly clear, I didn't need your mansplaining in your office about my body or my job, and I sure as fuck don't need it now about my shoes or sex life," I told him. "You have *no* right to pass judgment on someone you barely know just to get your jollies or whatever you think you're doing. So, if I ever see you again—which I probably will because the universe is a cruel, cruel place—kindly pretend I don't exist. For your sake and mine."

This time, he didn't follow me as I took off down the street, though I felt those dark eyes watching me the entire time. Not once did I turn around. I wasn't about to give him the satisfaction.

Before I reached the end of the block, however, my phone buzzed *again*. This time a text from Kate, outside our chat group.

> Kate: Are you on your way? If you don't make it today, I don't know if they will forgive you.

FIVE
WHY NONNA SHOULD STAY

#14 Becuz I need to eat!

In the end, guilt and duty got me good.

Two hours later, I stood outside the security lines at LaGuardia International Airport along with four of my five siblings, each of us taking turns kissing our grandmother on both cheeks. I'd met my family outside of the ticketing area after taking two trains and a bus all the way to the airport, still wearing the same wrinkled red shirt and black jeans. Nonna had just checked the three coffin-sized suitcases she was taking to Italy, and everyone was getting ready to say our final goodbyes. I got exactly four pairs of stink eyes that translated to, "where the hell have you been, Joni?" as I ran up, out of breath and knee throbbing.

Honestly, would JFK have killed her? At least I only had to take the E train from midtown.

"You take care of your family," Nonna told Matthew before muttering some things in Italian that the rest of us couldn't really decipher.

As the oldest, my brother had grown up hearing the dialects our grandparents spoke to each other, and after doing a tour in Sicily while he was in the Marines, he'd gotten nearly fluent. The rest of us, however, knew just Nonna's endearments and exclamations when we screwed up; I was pretty much only good for the swear words.

"Nina's sorry she couldn't be here," Matthew told her as he pressed a kiss to each of Nonna's lined cheeks. "She's not supposed to travel. Or get out of bed until the baby's born."

"*Dai*, of course," Nonna said. "She needs her rest before you don't get any more sleep, my beautiful boy." Then she turned to Lea. "And you, take care of our Michael and the babies, yeah? Like always, my good girl."

I rolled my eyes. I never understood why Lea was the favorite, Nonna's "good girl" when she had the sharpest tongue out of all of us.

Lea's eyes closed, almost as if in pain, while she squeezed Nonna tightly. "I don't know what I'm gonna do without you. But I hope you have the most amazing time. We'll visit soon."

Even I wasn't immune to the pain in Lea's voice. We all knew the likelihood of her and Mike schlepping four kids across the ocean for an Italian vacation was about as likely as the Central Park Fountain erupting with rainbow sprinkles. They'd only just barely made it work for Matthew's wedding last fall, and that was only because he and Nina had paid everyone's way.

For the first time, I really felt bad for my oldest sister. She was probably the smartest of all of us and was stuck in that crappy little house in Belmont with her mechanic husband and four kids. She swore up and down that she chose that life and loved it. Loved doing the books at Nonno's old auto shop while Mike fixed the cars. Loved chasing her kids around the park and carting them back and forth to school with her one-year-old on her hip. Loved cooking and cleaning and nagging and pinching pennies.

In some ways, it was true. I saw the way she looked at Mike when she thought no one was watching, and I saw the way he followed her around every room she was in, even after being together for close to twenty years. I knew she would never admit to wanting more for her life than what Mike was able to give her.

But she could have gotten it. It was hard not to imagine it for her sometimes too.

Well, when she wasn't pissing me off.

Nonna told Frankie to be careful in London and to see her after the baby was born, then hugged Kate and made her promise to visit her in Rome.

"You can count on it," Kate told her. "Hopefully in the spring. I want to hit up some sample sales and see what I can thrift for the shop, Italian style."

Nonna finally turned to me and reached out for my hands. She didn't say anything for a long while as her thumbs stroked my wrists, looking me over like she was searching for something to say. Something good. And finding nothing.

She tugged me close, and I had to lean down to hear her speak. Whatever she had to say, it wasn't for anyone else's ears.

"My baby Joni," she whispered fiercely. "You *find* yourself, okay? You find yourself, and you don't let go."

"Nonna," I started, but she cut me off with a fierce shake of her head that made her thick gold hoops sway from side to side.

"I know it's hard, *civetta*," she said. "But you have so much more than you think. I *know*, Joni. You just have to know it too. If you're willing to try."

My instinct was to avoid her stern gaze, those dark eyes that had always seemed to see everything I did, even if she didn't always say it.

She'd just always been there, from the time I was a baby when my actual mother went away and my father, her son, died.

Nonna was more my mother than a grandmother. And now she was leaving me too.

"You can do it, *tesoro*," she said. "I know you can."

Before I could help it, a tear slipped down my cheek. "I—okay. Thanks, Nonna."

I didn't want to say I would. I didn't want to make promises I couldn't keep. Doubt screamed through every cell in me, but I didn't want to voice that either.

All I could do was look into her eyes and try to absorb some of that hope she still had in me for some strange reason. And try to forget that starting tomorrow, I wouldn't be able to get it anymore.

Nonna stepped back to find that all of my siblings were fighting their own tears. After all, she hadn't just been a rock for me. She'd been the rock of our whole family. When things had gone to shit—which they had, too many times, in the Zola household—she'd been there, filling our house with love and lessons and a soft spot to land.

"I don't know why you're all crying," Nonna finally burst out, even as she wiped a few stray tears from her eyes too. "I'm just a few hours on a plane, not going to the moon!"

And just like that, we were all sobbing, huddled together in the kind of big family hug I hadn't experienced since I was small, since Matthew still lived at home and none of my siblings were married, and it was just us, the Zola kids and their grandparents, an unbreakable unit in a world that seemed to break everyone.

I buried my face in my sisters' arms, inhaled Nonna's gardenia perfume that I'd stolen when she thought I was cleaning, and relished the moment when no one was fighting or bickering.

I knew that love was at the heart of what it meant to be a Zola.

I only wished we could feel it a bit more.

"*Ciao*, babies!" Nonna called as she walked toward the gate.

We watched until she had gone all the way through security, until she gave us a little wave and vanished into the crowds.

AN HOUR LATER, we all emerged from Lea's minivan and piled into the tiny blue house she shared with her husband and their kids. There was barely room enough for the five of us in the living room, so I could understand why Lea hadn't allowed me to crash here. Her home was a shoebox.

"I could probably make a ziti if you're hungry," Lea said as she hung her keys on a rack next to the front door. That was followed by her coat and scarf on an already loaded row of hooks. "One last family dinner."

"No, I gotta get back to the shop tonight," Kate said. "I have a client coming in the morning, and I still haven't steamed all the things he wants to try."

"Xavi is going to be here in ten to pick me up too," Frankie said as she checked her watch. "The jet leaves Teterboro at seven."

"I'm driving back up to Boston tonight too," Matthew echoed. "I don't want Nina alone."

They all looked at me expectantly, expecting the final chorus.

Even Sunday dinners were finished, I thought bitterly. The Zola kids were splintering like kindling.

"Oh, don't worry about me," I said. "I have a busy schedule of staring at the ceiling in the shop's breakroom."

My siblings all shared meaningful looks. Then Frankie reached into her pocket and held out an envelope.

I took it. "What's this?"

"I told you I'd give you first and last," she said.

"I added a few extra too," Matthew said. "Nina and I wanted you to have enough to get some furniture or whatever you need."

"I popped a couple of twenties in there too," Kate said. "We were hoping you would have found a place today."

"Mike and I will help you move in," Lea added.

I swallowed as I took the envelope full of my siblings' charity and stared at the plain white exterior. "Overnight? Asking a bit much, don't you think?"

"Then use it tomorrow," Lea said, only a little too sharply. "Come over after the kids are at school, and I'll help you look. We can go into restaurants too, see if there's a hostess position open."

"With a toddler and a baby in tow? I'm sure that will really impress the landlords."

"Joni, come on."

"For your information, I *do* have a lead on a new job," I said. "Rochelle's waiting tables, and she invited me to join her."

It was sort of the truth. By way of omission. They didn't need to know what *kinds* of tables Rochelle was waiting, or the fact that I didn't really want to do it.

Because I felt bad about snapping at them all again, I waved the envelope at them. "Thank you for this, though. I will use it.

And...I am grateful for the breakroom, Lea. It's better than the street."

Kate sighed. "We'd never let it come to that, you know."

Did I? I wasn't so sure.

I accepted kisses from Kate and Frankie as they left, but Matthew lingered behind with Lea. Clearly, the two oldest had been planning something without the others.

"Spit it out," I said as I flopped onto Lea's saggy gray couch. I'd stay for a shower. God knew I needed one.

"Listen," Matthew said as he sat in Mike's ratty old armchair next to me while Lea hovered near the door. "I talked to Nina last night, and she's all right if you want to live with us in Boston for a while. Get a change of pace, and maybe get back on your feet. We can just throw your stuff in the back of my car and drive up tonight if you want."

I stared at him. "You want me to move to *Boston*?"

Matthew nodded. "It's not as bad as you might think. The pizza's garbage, and I'll cheer for the Red Sox when I'm dead in the ground, but I'm actually pretty happy up there."

"But there's no...there's like two dance companies there," I said. "What would I even do?"

"What are you doing here?" he posed back at me.

I couldn't answer that. And my brother knew it.

Instead, I made a face. "Isn't Nina about to give birth literally any day now?"

"Two months. But yeah, we're getting close."

Matthew looked unbearably proud. If I wasn't already so grossed out by my big brother making googly eyes at his socialite wife, I'd have been happy for him. He deserved a little happiness after taking care of the rest of us. But that didn't mean I needed to be the accessory to his life.

"I don't need to go to Boston just to be useless up there too and get in the way of your marital bliss," I said. "I'm doing just fine with that down here."

Not even a little bit true.

Matthew and Lea shared a long look as Lea moved to sit beside me on the couch.

"I'm worried about you," he said finally.

"Yeah, join the club," I cut back. "We *just* had this conversation last night."

"Which I hear went straight to shit after you stormed out," Matthew said. "But this isn't really about that. You want to live in the breakroom, live in the breakroom. You want to bartend and keep trying to dance, do that. But something happened this last year. You used to walk into a room and be the life of the party. Now you're just kind of…"

"A bitch?" I suggested.

My brother sighed. "I was going to say bitter, but if you want to roll that way, sure."

He pulled on the brim of the fedora he'd worn since Nonno had died. It was almost like a crown, if a crown could be an unbearably old-fashioned gray hat worn by pretty much every other grandpa in Belmont.

He was a good-looking guy. All my friends always had crushes on him when we were growing up. But to me, he would always be my big brother. The one who had basically been the next best thing to a father to me since I was a baby.

"You gotta get some decent threads, Mattie," I told him, with no other reason than simply to bug him. Because that's what baby sisters did. "You go home looking like this, and Nina is going to think she married a geriatric."

Matthew just cast me a long look with the green eyes all us Zola kids shared, and for the first time, I noticed the lines starting to form at the corners and the bits of silver appearing just over his ears. My brother wasn't a young man anymore. He had been carrying adult responsibilities most of his life.

"You'd get bitter too if the one thing you were put on earth to do became impossible," I said.

But Matthew shook his head. "It practically killed me to stop being a D.A., kid. Since college, I knew I was supposed to go after the bad guys. But now I'm working at a cushy firm, barbecuing on the weekends, and kissing my wife every chance I get. Sometimes, things change for a reason. I don't think it's just the knee that's bothering you. It's something else."

"After you left, someone named Shawn came by the house looking for you," Lea put in.

Goose bumps rose all over my arms. I was glad my jacket covered them.

"The change," Matthew said. "Does that guy have something to do with it?"

I stared at my hands, unable to look at either of them. I wasn't a bad liar, but my siblings knew every tell. It was imperative, however, that no one in my family ever know the mistake and former addiction that was Shawn Vamos. One that had started long before I'd ever thought I could dance on Broadway.

"Who is he?" Matthew pressed. "What did he want?"

Yeah, right. I wasn't about to tell my overprotective, former prosecutor brother about *that*. No way, no how. That shit was going with me to the grave.

I shrugged. "I don't know. Some guy."

On my other side, Lea snorted. "Probably another boyfriend of the hour. Is that where you went last night? To meet up with him?"

She looked over the clothes I still had on from last night. Judgment was practically oozing out of every pore she had. Again.

"For your information, that was a brand-*new* one-night stand, Lea. Don't worry. I don't remember the guy's name, but we definitely used protection. I'm not always as dumb as you think I am."

Lea and Matthew traded identically exasperated looks. Matthew stood up, clearly having had enough of this conversation. Or maybe he just didn't want to hear about his baby sister getting her fair share of tail too.

"I'm gonna go," he told Lea more than me.

She stood and crossed the room, then delivered a kiss to both of his cheeks, just like Nonna would. "Drive safe."

"Always do." He pulled up the collar of his wool overcoat and then turned to me. "The offer stands, Jo. Anytime you want a new place to land, let me know. I'll get you on the train before you know it."

The door closed behind him, leaving me in the room with only Lea while the sounds of crying children burst out from upstairs. She only shook her head.

"Sometimes," she said. "You don't have more sense than an empty piggy bank."

"MAMMMAAAAAAA!" cried a child I identified as Baby Lupe.

Lea sighed. "Come help me with dinner. If you're going to hang around, at least make yourself useful."

SIX

REASONS MY KNEE INJURY CAN FUCK OFF

#5 Mind over matter. Its only a Injery if I let it be.

"Please, Tom," I begged as I leaned toward my curmudgeonly old boss, reaching as far over the bar as I possibly could to give him a solid look down my shirt if he wanted it. "Just one itsy-bitsy, tiny little baby shift on the weekends. And then more when I blow your socks off."

Tom's gaze didn't even drop to where my cleavage was fully on display. "That only works on customers, kiddo. Stand up straight and listen for the twentieth time: the answer is no. You're not ready. And if you ask me again, you're fired."

I did stand up straight. And then pouted. Big time. Just like I'd been doing for the past six days, while I'd gone to look at four rooms in the Bronx, interviewed for five different waitressing jobs, and slept on the moldy old couch at the auto shop. Not one of the apartments was habitable. In two, there were mice walking across the living room floors like they were going for Sunday strolls. Meanwhile, none of the restaurants had wanted to hire me either, and unwilling to face Lea's sanctimonious puss after my failures, I'd settled for Snickers bars and stale coffee for dinner four nights in a row in the breakroom and showered at Rochelle's place when Carmine was at work.

I was done.

My sisters had had enough of me.

My friends had had enough of me.

I'd had just about enough of me.

Something had to give.

Tom just continued doing some kind of calculations next to the register while Carla, the other bartender on duty, just smirked from the other end of the bar. She was one of the full-time staff, worked Tuesday through Sunday, and collected all those delicious weekend tips. I was pretty sure they'd paid for her boob job too.

I should have known the girls weren't going to work on my boss. I wasn't sure if Tom even liked women—had never seen him even blink at his female staff or any of the near-naked go-go dancers. I should know. I used to be one.

So, I tried another tactic. Pity.

"Tom, *please*. I just really need the money. You don't understand —my grandmother moved to Italy, and I have to find a new place to live, like yesterday."

Tom stroked his gray mustache and gave me a side-eye. "Joni, you fed me that line four months ago when you wanted the promotion. And again two months again. And again last month."

"Yeah, but this weekend, it actually happened. Honest to God, Tommy, I'm sleeping on a lumpy sofa in my sister's auto shop right now. Please, just two extra shifts so I can stop smelling like motor oil and afford a room somewhere that's not also a rat's nest."

"I don't need the staff," Tom reiterated, though he pulled at his mustache nervously. "But…" He looked down at my knees. "One of my dancers did call in sick tonight."

I practically jumped. Well, I would have if I could have. "I'll do it."

One of Tom's caterpillar-shaped brows lifted. "What about your knee?"

"My knee can handle it for one night," I said. "I won't do anything crazy. Stick me on the end where no one really watches, and I'll just, I don't know, gyrate. I'll make standing around look like the best moves of the night. You know I will."

Before he could argue, I was already stepping out from the bar.

"Where are you going?" Tom asked.

I grinned and held up my phone. "Taking my break. I gotta call for some reinforcements so I can get ready to go on."

"ARE YOU SURE YOU CAN DANCE?"

Rochelle scanned me up and down with the same doubtful expression my boss had worn all evening. We stood in the middle of Tom's office while I put on one of the costumes she'd brought me from Diamonds, only ten blocks away. The silver booty shorts, matching crop top, and thigh-high boots were maybe a *little* more revealing than I would typically wear, but I figured if the outfit got through a pole routine, it would be fine for wriggling around on one of Opal's platforms.

"How can you move in this?" I asked as I tugged boots over the fishnet stockings, then pulled at the tiny silver top that barely covered my upper bits. "It feels like it would come right off. I'd rather be naked."

The boots were a little big—Rochelle's feet had about a size on mine. The shorts, however, were almost as small as my underwear, to the point where tugging them out of my butt was probably a losing battle.

"Well, that is the end goal," Rochelle commented wryly. "Not until I want it to, though."

I turned to the mirror to examine my appearance. My hair was pulled back into a tight ponytail, and I'd taken some extra care with stage makeup that wouldn't come off when I was sweating. It was a long way from the jeans, tank tops, and Vans I usually wore behind the bar. But the outfit felt like home to me. It was meant for the stage. Where I was meant to be.

"It looks good," she said. "And by the way, Kyle said he *does* need another server or two for the gambling clubs. Did you want to meet him?"

I bit my lip. I probably should have said yes. Frankie's money was burning a hole in my backpack, but no decent landlord was going to give me a place without more income.

Something was still holding me back, however. I couldn't quite make the jump from honest and poor to shady and, well, less poor.

"Ask me tomorrow," I said finally. "If my knee does all right tonight, I bet I can get Tom to give me back my platform Thursday through Sunday. Then, if I bartend a few other nights a week, that should be enough to get out of the breakroom."

Rochelle nodded. "Just let me know."

We packed up her stuff, and she walked me back to the bar, where things were already starting to pick up for a Thursday night.

"I'll wash the costume and drop it at your place tomorrow," I said as I rounded the bar to finish my shift before eleven, when I'd officially move to a platform for the first time in months. "You want a drink?"

Rochelle looked doubtfully down the bar. "Uh..."

"Shut up," I swatted through the air at her. "I can make you a rum and coke, bish."

She chuckled. "Let's see you try it, then."

I started pouring the drink, but already Rochelle was shaking her head. "Jo, that's bourbon, not rum. Try again, *mami*."

"Freaking brown liquor bottles all look the same," I said back.

"You look good, kiddo," Tom admitted when I sidled around him to grab another glass. "Like your old self."

I grinned up at him, cheeks tight with pleasure. "Thanks."

I couldn't lie. I was pretty damn excited, even if only to shimmy around like an idiot. For the last four months, I'd *ached* every time I watched the girls who had taken my place, knowing I could do better.

Last night, after sending out my sixth job inquiry, I'd gone for a long walk around Belmont. I found myself loitering outside the community center where I took my first dance classes. Through the windows, I could see the little girls in tutus fumbling their way through barre work. I envied every plié and port de bras.

So, I didn't care if this was a bad idea. I would have given *anything* to be on a stage again. I would have given my very soul.

I returned to where Rochelle was sitting and presented her with a finished rum and coke. My cousin took a sip and almost spit it out.

"Fuck, Jo, how much rum did you put in this?"

I eyed the beverage. "Um, I don't know. I just estimated."

"Well, it tastes like half the bottle." Rochelle took another sip and grinned. "Eh, I'll take it. Four buzzes for the price of one, am I right?"

Beside me, Tom groaned. "Joni, I told you, use the jigger until you really know your drinks. You're wasting liquor and costing me money."

I gave him another bright smile. "I'm sorry. Of course. I'll use the thingamajig—"

"Jigger," Tom said again. "It's called a *jigger*."

He stomped away, muttering something about "dumb kids" under his breath.

I just turned to Rochelle and giggled. "I can't say it. It sounds like a dirty word, don't you think?"

"You better learn, *mami*. Otherwise, you won't be able to keep this job neither." She stood up and grabbed her duffel. "I gotta go. If I don't start at Diamonds before midnight, the house fee doubles."

I made a face. "What does that mean?"

"Come dance with me, and I'll show you," she said. "Bye, baby."

We traded kisses, but when she straightened to leave, Rochelle froze.

"What is it?" I asked. "What's wrong?"

My cousin's mouth dropped open as she nodded toward the door.

"A stone-cold hottie just walked through the door, and he is staring right at you, *mami*," she said. "Something you haven't told me about this here job?"

I frowned. "What? No."

"Joni?"

At the sound of that familiar deep voice, something deep within my chest thrummed, like that velvety baritone called to the same part of me that hummed with excitement with every bass drop, every infectious beat coming from the DJ booth. I tensed—not, I realized, with dread or nerves, but because apparently, every cell in my body wanted to leap in the direction of the voice's owner.

Traitors.

I set the water glasses in front of my customers and turned. There he was, my very own Dr. McSteamy. Dr. Judgy-As-Fuck.

Nathan—excuse me, *Nathaniel*—Hunt. Looking at me like he had been searching for me my entire life.

SEVEN
HOW TO MAKE A GIN MARTINI

#4 Legit WHO CARES this drink is for old people

"Who," Rochelle said again. "Is *that?*"

I sighed. "No one." I leaned over and kissed her cheek one more time. "Go to work. I'll tell you later."

"Queen, you better." My cousin left, but not without giving Hunt a solid up and down as she walked out.

He didn't even seem to notice as he made his way to my side of the bar.

I checked the clock behind the register. Then my phone, just for good measure.

It wasn't even eleven.

He was never at the bar at this time of night. Usually showed up sometime past two, sometimes even three or four, closer to last call.

Instead of the basic, if immaculate, clothing he typically wore, this time, Hunt actually looked a doctor, with a pair of blue scrubs underneath his pea coat and the Hokas I'd seen him in before instead of shiny oxfords. He pushed his glasses up his nose as he stood at the bar and appraised me up and down, open but somehow without a drop of crudeness.

I had seen the way others noticed me the moment I emerged from Tom's office. There had been a whistle or two and plenty of men undressing me with their eyes.

Despite the fact that Hunt's open gaze lacked even a single of iota lewdness, his was the only one that affected me at all. As those brown eyes dragged back up my body, every bit of my skin seemed to flicker in response, like a candle that had just been lit.

Bastard.

"What are you doing here?" I demanded.

He swallowed and glanced around at the steadily growing crowd. Thursdays at Opal were usually somewhat crowded until about one thirty, which was why Tom shelled out for dancers to pump up the after-work crowd. It was probably a very different scene than the doctor was used to when he came in between two and three.

"There was a change at the hospital," he said, forced to speak louder to be heard over the noise. "I didn't have to work all night."

I crossed my arms. "I didn't ask you why you were here early. I asked why you are here at all. I told you to leave me the fuck alone."

He didn't answer right away but took his usual seat at the bar anyway. For some reason, I found it totally infuriating. What fucking game was this guy playing? Did he just get his rocks off all the time by torturing poor patients and bartenders?

Before I could ask him, a man in a blue striped shirt approached the bar. "Hey, gorgeous, can I get two gin martinis with twists?"

I sighed. "Right away."

Then I stood at the bar for a solid minute, trying and failing to look competent. What went into a martini again?

"Two and a half ounces of gin," Hunt said quietly enough that only I would hear him, though he appeared to be studying his fingernails. "Half ounce of vermouth. Twist of lemon."

I scowled. "I knew that."

He looked up, that gaze still forceful but open. Patient, even.

But he didn't say anything more.

Dick.

I finished the drinks and took the customer's card to close him out.

"Can I give you my number too?" he asked when I handed it back to him.

"Only if you want it in the garbage, baby," I said with a sickeningly bright smile. I knew this type. Men like him loved to be treated like shit by beautiful women, but only if you smiled while you did it.

It worked like a charm.

"Let me know if you change your mind," he said as he laid an extra twenty on the bar.

I swiped it up before he could change his.

Hunt didn't react to the exchange, but his dark eyes still followed me as I dropped the money into the tip jar behind the counter.

"Do you want your Macallan?" I asked him before helping several others waiting for drinks.

He shook his head. "No, help them first."

So he wanted to wait. Well, I had no problem with that.

Which he did. But not without quietly narrating the recipes for cosmopolitans, old-fashioneds, a mojito, a sidecar, and a lemon drop.

It was like having Siri talk me through a bartending class, if Siri looked like a movie star and spoke like a voice actor. I would have been annoyed if it hadn't been so helpful.

"How do you know all those drinks?" I asked once I was through the line and finally able to pour his whiskey.

Hunt accepted the brown liquid and swirled it under his nose. He took a small sip and set it back on the coaster. "My mother enjoys cocktails. We all learned the basics when we were children."

He didn't elaborate on who "we" were, and to my surprise, I found I wanted to know. Just like I wanted to know what kind of mother asked her children to mix her drinks regularly enough that they would memorize a textbook's worth of mixology.

I didn't ask, though, because I was also irritated that he piqued my interest in the first place.

And I did not want to be interested in anything about Nathan Hunt. Not at all.

"I'm surprised you wanted to show yourself in here," I said while

I took advantage of the lull in orders to wipe down the bar top. "Lower yourself to interact with an exotic dancer like myself."

Dr. Hunt blinked. "Did something change in the last week?"

God. Not him too.

"Not a thing," I lied with a fake, fake smile. "I'm walking on sunshine, can't you tell? It's always been my life's dream to show my tits to horny men."

Hunt looked confused. "I assume you're being sarcastic."

I huffed. He waited.

Fuck it. He already knew I was a mess, and I wasn't hiding anything. "This is just the face of someone who is running out of options."

I waited for him to ask me why. Drummed my fingers on the bar, tapped my toes on the ground, chewed my lower lip in anticipation of the next cutting remark where he would tell me I was an idiot or critique my increasingly inevitable career path.

I waited for his gaze to shift too. To drift down my body, openly eye my breasts, hips, legs, and everything else like a vulture ready to land on its carrion. I'd seen it too many times when other men learned I was a dancer and thought it meant the exotic variety. Once you crossed into that field, a certain—and large—portion of the world thought that meant every part of you was up for grabs.

But Hunt's gaze remained squarely on my face, pensive and unmoving. As solid as the building we were in. He stared, and I found myself staring back, the two of us caught in a tunnel of our own making. One that finally seemed to quiet all the noise that was constantly in my head. One that made my hands and feet still and my breathing come easier.

Then he pulled something out of his pocket.

"I stopped by to bring you something," he said as he set a package on the bar top.

"A present?" I joked, though something inside me squeezed. Why, I couldn't say. I didn't want *anything* from Nathan Hunt, much less a gift.

"Not really."

I opened the padded manila envelope and drew out a folded

sheet of paper and then a familiar garment: the emerald green bra I'd misplaced five days ago in his schmancy old building. "Where did you get this?"

Hunt tilted his head. "I found it."

"In your building? Oh my *God*, it was probably hanging off my clothes or something, wasn't it?" I slapped a hand to my face, imagining myself striding through that gilded lobby with my underwear hanging out from under my shirt.

He didn't correct me. Christ, that walk of shame went even worse than I had even realized.

"What is this?" I demanded as I shoved the bra back into the packet, then set it under the bar to grab later. "Some kind of messed up game? You don't have to show me the error of my ways, Dr. Hunt. I'm fully aware I'm a slutty bartender without common sense or any brains. My family, my boss, my friends—they tell me that all the time, so I definitely don't need some stuck-up doctor to point it out on a daily basis."

By the time I was done, Hunt's expression had barely shifted, though his brown eyes swirled with something like surprise.

"I—" He swallowed. "I wasn't trying to tell you that at all."

"Oh, *really*?" I snarked back.

He shook his head. "No. I assumed the bra was yours, so I brought it back when I found it. And…" He swallowed again, then pointed at the note. "The rest is in there."

I stared at the white piece of paper. I didn't want to pick it up. I didn't want any of this.

"I'm not always very good at saying what I mean," he continued. "Or at least what I…feel. It's an apology. For what happened in my office. And, um, the other day too, I suppose. I didn't understand that I'd offended you until I saw you exiting my building, and then I didn't know how to reach you otherwise, so I came here. That's, um, all."

"Hey, can we get a row of vodka shots, lady?"

"In a minute," I snapped. Then I picked up the note and took my sweet damn time reading it.

JONI,

PLEASE FORGIVE MY RUDE BEHAVIOR. IF I GAVE YOU ANY REASON TO THINK I WAS JUDGING YOUR PROFESSIONAL CHOICES, I APOLOGIZE. I RESPECT WHATEVER CHOICES YOU MAKE FOR YOUR BODY, YOUR JOB, OR ANY OTHER PARTS OF YOUR LIFE. MY ONLY CONCERNS ORIGINATE OUT OF FRIENDSHIP AND RESPECT.

SINCERELY,
NATHAN

His handwriting was small and neat—the opposite of what I would have expected from a doctor. He wrote with a mild cursive that I had to go over more times than I would have admitted to anyone to understand completely, so it took even longer than usual for me to get through it. But when I was finished, I didn't throw it in the trash. Instead, I folded it into a very small square and slid it into my shorts at my hip.

Hunt—no, *Nathan*—waited while I poured the vodka shots and made a few other drinks before I was finally able to return to him. When I did, he was staring at the note, the square visible through the tight silver fabric.

"You have terrible handwriting," I told him. When he held out his card to pay for his still-full drink, I shook my head. "It's on me."

"That's not necessary. I'm the one apologizing."

"So you did," I said. "And I appreciate it."

Nathan frowned. "That drink is very expensive. I don't want it coming out of your pay."

I didn't want that either, but somehow, tonight, it didn't feel right.

I thought about the note again. It contained words I'd so rarely heard from anyone. Respect. Friendship. Forgiveness.

And then I thought about the other word he said to me too.

"It's fine, really," I said. "I accept your apology. And, well, it's kind of hard to be mad at someone who tells you that you're perfect."

The noise seemed to die down as we stared at each other again. Even in the dark light, Nathan's eyes gleamed like silk. Full of promise. And something else I couldn't quite name that made me quiver like a plucked violin string.

"Well, I am sorry," he told me. "Please believe me. I was only surprised by your request." Tentatively, he took a sip of scotch, though his eyes maintained their focus on me.

"You're very intense," I said bluntly. "Do you know that?"

Nathan set down his drink. "I—yes. Yes, I'm aware."

"And it doesn't bother you that might put other people off?"

He seemed to think about that for a moment. "It does. I try to be attuned and adjust my behavior when necessary. But trying to be something I'm not capable of feels…uncomfortable. Painful, even. I don't do it unless I absolutely have to."

I swallowed. Yeah, I knew how that felt.

"So, you don't think less of me because I might be taking my clothes off for money in the near future?" I asked.

I was pushing; I knew. And rewarded when he almost spit out his drink.

But he didn't.

And I had to hide a smile myself.

"It's none of my business," Nathan managed after he finally swallowed. "It's your life, Joni, not mine. I would never judge anything you chose to do with it."

I adjusted the silver strap of the bra top, almost like I was bracing for a blow. If anyone else from my neighborhood had said something like that, I'd have thought they were joking. I felt like I was waiting for the punch line. Emphasis on punch.

"You don't usually dress like this at the bar," Nathan said, his gaze flickering ever-so-briefly to my skimpy clothes.

I looked down at them and back up. I thought I saw him looking at my legs, but it was too quick to tell. His eyes were as steadfast as ever, never drifting, never ogling. Not once.

Perfect, he'd said.

What did that even mean?

"I'm on one of the platforms tonight." I pointed to the staggered stages set into the wall above a row of VIP booths. "I used to dance there every weekend when I was in between gigs. The one in the middle is my old spot."

Nathan followed my finger like he'd never before observed the architecture of the bar despite having been here so many times. "Oh."

"Don't worry. Opal isn't that kind of club, so I won't *demean* myself by removing my clothes."

I couldn't help it. It was like picking at a scab covering a much larger wound, knowing that it would never heal unless I opened it up completely.

Nathan only shrugged. "Well, since you're not wearing very much right now anyway, I don't think it would make a difference. Although, at your other job, I suppose you'd need to be able to remove the rest easily, correct?"

I sighed. Why was it so hard to get under his skin? Especially when he was *so* good at getting under mine? "Ugh. For the record, I'm not a stripper, all right? Not that it would matter if I was, but I'm not."

Was it odd that I could almost hear a "yet" at the end of my own sentence?

I could practically hear Rochelle cheering from the Bronx.

Nathan turned his glass back and forth on the bar, almost meditatively. "Then why did you tell me you were? Or planning to be?"

This time, I couldn't quite meet his eyes. "Well, who knows what I'll be? And bigger boobs would come in useful here. You see what happens with a lot of the male customers. I figured I could turn that into some life-changing tips with the right equipment."

He frowned, like something didn't quite compute. "You want an augmentation to serve drinks *here*?"

"Oh my God, shout it, why don't you!" I hissed.

I grabbed a lime and started cutting it far too quickly, given how dull the knife was and the fact that I could barely see it through the tears suddenly clouding my vision. I could practically smell the desperation wafting off me like perfume. Could he? Could everyone in here?

A pair of large, capable hands descended on top of mine, stilling the knife. I looked up to find Nathan standing, having reached across the bar to steady me in my rage.

Every bit of anger fled, replaced by the electricity passing through our touch. And then something I wasn't prepared for at all. Something like peace.

"Joni," he said. "Please listen. And try not to slice your fingers."

I sniffed and shook a bit of hair out of my face, but released my grip on the knife. "What's the point?"

People around us were watching curiously by now. The other bartenders, dancers flirting with customers, even Tom through the window of his office. But Nathan didn't seem to notice or care. His gaze was as unwavering as ever, magnified by those simple silver frames, focused wholly on me.

"I'm not good at reading people's emotions," he said, just under the thump of bass vibrating across the lounge. "But when I know them well, I can read their bodies. Your eyes are very wet. You are about to cry. So I want to know why. I want to know what I did to make you so upset. Will you tell me?"

I blinked away the tears that were threatening more than ever. "You can't tell? Really?"

Nathan shook his head. "I know it's something I said, but I don't know what. You don't seem to like it when men look at your body and make sexually suggestive comments. At the same time, you move with—you hold yourself with so much grace, so much more at ease with your body than most. So, I didn't understand why you would want to change yourself that way. If it's what you really want, I won't say anything more about it. But I..." He released my hands then, only to push his glasses up his nose. One of his few nervous tics, I realized. "I don't think you really do."

I sniffed back a few more tears. "You don't know shit about me. You know I'm cute. You know I mix drinks. You know before that day in your office, I was nice to you. That's it."

For the first time, Nathan's full mouth twisted, like he'd tasted something unpleasant.

"I know more than that," he said. "I know you're kind to people when you don't have to be. That you have four sisters and one brother and you care deeply about what they think of you. That you live in the Bronx. There's more, but the point is that I listen when you talk, whether it's to Tom or another customer or sometimes to yourself when you're making mental lists of things to remember."

This time, I was the one who stared. How in the *hell* did he know all of that? Had I actually said those things over the past months? It wasn't impossible. But Nathan had never seemed like he was listening. And all this time he was paying that close of attention?

For what?

But before I could reply, the lights in the bar dropped suddenly, and the music changed from evening-friendly hip-hop to the more bass-heavy dance music preferred by the late-night clientele.

"Joni," Tom called from the other end of the bar. "Let's go."

I turned back to Nathan, then looked up to where other girls were starting to take their places on the platforms. "It's showtime."

EIGHT
STUFF I DO WHEN I'M NERVOUS

#8 Bite my nails. Stop it its so gross

I expected him to leave after that. I'd completely ignored his question, and let's be real: emotions aren't the hottest thing in the world, especially not to a man in the middle of a crowded bar where people came to escape things like insecurities and sadness, not to embrace them.

But Nathan stayed put on his favorite barstool, now sitting on his jacket while he held the scotch I knew he'd never finish. He was completely unaware of the effect he was having on nearly every woman within a five-foot radius, all of whom were openly eyeing the way the hot doctor's biceps stretched the confines of his scrub shirt.

I'd noticed too. Just like I'd noticed the way his butt filled out the otherwise shapeless blue pants. And the way his forearms had flexed when he'd held my hands.

I didn't want to notice.

But I did.

And now, I wasn't mad at all, and I couldn't understand why.

All I knew was that as I headed for the stage entrance inside

Tom's office, it was Nathan Hunt's beautiful brown eyes I continued to see. They were so warm, making me wonder about the rest of him. The way those broad shoulders might feel if I burrowed into them. How those arms might protect me from the rest of the world. If his breath might whisper warmth over my neck and ear as he stroked my hair.

In other words, I was even more ridiculous than usual, now fantasizing about a hot, pretentious doctor just because he had said the magic words no man had ever said: "I'm sorry."

Pathetic.

In Tom's office, I climbed the stairs that crisscrossed the wall, finding the door that opened to my assigned platform on the other side. Stupid, stupid, stupid. Caught up in Nathan's and my conversation, I hadn't even warmed up, hadn't even stretched. I was about to dance for the first time in months, completely cold.

Another dancer named Ella waved from where she was about to go on. "Hey, Joni. Glad you're back!"

I waved, though nerves danced in my belly, and my legs felt like a baby deer's. "Thanks, me too."

As I stepped out onto my platform, I couldn't help but steal glances at Nathan sitting at the bar, though now he was rotated outward to face the dancers. He sat straight and tall, a beacon of stability in the midst of all the chaos.

A remix of "Rhythm is a Dancer" by Snap! poured through the speakers, its strong baseline drowning out my thoughts and thrumming through my body. Tom had a thing for nineties electro-pop, which made people take to the dance floor like this was the Roxy, not a lounge that technically had no cabaret license. I started to twist and turn, feeling the eyes of the crowd on me. The stage lights from behind me transformed me into a seductive silhouette, a snakelike seductress moving for the audience's pleasure.

I spun and writhed, eager to show off. Okay, maybe this wouldn't be so bad. My body was remembering its tricks, sliding into the movements like riding a bike. I didn't have to be the sad, shitty bartender right now. I didn't have to be that sad girl with nowhere to live and no real life to speak of. This was who I was *supposed* to be, so why had I thought I couldn't do this anymore? The pain in my knee was barely a twinge.

I could do this. I *was* doing it. I was killing it.

I was falling to the ground.

With a vicious stab, my knee gave out just as I was playing with a pirouette-like move. I stumbled against the rounded wall of the platform and fell to the bottom, clutching my knee as pain scissored through me. I only narrowly missed rolling off the tiny stage completely, though I barely would have noticed.

Fuck, it really hurt.

"Joni!"

Nathan's deep voice thundered over the bass. Seconds later, he was there, hopping up onto the platform, lifting me into his arms, and cradling me against his chest.

It was even warmer and more solid than I could have possibly imagined.

"Honey, goddammit. Are you all right?"

Tom appeared below us, worry crinkling his brow. Behind him, some of the bar patrons were pointing and laughing, even though they hadn't stopped dancing.

"I—oh my God, it hurts!" I pulled my knee to my chest.

"She needs ice and elevation," Nathan told him. "Where can I bring her?"

"Back into my office. Second door off the bathrooms. I'll send someone back with a bag of ice."

Nathan carried me easily down the steps and into Tom's office, where he set me on the worn sofa in the corner. We were soon followed by Tom, who handed Nathan a bag of ice.

"I have her," Nathan said as he removed his coat and laid it over the back of the couch.

Tom looked him up and down, observing his scrubs. "Doctor, huh?"

"Surgeon."

Tom looked at me as he tugged on his mustache. "You good with this, honey? I gotta—"

"Get back to the bar," I finished for him. "I'm fine. Go."

With another glance Nathan's way, Tom walked back up to close the door to the platform, then left the office. As the door shut behind him, it muted the music out front, enclosing Nathan and me in quiet for the first time since he'd walked in.

"Hold this on it." Nathan positioned a pillow under my knee, then placed the ice on top of it. He frowned. "I should probably take you to the hospital."

"Absolutely fucking not," I said quickly, despite the fact that pain was tightening my voice. "I mean, no, thank you. It's the same injury; I just shouldn't have danced. It will be fine tomorrow. Good enough to stand on, anyway."

Nathan did not look convinced.

I rolled my eyes. "Do you have any idea how expensive a trip to the ER is? Why should I do that when I have a doctor here for free?"

"Joni, I'm a plastic surgeon, not an orthopedist."

"Yes, I am aware of that, Dr. Hunt," I replied. "It was a joke. But seriously, I'm fine. I'll be *fine*."

I would be, too. The pain was already receding, and while, sure, I'd probably have a bit of swelling for a day or two, I'd be back on my feet in time to serve drinks and look pretty by Tuesday.

Just no more pirouettes.

Probably never again.

The idea was like a hand flattening me to the earth. Just like always.

"You said one thing."

I blinked as Nathan's voice pulled me out of the shadow. "Huh?"

"In my office." His hand was still settled on the ice pack, a solid weight that I swore burned even through the ice. "You said your body was only good for one thing, and now that's gone. What did you mean by that? What was the one thing?"

"Oh. Um. Dancing. Which I obviously can't do anymore." I gestured at my knee.

He looked a bit confused. "Then why did you agree to dance tonight?"

"It's not the same. Up there, it's just club dancing. We only have to look hot and twist around on the platform. I ended up like this because I tried something I shouldn't have." I pinked, not wanting to admit I'd been doing that partially to impress *him*.

"But before you could do it…whatever it was?"

I nodded. "I used to be a professional dancer. The kind people work their whole lives to become. I was supposed to debut in *Chicago* a few months ago, but my knee blew out right before my first night. Some luck, huh?"

Nathan's eyes brightened with sudden understanding. "You sustained an injury. This same one?"

I shoved his shoulder. "You don't have to look so excited."

That dimple appeared again. "I like it when things make sense. Even better when the problems is potentially one I can solve."

"Don't get your hopes up. Other doctors have tried and failed. I'm just trying to accept the fact that I'm washed up at twenty-four."

Nathan seemed to ruminate as he looked me over. His gaze, however, didn't burn like it did before. For the first time, he was actually looking at me with that evaluating expression I'd seen on other doctors' faces before. One that likes a challenge.

"And you thought I was shaming you for dancing however you could," he muttered. Then to me: "What happened?"

I shrugged. I always felt like an idiot trying to explain it. "I was in rehearsal and tried this move I had no business doing. I wanted to impress the director. Tore my ACL instead. That was last August."

I was embarrassed to tell him I had only understood half of what the doctors had told me. That when they gave me the papers following my surgery, I couldn't understand most of that either. But then, again, what normal people could?

"I was supposed to mostly recover in two months, plus a while for extra physical therapy," I said. "And it did get better. Enough that I can walk, obviously. And stand. And even do some easy stuff, like I did tonight. But real performance is out. I can't jump or run. I can't do any complex turns. I ruined it and lost everything."

"Who was your doctor?"

"Um…some guy at Mt. Sinai West." I shrugged.

"My practice uses their OR. What's his name? Maybe I know him."

I shrugged again, feeling uncomfortable. "I don't know."

"You don't know who cut into your body?" Nathan sounded utterly dumbfounded. A lot like my sisters, actually.

I buttoned my lips shut. "I was in a lot of pain, okay? And it was late, and I'm already bad with names. They just gave me someone there, then scheduled a surgery with someone different. Maybe his name was Carver? Clinger? I don't know. I haven't been back since."

Nathan's big brown eyes somehow grew even bigger, magnified through his lenses. "What do you mean, you haven't been back since? What about follow-up? Post-op, physical therapy, future prognosis?"

I resisted the urge to turn away. "I missed an appointment, and they never rescheduled. I did see the PT for a while, but my insurance lapsed after I had to leave the show. Maybe you can afford a hundred and fifty bucks an hour for some massage and exercises, but I can't. Not with my income of three hundred bucks a week. Four if I'm lucky."

Nathan studied my knee under his broad hands for a long time. I took the time to study those hands. Surgeon's hands. Strong, yet dexterous. Steady and capable, just like the rest of him.

I bet he didn't struggle even a little to finish high school, much less college and medical school and whatever else he had to do to become a doctor. I bet reading books was as easy as breathing to him and that he could listen to his professors and remember everything they said. I bet he'd never had to beg anyone for work and live above *his* sister's auto shop just to survive.

Right now, Nathan seemed to be taking several deep breaths, clearly oblivious to the roller coaster of shame my brain was riding. Finally, he released my knee and sat back on his haunches.

"Well, your knee didn't heal correctly. ACL repair can take up to a year to recover, but I wouldn't expect a little turn like that to flatten you. You shouldn't be in this kind of pain after so long."

"No, I shouldn't," I said, pushing myself up on the couch. "Which is why I'm taking up another profession."

He surveyed me critically. "You mean taking off your clothes? Do

I have to point out that exotic dancers probably do the same thing you just did to hurt yourself?"

The fact that he said "probably" didn't escape me. Probably. As in, he was guessing. As this beautiful, wholesome man had never set foot in a place like Diamonds or its owner's dirty gambling rings and probably never would.

I didn't hate it.

"I am aware of that," I said. "Which is why I would just be serving drinks. *If* I take the job. But it's still an industry built on tips, you know, so looking hot is going to earn me something more."

Something like realization dawned on his face. "Ergo, a breast augmentation."

I rolled my eyes. "Come on, *Nathaniel*. You saw what I have—or, you know, *don't* have—down there. It's a good investment."

"An investment."

"Yeah, an investment. You're repeating yourself again. Why do you do that?"

He opened and closed his mouth several times before shoving his hand back through his hair. His other tell—one that seemed to be motivated more by aggravation than nerves. It made the curls bounce pleasantly and, for some reason, made him even more attractive.

"I do that when I'm trying to understand something difficult," he said finally. "An investment in what?"

I sighed. "People—and by people, I mostly mean the ones with testicles—like to look while I serve them drinks. Bigger tits, bigger tips, or so I've been told. You follow?"

His brows were furrowed so hard they basically made one across his handsome forehead. "How much?"

"How much for what?" I replied, more than ready to leave. My knee was numb, and I was cold. I didn't like the third degree from my own grandmother, and I sure as shit didn't like it from a guy who thought rescuing me from a fall gave him the right to interrogate my life choices.

"How much more would you make with larger breasts?" Nathan's full mouth twisted like he had eaten something sour. "Have you calculated a clear difference? How long would it take you to earn back the cost of the surgery? Is that number accounting for your other expenses?"

"I don't know, all right! A while. Six months, probably. But it doesn't matter because I need the extra money right *now*, and I wouldn't have had to sell my life away to pay for the stupid surgery to begin with. It was a dead end, just like everything else."

I turned my face toward Tom's cluttered desk. Nathan didn't need to know how horrible those questions made me feel.

"Why?"

It was so Nathan. Short and to the fucking point.

I swallowed. What did it matter if he knew the rest of it? No doubt he already thought I was pathetic. Just like everyone else.

"Because I'm basically homeless," I finally admitted. "Five days ago, I had to move into the break room in my brother-in-law's body shop until I can figure out something else. *If* I can figure out something else."

It was the first time I'd said it all out loud, just like that. And I'd never been more humiliated. Because it wasn't like I was confessing to one of my dancer friends, people who also barely had their shit together and who could just as easily end up in a situation just like mine. Nathan was a doctor. He lived in a fancy building on the river. He was clearly someone who'd had *his* shit together for years, probably his whole life.

"What do you mean, *if?*"

I sighed. There it was. The disbelief. Or maybe the realization. Everyone who knew me went through one stage or the other.

Usually, I was a good mimic. I had five siblings to learn from, after all. I knew the expressions Matthew wore when he was figuring something out, or how Marie, the consummate wallflower, appeared when she was listening really hard. I'd heard Frankie jabber on about books enough that I could nod along when people mentioned titles that I knew. I could generally pretend to be competent in polite conversation, at least to the point where people didn't generally know the truth.

But when anyone took the time to peek behind the curtain of my daily performances, they would always find the same thing.

Frenzy.

Chaos.

A complete and total mess.

I didn't know why I hated more than anything for this doctor I hardly knew to discover what everyone else already had, but I did. I really did.

Two fingers slipped under my chin, forcing me to look up. But when I finally managed to drag my gaze back up to meet his, there were none of the emotions I had feared. He didn't tell me I was an idiot or spoiled or that I needed to focus or grow up finally or any of the other things I'd been hearing for days and weeks and honestly my entire life. There was no pity. No disgust. Just open curiosity while he listened and then considered my story.

"I don't believe the word is *if* you find a solution to your problems," Nathan said with his particular brand of steady, no-nonsense factuality. "It's when. It's how. I don't know you well, but I believe in you."

I blinked. And stared. And wondered how in the *hell* I'd never heard anyone say those things before to me, but the reality was, I hadn't.

And so I did the only thing that made sense in my addled, confused brain.

I blinked at the handsome doctor who said I was perfect, who said I was worth believing in.

And I threw my arms around his neck and kissed him.

At first, it was a little like kissing a mannequin. A very warm mannequin with soft yet firm lips that gradually came alive under mine as I nibbled at the bottom one. Automatically, my tongue slipped out to meet his, and before I knew it, I was pulling him on top of me, threading my fingers into his curls, moaning into his mouth, and enjoying the way a deep groan emerged from the bottom of his chest as he gave in at last.

His lips met mine again in a way that was concentrated yet relaxed, full of the same intention that had filled every unmasked look, every direct question he'd given me. Nathan kissed me with purpose that was wholly within his control but also feral. Kind and still bordering on the edge of wicked.

Every muscle in his body seemed to tense, quivering like a bow waiting to be released.

I wondered what would happen if he did.

The thought made me shiver from head to toe.

Then he stopped. I tried to keep him with me, kissed along that impossibly sharp jawline, attempted again to suck his bottom lip between my teeth.

"Joni." Nathan's breath was warm against my cheek, slightly heavy, his voice a little hoarse as he managed to detangle my fingers from his shirt collar. Gradually, he unwound my arms from his neck and set my hands back in my own lap so he could sit up again on the edge of the sofa.

Realization flooded me. My stupid, rash decision making. My idiot brain.

"Oh, *shit*," I said. "Oh my God, I'm so sorry. You were just—you rescued me—and then you were here—and you listened—and you were actually nice, and—"

"And you're overwhelmed," Nathan completed kindly as he adjusted his glasses. "Maybe in a little shock, too. It's all right. It happens."

Through his lenses, I was surprised to find, once again, no sign of judgment. A little surprise, maybe. And an admittedly swollen mouth. Just kind understanding and a clear head while he looked me over with the same clinical expression he'd worn when he examined my knee.

Doctor Hunt. Nothing more.

I slapped my hands over my face. I wanted to shrink into a ball and roll away. I wanted to hide under my covers and never come out. Even if they were the ones in the breakroom.

"God, I'm such a mess," I moaned. "I'm sorry. So fucking sorry. See, this is why the question is *if*. Because this is what I do in a crisis. I kiss the nice doctor instead of thanking him like a normal human. I make rash decisions instead of acting logically."

"I don't, though." When I peeked through my fingers, Nathan tipped his head to one side. "As it happens, I've been told I can be too logical at times. But maybe that would be helpful right now."

"Oh, yeah?" I mumbled. "How?"

I watched as he rubbed his chin, then pushed his glasses up his nose again before saying the very *last* thing I'd ever thought I'd hear.

"You need a place to live. And as it happens, I need a new roommate. Therefore, you should move in with me."

NINE

REASONS I AVOID THE UPPER WEST SIDE

#1 Cant think of any but I def dont belong hear

"This is the service elevator. The co-op requires that all major deliveries go in and out of there, which would include your furniture if you take the room."

Approximately ninety minutes after I'd nearly face-planted off the platform at Opal, I limped after Nathan as he continued his tour around the lobby of 60 Riverside Drive, calmly pointing out things like mailboxes and doormen while I kept looking around, waiting for my one-night stand to pop out of one of the corners like a Jack-in-the-Box.

I had changed out of the silver hot pants back into my regular jeans, T-shirt, and leather jacket. My knee was throbbing but had improved after I'd swallowed a bunch of ibuprofen.

"All right?" Nathan asked when he realized I was lagging behind him on his way to the main elevator.

I nodded and slung the duffel bag full of Rochelle's clothes over my shoulder. "Just a little slow. I need to ice again, I think."

Nathan frowned at my knee, then took the bag without asking.

"Let's go upstairs. I have some cold packs in the freezer you can use while we discuss the rental agreement."

I barely paid attention to the quiet luxuries of the building as we walked back through the lobby to the main residents' elevator. And why would I? I'd been here only a week before.

Even so, I hadn't really paid attention then either. Had there always been two doormen to protect residents, plus two other men to operate the elevators? Were the prewar penny tiles in the lobby always as shiny as new coins? Or maybe it was only without a roaring hangover that I could appreciate the smear-free mirrors that circled the lobby or the refurbished art deco chandeliers hanging every ten feet or so. Everything screamed quiet, well-maintained opulence.

It was a far cry from my shabby old house in Belmont.

"So, why does a rich guy like you need a roommate anyway?" I asked as I followed Nathan into the elevator. "What's the catch?"

Nathan glanced at the operator, who acted like a piece of furniture. "No catch."

I narrowed my eyes. "I don't believe you."

Nathan shrugged. "Maybe I'm just making up for the fact that I offended you multiple times."

The elevator operator didn't even twitch. Talk about professional.

"By offering me a place to live?" I pressed. "That's a crazy way to say you're sorry."

"By doing you a favor," Nathan clarified. "I assume you'll want your own place eventually, so this wouldn't be permanent. I have a spare room that needs to be filled. When you find a better job that you actually want, you can save up and move out, and my conscience will be clean. Everyone wins."

I watched him as the elevator continued upward, looking for any indication of deceit. A twitching eyelid, a shifty gaze.

But Nathan only watched me right back until the elevator stopped, and the operator opened it onto the ninth floor.

"Come on," he said. "There are a few more amenities up on the general tour."

I stepped out, expecting to find a hallway like the one where I'd made my escape only days before. Instead, I found myself staring through several glass walls, each marking the boundaries of a few different exercise rooms available for residents.

It was the last thing I'd expected to see in a prewar building in New York.

The place had its own *gym*. Its own pool. A barbecue patio. A squash court.

It wasn't an apartment building. It was a freaking resort.

"There's a weight room and some cardio machines." Nathan ticked off the different areas as we walked down the hall. "A sauna down the hall and a pool on the deck that's open in the summer. And down there is a studio I thought you might be interested in."

I hobbled toward one of the glass doors. "A studio?"

Through the glass was a room lined with mirrors on both sides, a ballet bar affixed to them, with some various gym equipment and heavy bags stashed at the end.

It was a dance studio. Which Nathan had chosen to show to me. Tonight.

"I, um, thought you might want to use it sometime," he said. "To...practice."

"On my crappy knee? Doubtful." I eyed the mats in the corner. "I could do some Pilates and barre work, though."

Nathan dropped my bag on the floor, then leaned against the wall and crossed his arms, which made his muscles bulge distractingly, even in his pea coat. "It's none of my business if you continue dancing or not, but it seems like you want to. I'd assume you should keep up your strength as best you can. If you're not interested—"

"Oh, I am," I said quickly. "I—" I sighed. "Sorry, I'm just overwhelmed, and it makes me snappy. I haven't actually been inside a studio in months. The last time I did was after I was cleared by my PT. I fell even worse than when you caught me."

My cheeks heated at the memory—not of falling in front of half the New York dance community months ago, but of tonight and how it felt being carried around in Nathan's arms like I weighed literally nothing. The broad refuge of his chest and the brightness in his eyes when he'd offered to take me here.

Now, however, he was all business.

"Well, it's available if you want it."

Nathan paused, forehead crinkling with thought. Then he shook his head, and I found myself dying to know whatever he'd been thinking.

Or maybe I didn't want to know. Maybe it was the same as everyone else—that I was an idiot for even having that dream in the first place.

"I thought it might make up for…" Nathan straightened and rubbed his palms together. "The other misunderstandings between us. Moving in here will solve both our problems."

"Except for the one about how we don't even like each other?" I joked.

Nathan blinked rapidly. "We don't like each other?"

I mirrored his confusion. "We *do*?"

Nathan shuffled on his feet. "I—I'm sorry. I had no idea you didn't like me, Joni."

I coughed. "Nathan, I literally told you to fuck off. What did you think that meant?"

His hands pulled at each other, almost like he was cracking his knuckles, but with a more frenetic energy than I'd seen from him before. "That you were angry. I didn't—Jesus. I said I was sorry—what else—"

It was the first time I'd ever seen him this confused. And upset by it. Like he honestly didn't know what was happening.

"Hey." I set a hand on his shoulder, urging him to calm down. My touch seemed to help. "I'm sorry, man."

"No, *I'm* sorry. I had no idea I'd offended you so badly that you hated me."

"I don't hate you." I shrugged. "Or even dislike you. Anymore. Honestly, I don't really know you. But if it's any consolation, something has changed in the last hour. You went from being a stiff jerk to just kind of socially awkward." I glanced at the dance studio. "And nice. I have a feeling that underneath the weirdly direct questions lives a genuinely thoughtful person."

A warmth entered Nathan's eyes, and his mouth quirked, suggestive of a shy smile that I had a feeling would melt me into a puddle if I ever saw it emerge. "So, now that I've appropriately apologized, how do you feel about me now?"

That you're so…odd, I thought to myself as the list formed itself in my head.

How I Feel About Nathan Hunt

1. That by some miracle, he has no freaking idea how handsome he is.
2. That he's a walking bag of oxymorons: kind yet cold, warm yet clinical.
3. That he's really smart about some things and completely oblivious to others. Just like me.

"I don't know," I said finally. "But I think you might be a good person after all."

That hint of a smile deepened into a full-on suggestion, turning the dimple in his left cheek into more than just a hint. "Well, that's good. Especially since I'm not the easiest person to live with."

I sighed. Now, we were getting to the truth.

"I'll stay out of your hair," I told him. "Keep my mess to my room, leave my shoes at the door, and I will not touch any of your food or kitchen appliances without your consent. I promise."

Nathan huffed. "I—well, yes, all of that would be ideal, but that's not what I meant."

My brows popped up. "More house rules?"

He cleared his throat and pushed his glasses up his nose. It seemed to be a tell of his—almost like he was uncertain. Nothing about his face, his posture, or anything else would have told me that. But I was starting to notice that he pushed at his glasses whenever he was about to say something he wasn't sure about.

"Hey." I reached out and pinched his cheek lightly.

He started at the touch but didn't move away.

I pulled back my hand and offered a smile. "I know we got off to a rough start. But honestly, it doesn't matter what the rules are. You want me to scrub the floors every Tuesday with a toothbrush? Fine. I'll do it. You like to walk around naked after nine? You do you, man. The fact that you are offering me a place to stay at all is a godsend, so as long as you aren't a serial killer, I'll deal with whatever you need."

Nathan coughed. "I don't mean about the house rules. I meant… me. I've been told I can be sharp sometimes. Or unfeeling."

I snorted. "Nathan, I already knew that. Been there, told you off for it, remember?"

For that, I was rewarded with something that *almost* looked like the start of a smile. And for the first time, I wondered what it would look like if I got the rest of it. Just like I also wondered why I'd never seen it before either.

"I just want you to know that I don't intend it that way," he said. "And if I am, please tell me. Otherwise, I thought maybe things like the studio would make up for it. Because I am also…appreciative. That you're considering this, I mean."

I looked around the room with a new understanding of what it was. A gift. A sign that, for some crazy reason, Nathan Hunt feared deep down that he wasn't worthy.

I didn't know how or why that was possible. But that insecurity was there.

And that was something I completely understood.

Without stopping to think, I wrapped my arms around his neck and squeezed. Slowly, his hands found my waist, then slid up my back and returned the embrace.

I tried to ignore how good it felt as I lay my cheek on his big shoulder. How warm his skin was. How good he smelled.

"Thank you," I said, then pulled away before I wasn't able to anymore. "I appreciate it too. More than you know. Now, let's go back to the apartment. I want to get a look at my room before I sign my life away."

———

I WAS STRUCK with another wave of déjà vu when we stepped out of the stairwell on the eighth floor.

Well, of course, I was. I didn't remember the number of the apartment I'd snuck out of last week, but all the floors probably looked the same in this building. Maybe one floor down? Or one door over? Arden—Anders?—and Nathan were friends, or at least friendly enough that Nathan recognized the couch.

God, I hope I don't run into my shaggy one-night stand.

Nathan stopped outside a dark green door with a shiny brass 8F on the front and handed me a keychain with a little I Love NY fob dangling from the end.

"Try it," he said. "I just changed the locks, so you should make sure your key works. It's the same for the deadbolt and the bottom."

We stood close as I unlocked the door, trying and failing to ignore the scent of sandalwood and soap next to me. When he'd come downstairs to introduce me to the doorman, Nathan had looked as prim as ever in his glasses and just as sexy in a light blue T-shirt and gray joggers that hugged his legs *perfectly*. Even in scrubs at nearly one in the morning, the guy still looked like the teacher in an SAT prep ad in the subway—and it was embarrassing how stupidly hot I found that whole vibe. It wasn't fair, especially when I probably had raccoon eyes from all the stage makeup and was hobbling around like Tiny Tim.

The door opened easily, and Nathan held it open before following me inside and dropping my bag in the entry.

I didn't make it very far. Just past a shoe rack with two pairs of Hokas under a coat rack currently only bearing a rain jacket and Nathan's navy pea coat, then past a small round table in the foyer holding a familiar-looking fern and a bowl for keys. To the left, I stopped short at the living room entrance.

This was beyond déjà vu. I knew those windows and the view of the Hudson. I knew the painting over the fireplace and the photographs of classic New York buildings and Central Park on the opposite walls. Most of all, I knew that couch, the gray one with buttons and a neat row of *Harper's* magazines spread on the elegant glass coffee table.

This wasn't just a similar apartment. It was the *same* apartment.

I whirled around. Nathan stood by the foyer table, arms crossed, while he watched me with open curiosity. And expectation.

"I believe you've been here before," he said quietly.

I gawped. "This was *your* apartment the whole time?"

Nathan nodded. "I found the bra in my living room. When you mentioned the couch, I knew it was yours."

I whirled around, ready for the lurking ghost of Beardy One Nighter to pop out of one of the bedrooms and shout "gotcha!" at me.

"Aiden moved out. He couldn't live here anymore."

There was something more to that statement, but he didn't offer any more detail.

Jesus. I'd heard of men ghosting their dates, but I'd never heard of someone literally *moving* to avoid seeing me again.

Still, it was some relief to know I wouldn't run into him in the halls.

Then another thought curdled my blood. "Oh my God, you didn't, um, hear us?"

Nathan looked utterly confused. "When would I have heard you?"

My face blazed. "I, uh, well, I've been *told* I can be kind of loud."

Nathan continued to blink.

"While doing it," I elaborated.

Still no response.

"The deed. Sex. Fuck-ing." Lord, I really couldn't help myself.

Recognition finally flashed through those chocolatey browns. "*Oh.*" His cheeks flushed along with the tip of his nose, and I was rewarded with what it looked like to *finally* perturb Dr. Nathan Hunt.

He would have looked adorable if I wasn't mortified myself.

"I—no," he said finally. "I wasn't home that night. I worked late and went to the gym early, so I didn't return until you…woke up, I suppose."

It should have helped, knowing he wasn't here to listen in on the drunken, almost-sex I'd had with his former roommate. But somehow, it didn't. I wanted nothing more than to wipe the entire memory away.

"Well, Arvin—"

"Aiden," Nathan corrected me, like he almost couldn't help it.

"Is an idiot," I completed. "This apartment is amazing."

That almost-smile returned. "I'm glad you like it. Would you like me to show you the rest of it, or did you—"

"Please," I interrupted. "I, um, didn't see much last time."

Nathan blinked as my cheeks heated all over again. In the mirror, I had turned the color of a very ripe tomato.

"Okay," Nathan said as if I'd only commented on the weather that day. "Well, follow me."

It wasn't a long tour. I followed him past the living room and the eat-in kitchen, then through a formal dining room with the same river-front views. From there, the hallway split between two bedrooms, a luxe bathroom in the middle that was bigger than my entire bedroom at Nonna's.

"Eventually, I'll find a way to add a second bathroom, but for now, we'll have to share," Nathan told me.

"Oh, I'm *very* good at sharing a bathroom," I said as I explored the not-so-small space. The free-standing bathtub looked like a giant egg, and there was enough room that I could walk all the way around it before peeking into the two-person shower. "We only had one between six kids when I was growing up, and I always got the last of the hot water. I take the shortest showers in human history. You won't even know I'm in here."

"I doubt that." When I turned, Nathan looked visibly uncomfortable, keeping his eyes everywhere but on me. "And there is plenty of hot water. You can take however long you need."

It was a far cry from the shabby little house where I'd grown up or the bedroom I'd shared with Marie for almost twenty years. Nor did it in any way resemble the sardine-can situations so many of my friends had with two, three, or four roommates.

It was a grown-up's apartment. Tastefully decorated with classic furniture and shades of green, taupe, and white that was like a modernized take on the building's twenties vibe. It had things like a laundry room and linen closets and rugs that fit the rooms properly. A real home with stuff that wasn't purchased off Marketplace or dragged off a curb.

"Does it meet your standards?" Nathan asked when I followed him back to the bedrooms. "Have everything you need?"

"Are you kidding? It's giving Gatsby. The Baz Luhrmann version, but without all the gold. It's gorge."

Nathan tipped his head. "You do know that was originally a book, right?"

I shrugged, slightly embarrassed. Frankie was the reader in the family, not me.

"Well, this is your room." Nathan gestured toward the open door next to us.

I peeked into the bedroom where I'd slept literally one week earlier. Unlike the rest of the apartment, it was completely empty, painted white, with two windows that looked out onto the corner of West Seventh-Sixth Street and Riverside Drive. Nathan's room—the only room I hadn't seen yet—probably looked out to the river.

"You don't think it's kind of weird?" I said without thinking. "I was literally here a week ago doing...you know."

Nathan leaned against the doorframe and crossed his arms in a way that made his biceps bulge again. It was very distracting. "Do *you* think it's kind of weird?"

"Maybe a little." I crossed the room to look out one of the windows down to the sidewalk. The people looked a bit like ants from up here. Everything was quiet.

"It doesn't have to be. You slept with my former roommate. Sex happens."

I giggled. I couldn't help it. "Sex happens? You make it sound like a bill I forgot to pay. Or something you stepped in on your way to the subway."

That brow arched again. It was impossibly sexy. "Was it something special? Should I ask Aiden to come back? Maybe that will help you to remember his name."

His tone was still even, but Nathan was joking with me. Again.

Out of sheer joy, I grinned.

And for the first time, Nathan grinned back.

And ho-ly-shit. The guy had a smile bright enough to fuel all of New York. I almost fainted right then and there.

"I can think of more important things to remember," I somehow managed to say. "Like saying thank you. For letting me stay here."

Nathan clasped his hands together and nodded his acknowledgment. The movement was so immediate and bashful, he reminded me of a little boy for a moment. It was endearing.

"Any other house rules I should be aware of?" I set my bra on the window sill, ignoring the way Nathan's eyes darted in that direction. "Chores you want me to do? I'm really good at washing windows when I play loud music, but horrible at mopping floors. And counters are my nemesis, but I'll do my best when I have kitchen duty."

Nathan shrugged. "That won't be necessary. I have a housekeeper that comes in twice a week. I am a fairly neat person, so I'd appreciate it if you could make an effort to keep shared spaces picked up. That's about all, though."

A housekeeper. For a river-view apartment. That he apparently owned if he was planning renovations.

Something wasn't matching up. Men who had things like this didn't "need" roommates like me.

But when the lights of the city twinkled at me through my new bedroom window, I decided not to question my good luck. Don't look a gift horse in the...eye? Face? Whatever the saying was, I wasn't going to do it.

"Well, cool," I said. "And that's included in the rent too?" I dug into my purse for the wrinkled envelope of cash Frankie had handed me before she'd left. The one I'd carried with me everywhere all week in the event I finally found someplace to land.

Nathan nodded. "It is."

"Well, here. That should cover first and last. I think."

I crossed the room and held out the envelope. Nathan took it and thumbed through the cash, looking skeptical.

"Count it and let me know if it's enough. I should have the rest within two weeks. Hopefully sooner if I can find a second job."

Nathan still looked doubtful. A few seconds later, he handed the envelope back. "That won't be necessary."

I held it in my hand. What was happening? "What do you mean?"

He was staring at the money like it was going to burst into flames. "I can't take that, Joni. That would be unethical."

I swallowed. "But…that's what we discussed at the bar. At least, I think it is. I'll be honest, I'm pretty bad at math, but my sister said she gave me enough for two months in most places."

Shit. Shit, shit, *shit*. I knew this was too good to be true. I shouldn't have brought up the fact that I didn't have that job yet. Now, he was thinking I wouldn't be able to come up with rent and wanted me out. The whole arrangement was over before it started.

"No, I just mean, I don't need the money," Nathan said. "I'll wait until you can find another job and get yourself more secure. It's fine."

I stared at him, then at the money, then back at him. Was he for real?

"I can't do that," I said, holding the money back out. "It wouldn't be right. I won't—listen, I don't want to put myself in a position where I feel like I owe you something, but also, I can't take advantage of you that way either. If you won't take this, I can just look for somewhere else."

"Don't do that."

I opened my mouth to argue again, but Nathan wasn't listening. He removed his glasses and rubbed his face, almost like he was trying to get rid of a migraine. When he put them back on, I was still holding out the envelope. And he still didn't take it.

"What if…what if you paid me back another way?" he said.

Immediately, I straightened. It wasn't like I'd never heard *that* kind of proposition before. I was cute, often strapped for cash, and plenty of people in this city were willing to take advantage of that. More than once, I'd been offered parts by way of the casting couch.

I'd never accepted any of them, and I wasn't going to start now.

Goddammit. I knew it. I *knew* there had to be a catch. A dumb, dirty, totally predictable one. Were all men just shit? Was that the bottom line?

"Look, I know I went home with your roommate and have some rough plans to work in a strip club, but I'm really not that kind of girl," I said. "I'm sorry you got the wrong idea."

I started toward the door with the intention of pushing past him. Nathan, however, stopped me with a hand on my shoulder.

"That kind of—what are you talking—*oh!* Joni, no, that's not what I meant."

I crossed my arms and stared at the hand on my shoulder. "Oh, really? Look, I know I kissed you in Tom's office and everything, but that was a moment of weakness, not an offer to trade."

Nathan snatched it away like it was burned. "*Jesus,* of course it wasn't. I wasn't insinuating that you could trade sex for housing. I would never, ever suggest that."

"Well, then, what was that offer?" I demanded. "Because it sure sounded that way."

He sighed, leaned back against the doorframe, and shoved his hands through his hair. It made the curls bounce, and I resisted the urge to put my fingers in them too. I loved his hair, and secretly, I hoped he never tamed it with gel or wax or whatever else men used. It was the only thing about him that was at all messy. And annoyingly, it made him that much more perfect.

"Just say it," he muttered, more to himself than to me.

"Say what?" I prodded.

He sighed. "I—I need help with something too."

"Oh, and what's that? Getting your dick sucked?"

He reared like he'd been slapped. "Jesus, no. I need help with my social skills. As you've pointed out, they are fucking terrible."

After spitting out the words, Nathan grimaced like he'd tasted something bad. It was the first truly intense expression I'd seen besides the grin. And all of that had happened within an hour. I wasn't sure if that was good or bad.

"I've been diagnosed with social pragmatic communication disorder," he said quickly.

I frowned. "What is that? I've never heard of it."

"Most people haven't. It's sort of a cousin to autism. It only made the DSM-5 when I was just out of medical school. Prior to that, my family believed I had Asperger's Syndrome."

"And that's a type of autism, right?"

Nathan nodded. "But I don't have a lot of the qualities that would qualify me for an ASD diagnosis. So, they changed mine when Asperger's was removed from the DSM-5, and SPCD was put in." He shook his head. "Honestly, the label itself isn't as important as what it means. I struggle with social communication. I often miss basic social cues, jokes, idioms, or tone of voice. It stymies a lot of my relationships and sometimes makes socializing difficult."

"So, when you said you couldn't insinuate…you really meant it?" I wondered.

Nathan nodded. "That's correct. Or at least not without considerable forethought."

"No wonder you talk like a textbook."

He didn't laugh.

I tipped my head. "That was a joke."

Nathan just blinked. "I gathered."

"Then you should laugh."

He shrugged. "I only laugh when I think things are funny. When I was younger, I used to do it when I thought it was appropriate, but it seemed to make people even more uncomfortable. It's better this way."

Curious. Most people would laugh, even if it was just out of awkwardness. Oddly, I kind of liked that Nathan didn't. It was honest and open. More than most people.

"Fair enough," I said. "So, what does that have to do with rent?"

He sighed again. "I have an arrangement. With my family. I'd prefer not to go into it. But my parents worry about my socialization when I live alone, so I've promised them that I would always have a roommate while I live in New York. Or until I have a significant other to fill that void."

"So, you want me to, what, fill the void?" I asked.

How fucked up was it that even mad at him again, I still

wondered what it would take to fill the "significant other" void in Nathan's life instead of the roommate one?

What kind of person charmed a man like Nathan Hunt? What kind got to go to *bed* with Nathan Hunt?

Down, girl. Not the time.

Nathan shrugged. "In a manner of speaking. You can live here. And if you want, provide instruction on how to be better. With people."

"Why do you think I can do that?" I was dumbfounded. Of all the things I thought he would ask, this hadn't even occurred to me.

"You're terrible at making drinks, Joni. Genuinely awful. It took you three full weeks to get my drink order correct consistently, and I only ever get scotch neat."

"Gee, thanks," I said. "And that was sarcasm, in case you missed it."

Nathan just kept going like I hadn't spoken. "But no one ever seems to mind because you're so friendly—or maybe just charming. Your boss doesn't care, none of the bar patrons ever ask you to redo their beverages, and you still earn excellent tips despite the poor service. It's obviously because you're very good with people."

I perked up. "That's true. I *am* good with people." It was one of the few skills I could still claim.

"Well, maybe we help each other, then." Nathan's brown eyes softened on the other side of his lenses. "I can help you with a place to live. You can help me fulfill my promise to my family. Everyone gets what they want."

"They call that a win-win," I told him.

He offered another smile that did funny things to my stomach. "Yes, I know that."

I beamed. "Good. That's lesson one, then. It's a...a...what did you call it?"

"An idiom?

I grinned further. "Yeah, that."

Nathan's dimple appeared again. He looked like he wanted to laugh but wasn't sure how. I wanted to hug him.

"Thanks," he said. "I'll take notes."

We stood together in the doorway of my soon-to-be bedroom, like both of us were waiting for the other to speak.

I stuck out a hand for want of something better to do. "All right. Bedroom for friendship lessons. It's a deal, sir."

Nathan examined my hand for a moment, then stood up straight and took it in one of his. His paw practically swallowed mine, but his touch was gentle. Especially when his thumb brushed over my knuckles, tracing the bones within.

"It's a deal," he repeated softly.

I shivered and moved closer, almost like being tugged on a string.

Nathan's eyes dropped to my mouth.

Unconsciously, I licked my lips.

Slowly, I started to lean in, but before anything else happened, Nathan cleared his throat and stepped away.

God.

"When would you like to move in?" he asked.

I thought about the breakroom waiting for me. If I played my cards right, I would only have to spend a few more nights there. "Does this weekend work?"

Nathan nodded. "I have to work tomorrow, but on Saturday, I can help you bring things up."

I nodded. "Sounds good to me. I won't have much, and my family will probably help too." I grinned, considering one more thing. "Get ready for your second lesson, Dr. Hunt. With the Zolas, it's all about trial by fire. And unfortunately for you, my sisters take no prisoners."

TEN

SISTERS IN ORDER OF MOST TO LEAST ANNOYING (TODAY)

#1 Lea. Again

At exactly 9:14 in the morning, I was trying to unlock the door to apartment 8F with shaky fingers.

It was my fourth try. Only because I had the peanut gallery in the form of Lea, Kate, and Mike lurking behind me like ghouls and commenting the entire time.

"Does it have a chain?" Lea asked. "Maybe he needs to come unlock it."

"Of course, it has a chain," I said. "Every door has a chain lock."

"No one needs to use a chain in a place like this," Kate put in. "It's too fancy for petty larceny. Try your key again. Do you want me to try?"

"I got it!" I snapped. "Stop harping, and just let me do it."

"Why does he need a roommate again?" Mike wondered as he shifted a box of random books and art supplies from one hip to the other.

He peered around the hall with the same distrustful expression he gave everything that wasn't from Belmont. My brother-in-law was nothing if not a creature of habit. I honestly thought he had worn the same pair of jeans and rotating T-shirts since he had met Lea literally twenty years ago. Which…good for him. If, at forty, I can fit into the clothes I wore at twenty, I'll be over the freaking moon.

"Everyone needs a roommate in New York City," I said. "Even doctors. It's one of the most expensive places in the world. You know all know this."

"I know somethin'," Mike muttered.

I finally got the deadbolt to turn. "What does that even mean?"

Before he could answer, the door opened, and I fell into the arms of my new roommate.

"Hey," I said, somehow suddenly breathless.

Nathan peered down at me through his glasses, and I *thought* his full mouth twitched. "Hello."

God, he smelled good. Like soap and water and just a hint of coffee.

Nathan helped me stand upright, then took the heavy duffel bag I had slung over my shoulder without asking. "You shouldn't be carrying things this heavy with your bad knee."

"Well, you know what they say," I replied. "No rest for the…" I tapped my mouth, now wondering how that saying actually ended.

"Weary?" Nathan suggested.

"It's wicked," Lea called behind me while the word "wicked" literally echoed around the tiled interior of the building. "Originally a proverb from the Bible."

Nathan and I both turned to face her.

"It is?" he asked. "I didn't know that."

"Don't," I warned my sister. "Nathan, let me introduce you to some of my family. That's my sister Kate, my brother-in-law Mike, and the one giving us a Sunday school lesson is Lea. You can ignore her."

"Nice to meet you," murmured Nathan, though he didn't seem to think so.

I couldn't blame him when everyone was staring at him like a bad piece of meat the butcher was trying to pass off as fresh.

"It means that every sinner gets their due in the end," Lea clarified, instead of saying hello like a normal person. I mean, really. How anyone could look that imperious in faded skinny jeans and a Mickey Mouse sweatshirt? But that was Lea's magic power.

"Sort of God's way of saying 'fuck around and find out,'" Kate added with a mischievous grin that only expanded when I shot her a glare.

Shut it, I mouthed.

Make me, she mouthed right back.

To his credit, Nathan didn't seem to be disturbed by any of it.

"I'll keep that in mind," he said while he took the duffel bag from me. "I would have come down to help if you had called."

"I didn't want to bug you," I said.

Nathan only shrugged. "I set aside my day to help. It's no problem."

"A true gentleman," Kate remarked behind me.

"You can still help with the furniture, Prince Charming," Lea called. "Mike can't move it on his own. Now, can you let us in so we can put these things in Joni's room and inspect the place properly?"

Looking more than overwhelmed, Nathan stepped aside to let my family in, and instinctively, I stepped with him until we were the last to enter.

"Sorry," I said. "They're kind of like bulldozers. It's better not to stand in their way."

His mouth quirked again in that way that told me he thought something was funny but wasn't sure why. "It's all right. I have brothers too."

"You do?"

Huh. Nathan Hunt had brothers along with overbearing parents? The plot was certainly thickening.

"How's your knee?" he asked as we followed my siblings back to my room. "I restocked the ibuprofen if you need it."

Why, oh, why did a man buying me a Costco-sized container of painkillers make me blush?

"I'm all right," I said. "It's mostly back to normal if I'm careful. But thank you."

We walked down the hall and into the empty bedroom, where

my sisters were opening and closing closet doors while Mike inspected the windows.

I snorted. What were they planning to do? Bring me home if they found a speck of dust or a rusty hinge?

"So, *you're* the roommate," Lea said when she emerged from the double closet on the far side of the room. "Are you gay?"

"Lea!" I gasped. "What the hell?"

Nathan looked like he'd been slapped. "What?"

"It's fine if you are," Kate supplied. "We just need to know what's what between you and Joni."

Nathan blinked and pushed his glasses up his nose. "No. I'm not."

I wanted to squeeze his hand.

Lea looked Nathan over, clearly taking in what I and probably every other woman in New York noticed on a daily basis. The fact that the man was a legitimate fox who wore a plain pair of jeans and a T-shirt like a Calvin Klein model, even if he had no idea. I knew where she was going with this. If he was gay, it was one thing for me to be living here. But if he was straight, there was only one reason for it in her mind.

Maybe he'd say he was pan and really mess with her.

"Lea," I started again. "Cut it out."

"How did you meet anyway?" she asked. "Customer at the bar, right?"

"That's right," Nathan said. "Although we didn't really get to know each other until she came to my office for a consultation for a breast augmentation."

Every other head in the room immediately swiveled my way.

"You wanted to do *what*?" Lea demanded.

I gave Nathan a dirty look. "Thanks for that one."

"Joni, what?" Kate chimed in. "Aside from the fact that it's totally unnecessary, how were you even going to pay for something like that?

I shook my head. "I wasn't. I'm not. I thought about it for a second and changed my mind, all right? So just drop it."

I don't know why I bothered. Lea wasn't capable of dropping anything.

"So, what, you're her plastic surgeon?" she asked Nathan. "Here to make her into some little doll just like you want?"

"Lea!" I snapped. "*Stop!*"

"No," Nathan said. "I'm not. I actually advised her against doing the surgery. I didn't think it was necessary."

"Because you had the hots for her?" Lea pressed.

To his credit, he didn't back down. "Because I think she's perfect the way she is."

The sudden silence in the room was so thick I could have spread it on toast. There it was again. That word. The one that made my heart race in my chest and my lips swell with need.

Kate's hand floated to cover her mouth, Mike just looked bemused, and Lea looked like she'd been smacked upside the head.

"No." She shook her head so hard that the messy bun on top threatened to fall out. "And you're not staying here. You can take the couch at our house if you absolutely can't stand the shop, but I'm not leaving you here with an obvious predator."

"Predator?" Nathan asked. "Why am I a predator?"

"You're not," I assured him. "My sister is just being a bitch."

"Harsh, but maybe fair," Kate remarked to Mike, who had the good sense not to do anything but grunt.

"It's not a lack of manners when I'm just protecting you," Lea argued with a hand on her hip. "No offense, but you don't exactly look like you need a roommate, guy."

"His name is *Nathan*, you absolute brat," I snapped.

But again, Nathan just shrugged. "None taken. I don't."

"Nathan," I hissed at him this time. What was he doing? Giving the entire agreement away?

He ignored me completely.

"Well, at least he's admitting it," said Kate, now appraising him. "Anyone who wears The Row on moving day isn't hurting for cash."

Nathan looked down at the simple clothes that, yes, looked a lot more expensive than the thrifted overalls I used when cleaning houses for extra money.

She grinned. "I run a men's vintage shop in Riverdale. If you're ever looking to clean out your closet, I'll give you my card."

Nathan took it, looking puzzled.

"Kate, don't add to this garbage, please." As the fairest of my siblings, I at least expected her to be on my side.

"Doesn't care about his clothes either," she replied like I hadn't even spoken. "Classic rich guy behavior. Xavier is the same way," she remarked to Lea. "I noticed it the first time we met."

"Xavier is my other sister Frankie's husband," I filled Nathan in.

"And that one is married to a *duke*," Lea said meaningfully. "In England."

Nathan blinked. "Okay."

"A very powerful duke," she added.

He nodded. "The highest level of the peerage would automatically make him somewhat powerful."

"And very protective," she piled on. "Over this family, which he has adopted as his own. His youngest sister-in-law in particular."

I smacked my forehead. "For fuck's sake, Lea. You and Xavier barely even get along, so don't make veiled threats to my roommate on behalf of Frankie's husband. You have your own right here to help you bully my roommate."

On the other side of the room, Mike grunted again. This time, he looked like he was trying not to laugh.

"I want to be clear," Lea retorted.

Nathan was frowning now like he was trying to figure something out. "And you have a brother too, right?"

I sighed. "Yeah." Damn his good memory.

"Who is not going to like this," Lea said smugly. "Mattie will drag you up to Boston with him as soon as he hears about this nonsense."

"He can try it," I snarled back. "But at least Mattie knows to steer clear when the claws are out."

"True dat," Kate commented as she edged out of the room, clearly to snoop around.

"Amen," Mike muttered to himself, looking like he would rather be anywhere else.

Nathan now wore the same expression.

"I'm just saying," Lea continued. "Dr. Fancypants isn't the only one with a bit of money and some power."

"A lot of money," Kate's voice called from down the hall. A long whistle followed.

We all turned to find she was gone. We found her standing in the living room, staring at the painting hanging over the fireplace.

"My dude," Kate said to Nathan. "That's a Degas, isn't it?"

No one else in the apartment reacted, though Mike immediately dug out his phone.

"What's a Day-gah?" he asked Lea.

She shrugged. "The heck if I know."

"He was a famous painter," Kate told them. "We learned about him in art school. Lea, I'm sure you know at least some of his paintings. The famous ones about the ballerinas. Like that one. It's real, isn't it?"

Nathan's eyes jumped between all of us as he seemed to measure whether or not to answer the question. Then, his shoulders relaxed like he'd made a decision.

"Yes," he said as he pushed his glasses up his nose again. "It is."

Kate gasped, and now all three of my family members turned to examine the painting while I looked at it from the arched entry of the room.

Something about the painting did resonate. In it, a dancer lay on the floor, arms reaching toward her toes as she stretched. I smiled. The scene was familiar. She was clearly out of breath, and her dark hair curled around her neck just like mine did at the end of a long night.

Nathan moved next to me while my family took turns arguing about how much the painting was worth.

"I'm sorry about this," I muttered. "I told you, they're like jackals."

Nathan shrugged and offered me a shy sort of half-smile. "I think it's nice that they care so much. But are you all right?"

"Yes. Why wouldn't I be?"

He shrugged again. He did that a lot. "I don't know. You're typically very outspoken, but not usually as sharp as you were in the bedroom. Now, you're so quiet. This is the first time I've seen you stay out of a conversation."

I looked back at my sisters and Mike and thought about that for a second. Kate was telling the others about the composition of the painting, giving them a short lecture that I knew I wouldn't understand very well anyway. She would mention the painting at the next family dinner, and I'd feel like an idiot for forgetting everything she had said. It was better to act like I didn't care in the first place.

"It's hard to add to conversations like this when I barely know what they are talking about in the first place," I said. "Sometimes it's easier just to wait until they're done."

Nathan looked at me for a long time, like he was waiting for me to add something more. Then he crossed his arms. "I know what you mean. I often feel that way too."

I opened my mouth to ask how. And why. But before I could say anything, we were interrupted by Lea's obnoxious voice.

"This only brings me back to my original question. If he doesn't need the money, what exactly *does* he need in exchange for your new digs? What kind of 'payment' is he expecting, huh?"

Both Lea and Kate turned with their arms crossed to face Nathan and me. Next to them, Michael rubbed his forehead and muttered something like, "Come on, Tess." I recognized it as the nickname he'd used for years. Some derivative of Contessa when she was being particularly imperious.

"Did you ask my sister to move in with you because you want to sleep with her?" Lea demanded.

"Did you?" Kate prodded with her.

"Annnd, there it is," Mike muttered, though he seemed to watch me carefully for a response.

Nathan stared at Lea's finger, now outstretched toward him, until it dropped. Then he swallowed. "No, I did not."

"*Do* you want to sleep with her?" asked Kate, though she didn't seem as upset by the idea.

My eyes practically bugged out of my face. Just behind Nathan, I mouthed *SHUT UP*.

Kate just grinned.

Nathan looked between me and my three extremely nosy family members. To his credit, he didn't look the slightest bit disturbed other than the reddening in his cheeks. "That feels like a trick question. If I say no, I'd be lying since your sister is a very beautiful woman. But if I say yes, then it seems like I did invite her to live here with the intention of seducing her. Which, I assure you, I did not."

My hand twitched like it wanted to reach out for his. And I *thought* Nathan's twitched toward mine as well. I didn't know why.

Beautiful, he'd called me.

Also, he didn't deny that he wanted to sleep with me either.

Both ideas did something funny to my stomach.

Nathan glanced at me, and his brown eyes asked the obvious question: *Should I tell them?*

I shook my head in the tiniest possible way. *Absolutely not.*

He turned back to my siblings. "Joni is my friend. She needed help. And I'm in a position to offer it."

"Yeah, but—" Lea started.

"Oh, for God's *sake*," I spoke at last, stepping in between Nathan and my family. "Stop it right freaking now. Stop the picking and the intimidating and the speculating about Nathan like he's not even here, and just be nice. I mean it, Lea. Cut it out and act like a decent fucking human."

Lea opened her mouth, clearly ready to argue back, until her husband placed his hands on her shoulders and whispered something into her ear. Immediately, she softened against him, though she still had fire in her eyes.

"I still want to know why," she said, though not quite as loudly as before.

"I know you do," I said. "But this isn't your choice, it's mine. Now, for your information, Nathan is awesome. He's my friend; I've known him for months because he's a regular at Opal, and he has never been anything but kind and respectful to me."

Okay, so that was a bit of a lie. But maybe not so much, given what he'd told me last night.

"He found out I was in a jam, had an extra room, and offered it to me while I get my shit together enough to take care of myself," I finished. "He is beyond generous. And he deserves your respect and gratitude since none of you have to deal with me anymore."

Both my sisters seemed to look at everything in the room but me. *Take that*, I thought.

I knew it wasn't fair to be angry at them for leaving me to figure this out on my own. But I couldn't help it. Not completely.

"Anyway, it's just until I'm back on my feet," I said, reaching up to Nathan's shoulder. Surprisingly, he leaned into my touch. "Then Nathan gets his apartment back, and you can stop making up conspiracy theories, okay?"

His shoulder was warm through the soft cotton. I wanted to slide my hand down. Maybe slip it under his sleeve. Find out if his skin was smooth there or not.

Eventually, though, I had to remove it.

"The truck is double parked," I said as I turned toward the door. "If we all help, I bet we can make it in two loads."

TWO HOURS LATER, the truck that Mike had borrowed from one of his mechanics was empty. He and Nathan had brought up the battered, mismatched furniture left over from my room at Nonna's while my sisters and I had handled my clothes and boxes.

Kate and Lea seemed content to put the room together for me, and I wasn't going to argue with them about that, too. The room would probably be a mess in a week anyway, so if they wanted to fold my laundry for me, I wouldn't fight it.

The only thing I felt strongly enough about was a framed print of a painting called "The Star" that Nonno had given to me before he died. It was a picture of a dancer in arabesque on stage, with other dancers peeking through curtains behind her and a man in a tuxedo watching beside them. He'd given it to me when I first started dancing, and it had always had the place of honor just over my bed.

It was by the same painter whose actual art hung in Nathan's living room. In a funny way, it made me feel like I could belong here. Just a little.

While my sisters argued over the way to organize my closet, I slid out of the room in search of water. We'd been at it for hours, and I was parched. Just before I reached the kitchen, however, the voices of Mike and Nathan stopped me outside the door.

"I'd apologize for my wife's behavior earlier, but she is who she is," Mike was saying just before I heard the telltale crack of an opening can.

I snorted to myself. That was putting it lightly.

"Lea's protective. She practically raised Joni and Marie herself."

"Marie is the other sister who isn't here?" Nathan wondered.

I smiled. He had a good memory. Most people just remembered I had a giant family and that was it.

"Yeah, Marie's in France, learning to be a chef," Mike said. "She and Joni are only ten months apart. Basically twins. But the kind that are complete opposites. They fought like cats and dogs when she was around, but we all know Joni misses her. She hasn't been the same since Marie left."

There was a familiar twinge in my heart. It happened whenever I thought of my wallflower sister, off and living her best life in Paris. Maybe it was jealousy, like everyone thought. I was always the one who was supposed to shine brightest, but now *she* was out there like a moonbeam while I adjusted to life as a drudge.

But it wasn't jealousy.

Well, it wasn't *just* jealousy.

It was more missing the fact that we used to share everything. Marie and I didn't always get along. Okay, we *barely* got along. But she also knew me better than anyone. Even when she chimed in with the rest of the family's "shit on Joni" times, it wasn't the same. There were other moments, usually at night when we were falling asleep, where we would trade stories from our days. And she'd listen to my stories about the dumb comment I'd made to a teacher, the boy I'd let feel me up in the custodial closet, the newest dance move I was going to try. Sometimes, she'd tell me I was being dumb, but it was never without listening to the *whole* story. Maybe because, until recently, she didn't have that many of her own.

Marie always wanted to know the truth, not just some version that fit into the flighty, silly screw-up everyone else *thought* I had to be. Which meant that, in the end, she knew me better than anyone and accepted me for exactly who and what I was.

I didn't have that anymore. And when I'd lost dancing, the other part of my life that made sense, I'd realized just how badly I needed it.

I wished she were here right now. I would have given anything to know what she thought of Nathan and this whole setup. Oddly, I thought she would have liked him. They were a lot alike, now that I thought about it. Both were kind of shy, socially awkward, and fundamentally kind. They even both wore glasses.

Weird.

"Between you and me, I don't think it's all Joni's fault if she's a little immature," Michael was saying once I tuned back into their conversation.

I frowned. What the hell did that mean?

I could imagine Marie's face at that question. *Come on, Joni,* she'd say. *Let's not pretend you're not still fourteen at heart.*

Oh, God. Not even close. Even my imaginary sister had no idea about that.

"I've known her since she was maybe six," Michael continued after another audible sip of what I guessed was the six-pack he'd brought for after the job was done. "And the whole time, she's had every person in her family henpecking her to death, doing shit for her because they think she can't do it herself. They weren't doing her any favors. I can't say that to Lea, but it's the truth."

I scowled. I wanted to argue. But he...wasn't wrong. And I hated that just as much as I hated the fact that he was saying it to Nathan.

"Joni doesn't strike me as incompetent," Nathan replied. "Maybe a bit inexperienced. But she's still young."

"She is," Mike agreed. "Joni's seen things like all of us have in the neighborhood. Stuff no kids should have to. But her brother and sisters worked damn hard to shield her from whatever they could, so

BOYFRIEND OF THE HOUR   127

she's more naive than most too. Which makes her an easy target. Especially for the kinds of people who are used to having pretty things. And used to having what they want, when they want it."

Shawn flashed through my mind. I shook his face away. No, that wasn't what he was talking about. None of my family members knew about Shawn. No one except Marie, and she only knew the bare minimum and had never breathed a word.

There was a long silence while the men sipped their drinks together. I could easily imagine Nathan's face while he mulled things over. Probably wondering what the hell he'd gotten himself into inviting me to stay here. Probably thinking he'd made a huge mistake.

"Lea doesn't need me to say it, but I will anyway," Mike said just as I was about to walk away. "If you fuck her over, you won't just have all the Zolas to deal with—you'll have me too. And I can promise you won't like it."

"Why is that?" Nathan seemed honestly curious.

Mike snorted. "Do you actually *want* to fuck around and find out?"

His tone was as even and easy as it had ever been. Anyone else listening would never have suspected the threat laced with unspoken violence was like an invite to watch the next Knicks game.

But I knew my brother-in-law. Michael Scarrone was quiet and generally did whatever my sister told him these days, but when he made a threat like that, smart people took him seriously.

I hoped Nathan would understand the meaning there. I hoped he wouldn't have to find it out another way.

There was the sound of shuffling, then jingling of metal on metal before something hard was set down. Maybe on the counter.

"That's the key to this apartment," Nathan said, his voice just as low and serious as Mike's. "Take it. If I ever do a single thing to harm Joni in any way, you have my permission to come here and levy whatever punishment you think is necessary. I'll be here waiting for it."

I couldn't breathe. I couldn't even exhale the breath I'd been holding the whole time he'd spoken.

Mike was quiet for a long time, but I *thought* I heard the sound of him picking up the key. "You for real?"

Nathan's answer was immediate. "I don't make a lot of jokes."

Well, I knew that was definitely true.

There was another long silence. Then Mike chuckled lightly. "You know something? I believe that."

"I want what's best for her," Nathan said, almost as much to himself as to Mike. "I only want to help her. That's all."

My stomach clenched at his final words. I wasn't sure if it was relief in knowing he cared for me. Or with regret that he didn't, in fact, want anything more at all.

MONEY DOESN'T BUY MANNERS

"There he is. The prodigal son of Huntwell Corp."

Nathaniel Hunt sat down across from his brother in one of the leather barrel chairs at the Union Club on East Fourteenth Street, New York City.

He hadn't been to the pretentious men's club in a while. Maybe six months, maybe a year. The last time they were in town, his parents had told him to go, along with the list of other directives toward one clear goal: start acting like the eldest son and heir to the Huntwell Corporation or see other things he cared about disappear from his life.

Things from his past.

Things like Lindsay. Things like Isla.

"I hear you got yourself a new roommate," Carrick remarked as he swirled brown liquid around in a glass. "That's, what, lucky number forty?"

"Thirty-one," Nathan replied as he draped his wool coat over the arm of the chair. "And I'm just doing what they asked. Prodigal, however, implies I'm returning to Virginia. Which, I assure you, I am not."

Carrick didn't smile. Carrick never smiled. Instead, he bared the first six of his front teeth like a wolf and took a sip of his drink.

In some ways, it was like looking into a mirror. While their younger brother Spencer took after their mother's classical Aryan looks, Carrick and Nathan had both inherited Radford Hunt's more Gallic appearance, with deep brown eyes, unruly dark hair, and statures that had earned both of them unnecessary athletic scholarships at top universities.

That was where the similarities ended. While Nathan couldn't be bothered to cut his hair more than once every four or five months, Carrick kept his curls shorn close. He also spent, in Nathan's opinion, too much time grooming his ever-changing facial hair. This month it was a goatee circling his mouth and chin that, in Nathan's opinion, made him look like a cartoon pirate.

Carrick was also brash and outspoken, while Nathan tended to keep to himself. Carrick's charmingly manipulative personality was perfect for a life spent in politics, whereas Nathan's quiet directness was better suited for his pursuit of medicine. Carrick was a born leader; when he spoke, people listened. Nathan didn't typically speak at all unless he really had something to say.

Unfortunately, Carrick also had a temper that discouraged his audiences almost as quickly as he charmed them. Were it not for his tendency toward brash impulsivity, he might have had all the qualities needed in an eldest son.

That, however, was Nathan's job. At which he'd been a total failure for the last thirty-four years.

"Welcome back, Mr. Hunt. It's been quite a while. Can I get you a refreshment?"

The server, a middle-aged man named Bobby, whom Nathan had seen before, greeted him with a smile. Nathan didn't know why it was considered polite to smile so much. It didn't seem necessary when he knew the man wasn't excited to see him. He just wanted a good tip.

"It's *Doctor*," Carrick corrected Bobby. "Get it right."

Bobby's smile grew even broader. "Of course, sir. Please accept my apologies, Dr. Hunt."

"None necessary," Nathan told him. "And I apologize for my brother's manners."

The waiter had the good sense not to reply. Carrick smirked.

"I'll have a Perrier," Nathan said, if only to give the man something to do other than hover.

"Come on, Nate. One drink won't kill you. Live a little," Carrick cajoled, just like he had when they were in high school. And college. And at literally every family gathering or social event.

Nathan masked a frown. He also hated being called "Nate." Carrick knew that. Everyone in his family knew that. But they persisted because it was what his father had always called him, which meant his colleagues did too, as did everyone else within the greater Potomac region.

Or in Carrick's case, because he knew it would bother Nathan from the start of their conversation. At some point during their childhood, Carrick had appointed himself the emcee of Nathan's social development, constantly dragging him into uncomfortable situations where he generally came out looking like a fool or at least regretting things the next morning. It was because of him that Nathan had gone to his first party. Had his first drink. Kissed a girl the first time. And so forth.

Nathan had never been certain whether the guidance was actually to help him or just for Carrick's amusement. But it was now a nuisance that irritated him either way. At thirty-four, he didn't need his brother to teach him how to live.

He'd apparently hired a stunning twenty-four-year-old dancer to do that instead.

With a grimace, Nathan shook his head. "I have to go back to the clinic after lunch and then the gym. Perrier with lime, and the salmon with steamed broccoli and brown rice, please."

Carrick sighed, clearly disappointed. "The steak for me. Medium rare. Not that you were even asking, Bobby."

Nathan tried not to recoil. "Eating like that every day is going to give you heart disease. Possibly colon cancer. Diabetes."

"Maybe. But *I* like to enjoy myself." Carrick waved Bobby away. "Why are you still standing theer?"

"Yes, of course, sir." Bobby, now red-faced, wove his way back to the bar to submit their orders.

Nathan turned to Carrick. "Why do you always have to torment the staff?"

Carrick waved his hand as if he were batting away a fly. It made the overhead lights catch on the gold band of his watch. "It gives me something to do."

"Lobbying for Huntwell isn't enough?"

After graduating from Harvard Law at just twenty-three, Carrick had clerked for the Supreme Court before going to work for the firm that represented the family company's interests in Washington. He quickly realized he could do a far better job than any of the "hacks we hire out," and so returned to Huntwell to head up the government relations department that he invented for himself. Now, along with his position at Huntwell, Carrick sat at the head of the most powerful industry groups on the East Coast, and as the tax breaks benefiting Huntwell Corp rose, so did stock values.

Their parents were ecstatic. And since they had already talked Spencer back home by promising him control of the family's horse breeding operation, Carrick's return allowed them to focus their attention solely on Nathan. And after last week's brunch at Bergdorf's, they had made it very clear that he was expected to make some changes.

He had brooded on that the entire way home, which explained why he had literally run into Joni in the entrance of his building.

Carrick snorted. "It's playtime while I'm waiting for the bigger fish to fry. Speaking of which, I've been sent to reel you in."

Nathan frowned. The analogy was confusing. Did that make him a fish? Frying implied a sort of demise, didn't it? It was a poor analogy, considering Carrick spent the majority of his time cornering politicians to ensure the current legislation matched Huntwell's interests. Sometimes, that was accomplished with contracts. Sometimes with blackmail.

Perhaps his brother was just mixing metaphors. Most people didn't realize when they did that.

"I don't know why they sent you," Nathan replied. "I have a practice here. My work is in New York."

"Not if Mom has anything to do with it," Carrick replied. "I have to hear at least once a week about how many openings there are for plastic surgeons in the greater Potomac region. As of Monday, it's three, in case you were wondering."

Nathan nodded. "She's been sending me job listings for years. It's nothing."

"Yes, we're all aware where you inherited your stubbornness. Which is why you and I both know she's just going to keep sending me up here until you move back to Virginia."

Nathan shook his head. "You're mistaken. I just saw them a few weeks ago, and she didn't say anything about that."

Lillian Hunt had made her yearly Fashion Week trek to New York to put in her couture commissions. She was a lifelong Ralph Lauren customer, but generally had a few smaller houses she treated like pet projects.

"Dad read the paper while she informed me that they want me to resume therapy," Nathan continued. "Make more appearances at places like this. Keep working on my social skills. Nothing different."

The awkward brunch had mostly consisted of his parents' veiled threats about his life if he didn't do as they asked. That included resuming occupational therapy for his social skills, finding yet another unnecessary roommate, and making more appearances at corporate events in New York where, on top of his actual job, he was supposed to serve as a proxy vote on the Huntwell board in addition to his own seat and network on behalf of his father's interests.

None of that was a surprise. They went through this particular dance approximately once a year. Much like Carricks's attempts to draw Nathan away from his self-imposed rules, Lillian's efforts at converting her son into a "normal" person were intrusive but mostly just annoying. Unlike Carrick, however, she wasn't above using leverage to force Nathan to submit. Never too far, lest he try to leave again. But she was always trying to stretch the boundaries he'd carefully drawn between him and his parents.

It was a tug-of-war they'd been playing for years.

"That's not what they said," Carrick replied. "Why do you think they sent me to New York right after them? Half of success is in the follow-up, brother." He lazily drummed his fingers on the table. "Mom took one look at you and rushed right home to tell me all about it. Did you bang that waitress, by the way?"

"What waitress?"

"The one that slipped you her number on the check. Dad was impressed. And since they want you to find yourself some pussy, you might as well get there."

"Christ, Carrick." Nathan removed his glasses to polish the lenses that suddenly looked very smudged. Somehow, he never expected his parents to discuss his personal life with others, and yet, somehow, they always did.

It wasn't anything remarkable. As he and his parents had left Bergdorf's, the waitress had slipped Nathan her number.

That in and of itself was nothing new. Women did that frequently. Nathan didn't know why. He rarely paid any of them attention, but they did it all the time. Waitresses at restaurants, the barista at the Mt. Sinai coffee stand, even patients right after he had literally cut into their bodies to make them look younger or slimmer.

Unfortunately, this time, his parents had seen it. And had apparently approved, if only for him to "sow his oats."

Another metaphor Nathan didn't particularly like.

Because, as Carrick had pointed out, there had been *one* new request from his mother: that Nathan find himself a girlfriend. Otherwise, Isla would no longer be taken care of.

It was their only card to play, which Lillian did again and again without a shred of shame. The injustice of it felt like a hole burning in Nathan's chest. Unfortunately, his mother knew exactly what it meant to him and used it to her full advantage.

It was the only time he ever wished he could be more like Carrick.

But he wasn't.

Carrick leaned back as the server brought Nathan's Perrier, as well as a tumbler filled with scotch.

"I didn't ask for this," Carrick said, pointing at the brown liquid.

"I t-took the liberty of refilling your drink, sir." Bobby stuttered slightly under Carrick's harsh glare.

"Yeah, but if I wanted another glass of sewer water, I'd have asked for it. Send it back and bring me something better than the well crap you're passing off as Macallan. And if you want a tip next time, try not to be so obvious about defrauding your guests."

"I wouldn't—I wouldn't—sir, it was a mistake—" Bobby glanced between both brothers, obviously terrified.

"It's fine," Nathan told him. "Just bring a new one, please."

"Go," Carrick ordered. "And tell the kitchen to hurry up with our food. I don't have all damn year."

The server stumbled away while Nathan turned back to his brother. "Macallan Eighteen is your favorite drink. I'm assuming that's what you got, considering you drank it all. More games?"

Carrick shrugged, confirming his suspicion.

Nathan sighed. He'd be sure to leave an extra-large tip. The members of the Union Club paid well to do things like toy with the staff, but it was honestly one of the reasons he avoided the place. Men just like his brother. Men didn't actually say what they meant, spoke in veiled terms, and enjoyed the misery of others.

"Anyway, that's my point," Carrick continued once his drink had been replaced, and their food appeared shortly after. "When Mom is salivating over some random chick handing you her digits, you know she's getting desperate. They want you home for good. And you know the old man wants a grandchild before he finally croaks."

As always, the idea of returning to Virginia tensed Nathan like a pulled string on a bow. He sat up straight, then rolled out his large shoulders, trying to release the stress. It was very uncomfortable.

Virginia had never felt like a home, even when it technically was for the first fourteen years of his life. To many people, growing up on a horse farm might have seemed idyllic. Snowy winters and sun-blanketed summers spent roaming the fifteen hundred acres would have been a dream for most children.

But they didn't have Radford and Lillian Hunt as parents. For every hour spent on horseback, he had to spend two with tutors, occupational therapists, and etiquette consultants. When they came of age, all three brothers were sent to a boarding school during the week in Alexandria, an environment that was as overstimulating as it got. And yet the weekends under his mother's forceful thumb offered no reprieve.

"It would be easier if you just did what they want, you know," Carrick continued as he cut a piece of his steak and loaded it onto his fork, along with some potato and carrot. He was always putting too much food into his mouth at once. "Think of it as an investment. Once you're CEO of Huntwell, you'll make more money than you ever could at this little hobby of yours."

"Surgery isn't a hobby." Nathan paused as his fork pierced a piece of broccoli. "People don't do three years of medical school, six years of residency, and a two-year fellowship as a hobby. It's my profession. My life."

My brother shrugged. "A life that you should have never had in the first place. I never understood why you wasted your time with all that."

Nathan ground his teeth. He wasn't going to justify that choice to his family for what had to be the thousandth time since he'd announced as a college junior that he intended to go to medical school instead of Wharton. "I attend the monthly board meetings."

"And I smile in pictures. It doesn't make me a nice guy."

Carrick took another bite and continued speaking with his mouth full. Nathan knew it wasn't because he didn't know his manners. It was to bother his older brother even more.

"Face it, Nate. We're from a long line of hacks who give money to the people doing righteous things. We're not the ones who actually do them."

Nathan scowled. He couldn't really argue with him, but that didn't mean he liked it. Or was planning to change.

"Anyway, Mom told me to tell you that Isla's tuition won't be paid if you don't come home this spring. Or find yourself a real relationship. She said it's time."

"Why don't you or Spencer start procreating?" Nathan asked.

"You're already there. If Dad needs an heir so much, why does it matter which one of us produces it?"

"Because *I* am not the firstborn," Carrick said, his acid tone undercut with a layer of danger. "*I* am not the one whose name they want at the head of the company when Dad finally retires."

The brothers stared at each other. Nathan's grip on his fork tightened to the point where his knuckles turned white. The metal bent. Carrick glanced at the now-deformed utensil, then raised his hand. Bobby came jogging over.

"We're gonna need another one of those," Carrick said, nodding at the bent fork. "Preferably one that my brother won't Hulk out on."

Bobby had the good sense not to react. Nathan set the fork on the table, where it was promptly scooped up, then replaced it with a spare set of silverware from the server's apron pocket.

"Thank you," Nathan said, feeling his cheeks heat. Unlike Carrick, he didn't like losing his temper in public. "Please put it on my bill."

Carrick swallowed another noisy bite of steak as Bobby walked away. "You know, it wouldn't be an issue if you left her in the gutter where she belonged."

Nathan glared. "Don't talk about Isla that way."

"I'm just saying. I've never understood why you care so much about a seventeen-year-old girl you hardly know. Whatever went down between you and her mom happened a thousand years ago, and she's been in and out of boarding schools ever since. It's ancient history. You could just leave it in the past."

"Isla is *my* responsibility." Nathan shook his head. "I may not be fit to be in her life, but that doesn't mean I'm going to abandon her. If meeting our parents' ridiculous demands on my personal life means she is cared for the right way, I can deal with them. I have up until now."

Unbidden, Joni's face flashed through Nathan's mind. The porcelain skin with a hint of olive surrounded by the dark hair she usually wore in waves. The high cheekbones that made her tilted green eyes look almost feline. The knife-straight nose and rose-colored mouth that always seemed to be in a perpetual pout when she wasn't smiling.

He had, as promised, found another roommate, though he hadn't informed them who it was. Until now, all of the other short-lived denizens of the guestroom had been three primary things. They'd been financially solvent. They'd been quiet. And they'd been male.

Giovanna Zola was...none of those things. When he was thinking logically, Nathan couldn't understand why, exactly, he had offered her the room. He only remembered the look on her face when she'd told him her story. The intense feeling—the sudden *need* in his chest to do absolutely anything he could to make her feel better.

The kiss she'd given him hadn't clarified much either.

It was fine. He had a plan. The beautiful bartender from Opal needed a place to stay, and he needed to tell his parents he was making headway on their parameters.

But he hadn't anticipated the way Joni would look when she wished him good night after her family had left the apartment. She'd just come out of the bathroom, clean-faced, black hair tied up, and dressed in a short black nightgown that bared an expansive length of pale, creamy leg. Her green eyes had twinkled as she smiled, not because it was the thing to do, but because she seemed genuinely happy to see him and grateful for his presence. Her scent of gardenias had remained in the hall for a few more moments after she shut her bedroom door.

It had taken all of his self control not to start masturbating to her door, right there in the hall. Instead, he'd taken his third shower of the day while imagining her next to him, water running over her naked body. And had done it every day since, with no reprieve from this...*feeling*...in sight. It happened all the time now, thinking of everything he wanted to *do* to her. Sometimes, it was innocent, like staring—he found himself doing that a lot. But others were so degraded he couldn't even really call them daydreams. Dirty dreams. Despicable dreams. Dreams that made him wonder if he was genuinely crazy.

Carrick sighed. "I'm just doing you a courtesy. Mom's like a dog with a bone. She's not going to let up until you show a legitimate indication that her darling boy is coming back to the fold," Carrick continued after a long drink of scotch. "Seeing a shrink or having a yearly lunch at the Union isn't going to cut it. Maybe it's taking actual leadership on the board of directors. Maybe it's getting married or actually spawning another four-eyed baby for her to harass—I mean, dote over."

Nathan choked, nearly spraying sparkling water and salmon across the whole table. "I would not *spawn* anything. I'm not a fish."

Carrick waved away his shock. "Whatever. You know what I mean. It's why Mom is lining up every fucking debutante in the state of New York for the hospital gala now that you're actually going. She's planning to auction you off like a mail-order bride. After that, you can probably live in the OR, if that's what you want. Just as long as you get married first and give them a grandchild to train up. A real one, this time."

"So, what, I'm supposed to get engaged next weekend?" Nathan demanded. "That's absurd. All of these demands are absurd, but even if they weren't, a person can't change his life completely in a matter of weeks."

"No," Carrick agreed. "But you could start by bringing a date to the gala for once. Someone you actually like. And don't even think about faking it, Nate. Any other man in your position would just bite the bullet and hire an escort, but we all know you can't lie for shit." He took another bite of steak. "So, how about that waitress? It's a place to start."

They both chewed meditatively, watching the other as he ate.

Again, Nathan couldn't help thinking of Joni. Not just about how impossibly long her legs looked when she stretched in the living room last night, which had forced him into the shower yet again. Or the way she tended to chew on her bottom lip when she was thinking, which constantly made it look like a gumdrop waiting to be swallowed.

It was dangerous, this feeling. This tendency to catalog things about her, big and small. He already had multiple lists in the notebook he kept in his pocket most of the time. Hadn't stopped to think about why until they were already there.

JONI'S EXPRESSIONS
JONI'S FAVORITE JOKES
JONI'S FAMILY MEMBERS
JONI'S FAVORITE FOODS

The last was ongoing, but he'd already hunted down the amaretto cookies she said her grandmother used to make. And he started making her cappuccinos on the mornings when she got up with him just to see the third on his list of Joni's Smiles. It was the one when she was surprised but grateful.

The whole thing bordered on obsession, which was something that Nathan couldn't afford to have happen again. And yet, he couldn't seem to stop. Nor did he really want to, if he was being perfectly honest.

"Just tell Mom that I did what she wanted," he said after another bite of salmon.

Carrick leaned forward, eyes glittering. "So, you did nail the waitress, after all? Good for you, man."

Nathan rolled his eyes. "Jesus Christ, Carrick. I didn't 'nail' anyone."

"But you are finally getting some tail? Good. It's been too long since that model stomped all over your dick."

"Am I getting some...No. I only meant I found a new roommate."

Carrick sat back, as if examining Nathan. "Have you been listening to me at all? Mom won't care about that, considering the rate you go through them. I give him a month. Two tops if he's neat."

Nathan scowled. "I'm not that bad."

"Spence won the last bet, you know. He said your last one wouldn't last six weeks. I said ten. Little shit took ten grand off me."

"This one isn't going anywhere because she's my girlfriend," Nathan blurted out before he could stop himself.

Joni seemed to have that effect on him, he realized as he stared at his plate of half-eaten food. She made him do things, like shout about her perfection in the middle of his office, deliver apology notes like a lovesick schoolboy, and offer a place to live to someone he barely knew.

And, apparently, ask her to pretend to be his girlfriend.

Carrick, notably, was silent, though Nathan could hear the sounds of at least three more bites of steak before he finally managed to look at him.

It didn't make sense. His family was irritating, but Nathan didn't lie to them or anyone. As frustrating as they were, they were also the only people who knew exactly who he was. He didn't have to pretend around them, didn't have to come up with inane conversation just to put them at ease, smile when he didn't feel like it, or interpret their idioms and emotions. He could just be himself.

Maybe it wouldn't always just be them.

Yet again, Joni's face flashed through Nathan's mind, along with their strange agreement. He doubted that claiming her as a fake girlfriend was what she had in mind when she said she would help him with social interactions. But right now, that appeared to be what he needed.

Especially when Carrick was staring at him that way.

"Bullshit," he said when he had finally recovered from what Nathan guessed was shock. "You didn't find a girlfriend in the last week. It took you a year to even take your last one out to dinner."

When his brother had set him up with an angel (a term he gathered had something to do with modeling underwear), he had found her attractive enough that he wanted to sleep with her every so often, and since she seemed to expect the occasional dinner together, he provided that as well. But when she started talking about moving in together, he had broken things off immediately.

And yet Carrick seemed to think he was heartbroken.

That was almost a year ago now.

"Julietta wasn't ever my girlfriend. We just had an arrangement. But this one *is*." Nathan found himself insisting stubbornly enough that he could almost believe it.

"Oh, really? What's her name?"

"Joni."

"Joni what?"

But Nathan shook his head. "So you can ask your FBI friends to check up on her? I don't think so."

Carrick bared his teeth again. "It's the smart thing to do, Nate. It wouldn't be the first time this family was taken for a ride because you trusted someone you shouldn't. Isla is proof of that."

Nathan almost ruined another spoon.

"I told you not to bring her into this." His jaw was clenched so hard he was speaking through his teeth. "And Joni is not like Lindsay. Not even a little."

"So you say."

Nathan glared. "So I *know*."

This time, Carrick looked away first, as if he'd forgotten what it was like when his oldest brother was legitimately angry. "Fine, you want to be stubborn? Be stubborn. But I'll find out sooner or later. So, are you going to bring her to the gala?"

He should have said no. He'd already gone far enough with this ruse, and it was nothing compared to what would happen if his brother actually discovered the farce.

But for the fourth time that afternoon, another image of Joni appeared in the back of Nathan's mind. This time in an elegant dress, diamonds around her neck, her arm tucked into his elbow as he guided her into a room that looked a lot like the drawing room of Huntwell Farm.

She gazed around the black and white marbled floors, then turned and smiled in a way that was all for him. Her teeth were very white, but it was her eyes, so bright and daring while fringed with black, he couldn't look away from. Even in his imagination.

"Yes, I'll bring her," Nathan decided. He could make his apologies to her later. "So you can tell them to back off. We'll both be there. I'll see you in a few weeks."

ELEVEN
NONNA'S SPAGHETTI RECIPE

Note: By hand dosnt mean WITH your hand!!!

"K, so now you're going to julienne the carrots and roast them while the sauce cooks. They'll be good on the side."

"Who's Julianne, and what the heck does she have to do with carrots?" I demanded right before I dropped the two knobby carrots onto the wood cutting board.

The bespectacled face of my sister, Marie, blinked at me through my iPad screen. It was an expression that, up until last summer, I'd woken up to almost every day of my life. The one that wondered *How are* you *my sister?* right before we shared and then tore all our secrets apart between us.

I used to hate that look. Until it was gone. Which was probably why I'd begged her to teach me how to make Nonna's spaghetti via FaceTime two weeks after moving into Nathan's apartment. Homesickness appears in lots of different ways, and apparently, mine made me want to do more than make toast for the first time in my life.

Well, maybe homesickness wasn't the right word.

I didn't exactly *miss* Belmont per se, which surprised me. The people, definitely. But I was never getting my family back the way I wanted. Meanwhile, it was hard to miss a leaky house in need of cosmetic repairs and new windows when I was living in the lap of luxury with as much hot water as I could ever use. Since I could no longer hear the B60 bus through the night, I was also sleeping better than I ever had.

But there were certain things I wished were available. The amaretti from Gino's. My favorite prosciutto from the market. And Nonna's cooking. After weeks of grabbing cheap slices and microwave dinners, I needed some real food. And I knew just who I wanted to share it with.

"It's a method of cutting them," Marie said impatiently, then proceeded to describe how.

I frowned as her directions went in one ear and out the other. I never took oral directions well.

"How about I just do that?" I said, then whacked a carrot with one of Nathan's expensive-looking knives. "You know, that's prob-ably why I moved in with a complete stranger. He wears glasses, and he looks at me just like that when I say something silly."

"I didn't look at you like anything," Marie said as her dismay deepened while she watched me butcher the carrots. "Are you cleaning while you cook? It doesn't look like it."

I glanced around me at the kitchen, which was, admittedly, a disaster from my efforts. "Baby steps. Tonight, I learn to cook. Tomorrow, clean." I tossed the carrots in olive oil as she had directed and put them into the toaster oven on the counter. I'd clean up the drips of oil later. "Okay, carrots are in. What's next?"

"Check your sauce. If the tomatoes are cooked, you can take it off the heat and sprinkle the basil by hand."

I nodded. "On it. So, how's Paris?"

At first glance, Marie and I looked nothing alike despite sharing the same dark hair, green eyes, and olive skin as the rest of our siblings. In school, most people didn't realize we were related until they saw our last names. I was the coquette at the center of every party, who constantly tested the limits of dress code and curfew and had a new boyfriend every week. Marie was the wallflower who skipped every school dance, preferred Nonna's company to class friends, and had never met an ankle-length skirt she didn't like.

But in the six months since she had moved to Paris, I could already see some subtle changes. Her waist-length hair, which was always tied back in a mumsy bun, had been layered a bit to flow nicely around her face. The wire-rimmed glasses had been traded for some sexy librarian specs, and I *thought* I could detect a swipe of mascara and some lip gloss. She'd even gotten her ears pierced. *Finally.*

The wallflower was fading. Or at least thriving in a totally new garden.

I was happy for her. Mostly.

Marie just sighed. "All right. My French is actually getting halfway conversational. Enough that I could actually go to a market outside of the city last weekend and people understood me."

"Make any friends yet?" I dipped a finger into the sauce and tasted it. I didn't know what I was tasting for, but it seemed all right. Maybe a little bland. I added more salt.

"Don't put too much of that. And yes, I have some friends."

"Lost your virginity yet?"

Marie's face flushed. "I thought you weren't going to make fun of me for that anymore."

I sighed. "Sorry. Old habits."

"Bad habits."

"I'll add it to the list of the others I'm trying to break," I said. "But seriously, no guys? Or girls. Whatever floats your boat—I don't judge."

"Why does life have to be about them?"

I frowned as something occurred to me. "Mimi, you aren't into girls, are you? Or pan or something? It would be okay with me if you were, you know. I wouldn't care at all."

Marie just huffed. "Joni, just because I haven't slept with half of New York—"

"Or Paris," I added as I threw the mound of basil on the cutting board into the sauce.

"Or Paris—"

"Or anyone," I put in.

"Joni!"

I just chuckled. "Sorry. Go on."

Marie sighed. "I was just saying, that doesn't mean I'm not into men. Which…I am. I guess—Jo! What are you even doing?"

I looked up from where I had inserted my hand into the luke-warm tomato sauce past my wrist. "What? You said to mix in the basil by hand, so that's what I'm doing."

"Jo, that just means with a spoon, not shove your whole hand into the sauce. And I said *sprinkle* by hand, not mix. As a garnish." Marie smacked a hand to her forehead. "How much basil did you put in there?"

"Um, all of it?" I looked down at the sauce, now riddled with ribbons of basil that were quickly wilting into blackish wormy things. "The sauce is kind of brown now. Is it supposed to look like that?"

"Is marinara sauce supposed to look like brown sludge?"

I huffed. "Why do you have to be such a know-it-all, Mimi?"

The banter was purely out of habit; I was already moving to the sink to wash the sauce off my hand.

"Just put it back on the stove and cook it down. Maybe we can blend it up into a pesto-kind of thing."

"So, tell the truth," I said after I returned to the stove, where I could both talk and stir the sauce with a spoon instead of my hand. "You haven't hooked up with one French hottie?"

Immediately, Marie turned the color of a red, red rose as she turned away from her desk.

She'd given me a tour of her tiny French apartment, which had a great view from the top floor of her building but, as a former maid's quarters, was about the size of a shoebox. Right now, she was lying on her twin bed/couch, fiddling with a recipe she wanted to bring to class the next morning.

"Mimi, come *on*," I said when she didn't respond. "How can you still be a virgin in the city of love? Half the point of you going to Paris was to give it up at last."

"I came to Paris to learn to be a chef, you brat. And that's exactly what I'm doing. I don't have time to date."

"Is it that? Or are you still saving yourself for your boss?"

Her cheeks went from red to outright scarlet. "Daniel is *not* my boss."

"He's your boss's son, which is basically the same thing," I said, enjoying the upper hand.

My sister had worked for the extremely wealthy Lyons family in Westchester since she was sixteen, first as a part-time maid, then as an assistant cook. When their cook announced her retirement, the family decided to send her to Paris to train as her replacement.

They knew she was talented as a chef. What they didn't know is that she had been in love with one of their sons, Daniel Lyons, since she had first started working there.

"Let me ask: does he even know you exist?" I wondered. "Did you even say goodbye before you left?"

She was avoiding the screen like her phone was the one staring at her instead of me. "I did."

"Did you do what I suggested?"

Her glare was immediate. "Did I wait in his bedroom naked? Absolutely not. Not everyone is comfortable walking around in their birthday suit like *some* people I know."

I giggled. Just the idea of my prudish sister, who was generally more covered up than a nun, showing more than an ankle to her crush, was hilarious.

"It's called body confidence, dude. You should try it. It might get you laid."

"Not everyone jumps into bed with a person right after meeting them," Marie mumbled. "Maybe you should try *not* doing that for once. You might get more done in your life."

I opened my mouth to argue back but found I couldn't. I was too busy smiling.

"What is it? Are you laughing at me? It's not my fault you messed up the sauce."

I tipped my head. "Just enjoying myself."

I guess absence really does make the heart grow fonder.

"I did go to his room," Marie admitted just when I was rooting around Nathan's spice cabinet in hopes of finding something—anything—to save this dinner. "Daniel's, I mean."

I swung around with a sudden motion that sent oregano everywhere. "*What*? You never told me that! What happened?"

Marie shrugged while she toyed with a pencil. "I snuck up there on my last night after I'd finished cleaning up from the catering. The family was having a party, and it was still going on. But when he came up, he, um, had someone with him. The daughter of one of the guests, apparently."

"Oh my God, tell me they didn't—"

Marie shook her head, color high. "I can still hear her. She sounded like Nonna's old tea kettle. But I swear, there was no way to sneak out of there without being seen, so I just had to sit there, hiding between his suit pants while they did it."

"So you just listened to your crush getting it on with another woman? You are such a perv!"

"I am *not*!"

I slapped a hand over my mouth, unable to keep giggles from spilling out. The idea of my virginal sister crouched in a closet like a bystander in a bad porno was too much. No wonder Marie had agreed to stay in France for longer than originally planned. Pining or not, she undoubtedly had no desire to relive any part of that night.

"So, how did you finally get out? I know you came home that night. You were always back like four hours before curfew."

She sighed but let the insult slide. "They left right after."

"Ew, so he doesn't even cuddle? Sounds like a douche."

"Daniel is not a douche. They were just, I don't know, going to a party or whatever. Daniel was always going to parties."

I didn't comment on the wistfulness in her voice. It was the same way I used to talk about Broadway—a supposed pipe dream I couldn't help but chase while most people thought I was sad and pathetic for even trying for it.

Well, I showed them.

For a few weeks, anyway.

Then again, while I'd certainly never met Daniel Lyons, I'd seen more than enough of him in *Page Six*. The guy seemed to have a new model on his arm every week. They tracked him like big game hunters on safari.

It was yet another reason why Marie's crush on him was so sad. She was so far from the man's type, she might as well have been in outer space.

"Unfortunately, right before I left, his brother came in looking to borrow a belt and found me emerging from beneath a pair of Hugo Boss suits."

My jaw dropped along with my spoon, which left a big splat of brownish tomato goop on the hardwood floor. "The old one?"

There were two Lyons brothers—Daniel was the younger media darling, while the older one, whose name I couldn't remember, was a serious older man who ran the company, apparently.

"Lucas isn't that old. He just turned forty."

I made a face as I looked him up on my phone. "Old enough. And he looks at least fifty."

"It's the bow ties."

"Or the scowls." I shook my head and put my phone back on the stand so I could see Marie. "Too serious for me."

Is he?

The question chimed through my mind alongside Nathan's generally solemn face. Yeah, it was a bit hypocritical of me to be criticizing Lucas Lyons for being too serious when I was currently lusting after my own Clark Kent lookalike.

"So, what did he say?" I asked, if only to keep the conversation moving away from *that* train of thought.

Marie toyed with one of her waves that had curled into a loose corkscrew near her chin. "He just sort of stared at me. Then asked if he could help me find anything."

"And what did *you* say?" I prodded. I knew an invitation when I heard it.

Marie just blinked. "I didn't say anything. I was mortified and barely managed to scramble out of the room like a mouse."

"Marie. Come *on*. 'If you give a mouse a cookie'…she *needs* to eat the whole damn thing instead of running away from it," I recited, remembering our favorite book when we were little. "That man was making a play, Mimi. 'Can I help you with something?' means he wants to help you find his dick."

Two eleven-shaped lines appeared between Marie's brows. "*What?*"

"Don't do that," I said. "You're going to look like Nonna before you're thirty."

"But—he—what—no—I—" She was sputtering more than the boiling water cooking my pasta.

I smirked. "Try again, Mimi."

"Lucas Lyons was *not* making a move on me!" she erupted.

I snorted. "He was moving so hard, he was a moving *truck*. Eighteen-wheeler, sis. Ready to go cross country."

Marie just shook her head. "You're nuts."

"No, I'm right. It's too bad you're in love with his brother. You could have popped that cherry then and there."

Okay, fine, I was being obnoxious. But just like I missed Marie's face and her smudged glasses and her nun-like getups, I missed riling her up.

She was just another part of home I had a feeling I'd never get back. Not really.

"I think we should talk about *your* love life." Marie pulled me out of that line of thinking. "I hear your new roommate is a dish. Lea thinks he's going to break your heart, and Kate wants him to model for her shop."

"Lea can mind her own business. And Kate's mothball suits are too good for him."

"Is this dinner for him?"

I shrugged. "Maybe. I thought it might be nice. He's kind of throwing me a lifeline over here."

"That's a first. You giving back to someone like that, I mean."

I made a face at her, but I didn't argue. She wasn't wrong. Okay, so maybe my siblings were right. Maybe I was a little spoiled, though maybe it wasn't my fault. It was easier in a family of eight for the older kids to do stuff for Marie and me rather than waiting for their baby sisters to make it through small tasks at a painfully slow rate. It was why I didn't learn to tie my shoes until I was ten. Or why I'd never done dishes until Matthew, Lea, *and* Kate had all moved out. And it was why, yes, I barely knew how to make anything in the kitchen.

But I was a Zola, after all. Food was our love language. I could understand it just fine, even if I was just starting to speak it.

I didn't ask myself *why* I wanted to put in the effort all of a sudden. It wasn't because Nathan had been doing small things like this for me since I'd moved in two weeks ago. Every morning, I found a cup of espresso waiting for me in the fridge, ready to be poured over ice or a cappuccino on the days I managed to get up before eight. Which had been happening a lot more often.

It wasn't just coffee, either. Two days ago, I'd discovered that my shampoo, which had been down to watery remains, had been replaced. When I mentioned the fact that I struggled to sleep in the mornings after my late shifts, I came home the next day to find that blackout curtains had been installed in my bedroom.

I was being taken care of *as an individual* for the first time in my life. Rather than large sweeping moves meant to take care of six kids or help the youngers keep up, these small gestures were just for me. From Nathan.

"For what it's worth, Lea said Mike actually likes the guy," Marie said.

I nodded. "Yeah, Mike told me that too. Well, he sent me a three-word text. 'He's all right' is basically an essay in Scarrone."

Marie chuckled. "For sure. Lea's still worried, though."

"Lea's always worried."

"Promise me something?"

"What's that?" I looked up from where I was stirring the pasta. Had it been in the pot for ten minutes already? I'd forgotten to start the timer.

"Don't sleep with him."

I set down the spoon and glared at her.

Marie, however, didn't shy away. "Jo, I mean it. Don't mess up a good thing."

"What, do you think I'm just giving it up for room and board now?"

I didn't mention the fact that I had already imagined it more than once. Nathan was very clean, and it was hard not to imagine him in the shower running on the other side of the bedroom wall when I was trying to go to sleep. More than once, I'd let my hand drift down under the covers, and my brain meander where it wanted, which was imagining what the water looked like running over that big body.

Then, last night, I'd come out to get myself some tea and ran smack into him when he was coming out of the bathroom in nothing but a towel. Drops of water were still clinging to his shoulders and the solid patch of hair over his chest.

Turns out the muscles in those grab-a-girl shoulders extended right down his torso like a stepladder and disappeared beneath his towel in that strong, extremely lickable V-shape. Mother, *may I.*

I'd just stared, unable to pull my jaw off the ground. Nathan, unfortunately, had done the same thing, and so we'd just looked at each other like a couple of idiots, mouths hanging open while water drops fell to the ground from his wet hair, for at least a minute until someone's phone buzzed. I think it was mine. Maybe it was his. By the time I'd scurried back to my room, I'd been too distracted to check.

But my dreams had been *very* good.

"I know you," Marie persisted. "You like to be admired. I also know that when you feel down on yourself, you go looking for strangers to make you feel better. Or even worse, Shawn."

"Yeah, well, it's better than sitting in my room waiting for someone who doesn't know who I am."

I waited for another comeback, but none came. Well, that was a change. Six months ago, Marie would have cut right back at me. Now, she didn't even seem interested in the fight, even with a blow like that.

"Sorry," I mumbled. "That was low."

"It's also probably true," she said with a sigh. "But you're also worth more."

I shook my head. "It doesn't matter. I don't think Nathan is interested in me that way."

Nathan noticed me. He definitely thought I was attractive. I knew *that*. I knew it because he couldn't quite stop his gaze from traveling up and down my legs when I wore my admittedly small pajama shorts. And once, when I'd dropped a bunch of dried macaroni on the floor of the kitchen and had to pick it up, I'd looked up to find him staring down my oversized tank top and licking his lips. Only for a second. But it had still happened.

Yet whereas, every other red-blooded, hetero-leaning man in New York would have made a move by now, *especially* after we already made out once before, Nathan had been a perfect gentleman since I'd moved in.

It was as if the kiss in Tom's office had never happened, replaced with a deal that was saving my life. Now, I was just trying to keep my end of the bargain. For the first time in my life, I wanted to carry my weight as best I could.

Tonight, that meant dinner. And doing my best not to imagine my roommate naked.

I needed my sister to temper those urges. No one else shut down my crazy side better than she did.

"I miss you," I admitted.

"You do?" Marie looked legitimately surprised. Well, why wouldn't she? I had never been particularly nice to her.

But things were different now. Somehow, she'd stopped being my annoyingly shy older sister. Maybe I could be more than the family brat, too.

"Yeah," I said. "I miss my sister. You're the only one who tells me like it is but doesn't treat me like I'm stupid."

"I don't know about that. I've called you an idiot more than once."

"Yeah, but you never meant it, any more than when I make fun of you for being a virgin. It was just what we did. Lea…she means it. And Kate too. Matthew, Frankie, Nonna. They all do. To them, I'm just poor, dumb Joni, who can't get her shit together."

Marie sighed. "They don't think you're dumb, Jo."

"They do," I said bitterly. "And maybe they're right. But I don't want to be like that anymore."

Marie tipped her face on the screen. She didn't wear the same doubtful expression our other family members always had. It was something more like curiosity. As if she was waiting for me to figure out the last piece of a puzzle.

I wished she could tell me what it was.

"Well," she said. "If I can move all the way to Paris without knowing a soul, you can probably stand on your own two feet too."

I smiled. "You think so?"

"Of course. Out of all of us, you've always been the most fearless. It's annoying, really. Like there's nothing you can't actually do if you try."

I leaned closer to the screen. "Damn, Mimi. I didn't know you felt that way."

She just smiled back. "Me neither, as it happens."

I went back to stirring the sauce, if only for something to do.

"Joni?"

I looked up. "Yeah?"

"I miss you too."

Sister to sister, we watched each other through the screen for a little bit longer, neither of us talking.

Then the front door opened and closed.

"Mimi, I gotta go," I said. "Dinner time."

"Okay, but maybe strain the sauce to get out the extra basil," she suggested. "It will make it look less clogged. Oh, and don't forget the fresh grated Parm—"

"Thank you, bye!"

I ended the video and went to strain the pasta. It seemed a little too soft, but I figured it would be all right. No one was as picky about pasta as my family.

Nathan walked into the kitchen, looking like he had just gotten back from the gym. He had traded his typical button-down and slacks for athletic shorts and a synthetic shirt that clung to his muscles in a disturbingly hot way. The fact that he was still wearing his glasses only added to the Superman effect of the clothes—surgeon by day, bodybuilder by night.

Lord, I was in trouble.

He seemed to be on autopilot as he walked in, rubbing his chin but stopped exactly two steps into the kitchen.

"Hi!" I greeted him as I dumped the steaming spaghetti into a bowl. "Surprise! I made us dinner. You hungry?"

He looked around the kitchen, brown eyes growing wider by the second as they took in the mess.

"Joni?" His voice was hoarse, almost like he'd lost it. "What the hell did you do to my kitchen?"

TWELVE

PEOPLE I THINK NATHAN HAS SLEPT WITH

#4 Nobell Prize Barbie. If their isnt one there shoud be.

Nathan peered around the kitchen like he was expecting a bomb to go off. To be fair, it sort of looked like one already had. An effect that got…worse…the longer I looked with him.

Okay, so I had used almost every pot hanging over the island to make the sauce, cook the pasta, toast the pine nuts, and make a few other things that *really* didn't pan out. Broiling vegetables is actually kind of hard, okay? They catch fire in like a second.

Two pans were still on the stove while the others were piled in a sink along with the failed attempts at other side dishes. The white marble counters were, yes, littered with the ends of carrots, onions, tomatoes, and herbs along with too many utensils to count, several used bowls, and a variety of spices that had spilled when I was hurrying to measure them. Add a good amount of sauce splattered around for luck, and it was basically my preschool finger painting.

So I wasn't the cleanest cook in the world. I never said I wasn't going to clean it all up after.

"I cooked," I told him again, mustering my very brightest, "don't kill me" smile. "I thought it would be nice for you to come home to a hot meal instead of those premade things in the fridge."

Over the last few weeks, I'd learned that Nathan's meal planning was as regimented as the rest of his life. On Sunday, a box of prepackaged meals arrived, along with an accounting of their nutritional content and macros. They sat in the fridge in stacks, labeled with mealtime and ingredients, alongside a water filter and the cream he used for his coffee. The only vice in this man's life, so far as I could tell, was the scotch he barely drank at Opal every Thursday night.

Nathan's gym bag fell to the floor as he continued staring around the kitchen. The longer he went without replying, the more my cheeks heated, and it wasn't from the heat coming off the stove.

It really was a mess, but until now, I'd been sort of proud of it. This honestly might have been the first meal I'd ever made, top to bottom, all by myself, without Lea jumping in to dice the onions for me, Nonna scrubbing pots behind me, or Marie reaching over me to handle something on the stove. And I'd done it for him.

But Nathan couldn't know that. All he saw right now was the disaster.

And now all I saw was the mountain of things to clean up.

I swallowed. "Nathan?"

He finally looked back at me. And maybe a little bit of tension fell from his big shoulders. A little.

"It's just a thank you for taking me in," I said as I gave the sauce another good stir. "I noticed that most of your meals come from that service, but, come on, that's never as good as anything home cooked, am I right? It's giving lonely bachelor. I thought you might enjoy a change."

I was babbling, yes. Filling the space because he still hadn't said anything else.

At least he wasn't staring at the mess anymore. Now, he was just staring at me. Was I wearing something inappropriate? I glanced down at one of my favorite "at home" outfits: baggy black pants tied loosely around my hips and a vintage Lisa Frank T-shirt cropped above my navel. A couple of chains around my neck, a pair of black hoops, and some beaded bracelets around one wrist.

I'm all right there, I thought. He'd seen way more of me when I was dancing.

Maybe he was staring because I was almost as messy as the kitchen. My shirt was speckled with sauce, along with some water stains that wet the hem.

"You…have a bit of sauce…" Nathan stuttered as he pointed to my neck.

I turned in a circle but obviously couldn't locate something on my neck.

"Get it, will you?" I asked, skipping over to him with the sauce spoon in one hand and a dishrag in the other.

Nathan glanced around the room like someone was going to save him from the task. Eventually, though, he took the rag from my hand and tentatively dabbed it on my neck, just above my collarbone, then drew the wet cloth up to my jaw. His fingers lingered there for a moment, and he seemed transfixed by the spot.

I shivered when his knuckle brushed the sensitive skin under my chin.

"Thanks," I murmured, suddenly aware of his characteristically clean scent, now overlaid with a bit of sweat from his workout. Damn, he smelled good. It was all I could do not to lick him in exactly the same spot where he'd just touched me.

I wondered if it would taste like salt.

He still didn't speak.

God, he was so horrified he'd completely lost the ability.

I turned away and grabbed the two pasta bowls I'd set out to serve things up, conscious of the fact that Nathan still hadn't stopped staring.

Something was definitely wrong. In about five seconds, he was going to return to earth and kick me out for causing such mayhem. He was going to look around at what I'd done to his kitchen, possibly his whole apartment, and tell me the deal was off and he'd be better off learning social skills from the silent dude in the elevator.

The only way to fix it was to feed him. Nonna's sauce could fix anything.

"I really am sorry about the mess," I said as I started dishing up pasta, that admittedly looked kind of like overcooked glue, into the bowls.

"The mess?" When I turned around, Nathan blinked, then shook his head like he was falling out of a daydream. "I don't care about the mess. It's—Rita will clean it up when she comes in the morning."

I frowned at the mention of the housekeeper, who seemed to come and go from the apartment like a phantom, usually during the time I was asleep or at work. "No, don't make her do that. I'll take care of it."

Nathan looked unsure. But it was one thing to pay a housekeeper to do regular dusting and cleaning when the apartment was picked up. He couldn't know how it felt to be taken advantage of that way, but I did. And so did every other woman in my family.

"I'll do it," I said again as I spooned some of the sauce over each bowl. "How many meatballs?"

I bent down to remove a tray of meatballs from the oven. Okay, maybe they weren't quite as juicy as Nonna's usually looked, but they didn't smell awful. I bet they were all right.

Nathan eyed them suspiciously when I set them on the island next to the bowls. "Ah, two is fine."

"Are you sure?" I asked as I gave myself the same. "My dance instructor always told me to eat extra protein when we were building muscle. Did you lift or run today?"

Last night, Nathan had randomly told me his workout schedule, but I couldn't remember the order of things. Just that it was three days of sprint training followed by calisthenics to protect his joints and three of the heavier strength training that were responsible for his bulk.

Nathan was still studying his bowl. "I lifted." He looked like he was regretting it. "Three, then."

I dished up three, then scooped some of the carrots I'd baked onto each plate and grated Parmesan over them and the pasta, ignoring when some fell on the floor. I'd get it later.

With one finger, I scooped up an errant bit of sauce on the edge of my plate and sucked it off. Then I looked up to find Nathan staring again, this time at my finger as I pulled it out of my mouth.

Shit. Talk about bad manners.

"Er, sorry," I mumbled. "Hey, go wash up. I'll meet you in the dining room."

He started again but followed my orders without a word, mumbling something that sounded like, "Stop acting like an idiot."

I couldn't deny it hurt a little. But it was a fair critique.

When we met in the dining room, Nathan's face was red and slightly damp, like he'd washed it along with his hands. He offered a short nod as he took his seat at the table, which I'd set with napkins, silverware, and even a candle for good measure.

"Grace?" I asked, holding out my hand.

He took it but looked surprised. "I didn't realize you were religious."

I shrugged. "I'm not, really. But it's not a home-cooked meal if you don't say grace. Trust me, my nonna would approve." Quickly, I bowed my head to murmur the short prayer I'd heard literally every night of my life: "Bless us, O Lord, and these Thy gifts, which we are about to receive from Thy bounty, through Christ our Lord. Amen."

When I looked up, Nathan was still watching me, but now with a warmth I hadn't seen before. Something like fondness.

"Just a habit," I said, feeling oddly shy myself now.

God, he probably thought I was a baby. Saying my prayers like a little kid. I couldn't explain why I'd done it. It just felt right.

A brown brow lifted. "Next time, I'll join you."

I grinned. And to my shock, Nathan grinned right back.

"*Buon appetito*," I said in my admittedly poor Italian. If I was going to channel Nonna, I figured I should do it right. Or as right as I could manage.

"It's—" he stopped.

"What?" I asked.

He looked down at the steaming plate in front of him. "It's been a very long time since someone made me dinner. Thank you."

I poured some of his favorite sparkling water—he liked the

expensive stuff that came in green bottles—into the wineglasses I'd set out. "It's nothing fancy. Just spaghetti and meatballs with roasted carrots. I did sparkling water since you don't keep any wine in the house."

"Hypertension runs in my family," Nathan said as he accepted the glass. "I don't actually drink very much."

"I know. You barely touch your scotch at the bar."

At that, he frowned just as he was about to dip his fork into his food. "Then why do you bring it?"

I shrugged. "Because you always order it. Why *do* you always order it?"

Nathan shrugged back. "It just seems like what people do."

I nodded. "I get that."

And the weird thing was, I did. Sometimes I felt like life was a choice between acting like myself and pissing everyone off or doing what they wanted and feeling like an empty mask. In his own way, I had a feeling that Nathan felt the same.

"I'll make you something without alcohol next time," I said. "Perrier. I think we have it."

"With lime," Nathan said as that half smile emerged again. "Please."

We shared small, hidden smiles before we both had to look away. Why, I wasn't sure. But it was almost too much to handle.

"Can I ask you something?" I asked.

"Sure." Nathan looked up as he put a bite of meatball into his mouth.

"Do you have a girlfriend?"

He looked like he was about to choke. I wasn't sure if it was the meatball or my question. It did look a little dry. "I—no. I do not."

I pulled one knee up to my chest while I sat. It was something that always drove Nonna crazy, but sitting at a table like a normal person drove *me* crazy. "I didn't think so. You haven't called or mentioned anyone since I moved in. Plus, a lot of chicks wouldn't be too keen on a female roommate."

Nathan was suddenly very focused on twisting some spaghetti

around on his fork, blackened basil and all. "I—no. They probably wouldn't."

"Why don't you have one?" I wondered.

He paused just before he took a bite, then dropped the full fork to his plate. "A girlfriend?"

"No, an Academy Award. Of course, a girlfriend." I waved my hand at him, gesturing at, well, all he had to offer. Which was considerable. The bod. The job. The chiseled face and the charmingly rumpled hair. "You're a good-looking guy. Better than good-looking, if I'm being honest."

Understatement of the century, ladies and gentlemen.

Nathan, however, looked down at himself as if I'd told him his skin had just turned lime green. "I..." He looked back at me and picked up his fork again. "I tend to be very particular."

He then took a bite as if to punctuate the fact.

"Picky, yeah. I get that," I said as I started to twirl my own pasta around my fork. "My sister Marie is the same way. Twenty-five, never been laid, all because she's lusting after her boss, and no one can compare." Then something occurred to me in the middle of my rambling. "Holy crap, you're not a virgin, are you?"

As soon as it was out there, I regretted saying it.

"*What*?" Nathan mumbled through a mouth full of pasta.

My entire face heated like the sun. "Not that there would be anything wrong with that. I mean, it would be a little odd, a thirty-something guy with no experience. But I'm sure there are some out there, especially if you're super picky. Oh my God, are you saving yourself? Are you super religious, and I didn't know? Am I going to corrupt you living here?"

Oh, God, the babbling. I couldn't freaking stop myself. It was like I was a faucet that just. Kept. Running.

Until he set his hand atop mine, and the warm weight of it turned the faucet off.

We both stared at our hands, at the way his paw pinned my smaller one to the table. Then, gradually, Nathan pulled his back and went back to his pasta as if nothing had happened.

"For the record," he said. "I'm thirty-four, and I've had seven sexual partners. According to a 2019 NIH study, that puts me firmly within the average range for men my age."

I hadn't heard anything after the word "seven." Because at that point, women popped up in my brain like mushrooms. Seven stunningly beautiful, stupendously sexy, stupidly intelligent mushrooms.

Alongside my veritable forest.

I cringed.

What kind of women did Nathan Hunt go for? Were they blonde and curvy like Marilyn Monroe? Or was he more of a model aficionado who chased after the Bella Hadid lookalikes who roamed New York City like beautiful giraffes? Maybe he had a thing for female equivalents of himself: smart, brainy doctors who also happened to look like movie stars.

Whoever they were, they were probably nothing like me.

Not that it should have mattered.

It didn't. It *didn't*.

"Let me guess. High school girlfriend, college girlfriend, med school girlfriend, after med school girlfriend, plus a trio of regular booty calls or one-night stands?" I cocked my head as I counted my list with my fingers. "How did those go for you?"

"No one-night stands," Nathan replied calmly. Too calmly. "One college girlfriend, yes. We were engaged briefly, but it didn't work out. After that, the others lasted maybe a month or two during medical school, residency, fellowship. I didn't have much time for relationships."

I nodded. It made sense, I guessed. I didn't really know anything about doctors other than the ones on *Grey's Anatomy*, and they never seemed to leave the hospital. They were also horny as fuck and had sex in every available corner.

And now I was imagining Nathan running around in scrubs doing hot doctors in the break room. Great.

"Anyway," Nathan continued after he'd swallowed another bite. "Most of the women I've dated tend to treat me differently once they get to know me."

"How so?"

He busied himself with his pasta, taking his time with his words.

"I've been told I can be…cold. Unfeeling." He grimaced, like the next one was going to hurt. "It's been suggested that I don't have the capacity to love."

I blinked. "Well, that's fucked up. And obviously bullshit."

One brow lifted. "You think so?"

I nodded. "I do. Look at me. You took me in out of the goodness of your heart, and I'm practically a stranger. What kind of person can't do that if they don't have the ability to love? I think you just haven't met the right girl yet."

Nathan pushed his glasses up his nose and studied me for a long time. I sat up straight and looked right back. While I didn't *love* the idea of him being with other women for reasons I wasn't going to explore right now, I stood by my words.

"There are a lot of kinds of love," he said finally. "Not everyone is capable of all of them."

Well, he had me there.

"And then there is the matter of who my family is and what I do," he said as he went back to twirling another bite of pasta.

"I can't imagine that's an issue. You're hot enough that I bet plenty of women would jump you in a heartbeat. 'Specially if it meant they could bag themselves a rich doctor in the process."

Jesus. Had I really just said that? Of course I had. I barely had a filter, and it seemed to disappear when I felt awkward. Like right now.

"Is that what you would do?"

My head jerked up. Had he really just asked me that?

Based on the pinking in his cheeks, it seemed that way.

Something like shame flooded my system. Which was very confusing because he wasn't completely wrong. Had my sisters said something? Had one of them mentioned the fact that some version of that idea had been at least insinuated too many times to count?

Did he know that every time I had flunked out of school, my grandmother had sighed and said, "Well, at least you're pretty" as she patted my cheek?

"I may be a lot of things," I managed as I blinked back threatening tears. "But I'm not a gold digger."

Nathan sat back like I'd stabbed him. "Joni, I—"

"It's been suggested a few times," I admitted, feeling more idiotic by the second. This was supposed to be a friendly dinner. "Like that's what I should be doing to find success. Because, as you've probably realized by now, I'm too dumb to do it on my own."

Nathan put down his fork again. "Why do you keep saying things like that about your intellect? Your family made comments like that too when they brought your things. It was demeaning."

I shrugged and shoved a hand under one eye to push the tears away. "My family loves me, but...yeah. They know I'm not that smart."

"You seem intelligent to me."

I shook my head. "Trust me, I'm definitely not."

Nathan crossed his arms. "Explain."

I huffed. "Dude, you've lived with me for two weeks now—you must see I'm kind of a disaster. Yesterday, in the shower, I couldn't remember if I'd washed my hair, so I did it again. And then I got distracted by a song in my head, so I washed my hair three times."

Nathan's mouth quirked. "That just seems like excessive cleanliness. At worst, you might have some split ends."

"Yeah, well, it's like that with everything. I'm either so obsessed with my thoughts that I literally don't register anything else, or the world is so overwhelming I can't manage anything at all. I can't keep to a schedule, have to write things down at least five times to remember anything, and leave a trail of my crap wherever I go. You saw the kitchen." I waved in that general direction. "And that's my *best* behavior."

Nathan peered at me. "What does that have to do with your intelligence? Einstein had terrible hygiene. Plenty of bright people struggle with executive function."

I stared at my plate for a long time, suddenly wishing I could get up and go to my room. But if saying grace had been childish, running away would ice that particular cake. And for some reason, I didn't want Nathan to think that about me. He could find out I was an idiot and a flighty mess. But he didn't need to think I was a coward too.

"Well, I'm not bright either," I told him. "I'm pretty sure I graduated high school only because my English teacher had a crush on me, and two of my Spanish teachers made out with me after school. Pervs. They were so old."

Nathan didn't say a word; he just started eating again while I continued.

"School was never easy for me, unlike everyone else in my family. It took me a really long time to learn to read, and even now, I'm slower than most and can't spell at *all*. Math was horrible—don't ever ask me to recite my times tables. I wasn't trying to fail, but I could never seem to remember to do stuff. It was too much—the homework, the projects, the books, the classes." I dropped my foot to the floor, where it tapped automatically on the rug. "Things that came easy to others were always too hard for me. Not that bright. Get it?" I looked up. "Actually, I bet you don't. Doctors kind of have to do well in school, huh?"

Nathan seemed to take an extra-long time to chew and swallow. Then he sat forward and steepled his hands over his plate. "We only covered mental health for a few weeks in med school, but it sounds to me like you're neurodivergent. Possibly in multiple ways."

"Neuro-what?" He might as well have spoken Mandarin.

"It means your brain might work differently than others."

I blinked. "Oh. Well. Haven't I just been explaining that?"

Nathan turned to me like I was one of his patients. "Neurodivergence doesn't necessarily indicate intelligence deficits. I'm not a psychiatrist, but based on what you said and what I already knew about you, I'd guess ADHD, plus maybe a learning disability like dyslexia or dyscalculia. However, there are plenty of things that can interfere with different types of cognitive processing. Have you ever been evaluated?"

I shook my head. "Evaluated for mind issues? That would be a no."

"This can't be the first time anyone has suggested something like this. One of your teachers must have said something to your parents."

"Probably not, since my dad died when I was a baby, and my

mom was in and out of jail until I was twenty-one." Apparently, I was dropping *all* the bombs tonight.

Nathan frowned. "Who raised you, then?"

"My grandparents." I sighed. "Well, until my grandpa passed away. I was seven when that happened. Then it was just Nonna with six kids."

"She's the one who just moved to Italy."

I nodded.

He contemplated that for a minute. "And she never said anything?"

I snorted. "Did my conservative immigrant grandmother straight out of the nineteen-fifties say something about my weird brain? Ah, that's a big negative, man. Look, I don't know what school you went to—"

"My brothers and I all attended the Highland School, followed by Episcopal."

"Those all sound very fancy and maybe religious. Private?"

Nathan nodded.

"Figures." I toyed with my pasta but found I'd lost most of my appetite. Talking about this crap tended to have that effect on me.

Under the table, I tapped out the opening steps to my first ballet recital with my toes. God, I wished I could dance.

"Matthew, Lea, Kate, and Frankie all did elementary school at Our Redeemer—that's the local parish school," I said when Nathan kept waiting for me to fill him in. "But after my grandpa died, Nonna couldn't afford the tuition anymore, so Marie and I just went to the local public school in Belmont."

"That's in the Bronx?"

I nodded. "Yeah. They were fine. I guess."

"You guess?"

"I mean, as good as school is gonna get with thirty kids in a class-room, and half of them don't speak English." I picked up a shriveled carrot and let it drop back on the plate as I slouched around it. "The teachers had bigger problems to deal with than a little girl who couldn't read super well. Not when a lot of their students couldn't read at all. Skip to me barely graduating, then flunking out of community college twice. Cosmetology school too. Dance was the only thing I was really ever good at."

Nathan blinked, almost as if in recognition. "Dance. So that's what you meant."

Sadly, I nodded. "Pretty much."

He glanced back at the kitchen, then at me. Taking stock, no doubt, of the horrible mistake he'd made by inviting me to live with him. Joni Zola, The Great Disappointment.

"Well, for what it's worth," he said quietly, "I think you're smart. You're articulate and interesting and obviously very shrewd when you want to be. I also think you are much more than just a dancer. I think you are capable of just about anything."

I couldn't move. Couldn't even bring myself to look at him. If I did, I knew I'd cry.

"Would you ever consider being evaluated?" he wondered as he speared a carrot.

"What's that going to do now?" I wondered glumly.

"Well, for one, there are medications you can take for ADHD if you need them. If you have a learning disability, there are plenty of therapy options available, even for adults."

I chuckled. "Oh, Nathan, you're funny. I'll put that on the list right after the surgery I'm supposed to pay for with the two hundred dollars currently in my bank account. Well, one seventy-five after getting all the stuff for this meal. Sorry it's not organic. I can't afford it."

With that, I shoved my fork into my pasta and took the biggest bite I could muster. And immediately froze.

"Oh my *God*," I said, though it couldn't have been understandable through a mouth full of overcooked mush.

"What is it?" Nathan wondered, looking mildly alarmed. "Is everything okay?"

By some miracle, I managed to swallow the bite and not hurl it back up. I shoved my plate away, unable to bear it. God, it even smelled bad now.

"Nathan," I whispered. "This spaghetti is *horrible*."

Nathan looked down at his now half-eaten plate of food, then back at mine. "Well…yes. But I thought it was supposed to taste like this."

"You thought spaghetti and meatballs was supposed to taste like ketchup soup and garlicky cardboard?" Before I could stop myself, I fell back in my chair, laughing.

Nathan bit back a smile. "I—well, not generally."

Before I knew it, we were both laughing. It had to be a record. From tears to hoots in less than five minutes.

The best part, however, was that he was laughing too. I'd make him bad spaghetti anytime if I could listen to that warm, low chuckle whenever I wanted.

"Wait." I stopped laughing as another thought struck me. "You thought the food was terrible, and you ate it anyway?"

The pink in Nathan's cheeks flushed a bit darker. "What's that look? I don't know that expression yet."

I blinked and only *just* managed to close my mouth. "It's—I—I'm surprised, that's all. No one has ever done something like this for me before."

"You're surprised that I ate some bad pasta for you?" He was so obviously adorably confused. "Compared to whom? Why would anyone else have done that?"

"It's not about the pasta. It's about how terrible it is."

This time, I was the one to reach across the table for his hand. He gave it willingly and seemed unable to stop looking at them once they were joined.

"I grew up in a house where everyone just loves to tell each other what they're doing wrong," I said. "So, it's about doing something for someone else just because you want them to feel good. I…thank you, I guess. It's small, but it means something to me. I guess this look is happiness. In a way."

Nathan continued staring at our hands, this time with my long, thin fingers laid over his larger, solid ones. Gently, he turned his palm over, wove our fingers together, and squeezed.

"I have a favor to ask of you." His voice was low. The mirth was gone, but there was something gentler about it. An ease I hadn't heard before, even though he still sounded slightly nervous.

"What's that?" Right now, I'd probably give him anything. As it stood, I already owed him more than I'd ever be able to repay.

"I told you about my family, how they worry about me…socially." Nathan said the words through his teeth. The fingers entwined with mine tensed.

"Like how mine all think I'm an idiot," I said. "We have that in common, I guess."

Nathan nodded, and his hand relaxed again.

"My parents have recently become more fixated on my romantic life than usual," he went on. "They're convinced they need to find me a significant other at all costs."

He glanced at me like he was waiting for me to add something. Maybe object.

I only nodded. Some things were apparently universal. "You met my sisters, so you know I totally get it. Overbearing families are super annoying."

"They are," Nathan agreed. "Super."

I giggled. His brown eyes sparkled behind his glasses.

"There's an event I have to attend in a few more weeks. A gala for the hospital, then possibly some other events as spring approaches. My parents will be there, along with my brothers." Nathan paused as he ran his thumb over my knuckles. "In the spirit of 'helping' me with my social life, I wondered if you'd be willing to accompany me as…my girlfriend. At least, that's what I'd tell them to relieve the pressure. And in return, you can consider the next six months of rent paid, even if you decide to leave. It will hopefully give you the time to find a job you're suited to."

My jaw practically hit the floor. *"Really?"*

Nathan just squeezed my hand. "Yes, really. I'd be grateful. Clearly, I need some assistance when it comes to situations like these. Think of it as a lesson. I'll treat you like my girlfriend. And you can tell me all the things I do wrong. I…I think maybe we understand each other, Joni. Would you agree?"

Oddly, I did. I shouldn't have. We were about as different as it got. Nathan was a surgeon who was probably going to have a line of hot, equally accomplished women trailing after him the minute he said go. I was going to be lucky if I ever did anything besides serving drinks again. He was smart. I was...well, maybe I was too. But also, maybe not. I still wasn't sure about that one.

No matter what, though, he was right. There was something about this odd, awkward man I understood deep down. And even more strangely, he seemed to get me too.

"It's a deal," I said. Until I realized something else.

"What is it?" Nathan demanded immediately. "What's wrong?"

Dread lodged itself in my stomach like an anvil. "I can't go to a gala, Nathan. The only dresses I own are the ones I wear at the club. Everyone will think I'm your call girl, not your girlfriend."

Nathan recoiled, then looked me over, like my schlubby PJs were no different than Rochelle's silver outfit I'd worn just a few weeks earlier.

"Er—we'll have to get you a dress," he agreed. "I'll pay for it, of course."

I bit my lower lip. "Are you sure?"

I didn't want to take that too, but there was no way I could afford anything better than the ten-dollar sidewalk sales on St. Mark's Place.

"Call it part of your compensation," Nathan said as he took his hand back.

Relief coursed through me. "All right." Out of habit, I took another bite of pasta, and once again, could barely keep it down. "Oh God, that really is awful."

Nathan hadn't touched his. "Can I request one more favor?"

I took several gulps of water to wash down the horror show on my plate. "Depends on what it is."

"Please don't cook for me again. If you want to do something nice, I like the Greek place around the corner. They have very good souvlaki."

I grinned and was rewarded with yet another rare sighting of the Nathan Hunt light show when he smiled back.

"My dude," I told him. "That is a promise I can definitely keep."

THIRTEEN
THINGS A GOOD (FAKE) GIRLFRIEND SHOULD DO

#1 Uh...

"No, no, no. Try it again."

After the disastrous dinner I'd made him last week, we'd ordered dumplings and gone over a game plan to prepare for the gala I was supposed to attend. First, he was taking me to get a dress for the event and then wanted me to accompany him to dinner with some of his work colleagues as a sort of practice run for our fake relationship.

Before that, however, we had to get a few things straight.

And so, at approximately 2:04 a.m., Nathan sighed on the other side of the bar at Opal while I gleefully gave him lessons in acting like a believable boyfriend.

Not that I'd been looking forward to it or anything. Nor lit up like a glow stick at a rave when he walked in after his shift at the hospital.

Seriously, though. No one had the right to look that good in scrubs. Once again, his shoulders and ass made the shapeless blue garments look like couture.

"This seems unnecessary," he said as he produced a cloth from his jacket pocket and polished his glasses. "You're working. You don't even drink when you're working."

"Only because it makes it harder for me to count tips." I continued restocking the garnish trays under the bar. "You asked me to help you with this stuff, mister. So, for the third time, pretend we're on a date. Didn't you ever play make-believe as a kid?"

He replaced the glasses and lifted one eyebrow in a way that made my knees weak. And not in a way that was all that unpleasant. Yeah, I could take this role play we were doing to a whole other level.

No, Joni, no. Bad girl. Roommate, yes. Dr. Zaddy, no. Stop fantasizing about that stern, no-nonsense expression he is wearing right this second.

It really wasn't fair. People weren't supposed to get hotter the longer you knew them. Almost two weeks into living together, I should have started to resent things like how Nathan never left so much as a crumb on the counters or the fact that he absolutely refused to drink tap water. Instead, they just made him more attractive. I honestly wanted to jump the guy every time he watered his plants or glanced at me after polishing his glasses.

Like he was doing right freaking now.

I think you're smart.

It was that comment that did it. No one else in my entire life had ever said that to me. But Nathan Hunt, the biggest, hottest, cutest nerd on the planet…thought I was smart.

Maybe if he hadn't said that, I wouldn't have been sacrificing tips just to watch him sip club soda like a dude about to fall off the wagon. Instead, here I was, hanging on his every word.

I cut another lemon in half with a loud chop of the knife on the cutting board. "You're supposed to be practicing, babe. Let me hear it."

Nathan's big brown eyes rolled as he sat forward and clasped his hands. The action made his biceps stretch his thin blue sleeves to their limits. "Fine. I'll get you another vodka soda."

I set the knife down. "Dr. Hunt, what did we just discuss? If the girl says, 'Sure,' you don't just order her something, even if you think you know what she wants. You ask her first."

Nathan tilted his head in a way that made him look like a curious cartoon chipmunk. One rocking an indecently hot five o'clock shadow. "But you always drink a vodka soda. You avoid extra sugar when you can. If you were my date, I would have already figured it out."

I couldn't help but smile. "Aw, sweets, I love that you figured that out. And you should definitely work that into the conversation because it shows you see a girl and notice her."

Those big shoulders shrugged again. "I always notice you."

It was like he was commenting on the weather, but it still made me lose my breath. Nothing special, and yet somehow the most romantic thing I'd ever heard. Better than any shitty poem boys wrote in grade school, let me tell you.

> *Roses are red*
> *Violets are blue.*
> *Water is wet.*
> *And I always notice you.*

"That," I managed with a shaky exhale, "is exactly what you should say to any girl you're with. Right before you *still* ask her what she wants."

"This doesn't make any sense, Joni. It's just a simple observation."

"My dude, all women want is to be observed—to be *seen*. That's the stuff we love to hear, probably above all else. But we also want to speak."

His forehead crinkled adorably. "So you want to be seen and then heard."

"Exactly." I giggled. He wasn't making a joke, but it did sound the opposite of what old-fashioned people said about children. "So, try again."

Nathan huffed, clearly impatient. It made me want to jump over the bar and give him a hug.

"Fine. I noticed you enjoy vodka sodas. Would you like another?"

I grinned as if this small victory were as much mine as his. "Ten out of ten! And yes, sir, I would. Now, I'll pretend this glass of water is actually a drink on a date. See, it's that easy."

Nathan held up the glass of scotch he had, per usual, barely touched. "Cheers."

"*Cin cin.*" I touched my glass to his, smiled again at the clink, and enjoyed the dimple that appeared in his left cheek when he pretended to drink as well. "Now, you sit here and pretend your date is leaning over the bar to give you a peek at her cleavage while, in reality, I will serve the sorority girls down there another round of cosmos. Back in a flash."

Nathan's eyes followed me across the bar while I made a few more drinks and grabbed a few more empty glasses to put in the sanitizer. I didn't look back.

It wasn't because he was attracted to me. I knew that now. When I'd first moved in, I had thought that maybe there was something there, but I hadn't gotten one iota of that since.

Something else I was learning about Nathan Hunt: he liked to understand things. And he was a very quick study.

So that stare wasn't attraction. Nathan was just trying to figure me out.

"Notice anything good?" I asked when I returned to Nathan's end of the bar.

He tilted his head in acknowledgment of the question. "I'm curious why you called those women sorority girls. It didn't sound like a compliment."

I snorted. "It wasn't."

"Aren't you close to their age? What's the difference?"

I went back to chopping lemons. "There's a type. Girls who come to the city for school, usually because they have watched *Sex and the City* and *Friends* way too many times. They're not from New York, and they imagine their lives are going to be just like Carrie Bradshaw's. Hence the cosmos. And the dumb giggles."

As if on cue, the girls broke into a round of laughter. Nathan didn't even hide the fact that he was watching them while I spoke, and at least two of them were openly noticing him back.

One smiled at him and batted her eyes. She might as well have pulled up her skirt.

"Why don't you go down there? Try out your moves?" I suggested, though I couldn't bring myself to look at him while I said it. "College girls are smart. Right up your alley."

My throat felt tight while I said it. The idea of any one of those girls even touching my kind, brainy roommate made me want to do way more with this knife than chop lemons.

Nathan turned back to me. "I'm fine here with you."

The flood of relief tasted as sweet as chocolate milk.

God, I was an idiot. I had no right to feel this way.

"Can I ask you something?"

Nathan blinked. "Of course."

"Why scrubs tonight? Did something happen?"

Nathan glanced down at his surgical wear and made a face— well, as close to making a face as he ever got. "Surgical attendings typically wear scrubs in the ER, and I usually change when I leave. Tonight, I didn't."

"But why?" I pressed. "You've been coming here after your night shift for the last two months, but you're almost always dressed in work clothes or street clothes. See, I notice things too, Dr. Hunt."

He looked at me for a long time. Long enough that I felt frozen in place.

"I suppose I just wanted to get here first," he said when I was about to turn away.

It doesn't have anything to do with you, I told myself. Stop horning out over your stupid hot roommate. He was crunched for time. He's trying to learn how to be less awkward.

It's not because he actually likes you.

"Maybe we should do things differently," Nathan interrupted my cycle of neurosis.

I had never been so grateful. "How's that?"

"Maybe instead of this strange 'rehearsal,' as you called it, we can just make a list. What are the things that I need to be aware of to nurture a relationship?"

My eyes popped open. "Oooh, I love lists."

At that, Nathan smiled. Not at the dozens of awkward jokes I'd cracked nervously. The fact that I liked lists made him smile in a way that seemed to light up the entire bar, and I felt as bright as the Rockefeller Christmas tree right along with it.

"Me too," he said. He reached into his breast pocket and pulled out a small black book. "I write a lot of them here to remember things. Let's do one about relationships."

He opened the book and proceeded to flip through a bunch of pages, much too fast to see what was actually on them.

"I make lists *all* the time," I said with a grin and couldn't help but blush when I received one right back. "I just don't write them down."

Looking absurdly pleased, he pushed the book across the bar. "Would you be willing to start now? Maybe with things I should know about you. Favorite things, dislikes, major dates, etcetera. Information a boyfriend should know."

"On it!" I flipped the book around toward me and immediately began scrawling the first things I could think of.

Joni's Top Three
1. *Anything dancing. I will move to any kind of music.*
2. *Peonys*
3. *Pidgons*

Joni's Bottom Three
1. *Bobba tea. Tapioca is gross and way to sweet.*
2. *Homewerk of any kind. Reading, math its all horrible.*
3. *Stepping in ice puddels after it snow's*

I passed the book back to him. "My spelling sucks. Now you."

With an adorable glance over the rims of his glasses, Nathan quickly read through my lists. "Pigeons? Really?"

I nodded. "They're cute. I like it when the males get all puffed up and trot after the females. They look like little gray footballs."

With a wry smile, he set to work making his own.

NATHAN'S LIKES
1. VERY GOOD ESPRESSO
2. WHIPPED MASHED POTATOES WITHOUT ANY LUMPS
3. HARPER'S MAGAZINE INDEX

NATHAN'S DISLIKES
1. FOOT MASSAGES OR ANYONE TOUCHING MY FEET
2. SOCIAL MEDIA
3. SMALL TALK

"Looks about right," I said. "I'll remember not to rub your feet ever."

"Please don't." Nathan took back the book, turned to a new page, and wrote something across the top before passing it back to me. "If you don't mind."

THINGS A GOOD BOYFRIEND SHOULD DO

I looked up. "Really? This is only going to be for me, though. Everyone's different. My best advice is to treat every girl you date like a puzzle. Figure her out, and you'll be a good boyfriend."

Nathan swallowed but didn't look away. "Consider it a case study, then. I think it will help. Please."

I sighed. "All right."

THINGS A GOOD BOYFRIEND SHOULD DO
1. Let her pick the music and TV shows as much as u
2. Notise things about her nobody else does + listen to everything she sez. Even if you dont think it matters.

3. If you see something u like about her, tell her. Every time.

4. Always kiss her like its the 1st time.

I tapped the pen to my mouth, debating over one other item that had just occurred to me. Knowing Nathan, he'd probably take one look and leave. But in the end, I decided it was for the best. One day, some lucky girl was going to nab herself a surgeon who looked like Superman, and she deserved to get off too. Most men thought clits operated like start buttons, if they could find them at all. The fuck if my student here wouldn't at least know to figure it out.

5. Figure out how she likes to be touched. Its diffrent for everyone. And dont be stingey with your tung ether.

I passed the book across the bar to him. He read through it and looked up without a shred of embarrassment. Or, to my relief, criticism of what I was sure was atrocious spelling.

Now, I was the one who was impressed.

"I expected there to be more," he said when he was done.

I shrugged. "I'm not that complicated. And I didn't think I had to write down the Ten Commandments. Do you need to be reminded to be nice, not cheat, and not lie?"

Nathan shook his head solemnly. "No, I do not need to learn tenets of basic respect and honesty."

It was a joke, but he wasn't treating it like one. I *liked* that he wasn't treating it like one. That determined expression reminded me of the fact that most of my boyfriends had not learned this particular lesson ever.

He studied the list, and I had a flash of what he must have looked like in school, cooped up at a library, studying for his exams. And yeah, I won't lie. The image seriously did it for me. Especially when I could just as easily imagine myself pouncing on him in the back of a lonely, isolated library stack.

Stop it, Joni. He is your roommate and fake boyfriend. Emphasis on *fake*.

"As a doctor, I'm also very familiar with the female anatomy," he continued like I wasn't combusting in front of him. "And I make it a point to make sure my partners receive as much pleasure as I do from our sexual encounters. Anything less would be unethical, don't you think?"

His brown eyes met mine, and for a split second, the noise in the bar faded away, and once again, I found it hard to breathe.

"I—definitely not," I managed without a stutter. Just barely.

"It's also just enjoyable," he added.

"Oh?" Why did my voice sound so breathy?

"Yes. Every body is different, whether it's one of my patient's or belongs to someone I'm seeing. They all respond differently to various stimuli or treatments. Figuring out which ones and how is like a puzzle. I've always liked puzzles. I'm good at them." He seemed to refocus on my face again. "Are you all right? You don't look like you're breathing properly."

That's because I'm imagining *exactly* what you do during your "sexual encounters," Dr. Hunt. Or how you would solve *my* puzzle.

My God, he had said it just like that without the slightest suggestion or game at all. Like he didn't know the way it would make my thighs squeeze or my nipples poke through my shirt.

"I'm fine," I managed. "I—I'm glad we're on the same page, I suppose. Less, um, to teach you."

Nathan looked down at said page, then back to me. "Well, you're a good teacher. I appreciate it."

I focused back on the lemons, willing my cheeks to return to a normal temperature.

My reaction didn't make sense. He wasn't overtly coming on to me. Between being a dancer and just being a red-blooded teenager growing up in New York, I'd experienced more than a lifetime of that kind of stuff. I'd been on the receiving end of catcalls since my tits had popped out, had been sneaking out to nightclubs before I could even drive, and had learned the art of flirting in a bar as soon as I got my braces off. Kids in New York grew up fast, and I was no different.

But this was different. I shouldn't be reacting to what was, on his end, just a basic conversation about anatomy.

It occurred to me that these lessons were bullshit. Not because Nathan wasn't socially awkward—he was. But I didn't know how to tell him that his lack of game and absence of pretense was sexier than any line I'd ever gotten. There was something so unbearably hot about a man who looked at you without a shifty, unpredictable gaze. Who just straight out said he wanted to be with you instead of spitting games or shouting catcalls. Who didn't try to hide it at all.

Nathan didn't need to learn to flirt. He just needed to find a girl he really liked and tell her straight out. If she didn't appreciate his brand of honesty, then she didn't deserve him.

The idea of him with another woman struck a nasty chord of *wrong* through my stomach. I pushed it away and was about to tell him to throw all my advice out the window and just be himself when we were rudely interrupted.

"Joni?"

A deep voice I had genuinely hoped I'd never hear again echoed through the bar and down the little path it had created in my soul over the last eight years.

It had been four months since I'd heard it. Since that shifty gaze and insinuating smile had last landed on me.

Back in my life.

Again.

Fuck.

"Who is that?"

Nathan had turned on his stool toward the owner of the voice, who was currently making his way through the bar.

I ground my teeth and nodded in the direction of the voice.

"That's...Shawn," I said with a heavy sigh. "He was sort of...my boyfriend. Or something like that."

FOURTEEN
WHY SHAWN VAMOS SHOULD WALK OFF A BRIDGE

#28 That naked lady tatoo on his butt. Wy have a butt on your butt??

"**Y**ou have a boyfriend?"

Momentarily, I was reminded of Wiley E. Coyote after he'd been run over several times. Punch drunk—I supposed that's what you would call Nathan's expression.

Addled.

Or maybe a little heartbroken.

I shook the thought away. It was ridiculous. Nathan and I were friendly roommates with a weird kind of arrangement. There was absolutely no reason for him to be sad if I was involved with someone else.

Which I wasn't. Not really.

Or maybe I was.

"Er, had. Not exactly, but, um, sort of—" I started to say, but couldn't make it any further before I was interrupted by the bane of my existence—otherwise known as Shawn fucking Vamos.

"Joni, what the fuck?" Shawn stepped up to the bar right next to

Nathan as if he and every other person in Opal were just another piece of furniture.

It was what had attracted me to him in the first place. I'd never seen anyone do that—walk into any room like they owned it without breaking a sweat.

That particular talent hadn't changed in the years since we'd met, and neither had his typical uniform of ripped jeans, a designer T-shirt that revealed two arms full of tribal tattoos, and a thick silver chain that gleamed against his smooth chest. His short black hair and groomed stubble also remained constants. The only real differences now were in the way his shirts were a little tighter around the midsection and the new filling that flashed gold with the others when he smiled, matching the two small hoops in his left earlobe. At fourteen, I'd thought his teeth made him look like a pirate, but now I recognized them as a marker of bad dental hygiene.

"I've been trying to reach you for weeks," he said in his thick Newark accent. "Even went all the way up to your grandma's shitty house, but apparently, she doesn't live there no more, and neither do you. What the fuck happened?"

He slid onto the barstool next to Nathan and folded his hands together into one large fist. The motion made his elbow bump into Nathan's.

Nathan didn't move at all, barely even turned to look at Shawn. But I could tell he was watching and thinking. By the way a muscle at the corner of his jaw was starting to tick; I doubted it was anything good.

Shawn scowled at Nathan when he didn't automatically give up the space. "You mind, guy? I'm talking with my girl."

"Nathan stays where he is," I suddenly found my voice.

Both men turned toward me, and the forces of both of their expressions—so different and yet equally powerful—had me backing up against the sink behind me. I reached out on either side to grip the edges of the bar, like I was on a teetering ship threatening to toss me overboard in a storm.

"He's a paying customer, Shawn," I said. "You're not."

Nathan's brows lifted above his glasses, and I knew what that meant. A customer? Really?

Shawn turned back to Nathan to give him his patented look-over, the one that most men understood as nothing good. It was a look that weighed the competition. Calculating just how many punches it would take to throw the sucker to the ground.

Anyone else would flinch under that black gaze.

Nathan didn't move a muscle.

To my surprise, Shawn turned away first, then offered me a smug grin that had always reminded me of a shark's. "Well, you always did like an audience, baby. Speaking of, you dancing tonight? I wouldn't mind watching a little show myself."

Nathan frowned, obviously confused, as he glanced down at my knee, then back at Shawn. His confusion was clear, and it made sense. After all, if Shawn was my boyfriend, wouldn't he know about my knee? Or that I'd moved out of Nonna's? Or where I'd actually gone?

This wasn't the time or place to explain everything to him. Especially when I'd never explained it to anyone. Not even Marie knew the whole story.

"My knee's busted," I said.

"Still?" Shawn sounded annoyed.

"Just like it was the last time I saw you."

"Hey, you can't blame a guy for not wanting to hang around no cripple, gorgeous. I'm too busy to play nursemaid. I'm sorry if that hurts your feelings, but it's the way the world works."

Nathan's eyes flared, but he still didn't say anything. Instead, he took a very long drink of his scotch. Under normal circumstances, I might have grinned at the way his eyes reddened at the unfamiliar sharp bite. But right now, I had no more sense of humor than he did.

I sighed, then picked up a cloth and started rubbing a spot on the counter that was already clean. "What do you want, Shawn?"

Shawn's smile disappeared. "I already asked. Where you been?"

"Around," I replied sullenly. "I moved out. Listen, do we really have to do this here? I'm at work."

Shawn drummed his fingers on the bar top and gave me another predatory grin. "I'll behave if you can, Sunshine."

It was a dare. And maybe one I might have responded to long ago. Back when Shawn used to rescue me from a chaotic house, sneak me into clubs I had no business going into, cheer me on as I danced on tables, and let him feel me up under them. Back then, it often felt like we were either fighting or fucking. There was a certain high to both.

A certain crash too.

"I told you in the fall I had to move out," I said with short, clipped consonants. "Nonna went back to Italy, so she rented the house. You'd know all of this if you hadn't dumped me and then gone straight to Diamonds. Chelle works there. How could you possibly think I wouldn't find out?"

Shawn just grinned. "I knew you would. I made sure of it. Honest, I thought I might run into you that night."

I scoffed. "In a strip club I never worked at? How dumb do you think I am?"

Another sharp grin. "You really want me to answer that, baby?"

My entire body flushed under that knowing gaze. And not in a good way.

Shawn sat back, hands up as if in surrender. "Hey, hey. I'm just being honest. What do you want me to say, you're a rocket scientist? Sure, if that's what you want to believe, you're a fuckin' Nobel Prize Winner."

"You know what?" I snapped. "Fuck you. You're just the same as you always were. An asshole."

Nathan's knuckles turned white around his glass as he glared at Shawn.

"An asshole who tells it like it is. Which is how you know I'm still telling the truth when I say you're as beautiful as ever, and I miss you. There's no one like you, Sunshine." He leaned across the bar and drifted a hand across my cheek. "I don't care if you're a little slow, sweetie. I like you just the way you are. Always did."

And that, in a nutshell, was every conversation I had ever had with Shawn Vamos. One part insult. Two parts compliment. A snakelike ability to twist every insecurity I had around his fingers so he could tug, and I'd do his bidding.

I hated that it was working. That I was sliding back into this give-and-take so easily.

"Besides," Shawn said as he sat back onto his stool, looking satisfied. "I was just looking at Diamonds, not touching. And any man who doesn't do that every now and then either has his balls cut off or he's lying. There's no in-between."

Beside him, Nathan grunted. Or growled. It was hard to tell which.

But it was enough to yank me out of this cycle.

"I don't know," I replied as I went back to wiping the bar. "Nathan, do you enjoy visiting strip clubs?"

In a blink, Nathan erased the scowl he'd been wearing since Shawn walked in. He glanced between us both. "I do not."

Was it messed up that I was relieved?

Or was I stupid for believing him in the first place?

"See? Liar." Shawn seemed to echo my thoughts as he pointed a thumb toward Nathan. "Or gay, maybe. Whatever spins your wheels, my man."

"I'm neither," Nathan said through his teeth. "I've just never needed to pay women to put their bodies on display for me."

"Nathan's a doctor," I added, though I couldn't have said why.

Maybe it was just to make Shawn feel less than since he was so good at doing the same thing to me. You want to call me stupid? Well, here's a smart-as-fuck guy who thinks I'm smart too.

Shawn gave Nathan another once-over, then turned back to me. "Whatever. Besides, it didn't mean nothing. You know that."

"It meant something to me," I snapped back. "We said we were exclusive. Pawing girls named after cocktails is not included in that arrangement. *That* is why we had to break up for the thousandth time."

At that, the cocky smile on Shawn's face finally disappeared as he leaned across the bar, clearly wanting me to come closer. Or maybe run far, far away. I could never decide which when it came to him.

I stepped back again, and when I did, he smiled like he'd planned it all the time. Dammit.

It didn't help that Nathan was looking at Shawn like he wanted to flat-out murder him. Or that I found the expression annoyingly hot. What was wrong with me?

"I don't remember no break up, Sunshine," Shawn said in a low voice meant only for me. "I don't remember a single fucking word about it."

I couldn't help the way the hair on the back of my neck stood up at the sound of that low growl. Or the way that nickname, Sunshine, called to me while at the same time made me want to leave this city and never look back.

How could one person make me feel so many things at once? One look from Shawn, and suddenly, I was at war with myself all over again.

"That's only because you wouldn't take any of my calls or texts," I mumbled. "You disappeared, just like you always do when you screw up."

"But that's just how we roll, baby. We're free spirits, you and me. We never could be tied down, and that's why we worked. It's why I'm always gonna be your man, too. Isn't that right?"

I chewed on my lower lip. *Say no*, I told myself. Tell him he's wrong. Tell him to leave. Tell him he's not your man.

Nathan was still watching us carefully. Mostly me now. Mostly like he was waiting for something too.

"Can I get a Tito's and tonic?"

I welcomed the distraction of another customer. Even welcomed her, pointing out when I poured Sprite instead of tonic. Twice. It kept me from looking at Shawn's leering face. Or seeing the disappointment that must have been scrawled all over Nathan's.

"Damn, you look good now that you're out of that brace and shit," Shawn said when I turned around after the woman had left with her drink. "Fuck, real good, baby. That shirt is fire. Looks even better on the bedroom floor, though."

I glanced down at the clingy black top that wasn't anything special but seemed to get me a fair amount of attention. The jeans too

—the second-skin 501s I'd found at a thrift shop. It was a look straight out of a nineties Calvin Klein ad. Something that was last popular before I was even born. But a classic was a classic.

After all, it had kept Shawn looking at me like that for over a decade, hadn't it?

I just wasn't sure if that was a good thing.

I turned to find Nathan studying the list I'd made earlier. Was he taking notes? Looking to see if I'd included shallow compliments like that?

I wanted to tell him not to listen to Shawn. That, as nice as it felt to hear men say I was pretty, it was the same shit I'd been hearing since I was a kid and pretty much *all* I'd heard since. I was finally starting to value the idea that someone might actually want me for something else. Maybe even believe it.

And he'd done that over an awkward meal and some untouched drinks.

Suddenly, Nathan stood. His stool screeched on the battered wood floor loud enough that both Shawn and I jumped.

"Jesus, guy," Shawn said. "Give a warning, why don't you?"

Nathan ignored him. "I'm going home," he told me. "I'll see you—"

I cut him off with a subtle shake of my head. The last thing I needed was Shawn figuring out where I lived. Who I lived with.

Well, maybe not the last thing. That was still a threat. And he was thankfully busy on his phone.

"Um, hold on. Let me close you out," I said.

He waited, obviously confused, as I went to the cash register, and after a quick glance to make sure Shawn still wasn't watching, jotted a quick message on a piece of blank receipt paper.

Please stay til he leeves.

I knew the spelling wasn't right, but I didn't have time to check it on my phone.

"Here's your check," I said loudly as I placed the note, folded like a tent, in front of Nathan. "Unless you want something else."

Nathan opened the receipt, frowned immediately as he read it, then darted another worried glance at Shawn before shoving it in his pocket and immediately returning to his stool.

I hadn't realized how fast my heart was beating until it finally slowed down.

Safe. That's how Nathan made me feel.

I also hadn't known that until now.

"Actually, I'll have another drink," he said. "My regular."

I offered a grateful look and nodded my thanks before turning to pour him a glass of scotch I knew he wouldn't even drink.

"I'll have one too, baby," Shawn said as he set his phone down. "Same as four-eyes right here. You don't mind a little joke, do you, guy?"

I sighed but poured two of the same drinks.

Nathan stared at his, while Shawn took a long, noisy slurp. "Thank you," he said quietly.

"No, thank *you*," I murmured back. I hoped he knew what I meant by it.

"Yeaaaaah," Shawn crowed after downing nearly half the very expensive scotch. "That's the good stuff. Only Macallan for me."

"You can close me out," Nathan said again. "Um, again, I suppose."

With a small smile, I took his credit card. Shawn, however, did not offer any form of payment. I waited. And waited.

He sipped on his drink and just smiled wide enough to show two of his fillings.

I sighed. Tom was at the other end of the bar, clearly watching the whole episode and distinctly making sure I wasn't about to comp his nicest liquor to one of my admirers. And I wasn't, either. I made that mistake on my very first night. Ended up spending my whole paycheck in an hour.

"I—do you want to—it's about—"

God, I hated the way he made me stumble over my words, like I was ten again, struggling to read in front of my class. I barely did this anymore. Not even when customers had me check the math on their tab.

"Spit it out, Sunshine," Shawn said with another knowing grin. "You know I hate it when you stutter."

My face burned. "I—"

"I don't mind it."

We both turned to Nathan, who was swirling his drink meditatively.

"A stutter," he clarified. "It doesn't bother me at all."

His chocolatey eyes were so open and kind, and I wanted to dive into them just to escape this horrible bar. This horrible person beside him.

Again, however, I shook my head with a silent message. *Don't.*

Nathan's brow crinkled slightly, but he didn't say anything more.

"The drink, Shawn," I mumbled. "It's—it's expensive, so I can't c-comp you. My, um, boss is right there, and he'll dock my wages."

Shawn looked over at Tom, then rolled his eyes. "Is that all? Fine, what do I owe you? Twenty?"

I sighed again. It was just like him. Play the nice guy but take advantage where he could. Shawn always loved a good "connection."

"It's a hundred dollars a pour," Nathan supplied. "One twenty with tip."

Shawn turned, and his gaze took in Nathan's arms and shoulders, and I enjoyed the way it kept going up several inches as if he only just realized how big Nathan really was.

I took particular pleasure in the fact that, after their eyes met, Shawn looked away first.

"Thanks," he said stiffly. "But Joni's my girl. She'll hook me up."

Nathan turned back to me, his expression sharper now. "That's right. He's your boyfriend."

"It's complicated," I murmured. I didn't know what else to say.

"That's one way to put it." Shawn chuckled like I'd just said something funny.

Nathan looked like he wanted to take him by the collar and throw him out of the bar.

"The-the scotch?" I continued sputtering like a broken speed boat. "It is, um, actually really expensive, like Nathan said—so I can't give you a discount, see, and—?"

God, why was everything out of my mouth suddenly a question?

"Joni."

I turned toward Nathan's deep voice, calm and velvety. He nodded toward the card in my hand.

"Just add it to my tab," he said. "I don't want it to come out of your wages."

I blinked. "How did you know that it would…"

"You just mentioned it," he replied, then tapped a finger on the pocket of his scrubs, where he'd tucked the list. "And you told me before. 'Listen, even if you think it doesn't matter,' right?"

Shawn glanced between us like we were engaged in a tennis match. When his gaze landed back on Nathan, he was scowling.

Crap.

"I got it," he said as he extracted a hundred-dollar bill from his wallet. He set it on the bar top and slid it toward me. "There you go, baby. You know I'll always take care of you." Then, as if he was bored of the whole conversation, Shawn downed the rest of the drink like water and then stood up, smacking his lips. "Well, as much as I want to sit here wasting the night away, some of us have to work in the morning."

He leaned across the bar to grab my wrist and tug me as close as I could come with the barrier between us. I didn't dare twist away. Part of me didn't actually want to as the scent of his, the blend of Sauvage cologne, scotch, and a hint of tobacco, slithered around me like it was a chain around my body, locking it up tight.

But another part of me froze as he pressed a loud kiss to my closed, unmoving mouth. I didn't even move as he squeezed my ass. Couldn't until he'd stepped fully away, having marked me as his for everyone—for Nathan—to see.

I wrapped my arms around my waist as a sudden chill swept over me. Wrong. Everything about Shawn felt so…wrong in a way he never had before. Even when I was so mad at him I could spit, his touch had never made me shrivel like this.

Nathan still hadn't moved.

I didn't dare look at him.

"I'll call you," Shawn said as he pulled on his jacket. "We'll make up right next week. I promise."

I prayed he'd break that promise, just like so many others. Unfortunately, I had a feeling he wouldn't. He never did in the beginning.

"See you, Sunshine," Shawn called, then grabbed his coat and wove his way around the remaining bar patrons.

Nathan and I both watched until the door had closed behind him, leaving us in the bar with the few remaining customers as Tom switched on the music for last call.

Eventually, though, I managed to exhale. And finally met Nathan's eye.

"I think he *is* your boyfriend," he said. "Not *was*."

I deflated like a balloon. "I'll explain at home. I promise."

Nathan's gaze was hard and searching. "Yeah, I think you'd better."

FIFTEEN

REASONS I'VE NEVER HAD A REAL BOYFRIEND

#1 Shawn Vamos. Thats probly it.

The next morning, just before noon, I stumbled out of my room in search of coffee, where I found Nathan looking equally sleepy as he made himself an espresso, though he had clearly already been to the gym.

We hadn't talked much after Shawn finally left. Nathan had sat quietly at the end of the bar while I made excuses *not* to hang with him there. For once, I was a model employee, doing everything I could to help Tom finish last call and clean up. We even managed to close up fifteen minutes earlier than usual.

Nathan had stayed to walk me home, and even then, he didn't ask any questions about Shawn or demand further explanation. I didn't offer any either. We were both tired, I said. We needed some sleep.

Now, though, I didn't have sleep to fall back on. And the minute Nathan saw me walk into the kitchen, I knew he wasn't going to take any other excuses to avoid this conversation either.

Fantastic.

"Here," he said, handing me the cappuccino he'd just made for himself. "I'll make another. And after, we should talk."

There wasn't much more I could say to that.

Ten minutes later, we were both sitting in the living room, facing the Degas painting, while one of us got up the nerve to speak first.

"All right," Nathan said, finally. "It's not really any of my business if you have a boyfriend. But I do feel misled, given the agreement we came to. It doesn't seem appropriate for you to act as my significant other if you're already involved with someone else."

"I'm not involved with Shawn anymore," I said as I folded my legs underneath me. I was still in my pajama shorts, but the throw blanket was on the other side of the couch.

"That's not what you said last night." Nathan's eyes sharpened as he reached over and handed me the blanket. Without me asking.

I bit my lip but took it gratefully. He really was too good for me.

"That was…habit, I guess," I said. "It's what he expected to hear, and when it comes to him, it's easier just to give him what he expects sometimes. He never liked it when I called him my boyfriend, but he didn't *not* like it either. You know?"

"No, I don't know." He frowned. "So, he's your boyfriend that you're not involved with? Or you are, and he isn't? I don't understand."

"I don't know what you want me to say," I mumbled, staring at the silky foam atop my cup. Nathan had made the shape of a leaf with it.

"I just want the truth. Whatever it is."

I took a long drink of my coffee. It was perfect. Just like him. And very *not* like me.

"You want the truth?" I sighed. "The truth is, I'm a mess. But you already knew that."

Nathan only blinked. Waited in his patient way. The one where I couldn't exactly tell what he was thinking, but somehow, I knew he wasn't judging me.

I wasn't sure how that was possible.

"Shawn isn't my boyfriend."

"But you said he was."

I sighed. "He—I guess he always sort of is, but only because he won't let me break up with him completely. I hadn't seen him in more than four months, but that's not unusual. I was hoping he wouldn't show up this time, but I'm not that lucky. He's just a bad penny. A *really* bad penny."

Nathan sat back into the couch. "Explain."

I pulled the blanket up to my chest, wondering how in the hell I could put the tale of Shawn Vamos together. It wasn't a story I'd ever told to completion. Rochelle knew a little, considering she was there when we met. Marie figured out bits and pieces when he picked me up from school once, but she never pressed me for more than I wanted to share. The rest of my siblings, or even Nonna, were completely oblivious to his existence.

Because that's the way he wanted it. Said our relationship was just for us.

And like a fool, I'd believed him.

"We met about ten years ago. No, wait, almost eleven. Jeez, I'm getting old."

Nathan gave me the same look I sometimes got from my older sisters when I made similar comments.

I chuckled. "Okay, maybe not. Anyway, he saw me dancing once. I was in this troupe that did a performance at a mall in New Jersey. Kind of lame, I know, but I was the lead soloist. Shawn was there and came up to me afterward. And he was nice. Hot, for an older guy. Well, to me, he was older. Twenty-two at the time, I think. Maybe twenty-three. I thought he looked like one of the guys from One Direction."

I could imagine it like it had happened yesterday. Shawn was a boy band lookalike with arms covered in tattoos, holding a bag from the Gucci store in one hand while the other was wrapped around a gorgeous-looking blond girl. I was waiting in line to be shuttled back to the bus with the rest of the girls in my troupe. Even now, I remembered seeing that hand on the woman's waist and wondering when I'd ever find a boy who would touch me like that. I'd never even had a boyfriend. Had gotten my braces off maybe two months earlier.

Shawn had sent the woman on her way and beckoned me over to

talk to him. As if in a trance, I'd followed. We spoke just long enough for me to tell him my name and where we were from before my teacher had called me back.

He'd smiled with blue eyes the color of the ocean and said goodbye.

I expected…well, I don't know what I expected to see on Nathan's face as I described it. Disgust? Horror? If he and I went on a date, no one would blink an eye at the age difference between us. There weren't even ten between Shawn and me, but when the younger person is only thirteen and the other one is in his twenties, people are going to talk. And judge. A lot.

I certainly would.

Nathan, however, didn't change his expression. He just sipped his coffee and listened.

"It wasn't anything. Just a chat. But then he started coming to the studio every now and then. Happened to run into me on the street. Said hello. Kept coming back." I shrugged. "It was all harmless. And I guess I developed kind of a crush."

It was so odd to remember. I was at that weird age where my body looked almost like an adult's, but my brain was more like a child's. All my siblings were growing up, and I was sure I was right there with them, so when this nice older guy that looked kind of like Zayn Malik was paying me all sorts of attention and compliments and talking to me like an adult, I thought that proved my point. It was innocent. And it felt good.

So I never thought anything of it when he started bringing me presents too. Little things, like a flower from the bodega. A cheap necklace from Forever 21. Nothing big. Nothing crazy. Just things he said made him think of me.

No one had ever done that for me. Half the time, even my Christmas gifts were hand-me-downs originally bought with someone else in mind.

So, yeah. I developed a crush. A big one.

"Then things started to get really bad at home," I said as I hugged a pillow to my chest. "Mostly because of school. Everyone else in my family is smart, see. Really smart. My brother is a freaking lawyer.

Lea got a degree, too, before she had kids. Kate did fashion school and built her own business, Frankie was valedictorian, and Marie was already becoming this brilliant chef. And then there was me. Flunking out of ninth grade. Nonna was *so* mad. She said my grandfather was rolling in his grave right alongside my dad, and that they would both be so ashamed of me. That *she* was ashamed of me."

For the first time, Nathan's brow furrowed. "I understand that feeling."

I snorted. "Yeah, I bet your family's really ashamed that you became a surgeon. Real stain on their legacy."

Nathan's big shoulders just rose and fell. "It wasn't the path they planned for me. Among other things."

His brown eyes met mine, and I saw truth there. A pain that mirrored mine. I didn't know how or why, but somewhere along the line, Nathan Hunt had experienced the same kind of berating, shaming, and humiliation from his family that I had.

Just the idea made me rage inside.

"So, what happened with him after that?" he asked, pulling me out of my anger on his behalf. "How did it become…more?"

I cleared my throat and released the pillow I only just realized I'd been squeezing half to death. "Oh, well. About what you'd expect. I was angry with my family. And sad. And Shawn was…there. He started picking me up and taking me to dinner. Helping me with my homework when I needed it. Making sure I got to and from dance class. Just, you know, taking care of me. He made me feel like it was just us against the world, and I believed him. And when he finally kissed me, I felt like the luckiest girl on the planet, you know? I would have done about anything for him at that point."

And I had, but I wasn't about to describe all of that to Nathan. How Shawn had confessed his feelings to me as if he had some terrible disease, and only I could provide the cure. Convinced me that we needed to stay a secret, that we were soulmates who just needed more time.

I lost my virginity four months before I turned fifteen.

I thought I was in love.

Because I thought I was his.

But when you don't have anyone to talk to about these things, you also don't have anyone to tell you you're being an idiot. So, I also didn't have anyone to tell me that the inevitable was going to happen. That Shawn would tire of me and become alternately distant and controlling. That I'd never be able to reach him—only he could reach me. That I'd live for the days when I'd spot his red Mercedes turning the corner by the dance studio, knowing he'd take me for dinner like a grownup, then to motels that eventually grew less and less pretty as the years went by. That some days, I'd feel like the center of his world, and others, I'd feel like he kicked me out of it.

That I'd never be his girlfriend. Never be anything real.

But that every time I'd try to break it off, he'd worm his way back in all over again until I'd give in.

"It went on like that until I finally graduated high school," I said. "Then he sort of lost interest for months at a time. I knew he was always seeing other people. He said we defied labels."

I could hear myself practically parroting the same line Shawn had fed me last night, like I was still that idiot teenager. He still looked almost the same. And I had felt the same. The second he walked into the bar, every bit of lightness I'd felt had vanished, swallowed by that dark shadow of inevitability.

"But even then, he'd always come back. But by then, even though I didn't want him to, it was just easier to wait until he was bored again. Shawn gets angry when he's rejected, and he knows things. An angry Shawn is a scary Shawn. And I don't ever want anyone else to know about him, Nathan. No one."

The unspoken question, of course, was why I had told him then.

Because I had to.

Because I could.

Because, somehow, Nathan was still looking at me like he always had, without judgment or contempt. Like I just was.

"So, let me paraphrase," he said once it was apparent I was done talking. "When you were thirteen, a twenty-two-year-old man started grooming you—"

"Dude, I'm not a dog," I cut in. "He wasn't *grooming* me."

"It's just the term for when an adult manipulates a child into an inappropriate relationship," Nathan explained quietly. "I didn't mean any disrespect."

I took another long drink of coffee. I knew that. I'd just...never wanted to say it out loud.

"He started a relationship with you," Nathan rephrased, then looked up as if to say, *Is that better?*

I nodded shortly. He went on.

"He made you dependent on him, built an attachment, cultivated a sexual relationship with a minor—"

"It wasn't illegal," I muttered. This right here was why I never told anyone this story. "The age of consent in New York was fourteen until a few years ago." When Nathan's eyes flashed with something dangerous, I shook my head. "Don't ask me how I know that."

Undoubtedly, he already did. Because Shawn had known. Had explained it thoroughly the one time I questioned whether or not someone his age should be kissing someone as young as me.

"That was for marriage, not sexual activity, which has always been seventeen," Nathan said just as quietly. His eyes flashed again. "It made the news when it was finally changed."

My voice caught as I realized I had been fooled by yet another one of Shawn's lies.

He'd said it was fine. That no one could get into any trouble.

I'd believed him. But I'd known no one else would think so.

"I'm not fourteen *now*," I said in a way that I somewhat sounded like it. "*Or* seventeen."

The flash in Nathan's eyes softened. "No," he said in a voice that was slightly husky. "You are an adult woman capable of full consent."

I nodded. "Yes, I am."

There was an awkward silence as we stared at each other across the room. I was suddenly aware that I hadn't bothered to put on a bra this morning when I'd woken up and that this T-shirt was very thin. Almost as thin as Nathan's, which was doing nothing to hide the shape of his muscles he worked so hard at the gym to maintain.

Grown woman meets grown man.

Nothing illicit at all.

Yet something that I had no business thinking about.

Nathan cleared his throat. "So, what happened since? You got back together at some point?"

I shrugged. "Yes and no. Whenever he's lonely, he sniffs around looking for company, and I've been a safe bet for years."

Nathan looked confused. "Is that what *you* want?" How could I explain this the right way? The answer was generally no, although sometimes it was easier to say yes.

And then there is the other reason. The reason I wasn't even going to mention, much less think about.

"Like I said, it's easier just to give him what he wants," I said simply. "He's like an ant infestation. He'll just keep showing up until he finds a better source of sugar."

"And why do you let him? Ants can be exterminated."

Yeah, I wasn't going to tell him that. I wasn't ever going to tell him, or anyone, *that*. "Because it's not worth the fight, that's why. Shawn's a baby. I can handle him."

Nathan was quiet for a long minute. A thick silence filled the room, and I found myself looking around at all the things my sisters had noticed. The custom curtains. The plush furniture. The painting on the wall of the dancer.

She was by herself, stretching on the floor. She looked focused as she reached toward her toes.

But also lonely. As lonely as I felt whenever I thought about Shawn. My family. The whole stupid story of my life, empty of accomplishment.

God, what I wouldn't give to be her again, with something, *anything*, to focus on. That familiar space with the springy wood floor, where I'd been able to release all the noise in my head without thinking. The only place I'd ever felt free. And purely myself.

"But what do *you* want?" Nathan asked, almost like he was reading my mind.

I looked up, yanked out of my thoughts. "I used to want a lot of things."

"I mean with him. Shawn. There's history there. Do you want there to be more?"

"Oh." I played with the ends of my hair. "If I'm being honest, I wouldn't mind never seeing him again. Shawn never brings anything but trouble. But I doubt that anything less than me walking down the aisle with another man would put him off."

"Really?" It was meant to be a joke, but Nathan seemed to take the idea seriously.

"Dude, no," I said. "I mean, yeah, probably, since he's about as commitment phobic as it gets. But no. I don't need to get freaking married for him to leave me alone. Probably just be in a real relationship. Preferably with someone who could beat him up. He can throw a punch, but he doesn't have a lot of muscle."

Just the idea felt like a bad trip. Even more when the image of Nathan in a tux standing next to me in a veil popped into my head for absolutely no reason.

My stomach did a somersault.

God, what was wrong with me?

"But has he ever seen you in a serious relationship?" Nathan pressed.

I snorted. "I'd have to have had a serious relationship for that to happen."

I should have been able to say yes. Because I knew how lame it was, that at twenty-four, I'd never had a relationship last more than a few weeks. "Joni's Boyfriend of the Hour," like Lea had said too many times to count. She also liked to sing that old song "Maneater" whenever I had a date.

It was supposed to be funny, and maybe it was. But deep down, I wondered if they were right.

And then I wondered if the real reason none of my relationships seemed to last was because of one core reality: I just wasn't worth it.

Nathan looked thoughtful. I fought the urge to bury my head in the couch cushions. Instead, I sat up straight, remembering the posture lessons that Mrs. Suarez had practically beaten into me.

That made me feel a little better. Dancers don't shrink. They stand tall and hold their bodies with inner strength.

Even when shit gets really hard.

Maybe I wasn't a dancer anymore, but at least I could do that.

"I think maybe the charade we agreed to might benefit us both," Nathan said finally.

I frowned. "How do you figure?"

He sat back in his chair and drummed his fingers on the arm. "I think we should just pretend to be in a relationship...all the time... starting now. You'll come with me to work and family events. Be my date to things and, ah, 'coach' me, like we discussed. I'll pick you up from your shifts at the bar, accompany you wherever else you need, and help you earn some respect from your family and put off this...predatory person in your life." He tipped his head in that way I'd come to recognize. It meant he was feeling amused. Maybe a little mischievous. "Do I look like someone who could beat him up?"

I worked a corner of a throw pillow between my fingers. It sounded good. Maybe too good. A gorgeous apartment and stupid hot "boyfriend" falling into my lap just when I was hitting rock bottom.

There had to be a catch.

"I don't understand why you would do all of this for me," I said.

He tilted his head, causing a mussed curl to fall over his brow. "It's not just for you. It's for me too. We discussed this."

"Yeah, but I'm a legit mess, as we've also discussed. You have way more to offer. I know you said you have that social disorder thing—"

"Social pragmatic processing disorder," he corrected me gently.

"That, yeah. But to me, it doesn't seem like that big of a deal. I don't for one minute believe that you couldn't get a girlfriend—a real one—like that." I snapped my fingers to demonstrate.

Nathan didn't argue with me. Which told me I was right. I could easily imagine it—women falling all over themselves to give the hot doctor their numbers. His own patients probably came onto him at all hours of the night.

Messing around with me was a waste of his time. We both knew it.

"Maybe I just like you better than most people," he said. "Have you considered that?"

I laughed. "Come on. I'm not that dumb fourteen-year-old anymore."

At that, he looked visibly angry for the first time. The hard glare in his eye shut me up immediately. All irreverence ran right out the front door.

"Do *not* compare me to that piece of shit, Joni," he said through clenched teeth. "If you think I'm no better than a pedophile who preys on innocent young girls, then you're right. This isn't going to work at all."

My mouth fell open. I was about to argue with his description of Shawn but found I couldn't. For the first time in my life, disgust slid down my back like a snake when I thought of him. Thought of me. Thought of how young I was when I gave him so much of myself.

And thought of how impossible it would be to get any of that back.

"Okay," I said. "I shouldn't have said that. I don't think that of you at all. I think you're...I actually think you're amazing if you want to know the truth. I wasn't lying when I said all those nice things about you to my sisters. I meant them."

We stared at each other for a long time as the sharp edge in the room faded away, leaving just the two of us, and the fact that we both seemed to, frankly, just really like each other to sink in.

Maybe it really was as simple as that. Nathan liked and respected me, and I felt the same about him. I didn't know why that was such a rare combination, but apparently it was. For both of us.

"You were too young," Nathan said in a softer tone now. "I don't know you all that well, but I know that. Just like I know that right now, you deserve a lot more than the way people in your life seem to treat you. But you're smart and kind, and you're my friend. You need some help. We both do. I'm open to trying if you are."

I blinked. I honestly wasn't sure what to do with this. An honest exchange. How novel.

"Speaking of, that dinner with my colleagues is next week," Nathan said. "We should probably buy you something to wear to that too."

I looked down at my clothes, which currently consisted of one of

Matthew's old Marines T-shirts over a pair of threadbare striped pajama shorts. "This isn't it, but I do have nice enough things for dinner. You've seen my other stuff."

Nathan shifted in his seat. "Transparent lace is fine for a bar, but you can't show up to dinners with my partners in a see-through shirt. I don't personally care what you wear—"

"Except for my shoes," I put in playfully.

That earned me a small smile. "Except your shoes that don't provide you any arch support, yeah. But the rest..." He waved a hand around. "It's just about meeting social expectations of particular class environments. Most people are shallow enough that things like clothes and appearance trigger certain prejudices. Ones you don't deserve."

"I thought you weren't good at social stuff," I said.

I was joking again, but the comment cast a shadow across Nathan's face.

"People who are raised by Lillian and Radford Hunt are acutely aware of class-based social mores such as wardrobe and table manners," he informed me. "My brothers and I suffered through years of those 'lessons' together."

It was one of the few pieces of information he'd offered about his life outside of New York. I wanted to know more. I'd spilled my guts to him—now I wanted Nathan's stories. I wanted all of them.

But before I could ask for any, Nathan checked his watch and swore under his breath. "Shit. I'm late for clinic. But I'll be back at five. That should give us a few hours to shop."

And before I could answer, he stood up, ready to go to his room and change, I supposed.

"Wait," I called as I followed him into the hall.

He turned, one hand shoved impatiently into his curls. I found myself wishing I could replace it with mine. They looked so soft. So inviting.

"What is it?" he asked. "Is there something else you need?"

Wordlessly, I stepped forward and wrapped my arms around his neck. "Just to say thank you. For everything you're doing, Nathan, really. I don't know where I'd be right now if you hadn't dropped into my life like some kind of guardian angel. I'll pay you back one day. I promise."

His big, warm body stiffened under my grasp, though he didn't move away.

"Nathan," I said into his chest. "This is a hug. When you receive one, you're supposed to give one back."

His hands landed awkwardly on my hips. "But no one is here right now. Here, we're just friends. Roommates."

I wished the uncertainty in his voice didn't make me feel so... hopeful.

"Friends hug," I told him. "Roommates can too. And boyfriends definitely hug. Like all the time."

"Is that right?"

I looked up to find him smirking down at me. It was fucking adorable.

"Yes, it is." I pulled him closer, telling myself it wasn't because his body, safe and secure, made me also feel safe and secure. "And they don't let go until their girlfriends do. Ever."

This was a lesson. Nothing more.

Nathan's hands squeezed my waist, then slipped around on either side so he could wrap his arms fully around me, holding me tightly enough that almost every part of our bodies met, separated by only a few thin layers of clothing.

"Is this all right?" he murmured into my hair, which he stroked gently with one hand. "Not too tight?"

I buried my face into his neck, inhaled his clean, sleepy scent, and sighed, suddenly as content as I'd ever been in my life. "It's perfect."

It wasn't until much later that it occurred to me, I wasn't just talking about the hug.

SIXTEEN

RICH MEN'S WIVES WHO STARTED OUT NORMAL

#8 Karlie Kloss

Nathan Hunt was holding my hand. He was holding my *hand* and had been since he'd picked me up from our apartment at 5:05 p.m. and ushered me into a cab that was waiting at the curb.

He'd done it in front of the weekend doorman, Turo. He'd done it in front of two of his neighbors, whom he'd greeted by name and introduced me to as his "girlfriend, Giovanna." And he'd done it in the cab all the way to the Upper East Side, where he'd tugged me out on the sidewalk and led me across Fifth Avenue and through the revolving glass doors of Bergdorf Goodman.

He was just following through. But I hadn't expected our agreement to start the moment he'd returned home after the clinic. I'd spent the afternoon taking a long bath in the oversized tub, scrubbing and moisturizing every inch of my body, then doing my physical therapy exercises before coming up with a million reasons why pretending to date Nathan Hunt was a very bad idea. They all boiled down to the same basic three, which I scribbled on the back of a receipt along with a few others:

Reasons Nobody Will Buy This Fake Relationship

1. Rich handsom men only scrwe washed up dancers.
They dont bring them home.

2. Your going to emberess him. Nathan can keep his
Mouth shut. U cant.

3. ur life is a mess. Hes going to get sick of cleening
it up.

By the time he rushed in from the clinic, still wearing the pressed slacks and maroon-striped button-down that made my mouth water, I was ready to call it off and get packing. Then he grabbed my hand, and every single reason evaporated into thin air.

"This really isn't necessary," I said for what was probably the tenth time since we'd entered the luxe, marbled interior of the famous department store.

Bergdorf's was one of those places I'd always known existed. Theoretically. It was a New York landmark, like the Plaza or the Empire State Building, so I'd probably even walked by it—maybe on a class trip to see Rockefeller Center or Central Park. But I'd never been inside. Because why would I, a broke dancer, sixth child of a lower-middle class family, ever have a reason to mingle with the too-rich-to-be-famous people who shopped at a place like this?

"I'm telling you, I can get ten-dollar knockoffs of all this stuff on Lennox," I said as we strode across the fourth floor past whole sections filled with couture. Things seemed to get more expensive in this store the more stories you climbed. I was legitimately wondering if they held a second Fort Knox on the floor above. "Or St. Mark's if you don't want to go uptown."

Nathan just shook his head as he towed me toward the back of the floor. "This is easier. They'll know what you'll need for the next few months."

Few months, huh?

Was that the amount of time he thought it would take to get rid of my parasitic ex and throw his family off his reclusive ways?

I should have added another reason to my list. Considering my past relationships, Nathan Hunt was going to get sick of me way before then.

"Hello, Andrea," Nathan greeted a petite woman standing in the center of an empty department with the words "Personal Shopping" mounted in big brass letters on a beam over the entrance. "I apologize for our tardiness. There was a bit of trouble getting across town. This is my girlfriend, Giovanna."

He kept using that name, and I kept letting him. Like it helped me get into character as the type of woman who would actually be Nathan Hunt's significant other.

"It's no problem, Dr. Hunt. You know it's always our pleasure to work with your family." Andrea turned to me. "It's lovely to meet you, Giovanna."

Andrea looked like she belonged here, with her pinned-back blond hair streaked with silver, shiny red loafers and a sleek black outfit that wasn't too tight or too loose. Perfectly fitted in that way I'd never achieved in my life.

I glanced at him. His *family*?

"My mother likes to shop," Nathan told me. "I get fitted at the men's store across the street. It's why I knew they would know what you'd need."

I reared. "Nathan. I don't want to look like your mother."

It was out of my mouth before I could stop it. Exhibit #1017 of Joni running her mouth.

That list was coming to life before my eyes.

Andrea, to her credit, didn't even giggle as she set a kind hand on my shoulder and smiled. She was probably a little older than my sisters, sweet in that way I'd expect my mother might have been if she hadn't been ruined by alcohol and a criminal past.

"I think he just means I'm familiar with the sorts of events his family attends, dear," she said kindly. "And he would be right. I've been dressing Lillian for close to twenty years now. You boys too, isn't that right, Dr. Hunt?"

We both swiveled toward Nathan, who just bobbed his head. "Er, yes. That's right."

His cheeks pinked when he caught me gawking at him—Nathan

actually looked embarrassed. I made a mental note to tease him mercilessly about needing to be "dressed" like a doll.

Or could I? After all, I was here for the same reason, wasn't I?

"So, what do we have coming up, dear?" asked Andrea.

I blinked. Was she talking to me or Nathan?

"There's a charity gala coming up—The Sinai Children's fundraiser," Nathan said.

Andrea nodded. "So we'll need an evening gown, then. Anything else?"

"She'll also need some clothes for dinner with my colleagues. Possibly a few small events at the Union. Cocktail hours, parties with her friends, things like that." Nathan was barely paying attention as he thumbed through his phone. "We might go down to Virginia for the races too, so really, just help her pick out anything she likes."

My mouth dropped. Cocktail hours? Parties? Virginia races? None of those were part of the original plan. "Nathan, that's really not—"

"Just do it," he cut me off again, speaking directly to Andrea. When he finally met my gaze, he shoved his phone into his pocket and made directly for me, even taking my hand again, like he needed the contact. "Let me do this for you, please."

I shivered at his touch. Or maybe at the slight yearning in that otherwise stoic voice. Either way, I didn't let go.

"I'll just start gathering a few options," Andrea said, glancing between us curiously. "What are you, Giovanna, a size four?"

"Sometimes a two. Depends on the brand," I murmured, unable to tear my gaze from Nathan's deep brown one. "And you can call me Joni." There was no way I could keep character with someone essentially the costumer for this little show of ours.

"We'll take measurements after I come back with some options." Andrea had the good sense to make herself scarce while Nathan pulled me to face him.

Our fingers were still intertwined. But that was because there were still people around, right? Not because he actually wanted to touch me like that.

"Nathan," I tried again. "We were supposed to just get one or two dresses. Not a whole new wardrobe. This is totally unnecessary. You don't have to do this."

"I think I do." His hand squeezed mine like he was trying to communicate something else. Then he leaned in, his lips brushing my ear as he murmured into it, "'Reason Number Six: he looks like a magazine ad, and I bet his family does too. You look like you rolled out of a donation bin.'"

I reared back. "You saw my list?"

"Well, it wasn't hard when you left it crumpled on the couch."

I huffed. So, maybe I had. That didn't mean he had to go reading the stupid thing.

Nathan tilted his head with a sly half-smile, then pulled from his other pocket a little leather-bound book and handed it to me. It was identical to the one he had, but red.

"Thought you might want to start keeping your lists in one place too," he said. "It helps me. And I promise not to snoop."

I took the book and stared at it for a moment. Another gift. One I had a sneaking suspicion I didn't deserve at all. "Thank you."

"You're welcome." He watched while I tucked it into my purse. "As for the clothes, I do think it's necessary. If we're going to pull this off, I don't want you to have any doubts about fitting in. Not that I think you should."

"You were the one who told me I can't wear my normal clothes around your family," I said bitterly. "I wouldn't have even thought otherwise until you said that."

Nathan seemed to think about that for a long moment. "What would a good boyfriend say at this moment?"

I blinked. "I—what?"

I hadn't expected *that*. An argument, yes. Being told I was overreacting, sure. But not asking what he should say.

Nathan just came even closer. "I'm trying to do something helpful, but it's not working. Or at least it's coming off in the wrong way. So, help me understand what the right thing is." He looked over my outfit, which currently consisted of my favorite pair of vintage Levi's, a cropped leather bustier, and purple Jordan Ones I'd found at a garage sale last year.

It was my favorite outfit and the polar opposite of Bergdorf's. And him.

"Don't just say I can do what I want. Tell me something you like about my clothes. And don't bullshit me."

Again, he looked over my outfit, but this time, his gaze burned a little. And not in a bad way.

My heartbeat seemed to drop somewhere between my legs.

"I like what you're wearing a lot," he said. "Especially that." He pointed at the bustier. "What is it called?"

"A b-bustier," I said.

He nodded and silently mouthed the word. "It's very flattering. I like the way it reveals your hips and how it creates a different shape to your décolletage that is very, um, tempting." His eyes looked like they wanted to drop to said body part but didn't. Instead, they burned even brighter when they met mine. "Is that adequate?"

Slowly, I nodded. "That's, um—" I cleared my throat of a frog that seemed to have come out of nowhere. "Yes, that's just fine."

"Good. Now, we're supposed to have dinner at Per Se on Friday with my colleagues, like I said. Would you wear something like this? Because honestly, if that's what you want, I'm fine with it."

From anyone else, the question might have sounded condescending. Utterly preposterous and designed to make me sound like a total idiot. In those circumstances, too, I would have thrown a fit. Told the speaker to fuck right off, that I wore what I liked, and they could go screw themselves if they didn't like it.

I'd done it more than once to Shawn. Other men I'd "dated." My sisters. Even Nonna, though with maybe more appropriate language.

But right now, I didn't see a shred of that condescension in Nathan's eyes. He wasn't judging me. He just really wanted to know what I preferred. What *I* wanted.

"Is—is that a nice restaurant?" I wondered lamely.

Nathan nodded. Again, without a drop of shame. "It has three Michelin stars."

Well, I knew that was good. Having a famous chef for a brother-in-law had at least taught me that much.

"Well, then, no," I finally said. "I wouldn't wear something like this." And then I admitted something I probably never would have admitted to anyone else. "At least, I don't think I would. I don't really know what to wear. I've never been to a restaurant that nice."

"So, what do I say here?" Nathan gave my hand a little shake. "What would a good boyfriend say? I don't want you to feel bad about this. I just want to help."

And he did. Finally, I could see it. Nathan wasn't trying to make me into something I wasn't or tell me I wasn't good enough. He was as lost as I was, trying to do his best.

"A good boyfriend would say exactly what you just said," I told him honestly. "And then, you know, we'd probably have some crazy makeup sex in the dressing rooms."

Immediately, Nathan's face flushed the color of the bright red dress hanging from one of the mannequins.

"But we can skip that part," I quickly amended. "Don't worry, I won't jump you. Again, I mean."

"Do you, ah, want me to kiss you?" Again, he didn't look like he was joking.

And, of course, he wouldn't. Stupid me, I should have remembered. Nathan didn't joke much. Or at least didn't really understand *mine*.

"Uh—Well—I—" The moment couldn't have needed clear communication more. And here I was, stumbling over every word.

"It's probably not a bad idea," he said like he was thinking through the weather. "We'll probably have to kiss here and there in front of people to seem genuine. Nothing profane, of course, but we should probably practice a few times, so it isn't awkward." He blinked. "Don't you think?"

I shrugged, though every cell in my body was suddenly dancing in place at just the idea of kissing this gorgeous man again. On purpose. And, you know, without being in the middle of a nervous breakdown.

Don't get carried away, Joni. It's just *pretend*.

I could pretend-kiss. I'd done it before onstage and kissed plenty of other people I barely knew, so I could definitely fake kiss someone as beautiful as Nathan Hunt.

So I popped up on my toes and smacked a quick kiss on Nathan's cheek, surprising him right out of holding my hand, even into taking a few steps back in shock.

I grinned. "There. We kissed. All made up, just like if this was a real relationship."

At that, he frowned. "I think we should keep that between us in public. Don't you?"

I bit my lip. "Right. Sorry."

We stood there for a moment, shifting awkwardly on our feet. I wasn't sure what to say, and he was just watching me.

Where the heck was Andrea with the dresses?

"Is that how you would have kissed...him?" Nathan wondered.

I didn't have to ask who he was referring to. Something like jealousy flickered through Nathan's otherwise calm exterior at even the barest insinuation of Shawn. No, not jealousy. Something stronger but less toxic. Wariness. Protectiveness.

"I—no," I admitted again. He really was getting all my secrets out of me. "Probably not."

Nathan studied me a moment more. "I don't want to make you feel the way he did either. I don't think he was a good boyfriend."

I shook my head. "Ah, no. He definitely was not."

Nathan nodded like something had been confirmed. And then, looking much more determined, he placed his hands on my cheeks and set his lips back on mine.

Obviously, I'd been kissed before. Kisses in games when I was still in middle school. Kisses on the subway or buses or the back seat of a car. Kisses on street corners or as I tumbled into a stranger's bed, or kisses through a music-riddled haze at the back of a party. Kisses from Shawn, of course, and kisses from other dates, too. Kisses from too many people to count, to the point where they all bled together, and I couldn't really remember any of them clearly.

Every detail of this kiss was as vivid as a brand-new Crayola box.

Nathan's firm mouth, a quick touch of tongue to tongue, insistent but not forceful, a nip of his teeth as they drifted over my bottom lip.

It was enough that I bit back. Just a little. It was like turning on a light.

The kiss went from zero to sixty instantaneously. His hand slid around to cup the back of my head; he slanted his mouth over mine, and his tongue twisted with such intensity that I didn't just forget where we were—I all but forgot my name.

It lasted only a few seconds, but that was enough to leave me breathless and Nathan sucking in air like he'd just run a marathon. When he stopped, his color had returned to normal, but those eyes were even darker than before. Deeper. Begging me to jump in and see just how sweet the rest of him really was.

That was when I knew that in a sea of fuzzy watercolor memories, my first kiss with Nathan Hunt would be crystal clear from this moment forward.

And I would never forget it.

"Holy shit," I breathed when he finally let me go. "Where in the hell did you learn to kiss like that?"

He frowned. "You didn't like it."

He looked so concerned, I almost laughed. But instead, I grabbed a handful of his shirt and pulled him back to me.

"No, I liked it a lot," I told him and kissed him again.

He startled but caught up soon after, wrapping a large hand around my neck, another at my waist, and started giving as good as he got. I hadn't made out like this with anyone since high school, and back then, it was a sloppy mess. Nathaniel, though, knew exactly what he was doing.

He wasn't kissing me like I was a nobody, a fling, a one-night stand. Or, I thought, like someone he hired to pretend.

He was kissing me like I was forever.

Like he wanted to steal that forever for himself.

"Whoa," I gasped when we broke apart at last.

Nathan was breathing hard too. "What?"

I swallowed. "Nathan, you kiss like a pirate."

One brown brow rose quizzically. "A pirate? Is that a good thing?"

"It's a very good thing." Lord, I could barely feel my lips. Or the cheek that he was currently stroking. "It's perfect."

More, the rest of my body cried out. Like an addict, every part of me was screaming for the rest of where that came from.

"Well, I pulled several things that you might like, dear—oh, how sweet."

We sprang apart at the sound of Andrea's voice. She smiled at us as if she was keeping a secret right along with us.

Lord. She had *no idea*.

"Ah, thanks, Andrea," Nathan said as he stepped to the side, though his hand lingered on my waist.

"Good to see you happy, dear," she murmured to Nathan as he took a seat.

He didn't answer. But when his brown eyes met mine again, they shone as bright as stars. Just like I was certain mine were doing too.

"Just tell her what you like and what you don't," Nathan said from the sofa while he stretched his arms across the back as if preparing for a movie marathon. "Then you can try things on while she looks some more. I'll help."

I blinked at the rack of dresses. A glance at one tag told me each cost more than I made in a month at Opal. Some of them, two or three times that much.

"I think Karlie Kloss wore this one," I murmured with a glance at Nathan. "I saw it on POPSUGAR."

I sounded like an idiot, bumbling about like I hadn't just had my face kissed numb in a room full of couture.

But neither Nathan nor Andrea said a word about it.

He just shrugged and pushed his glasses up his nose. "I've only met the Kushners a few times."

Well, it was close. In the same world.

The thought was actually kind of uplifting. If Karlie Kloss, the model who grew up in St. Louis, could make herself at home in this world, maybe there was hope for me.

"This one too," I said, pointing to a slinky green number that would undoubtedly match my eyes. "And that one. Ooh, that's nice."

Andrea smiled and set the ones I'd indicated into a dressing room. "That's a good place to start. Try on a few more, and then we'll really have some fun."

HOW TO MAKE MONEY FAST

#9 Stripping. Dammit.

"It's just an interview," I told Rochelle for what was probably the tenth time since I'd shown up at Diamonds that afternoon. "And I don't see why I can't go to one of the actual pop-ups for a trial instead of doing it here. Kyle knows I'm not planning to get on the pole, right?"

On Monday morning, I'd woken up to a call from one of the lobby doormen, who'd informed me about a delivery coming up from Bergdorf's. But instead of the two dresses I'd picked out with Andrea, a messenger had rolled in two full racks of clothing, plus more bags, shoes, and accessories than I could count.

Nathan didn't pick up the phone when I'd called—he had back-to-back surgeries all morning. He had, however, responded with his typical straightforward literalness to my texts once he was out.

> I don't know if you are aware, but it looks like all of Bergdorf's was just delivered to your apartment. And charged to your credit card. You may be a victim of identity theft.

> Nathan: It's not the entire store, only the things you said you liked. I also told Andrea to add any other accessories she thought were necessary, so if something is missing, just let her know, and she'll have it sent over.

> I don't know what to say. It's beyond generous. And way way way too much.

> Nathan: It's necessary.

He reiterated that he was serious about this arrangement of ours and wanted me to be prepared for anything.

I didn't know what to think of it. Of him being so generous. Of how he didn't seem to think it was generous at all. Or of how much money a person had to have to feel that way in the first place.

And then there was the small but not insignificant fact that I couldn't ever hope to pay him back for all of these things.

I had spent the rest of the morning putting the clothes away in my closet and trying not to have a heart attack whenever I saw the price tags.

Then I'd immediately called Rochelle and asked her to get me that meeting with her boss.

It wasn't the clothes themselves exactly that made me call my cousin. It was what they represented. This weekend, I was supposed to act like Nathan's girlfriend, someone who wore things like these to galas and fancy dinners, who could talk about literature and art the way Matthew, Kate, and Frankie had always been able to do.

But it was more than that. People like that knew how to act in those situations too. Xavier, Frankie's husband, and Nina, Matthew's wife, were proof of that. They knew which forks to use at a fancy restaurant. They had impeccable grooming and museum memberships. Had traveled the world, stayed in five-star hotels, knew exactly how much to tip bellhops, and collected art like my nephews collected Pokémon cards.

It was a different world, and learning how to navigate it would cost money. And since Nathan had clearly paid way more than I ever would have accepted, the rest had to be up to me.

So, I was doing what I had to do.

Sitting beside me in the Diamonds locker room, Rochelle just smirked as she helped me apply false eyelashes over a thick cat eye. "Kyle's not going to take you to one of those unless he knows you're legit. This is your audition."

Diamonds was no different from any of the other strip clubs still left in Manhattan. Past the theater district and close to the river, it was in the part of midtown that still hinted at the darker New York that existed before I was born, when Seventh Avenue was dotted with peepshows instead of Disney stores and restaurants. The building itself was a converted walkup that had been painted black up and down the brick exterior and over the windows. The entrance was covered by an awning lit with a neon sign bearing its name and an animated woman's leg kicking toward the night sky.

"My sunny personality isn't enough to wait tables?" I asked. "I have to take my top off so he can make sure my tits aren't different sizes too? Everyone's are, you know."

Rochelle snorted. "*Mami*, last year you skinny dipped for two hours in front of fifty people that night Carmine snuck us into the pool during the heat wave. I've seen you perform in nothing but a thong and body paint. Why are you getting shy now?"

I pressed my fingers to the edges of my lashes, waiting for them to dry. "I'm not."

That was a lie. I actually had a very good reason for getting shy. A six-foot-four hulk of a reason with an adorably sweet smile. One that wore glasses, kissed like a god, and said the word "perfect" with a growl that made my toes curl.

Then I sighed with my eyes still firmly shut. "I just don't want to do it here."

"Why, you want to serve drinks topless at your regular job? I think you might get arrested."

I shook my head. I didn't want to ask. But at the same time...I knew I had to. "You haven't seen Shawn here recently, have you?"

There was a long silence. Longer than the remaining seconds needed for the eyelash glue to dry. Gingerly, I removed my fingers and blinked. The lashes stayed put. Good.

Rochelle, however, was looking at me like something was very, very wrong. "Please tell me that motherfucker isn't back in your life."

My family barely knew anything about Shawn Vamos, but the same couldn't be said about Rochelle. It had always been hard to hide from her, especially since she'd been with me on the day Shawn and I met. And for a long time, served as an alibi when I needed to claim a "sleepover." She'd enjoyed attention from some of Shawn's friends too, so it's not like she had ever judged me for him.

But unlike me, my friend had easily grown out of that part of our lives. Out of the clutches of men like that.

For me, it hadn't been so easy.

I gave a half-hearted shrug. "He showed up at the bar on Thursday."

Rochelle swore under her breath. "Fuck, Jo."

"Hey, I can't stop him from just showing up places. He really is a bad penny."

"A demon penny," she concurred. "Why don't you file a restraining order or something? Get him off your back permanently."

I gave her a look. "You know why."

Rochelle had the decency not to voice the reason out loud. "I still think you should tell your brother about that."

"I am not telling Matthew or anyone in my family. You know that."

"Yeah, but Matt would sic the entire NYPD on his ass," Rochelle said. "Get him locked up for what he did to you."

"I was legal at the time." My voice was a monotone. I hated talking about this. "Technically, he didn't do anything wrong."

"Yeah, but I bet others weren't. No offense, baby, but you weren't the only girl Shawn fucked with."

The sick feeling in my stomach grew. I couldn't argue with that. I didn't even want to anymore.

And yet he still held me hostage. I'd accepted that he always would.

Didn't mean I liked it.

I closed my eyes and saw Nathan's face. The confusion that crinkled his brow when he learned the basics of my story with Shawn.

The shame that clouded my vision and made me sick every time I imagined telling him the rest.

No, he would never know.

No one else would.

I'd take that shit to my grave, no matter the cost.

"Well, what does he want?" Rochelle asked.

That wasn't so easy.

"I don't know," I admitted. "He sat down, had a drink. Gave me some shit for disappearing for a few months—"

"When he ghosted you after your surgery," Rochelle added while she applied some silvery eyeshadow.

"After that, yeah. Then he and Nathan got into a weird sparring match over paying for his drink, and then he left."

Rochelle stopped with only one eye done. "Wait, your sexy room-mate was there too?"

"Um, yeah. Except now he's sort of my boyfriend. I guess."

What should have felt good to say out loud instead just felt dirty. It was one thing to play a part for Nathan's family and coworkers, for stuck-up people I didn't even know. It was another thing completely to lie to my closest friend.

"I knew he wanted that ass!" Rochelle crowed. "I knew it wasn't just him being a 'nice guy.'" She shook her head. "Rich men don't help pretty girls for nothing. So, I hope you're being careful."

I sighed. "It's really not like that. We haven't even…you know. Just a couple of kisses."

I wanted to tell her everything. I wanted to reveal the whole arrangement, partly so she wouldn't think he was a dog just like everyone else, but partly to get some perspective on the cloudy hotness that had occurred in the department store. How could something that was just pretend feel so confusingly real?

But I couldn't. Because the agreement was between me and Nathan, who was literally saving my ass. I couldn't betray him like that. Not even to my best friend.

Besides, for the plan to work for both of us, I needed her to spread the word. And Rochelle was a very dependable gossip.

"Well, if Shawn does come by here, you can tell him, or any of his friends, that I'm not available anymore," I said.

It had worked for her, once upon a time. Back in high school, Rochelle and I had both been tied up with Shawn and his friends. We were the young girl arm candy they took to Yankees games and parties and too many places sixteen-year-olds had no business being.

Then she met Carmine, and we found out how those men felt about used goods. They lost interest in Rochelle completely. And she'd never looked back.

I prayed it would work the same for me.

"If Shawn shows up here, I'd probably nail his dick to the door before asking the bouncer to throw him out," Rochelle replied as she went back to doing my other eye. "But I'm happy for you, *mami*. Just be careful, all right?"

I nodded. "Always. All right, fit check."

I stood up and looked myself over in the mirror. I'd done my hair and makeup in essentially the same look I used as a go-go dancer— dark eyes, false lashes, overlined lips, and heavy contouring, all with stage makeup that was impervious to sweat. Not bad. I wasn't much for the caterpillar lash up close, but it would look good under the dimmed lighting of the strip club.

The look wasn't quite on par with the elaborate outfits the other girls were currently putting on, but Rochelle had assured me that the mesh tunic over my skimpiest bikini was more than appropriate, especially when paired with the mammoth heels called Teasers, she was lending me until I could buy my own. So long as I could move and flirt, I was good to go.

"You look hot," Rochelle said as she started pulling out her own stage wear for the evening. "Like Velma Kelly before she goes to jail."

I had to grin. On any other day, namechecking my favorite character from *Chicago* would have just been depressing, but that was exactly the image I was going for. Dark, glam, and without any fucks to give. I hadn't seen this girl in a while. Granted, I never brought her out expecting to audition in a place like this, but what the hell? Money was money.

"Word to the wise," Chelle said as she adjusted her tight blue bodysuit. "Tip Kevin—that's the other doorman—well. He walks girls to the train."

I nodded. My cousin had already explained to me that the dancers and servers were expected to pay a small bit of our tips to the bar staff, similar to how the dancers at a club like this paid house fees and tips to the rest of the staff. Depending on the number of players and how well they did, the percentages varied. Honestly, the numbers made my head...hurt. But I'd figure it out when the time came.

"Did you pick a stage name yet?" Chelle asked while I fluffed my hair a bit more. "I don't give anyone my real name. No stalkers, please."

I sighed. It wasn't a bad idea—it would actually make the whole getting into character thing easier. But I'd been completely blocked since she'd suggested I come up with one this morning. "I can't think of anything. What's yours?"

Rochelle grinned as she started pinning up her tight curls. "Coquita."

I laughed. "Like the drink?"

She just grinned harder. "They always did call me a coconut back in school. I might as well use it."

I guffawed. "It's perfect." I turned back to the mirror. "Should I just be lazy and call myself Velma? Or is that too Scooby Doo?"

Rochelle made a face. "You gotta do something sexy, babe."

"Gigi it is," I said, thinking of another famous musical character, this one a bit closer to my actual name. If I was going that direction, I might as well stick with it.

FIFTEEN MINUTES LATER, Rochelle took me up two sets of stairs and down another long hall to the manager's office on the top floor of Diamonds.

"Good luck," she said just before knocking on the open door and blowing me a kiss. "Kill it."

"Kyle?" I entered the room, where a thin, middle-aged man with slicked-back hair and a chain around his neck the size of my belt stood from behind a big black desk. "I'm Joni, Rochelle's cousin."

"Joni," he said as he extended a greasy hand with two gold rings on his thumb and pinky finger. "Good to meet you, honey. Rochelle says good things. Can't wait to see you in action."

I crossed the leopard-printed carpet to shake his hand and looked around the room. On one wall were a number of screens. Some were looking into a few private rooms, all currently empty, and a few others were tracking other parts of the club. The far wall of the office was just one big window that looked down into the main club. The lights were on, and there was no music playing, but I saw signs of activity as waitresses, bartenders, and other club employees floated around, getting the place ready for it to open at two.

"My knee's still out," I said. "But I can move a little and wait tables, serve drinks."

"Lap dance?" Kyle asked, his beady eyes giving me a thorough once-over.

I nodded. "That won't be an issue."

He nodded. "Well, you look the part, honey." His eyes stopped at my chest, and he didn't even try to hide the fact that he was eyeing my breasts like chicken cutlets. "Did you ever see that surgeon? I sponsored your cousin's work, you know."

I sighed. "I did. But I don't think it's for me."

Because you're perfect just the way you are. I could practically hear that low burr brushing against my cheek.

Kyle shrugged. "You change your mind, you let me know. We're always happy to take on real talent here, and Rochelle says you're the real deal."

I nodded. "Sure. Thanks."

Kyle then proceeded to lay out the rules for working for him, counting them with his thumb, index, and middle finger as he went. "We got three. No drugs. No stealing. No sex. Some of the girls might tell you differently about what can happen in the private rooms, but I run a straight operation at my clubs and my parties. Topless only. You can let 'em touch what you want, but nothing under the panties. They want more, you take it out of my place of business. If my liquor license is revoked because you're turning tricks, you're gonna owe me a whole lot more than house fees. You got me?"

I barely managed not to grimace. "I have zero problem with that."

"Anyone gives you any grief, you talk to Kevin or one of the other security guys. I usually keep at least three at every game, more at the club. Take care of my money; take care of my girls. No matter what."

For a fee, I expected, remembering Rochelle's explanation. Which I fully intended to pay. I just hoped it wasn't too much.

"All right, then," Kyle said. "Let's head downstairs and get your audition done before we open. Afterward, we can take care of the paperwork. If everything goes all right, you do a few trial shifts here, and then maybe you can serve at some games next week. I got a hot game going on uptown."

I grinned. "Sounds good to me."

I followed him out of the office and down to the main floor, which was lit a bit darker now as the staff got the place completely ready for the evening.

"Stage sets are usually three songs," Kyle said. "Most of the girls working the games do at least one per night, on top of serving drinks. That all right, honey?"

I looked down at my knee.

"Nothing fancy," he assured me. "I just need to know you can move. It don't take much."

This was probably a terrible idea. But suddenly, it didn't matter as I walked up to the stage—a long platform scattered with poles that wound through the center of the room.

"I guess she's ready," Kyle said with a laugh as he took one of the leather chairs near the stage. "Any song you want?"

I drew a hand down the pole, then back up. I wasn't super experienced with this form of dance, but I'd taken a few classes out of curiosity a couple years back. Enough that I thought I could come up with something simple, mostly favoring my good knee.

Hell, my body was itching to move.

"Cardi B," I said. I figured if I was going to do this, I was going to do it right. "'Money.'"

Kyle chuckled. "You're aiming high, girl. I'll give you that."

But by that point, I no longer cared about anything he had to say.

The room was empty. There was no one else but me up here. And I was going to make the stage mine.

I turned on my good knee, wrapping myself around the pole like a kitten around a stranger's leg. The pounding piano chords vibrated across the room. And that was all it took.

I was already a dancer when I got on that stage. But the second I grabbed that pole, I became something else entirely.

EIGHTEEN
COURSES ON A TASTING MENU

#1 Amuse boosh. Also wtf is that??

"You can do this," I whispered to myself. "It's just another part."

Four days, two shifts at Diamonds, plus my regular shifts at Opal later, I stood outside the blue-doored entrance of Per Se on Friday night. The shopping center at Columbus Circle was yet another New York semi-landmark I'd never entered, and it was clear walking through it that it was yet another place for people who made more in one day than I'd ever hope to earn in my life.

At least I had a little extra cash in my purse. Clutch? Baguette? I honestly didn't know what to call the little gold thing hanging from my wrist. It barely held my phone, ID, and what was left of the wad of cash I'd made this week.

I'd served two full shifts, and both had gone well. Kyle had promised to bring me on to serve at his game nights with Rochelle. That was apparently where the big money came in. Meanwhile, I could continue serving at Diamonds any other night I liked.

It wasn't the greatest work in the world. The customers were handsy, my knee was sore after too many simple yet taxing twists on customers' knees, and I had to give almost half of what I'd made back to the house at the end of the night. But the extra money had paid for a classy soap manicure like my sister-in-law Nina preferred, plus a blow-out at a swanky salon near Nathan's apartment. I'd also had my eyebrows threaded, watched about a dozen YouTube videos on table settings, and felt about as prepared for tonight as I could be.

Deep breaths, I told myself. Just like you were about to go on stage.

I pulled at the hem of the silk dress, so dark green it was almost black, that slithered down to my knees, revealed my shoulders with a demure boatneck, and showed a hint of leg through a slit that ran only a few inches up one thigh. My jewelry was simple. I'd traded the hoops and costume jewelry for the gold studs that had first pierced my ears at ten, paired with the simple gold chain and St. Mary medallion I'd received for my confirmation. More YouTube tutorials produced a simple French twist that was a lot harder to achieve than it looked and clean makeup instead of the dark liner and lash extensions I probably would have chosen on my own.

If this was another performance, then my character was the ingenue making her debut in high society. But the conservative fit somehow made me feel more naked than anything I'd worn on stage. Even at Diamonds.

And this little dinner with Nathan's colleagues was only a dress rehearsal for the gala I was supposed to attend with his entire family in another few weeks.

I opened the clutch and pulled out the little red book Nathan had given me. On the sixth page was the first list I'd written for tonight.

Things to do at dinner as Nathan's pretend GF
1. Think before you speak. dont talk about shit you dont understand.
2. Also dont swear so much. BE A LADY.
3. Keep your elbows off the table.
4. Dont spill anything on these Fancy cloths in case he wants to return them.

5. *Good postur. Walk like the dancer you* ~~used to~~
~~be~~ *ARE.*

All good advice, most of which came from internet searches on "how to go to a society dinner," which led me down a rabbit hole of finishing school websites and TikToks about debutantes.

There was a lot about curtsying and people wearing books on their heads. I figured I could at least handle the posture. The rest of the rules I'd cobbled together the best I could.

"Just do it," I mumbled to myself.

Like it was waiting for me to quit stalling, the doors opened as a few diners exited.

Well, that was my cue.

I strode into the restaurant like I owned it, conscious of the turning heads (most of them belonging to men) as I made my way toward the bar on the far side of the neutrally decorated space dotted with linen-covered tables and views of Central Park. The place was crowded—every table was full, and the bar itself was jammed with people, even at only six thirty. The elegant notes of a grand piano being played in the far corner floated over the crowd, creating the perfect atmosphere of ease and elegance.

For the first time, I understood why Nathan had insisted on the new wardrobe—and was eternally grateful. Everyone in the restaurant also dripped money. If I'd shown up here in my jeans and Vans, I probably would have been given a dollar and sent to sit on the sidewalk with the other panhandlers.

I searched the crowded bar and eventually spotted Nathan sipping on what I would have bet was a soda water and lime out of a rocks glass. No scrubs tonight—of course, why would there be? Instead, he was wearing one of the countless pairs of wool pants he preferred for clinic days. This time with a matching suit jacket, tailored perfectly to those big shoulders, over a light blue shirt that complemented his eyes and a dark blue plaid tie. He was facing another man who was speaking, nodding every so often while he listened.

There was something missing, though. When he came to my bar, Nathan was generally so much quieter than he appeared to be here. When we weren't making idle conversation, he generally just sat with his overpriced scotch in front of him and studied everything and everyone around him, making no attempt to hide his interest.

Now, I saw none of that intense attention on his face. If anything, he looked like I probably did when I was forcing myself to pay attention in class, knowing the information was going in one ear and out the other, and unable to do anything to help it.

Because he was faking it, I realized. The interest, the slightly stiff smile, the courteous nods. I didn't know how I knew he was putting on as much of a show as I was, but I did. Which made me wonder how often Nathan felt like he had to be someone he wasn't just to fit in. Just like me.

And you know what? I kind of hated it.

I wanted *my* Nathan. The one who couldn't care less if people thought he was cold or slightly off. The one who only asked questions when he was truly interested and stopped talking completely if he wasn't.

I liked the Nathan who was one hundred percent genuine and didn't feel the need to hide his idiosyncrasies. Especially since I liked those too.

I raised a hand, trying to get his attention. "Nathan!"

The man he was speaking to turned with him and mouthed "Wow" before nudging Nathan in the arm. A few other people around them also turned to see who was calling out—two other men standing next to women in outfits even more elegant than mine, plus another woman with bobbed brown hair standing just beside Nathan, who didn't seem to be attached to anyone.

Though she was looking at me like she wasn't particularly happy I'd shown up.

Showtime.

"Hi, babe," I said as I strode up to my fake-boyfriend and laid a kiss on his cheek. "Sorry I'm late. I couldn't get a cab."

That wasn't *technically* untrue. Since I couldn't afford a cab, I couldn't really get one. It was kind of funny watching the reactions of people on the subway. People who wore clothes like this didn't take public transportation.

"Oh, I completely understand," said a blond woman I assumed was someone's wife, judging by the diamonds circling her left ring finger. "It's just murder getting across town this time of day, even just coming down Park. See, George, this is why I think we should have our own driver."

I congratulated myself on my excellent improv. Scene One in the Tale of Nathan Hunt's Girlfriend: establishing common ground with the rich and impatient. My first leading role, and I was already killing it.

Nathan, however, was forgetting his lines.

Instead, he was still staring at me. His eyes had lost that look of faux interest as they traveled over my clothes and my hair, lingering a half-second longer on my exposed shoulders. His mouth had also fallen open. Just a little.

I preened like a freaking swan.

Yeah, spending a few nights at Diamonds was definitely worth that exact reaction.

"Nate," said the man standing next to us. "How about an introduction to your lady friend?"

"Showtime," I whispered into Nathan's ear and turned to flash my brightest grin at his friend. "Sorry, I just couldn't wait to see this one."

I wasn't sure why he used my full name. Maybe it was just easier to keep my character straight. Or maybe it was the fact that Nathan said he liked the way it rolled off his tongue.

Nathan cleared his throat. "Ah, yeah. Giovanna. My, um, girlfriend."

"Joni," I corrected, then purred, "This one's the only one who calls me Giovanna. And that's only when he's flirting with me. Isn't that right, babe?"

"Can't blame him for trying," the man said as he stretched a hand toward me. "I'm Jordan."

Nathan seemed to wake up at the sight of Jordan's hand touching mine. "Yes, I apologize. Joni, this is Jordan Palmer, one of the chief surgeons at my practice, and his wife, Tracy. The others are Boon and his wife, Adele; that's Dwight and his fiancée, Reagan; and this is Charlotte Mueller, our newest surgeon."

As Nathan gestured toward each person now standing around us in a semicircle, they offered a polite nod or smile. All except the final woman—the one with the neat brown bob—who only barely managed a tight grimace.

"Wonderful to meet all of you," I said with another smile. "Nathan has told me so much about you."

One of Nathan's brows arched at that, but he didn't correct the obvious lie.

"So what do you do...Joni?" asked Charlotte. "We haven't heard a *thing* about you."

"Oh, I'm looking for a new position, actually," I said. "Right now, I'm working at—"

"Joni's in recovery after an injury," Nathan put in before I could finish. "Before that, she was in *Chicago*."

"On Broadway?" asked the woman named Reagan. "Oh, that's such a good show!"

I nodded with a smile, ignoring the tightness in my chest at the mention of it. "Yes, it is."

"It must be so exciting to dance on Broadway," said one of the other women, whose name I had already forgotten. Drat. "You must be very talented."

I opened my mouth to say I really didn't know, since I hadn't even made it to my first performance when my knee decided to break, but Nathan stepped in again.

"I think our table's ready," he said. "The maître d' is waving us over."

The little party immediately followed a host, who started leading them to our table. Nathan and I followed, and I took a moment to hang back.

"FYI?" I whispered into his ear as we walked. "Boyfriends usually touch their girlfriends. A little PDA isn't just for department store clerks."

That brown brow lifted again. It did funny things to my insides. "PDA?"

"You know, public displays of affection." I smiled. "Just a little since they're your coworkers. No need for full tongue. But they're not going to believe we're actually involved if you don't touch me at all." I nodded toward one of the doctors. "See the way he has his hand on his wife's back, guiding her around? I bet he lets it rest on the back of her chair when they sit down too. Maybe plays with her hair if he likes her a lot. That sort of thing."

Nathan seemed to look around the rest of the restaurant as if searching for further evidence. He'd find it, of course. It was a fancy place, but when couples weren't eating, they were generally touching, at least a little. The ones who weren't...well, they'd probably been together for eons or were on their way out.

"And women like that?" he asked.

I nodded. "Most, probably. I know I do. Just like they like being told they're pretty when they make an effort or petted like a cat."

He blinked but didn't hide his smile. "Like a cat?"

I shrugged. "Don't blame a Leo for being a lion, man. We like to be the stars of the show. All you need to do is pet me and tell me I'm pretty, and I'll be yours forever. Sad but true."

The smile quirked. "I'll keep that in mind."

His palm found the small of my back, fingers touching my spine. A shiver went straight up it as he guided me through the restaurant with a strong propriety, not unlike my dance instructor had in the sixth grade when I took a year of ballroom just for the fun of it.

I didn't know if Nathan Hunt knew how to dance, but if he did, I was willing to bet he was a hell of a lead.

"And you look very beautiful, by the way." His voice rumbled beside my ear as he pulled a chair out for me. "I would have said it earlier, but I thought I'd lost my voice."

He pulled out a chair, and I sat, but not before Nathan captured my hand and pressed a kiss on my knuckles. His breath was warm, and my insides danced again.

"Better?" he murmured as he took a seat beside me.

I smiled. "You're a quick study, boyfriend."

If I wasn't mistaken, those chocolatey eyes definitely twinkled.

I decided that maybe this whole pretend relationship gig wouldn't really be that hard. Then I looked at the menu and barely understood a thing.

Quail eggs. Foie gras. Wagyu.

It was a foreign language.

This was what it meant to be a part of high society? What was wrong with pasta and salad?

"Oh, there's one," I murmured with relief as I spotted something familiar. "Okay, I'll try that."

"What's that?" Nathan asked.

I pointed to the rigatoni. And uni with truffled black pearls, whatever those were. Anything was good with pasta.

Nathan glanced at the item, then looked up at me. "Oh. Actually, it's a tasting menu, so you'll get to try everything. They just give you this so you know what's coming."

"Oh."

I went back to studying the menu again. I wasn't able to get through it as fast as everyone else, so I set it down, not wanting questions about why Nathan's dumb date couldn't read a menu without murmuring the words to herself or tracing the lines with one finger. I did, however, spot a number at the bottom. One that made my mouth drop open.

"Nathan," I whispered when everyone else was busy chattering about their latest stock portfolio or whatever rich people like to discuss.

He turned to me again. "What?"

A few of his colleagues looked at me curiously. I didn't want to embarrass him, so I pointed at the number.

"It's…a lot," I said quietly. "And that's per person?"

He nodded.

I gulped. "Are you sure we can afford this?"

To his credit, Nathan didn't laugh. He didn't even smile. He just examined me for a moment, then plucked the menu from my hands and set it on the plate in front of me.

"Just enjoy yourself," he said as he slid his arm around my chair.

His fingers grazed my neck, toying with the curl that I couldn't quite keep pinned in place.

I shivered again. And not unpleasantly.

"Welcome to Per Se," said the server who had just arrived at the table. "I see some of you already have drinks, but can I refill a few cocktails or get anyone a different beverage?"

"We'll probably get a bottle or two for the table if there is something you'd recommend with the menu tonight," said one of the doctors. Shoot, I couldn't remember his name.

"Giovanna would like something," Nathan said. "A vodka soda —" He broke off and turned to me. "Isn't that right?"

I couldn't help my grin. He'd remembered. Not just my drink, but to ask.

I nodded. "Yes, please."

"Top shelf," Nathan said to the server, who left before I could protest that the house vodka was just fine for me.

But maybe that wasn't just fine for *Giovanna*. She would have been used to the finer things in life.

"Doesn't it look good?" said the woman whose name was... Reagan. Yes, that was it. "I've been dying to come here ever since this one told me about it."

"I don't know," said the woman named Charlotte, who was looking kind of bored as she peered around the restaurant. "I was kind of disappointed we couldn't find a table at Chez Miso."

"It's been booked solid since it opened," said Jordan. Yes, that was his name. "I've been having Brenda call weekly."

"I could probably get you a table there," I put in. "I'll just call the owner. The food is super good—totally worth trying."

The entire table swung toward me, more than one mouth agape.

"*You* know Xavier Parker?" asked the one I thought was named Boon.

I nodded as the server set down my drink. "He's married to my sister."

The rest of the jaws dropped. Besides Nathan's, that is, though the fingers at my nape had stilled.

"The Duke of Kendal is your brother-in-law?" asked Reagan.

I nodded again. "You know who he is?"

"Honey, everyone knows who Xavier Parker is," Charlotte put in like I was an idiot. "He was the toast of the city last year."

I didn't like her tone.

The divot between Nathan's brows appeared.

Charlotte continued. "My mother couldn't stop talking about him for months after he ran off with—I mean, reconnected with your sister. A teacher, isn't she?"

I flushed. This was kind of odd. Frankie had told me that she and Xavier were a hot topic of conversation and that more than one stuffy uppercruster had hated on her and Sofia, my little niece, since she and Xavier got back together. I'd just assumed it was happening on the other side of the pond and New York was safe for them.

Apparently not.

"Our parents know his stepmother, Georgina," Charlotte informed Nathan. "Huntwell Farms provided a stud for her horses a few years ago, remember?"

Nathan shook his head. "Spencer manages the breeding operation. I wouldn't have met her."

Races? Breeding? Mothers?

What in the crazy horse farm was Nathan's life?

And why hadn't he told me about Annie-Get-Your-Man in his office?

"It's crazy, I know," I said. "He and my sister had a fling years ago. Then he went back to England, she had his baby, they ran into each other at a party five years later, and abra-ca-damily, there's your new family. They got married last year, and I'd be stupid jealous if I didn't love my sister so much. But Xavier is crazy about her. They are legit fire together."

I turned to find Nathan watching me closely and mouthing "legit fire" to himself with an adorable smile.

"Right?" I said with a knowing glance.

After all, if we were in a relationship, he would know these things.

That seemed to pull him out of whatever trance he was in. "Oh, right, yes. They are very happy."

Charlotte looked between us. "I'm surprised you never mentioned you have a new connection there, Nate. Your parents must be thrilled."

She did not sound like she enjoyed that particular possibility.

"That's amazing," Reagan said whole-heartedly. "What a fairy tale, huh, hon?" she asked her fiancé, the one named Dwight.

He was quiet like Nathan. I hadn't yet heard him say a word. Her, though, I liked.

"It really was," I said. "She's expecting their second this spring."

As if on cue, the wives and girlfriends at the table all broke into a chorus of oohs and aahs while their men eyed me curiously as if to wonder about the genetic code I carried that attracted someone like Xavier Parker.

I didn't tell them I was nothing like my sister except for the dark hair and green eyes. Frankie was petite and curvy, while I was taller and almost too thin. She was bookish, smart, and could offer far more in conversation with these people than I'd ever be able to. Of course, she fit into Xavier's world. That was where she belonged in the first place.

Unlike me.

But tonight, apparently, you wouldn't know it. I was killing with this crowd. Well, most of them, I thought as I caught Charlotte giving me the evil eye.

I just smiled sweetly and took a drink of my cocktail.

"We tried to get the head chef to cater the Brooklyn Museum benefit," said the blond lady whose name I thought was Stacy. Or Pacey. Crap. "Maybe you can ask your brother-in-law about that too."

"Oh, I've been to that benefit!" I exclaimed.

Maybe I was a little too eager, but I was honestly just excited that I actually had something in common with these people.

Again, a table full of surprised looks turned my way.

"Well, not as a donor," I admitted when even Nathan looked doubtful. "I was in the dance company that did a production of *Giselle* as flowers." I grinned at Nathan. "I was the peony."

His mouth had fallen open in the most adorable way while he looked me over as if with new eyes.

"Your favorite," he said.

I grinned. "You remembered."

Nathan picked up my hand and feathered his soft lips over my knuckles without breaking his gaze. "I'd never forget."

"I remember that too!" the blond woman put in. "Oh, you were exquisite! No one in the room could even speak while you did your solo. Nathan, have you ever seen her dance?"

Nathan's eyes didn't move from me while he replied. "I have."

I bit back a smile. The fact that it had only been on a platform before I literally fell into his arms was our private joke.

"And she is exquisite," he agreed.

It was a fake compliment. I knew that. A complete and total farce.

But every cell in my body seemed to shimmy with pleasure in response to it.

"Where did you study?" Charlotte interrupted our little moment. "A conservatory, I assume? That is, if you're *so* accomplished."

Her face was pleasant, but I could hear the snarl in her voice. Even if no one else seemed to.

"Ah, no," I said. "I grew up in the city, so I learned mostly at local spots. I've been auditioning since I was twelve or so, though."

"Did you attend LaGuardia?" asked the blond woman, who, even if she was nosy, was reasonably nice. At least her interest was genuine.

"Tracy, don't pester the girl," chided her husband, whose name I barely remembered was Jordan. "I apologize. She's like a child with a new puppy. Just crazy about the arts."

"That's okay with me," I said, though my face was growing hot with everyone's eyes on me. For some reason, this felt harder than the thirty-two fouettes in *Swan Lake*. "Um, no. I studied mostly at a studio near Fordham. And later worked with some teachers in Harlem, too."

"The Bronx, really?" said Jordan to his wife and really everyone else at the table. "I suppose there's more than meets the eye to this one, isn't there? Congratulations, Nate. You've really found yourself a rose out of concrete."

Was the compliment more than a little condescending?

Yes.

Did I still beam?

Absolutely. More because Nathan was still watching me with admiration. And that meant more to me than what any of these people would ever have to say.

On the other side of the table, Charlotte eyed me a second longer than was comfortable before taking a long sip of her wine.

"Giovanna is full of surprises," Nathan said. "That's one of my favorite things about her."

He brushed a hair out of my face, pulling my gaze back to his as his finger lingered around my jaw. To my surprise, I found humor there. And something else I'd only ever seen on the faces of a few men, all of them in my family: my grandfather, my brother, and my two brothers-in-law. And only when they were looking at their wives.

Adoration.

It almost made me drop my glass, so I took another sip of the impossibly smooth vodka instead.

"Lucky bastard," said Jordan to one of the other doctors, who chuckled in response.

I didn't know who it was. I couldn't look away from Nathan's warm gaze.

Nor, it seemed, could he look away from mine.

NINETEEN
WOMEN WHO PROBABLY WANT NATHAN HUNT

#1 Charlotte the Mule.

As dress rehearsals go, the dinner went more smoothly than most.

See, the point of a dress rehearsal is always to work out any remaining kinks in the production. It's where you figure out that someone is entering the stage from the wrong mark or that the light blocking doesn't match the choreography for the second scene's entrances.

So, in a way, it was a good thing that someone like Charlotte Mueller was sitting across from me at dinner, watching me try not to look lost when someone discussed a difficult surgery Nathan had had last week or pretend that I'd "forgotten" basic things about my boyfriend like his birthday or the fact that his brothers' names were Spencer and Carrick (rather than not knowing these things at all). Her ladylike snarls and curt questions pointed out the holes in our production in a way Nathan's other coworkers, who barely seemed to know him at all, could not.

Clearly, there were some things we needed to fine-tune.

Didn't make it fun, though.

BOYFRIEND OF THE HOUR 241

Otherwise, I managed to fake my way through the rest of it, including a meat course served through a cloud of smoke and soup offered in the form of a bubble. In a way, Nathan had done me a favor by bringing me to a restaurant where you didn't have to order. The silverware was changed out for every course, so I didn't have to worry about which fork to use. And since everyone was eating the same things, I could just wait to see how other people portioned out their food before I attacked mine. By the end, I was surprisingly full, which was more than I expected from courses consisting of approximately two tablespoons of food each.

"So you'll be at the gala?" Reagan asked as we waited outside Columbus Circle for cabs.

I smiled at the smaller woman with braided hair. Reagan and I had hit it off fairly well—probably because she'd grown up in a neighborhood not far from mine, near Yonkers.

"Yes, we will," Nathan confirmed beside me, where he had secured my hand in the crook of his arm. "But we'll be sitting at the Huntwell table. We're chairing the event this year."

For probably the twentieth time that evening, I tried not to look surprised. He hadn't mentioned the part of the "gala" where I was the date of the head honcho.

On the other side of us, Charlotte eyed Nathan with something that looked a whole lot like lust. Which turned to disdain as her blue-eyed gaze landed on me.

"Great," Reagan said. "There's never anyone fun at these things, right, baby?" She squeezed Dwight's arm.

He just nodded as several cabs pulled to the curb.

"We'll see you then, Joni," said Jordan and his wife hummed her approval as she traded air kisses with me. He was a bit older than the rest of the crew—I gathered he was the original doctor at the clinic and had been a bit of a mentor to the rest of them. There was something fatherly about the way he looked over Boon, Dwight, and Nathan before turning back to me with a kind smile. "I'm glad you're bringing this one out of his shell. It's about time."

We watched as each couple got into their own cabs, all departing for what I was sure had to be their massive apartments and townhomes scattered all over Manhattan. None of them had that look on their faces, the invisible weight of people who didn't know where their next rent check was coming from or how they were going to pay their cell phone bill next week.

What must that be like?

"I need to pick something up at the clinic," Nathan said after everyone was gone. "Do you mind walking? It's only a few blocks from here."

I nodded. "I'm all yours."

He blinked, almost as if startled, but didn't argue as he led me down the street.

"I THINK your coworker has a thing for you," I said as Nathan unlocked the elevator panel of the charming brick building off West Sixty-Fourth Street. "The single one with the short brown hair."

I'd been here before, of course. That humiliating appointment seemed like eons ago.

The elevator doors closed, and he appeared to consider the idea as we rode up to the fourth floor.

"Charlotte? Yes," he finally said as the doors opened.

I waited for him to expand on this as we walked into the empty clinic. When he didn't, I tugged on his wrist just as we reached his office. "Explain."

Nathan sighed as he unlocked the door. "Why?"

"Because you made me spill my guts about Shawn. And also, because it seems like something a girlfriend would know if she were in a trusting relationship."

Not, I told myself, because I was actually jealous. That wasn't the case at all.

I followed him into the darkened office, and when he sat down in his desk chair, I leaned against the desk in front of him.

Nathan looked up at me. "Charlotte joined the practice last year, but our families have known each other since we were children."

"I picked up on that. She likes to name-drop your mom."

"I don't know why. I don't really get along with my parents." Nathan shrugged. "But I don't think she was particularly happy you joined us at dinner. I've gotten the feeling she would prefer to be my date for the gala and any other events I might have to attend."

I snorted. "You think? Real talk: I kept wondering if she was going to shiv me with her steak knife. I also don't think she believed we were a couple. She was quizzing me all evening."

For that, I received an adorably wry look. "I don't think Charlotte would 'shiv' anyone."

"Just one more difference between her and me, then."

"What do you mean?"

I swallowed a grin. His obliviousness was sometimes too cute to handle. "Just that...well...let's just say that if you were really my man, I wouldn't have put up with a snooty brat like that, making eyes at you all night long."

That brow lifted again. "Oh, really? What would you have done differently?"

"Probably called her out in front of everyone. Told her off, maybe thrown the dessert all over her blouse for good measure. I doubt raspberry chocolate mousse comes out of white silk."

I giggled. I was only half serious, of course. Okay, maybe more—my temper had gotten the best of me more than once, and the idea of prissy Miss Charlotte scraping poo-colored dessert off her perfect clothes was more than a little funny.

"Should I have done that with Shawn?"

And just like that, the laughter was gone. "What?"

Nathan stood suddenly, his big body blocking the lights of the city while he caged me between him and the desk. Not so close I couldn't escape. But several steps beyond regular decency, none-theless.

"I didn't like the way he was looking at you or the things he was saying at Opal. And at the time, I didn't even know who he really was." Nathan's voice seemed almost an octave lower. A rumble that reminded me quite clearly of a lion on the prowl. "If we see him again, are you suggesting I throw hundred-dollar scotch on him the next time he calls you 'Sunshine'?"

I swallowed. "Only if you wanted to be punched in the face. Shawn doesn't hold back."

Nathan considered this. "I don't start fights, Joni, but I have ended a few. I doubt it would last long with him."

We blinked at each other in the darkness. There was that stare again. The one he had been hiding all evening. The one he only seemed to use with me.

"Well, then, I suppose it's a good thing we're not actually in a relationship," I said with a suddenly scratchy voice. "I'd hate for you to start your first one."

Nathan looked at me—hard. His gaze dropped to my mouth before returning to my eyes. "You'd be worth it."

We were both quiet for a long minute. I opened my mouth to speak, not exactly knowing what I would say.

And just then, the elevator door opened with a ding.

"Nathan?"

My eyes popped open. She didn't. That bitch. Had she followed us here?

"Nathan? Is that you?"

I turned as Charlotte's voice rang out through the empty clinic. Nathan's hand, suddenly cuffed around my wrist, held me in place.

"Easy," he murmured.

"Where's that raspberry mousse when I need it?"

"Or a shiv?" He chuckled before calling out over my shoulder. "Hello, Charlotte. I'm just here picking up a few patient files to review. I thought I'd show Joni around since she's with me."

Charlotte's heels clipped the wood floors of the clinic as she approached. "Oh, I see. I needed to grab a few things as well."

Liar, I thought. You heard him tell me he needed to come here and thought he'd be alone.

Yeah, Nathan was *really* lucky I wasn't his actual girlfriend.

I twisted around to smile at Charlotte, though Nathan still had my wrist pinned to my side, warning me not to move. He stroked the sensitive skin just over my pulse with his thumb. Nothing Charlotte would notice. But something everyone in the room would sense anyway.

"You should do that, then," he told her, which was a dismissal if I'd ever heard one.

Charlotte seemed a bit taken aback. I offered a haughty grin. That's right, get the hell out.

"I...all right." She bobbed her head and went back down the hall to her own office, but not before shooting another glare in my direction.

I turned to Nathan once she was gone. "You know, this only proves my point."

He sighed. "It doesn't look very good, does it?"

Part of me thrilled that he didn't like her attentions. But only part. The other was saying something else completely. Something I knew I had to say it out loud.

"She would probably be a better fit for this little job we're running here," I murmured, though it was hard to think straight with his thumb still tracing gentle circles over my wrist. "Given the fact your family already likes her, especially. She already has an 'in' there."

The thumb stopped. "Job? Oh, you mean our relationship."

"Our *pretend* relationship, yeah. Except with her, it wouldn't have to be pretend."

Nathan shook his head. "I don't want a relationship with Charlotte Mueller, pretend or otherwise."

"Why not?"

I was pressing. I couldn't help it. I told myself it wasn't because I was jealous, that I wasn't being that girl who forced her boyfriend to denounce another pretty girl just because she couldn't handle it. There was no point. Not when this wasn't even a real relationship, to begin with.

I was also lying to myself.

He took a step closer, forcing me to sit completely back on the desk. "Because she isn't..."

His chest brushed against the front of my dress. I wondered if he knew how sensitive I was to just his presence. If he knew I wasn't even wearing a bra with this dress, and if he looked down, he'd see exactly how he was affecting me.

This wasn't right. This didn't feel like pretend anymore. Charlotte wasn't in the room. None of his coworkers were present.

I wasn't sure I cared.

"She isn't what?" I dared him, tugging lightly on his tie.

I looked up and found Nathan's deep brown eyes pinned to my mouth.

He licked his lips. "She isn't you."

His lips descended on mine, this time accompanied by a hand at my back and another that slipped into my hair and pulled just enough to make me moan. Nathan seemed to take it as an invitation as his tongue slipped in to greet mine, dance with it a bit, before he explored the rest of my mouth, sucking, licking, biting at my lips until I was panting into his.

The hand in my hair slid down as we kissed, wrapping around my neck, flattening over my sternum, and then slipping beneath the cowled neck of my dress to close over one breast. His mouth traveled over my jaw, licking and biting at my neck while his hand squeezed and kneaded my breast with a tight, consistent rhythm.

Nathan's entire body shuddered.

I couldn't help but quiver right back in response.

"Perfect," he mumbled against my skin. "So. Fucking. Perfect."

I purred as my hands slipped into his hair, curls so soft and lush. My God, his mouth was perfect. His touch, too. Most men veered too far in one direction or the other, but Nathan's hands, a surgeon's hands, were trained in finesse. Equal parts rough and tender.

The thumb that had previously tortured my wrist now brushed delicately over my nipple, toying almost reverently before he tugged the loose neckline down with a slight tear and took the nipple into his mouth.

I gasped.

Worship.

There was no other word for what Nathan was doing with each flick, each suck of his tongue and lips.

This was no boy bumbling around in the back of a friend's car or a drunken fumble after too many drinks at the bar. Nor was he some preying older man looking for one thing from an innocent young girl.

This was a man, pure and simple, doing what so many of them could never manage in the presence of a woman.

Adoring her.

Revering her.

Worshiping her with every nip of his teeth, every swirl of his tongue.

I fell back, only to be caught by Nathan's other arm, suspended at his mercy as my legs fell open, urging him to grind his erection into me through the wool of his pants and the thin lace of my new lingerie.

I realized at that moment that I'd never understood what real passion was. Never with any partner—not even Shawn—had I really felt what it was to be prized. Cherished. Not until this night, this moment, in this office, with this boyfriend.

Fake boyfriend.

Fake.

"Well, good night—oh!"

Whether it was the word echoing through my mind or the sound of Charlotte's voice, I suddenly felt like a bucket of cold water had been tossed over me. Nathan froze, then immediately straightened, taking me with him as he pulled my dress back into place.

I didn't dare look in her direction, choosing instead to lay my head on his chest and stare at the wall. She'd see everything written across my face.

Desire.

Guilt.

Lust.

Lies.

Nathan, however, was as cool as ever. The only signs that he'd just been devouring me like a bodega buffet were his mussed hair and slightly swollen mouth that was probably only visible to me.

He pushed his glasses up his nose and nodded. "I'll see you tomorrow, Charlotte."

The hand at my back kept me sitting upright while I flapped my hand over my shoulder, hoping that would suffice as a polite goodbye.

I kept my cheek pressed to his lapel as her footsteps retreated. And the elevator door chimed open. And then finally closed.

Then and only then did the hand at my back retreat.

I stifled a whine at its absence. No, come back.

Nathan stepped away to adjust his clothes, which were barely out of place. His erection was still obvious, but he adjusted that too, so it wasn't *quite* so present. But he couldn't hide something that large.

Not really.

Nathan's eyes met mine, unfathomably deep and dark in the dim light. "Do you think she believes it now?"

I coughed. "Does who believe what?"

He nodded toward the elevators. "Charlotte. Do you think that worked?"

My stomach dropped. God, I was an idiot.

That was just part of the act. Another scene in the play. A kiss that had felt so damn real, I'd done the worst thing a performer could do —gotten lost in my character.

Still breathless, I nodded.

"Good. She'll gossip with her mother, and it will get back to mine."

I nodded again, then bit my lip, wondering if Nathan might kiss me again for good measure. You know, just to make sure, in case she came back in.

But he didn't.

I wondered if he ever would again.

Or, more importantly, if he should.

"What about your friends?" he wondered.

I blinked. "Huh?"

"This isn't just for me. Who needs to see us together for it to get back to him—to Shawn?"

If Charlotte was a bucket of water, hearing Shawn's name was like plunging into an ice bath. I honestly hadn't really even thought about it beyond talking to Rochelle.

But Nathan had a point. To take myself off the market, word

needed to get around. Which meant that I needed to bring him into my world as much as he was escorting me through his.

I took his hand. "Up for a late night?"

He tilted his head to the left. "I suppose. Where are we going?"

I looked him over, took in his buttoned-up persona and the perfect face, and considered how no one who really knew me would ever believe I'd have snagged a dude like this.

For the first time, I wondered if that meant they didn't know me at all.

"Brooklyn," I told him after texting a few friends. "We won't be long. But we'll need to stop by the apartment to change clothes first."

TWENTY
SURPRISING THINGS ABOUT
NATHAN HUNT

*#17 The way he weres tshirts like coture. But those
arms tho*

An hour later, the cab Nathan had insisted on hailing pulled up to a warehouse in Brooklyn that had a life-size giant octopus alongside a wooly mammoth painted over the entrance.

I'd have gone for the train myself. But while he had allowed me to force him into jeans and a plain black T-shirt, my fake boyfriend had steadfastly refused to subject himself to New York's subway system.

"Do you have any idea how many pathogens exist on one seat in the subway?" he'd called from his bedroom.

"Do you have any idea how many live on the seats of New York City cabs?"

He just chuckled but didn't relent. And so, one overpriced cab ride later, we found ourselves in Bushwick.

"Huh. They changed it," I said as I took in the mural, which served, in my opinion, as a festive intro to the performances I could already hear warming up inside.

"It changes?" Nathan wondered as he looked it over.

I grinned at him. "Oh, all the time. Casper can't deal with looking at the same thing for too long, so they swap it out at least once a month. Two months ago, this dude was an orc surrounded by Barbie dolls. Before that, I think it was a collection of pegasuses doing lines. Or just pegasus?"

"Pegasi." Nathan looked up at the octopus as if he was struggling to imagine either option in its place. "And this is the type of place where he—Shawn—would come?"

I wrinkled my nose. I honestly did not want to think about my ex this evening. "Shawn goes wherever the party is, and Casper's been the best party in town for years. If he doesn't actually see us here tonight, he'll hear about it. And that's almost as good. Maybe even better."

At least it would be easier. If I could keep communication between Shawn and me as hearsay for the rest of my life, I'd be a very happy girl.

"Come on," I said as I tugged Nathan up the steps. "Let's see what's happening tonight at Peek."

Inside, the entry of the warehouse was more like a speakeasy, with a makeshift bar in one corner that essentially paid for the whole project and slouchy chairs and thrifted tables set up where people of all walks of life were clearly enjoying themselves. Two hallways led in completely different directions—one toward Casper's living quarters and the rooms they sometimes lent to artists who were particularly and amorously "inspired" on given nights, the other into an enormous performance space where a band was getting ready to play.

"Darling Joni, my love, where have you been? It's been a million years, and I *will not stand for it!*"

We turned toward the owner of the squawky voice I knew and loved. Immediately, I flung my arms out to accept a hug from the one and only Casper LaVoe.

Casper LaVoe—a name that I was ninety-nine percent sure was fake and one hundred percent didn't care was fake—was a friend I'd known since I was about fifteen. We'd met at a master class sponsored by Alvin Ailey for kids in the Bronx. Everyone we knew thought Casper was crazy when they quit their job at the Metropolitan Opera to rent a leaky old warehouse in Bushwick. But when they renamed it Peek and started throwing some of the most innovative gatherings in the city, it quickly became *the* place for artists to gather and share their work. And party really, *really* hard.

"You look amazing," I said when Casper finally released me from an eons-long hug. "Love the new braids. The color is hot."

Casper acted like they were fanning themselves, then picked up one of the multi-colored braids that reached their waist. "Just about raped my bank account, but I had to do it. Blair and I are deconstructing *Joseph and the Amazing Technicolor Coat* next week, and *I'm* going to play the coat. Oh! I have the best part just for you if you want to do it." Casper looked down at my leg. "All better, I hope?"

I made a face, and Casper wilted like a flower left out in the sun too long.

"Tragic," they said to no one in particular. "She really was an artist on stage."

Even though I knew Casper was just as dramatic with everyone, I still loved the fact that they really understood what it meant to be robbed of my ability to dance.

Casper was right. It really had been too long since I'd been here. Or around performers in general. My people.

"Darling, what is this we're wearing?" Casper asked as they twirled their finger, asking me to spin. "This garment. Is that silk? You look like the river at night and in the best possible way—all flowing and mysterious. I want to dive into you and soak for hours."

The attention made me bloom. I'd kept on the dress from dinner but had taken down my hair and brushed it out to look a little edgier, along with a generous helping of eyeliner and some dark lipstick that made me feel like an underworld fairy.

This was half the reason Casper and I always got along. We were both prone to the same sorts of dramatics when things weren't going our way, but we also knew exactly how to stroke each other's egos when they were.

"And what have we here?" Casper demanded as they looked

Nathan over with blatant appreciation. "Did someone find herself a bona fide Beatnik? Will we hear him 'Howl' in the night for us, hmm?"

Nathan didn't balk at Casper's overt inspection. "Are you saying I look like Allen Ginsburg?"

"Who's Allen Ginsburg?" I wondered.

"NOW HEAR THIS!" Casper crowed, gaining the attention of at least four tables. "Our lord and saint, Allen Ginsberg, was only one of the greatest queer poets ever to grace this world and I'm sure many others. 'Visions! omens! hallucinations! miracles! ecstasies! gone down the American river!'"

Casper said it with such flair that the room spontaneously broke into applause. They took a quick bow, then turned back to Nathan and me.

"Allen Ginsberg wrote 'Howl,'" Nathan clarified for me. "I'm pretty sure that was a direct quote." He turned to Casper. "I don't write poetry, though."

"Maybe not, but you do have excellent taste in eyewear," Casper said with a nod toward Nathan's glasses.

I grinned. I might not have known the poet, but I did know who the Beatniks were, since I'd probably seen *Funny Face* at least twenty times with Nonna. I'd told Nathan to put on the most casual things he owned, and he'd emerged in some dark jeans that did dangerous things to his ass and a black T-shirt that made his biceps look about twice as big as usual. With the glasses, he did indeed look like some kind of bad boy philosopher-poet getting ready to seduce Audrey Hepburn.

"I think Casper's just saying they like your outfit," I told Nathan as I reached for his hand. "Casp, this is my boyfriend, Nathan Hunt."

I almost stumbled over the word, but the squeeze of his hand around mine kept me centered. Nathan didn't blink or tremble or look away from Casper at all. Damn. He was as good a performer as anyone in here.

"Boyfriend?" Casper gasped. "Is it…"

"It's serious," I lied. "You know I wouldn't bring him here if it wasn't."

Nathan couldn't read the surprise on Casper's face, but I could. And it was exactly the reaction I was hoping for. Shock, yes, that I would ever call someone that, or at least bring someone other than Shawn here in that role. But also maybe some eagerness. Like they couldn't wait to share the news.

"Lovely to meet you," Casper said as they deposited twin kisses to each of Nathan's cheeks. Suddenly, it was like they couldn't scurry away soon enough. "Let's chat soon, darling. Oh, do you want?" They materialized a baggie of small white capsules and dangled it in front of us. "An unsinkable Ms. Brown for the evening?"

I glanced at Nathan. "Er—"

"Ms. Brown?" he asked.

"Molly," I clarified. "You don't have to."

His brows relaxed with recognition. "Oh, MDMA."

Casper nodded as he shook the baggie like a demented maraca. "Only the best for my friends."

I knew I shouldn't. And six months ago, I wouldn't. It's not that I didn't have plenty of options for it or that other dancers I knew weren't partaking. Cocaine blew through Broadway like a snowstorm.

But dance was the only thing I was ever good at. I could never bring myself to jeopardize that, even for the occasional night out.

Now, though…why the hell not?

Impulsively, I grabbed one of the pills, popped it in my mouth, and swallowed it quickly. Then I turned to find Nathan watching.

"You don't have to—" I repeated, but before I could finish, he'd already taken one and followed suit.

I gaped. "*You* want to do ecstasy?"

Nathan only smirked. "No surgeries until Wednesday. I believe this is the definition of 'When in Rome, do as the Romans do.' Isn't it?"

"*These* Romans like to fall in love," Casper told him with a gleeful grin before floating away to greet some other new arrivals.

"Come on," I said as I pulled Nathan toward the performance space, where a band was starting to play in front of the typically diverse crowd that Peek attracted.

The musicians were attempting something best described as a mix of down tempo, folk-country, and acid jazz. They weren't *good*, exactly, but they were trying hard, and the audience, a wild assortment of all varieties of gender, ethnicity, sexuality, body adornments, hair color, fashion sense, and enthusiasm, seemed to appreciate that fact. Some were dancing wildly, others just swayed from side to side, lost in their own worlds. Many chatted in groups of two, three, or four as they watched the musicians, while some near the front appeared to be spontaneously choreographing to the beat. Five people were constructing a sort of human pyramid at the back of the great room, from which they were attempting to hum and vibrate along with the band's melodies.

I searched Nathan's face for any signs of disapproval. It was always a sort of litmus test, bringing people to places like this. Not everyone could vibe with this sort of crowd. Casper and their ilk avoided labels like the plague, and Peek had been created for anyone to be anything they wanted without judgment, provocation, or limits on their art.

To some, that concept was very uncomfortable. Others embraced it fully.

I'd never brought anyone from the neighborhood here. Not even Rochelle. Certainly not my family, although a few times I'd wanted to bring Marie just to see if she'd crawl into a hole or if she'd surprise me by liking it. But I never had. I knew, that in my heart, I was one of the lonely souls in this city who sometimes needed a space like this to escape and just *be*. And I couldn't bear it if someone I loved looked at me differently because of it.

Nathan, however, was nothing but curious as he perused the room and watched everything happening, hand still firmly wrapped around mine. If anything, he was just as content as anyone else. He was fine with it all. Fine with *me*. He wasn't going anywhere.

"So, your family," I called out once I had started to relax.

He turned. "What about them?"

"Horses? Really?"

His shoulders tensed slightly. "I grew up on a horse farm about an hour from Washington, DC. My family breeds racehorses as a side project."

"That's what they do for fun?" I was legitimately shocked. I liked to go thrift shopping for fun, not collect multi-million-dollar animals.

I'd known Nathan was wealthy, but not like that.

Or maybe that was just his parents.

"Don't you think I should know a little more about this kind of stuff?" I asked when he didn't answer my question. "It's going to seem weird if I meet your parents and I have no idea who they are."

He turned again, appearing visibly pained. "No, you're right. I've been putting it off."

"Are they that horrible?"

He shrugged. "Yes. No. I don't really know. I left Virginia to find some space from them. But also, I don't like talking about them because people tend to treat me differently when they find out who they are."

"And that is?"

Nathan sighed heavily. "My parents are Lillian and Radford Hunt."

I blinked. And waited for some epiphany to fall over me, as it was obviously supposed to. It didn't. Which meant that, yet again, I was a clueless idiot.

"You're not saying anything," Nathan said.

"I...don't have anything to say," I replied. "Are those names supposed to mean something? You've mentioned them before, you know."

"Most people know them." He tried again. "Until last year, my father was the CEO of the Huntwell Corporation."

Again, nothing. "So, your family owns a big company? What do they do?"

Nathan appeared genuinely surprised by my response. "Mostly venture capital, although my father has always had a soft spot for mining—do you really not know who they are?"

I shook my head. "I don't follow finance, man. Too busy pouring drinks and shaking my ass."

"Until he retired, my father was one of the leading venture capitalists in the country. Sort of like Warren Buffet."

When I didn't answer to that, he continued with more names.

"George Soros? Peter Thiel? Larry Fink?"

I shook my head three more times. "Nope, nope, and nope. I'm assuming they're all super rich, probably white guys, but beyond that, they're just names."

Nathan looked honestly bewildered. "These are some of the wealthiest people on the planet, Joni. The decisions they make affect everyone. When they invest in something, it changes the world."

"Which is amazing," I concluded. "And I'm sure I've paid attention to things they've done. But the names just aren't important to me. Like this dress. I couldn't tell you who designed it. I think I saw it on Bella Hadid once, on *Page Six*. But mostly I just think it's pretty and I like it. I feel the same about the vintage Steven Madden dress I found in the bargain bin at the Goodwill."

Nathan remained quiet, digesting my words.

"So, your family's rich," I pressed on. "And given our arrangement, obviously overbearing. Question, though, why do *you* know so much about these guys when you're a doctor, not an investment banker or whatever?"

Nathan squinted like he was physically pained by that question. "I double majored in business. And I still have to maintain a seat on the company's board. It's part of the...arrangement...I have with my family."

"I see." I considered. "Anything else I should know before I meet them?"

Slowly, however, the pain faded from Nathan's face. And eventually was replaced with something closer to appreciation.

Which was odd.

But I'd take it.

"Yes," he said finally. "I have two younger brothers."

"Spencer and Carrick," I said, remembering dinner.

He nodded. "That's right. Spencer is the youngest, and like I said, he manages the breeding operations. Carrick works for the company, representing their interests to Congress and things like that. He and I are less than a year apart—"

"Like me and Marie," I jumped in. "Are you close?"

Nathan shook his head. "Generally, we don't get along. Our relationship is fairly antagonistic."

I nodded. "Yeah, Marie and I were like that too. But you know, things can change. Ever since she left for Paris, I actually miss her. A lot. Sometimes you need a person who will tell you exactly like it is, you know? She's the only one in my family who does that for me. Good and bad."

Nathan seemed to think about that for a moment. "Carrick is also very blunt."

I grinned. "So are you. See, you already have that in common."

For that, I received a wry smile. It was quickly becoming one of my favorites of his expressions. Nathan seemed to like it when I picked out personality traits of his that I suspected others didn't see. Or else were too intimidated to name.

"My father's greatest wish is for his eldest son—that's me—to return to Virginia and resume his seat at the head of Huntwell," Nathan said as he turned his attention back to the band, which was currently playing a very strange dancehall version of "Jolene" while the performers in the front attempted something like tango-meets-krumping.

I turned. "They want you to stop being a surgeon?"

I honestly couldn't imagine it. In the short time I'd really known him, I could see that his job was the most important thing in his life. Everything revolved around his surgery schedule. The man was a machine about it.

Nathan nodded. "I double majored in finance and pre-med, so I suppose I technically have some business savvy. And my parents are convinced that living here hasn't been good for me. They want me home, where they can force me to marry a vapid debutante, procreate, and eventually take over my father's position as CEO at Huntwell."

Things were becoming clearer. "So that's why you want to introduce me to them as your super serious girlfriend. You think that if you can show them you're happy here, with a solid social life and all the things they say you can't do without them, they won't pressure you to come home and join the family business, yeah?"

Nathan almost seemed embarrassed. "I suppose that's the majority of it."

"Why not just tell them no?"

Nathan gave me a look. "Would you believe I've tried that?"

I didn't answer. This time, it was my turn to deliver snarky expressions.

"My parents are very stubborn. And very...controlling." He pushed his glasses up his nose. "I honestly think the only way they will believe I actually enjoy the life I've built on my own is to show them I've met their terms."

"Well, are you?" I asked. "Happy?"

"I am...content with my life in New York," he said after a moment. "It's a life I chose for myself. That's more than I can say about anything in Virginia." And then his deep brown gaze fixed on me, and my heart thumped in response. "I'm happy here with you. Right now."

We watched each other for a good long time while one strangely written song bled into another, and the rest of the room seemed to blur a bit.

The down tempo element in the music dropped a few beats in tempo as the band launched into a sensual cover of a Metallica song.

Honestly, it wasn't bad.

Kind of pretty, actually.

"So, how do we do this?" Nathan wondered, pulling my attention back.

"What do you mean?"

"Well, at dinner, it was easy. I don't date often, so just coming to the restaurant—"

"And making out in your office?" I cut in slyly.

His mouth quirked. "Er—yes, that. That was all that was needed. Or all that was needed for most people who know me to believe I'm in a relationship. But for you..."

I put a hand on my hip in mock outrage. "What are you saying, sir?"

Nathan rolled his eyes. "Joni, I ran into you after you had a one-night stand with my former roommate. Forgive me for saying so, but it didn't seem like unusual behavior."

Just like that, the air was punched out of me. Nothing kills the mood like telling the girl you're with that you noticed she's kind of a slut.

No man likes a girl like that. I don't care how "happy" he is at the moment.

"For the record, I couldn't care less."

That did it. I scowled. "Oh, no?"

Nathan shook his head. "It wouldn't matter to me where you've been or who with before me. Just as long as you're with me now." He stepped closer. "Are you with me now?"

There was no insecurity in those big brown eyes. No uncertainty. Just a question, plain and simple. Honest and direct.

So, *so*, Nathan.

"I'm with you," I confirmed.

He nodded. "Good." Then he looked around. "But my question still stands. What do we do now that will convince people I'm more than another one-night stand?"

"You mean how do we convince them we're in love?" I wondered, though for some reason, the idea made me feel embarrassed.

I didn't stop to wonder why I thought the idea was so ridiculous. Why imagining myself the object of someone's continuous adoration and desire was absurd enough to make me blush.

Nathan nodded again. "Your friend obviously went off to share what you said, but this is a performance space. I imagine these people enjoy a good show."

I had to think about it. I mean, I *really* had to think about it.

Because the truth was, I may have had my fair shares of partners, but I was increasingly certain I'd never actually loved any of them.

Even Shawn.

Maybe, especially Shawn.

"I think the MDMA just passed the blood-brain barrier," Nathan said as he looked around, brown eyes now slightly dilated. Then they landed back on me and took on a hazy sort of expression.

My fingers were starting to tingle. And his skin looked *so* soft.

His hands, though, weren't exactly soft or hard. And I knew that now, from holding his hand and also from having him touch me—really touch me—in his office only a few hours ago.

He had calluses on them from the gym, but he kept them incredibly clean, probably because of all the time in surgery. Right now, though, the rest of my body tingled with the memory of those hands, the way they felt when they moved up my waist, the slight scuff of his fingernails when they dragged my dress down...

"Pick me up," I said abruptly.

Nathan also seemed to be caught in a daze as he turned toward me, close enough that our bodies were almost touching. "What?"

I leaned back to look him in the eye, though my hips seemed to move toward him. "Pick me up. And then twirl me around slowly. Like a princess in a movie."

His confusion was adorable. "Why would I do that?"

Even as he spoke, his hands already found my waist, locked into the curves like they belonged there.

I grinned. "Joy, silly. People do dumb things when they're stupid happy. If we were really in love, you'd be so overcome with it that you couldn't help acting silly. You'd have to let it out. So you'd kiss me until we were both giddy and then you'd pick me up and swing me around until I was shrieking with happiness too. Then we'd break down in giggles together, and you'd kiss me again. And this time, you wouldn't stop."

Nathan took a moment to digest everything I'd said. Undoubtedly, he thought it was stupid. But his hands remained on my waist. He stared at them as if weighing his choices. Keep them there and go with the flow. Remove them and end the whole thing.

Then, before I could say another word, he lifted me as easily as any partner I'd ever trained with. My arms wound around his neck, my hands into his thick curls, while he pressed kisses into my bare neck and collarbone. I could feel his smile against my skin. Joy sprouted from deep in my gut, and I laughed with the kind of unadulterated glee I'd just described, except none of this was an act. Maybe it was the drugs, but I had a feeling I'd respond the exact same way if Nathan picked me up on a street corner.

Maybe even more if we were alone.

"Good?" Nathan asked when he finally set me down.

He was grinning so hard that his left dimple was joined with one in his right cheek, and a thin sheen of sweat had appeared over his brow. Those chocolatey eyes flashed with the delight I knew was reflected in mine, and before I could stop myself, I clasped his face between my hands and kissed him, long and hard.

For the second time that night, his lips met mine, soft yet firm, tentative yet full of impact. And then he was devouring me, growling softly while his tongue and lips and teeth explored the terrain of my mouth. His hands slipped lower, taking firm handfuls of my ass, pressing me into him, into that considerable length that still teased even through his jeans.

When we broke apart, he was sucking in harsh breaths. His eyes were almost completely black as he searched my face for something.

"Good?" he asked again.

"Very good."

I pressed one kiss to his upper lip, then another to the bottom. He shuddered with each one, his hands gripping my skin harshly, shaking through the fabric of my dress.

"Now," I said, just before I swiped my tongue across his lower lip. "Do it all again. And this time, don't stop."

FAMILIAL PATTERNS

Nathan's lips were burning. They had been prickling for weeks, but the slow burn had intensified considerably since 9:42 p.m. last night.

It wasn't an uncomfortable burn, like when he drank coffee too quickly or forgot to use sunscreen on a hike.

This wasn't even a nuisance. It was pleasant, even. A frisson that tingled over his mouth during waking hours and augmented whenever he saw Joni.

Or thought about Joni.

Or more specifically, thought about Joni's mouth.

Which happened a lot.

He was up to three showers a day.

"Nathaniel?"

It had started with kissing her in the middle of a department store. Actually, that was incorrect. It had started the first night they'd met at that damn bar, when she'd popped up on her toes to "pay him back" for his kindness with an innocent kiss to the cheek but ended up smashing her lips to his instead.

That spark had been blown into embers in her boss's office when she'd kissed him the first time, and Nathan had all but mauled her right there on the couch.

He still couldn't believe he'd lost control that easily.

Kindling had been added with that "practice" kiss at Bergdorf's. Blown into a flame at dinner, where watching Joni savor ten courses worth of fine dining with those absurdly luscious lips was no better than pornography. Fanned considerably in his office last night (he'd legitimately considered fucking her on his desk even with Charlotte Mueller in the next room) and blazed into a full-blown inferno at… whatever he should call that place Joni had taken him in Brooklyn. By the end of that damn party, Nathan's entire body felt licked by flames.

And yet he wanted to walk straight into the fire and let it consume him.

Every instance had been a taste. A step toward completing the ruse they had set up together—however oddly determined and almost certainly ill-advised it was. He still wasn't sure why exactly he had thought it was a good idea to propose such an insane idea. But even now, in the cold light of day, with his head pounding and body aching after maybe an hour of sleep on that shitty warehouse couch, he still wouldn't do anything differently. He only knew it was better than the alternative: Virginia. His parents.

And then, of course, there was Isla to worry about.

"Nathaniel! What is the matter with you?"

The sound of his mother's peevish voice, the faint Virginian accent sliding over her vowels, was enough to yank him out of his fantasies. For now, anyway. At the moment, he wasn't in a place to consider further self-immolation in the form of kissing Joni Zola, but in fact, he was about to have his second brunch in two weeks with his parents, who had just arrived in the city in anticipation of the Sinai Children's benefit on Friday.

"Hello, Mom." He greeted his mother with a perfunctory kiss to the cheek, then nodded to the man next to her before sitting down at their table at BG Restaurant on the seventh floor of the Bergdorf's department store. "Dad."

"Nathan." Radford mirrored the same abrupt gesture without lowering his newspaper.

Much like Nathan, his parents—especially his father—were creatures of habit. Radford Hunt had enjoyed the same breakfast, lunch, and dinner for most of his eighty-three years. His days followed the same routine no matter which of his houses he was occupying. And when he did divert from those routines, they were only to other well-established paths of travel.

Bergdorf's was one of them and had been since before Nathan had even moved to the city as an intern. It didn't matter if the eggs were sometimes rubbery or the coffee a bit weak. Radford liked to read the *Wall Street Journal* with a view of Central Park, and Lillian liked her single crab cake before meeting with Andrea, her favorite personal shopper, on the fourth floor.

"Nathan, where have you been? We were expecting you thirty minutes ago. And whatever are you wearing?" Lillian Hunt sniffed. "Is that patchouli?"

Nathan offered the grim smile his mother called his "mopey face" (whatever that meant). He was aware of the irregularities. Tardy when he was always on time. Dressed in last night's wrinkled jeans and a dusty T-shirt instead of the tailored clothes his mother typically sent from Milan or Paris when she went. Reeking of the strange Brooklyn warehouse where he had spent the night on a stained floral sofa with Joni wrapped in his arms instead of alone in his three-thousand-thread-count sateen sheets.

The MDMA had been strong, and they hadn't been able to stop touching each other once it had set in. Nothing more than that, as if by some unspoken agreement, they both knew it would violate some basic rule of consent. For some of the party-goers, the public space hadn't stopped them from enjoying each other more thoroughly in the darker corners. Nathan, however, hadn't minded keeping his hands over her clothes and his lips above her collarbone. He and Joni had remained fused on that dance floor, touching, dancing, twirling, and, yes, kissing, until they'd finally collapsed on a couch in the corner and drifted off to the sounds of that terrible band reinventing bossa nova as punk rock.

It was unequivocally the best night of his life.

And maybe one of the best mornings too. Nathan had woken with a half-asleep arm and a sore neck, the snoring of multiple people buzzing in his ears, and Joni's face smashed on his chest. She hummed lightly in her sleep, a nondescript song that had no real melody; one hand curled into his shirt, her black lashes fluttering over opalescent eyes as she approached consciousness. Nathan swore he had known that song before he had ever heard it.

When she woke, she'd looked up at him, her typically bright, if slightly sad, green eyes full of something sweet and light. Something like hope. Something so indelibly *right*.

And he hadn't been able to breathe.

His lips, however, still tingled as if just the memory of her face set them alight all over again.

He still couldn't make any sense of it. He wasn't sure he wanted to. And certainly not to the people sitting at this table.

Nathan perused the menu, which was written in blurry script that wasn't helping his headache. He'd just order the same thing he always got. His parents were still staring as he removed his glasses and massaged his forehead.

Once again, those bright emerald-colored eyes flashed in his mind, her sly, slightly crooked smile curving under the multicolored lights strung across the exposed rafters of the warehouse. That perfectly proportioned mouth opening just under his, back arched as his hands slid up her ribcage, daring to cup her impeccably petite, exquisitely round, utterly grabbable breasts—

Nathan cleared his throat and replaced his glasses. His parents were staring at him like his skin had turned blue. Lillian was ignoring her mimosa while Radford had actually set down the financial section of the *Journal*.

"I had a long night," Nathan said, realizing they were still waiting for an answer to his mother's comments.

"At the hospital?" his mother wondered.

Nathan didn't answer, and she seemed to take that as confirmation. His father's shoulders relaxed a bit.

"Not sure how any son of mine ended up working a night shift," grumbled Radford as he snapped the paper in front of his face again. "Absurd is what it is."

"People have emergencies at night too, Raddie," Lillian said. "Although they are running you ragged, Nathaniel. You know your father is good friends with the chairman of Georgetown's board, and he has personally assured us that you would get to choose your hours at the hospital to fit your needs. It's just a phone call away, honey."

"I'm not looking for a different job," Nathan said as he raised a hand toward a server.

His parents shared a glance. But before either of them could reply, the waitress arrived.

"Welcome to BG," she said with a broad smile that revealed slightly too many teeth. It wasn't bad, but it wasn't Joni's, whose smile—every iteration—was perfect. "My name is Emily, and I'll be your server. Can I start you off with anything to drink?"

"Club soda and the salmon salad," Nathan replied shortly.

"Are you sure?" Lillian pressed. "The specials did sound very good. Perhaps you should hear them."

"Lillian, don't pester the boy." Radford's voice was typically sharp. "He orders the same thing every time, just like we both do." He flipped the paper back up while he spoke to the server. "He'll have that salad like he always does. My wife will have the crab cake, and I'll have the croque madame, no parsley."

With one hand, he waved the server away. She stole an extra glance at Nathan, and after he nodded, she disappeared, leaving him and his parents in silence while the rest of the restaurant chattered.

"You're looking well," Mom said finally. "Other than..." She waved a manicured hand toward his clothes. Today, her nails were the color of the pink seashells he and his brothers used to collect on the North Carolina beaches.

Nathan glanced into one of the many mirrors mounted on the walls, if only to determine what she saw. Aside from his disheveled appearance, he looked identical to when she'd seen him only two weeks ago. Worn out and dirty, but otherwise, there was the same brown, curly hair that flopped over his forehead because he hated the feel of hair products. Same brown eyes he'd inherited from Lillian and the long, straight nose with the crooked bridge granted by Radford. Same large body maintained at the gym every day except Thursdays.

Same, same, same.

Except right now, everything felt different. And Nathan still didn't understand why.

Joni's green eyes blinked in his mind's eye, and his lips burned a bit more in response.

"You've got to take better care of your wardrobe, Nathan," Lillian said as she took a sip of her mimosa. "Denim's for the farm, dear, not Bergdorf's. Those jeans belong in a donation bin. Where are the Stefano Riccis I sent?"

"I have no idea. Probably in my closet with everything else you sent."

Nathan already knew there was no way he would ever get rid of the jeans Joni had approved for him last night. Jeans he had never worn before then.

His mother sighed but wisely didn't press. She probably knew this line of questioning wouldn't go anywhere.

Nathan looked around the table expectantly. His parents had invited him to brunch this morning because the family was all arriving early before the gala at the end of the week. He'd expected his brothers to be there too. But there were no other jackets on the backs of chairs, and the table was only set for three.

"For God's sake, Nate," Radford said as he turned a page of his paper. "You obviously have a question. Just ask it."

Nathan frowned. He didn't have a question. Maybe some musings. Generally, he didn't ask questions unless he really needed to know the answers. Sometimes, he still forgot that it was a typical part of a conversation.

His father knew this, but Radford Hunt had never been a particularly forgiving man. Nor a patient one.

So Nathan asked, "Where are Spencer and Carrick?" mostly to put his father at ease. He honestly didn't care where his brothers were.

"Carrick arrives Monday night." Behind the paper, Radford took an audible sip of his coffee. "He's whipping votes for the next bill that includes some important earmarks."

Despite having retired from Huntwell, Radford seemed to have his fingers in the business more than ever. According to Carrick, Radford had left before the board could vote him out, but not before installing an interim CEO he could manipulate from home.

It wouldn't last forever. Which further explains his parents' sudden intensified desire to bring Nathan back into the family fold. Despite his best efforts, he had a feeling they would never give up hope that he might take his father's place at the company, if only as a puppet.

"And Spencer's in Warrenton until Friday," Lillian added. "There's a new stallion arriving. You should come down and see it, hon."

Nathan nodded. There wasn't much about Virginia he cared about anymore, but he did miss the horses. The occasional ride in Central Park couldn't compare with a gallop across Huntwell Farm's fifteen hundred acres. It was the largest original patent left in Virginia, land that had passed undisturbed through generations of Hunts since granted in the wake of the Revolutionary War.

His family all still lived on the old plantation that had been converted to a thoroughbred breeding operation near the last turn of the century. Thanks to Spencer, what had originally been a family hobby had become profitable enough that he was able to make it his full-time job while Carrick worked on behalf of Huntwell Corp. in Washington. In that way, at least, Nathan was grateful for both his brothers. Their willingness to take on parts of the family business was why Lillian and Radford had begrudgingly allowed their eldest son and assumed heir to become a lowly doctor.

For a while, anyway.

"Cary said you got yourself a new roommate," Lillian said after the server had brought Nathan's drink and refilled his parents'. "And that you're bringing her to the gala."

Radford emitted a groan, though Nathan wasn't sure if it was in response to Lillian's question or to something he'd just read in the paper, which he set back on the table.

"Girlfriend," Nathan corrected her. "She's my girlfriend. Not just a roommate."

"A girlfriend," Lillian repeated. "That you're living with."

His parents shared a look that he couldn't read. He hated it when they did that, mostly because they knew exactly how difficult it was for him to interpret their faces.

Not like Joni, whose face was an open book. Like Nathan, she almost always said what she was thinking. He had learned her expression faster than anyone he'd ever met, and while she seemed to think her lack of self-censorship made her a "mess," it was honestly one of Nathan's favorite things about her.

Joni was Joni. Nothing more. Nothing less.

Perfect.

"Well, go on. Tell us about her," Lillian prompted.

Nathan ground his teeth, though he had known it would come to this. "Her name is Giovanna, although she goes by Joni. She's a dancer, originally from the Bronx, who is currently bartending while she recovers from a recent injury to her knee."

It didn't seem adequate, this description of Joni. These were the things that might be listed on a brief bio, maybe a cover letter. But they were so unimportant when compared to all the traits he had learned about her over the past month.

But was he supposed to tell his parents about the way her green eyes changed from emerald to almost jade when she thought something was funny? Or the way her lips curved at the edges when she daydreamed, like she had a secret to share with only him? Would it even matter that she moved like a piece of art, had a laugh like a song, or had a way of making any person in the room feel like they had the most important voice in the world when she listened?

Or should he point out the obvious, which was that he was only able to notice these things in her and no one else because of his dangerously growing obsession with her?

And it was an obsession. He could admit that now to himself. To the point where he was taking three showers a day, regretting that he had ever given her bra back, and could not get the memory of the exact shape of her nipple against his tongue out of his mind.

While he was at it, maybe he should also mention that she wasn't really his girlfriend, just a young woman desperate enough to play along in exchange for free rent and his help chasing away an ex. That he couldn't bring himself to ask her if she actually liked kissing him of her own accord or if she was only doing it because others might see them and support their charade.

It was the truth. But that didn't seem right anymore either.

His parents again traded looks, and this time, even he could tell they weren't impressed.

"A dancer. Really?" His father almost looked bored by the idea. "I went out with a dancer once. When I was a nineteen-year-old grunt in the army, not a respected man of business."

"You think she…might enjoy an event like the benefit?" his mother added. "A girl like her?"

Nathan frowned. "Why wouldn't she?"

Radford rolled his eyes and grumbled something before taking another sip of coffee.

"Just that it might be a little…lonely for her with all these strange people," Lillian said.

Nathan only blinked. "She won't be lonely. She'll be with me."

"What about Charlotte Mueller?" his mother wondered far too nonchalantly. "Her mother is an absolute darling. Debbie joined the DAR last year, and you know she's a dear friend. She said Charlotte's enjoying her work with you, and she's already attending the gala with the rest of your doctor friends. You would make the perfect escort. And don't you remember how well you two got along when you were little?"

"*Joni* is my girlfriend," Nathan said clearly. "She's who I'm bringing, and she's important to me. I'd like you to meet her."

He found no trace of a lie in any of the statements.

"Nathaniel, there's no need for that tone. I'm only trying to help."

"Like he'd ever appreciate it," Radford muttered.

"Radford, hush," Lillian told him. "That's why we're here, isn't it?"

"What do you mean by that?" Nathan figured his father should be happy. He was asking a direct question. "You're here for the hospital gala."

Lillian sighed and twirled a bit of her ashy blond hair between her fingers. "I mean, here without your brothers. Your father and I wanted to see you alone because we're still worried about you, honey."

Nathan frowned at the endearment, which was used multiple times now. His mother only used pet names like that when she had bad news to share. Or requests she knew he wouldn't like.

Nathan remained quiet when the server appeared with their orders and waited patiently for his mother to explain, as he knew she would eventually.

"Look at him," Radford finally said. He had set down the paper again to cut up a few bites of toast, cheese, ham, and egg. "Say something like that to anyone else, and they want to know why. They ask questions. They respond, for God's sake. From him, it's nothing."

"Raddy, please," Lillian chided. "He's made progress. Not like when he was a child, you remember. He barely talked at all back then."

"I'm also still here," Nathan added shortly as he picked up his fork. He hated when they did that—talked about him like a zoo animal. "I'm just listening. You're apparently still worried about some nonexistent issue with my social skills. I suppose you'd like to tell me why and what you'd like to do about it."

Lillian took a large sip of her mimosa, looking a bit like she wished it were something stronger.

"Your father and I have decided…that it's time for Isla to go back to North Carolina."

Nathan froze, fork poised over the filet of grilled salmon, and looked up at his mother. He could have sworn she flinched. But only a little. "Say that again."

It wasn't a question. It wasn't even a request.

"She's in school," Nathan said. "And she's making progress. You'll ruin all of that."

"It's inappropriate," Radford said. "The press is going to find out about her, and that's the last thing we need after what Carrick put us through last year."

"Isla has nothing to do with Carrick's indiscretions with senators' wives," Nathan said. "She's a child."

"She's seventeen."

"With the social skills of a seven-year-old. You know this." Nathan couldn't help the way his voice heightened. He tried never to lose his temper because when he did, it seemed to scare people. But Isla was a pressure point his parents like to find.

"And that damned school is saying she'll need to stay there for another five years or more," his father bit back. "When we signed those forms, no one thought it would take this long."

Nathan stared at his plate, fighting the urge to throw it to the ground just to hear the porcelain shatter. "You promised. I've done everything you've asked of me, and you *promised* you would take care of her."

"Sometimes promises have to change." His mother's voice was trying to be kind. He could hear that. But it wasn't working. "We just don't have the bandwidth to continue overseeing her like this. Of course, if you came home...perhaps you could take over. She could visit the farm. Really be part of the family, since that's what you want so badly."

Silence descended over the table like the thick bechamel sauce oozing from Radford's toast, cloyingly rich and far too heavy.

Nathan stared down at his salmon, weighing a bite. But suddenly, even the texture of the salmon looked wrong. His stomach roiled, and it had nothing to do with the hangover.

He set down his fork and pushed his plate away.

"That's impossible," he said. "The court said it's impossible. Because of you."

"The court ruled that you have no legal rights with Isla," his mother said. "But since your father and I were able to procure guardianship, we do. Including deciding what's best for Isla's imme-diate future." She looked at Radford. "I think we can oversee them both in our own home, don't you, Raddy?"

Radford gave a curt nod.

"Then it's settled," Lillian said with a bright smile. "You'll sell your shares in that bitty little practice, split your time between Georgetown and Huntwell, and come home where you belong. Isla can stay at Ferndale, and she'll relax knowing you're close. Everybody gets what they want."

She looked around the table. Nathan wondered if she was expecting applause.

Unfortunately, by the time she was finished speaking, Nathan's hands were shaking in his lap, fingers pinching his thighs so tightly his knuckles were almost white.

Rage. That's what this feeling was. Pure, blinding rage.

"Nathaniel?" Lillian seemed very far away. "Doesn't that work out just fine?"

Nathan closed his eyes, counted to ten, then opened them. He had to do it four more times before he could unclench his teeth.

"Nate," his father barked. "For God's sake, *speak*."

"Since I was a child, I have done everything you have ever asked of me." Somehow, Nathan managed to keep his voice even. Kept it from shaking.

Radford snorted. "That's a fairy tale I haven't heard before."

Nathan's eyes were as sharp as knives. "It's the truth. I'm sorry I haven't been the son you wanted. I genuinely am. None of us turned out the way you planned. You needed smart, charismatic leaders to take over once you retired. Instead, you got Spencer, Carrick, and me."

"Dr. Doolittle, Gordon Gecko, and Rain Man," his father muttered. "Lucky fucking me."

"Radford!"

"Well, it's true," he snapped at her, and Lillian obediently quieted.

Nathan didn't bother arguing with him. He'd heard enough versions of that insult over the years that it no longer stung.

"Yes, Dad. You wanted an acceptable heir to your self-made throne," he continued. "And while I admit I have never become exactly what you wished, I have, in fact, done nearly *everything* you requested over the last ten years. You wanted me to attend board meetings while I was in the middle of my residency? I spent hours reading quarterly reports instead of sleeping after thirty-six-hour shifts. You demanded I see a therapist that *you* chose? Dr. Mitchell is officially my longest adult relationship. You insisted I still live with a roommate? I've spent my thirties acting like Bert and fucking Ernie despite being one of the highest-paid surgeons in the city."

"Nathaniel," Lillian said as she set a hand on his shoulder. "You just struggled so much as a boy, as a young man. We saw you needed the push, is all. We have only ever done this for your own good."

"You did it for yourselves," Nathan snapped back. "And I did it for her. For Isla. Because *you* said you would take care of her when the court ruled I could not."

"And whose fault was that?" His father spoke through his teeth, his gray eyes somehow darker than the steel on the table.

"Mine." Nathan's response was immediate. "I was twenty-one and barely able to speak after what happened. As you never cease reminding me. But this…" He shook his head. "So, now you'll sacrifice a young girl's future just to get what you want. And you'd have me throw away an entire life I've built for myself just to control me. Why can't you shape Carrick or Spencer into what you need? They're already in Virginia with you."

"Because Carrick and Spencer are parasites without a lick of sense between them, and you know it," his father finally burst out, his silverware landing on his plate with a clatter. A few tables next to them went quiet. "You might be a social idiot, but you're smarter than everyone else in this family. You're the only one of my sons who can take over my life's work."

"And what about my life's work?" Nathan asked.

"You're only thirty-four. You don't have a life's work."

"It took me a decade to become a surgeon. It's what I'm supposed to do."

"No, what you are *supposed* to do is be a goddamn Hunt," his father barked. "It's a fact, not a choice. And the sooner you get it through your thick head, the better."

They stared at each other for a long time. Minutes passed while the clamor of the restaurant merged with the roar in Nathan's head.

Eventually, though, the roar quieted into a low growl of resignation. One that, unfortunately, Nathan knew well.

"I need time," he said as he sat back in his chair and stared at his full plate of food. "A few months, at least. To sell the practice. Finish the surgeries I've already committed to doing. Transition patients. I can't just leave."

Lillian glanced at Radford, who had already gone back to reading his paper. "I should think that would be just fine, don't you, Raddy?"

Her voice sounded like a children's song. Far too happy in the face of unbearable tension.

Nathan's father only grunted.

Lillian turned to Nathan with a brilliant smile. "There you have it. Let's see, two months would put us right at the Gold Cup, as luck would have it."

"That's not luck," Nathan said to the table. "It's a calendar."

"We'll have you home right at the start of the season." Lillian beamed. "We'll celebrate your homecoming then. A family reunited."

Nathan didn't respond. His mind was too busy working.

Because he had two months, starting now, to figure out how to take his life back from the people who had owned it from the day he was born.

And he wasn't sure if Joni would like what he had in mind.

TWENTY-ONE
TOP TEN BILLY JOEL SONGS

#1 ~~New York Stat of Mind~~ Just The Way You Are

"What about this one?" I asked as I strode into the living room for what was probably the sixth time on Monday evening.

"Hold on."

I waited while Nathan finished typing something into his computer. Probably something called "charting," whatever that was. I knew he had to do it every night after he got home, and that it was something to do with his job.

He looked absurdly handsome in his preferred at-home clothes: glasses, of course, a soft heather-gray tee that did nothing to hide his muscled arms and the chest I'd blissfully slept on in a Brooklyn warehouse, black joggers that made me sneak glances at his butt more than I wanted to admit, and socks with pictures of Einstein sticking out his tongue on them. He had surprised me tonight by wearing a baseball hat too, completely unaware of how the sight of it pulled backward turned me feral.

I smiled and made a mental note to write a new list.

Things that Surprise Me about Nathan Hunt

1. He's a terrible cook. Maybe even worse than me. Which is shocking because he seems really good at everything else.
2. He's a *Dune* dork. Apparently, he's read the series five times. He reads a little every night before he goes to sleep. A lullaby of giant sand worms.
3. He has a thing for weird socks. So far, I've seen crazy scientists, raccoons, and Sasquatch.

We made a surprisingly domestic fake couple, spending the rest of the weekend recovering from the party together despite not having an audience or any real reason to be. We worked out together in the top floor gym, made dinner (which mostly consisted of me watching from the kitchen island while Nathan heated up premade meals), and lounged in the living room, Nathan reading a book while I watched Netflix on my tablet or scrolled on my phone. Once, we took advantage of a break in the wintry weather to walk up Riverside Drive. Outside, Nathan held my hand just because. I didn't stop him.

I just liked being around him. The stark differences between us didn't seem to matter. Nathan didn't care that I wasn't up to speed on Nobel Prize-winning novels or that I indulged in scanning celebrity gossip sites while I drank my coffee, and I didn't care that he barely knew who Taylor Swift was or why people were so obsessed with her love life.

Sometimes, we talked, and sometimes we didn't. I didn't have to figure out how to sound extra charming to make him forget I wasn't that smart. And I thought he felt some of the same relief in not having to paste on that awkward smile he wore throughout most of the dinner with his colleagues.

We could just be.

And it was really, really nice.

Nathan finished his notes, but when he looked up at me, he jolted and barely caught his computer from slipping off his lap.

I grinned. "That good, huh?"

I twirled around in a red satin dress that barely went past my butt. It was one of the many pieces from Bergdorf's, and I'd put it on just to see that look on Nathan's face.

Mission accomplished.

Nathan set his computer aside, and I watched with satisfaction as the muscles in his neck fluttered while he swallowed.

"I—do you know what black tie means?" he asked, though he wasn't quite able to tear his gaze away from my bare legs.

"It means *you* have to wear a black tie, right?" I quipped as I twirled around, enjoying the way he didn't blink. Not once. "I figure this will make a splash. You want people to know I'm there. Arriving in something shorter than an ice-skating costume will do it, don't you think?"

I was playing with fire, I knew. I had no right to flirt with this man like this, especially when he didn't seem to pick up on half the cues anyway.

But I couldn't help it. I already liked it when people looked at me. But Nathan's dark-eyed smolder seemed to matter more than most.

Finally, he managed to close his mouth. "You're joking. This is a joke."

"Yes, you dork, it's a joke." I flopped onto the sofa next to him and set my feet on the coffee table. "Can you imagine what people would say if I showed up in this? I think it might actually be lingerie. They'd probably think I was a call girl."

Nathan looked more than a little uncomfortable with that idea but didn't say anything.

"And for the record, I know what black tie means. I had a prom too."

I nudged him in the shoulder. He didn't move away.

There had been a lot of that over the weekend. "Accidental" touching. In the hall. The kitchen. Brushing arms when we reached for a mug or getting caught in a doorway together when no one moved first.

Maybe I wasn't the only one walking a fine line between real-life flirting and this pretend play.

"Hey, how about some music?" I asked as I got up to try on

another dress. "Or would that disturb your work?" I looked around. "Is there a speaker in here?"

"There's a Bluetooth one on the bookshelf," Nathan said, already pulling out his phone. "I'll put something on while you change."

When I returned in another dress—a long yellow one this time with an almost indecent slit nearly to my hip—Nathan was nodding in time to the tunes.

He brightened when he took in the dress. "That one's nice." His gaze dropped again to my bared leg, and I could see his Adam's apple move when he swallowed. "Very nice."

"I think it's a little too 'Leg or breast'? Plus, I sort of feel like Big Bird. I think I should look a little more sophisticated when I make my debut as your lady friend." I perked my head at the familiar piano riff. "Is this Billy Joel?"

"Would you prefer something else? I can change it."

I shook my head. "No, it's fine. I like him too. I was just… surprised."

Nathan cocked his head. "Why? He's a very popular artist."

I giggled. "No shit, Sherlock. He's one of the bestselling musicians of all time. Just a little before *our* time, wouldn't you say?"

His big shoulders shrugged. "Maybe yours. I was born a bit before you. And my parents listened to these albums a lot, so I suppose I find them familiar."

At that, I softened and went to sit next to him on the couch, taking his phone so I could look through the playlist. He stiffened as our shoulders touched again, but then relaxed, almost as if he welcomed the warmth.

I swiped through all the albums available on his streaming service.

"I like Billy Joel too," I said. "It reminds me of my dad, even though I never knew him. He had all these albums. We used to play them on Nonna's record player." I pointed to *The Stranger*. "That one is my favorite."

"Sometimes music provides a way to connect that still feels… safe, I think."

A chill traveled down my back. Such a simple statement, but too true.

I wondered what he used music to avoid in his relationship with his parents.

Nathan narrowed his eyes as if studying the black-and-white album cover would tell him something critical about my choice. "Why that one?"

I just shrugged. "Have you ever heard the way he writes about the women he loves? They're full of flaws but perfect to him. Who wouldn't want to be adored like that?"

Nathan didn't reply, just tipped his head in that way he did when he was listening really hard, watching me like I was this hard puzzle he was trying to sort out. I didn't know why. I wasn't complicated or anything. Just a little girl who wished she knew her daddy and wanted someone to love her.

"Even though I never knew my dad, when I was lonely, I'd put these songs on and imagine he was there hugging me," I went on, closing my eyes as the opening chords to "She's Always a Woman to Me" came on. "And that was him telling me all those things I wanted to hear." I tipped my head back at Nathan. "Who doesn't want to be told 'I love you just the way you are'?"

Just like it always did, the mention of Leandro Zola made my gut squeeze a little. And something prick at my eyes. I only knew him through pictures, most of them from before I was born. A dark-haired twin of my brother who often wore a Yankees hat, always had a drink in his hand, and had a smile like the sun. My older siblings said he had a much darker side, mostly brought out by alcohol, but I chose to think of him more like the version in my head. The dad I'd always wanted but never got to have.

I shook the memories away before they made me cry in this pretty dress. "It's weird, huh? Missing someone you never knew?"

"How old were you when he died?"

"Nine months. So, obviously, I don't remember him at all. But I do miss him." I shook my head. "It's ridiculous, isn't it?"

Nathan frowned, causing that adorable divot to appear between his brows and the skin around his jaw to tighten. I wanted to kiss that divot. I wanted to smooth out the lines.

No, Joni. You're roommates. Just his *pretend* girlfriend. That's all this is.

"Did you know that cells have memories?" Nathan asked.

I blinked out of my thoughts. "Huh?" It was such a random thing to say at this particular moment.

He kept going. "Our cells are actually incredibly intelligent. There's a lot of research on the matter. They've shown, for instance, that stem cells in the skin actually keep track of previous inflammation to better aid healing. Skin cells that have already been scarred actually heal two point five times faster than skin that has never been hurt before because they already know what to do. Or T-lymphocytes—that's a type of white blood cell—will actually impart memories of previous infections to daughter cells that last up to ten years, which helps fight similar infections should they return. But they have daughters, and they have daughter cells, and so really, we don't know how long those memories actually last, but they probably exist on some level for the rest of our lives, even if they weaken with time—" He looked up suddenly, cutting himself off. "Sorry. I didn't mean to go on like that. Some people find it annoying when I don't provide breaks in a conversation."

I smiled. He said it was annoying, but honestly, Nathan's tendency to go off for a while about random bits of information was already one of my favorite things about him. He knew so much about so much. It was kind of like hanging out with Frankie or maybe one of my teachers, but he didn't care that I didn't know as much as him. There were no judgmental looks or bad grades on quizzes. It was like living with a really nice encyclopedia. He made learning fun.

It also turned me on. A lot.

"You don't ever have to apologize for teaching me things," I told him. "I like it. Although I'm not sure what cell memories have to do with Billy Joel and my dad."

Again, that crooked smile made an appearance—the one that revealed the dimple in his left cheek.

God, he was gorgeous. So, *so* gorgeous. And he really had no idea.

"I—well—um—" For once, he didn't seem to know what to say. Then he pushed his glasses up his nose and tugged at the backward brim of his cap. "Science hasn't really pointed to it one way or another, and I'm not saying it's supported by any legitimate research at this point—" He cut himself off again as if he realized he was starting to go on another tangent. He took a deep breath, then continued. "I just mean to say, maybe some parts of you do remember your dad. Even if it's just in your skin. Or your cells. So it's not ridiculous that you miss him. Not at all."

When our eyes met again, this time, I was the one to look away first. His eyes were just so brown. And with this lovely music and the idea that maybe my fantasies weren't just fantasies after all...

How could this person who barely knew me manage to tell me exactly what I needed to hear?

"Did I upset you?"

I looked back, this time with my vision clouded a bit by more tears. I laughed and wiped them away. "No, no. These are happy tears."

Again, Nathan's head cocked. Again, he was just so freaking cute. "Ah. Happy tears."

I nodded. "Happy tears," I confirmed. "Cell memory. I like it. Thank you for telling me about it."

Again, that shy smile made an appearance. "You're welcome."

"So, what about me?" I pressed, suddenly eager to change the subject. "Do I get a fashion show too?"

He shook his head as he rested an arm behind me on the couch. I leaned back against it, and once again, he didn't move it away.

"I own a tuxedo that's adequate," Nathan was saying as his fingers brushed my shoulder.

I nodded. "I bet renting would be tough. Big arms and all." I gave his biceps a squeeze for good measure. It didn't even squish a little. "Why *do* you look like this? You don't see a lot of doctors that could play for the NFL."

Nathan adorably peered down each of his arms as if they had only just grown from his body. "I played baseball, not football."

I gawped. "You did?" That explained the hat.

He tugged on the brim. "In college, not professionally. Although my coach wanted me to go to the Combine instead of medical school."

Despite his size, the idea seemed absurd. Nathan was the opposite of what I imagined a typical jock to be. He was generally quiet, shy, and a total brain—not like the loud, shouty meatheads that traipsed the halls of Belmont Prep. Granted, our school wasn't exactly known for producing baseball players, but there was always that contingent.

He shrugged. "I played for Duke. It was a good way to get out of Virginia." His mouth tugged into an impish half-smile. "My father attended Georgetown, and we were all expected to go too—he wouldn't pay for anywhere else. Spencer and Carrick went, but I… did not."

I grinned. "I never knew you were such a rebel."

"Never on purpose," came his wry mutter.

We watched each other a moment more: the closeted rebel and the consummate flirt. Nathan's eyes dropped to my lips, and I found myself leaning in. Maybe we could share a kiss that was just for us. Maybe it didn't have to be all for show.

His lips were maybe an inch from mine when we were interrupted by a loud knock at the door.

Both of us flew to opposite sides of the couch.

"Expecting company?" I wondered.

Nathan frowned as we both stood. "No."

"Nate!" Several more loud knocks shook the door. "Nate, you little shit. I know you're home. Open the damn door before I make a scene for the neighbors."

"Fuck," Nathan muttered as he checked his phone, which had several messages left unanswered. He'd had the ringer turned off. Apparently, he'd been more absorbed with his work than he'd realized.

I didn't dare think that maybe he'd wanted to shut out the world as much as I did.

"Who is that, the IRS?" I joked as Nathan went to open the door.

"No." He turned to me with apology in his eyes. "It's my brother."

TWENTY-TWO
WHY CARRICK HUNT SUCKS BALLS

#5 he calls me sweethart. ewww

"What in the *actual* fuck? It's a goddamn blizzard out there, and only half the streets are plowed. Fucking New York. This is why I never come here."

Peeking around the corner from the living room, I watched a man who could have been Nathan's body double march into the foyer with the grace of a tank, shake snow off an ankle-length wool coat, and turn around with a face that looked almost exactly like Nathan's, but for the missing glasses and lack of underlying kindness.

Those eyes might have also been brown, but everything about them was glacial.

"Well, well, well. What do we have here?" The man stripped off his coat and tossed it to Nathan, who hung it on one of the hooks near the door. "This the dancer that's giving Mom conniption fits?"

"Carrick, this is Joni, my girlfriend. Joni, this is my brother, Carrick Hunt." Nathan sounded less than excited to make the introduction.

"Nice to meet you," I said with a little wave.

Carrick's smile lacked any warmth whatsoever. "You too, sweetheart." He turned to his brother. "Nate, seriously. I need a drink, and I need it yesterday. My toes are about to fall off."

Nathan rolled his eyes. "There's a bottle of Macallan in the kitchen."

With a grunt, Carrick turned in that direction.

I looked down at his shoes, which were tracking water and ice down the hall. "Do you mind leaving your shoes at the door? We try to keep the floors clean."

Was it me, or did Nathan's eyes sparkle when I said that?

"As it happens, yes, I do mind," said Carrick before he bared a set of bright white teeth in a wolfish grin. "I'm a grown man, so I don't pad around in my socks like a fucking toddler."

"Then you must be ready to mop up after yourself since I'm not going to fucking do it," I retorted before I even considered speaking to Nathan's brother with a little more respect.

Everyone in the hall froze. Carrick stopped halfway to the kitchen as if he saw me for the first time. That icy gaze pulled down my body, pausing on my bared leg.

"You sure about that, sweetheart?" he asked. "I bet my brother wouldn't mind watching you bent over, doing a little scrubbing in that dress."

"That's enough." Nathan shoved a hand on Carrick's chest and pushed him back toward the door. "There are slippers for guests in the hall closet. And if you talk to Joni like that again, you'll need to leave."

"Not before I slap him in his smug face," I muttered, though they both clearly heard me.

To my surprise, Carrick's grin only widened. "I like this one," he said as he shook a finger toward me and retreated to the closet to find Nathan's spare slippers. "Mom's gonna love her."

I frowned. What was *that* supposed to mean?

"Joni."

I looked up to find Nathan making a small gesture toward my dress.

"Do you maybe want to change?" His ears turned a little pink, right on the lobes. "Not that I don't like the dress, but, um…"

My eyes popped open. "Right! Yes. I'll be back."

"I'll make you a drink too," Nathan said as his brother lumbered toward the kitchen, likely in search of something similar.

I nodded. "Thanks. I have a feeling I'll need one."

Ten minutes later, I reemerged from my bedroom in a more, well, if not respectable, then at least more conservative set of tie-dyed purple sweatpants and a vintage I Love Lucy T-shirt. I found Nathan back on the couch, his brother sipping scotch in the armchair, and both of them half-watching a Knicks game on silent. A neatly made drink was waiting for me on the coffee table—a vodka soda, by the look of it.

I smiled. Nathan really did notice the small things.

"What are you doing here anyway?" Nathan was asking Carrick when I joined him on the couch. "Why aren't you staying at the house in Westchester with Mom and Dad?"

He was reaching across the back of the sofa, and this time, I let my body curl into his, the way I might if he were *really* my boyfriend. His arm fell naturally over my shoulder, and his thumb brushed my neck as he played with the pieces of hair escaping from my bun.

Carrick's eyes darted over us, appearing to take in every little detail of our ruse. He didn't even bother to hide his surprise at the way his brother touched me. Our affection and familiarity must have been uncommon.

My heart squeezed a little at the thought. Nathan deserved affection. The idea that he hadn't given or received much of it made me sad. And more than a little bit angry.

Carrick just made a face at us. "Mom's on a warpath. I needed a break. At home and here."

"Did something happen to the townhouse in Georgetown?"

Carrick took a long slug of his whiskey. "No, but she's been following me there too. I woke up last Monday with a girl in my bed, listening to Mom making coffee while she yelled at NPR."

I listened curiously, gathering the small facts about Nathan's family like Easter eggs. After he'd told me a little about them, I had, like any self-respecting human being, done a Google search. And discovered that his parents weren't just "investors," but that his family's overall worth was more than a hundred billion dollars. And that after a childless first marriage, Radford Hunt and his second wife, Lillian, had had three sons that, yes, he very much wanted to take over his legacy now that he was in his eighties. Specifically Nathan.

One hundred. *Billion*. Dollars.

It was one thing to see it on Google. It was another thing completely to fathom that my calm, unpretentious Nathan was worth that kind of dough.

Or maybe he wasn't. Maybe he'd rebelled more than he let on.

It did make me feel better about accepting all the clothes, though. Talk about a drop in the freaking bucket.

Even so, it had all seemed theoretical until now, listening to Nathan and his brother talk about houses like they were pieces of plastic on a Monopoly board or couches they'd crashed on when visiting from out of town. But we also weren't that different. They complained about their mother's meddling the same way my siblings and I bitched about Nonna when we were teenagers. The way I still griped about my siblings even when I yearned for family dinner.

There was a pang in my chest at the idea of those dinners. I hadn't been to Mass in weeks—hadn't had my grandmother to drag me there. I'd barely spoken to any of my sisters besides Marie. Hadn't even gone up to check on my nephews.

My family was messy, yeah. But they were my mess.

"You know, one day, your mom won't be there to pester you, and then you'll miss it," I said before thinking. "Then where will you be?"

Both men blinked at me like they'd almost forgotten I was there. Only then did I think that maybe commenting on my fake boyfriend and his unfriendly brother's relationship with their mother maybe wasn't the best way to make a first impression.

Carrick gave me a hard look, then turned back to Nathan. "So, how did you love birds meet?"

I shrank into Nathan, whose hand tightened on my shoulder.

We'd discussed a story, of course, but he knew I was terrible with details, and frankly, I didn't trust myself not to screw things up. In the end, we'd basically settled on "stay as close to the truth as possible and follow Nathan's lead" if this line of questioning happened.

Looked like that time was here.

"At a bar," Nathan said. "Joni mixes drinks at a lounge near the hospital. I stopped in after my night shift, and we talked."

Carrick looked dumbfounded. "*You* stopped in for a drink? And *talked* to a stranger?" He looked around the room like he thought someone might jump out from a curtain with a camera. "Who are you, and what did you do with my big brother?"

I nuzzled into Nathan. "He can be chatty under the right circumstances."

Carrick snorted. "Like what? The end of times?"

"It was a bad night," Nathan put in. "I'd just lost a patient. Joni helped."

"I didn't know that," I murmured and reached over to pull his hand into my lap.

Vaguely, I remembered him being upset that night. Now, I was kind of annoyed I'd never thought to ask about it. Too wrapped up in my own stupid self, like Lea said.

Nathan's eyes met mine, large and mournful, as his fingers tickled my nape. "It's not something I like to talk about when it happens. It's rare, but it's always a risk."

"Who was it, another mommy makeover?" Carrick snickered. "It's gotta get old staring at so many saggy tits, man."

I glared at him. Asshole.

Carrick seemed to think that was even funnier.

"Cosmetic surgeries are only about half of what I do, as I've told you several times." Nathan's tone was cold, but his hand clutched mine hard, full of heat. "Most of my days are spent dealing with burn victims."

I looked up at him again. "Really?"

His eyes warmed when they met mine. "Really. I specialize in reconstruction."

Another piece of the puzzle that was Nathan Hunt clicked into place. The fact that he didn't just spend every day enabling women like me to get bigger breasts for bigger tips, but actually helped people recover from major trauma, made a lot more sense, given his personality.

But it still didn't explain why he had chosen this path rather than following the one his family had set out for him. The one they still wanted him to follow.

"How long ago was that?" Carrick asked as he slouched back in his chair.

"Almost five months," I supplied cheerily since, apparently, we were telling the truth. "If you count the first four after we met when we barely spoke."

"Five *months*?" Carrick looked between us, glass halfway to his mouth. "And she's already moved in?"

Nathan shrugged. "Neither of us has a lot of free time, so when her living situation fell through and Aiden moved out, it made sense for her to be here. I like having her around."

I grinned up at him. "Aw, babe, I like being around you too."

I found myself searching for the lie. For any sign that it was just an act. Because it *was* an act. I had to keep telling myself that.

Nathan's full mouth curled in a mischievous half-smile, as if he was enjoying playing this game as much as I was.

Unthinking, I toyed with the hem of his shirt, playing my fingertips over the ridges of his lower stomach. It was nothing I wouldn't have done in a typical relationship, but it clearly caught him by surprise as the muscles contracted immediately under my touch.

Nathan leaned down to put his mouth by my ear and speak in a gruff, low voice. "Unless you want me to molest you in front of my brother, you need to stop doing that immediately."

I froze and pulled my hand away. "Oh. Sorry."

His other hand closed over mine again, keeping it where it was— on top of his clothes but still on his person. "Don't be."

We blinked at each other for a moment.

On impulse, I kissed him. Just a stamp, barely a peck, but the hand at my nape threaded into my hair and held me a second longer than I planned.

His tongue touched mine, but only just. When I pulled back, my face was heated. His cheeks were also pinked.

We both turned back to find Carrick watching us. Unfortunately, he looked more suspicious than ever.

Was it that strange to be seeing his brother kissing a girl?

"Sounds like you're positively stewing in domestic bliss, brother," he said as he rotated his glass in his hand. "And what do you guys like to do with all this 'free time' you have together now?"

"Reading," Nathan said at the same time I spouted, "Netflix and chill."

Our eyes met in a collision of awkward.

"Um, right," I amended. "Yeah. Reading. Love it."

Under my hand, Nathan chuffed like a tiger. He knew *exactly* how much I liked to read.

"Is that right?" Carrick asked. "Got a little book club going between you?"

"Actually, yes," I said a little too quickly. "We just read, um…"

"The Great Gatsby," Nathan supplied. "It's a classic. In honor of the apartment."

I snorted, unable to keep back the laugh. He really did remember every little thing.

"Nate's favorite book, huh?" Carrick replied, looking at me.

My eyes bugged. "Oh, yeah. Man, it's so good, don't you think?"

I was *terrible* at this. I hadn't been able to fake book discussions in high school either, so why had I chosen to lie about one now?

"Joni had never read it, so I read it to her," Nathan said smoothly as he went back to playing with my hair.

The calming effect was instant.

"Oh, yeah? What was your favorite part, Joni?" Carrick asked. "Hope you paid attention. Nate was obsessed with that book in college."

Oh, Nathan, you adorable, beautiful dork.

"Well, the part about Gatsby, of course," I replied, fully conscious of how lame my response was.

"Who is…?" Carrick pressed.

I frowned. What was this, a book report? I never passed those either, even when I had legitimately tried to read the book. "The main character, obviously."

"The one who defrauds people into thinking he's someone else," Nathan put in. He looked down at me. "It doesn't matter how rich he is, how many parties he throws, he can never be something he's not, which is really just a man from North Dakota."

"It's a good lesson," Carrick remarked, looking at me. "There are some worlds you just can't break into. No matter how good the costume."

I blinked as remnants of the plot—at least the one I knew—came back to me. "Oh, *right*! Yeah, the movie version was kind of crazy, though. Leo DiCaprio is hot enough to play that Gatsby guy, but I did not think Beyoncé fit the twenties."

"We like to compare the adaptations to the books," Nathan confirmed oh-so-naturally. Which, for him, was about as stiff as one of his cutting boards.

As lies went, these weren't our best. Nathan didn't seem to have any experience at all with bullshitting people, and I had a feeling his brother knew that very well. Which was why I threw my legs over Nathan's knees and pulled his face back to mine for another kiss, this one with enough tongue to last a solid minute.

Or at least until Carrick was uncomfortable enough to clear his throat.

Twice.

When I sat back up with a satisfied grin, Nathan looked a bit dazed. He shook his head and smiled. I was full of grins.

Carrick glowered at both of us.

"If you're done," he said. "It's getting late."

Nathan sighed and gently removed my legs from his. "Did you get a room at the Waldorf or the Plaza? I'll have the doorman call you a car."

Carrick was still eyeing me like I was about to grow a nose like Pinocchio. Whatever we thought we were doing, it wasn't working. Not with him.

"Actually, I think I'll just crash here," he said. "Avoid the snow. Spend some time with my brother. Get to know his girl."

Dread sank to the bottom of my stomach as I stood too. "Um... well..."

Carrick leered. "That's okay, isn't it? I assume you're sharing a bedroom, so there's a free room, right?"

Nathan and I traded petrified glances. There was absolutely no way out of this.

"You don't—" Nathan started to murmur before I cut him off with another pasted-on smile for Carrick.

"Of course," I said. "I just need to make up the bed and put my clothes away. Nathan's closet is too small for all of mine. You understand."

Carrick held up his glass as if to cheer my words. "Take your time, sweetheart. I got all night."

I nodded and left the room, only barely hearing Nathan mutter something about needing to help me before he followed me into my room and shut the door.

"We don't have to do this," Nathan said as I immediately started hanging the dresses I'd been trying on back into the closet. "I can come up with something else. Tell him I'm ill or something. Or just that I don't want him here, which is actually true."

"And give him another reason to think this is all fake?" I started stripping the bed. "You're a shit liar, by the way."

Nathan smirked. "And you're any better?"

I chuckled as I tossed my used sheets onto the floor and grabbed the spare set from the closet. While I didn't love this situation, I did enjoy the fact that Carrick would have to spend the night in my tiny twin bed wrapped in Strawberry Shortcake bedding that was bought circa 1988 and had made its way through *five* Zola girls. Nosy bastard deserved it.

"Look, it's a bed, not a pit of lava," I said. "We can share it for a week, don't you think?"

Nathan did not appear to share my optimism.

"I don't bite," I tried again. "And you could fit a family of five on your mattress. You won't even know I'm there." I stopped, arms full of my duvet. "Unless you want to call this off. Which, I wouldn't blame you. Lying to your family isn't easy."

That seemed to shake him out of it.

"If they find out you're not really my girlfriend, I'll never hear the end of it. Among other things." Nathan grabbed a pillow and started tearing off the case. "You can sleep in my bed until he leaves. With luck, it'll only be for the night."

TWENTY-THREE
THINGS THAT APPARENTLY TURN ON NATHAN HUNT

#3 me in a tshirt???

"Are you dressed?"

A quiet knock sounded on Nathan's door, and then it opened. He popped his head in, eyes covered.

"Like a nun," I called from where I sat on top of his king-size bed, scrolling on my phone and enjoying the view of the Hudson River and the Gutenberg, New Jersey skyline twinkling from the other side. "Come on, get in here. Your brother's going to think it's weird that you're knocking to come in to a bedroom we supposedly share."

Nathan edged into the room and uncovered his eyes. "What are you wearing?"

I stopped scrolling and looked down at myself with a frown. "Oh, no, did I get toothpaste on me? Lea says I'm a disaster in the bathroom."

"You're—well, yes, you are, but it doesn't bother me—still, that's my—Jesus."

I looked back up to where Nathan was standing at the end of the bed, one of his oversized pillows pressed to his front, and his eyes squeezed shut as if he were in pain.

"What?" I asked. "What's wrong?"

"Joni, that's my shirt. *Just* my shirt."

I looked back down at the Columbia Medical School shirt I'd found neatly folded in his top drawer. It was enormous. Because Nathan was enormous. And it smelled like him too—like sandalwood and coffee and very clean soap.

In other words, like heaven. I was considering wearing it forever.

"Well, I have underwear on too," I finally said. "I didn't think you'd mind if I borrowed something since I cadn't exactly go back into my bedroom and ask Carrick for some pj's. It would give the whole game away, don't you think?"

Nathan just groaned and mumbled something unintelligible to himself. "I—it's fine. I just didn't realize…"

I grinned as I looked him over myself. "Aw, you're so cute in your full pajamas. My nonno used to wear ones like that. But won't you be kind of hot?"

The apartment wasn't an oven or anything, but Nathan had a pretty heavy-duty duvet. I already knew a T-shirt and underpants were going to be plenty for me.

Nathan looked down at the blue and red plaid flannel set he had changed into, then back at me with a frown. "I thought you'd appreciate some extra clothes. My mother gave me these a few years ago. I've never worn them."

I snorted as I looked back at my phone. "Please. Don't incinerate on my behalf. What do you usually wear to sleep?"

"Typically just my underwear. I keep the apartment at sixty-four degrees at night. Studies show the body maintains a more natural circadian rhythm when it sleeps at a temperature below sixty-five."

I'm not going to lie. My nipples popped right out when he started nerding out like that. He really had no idea the effect it had on me.

So I continued to stare at my phone, pretending to examine a video about cat zoomies so my body could calm the heck down. No need to be flashing my headlights at the poor man right before bed.

He was obviously uncomfortable enough with this arrangement.

"Well, don't melt," I told him. "Even if you sleep naked, it's just a body. We're already not getting enough sleep as it is."

He seemed to think about that for a long minute. Then, while I was specifically *not* looking, I couldn't exactly miss it when he unbuttoned the shirt and removed it. Or when he took off the pants, revealing tight black boxer briefs that left very little of what was obviously a considerable package to the imagination. Or flashed a stupidly ripped set of muscles and a generous patch of curls over his chest before he slid under the covers.

Nathan took off his glasses, set them on his nightstand, and closed his eyes all over again.

"Everything okay?" I asked, looking up from my phone as if I hadn't just been ogling him via my peripheral vision.

"Yes, I—" he cleared his throat. "This just isn't what I expected to be doing tonight."

"Babe, I don't think either of us was expecting a sleepover, but here we are." I put my phone on the bedside table and pulled my knees up to my chest. "I'm on the right side, aren't I?"

He coughed. "Uh, yes. You're on the right side."

"Then...are you going to open your eyes? You're acting kind of weird."

His eyes remained closed. "That's because *this* is kind of weird."

Well. Couldn't argue there.

"It's not *that* weird." Okay, maybe I could argue a little.

"It is. You're my roommate. And my pseudo-girlfriend, who should be sleeping in a different room. This was only going to work if we had clear boundaries. Instead, you're in my bed, and you don't have pants on, and we've kissed multiple times."

By the time Nathan was done, he was scrubbing his hand over his face so roughly, his cheeks were red.

I honestly didn't know what to make of it. Okay, sure, things were a little muddled. But he didn't seem to hate kissing me. And he also seemed to like my legs, or at least looked at them like he did. We'd spent half the evening curled up together on the couch. Why did a bed have to be so different?

Was I that disgusting? Or maybe just embarrassing?

"Those things...are all true," I started slowly. "But they only have to be weird if we let them be."

One brown eye opened. "Explain."

"Well, those kisses were just for show, weren't they?"

No response. So, I went on.

"And, come on, haven't you ever had a sleepover before?"

The expression in that eye let me know he wasn't a monk.

"I don't mean like *that*," I said. "I mean, like…I don't know. Didn't you ever spend the night at a friend's house when you were a kid? Or have to share a bed with one of your brothers or something on a road trip?"

The thought made me giggle. The idea of Nathan and Carrick, two linebacker-sized men, wedged into a double bed at a roadside motel, was too funny not to. Lord, I bet they were enormous as teenagers. All arms and legs and glasses and growls.

The other eye opened, but neither of them seemed to understand what I was talking about. "Ah, no. I can't say we ever had to share a bed when we traveled or any other time."

I almost asked why, but then I remembered. Right. Nathan was rich. At least his family was rich. He had probably never even been to a roadside motel, much less had to share a bed in one. Or at home, for that matter.

"Well, I did," I said. "Marie and I shared a bed until I was eight, and my brother moved out. My older sisters fought like alley cats over who was going to get the attic. Me, I was just excited to have my own mattress." Suddenly, I was done playing games. I huffed and threw back the blankets. "Just explain what is the freaking matter. You're acting like I'm a leper, and if you even look at me, you're going to get some horrible disease. Is it that bad having me next to you? Should I sleep on the floor? Or go back to my sister's break room?"

"No!" The word came down like a hammer, slamming between us. "It's fine. I'm fine."

"You're obviously not fine. You're so stiff, you're basically a Lego Man, and you look like you're in pain. What is going on?"

"Jesus, Joni, if you must know, it's because seeing you in that gave me an enormous fucking erection, and it's not going away!" Nathan exploded, face toward the ceiling, the wall, literally anything in the room but me. "I'm the one who suggested this charade, and now I'm sitting here like a thirteen-year-old boy who just saw a pretty girl's bra strap. It's fucking embarrassing."

My mouth fell open. I honestly had no words. And that was a first—I *always* had something to say.

I looked back down at myself, trying to figure out what exactly was so appealing. I was ready for bed in the oldest T-shirt I could find in Nathan's drawers, plain black underpants that wouldn't impress anyone, makeup scrubbed from my face, and my hair tossed up with a bright pink scrunchy.

"*This* is what does it for you?" I asked, genuinely shocked. "Not the pretty dresses or the red slip, but a ratty T-shirt and underwear?"

"Apparently." The word was mumbled through his fingers. "I'm a surgeon, for Christ's sake. I've seen literally hundreds of bodies."

"I mean…how big a boner are we talking?"

It was the best thing I could think of to break the ice. Because that's what you should do when the beautiful, socially awkward man pretending to be your boyfriend confesses to having a giant hard-on just from the sight of your legs and how you look in his shirt. Ask for his measurements.

"Like this?" I held my hand about four inches apart. "Or this?" Six inches. "Tell me when." I kept going. And going. And going.

All I received was a brown-eyed glare that made me want to cover that face with kisses.

"Big. Dick. Energy," I whispered before slapping my hand over my mouth as another giggle escaped.

His head jerked toward me. "*What?*"

"Nothing!" I sang out. "I'm just being twelve!"

"What did you say?" he demanded. "Are you making fun of me?"

"No," I said through an avalanche of giggles. "Yes. But no, not really. I just…well, I fucking knew it!"

Nathan's deep scowl only made me laugh harder. "What the hell did you know?"

"You got that swagger, baby. That B.D.E. You don't even know— oh my God, just call me Ariana Grande!" I could barely speak through the laughter. Tears were starting to stream down my face, and before I knew it, I was whooping into a pillow. "Oh, God! Oh my *God!*"

"Who?" Nathan demanded again. "What the fuck are you talking about? Just explain!"

Before I knew it, we were playing some kind of demented game of tag in his giant bed, both of us half-laughing, half-shouting while I wriggled helplessly, and Nathan seemed to alternate between wanting to shake me in frustration and sit on his own hands to stop himself. In the tussle, the blanket fell off us both, once again revealing my bare legs (and apparently Nathan's kryptonite) and Nathan's shameful response to them through his boxer briefs. Which, if I was being honest, was nothing to be ashamed of. Not. At. All.

My eyes practically bugged out of my head. "Holy guacamole, Batman."

Nathan turned about the color of a beet while he scrambled to right the covers. "You're impossible. What the hell is 'big dick energy' and what does it have to do with a pop singer?"

I sighed as I sank back into my side of the bed, squeezing my legs together and now realizing that it was, indeed, going to be a very long night. "It means you have a really big cock, Nathan. And it means I appreciate it. You're welcome."

There was a long pause beside me. And then I felt, rather than saw, him relax a little. "Oh. Thanks. I guess."

I nodded as I stared at the ceiling, trying and failing to catch my breath. "Anytime, baby. Someday, you're going to make some nice woman *very* happy. Is that clear enough for you?"

Now, I was the one who couldn't look at him. Not when my mouth was completely dry from hanging open, panting like a dog. Or when I was sure lust was probably scrawled all over my face. Even Nathan couldn't misinterpret that expression.

When my heart had finally stopped banging like a drum, I got up the nerve to look at him. Nathan was watching me intently right back. Watching my whole face. My eyes, yes. But also my quivering chin. My bottom lip tucked between my teeth.

He leaned closer. "I think you…"

I sucked in a breath. "I what?"

Nathan's eyes dilated as they focused on my mouth. "That you…"

But before he could finish, there was a loud knock on the door.

"What?" Nathan barked as he yanked the blankets up to his chest. I did the same, even though I was covered.

The door opened, and Carrick's head popped around it, one hand pressed to his eyes.

"Look," he said curtly. "As happy as I am that you're finally getting laid, you think you can wait until I'm gone to make your woman lose her mind? Otherwise, get some fucking soundproofing. Generally, I'm down, but not when it's my goddamn brother playing dirty Dom in the room next door. You got me?"

I folded my mouth but couldn't help but collapse into another fit of giggles, this time shoving my face into Nathan's deltoid while my body shook uncontrollably.

Nathan's sides shook as, once again, he rubbed his forehead like he was about to lose his mind. "We understand."

"Good."

The door slammed, and we listened to my bedroom door close a moment later.

Nathan turned to me. Something like humor danced in those big brown eyes. "This is going to be a really…hard…week, isn't it?"

I bit back a laugh. "You and your jokes."

That quirk turned into a grin. It made me feel like I was floating in the middle of the room.

"It's gonna be rough," I confirmed as I grabbed Nathan's face and stamped a kiss on that chiseled cheek. "But don't worry, babe. My nonna always says misery loves company, and there's no one I'd rather be miserable with in this bed than you."

TWENTY-FOUR
WAYS I COULD MEASURE NATHAN'S DICK

#5 compear it to a pensil when hes sleepng. Or some-thing alot bigger

I awoke to the sound of birds chirping.

Birds chirping. In Manhattan. In January.

Slowly, I blinked my eyes open to find a bright red bird sitting on the window sill, pecking at a feeder hanging from the fire escape and occasionally bursting into a song loud enough to be heard through the double-paned windows. Like I was *Sleeping Beauty*, and he was here to escort me through the concrete jungle I called home.

Birds, I realized. Nathan had a thing for birds. Enough that he had taken the time to purchase and install a feeder for them outside his window, in the exact right place for him to watch them when he woke up every morning.

For a split-second, I imagined him tromping through Central Park with a pair of binoculars and one of those utility vests with thousands of pockets. Maybe he would be wearing a backward base-ball cap for good measure, and every so often, he'd turn around and point out a whippoorwill or a chickadee or whatever the heck else was roaming the woods in the middle of the city.

I'd have to add it to my list of Nathan's surprises.

I didn't know why a bird fixation only added to his general appeal, but it did. It really did. So much so that my lips suddenly felt swollen with the desire to kiss him, and my heart seemed to beat right between my legs.

That was when I realized that ache wasn't just because of the nerd porn playing in my head. And I wasn't just warm because of the cloudlike duvet protecting me from the otherwise chilly morning air.

There was a muscled arm slung over my waist. Another wedged under my neck and pillow. A broad chest pressed against my back, and a heavy leg draped over my hip.

I peeked under the covers to discover that, yes, I was completely and totally wrapped up in Nathan Hunt, who was currently still dead to the world, his long nose buried in the back of my hair while his breath whispered along the nape of my neck.

Was I surprised to wake up spooned by my fake boyfriend?

Yes.

Did I hate it?

Not even close.

I shifted slightly, and—*What is that?*

I froze as I realized that, yes, the erection I'd teased him about so mercilessly the night before was definitely wedged between my legs. Not only that, but it appeared to be taking its revenge for me being a brat about it. Somehow, it had popped out of the opening in his briefs and slipped directly between my thighs. Which were also not helping things by quickly, er, lubricating the situation.

The arm around my waist tightened as if in reflex, and a low growl emitted behind my ear as Nathan pulled me against him in his sleep. His hips tilted into my ass, and the entirety of *him* slipped another inch closer to home.

I should have jumped up. I should have shouted, "OH MY GOD, IT'S A CARDINAL IN THE WINDOW," hit Nathan with a pillow, and launched into the tap dance routine I did for my eighth-grade production of *The Music Man*. Literally, anything to break this horrible, torturous, delicious tension. Something other than lying here, breathing hard, and trying *not* to spread my legs just enough for the tip of him to find me. The last thing he needed was to wake up already having sex with the woman he'd said quite clearly was *not* a person he wanted to date in reality.

Just pretend.

We were just pretend.

And this...wasn't pretending.

Nor was it consenting.

I squeezed my legs together—which did not help my problem, by the way, since now I could feel the entire length of him wedged between my thighs.

Nathan groaned, and the hand at my waist moved up to cup my breast. "Need you," he mumbled, his deep voice thick with sleep.

It wasn't me. I just had to keep telling myself. It wasn't *me* his body wanted like this first thing in the morning. Just like it wasn't *me* that he'd gathered in his arms while he slept.

He'd had a serious relationship once, before he became an eminent surgeon. Maybe it was her who sparked dreams like the one he was currently having.

An unreasonable pang of jealousy sprouted in my gut as I wondered what kind of woman would inspire that in Nathan. She was probably just like him—someone accomplished, intelligent, self-assured. Someone who had her shit together. Someone who deserved his brand of frank compassion and kindness.

Someone who had let him go. Because I was somehow sure that's what happened. I didn't know Nathan well, but I knew he was loyal. I knew he made commitments and didn't go back on his word. I knew he was there for others, even when he didn't want to be. I knew he worked hard to please his family and the people he loved. And that if he had loved someone else, he would have never left her of his own accord.

Which meant she had left him.

For a moment, I hated her. I hated this woman who had, in some way, treated this quiet, incredible man like garbage. I hated her for not knowing what she had because if she did, she would have never tossed him aside like he was nothing.

I hated her because, for just a moment, I wished I was her.

I wished someone like me could ever have a legitimate chance with someone like him.

And then I hated myself for knowing I never would.

"Come here," Nathan rumbled, clearly still asleep.

Just like he was still in dreamland when he nuzzled behind my ear and thrusted his hips against my ass again as the hand over my breast kneaded softly. His cock slipped further between my thighs, and this time, I couldn't help but moan as it tickled my slick entrance.

The effect was immediate. The hand on my breast squeezed just before he flipped me around in his arms, slipped a hand around my nape, and kissed me. Hard.

I moaned again, knowing I should break the kiss, but unable to do it. His mouth was so warm and insistent, even in sleep. His grip so intense. Addictive, even.

Then Nathan's eyelashes blinked against my cheeks. And he proceeded to fly off me like a bat out of hell. "Jesus!"

I remained curled up in the other direction while I listened to the sounds of him scrambling off the bed, swearing lightly to himself, then quietly pulling some clothes out of his dresser. I didn't dare move. Not until I could get my expression together and convincingly play the Girl Who's Been Asleep the Whole Time.

I rolled over just as Nathan had put on his glasses and was making for the door in nothing but his plaid pajama pants.

With daylight dappling his bare chest and stepladder abs, the man looked even more delicious than he had last night, even half-asleep and clearly freaked out. His hair was mussed, and his lips were swollen from the kiss.

I wondered if they were throbbing like mine.

"Good morning," I said, with what I hoped was a very sleepy, slightly confused smile. Not a been-turned-on-for-the-last-fifteen-minutes smile. More of a what-just-happened? smile.

Though if anyone could stay asleep through a kiss like that, she was probably dead.

Nathan's face was bright red as he looked at everything in the room but me. "Uh, hello. Yes, um, good morning."

I propped my head up on one hand. "Sleep all right?"

Nathan nodded and shoved his glasses up his nose. "All right. Sure."

Liar. I only knew that because it had taken me a full ninety minutes of staring at the ceiling to drift off, fully conscious of the two hundred or so pounds of absurdly good-smelling man next to me. And Nathan had been spinning like an egg beater the whole night, as though he absolutely could not get comfortable with me next to him.

I smiled wider. He blinked like an owl, like he was waiting for me to do something. Scream, maybe?

Or invite him back to bed?

I almost did it. God knew I wanted to.

"I'm, um, going to make some coffee," he said. "Would you like some?"

I nodded. "Please."

His gaze drifted over me. I was still clad in his T-shirt and my underwear, though in his flurry to escape the bed, the duvet had been pulled off one of my legs.

He managed to drag his eyes back to my face. "There's, um, a, uh, robe of mine you can borrow in the closet. Because of Carrick."

Again, I nodded. I'd have to sneak some things in here later today. Hopefully, Carrick had errands to run.

Five minutes later, I was up and swimming in Nathan's bathrobe, an absurdly cozy cashmere thing that made me want to curl up like a cat in a window sill and look through a fashion magazine.

I padded down the hall toward the kitchen but stopped just outside when I heard Carrick's voice.

"I gotta say, well done, brother. Well fucking done."

I frowned and clutched the collar of Nathan's robe close. I knew I didn't like Carrick.

There was a pause while Nathan ground the espresso beans. "What exactly are you congratulating me for?"

"Just, you know, good for you. It's about time you moved on."

Moved on from who?

Her, my subconscious told me. There was only one person it could be. His college sweetheart, the one who'd broken his heart. At least in my imagination, that's what she did.

I listened to the familiar sounds of Nathan working his espresso machine. "I didn't need to 'move on' from Julietta. We were never even a little bit serious. It's not a big loss or anything."

Okay, so not *her*. One of the flings, then. Someone more recent, apparently.

I didn't ask why that made me want to claw her eyes out.

On the other side of the wall, Carrick just chuckled. "Nothing sticks to you, just like Teflon, eh? Better way to be, even if she was a supermodel. Still, not a bad piece of ass for my shut-in brother."

Again, I scowled. He made Nathan sound like a creepy hermit, but he wasn't that at all. He was shy, was all. A little reserved. He didn't deserve to be treated like a weirdo for it.

"Anyway, this one's a nice little rebound, but did you really need to give her a room to get some pussy?" Carrick went on. "Based on her stuff, she probably would have settled for five hundred bucks and a smack on the ass. I think that bed frame is older than Mom. Squeakier too."

I winced. Asshole. But more importantly, apparently, our pretend game wasn't working so well. Even spending the night in Nathan's room hadn't convinced his brother that we were actually a serious couple.

"Don't talk about Joni that way," Nathan said, his tone sharpening in a way I hadn't heard before. "It's not like that."

"Nate, come on. You can't possibly think she's a long-term prospect. Girls like that are good for one night, not forever." Carrick snorted as loudly as a horse. "Or ten years, depending on your theory of marriage. Keep it on the side, brother. Or maybe just as an appetizer. Definitely not the main course."

Tears pricked my eyes as I slumped against the wall. Okay, so maybe this served me right for eavesdropping. It wouldn't have been the first time I'd heard people—mainly my own family members—saying harsh things about me when they thought I wasn't listening.

But that didn't mean it didn't hurt. And for whatever reason, Carrick's nasty words hurt a lot.

Or maybe it was just the fact that Nathan wasn't arguing with them.

"I swear to *God*, though," Carrick went on. "If you fuck again while I'm on the other side of the wall, I will come in there and watch, you pervert. Or else she can come next door after if she's willing."

Suddenly, there was a crash, and when I got up the nerve to peek around the corner, I found the two brothers thrashing around the kitchen. The two stools from the kitchen island toppled to the ground while the copper pots hanging above swung from side to side, clanging into each other. Nathan's face was etched with murder as he whipped his brother around into a full nelson, then pinned him against the counter.

Carrick, however, seemed to be enjoying himself. Laughing, even.

He really was unhinged.

"You sneaky little fuck," he wheezed as Nathan shoved his forearm into his windpipe. "I didn't know you still had it in you."

"I said *stop*," Nathan ground between his teeth. "I meant it."

Well, now I knew how he learned to finish those fights he mentioned. I also know who picked them.

"Um, good morning?"

Both men's heads jerked to me as I picked up the stools, then sat on one, keeping the counter squarely between me and the brawling brothers.

"Good morning," Nathan said again. He didn't, however, release his brother. "Would you like a pour over or a cappuccino?"

I nodded. "Uh...whatever's easiest is fine."

He turned back to Carrick, who honestly seemed to be entertained in his struggle to breathe.

"Apologize," Nathan ordered through his teeth. "Now."

Carrick darted a narrow glance at me, then looked back at his brother. "For what? She didn't hear anything."

"I don't care," Nathan said in a tone that was as even and low as it normally was, but still somehow made the hairs on the back of my neck stand up. "She's here now. So now you're going to apologize, or you're going to get the fuck out of my apartment. Your choice."

"Is that right?"

Carrick glanced between the two of us with sharp, calculating eyes. Then he offered me a smile that was anything but kind. It reminded me of the Bible stories of the serpent. Exactly how the snake had probably looked before he tempted Eve with the apple.

"I apologize, Joni," he said. "For anything I might have said that was inappropriate." He looked back at Nathan. "Now, let me go, you big fucking bully. I have a meeting across town in forty minutes, and you're creasing my suit."

Nathan released his hold on Carrick, who immediately strode for the kitchen exit, though he stopped beside me as if to look me over one more time.

"Interesting," he said as he took in the bathrobe, my messy bun, and the chipped polish on my nails. "Very interesting."

I didn't ask what. I wasn't sure I wanted to know.

"Have a good day," I called as he left. Or don't, you dick.

"And get a hotel room while you're out," Nathan called after.

"Not on your life!" came Carrick's shout just before the front door slammed behind him.

It echoed around us, along with Carrick's veiled comments.

"I'm sorry about that," Nathan said mildly as he returned to the espresso machine and started the process of making us both drinks.

I'd watched him do this several times at this point, and there was something about the way his big hands moved capably over the machine, pulling shots and pressing the beans, all to produce such a delicate drink. This was why he was a surgeon, I realized. He approached everything with finesse.

My right breast tingled, remembering the exact feel of that deft touch. Even in his sleep.

"Which part are you sorry for?" I wondered as Nathan set a mug in front of me. He'd poured the design of a flower with the milk this morning. "The spontaneous fighting or the part where your brother compared me to antipasti?"

Nathan grimaced as he took a sip of his coffee. "You heard that."

"I did." I patted his hand. "Don't worry about it. I've definitely heard worse."

That didn't seem to help. He grabbed my hand and tugged lightly, as if to beckon for my attention. "I hate that you've been treated like that by anyone. My brother is an asshole."

"Well, not totally," I said with a grin. "His body has other parts too."

The joke didn't land. Nathan just released my hand and shook his head. "About this morning…if I did anything inappropriate…"

"You mean the part where you woke me up with full tongue?" I took a big sip of coffee, if only to hide the grin I couldn't quite stifle at the thought of that kiss. Under the counter, I squeezed my legs together, grateful he couldn't see.

Nathan just grimaced. "You were awake."

"Kind of hard not to be when someone tries to maul you first thing in the morning." I shrugged. "Don't worry about it. I've also definitely—"

"If you tell me again you've experienced worse behavior that way too, I honestly might hunt the perpetrator down today instead of going to work," Nathan said without even looking at me.

There was no levity in his voice. Not even a hint of sarcasm.

I put my coffee down.

"Don't do that," I said just as solemnly. "I was making a bad joke."

When he looked up, the intensity in his eyes made my whole body quiver in response.

"I don't like those jokes," he said quietly. "I don't like jokes about anyone mistreating you. You don't ever deserve to be hurt."

Something in my chest tightened at his words, and I found it difficult to swallow. It was such a simple thing to say that no one should hurt me. You'd think I'd have heard it plenty of times, with a giant family who supposedly loved me and five siblings to watch my back.

But no one ever had. Not out loud. Not like that.

"Thank you," I said just as quietly.

"You're welcome."

"And I...well, I was just trying to lighten the mood. The truth is, it wasn't bad at all. Waking up with you, I mean. Or the kiss, even if it wasn't me you were kissing, exactly. Whoever you were dreaming about...she's a lucky woman."

Nathan's gaze met mine with such force, I almost fell off my stool. It was an expression I'd never seen before. Confusion, maybe. Mixed with something almost like grief.

He must really miss her, whoever she was.

The mystery women from years past.

His long-lost love.

For whatever reason, the idea suddenly felt unbearable.

I slid off my stool and picked up my drink. "Thank you for the coffee. I'm, um, going to get ready for the day." To do what, I wasn't sure. I wasn't working until tomorrow.

"Wait."

I turned. Nathan was still staring hard at me, but he shook his head and rubbed the spot between his eyebrows.

"You don't have to go," he said. "To the gala. Carrick...he's just a preview of what my parents are like. If you don't want to put up with it, you don't have to. I can make it work."

I considered him for a long moment. I wasn't going to lie. After interacting with Carrick and learning a bit too much about Nathan's family, the entire idea was starting to feel like an icicle shoved through my chest.

"But...wasn't that the point of all this?" I asked. "To show your parents and these business people that you're actually well-adjusted and happy? Unless you think Carrick is going to blow things..."

Nathan sighed, obviously not thrilled with the idea himself. "He'll behave himself in public. Spencer usually does too. And my parents won't misbehave in front of board members."

"But what if Carrick tells them what he said to you?"

Nathan nodded. But still looked uneasy.

"What? What is it?"

He bit his lip. "I think it's going to take something...more...to convince my parents I should stay in New York. Not just a room-mate. Or a girlfriend."

I tipped my head. "Shit. It's not working?"

He sighed. "My mother wants all of her sons close. But there is something my father wants more."

"What's that?"

He swallowed thickly. "An heir. In the form of a grandchild."

I stilled. "Dude. Um, I don't think we can fake *that*."

Nathan gave me a look. "I know that. But if you're willing—and you can say no, Joni. You can *always* say no with me—it might be more convincing if you weren't just my girlfriend. But maybe my fiancée too. If we told them we were getting married. And that we wanted to start a family soon."

I couldn't move. Now, he wanted people to believe we were truly in love? That we wanted a whole life together, with a house and kids and the whole nine yards?

I could pretend that. I could probably *live* that for real.

The thought was terrifying.

"After what Carrick said, do you really think anyone would believe it?" I had to ask. "Do you really think they would believe someone like you would want to *marry* someone like me?"

I hated that I had to ask. But the question was too obvious not to.

Nathan seemed to think on that for a long moment too.

"If they don't believe I care for you, then it's because they don't want to believe it," he said finally.

"Or maybe you're just not a very good actor," I said, half-jokingly. "It's a good thing, Nathan. It means you're honest."

"So are you."

Was I?

Right now, I wasn't so sure.

But I did know one thing.

"You asked me to be there, so I'm going," I said. "We have a job to do, and I'm going to see it through on Saturday night. Apparently, with a ring on it."

I touched my hair and examined my empty fingers and the nails that were already starting to chip. I was running out of funds to keep up with these engagements.

"I'll get one," Nathan said. "Something nice. Something you can keep later. For…whatever you need."

I didn't even want to ask how much that would cost him. Or admit to myself how good it might feel to wear something like that from him.

Even if it was just a costume. Even if it was just pretend.

"Okay," I said as I pulled out my phone to text Kyle.

After I'd served drinks at Diamonds a few nights last week, he'd offered me a chance to serve at one of the gaming nights with Rochelle.

I wasn't sure I was going to take it. I was honestly hoping I wouldn't have to.

But a new manicure and a blowout weren't going to pay for themselves.

And I didn't want to give Carrick or anyone else at that event a reason to think I didn't belong there.

At least on the outside. I already knew the inside was a lost cause.

TWENTY-FIVE
WORST BARTENDERS IN NEW YORK

#1 Mac whatever his name is

"One girl per table. Tips are yours minus twenty percent to the house. If there's a problem, we'll switch you around, but there should *never* be a problem. You got that?"

I nodded for what was probably the tenth time in the last ten minutes as Kyle, the owner of Diamonds strip club and the manager of what I suspected was only a semi-legal underground gambling operation, finished showing me around the basement of a nondescript brownstone on East 125th and Pleasant Avenue, at the very edge of Spanish Harlem.

It wasn't exactly what I'd expected when Kyle told me it was a "casual" get-together. In its way, this place was busier than Opal, except it was full of men ready to see me serve them their highballs tits out.

"Rochelle, you're tables three and four. New Girl, tables five and six. Leave your things in the coatroom. Beto will take care of them."

Kyle rubbed his goateed chin and glanced through the doors toward the crowd gathered around a variety of game tables. He seemed a little more nervous than when he was at Diamonds—

constantly moving and fidgeting. These were obviously some high rollers.

"They just sat down, so they need drinks ASAP. And whatever else they want. Company, a blow on the dice, a lap dance—they ask, you give, all right?" He looked me over. "You look good. I knew that size would be better."

I looked down at my outfit—if you could even call it that. The "uniform" Kyle had given all the girls consisted of black hot pants over fishnet stockings, black high heels, a bow tie...and that was all. He'd insisted I would fit into shorts a size smaller than usual, and they were riding up my butt a little. Apparently, that was the look he was going for.

"Yeah," I said. "But...I thought we didn't have to go topless if we don't want."

But Kyle was already gone. Rochelle just shrugged at me as she took a tray of drinks from the bartender. "You can put your bra back on. But you also probably won't be asked back either."

I scowled. I'd been hoping to keep my top on tonight, but apparently, that wasn't in the cards. But neither was getting my hair and nails done this week with the hundred dollars currently in my bank account.

"Fine," I said as I took a tray of drinks for myself. "Where is table five?"

I followed Rochelle into the smoke-filled room, which looked and sounded more like a speakeasy in the nineteen twenties than a grungy basement. The walls were papered in silk florals, with maroon wainscoting reaching up from the floor. Wrought iron chandeliers with glinting glass prisms dangled over men seated in leather chairs around green felted game tables—the only things that didn't look like they were permanent fixtures in the room.

It wasn't exactly a small operation. There were about a dozen tables, each surrounded by six or so men plus a dealer, most of them wearing suits or at least pieces of them, with ties untucked, jackets off, and sleeves rolled up.

Rochelle and I weren't the only servers here tonight. Two more I recognized from Diamonds were already strutting around the room with drinks. Another was sitting on the lap of an older man in the corner, grinding on him while the others around the table leered and laughed.

"You ready?" Rochelle said. "Come on, *mami*. The money's out there."

I straightened my back, just like I was waiting in the wings for my cue. It was another part to play. Just another part.

"Ready," I said and followed her toward table five, where four men sat waiting for cards to be dealt.

"Gentlemen," I greeted my customers for the night. "Can I get you anything?"

The men all turned while the dealer shuffled, each openly appraising my body.

"Nice, a new face," said a barrel-chested man in a striped shirt and paisley tie. He had a mustache that reminded me of old pictures of my grandpa when he was young, but he spoke with a thick Eastern European accent.

"New attitude too," I said with a wink, earning more than a few chuckles and a low howl.

"Boys, this is…" Kyle appeared behind me with a cue I recognized. Was I giving a stage name or my real one?

I flashed the smile that always won over customers like these. "Gigi. How're you boys doing tonight?"

"Better now that you're here, honey," said another gray-haired man beside the first.

"That's for sure," added a third who looked like my uncle Tino.

The fourth man at the table, who was younger and vaguely resembled the older one in the paisley tie, just cast a blank glance toward me before picking up the cards set before him.

I kept the grin pasted on my face but made a mental note to focus on the others. Obviously, this one wouldn't be the biggest tipper.

"Well, let's keep that going," I told them. "We got some shots of bourbon for you on the house." I set down the shots in front of each man, allowing them each an up close and personal view of my bare chest. I didn't have much, but what I had looked good. They seemed to appreciate them, anyway. "Now, what else would you like?"

Each of the men placed their orders, one with an extra fifty for a lap dance later.

"And I'll have a whiskey on the rocks."

The voice was like a wet finger drawn down my back on a very windy day. I turned and found the very last person I would have expected. Or wanted to see at all.

Shawn Vamos smiled, revealing that gold filling again among stained teeth. Regrettably, I had to admit he was still handsome, though The sooty black eyes that had charmed me at fourteen were just as sooty and mysterious, the grin just as devilish.

"You know what I like, baby," he said.

"Shawn, you know her?" asked the large man in the tie.

Shawn nodded. "Yeah, Lis, this is my girl—"

"Gigi," I interrupted with a wild look. "It's Gigi."

Shawn's sharkish smile spread with an acknowledgment of our little secret. "That's right. Gigi." He turned to the men. "We go way back. You boys need anything, she'll find a way. And I do mean anything."

The leers at the table grew a bit more familiar. A bit more expectant.

Dread landed in my gut like an anvil.

"I'll be right back with your drinks, fellas," I told them, then turned, conscious of all eyes on me, while I made my way to the bar.

Shawn, however, did not sit down. Instead, he followed me back to where I submitted the orders for the table and waited while the bartender, a large man who simply went by "Mac," went to work.

"What do you want?" I asked without looking at Shawn, who had made himself comfortable right next to me. "What are you even doing here? You've never been into gambling."

"I could be into gambling. I could be into anything." He leaned back against the bar and lit a cigarette. "But I don't think that's the question, gorgeous. What are *you* doing here?" He toyed with his lighter, flipping the flame on and off. "What happened to your boyfriend?"

"What boyfriend?" I played dumb. Sometimes it worked. But not tonight.

"You know who. I heard you were all over some guy at Casper's last weekend. Spent the night on the couch. Was it that four-eyed gorilla from Opal?"

"Word travels fast." Apparently, our plan had worked, in my favor, at least. "Yeah, that's him. Although I don't see why it should matter to you."

For some reason, I didn't like admitting that I was in a relationship with Nathan out loud. Not to Shawn. Not like this.

Fake.

Not. Real.

But that was the point of this whole little performance, wasn't it? To make Shawn think I didn't matter anymore. That I was taken.

"It matters when it comes to my assets."

I bristled. "I'm not a fucking bank account, Shawn. Or one of those fake Fendis you used to hawk out of the back of your car."

Shawn's easy smile curled into a snarl, just like it always had. "Watch it, baby. Don't let that temper run away with you now. Things are just starting to get fun again."

I smiled at the bartender, who glanced at Shawn but was wise enough to say nothing while he mixed an old-fashioned.

"Four-eyes know you're working here?" Shawn asked, first nodding out at the crowd, then making no effort not to ogle my breasts. "Rubbing yourself down with baby oil like a piece of meat for these old men?"

Then he looked away in disgust, like my body meant nothing to him. Like I was old news.

I supposed I was.

"Who?" I asked again as I watched Mac start on a gin martini. He was a lot faster than me, but I wished he could go faster just so I could escape this conversation.

"Don't play dumb, Jo. Your boyfriend." One black brow lifted. "Is it serious?"

I shrugged. "Serious enough. We live together." I turned. "And we're getting married."

The lie tasted like the biggest pill I'd ever had to swallow. I literally almost choked.

"And he doesn't want to control my job, unlike you," I added. "*He* actually trusts me."

"Married, huh?" Shawn looked me over again. "If you needed a job, honey, you know I'd always help you out."

I turned, unable to keep the glare off my face. "I don't need a pimp, you asshole."

Shawn looked me up and down. "You sure about that?"

It was everything I could do not to throw one of the drinks in his face.

"*Yes.* Now fuck off, and let me get back to work."

I tried to turn away, but before I could, Shawn snatched my wrist and whipped me back around to look at him.

"You and your smart fuckin' mouth," he bit out. "I can tell you one thing: he ain't ever gonna marry *you*, Sunshine. No man wants to come home to used goods for the rest of his life. I sure as shit wouldn't."

"Didn't stop you before," I snapped back.

His hand gripped even tighter. "You think you're better than me? You always did, didn't you? Well, you're not, and you *know* I have the proof. You think your fancy man in glasses is gonna want you when he knows you've done way more than shake those titties around?"

"Don't," I gritted out. "Stop."

"All I gotta do is click a button, gorgeous. Then your face is all over the internet, moaning for more while you take it good and hard for the camera."

Shame flooded me as my face and body heated like a flame. "You promised you wouldn't."

"And you promised you'd always be mine," Shawn cut back. He looked me over again like a car salesman valuing a trade. "They'd be crazy for you over on OnlyFans. That body could still be good for something, after all."

I stared at the bar top, then over to Mac, who was still pouring drinks, somehow even more slowly, as if he were enjoying the show.

"Don't," I said again, though my voice had lost its edge. Then, "What do you want?"

Shawn glanced back at the table, then returned his smarmy gaze to me. "Nothing. For now. Just for you to remember who you *really* belong to."

When Mac placed his drink—basic scotch on the rocks—Shawn picked it up and raised it in my direction.

"One of these days, I'm going to need that charm again, Sunshine," he told me. "Especially with this crowd. Lis seems to like you. So have fun with old four-eyes, but when I call, you're gonna come. Or else that video is going up everywhere, and you can kiss your boy toy goodbye."

He raised his glass to me as if in salute, then sauntered back to his table.

Shaking, I waited for Mac to make the last two drinks while I stared at the bar top and tried to calm my breath, my heartbeat, and literally every cell in my body that was screaming at me to *run*.

But that I couldn't do.

Because Shawn had always been a predator.

Which meant if I ran, he was guaranteed to chase.

Faking a relationship was never going to work—if anything, I should have known it would make him pick up the scent that much more.

Eventually, my breath calmed to the point that I could gather the drinks. I turned to bring them back to the tables but found someone else had joined the men at table five. And to my horror, it was yet another face I would have preferred to never see again.

Carrick Hunt's dark brown eyes darted between Shawn and me, and I knew he'd seen our entire interaction at the bar. The difference between them was stark. Both were predators, but while Shawn was about as hapless as a puppy at this table full of full-grown wolves, Carrick had the confidence of a pack leader.

Or maybe one that was even more dangerous and unpredictable. A lone wolf.

I took a deep breath and plastered on a smile. Took one step forward and then immediately set my tray back on the bar and made for the exit.

"Hey," Kyle called out just before I reached the coat room. "Where do you think you're going?"

I turned. "Kyle, I'm so sorry, but there's, um, been a family emergency. I have to go."

"Lemme guess, your grandma's in the hospital," Kyle jeered. "Get back to work."

"Kyle, *please*. I really can't go back in there. My table is—"

"Your table is full of some of the biggest Gs in the city," Kyle cut in through his teeth as he grabbed my arm. "I went out on a limb to hire you here tonight, so you can't just run out and leave me hanging, kiddo. You promised me hours."

I clutched my shoulders. This wasn't performance. It was torture.

"I'm sorry," I tried again. "I'll come back to Diamonds if you need. Tonight, I just…I don't think I can do this."

"And I don't think I give a shit. Get your ass back in there and get to work. Now."

I knew that tone. I'd heard it enough in the voices of hardscrabble men in Belmont. In bouncers and doormen, and even policemen, from time to time.

It was the one that said "don't even try it" to kids like me who wanted to break the rules.

I didn't want to try. I didn't want any of this.

So I lifted the tray and followed my ex-boyfriend back to the table and delivered the drinks.

It was just another part. Just another role, I told myself.

And in a few hours, this show would be over.

TWENTY-SIX
BEST SUBWAY LINES

#4 F train—cutest construction workers

I used to think nothing would ever be as bad as forgetting the choreo to my very first lead role in a play, versus a dance-only production.

At fourteen, I had the part of Lola in my high school's version of *Damn Yankees*. I was a reasonably good singer, but it was the dancing that got me the part. Which was why when, in my stress over learning my lines and remembering the lyrics, I completely forgot the steps to the first number, "A Little Brains, A Little Talent." I froze right there on stage, then forgot the lyrics too, and then my lines until Louis Martinez, the kid who played Applegate (e.g., "the Serpent"), whispered the next one to me. I was barely able to mumble through the number while I shimmied around the stage.

I thought that nothing that bad would ever happen again.

I was wrong.

Serving drinks topless and giving lap dances to my ex-boyfriend and his cronies while my fake boyfriend's brother watched for five hours was worse. *So* much worse.

So, it was with undying relief when sometime past three, the room emptied out, and I was finally able to leave, fully clothed, counting the two thousand dollars I'd made that night just from packing on the smiles, shaking my tits, and grinding on a couple of middle-aged men's knees and half-hard dicks.

Rochelle wasn't kidding when she said it was easy money. But I couldn't say it was worth it. Not with Shawn and Carrick watching me like hawks the entire time.

After that, the other servers and I paid out from our tips and left; I took a short cab ride to the 1-train station on 116th. I was dangerously half-asleep on the platform when I heard the sound of footsteps behind me. The hairs on the back of my neck prickled up with the knowledge that someone was there. Someone was watching.

"Well, hello there, *Gigi*."

I jumped, dropping my duffel bag full of clothes on the ground, and when I picked it up, I found Nathan's brother leaning casually against one of the tiled pillars in the tunnel, looking me over like I was a car he was planning to test drive.

He was completely out of place in the dingy tunnel, still wearing the three-piece suit from this morning. That was another key difference between Carrick and Nathan. Carrick wore suits the way warriors of the past probably donned armor, as uncomfortable, but necessary protection. Nathan, on the other hand, looked perfectly at ease in his rotation of casual but tailored menswear, hospital scrubs, and gym clothes.

I realized I much preferred the latter. Armor meant there was something underneath that was being protected. Something real. Armor wasn't something you could trust.

"Jesus," I said, pressing a hand to my heart. "Did you follow me here?"

Carrick shrugged and walked closer. "It seemed like the easiest way to get a word without any other...interested parties listening in."

I didn't have to ask what he meant. Whether it was the people in the gaming hall, Shawn, or just Nathan at home, there were plenty I didn't really want listening to the conversation I knew Carrick and I had to have.

"Plus, I don't think my big brother would approve if I didn't at least see his lady home after a long night of jiggling her tits."

"I—um—" I cringed. "Fuck."

Carrick smiled in that unnervingly canine way of his. "Sounds about right. Did you?"

"Go to hell." Something in me shriveled at his harsh words, but I forced myself to stand up straight. "What else do you want me to say here?"

Carrick stood up straighter, a fair body double for his brother. Just as tall. Just as broad.

But not quite as intimidating.

Maybe it was because I knew his intimidation was all bravado. The intensity of a man who wanted people to be scared of him. Nathan just didn't fucking care what people thought. And that had to be as intimidating as hell to a man like Carrick, who probably knew he could never quite measure up to his older brother.

The thought made me smirk.

"I'm surprised you ventured into the gutter," I said, gesturing around the empty subway platform, typically coated in grime. "Aren't rich assholes like you too uptight to get your hands dirty?"

"Nathan's the one who doesn't like to get dirty," Carrick told me before baring his teeth a little. "I always figured it was part of life. Sometimes, dealing with a little filth is necessary to get what you want." He looked me over; that blackened gaze dragged up my clothes, making me feel like I was a part of that filth. "Nice outfit, 'Gigi.' Is that your real name?"

I'd been too tired to change out of the hot pants, so I'd thrown on my coat over the uniform Kyle had given me and left. The coat, however, was currently hanging open in the dank pressure of the underground tunnel.

I scowled as I yanked it closed. "It's a job, you pretentious dick. And for the record, Gigi is short for Giovanna. I use it so men like you don't learn my real name and stalk me."

"Too bad I already knew it. So did that shit stain. What's his name? Vamos?"

I wrinkled my nose. Apparently, we really were doing this. "Shawn. Yeah. We, um, know each other from a long time ago."

"Know each other how?" Carrick's posture was still casual as he watched a mouse traverse one of the train tracks, attentive like a predator tracking his prey.

I shrugged. "We were sort of involved."

"Involved how?"

"You know, I don't think it's any of your business."

"Tonight, I found my brother's apparently 'serious'"—Carrick mimed air quotes as he said it—"new girlfriend serving drinks topless at an underground gambling club. Call me a concerned citizen."

I sighed. I wanted to fight him, but I didn't quite have the energy.

Also, I could see his point. Carrick was an asshole, but he was standing up for his brother. I'd probably give him the same third-degree if I'd been in his shoes. God knew my family had given Nathan grief for a whole lot less.

"This, when she's supposed to parade around our family and half our board of directors in a few days dressed like a Stepford Wife," he continued. "If word of this gets out, every deal I've made in Washington goes to shit, not to mention the family's good name. So, yeah, I think it's all my business, babe."

And now that feeling was gone.

"You're an asshole," I snapped.

"Yes, I am," Carrick bit right back like the wolf he was as he turned fully toward me. "But if you want me to keep this little secret of yours, you're going to tell me what I want to know. What exactly is your connection to Shawn Vamos?"

I paused, examining him a bit longer. But Carrick wasn't going to let me off easy.

"Shawn used to...do things for me," was all I would say. "We met when I was younger, and, I don't know, we were kind of together. We'd hang out. Now, we don't. That's it."

"Well, that's a bullshit story if I ever heard one," Carrick said. "What do you know about the Antoni Regime?"

I blinked. "The what?"

Carrick rolled his eyes. "Don't play dumb. Your boy Shawn rolls in with some of the toughest gangsters on the East Coast, and you don't know any of them? I just watched you give Lis Antoni two lap dances. It was all I could do not to vomit all over my cards."

I cringed at the memory. It hadn't been my finest moment either. But I'd had to give several lap dances tonight, and I still didn't know any of the recipients' names, much less whoever this Lis Antoni guy was.

"I don't know who you're talking about," I said. "I work for Kyle, the organizer, and this was my first night. I wasn't expecting Shawn to be there any more than I was expecting you. He and I have barely talked in months. I was just doing my job."

Carrick looked at me for a long time. "Are you serious?"

"Yes!" I exclaimed. "Look, man, some of us weren't born with trust funds and giant houses. Some of us have to do whatever's needed to pay our way in the world. Nathan knows and accepts that about me, so I don't see why you shouldn't either."

I lifted my chin, waiting for him to cut back or start another interrogation. But Carrick only continued to examine me before he finally shook his head and muttered, "Goddammit. Not again."

I scowled right back at him. "What does that mean?"

"It means my brother has a fucking type," Carrick spat. "God, this is some kind of déjà vu. It really is. And I am not going through this shit again with him. It was hard enough the last time."

I opened my mouth to ask him to elaborate, but before I could, our conversation was swallowed by the rush of the incoming train. The doors opened, and I stepped in, not even looking to see that Carrick was following me.

We took seats on one of the long plastic benches in a car that was empty except for a bum sleeping in the far corner. This was about as private as it got in New York City.

"What 'last time'?" I pressed once we were moving. "What are you talking about?"

Carrick huffed under the harsh fluorescent lights. "What, he didn't tell you? And I thought you two were so serious."

Maybe it looked bad, but now wasn't the time to pretend I knew what the hell he was talking about.

"I don't know *everything* about your brother," I said. "So if there is something important, maybe just quit the bullshit and give me the truth."

Carrick turned, his wide shoulders blocking out the subway tunnel passing by the window. "You want some truth, twinkle toes? All right, here it is. You're not the first gold-digging gutter mouse our perfect Nathaniel has dragged home. Thirteen years ago, he got wrapped up with another so-called 'dancer' who was addicted to anything she could sniff or snort. She had all sorts of 'friends' just like your Shawn Vamos too."

I stiffened in my seat. "Nathan's never been involved with anyone like that. He had a girlfriend in college, and was engaged once, but that's it."

Carrick stared at me, disbelief coloring that unnervingly handsome face, so similar to his brother's and yet so icily different. "You don't know. Holy shit, he hasn't told you *anything* about himself, has he?"

I bit my lip, wishing I had changed back into more substantial clothes. It was freezing under that soulless gaze.

"The college thing is right. Nathan met Lindsay when he was at Duke. At a strip club, actually, when the baseball team took him there for his twenty-first birthday. Stupid idiot fell for the first girl to shake her tits in his face, then let her bleed him dry for *months*. Meanwhile, he had no clue it was because she was hooked on meth and had a kid to take care of. Nate was nothing but an easy mark."

I bit my lip. As much as I hated to admit it, I could see it happening, especially before Nathan was a doctor with enough knowledge to spot things like addiction. He missed all sorts of cues other people noticed first. I could easily imagine him as a naive twenty-one-year-old. Handsome, shy, and kind—an easy target for someone like that.

Carrick shook his head like he still couldn't believe it either. "She died trying to cook that shit herself with her dealer. Blew up a trailer and almost killed her daughter too. Isla still looks like she went through a war zone. It's because of *her* that Nathan's a fucking plastic surgeon instead of working at Huntwell, where he belongs. Dumb motherfucker is more interested in skin grafts than his own family's legacy. Thinks it's his 'calling.'"

By the time he finished, my head was spinning. This explained so, *so* much. "But-but I'm not a drug addict," I managed to stutter. "And I don't have a kid."

"Yeah, you must be a real jackpot then," Carrick said dryly. "Let me guess, you're a stripper with a heart of gold, putting yourself through a Ph.D. program for that secretly massive brain of yours. Not it? Then maybe you're paying for a sick relative's cancer treatment. Still no? Hold on, I got this." He snapped his fingers with a loud crack. "You're a secret agent on a mission to expose the dark underbelly of New York. Am I on to something?"

I remained silent and stared at my knees. He knew none of that was true.

"Or maybe it's like this," Carrick went on mercilessly. "You're a two-bit dancer from a broken family who've mostly given up on you. You barely graduated high school, and now you can hardly keep a job because you don't have any real skills. Then my brother comes along, looking real nice, like a lottery ticket in glasses. Am I warm?"

I squeezed my eyes together, willing the tears that pricked to go away. How did he even know all that? Was it that obvious I was such a complete and total loser?

"Thought so," Carrick said, appearing to take my silence as a confirmation. "Your 'friend' Vamos back there sings like a fuckin' canary after he's done a few lines. Even says you think you're going to marry Nathan. I'm here to tell you, it's *never* going to happen, sweetheart. Not on my watch."

I bit my lip harder, willing the tears in my eyes to die down. I would not cry in front of this asshole. I would. Not. Cry.

"I'm not...I'm not like her. Lindsay," I barely managed to whisper. "And I'm not using your brother. I'm *not*."

I wasn't like her, I told myself. I *wasn't*. But even I had to admit, some of the similarities were close. Too close.

"Maybe not," Carrick said as he settled back into his seat like it was a throne, not a dirty bench on the subway. "But maybe Nathan sees something in you he wants that he couldn't have back then."

"What's that?" My voice warbled.

Carrick almost looked pained to say it. "Redemption. Justice. Once he gets it in his head that something is the right thing to do, he can't ever let it go. Some might call it obsessive. I just call it naive."

I didn't answer. I couldn't. This was ten types of fucked up.

"I should have known the second he said you work in a bar." Carrick shook his head. "He couldn't save Lindsay, but maybe he thinks he can save you. Well, I'm here to tell you and him he can't. Some things, some *people*, are beyond salvation."

A tear streaked down my cheek before I could stop it. Was that all this ploy really was? Not a joint venture to free ourselves from limited futures, but a secret attempt by Nathan to make up for the past?"

Was I just a useless charity case to him?

A pathetic second chance to redeem himself?

"Where does he really think you were tonight?" Carrick's gravelly voice cut through my self-pity. "That lounge where you met? Out with friends? Or does my strait-laced brother actually know that his so-called 'fiancée' spent her evening serving body shots and shaking it for gangsters?"

The look on my face clearly told him everything he needed to know.

"He wouldn't care," I mumbled. "He said he wouldn't care."

Carrick snorted. "That's what all men say when they're drunk on pussy."

At least he thought we were actually sleeping together. It was probably the only part of the charade people did believe.

"You don't understand what it's like. I need this money. Not because of drugs or kids or anything like that. But because of *him*." I picked at my threadbare coat and toed my Vans on the floor. "Do you have any idea how much it costs to fit in with people like you? I made him a promise, and I won't go back on it. It's only for—"

I cut myself off before I could babble any further. Before I told Nathan's secret. Before I told mine.

"I just want to help him too," I said quietly. "And all he wants is his family's support, so I'm here to help him get that. That's all. What I do with the rest of my time is my own business. Not yours. If you care about your brother, you won't hurt him with it either."

Carrick seemed to peer right through me with those black, soulless eyes. And for several moments, I honestly thought he was going to tell me to fuck off. I was ready for him to deliver a threat. Say I wasn't good enough for his brother and that if he saw me with Nathan again, he'd share with the whole world what I was doing, not just his brother.

God, I was tired. How many more men were going to use my secrets against me tonight?

In the end, Carrick just relaxed in his seat as the train came to a stop.

"You need to tell him," he said as we both stood. "I'm not cleaning up his mess again, and you've got catastrophe written all over you. You'll learn one thing quick about the Hunt family, little girl: we're aptly named. When it comes to protecting our own, we shoot to kill. And we hit our marks every time."

TWENTY-SEVEN
REASONS SHAWN VAMOS SHOULD WALK OFF A BRIDGE

#34 he dosnt take no for an ansewr

To my surprise, Carrick didn't walk home with me, but instead veered down a side street in search of "more fun." I wasn't sure what he was looking for at this hour, but I had a feeling it would come with a hotel room. I couldn't help being relieved that I didn't have to continue our conversation. I had enough to think about besides trying to act at least a little competent in front of Nathan's bully of a brother.

It was almost four in the morning by the time I rounded onto Riverside Drive. Across the river, the few lights glimmered off on the New Jersey side of the Hudson. They looked so peaceful. As if they were calling me to join them.

"Reminiscing about the good days, Sunshine?"

The voice startled me as I turned and saw Shawn Vamos step out of a shadow cast against Nathan's stately brick building.

I stepped back. At this time of night—or early morning—the street was fairly empty. Riverside didn't get much foot traffic, and while cars still flew by on the parkway, no one else was around to see our conversation except maybe the occasional garbage trucks getting to work.

Right now, it was just us.

Every tiny hair stood up on the back of my neck. "Shawn. What are you doing here?"

Shawn shrugged as he shoved his hands into the pockets of his leather jacket. "I wanted to make sure you got home safe. Since your *boyfriend* didn't."

I stepped back. Something in his voice didn't sound right. His eyes didn't look right either.

"You're drunk," I told him. "And probably high."

Shawn barked a laugh, too loud and intense. "Brain surgeon over here," he joked to absolutely no one. "What other gems you gonna point out, Sunshine? The sky's blue? Grass is green?"

"How about you're a dick?" I snapped.

"You already knew that one," he said, making a sudden grab for my wrist and pulling me to him. "Never stopped you before. In fact, I think you liked it."

"Well, it's stopping me now," I said as I tried to shove him away. "What don't you get here? I don't want you anymore. I don't care about the tape or whatever else you have on me. I'm taken, and he won't care about that anyway. You always said you don't want another man's sloppy seconds, so keep one shred of your dignity, and let me go."

"I don't think so."

The duffel dropped to the ground as Shawn pushed me against the darkened wall, where he'd been standing before, hard enough that my head smacked the brick, and I saw stars. His hands roved all over my body as he pressed rubbery lips to my neck and mouth.

How I'd *ever* been attracted to this, I couldn't fucking imagine.

"No," I said as I struggled in his grasp. "No!"

"You asked me what I want," he slobbered into my ear. "And I thought about it. I said you belong to me, Sunshine. I think you need to be shown."

"Get off!" I shoved him back, but it did no good. Shawn wasn't a bodybuilder, but he was still stronger than me.

He shoved one hand under my coat, groping like a teenage boy while his teeth bit into my neck like a clumsy coyote. He smelled like cigarettes and cheap booze, and his breath rattled like it was trying to keep up with a heart beating far too fast. I struggled, tried to kick out, but it was no good. I was pinned with nowhere to go.

It hadn't always been like this. In the beginning, he'd been sweet. Suave. Careful, even in the back of his car. Fingers that teased, a voice that crooned, convincing me that he was safe in ways no one else could be. That version of Shawn came and went over the years, but it was always in reserve, waiting in the wings to bring me back in after this version chased me away.

It had all been a game, this give-and-take. A ploy to manipulate a young girl the same way a charmer might hypnotize a snake.

And now it made me sick. And enraged.

"*Get off me!*" I shrieked again, this time directly into his ear.

I was quickly rewarded by a hard slap across the face.

"You need to shut the fuck up and remember your goddamn place, you little whore!" Shawn shouted.

"And you need to take your hands off my fiancée."

Nathan's deep voice thundered into the night, and before I knew it, Shawn's body was whipped off mine and smashed into the brick. Two quick punches to his gut, and he was crumpled over, gasping for breath just before Nathan pinned him by the neck with a powerful forearm.

I recognized the move—it was the same one he'd used on Carrick. But while that little tussle had been a warning, playful enough that Carrick had enjoyed it (and, I suspected, baited Nathan into it), this one was more than a threat. It was pure violence. Death balanced on a knife's edge.

Nathan quickly restrained Shawn's other hand above his head, a fucked-up parody of intimacy against a wall.

"Listen well, you worthless, predatory *fuck*," Nathan gritted, his voice barely intelligible in the dark night air. "Joni isn't yours. She doesn't belong to anyone. But she does, however, have my protection, which means that if I ever see you breathe in her direction again, I will snap your neck and throw you into the sewer for the rats to eat. You touch her again, you die. Do you understand?"

Shawn wheezed, eyes bulging.

Nathan, however, was unforgiving as he rammed his arm harder against Shawn's neck. "Do. You. Understand?"

The air seemed so stiff, I could shatter it with a hammer as I watched Nathan, and Nathan watched Shawn. Shawn's gaze, however, bounced between the two of us, but eventually, he nodded and flapped his hands in a weak sign of surrender.

Nathan loosened his hold just enough for Shawn to speak.

"S-sure." Shawn's voice was hoarse, like he'd been screaming instead of being strangled. "You got it." His blue-eyed glare alighted on me. "We're done."

I straightened and crossed my arms. "Fine by me."

Nathan finally released him, but not before shoving him against the wall once more for good measure. "Go. Don't let me see you again."

"Yeah." Shawn lumbered off into the night, clutching his waist where Nathan had drilled into his kidneys. He glanced back once more before he turned the corner and was gone.

Nathan looked like he wanted to start in his direction, but stopped when I grabbed his hand and pulled.

He turned and looked down at our joined hands. Immediately, I let go.

His brown eyes flared, his chest rising and falling with heavy breaths.

"How did you know I would be there?" I wondered.

"Carrick," he said curtly. "He sent me a text saying you were on your way. I didn't want you alone on the street."

His fists opened and closed, and I recognized the signs of someone practicing measured breathing. In, two, three, four. Out, two, three, four. I could practically count the beats along with him.

"Nathan, I—" I started, though I had no idea what I would say. How I would explain Shawn's presence.

"I don't want to know," he interrupted. "I can't—I can't talk right now, Joni. I'm too upset."

I hung my head, feeling utterly guilty. It was my fault he was in this situation. My fault he had been forced to assault someone outside his apartment building at four in the morning. My fault he was so overcome with anger he couldn't even speak.

Maybe Carrick was right. Maybe I was bringing nothing but chaos into Nathan's life, and I needed to bow out before I could do any further damage.

But the idea of roaming alone in this city, which suddenly felt dangerous in a way it never had before, kept me where I was.

"Let's just go upstairs," Nathan said, holding out a hand toward me, though he still couldn't look me in the eye. "I have back-to-back surgeries, and I have to be up again in an hour and a half. I need to get some sleep."

I nodded and let him walk me inside, his grip as gentle as ever. As we rode up in the elevator, I resisted the urge to burrow myself into his chest, to beg for him to wrap those big arms around me, providing shelter in a way I was starting to suspect only he could.

By the time we got to the apartment, I was shaking. Nathan hadn't looked at me once. He released my hand as we took off our shoes, then walked down the hall in silence, socked feet heavy on the hardwood floors.

He paused outside the bedroom door. "Are you coming?"

I looked up from hanging my coat on the rack in surprise. I'd honestly wondered if I should just spend the night on the couch.

"In a minute," I replied. "I'll be in soon."

He gave a curt nod and disappeared into the bedroom.

I showered quickly, changed into the T-shirt still in my bag, and tiptoed into Nathan's room to find the bedside light on for me. My fake boyfriend—fiancé—whatever he was…was already fast asleep. I watched him for a moment, enjoying the peace on his face while he slumbered. The anger, the confusion, and the tension were erased in his dreams.

Good for him. He deserved it.

As soon as I slipped into the bed, I was once again gathered into his chest while he slumbered. He nuzzled my neck and threw a heavy leg over my hip. His scent of sleep and soap and warmth wrapped around me as securely as his blanket.

"Come here," he murmured into my ear, though his breathing was heavy enough that I knew he was already asleep.

Her, I thought, even as my body naturally relaxed under his heavy, secure weight. He was thinking of her.

Not the woman Carrick told me about, but the one he had almost married.

Undoubtedly, someone who wasn't parading around in front of men for tips.

Someone who wasn't hiding her worst side from him.

Someone who didn't have secrets like me.

Still, I didn't move. I knew there was a good chance this might be the last night I'd ever spend in this bed, with this man, in this space where I knew I belonged.

I shouldn't have taken it.

But I never claimed to be a good person.

A flirt, maybe. A charmer.

But never good.

I was definitely not that.

TWENTY-EIGHT
WHY I NEED DANCING

#2 it makes everything else in my head quiete

I t was almost three in the afternoon when I finally woke up, sunlight blazing through the window on an icy winter day. Nathan was long gone, off to perform life-altering surgeries and then finish his usual clinic hours.

I spent an hour lying there, smelling his sheets and wondering if that ghost of a goodbye kiss on my cheek actually happened or was just a figment of my imagination. Then I laid there for another hour, debating whether or not I should just cancel my appearance at the gala. Whether I should just cancel the whole arrangement and go back to Belmont, where I belonged. After all, Carrick was probably going to spill what he'd seen to Nathan anyway, so there was no reason for this to continue.

But in the end, I kept seeing Nathan's big brown eyes blinking at me from across the bar. I remembered him saying he didn't care what I wanted to do, as long as it was my choice.

And I imagined the disappointment coloring his features if I bailed on the one promise I'd made to him in all of this: just to be there.

That alone got me out of bed.

When I was little, I often had a hard time sleeping in the room I shared with two of my sisters. Frankie snored, and Marie kicked me in her sleep. More nights than not, I'd sneak out after bed and crouch at the top of the stairs so I could peek at whatever my older siblings were watching on TV.

Soul Food was one of the few movies Lea and Kate could always agree on with their friends. Not exactly appropriate bedtime fare for a six-year-old, but I usually fell asleep on the stairs before the Big Mama fell into her coma. I usually tried to stay awake until my favorite scene, though. The one where Faith, the wayward cousin, does her dance audition to a piano version of "Don't Leave Me" by Blackstreet. She was the bad one in the family. The one who stole everyone's man. The fuckup and nothing else.

In that scene, though, she dances and comes alive, and everyone watching knows it. They don't think she's a screw-up. They think she's an artist. A person with real merit. And it was to those beautiful, butter-smooth piano riffs.

Even at that age, I could relate.

It was the reason I started dancing in the first place. I rewound the VHS tape and taught myself her choreography until Nonna finally put me in dance classes just to stop hearing the music.

That day, when I finally got myself out of bed, I didn't go for a walk, look for a job, call Nathan, or do any of the things I knew I *should* prioritize. Instead, after seeing that Carrick was also not in the apartment, I changed into dance clothes—*my* clothes. Faded cropped leggings, a stretched-out leotard, and the pair of soft black ballet shoes I hadn't worn in months. Then I fled to the studio on the top floor.

It wouldn't feel the same. I knew that. There were things I couldn't do, moves my knee just couldn't handle. And since I had no desire (or money) to go to the ER, I had to hold myself back at least that much.

But the rest of the routine...it had been too long. A quick bout of good cardio, followed by some light ballet work and stretches on the floor and against the wall. Then I put on my favorite playlist, the one that included everything from the Chopin barre music Mrs. Suarez played in her studio to the old-school Sinatra Nonna used to teach all her grandkids the box step, to show tunes and hip hop and everything in between. Every number I'd ever loved, every routine I'd ever given myself to. I selected "Don't Leave Me." And I danced.

THREE HOURS LATER, I was covered in sweat, and my knee was throbbing, but I felt almost at peace and happier than I'd been in months as the final song in my playlist came on: Billy Joel's "She's Always A Woman."

I smiled. This was a new addition. Mostly because I thought Nathan would like it. When I'd added it to the list, I'd imagined how he might sit and watch me while he listened.

Moving in time to the familiar piano, I wove my body into spontaneous patterns around the room, taking up as much space as I liked with arabesques, leaps, and pirouettes onto my good leg, and too many other movements I didn't have names for but only did because they felt good and right. By the time the song was on its final bars, I ended with a deep bow down to my toes, folding into myself like a butterfly returning to its chrysalis instead of going out into the world. It's what I wished I could do. I didn't want to fly. I wasn't ready. All I wanted to do more than anything else was go home where it was safe.

But home didn't exist.

And so I was here.

"You have to dance."

A deep voice that warmed every cell in my body echoed through the room. I jumped and straightened, then found Nathan's reflection in the mirror.

He was standing in the doorway, still impossibly handsome in his scrubs. His glasses were a little smudged, and his hair looked like he'd been running his hands through it again. Like he had been too busy to change, too much in a hurry to take care of these little things the way he usually would, all because he wanted to come home to me.

My heart ached in response.

How I wished it were true.

I turned, feeling suddenly awkward. "Um...hi."

"Hi." He took a step into the room. "I got home, and I couldn't find you." He looked around the studio. "Now I know why."

I crossed my legs, suddenly shy in my dancewear. I didn't know why. He'd seen me in far more revealing things at the bar. Or even his bed.

Maybe it was because out of all the clothes I'd worn in front of Nathan, whether they were costumes for a platform or for his parents, these worn-out dance clothes weren't a costume. They were just me.

"It's where I needed to be," I said quietly. "How did you think to come here?"

"Just a guess. I was about to call your sisters, but I thought I'd check here first." He shoved a hand through that thicket of hair again and shook his head like he still couldn't believe something. "I didn't understand until now. But you're...Joni, you can't stop doing that. Dancing, I mean. You're too good."

I deflated a little, though the acknowledgment felt nice. He couldn't know how much of a shadow I was of my former self. How completely absurd it was to think *this* was what I used to be capable of.

"Oh, Nathan," I said sadly. "I had to stop. You know that. This..." I waved a hand toward the room. "This was just messing around."

He shook his head stubbornly. "It didn't look like it. That was... that was fucking amazing. I am *literally* amazed."

"No. I had to skip so much of that routine."

Nathan openly gawked. "There's more?"

I nodded. "Oh yeah. But my knee..." I flapped a hand toward my scarred leg.

His eyes darted quickly down. "Right. Your knee."

He didn't say anything more, though his gaze didn't move. His focus remained on my legs and seemed to grow hotter with every passing moment.

I fought the urge to cover up. More from my own yearning than from that heated expression.

"About last night," Nathan started. He managed to tear his gaze up from my legs, and his brown eyes met mine, looking almost nervous. "Did Shawn follow you home from the bar?"

I gulped. But as easy as it would have been to let him think that, it would have also been the same as lying.

And I didn't want to lie to Nathan. Maybe I even felt like I needed to tell the truth.

Or as much as I could handle telling.

I sighed. Might as well get it over with.

"I...I have to tell you something," I said. "I wasn't at Opal last night."

"I didn't think you were," Nathan said, to my surprise. "You only work Tuesdays and Thursdays, and I've heard Tom refuse to give you more shifts at least ten times."

I should have known he would remember that. Nathan noticed *everything*.

"I was working somewhere else," I said.

Nathan perked up, obviously curious. "You got another job? That's great. Where?"

"I don't know if I would call it great," I muttered as I sank down to the ground. I pulled my knees close to my chest and swallowed hard. Why was this so hard to say? "I was working for this guy named Kyle. He's the, um, manager at Diamonds."

"The strip club?" Confusion colored Nathan's face, but not, I was grateful to see, anger.

"Yeah," I admitted. "He took me on for a couple of shifts there a few weeks ago, serving drinks, but it was a trial for these...parties he runs."

Nathan was quiet for a long moment. "I didn't know you had decided to do that after all," he said finally.

"I'm not actually stripping...but I was topless. And had to give lap dances and things like that."

Every bit of the description that, in my mind, hadn't been that big of a deal felt dirtier the more I recounted it. The windowless walls. The cluttered green tables. The harsh laughter of the men with oily stains on their teeth as I worked their bulging pants.

If I'd liked it, it would be one thing. If I was even apathetic about it, that would be another.

But I hated it. I hated every bit of it.

"It was shady," I said. "Shady enough that I'd rather get on the pole than do it again, if only because it's legal. I'm pretty sure this place wasn't, and I won't be going back. But I needed to tell you, partly because I just don't want to mislead you, and partly because Shawn was there, and also…Carrick."

Immediately, Nathan's whole body tensed. "What did he do?"

I sighed. "Nothing. He did nothing. But he saw me…you know, and then we rode the subway back to this neighborhood together."

"Well, that explains why he texted me last night," Nathan said wryly as he removed his glasses and rubbed the spot between his brows. "He knew where you were coming from."

Curious. Carrick certainly hadn't given off the "walk a gal home safe" kind of vibes. He had, however, given off the "I don't want my brother to kick my ass" ones.

"He also met Shawn. Who I did not know was going to be there, Nathan, I swear it. He just showed up with these gangster dudes, but I did *not* ask him to come. And I told Shawn…and he told Carrick that…well, I sort of said we're engaged."

Surprise colored Nathan's face. "You did?"

I bit my lip. "Was I not supposed to?"

He shook his head. "No, it's fine. I only…I suppose I thought it was primarily for my parents' benefit." He shrugged. "I didn't think you'd want your friends to find out about that too."

I gave a half-hearted shrug. Honestly, that hadn't even occurred to me, even with Rochelle there. All I'd known was that I wanted Shawn to leave me alone. That I wanted him to know once and for all I was not available for him anymore.

"It didn't work, though," I said as I lay my cheek on my knee.

Nathan's face hardened with the recollection. "Because he followed you home."

I gulped. "Er, yeah. Apparently. But I didn't want him to do anything—"

"Of course, you didn't want him, Joni. I heard you yelling before I was even outside."

"Oh, um. Okay. But I didn't want to talk to him ever. Honestly, I just needed to make some extra cash, and working for Kyle seemed like the easier way to do it, and now everything is a mess, and I just...."

I trailed off as I waited for the next interruption. Maybe some yelling. A bit of name calling. Shaming for good measure, followed by a solid lecture on how stupid I was before ordering me to get the hell out of his apartment.

But instead Nathan just said, "Okay."

I looked up. "Okay?"

Nathan inhaled and exhaled deeply. "I don't want you to see Shawn Vamos ever again."

I wilted. So he did blame me. "Nathan, I promise I'm not trying to contact him."

One hand waved the comment away like a fly. "I don't mean that way. I mean that you need to file a police report about what happened so we can get a restraining order. He assaulted you last night. It *can't* happen again."

My mouth dropped. He couldn't be serious. If last night had taught me anything, it was that poking the bear was more dangerous than waiting for it to go back to sleep. Serving Shawn with a restraining order would basically be like using a really big stick.

"I could have killed him last night," Nathan admitted. "Part of me wanted to. For touching you that way."

This time, the shame I heard in his voice was for himself. Not me.

It took everything I had not to get up and hug him. "Nathan, you do *not* need to feel bad about that."

"Don't I?" He rubbed his face. "I just want you to be okay, Joni. I would have given anything at that moment to get him away from you. It's almost compulsive, this need I feel to keep you safe. Obsessive, even."

We remained there together, pondering just what had happened and the gravity of Nathan's admissions. I rubbed my own face, considering how much I liked them. How much I wanted to believe them too.

He was obsessed with me a little bit? Well, I was kind of obsessed with him too.

And that was a very dangerous and addictive thing.

"And as for your job, I won't pretend I wouldn't have preferred to know where you were working before my brother did," Nathan said carefully. "Mostly because I don't like being the last person to know things. My family did that a lot. Kept things from me. Manipulated me because of it." When he looked at me again, his eyes were impossibly big. "They still do."

My heart twisted. God, I knew how that felt better than anyone. "I never wanted to keep things from you. I just...I don't want you to be ashamed of me."

He tipped his head. "Joni, if you needed money—"

"It wasn't about the money," I cut in, maybe too sharply. "Well, it was. But it was also about...ugh, I don't *know* what all it was about. What it *is* about. All I know is that I don't want you to think I'm taking advantage of you."

I flopped backward in frustration, kicking my feet out like a child. Nathan took a few broad steps toward me, then slowly sank down next to me, right there on the floor.

"Is that what you want to be doing?" he asked without a trace of derision or contempt. "Because I meant what I said, Joni, if it's what you want, I don't care. I really don't."

"Oh, you'd want your fake fiancée to be a glorified stripper when she's not working at a shitty bar?" The words tasted bitter, like unsweetened chocolate. "Makes me a real prize to introduce to your parents."

It wasn't a fair question. I knew it wasn't fair. Because I wasn't actually his girlfriend or fiancée or anything remotely close enough for him to protect or possess or whatever else I thought was supposed to happen.

Which wasn't even what I wanted.

Was it?

"I don't..." Nathan sighed. "Well, I admit that I would prefer that the woman I'm seeing not sleep with other men."

"That's not what I was—"

"I'm not finished."

I buttoned my mouth shut. And forced myself to listen.

"And I hate the idea of people touching her without consent or treating her poorly because of what she does."

He practically growled that one. I wasn't sure if that was a response to me or maybe *her*. Lindsay. Something he'd seen long ago.

"But," he finished, "the idea that I could ever put limits on what she wants to do, stifle her in any way...no. No, that's not something I'd ever want to do."

"Is that how you felt about *her*?" The question toppled out of my mouth before I could stop it.

Nathan turned sharply and stilled. "Who?"

I peeked up at him. "Your real fiancée. Or maybe Lindsay. And... Isla."

Nathan braced his arms over his knees but folded his hands together hard enough that his fingertips turned white. "Carrick." He spat the name.

"He said...Lindsay was like me. That you fell in love with her in college, and she took advantage of you and wanted you to help her and her kid. And that she died in a fire, and I'm basically just your second chance at the same thing." I said the words quickly. They tasted bitter on my tongue. "That I'm a pathetic version of the real thing. Redemption."

My fake boyfriend was quiet for a long time. A *very* long time. Long enough that I wondered if he was going to speak again.

When he did, though, it wasn't at all what I thought he would say.

"You are *nothing* like Lindsay Frazier."

I bit my lip. Frazier. Her last name made her seem more real, somehow. "But Carrick said—"

"Carrick was twenty years old and more interested in frat parties and binge drinking at than my life during college," Nathan interrupted. "He has no real understanding of what happened between me and Lindsay. He didn't even know about her until I asked him to come to her funeral."

"So…what did happen, then?"

At that, Nathan sighed and removed his glasses to rub the spot between his brows. Oof. If he was taking them off, it must be really bad.

"I have a story for you too," he said. "You're not the only one with secrets."

TWENTY-NINE

MOST IMPORTANT THINGS TO NATHAN HUNT

#1 Isla

"Some of it is true," Nathan said after we had scooted back to lean against a mirror, side by side under the barre. He stretched out his long legs, big feet flopping to the side. "She was a dancer like you, yes. And I did meet her in the strip club where she worked." He looked adorably bashful. "Some of the players on the baseball team took me when I turned twenty-one."

"Carrick told me that part," I said. "And no judgment, really, if that's your thing."

I received a sidelong glance. "It's not."

I chose not to fight him on that. I found I liked him better for it. "So, what, you fell in love?"

Nathan immediately shook his head. "Definitely not. I…" Almost unconsciously, he picked up my hand and started tracing his thumb over my knuckles while he spoke. "I wasn't very good with girls. With women. I'm still not."

"I don't know about that."

For that, I only received another very dry look that made me giggle. Nathan cracked a smile, which made me laugh harder.

"Maybe there is some truth to Carrick's version," Nathan admitted. "But I don't know if Lindsay knew I had money when we first met. I doubt it. I would have just looked like another college student."

I sincerely doubted that, but didn't say it. Even in casual clothes, Nathan carried himself with the confidence and poise that I suspected only came from the highest levels of breeding. A quiet pedigree, but a pedigree, nonetheless.

"I think she liked that I was the only person in our party who didn't order a lap dance," he went on. "When my teammates bought me time with her in a private room, we just talked. She didn't seem to mind that I wasn't outgoing or that I was content to let her speak. When she asked at the end of the time if I would be interested in a date, I said yes."

"You didn't care that she was a stripper?"

"It's a job," he replied with a shrug. "As long as she was happy and treated well, why should it matter? Although, to be fair, when I turned twenty-one, I still hadn't had intercourse with anyone yet, and I really wanted to."

I blinked. A few months ago, I would have been shocked by that information. If Nathan had been one of the nerds at my high school, I probably would have cornered him under the bleachers and never let him go.

But now that I knew him, I could easily imagine how hard it would have been for him to talk to girls at that age. Flirting was all about innuendo and facial expressions and unspoken hints—all things he struggled with.

He kept going without an iota of shame. "We saw each other for a few weeks before she told me about her daughter. And at first, I thought it wasn't a great idea to date a single parent. Additionally, even before I realized that Lindsay struggled with addiction, I knew she wasn't someone I would ever have a serious relationship with. We were too different."

I frowned at our joined hands, now resting on Nathan's thigh. "We're different."

"In some ways. But...I believe I understand you, Joni. And I think you understand me."

My knee-jerk reaction was to argue, but I couldn't. In the space of a month, Nathan had transformed from an abrupt, imperious doctor and grumpy customer into one of the kindest, most genuine people I'd ever met. He said what he meant and meant what he said. He expected and even valued the same from others. He didn't need flashy fashion or flirtatious grins or suggestive comments to make him happy.

He just needed the truth.

Huh. Apparently, we did have something in common. Something big.

"I was going to break up with her the day I met Isla. Lindsay and I were meeting at a park, and she brought her daughter. This very small, very smart little girl who seemed to struggle with certain things, like new spaces and certain noises."

Isla, it turned out, was autistic. As Nathan told it, she also struggled with a lot more than the communication issues he dealt with, although that was certainly part of it. She also had intense sensory issues that often prevented her from eating enough, could not tolerate many changes to her routine, and suffered from extreme anxiety for someone so young, among other elements of the spectrum.

But she liked Nathan. A lot.

"I didn't think I could break up with her mother with her there. But every time I saw her after that, Lindsay always had Isla with her. And eventually, Isla became attached."

"Of course she did," I said. "Who wouldn't?"

"Most people," Nathan said dryly.

"Then most people are idiots." I gave his hand a shake. "You don't know how wonderful you are."

He was quiet a moment. "Thank you."

"You're welcome. Now tell me the rest."

He sighed. "At some point, it became clear that Lindsay had a drug issue, which wasn't good for Isla for obvious reasons that were even more intense because of her ASD diagnosis. I finally figured it out when I got a call from Isla's school asking me to pick her up because her mother couldn't be found. I was listed as the emergency number." He huffed. "We found Lindsay at her apartment. She was in the middle of pulling her car apart on the street. The dashboard had been pulled up and was on the sidewalk." He looked at me. "She was searching for a rock."

"I'm assuming you mean meth." People didn't tear apart their cars for pebbles.

Nathan nodded. "That was when I knew I couldn't just leave her. Isla, I mean. So I stayed. I tried to help her and her mother too. Lindsay and I even got engaged so I would be able to provide them both with healthcare as a domestic partnership. Rehab for Lindsay. Occupational therapy for Isla."

"So…that's who you said you were going to marry?" I said.

Nathan's eyes swerved to me, dark and sharp. "I said we were engaged. I never said I was going to marry her. It's different."

"Not to most people."

"Well, it was to me."

What did that mean?

"You couldn't just…pay for the health insurance?" I asked instead of the question I really wanted to know. My thoughts were dancing all over the place. This story had me reeling.

Nathan shook his head. "My parents have the money, not me. They had cut me off just for going to Duke, so at that age, I was surviving on scholarship funds and what I earned working at a stable in Durham. I didn't come into my trust fund until I was thirty, and even then, it was most stocks in the company. The apartment and everything else I have now belong to me. It's what *I* have earned for myself."

"That's a lot for a twenty-one-year-old to handle," I remarked, though I couldn't help thinking of my brother or Lea, taking care of the rest of us when we were small. Or Frankie, who had Sofia on her own at twenty-three. "Your parents wouldn't help you?"

Nathan shook his head. "Absolutely not. We weren't speaking much during those years anyway. They definitely didn't approve of Lindsay."

Jerks. I hadn't even met Nathan's parents yet, but I had a feeling I wouldn't like them when I did. This was a little girl we were talking about. Someone their son obviously cared about, and they hadn't lifted a finger for her.

"It wasn't enough, though," he said. "Isla was with her mom when Lindsay died. She took her with her to her dealer, some man in a trailer in the woods that I guess Lindsay was also working with. There was an explosion. Isla managed to get out, but she was badly burned. She's had several surgeries over the years to repair the damage, but it was quite disfiguring."

So that part was true too. Jesus.

"None of this sounds that different from the story Carrick told me," I admitted.

"There are some differences."

"Like what?"

"For one, I didn't love Lindsay." He looked at me, his brown eyes wider than ever. "I never loved her. At all. I told you I was engaged in college, and it's true. But it wasn't because I loved Lindsay. It was because I came to love her daughter."

I digested that for a moment. Went back over the relationships he'd listed. If Lindsay and the fiancée were one and the same, that meant the woman I'd imagined was the one who was fake. A complete figment of my overactive imagination.

So, who was he asking for in his sleep?

Was it still this girl's mother? This woman he never really wanted to be with?

It didn't make sense.

"So what happened to Isla?" I pressed. "Where is she now?"

Nathan sighed. "She's seventeen. I pay for her to attend a boarding school in Virginia for autistic children. She's doing well. Enough that I think she'll be able to attend college with some accommodations." He looked at me with a pride that could only be described as paternal. "She's very bright."

"So you said," I said. "Seems like everything is all right now."

"It will be after she turns eighteen." Nathan sighed. "Until then, things are...complicated."

"Complicated, how?"

He turned. "After Lindsay died, my parents used their connections in the North Carolina court system to become Isla's foster parents. And then, eventually, her legal guardians."

"They adopted her?"

Nathan shook his head. "No. They just make her decisions officially since when her mother died, the courts said I was too young to become her guardian. I pay for everything, but they have to consent and sign the papers. And right now, they are proposing to send her back to North Carolina to live with some of Lindsay's distant family. In a trailer park. The effect of that kind of change on someone like Isla, being ripped from everything she knows, placed in an environment like that, would be disastrous."

Suddenly, everything made sense. The strange hold Nathan's parents had on their thirty-four-year-old son. The fact that this man, who so staunchly marched to the beat of his own drum, was willing to go so far as to fake a relationship to appease them. Isla's guardianship was clearly the tool they used to get what they wanted from the son, who otherwise wouldn't come to heel.

No wonder he was so intent on giving them what they wanted. It wasn't for them. It was for her.

If only I didn't mess it up.

I turned. "Nathan, I think you need a different fake girlfriend. Or fiancée. You know."

His head whipped around. "What?"

"I think...no, I *know*...I can't...the stakes are too high." I scrubbed my face, willing myself to find the words that just wouldn't come. "I don't want to mess things up for you, and I think I already have. Your brother knows what I do, and obviously, your parents won't be thrilled with it either. You need someone they won't find issues with, you know?"

"Joni."

"Maybe that Charlotte person," I rattled on. "We already know she likes you, and she's pretty. I bet she'd play arm candy in a hot second, even if she knows it's just a ruse, and then maybe you'll come to—"

"Joni, *stop*."

"I won't!" I was practically shouting now as I jumped off the ground and started pacing around the studio. "It's too important. You can't tell me a story like that, show me that a girl's whole future literally depends on me playing a part, and then expect me, of all people, to not fuck it up."

"Why?" Nathan demanded as he stood himself and started pacing with me. "Give me one good reason you can't do this."

"I don't have one reason, I've got a million."

"Tell me."

"No," I said as I whirled around in a corner.

"Why not?"

"Because you don't want to hear them all!" I shrieked. "Trust me, you *don't*. You don't want to hear that I started school a year late because my grandma thought I was too stupid for fucking kindergarten. You don't want to hear that I made out with at least three different teachers just to pass high school or that I lost my virginity at fourteen to a twenty-three-year-old man who still holds more power over me than the IRS. And you don't want to hear that, yes, I let rich men look at my tits while I serve them drinks because if I can't dance, it's the next best thing my body is good for in a world that didn't give me anything else to work with."

Nathan remained silent. I waited for him to answer. To say *anything*. And when he didn't, I collapsed against the mirror as I wrapped my arms around my waist.

"But here's the main reason," I said, voice choked through my quiet, chest-wrenching sobs. "I can't pretend anymore with you because it's not pretend for me. I will mess this up. I will. And then Isla's life will be ruined, and so your life will be ruined, and I won't do it, Nathan, because I lo—because I c-care about you too much to hurt you that way."

We stood like that for a long time, each at a different side of the studio, our reflections bouncing off into a million different versions of the same horrible impasse. The same space between us, filled only with my silent tears and the feeling like my chest was being ripped apart from the inside.

God, what I wouldn't give for that space to close. For one more night in his arms, even if I never got anything else. These feelings were too much to bear otherwise.

Please, I begged God, the universe, anyone who was listening. I'd said what I needed to stay. Now, I just wanted this pain to stop.

And by some miracle, the universe heard me.

Nathan started to walk across the studio, one step at a time, until he was standing in front of me. Then he took me by the shoulders and wrapped his big arms around me, one hand at my waist, the other cradling the back of my head as he pressed it into his shoulder and rocked me lightly until my sobs subsided into the occasional hiccup.

A low hum vibrated in his chest. Not music per se, but just as melodic and calming. At least to me, while I poured my heart out into that broad, sandalwood-scent chest.

Finally, when I had stopped crying enough to speak again, I pressed back to look up at him.

"You don't need another burden," I whispered. "And that's all I am. That's all I'll ever be to anyone."

Slowly, Nathan reached out and, with his thumb, wiped away a final tear I didn't even know was falling down my cheek.

"You're not a burden, Joni," he said almost as softly but clearly. "You're a gift."

"A gift of what?" I couldn't find it in me to joke. But I couldn't for the life of me see what he meant.

He was quiet a moment more, which I was learning just meant he was gathering his thoughts. I wondered if he was like me, and they ran crazy in his head too. I wondered if I could learn to pause like that one day. If it would make me a comfort to someone else the way he was to me right now.

"All my life, I've known I wasn't like others," he said at last. "It's the first thing people say about me. How serious I am. How unfeeling. There have been exactly two people I've ever met who never cared that I was different or said anything about it because they accepted me exactly as I am. One of them was a four-year-old child with autism. And the other is you." He reached out to cup my cheek. "I think I give you the same, don't I?"

I thought about it as I blinked back tears. And the more I thought about it, the more I realized he was right.

There was one thing that we could both give freely to each other. Something that was nearly impossible to get in this cruel world. Something I'd never had from my family or my friends, let alone boyfriends.

Acceptance. Simple, pure, and true.

Somehow, in this crazy process, Nathan and I had become something even more important than lovers.

We'd become friends. Deep and real friends. The kind I'd never had.

But as soon as the warmth of that realization wrapped around me, a different realization sliced it away. Something truly awful. Something that would end this friendship as soon as it had started: acceptance wasn't enough.

"Do you say everything you mean to me?" I asked, mostly because I had to. "Really and truly, all the time?"

Nathan looked at me for a long time. "Not all the time," he admitted. "There are some things I keep to myself."

"Good things?"

I was sort of teasing, but he nodded, serious as ever.

"When you think them, you should say them," I said. "Rule number three, remember? 'If you see something you like, tell her. Every time.'"

Nathan's eyes were deep. Mournful.

"You don't want that," he said. "No one would want that."

Heart thumping, I clasped his face, forcing him to look at me. Forcing my hands not to shake while I asked, "Why is that?"

His chin quivered. "Because with you…" He swallowed thickly. "With you, I think them *all* the time."

"You—you think what?" I stumbled. It couldn't be. There was no way.

But he only pulled me closer so he could frame my face with his hands just as I was doing. Making sure I was listening. Making sure I heard him.

"I don't care what you do for work," he said. "And I don't care if you can't clean up a kitchen. I don't care if you were good at school, or dance, or anything else you tried. I just want you to be exactly as you are. I like you—honestly, I'm kind of obsessed with you, Joni, just the way you are."

I sucked in a breath but found I was shaking so hard I could barely exhale.

"You—you are?"

Nathan's eyes glimmered with promise. "I am. And I'm not pretending anymore either."

Then he kissed me. Without an audience. Without a single soul to convince.

And this time, he didn't stop.

THIRTY
TYPES OF KISSES

#16 the i need you right freaking now kiss

W as it true?

Was I really here, in his arms, accepted for exactly who and what I was, while Nathan Hunt kissed me in the middle of a dance studio? *My* place?

My mind couldn't quite believe it, but my heart was more than willing as I wrapped my arms around his neck and pulled him closer.

The kiss was just as intense as our first, as any other we had shared. His mouth was soft and tender, lips firm but patient. He tasted like home.

That was Nathan.

My Nathan, I thought as I pulled lightly at his curls. A growl emerged from the back of his throat, and suddenly, I was flipped around and shoved against the mirror.

Maybe not so patient.

Right now, I was okay with that.

His mouth trailed down my throat, teeth nipping and biting all the way to the low neckline of my leotard.

"Is this all right?" he asked again and again when his hands traveled over the rest of me. Molding to my breasts, my waist, my ass, my thighs, taking full, lush handfuls, squeezing, kneading, memorizing my shape. "Is this okay?"

"Yes," was all I could manage. "Yes, yes, yes."

And then it wasn't. Because I needed more. Needed the barriers of cotton and Lycra and anything else separating us stripped away. I needed his hands on my skin and his mouth everywhere. I needed to touch that hardened length of him currently pressed into my hip. Fuck, I needed to do way more than that.

It wasn't enough, this room, open to whoever might walk in. It was hot, sure, and as a performer, I'd always had more than a little exhibitionist streak.

But I needed Nathan unfettered. I needed him raw.

He lifted me then, and my legs found their way around his waist, locking us hip to hip as he ground into me with a pained groan.

"Joni." He sucked on my lower lip hard enough that I winced. "I need...I want to go...*ahh*."

"Downstairs," I agreed. Then I took his chin and forced him to look at me. "Take me home."

Something locked between us with that word. I couldn't have said what. Those chocolatey eyes contained depths I couldn't hope to explore completely, yet I knew, at that moment, that I never wanted to stop trying.

For the last month, I had missed my old home so much it hurt.

I missed the sagging brown house, the front porch with the squeaky step, the room I'd shared with my sister, the friendly noises of the neighborhood, the chatter of my siblings, and my grandmother cooking dinner each night.

But right now, the only home I saw was in those big brown eyes. All the homesickness I felt for Belmont faded away because I was here. With him. Where I belonged.

Nathan kissed me again, then proceeded to carry me, our mouths still fused, out of the room and to the bank of elevators. He was incredibly strong—his muscles didn't even shake as he held me securely in his arms.

"My phone." I gasped just as the elevator doors opened. "My speaker."

"Later." He kissed me again as he carried me inside, then managed to press the button for our floor. "I'll get them later."

"But they...could be...stolen..." His mouth was so insistent, so hypnotizing, that I could barely think straight.

"Joni."

His voice pulled my attention back to him. Back to those big brown eyes. Back to home base.

"Hmm?"

"I'll buy you a new phone and speaker," he said in a voice graveled with want as he shoved me into the wall. "But right now, I am not exaggerating when I say I really might die if I'm not inside you immediately." His forehead touched mine. "That means right fucking now."

I quivered in his arms, and when my legs squeezed his waist involuntarily, Nathan's entire body shuddered.

"You're right," I said just before my mouth found his again. "Fuck the phone. Get me naked yesterday."

I barely heard the elevator doors open. Barely registered the walk to our apartment, a neighbor's door opening, followed by an "Oh my!" Didn't even notice that we were inside the apartment until Nathan tore himself away long enough to look down the hall as my feet dropped to the floor.

"Carrick, if you're here, *don't be!*" he shouted right after the door slammed shut behind us.

We both waited for an answer.

There was nothing.

We turned back to each other and lunged.

And then we were everywhere. Against the front door as Nathan kicked off his shoes. On the foyer table, sending the vase of gardenias crashing to the ground when his mouth latched to my breast. Scrambling down the hallway as he chased me like a man on the hunt, the first sign I'd seen that he lived up to his predatory name. I was more than willing to be his prey.

His hospital shirt landed somewhere near the living room. His scrubs bottoms halfway down the hall. Lord, he was beautiful, as big and brawny as a bear, rippled with lean muscle and the perfect smattering of hair across that broad chest.

He caught me just inside the bedroom and tossed me onto the bed like I was no heavier than a sack of groceries.

"Take it off," he ordered as soon as the bedroom door closed. "Take everything off."

I grinned and yanked off my leotard, then shimmied out of my tights and underwear. No sexy striptease needed here. No putting on a show.

He could have it if he wanted. Another day, another time. As a performer, I was a chameleon—I could be a thousand different women if that was what he wanted, and I looked forward to taking on that challenge one day.

But here in this room, as Nathan looked at me in nothing but my skin, I just wanted to be myself.

Just Joni.

"Perfect," he murmured as I lay back on the bed, displaying myself for him while I took in his own beautiful form.

Though I preened from his words, doubt slipped through my thoughts. "Oh, Nathan. I'm definitely not perfect."

His eyes drew back up my body, lighting a trail of fire in their wake. "You are to me. You've always been perfect to me."

That was all I needed to hear as I nestled back into the pillows. "Come here."

He did, but instead of covering my body with his, he knelt between my legs and trailed a finger over them.

"What are you doing?" I asked. "I said *come here*."

But instead, I was rewarded with an uncharacteristic smirk.

"Number one," he said as he drew his hand up and down my inner thigh. "'Let her pick the music and TV shows.'" He tipped his head. "I think I do pretty well with that one."

I frowned. "What?"

"Number two, 'Notice things about her no one else does and listen to everything she says.'" He kissed the side of my breast. "Even if you don't think it matters."

I opened my mouth, but nothing came out. This was sounding familiar.

Nathan bent down to hover his mouth over my ear. "You don't have to worry about that. It all matters to me."

It was the list I'd scrawled in the bar. In his notebook, the one that twinned with mine.

He pulled back a bit to look me in the eye; the smirk growing now. "Rule number three, well, we covered that one upstairs. Right now, I like everything about you. I like this." He kissed my neck. "And this." Another to my left breast. "And this." Now my stomach. "And this." He returned to my mouth.

And stayed there for a long time.

"Number four," Nathan murmured against my lips when I came up for breath.

"Always kiss me like it's the first time," I echoed.

Nathan smiled. "I'm trying."

He kissed me again, tongue twisting, hungry and intense, like he wanted to swallow me whole. When he was finished, we were both breathing hard, and the space between my legs was aching for more.

"You're succeeding," I informed him, barely able to speak. "Pirate."

The smirk morphed into a smile. "Good. Do you remember number five?"

I blanked. I could barely think at all right now, much less remember everything on that stupid list. "I...no." And then I did. "'Find out how she likes to be touched.'"

Nathan's eyes lit up. "I've been looking forward to this one."

He sat up on his knees, giving me a full few of his stacked physique while he spread my legs like a man surveying a field. He floated his hands over my body, then drew his fingertips ever so lightly, up and down my torso, my legs, my neck, my breasts. Testing my responses. Figuring me out.

I was imprisoned by his exploration. I didn't say anything; I knew he was mentally noting every shift in my body as he discovered the places that made me hiss and others that made me moan.

I wondered if he would write a list about it later.

. . .

WAYS TO MAKE JONI COME

I BET he'd need a whole new book.

I intended to fill one up about him.

"Here?" His finger drifted over one nipple, then pulled lightly, making me mew. "Or what about here?" His other hand drifted down the inside of my thigh, and my hips jerked toward him.

"You're evil," I told him between panting breaths.

"I assume that's a joke." His finger drew up my center, toying gently there, teasing the space without penetrating. Drawing patchy breaths and the occasional gasp in response. "But I'm not feeling very funny."

Then he lowered his head and pressed a kiss to my inner thigh. And the other one before he removed his glasses and set them on a bedside table.

"There was a second part to number five," he said as he leaned back down, close enough that I could feel his breath heating the sensitive skin of my thighs. "An addendum, if you will. Do you remember?"

He licked straight up. I moaned in response.

"'D-don't be stingy with your tongue,'" I recited, eyes squeezed shut in anticipation.

I could feel that delicious smile against my thigh. "I don't intend to."

And then he set to work, placing my legs over his big shoulders so he could splay me open for him while his mouth sampled my darkest spaces, licking, nipping, even slipping his tongue inside me to taste it all. I moaned without a care, grabbed for the curls that were everything I'd dreamed they'd be, ground my hips against that intrepid tongue, even more when it was replaced by a finger, then two. His lips closed around my clit, and he sucked gently, then a little harder as his fingers curved inside me. Every part of me squeezed as a squeal slipped from the back of my throat.

Soon, I was practically singing as his hand worked harder in tandem with his mouth. It was too much, all too much. The pliancy of his lips, the delicate swipe of his tongue, the slick pressure of his finger, the scrape of stubble on my thigh. I wanted it all but needed more as he drove me higher, higher until I couldn't help but explode in light and desire around him.

"NATHAN!" I shouted as I came hard enough that I swore the walls of the apartment shook right along with my body.

He didn't stop, though his movements gradually ebbed along with the pleasure pulsing through me. When I was finally able to see clearly again, I looked up to find him watching me with a hazy expression.

"So beautiful," he murmured. He leaned down to kiss me. "And you taste so fucking good."

I arched into his words, into him, then reached down to pass my hand over the *very* obvious bulge in his black boxer briefs. "Take these off. It's your turn."

Looking almost bashful, Nathan stood and removed his underwear. His erection fell out, heavy and long. My mouth literally watered.

He was big. Even bigger than I had thought, having seen him once through his shorts and feeling him half asleep. For a split second, I wondered if I could take him.

My heart pounded between my legs with trepidation and desire.

"We could stop now," he said, obviously noticing my shock.

I looked up. "Don't make jokes like that, sir. You can't tease me with that thing and just walk away."

For that, I was rewarded with another blinding smile as he hauled me up from the bed for another soul-searing kiss.

"I want you," he said against my lips. "I want to own this body, Joni. I want to sink into you so deep I forget my name. Forget my entire fucking life."

That was all I needed.

"Number six," I said. "Talk to her every single time. Just like that."

"I'll remember that."

Nathan gently pushed me back onto the mattress. And then he was there, a heavy weight putting on a condom, then a solid rod teasing my slick entry, nudging its way in, inch by massive inch.

He took it slow, giving me extra time to get used to the sheer size of him. I sucked in a breath as he used his weight, angling one of my legs over his arm so he could go deeper, then deeper still.

"Fuuuuuuck," I hissed once he seated himself fully.

I was so full, so unbearably, deliciously full.

"All right?" he asked again.

"Yesssss." I couldn't manage any other words, head thrust back, chest up as I breathed through that ache, that overwhelming fullness.

Then he began to move. Slow, at first, a delicious withdrawal, followed by an equally controlled, patient thrust. I was already flailing and would have thought him unaffected if I hadn't looked up and seen desperation in those eyes, along with sweat dripping down his temples. He was struggling as much as I was to keep himself under control.

I spread my legs farther, then used all those muscles, so carefully trained from years or dance, yoga, Pilates, and any other training I could find. And I squeezed.

Nathan choked in response. "Jesus. Joni—"

I reached up and pulled him to me for a kiss, sucking on his bottom lip.

"You can let go now," I told him. "I can take it."

Nathan surged forward on a groan. His hands found mine, pinning them to the bed as he really began to move, transformed into the beast I never knew he could be.

"Joni," he said as he thrust harder and harder still. "Fuck, *Joni!*"

"Give it to me," I begged, head thrashing from side to side.

"You'll take it," he grunted, working harder now, every muscle flexing as he worked my body mercilessly. "Fucking take *me!*"

Then he was gone, and I moaned until he flipped me over in quick, efficient movements, then entered me from behind in one harsh thrust. Again. And again. Deeper still. Impossibly deeper.

I grabbed for pillows, bedding, anything to help me brace against his onslaught. But there was only Nathan, his heavy weight covering my body, one hand reaching between my legs, finding that spot he'd already worshiped with his tongue.

"Does it feel good?" he demanded. "Does my dick feel fucking good to you?"

I couldn't answer. I couldn't even think. All I could do was feel the onslaught of sensations. The teeth scraping my neck, the fingers toying with my clit, another torturing my nipple as he pounded harder and harder still.

"Fuck," Nathan gritted out. "Fuck, I'm going to come. Fuck, I'm going to come so. Fucking. Hard."

As it happened, his words were my undoing. My body stretched and tensed at the same time, taking him as far as he could go as I exploded around him on a shout.

Nathan roared as he surged forward, caging me to the mattress as we both shook out long, blinding orgasms. Our bodies quivered in time, pulsing, shocked by the intensity of pleasure.

I wasn't sure where he started and I left off.

I wasn't sure where I was.

I wasn't even sure of my name.

And at that moment, I doubted he knew his either.

Gradually, the room came back into focus. A cool breeze feathered over my back as Nathan pulled out and disposed of the condom. When he came back, I was turned in his arms, my noodle limbs wrapped around his as he pulled me into his chest, where I could feel his heart still thumping against my cheek.

His mouth rested in my hair, which he lightly stroked. "Are you...okay?"

I almost didn't register his question, but when I did, I almost laughed. "Am I *okay*?"

"Yes." He angled his head back so he could look at me. "Please answer. I don't generally lose control that way."

He was genuinely concerned.

I touched my nose to his. "I am more than okay, babe. I am swimming in a pool of bliss." I kissed him for good measure. "You can lose control like that any time you want."

Nathan relaxed, and I went back to resting on his chest.

"I didn't know," he said as he stroked my hair. "I didn't know it could be that way."

My heart was still beating in my head, thoughts jumbled. Faces flashed through my mind. Other people. Other partners. Even Shawn, whose early kisses and touches and so much more had shaped my sexuality so thoroughly that, at one point, I had felt hostage to his knowing touch, wondered if anyone would ever know my body the same way.

They all splintered in my mind's eye, rendered dust by what had just happened.

"Maybe it's only like that for us," I said and knew it to be true.

I ignored the fear stabbing my heart when I realized what that meant.

If it was only like that for us, I was ruined for life.

Which meant if I lost him—and I inevitably would—my heart would be ruined too.

No, I told myself. He said it himself. He likes you just the way you are. There's nothing that would make him leave now.

The words became a mantra as I drifted off to sleep in Nathan's strong arms, no different than the fairy tales that danced in my head after bedtime stories as a child.

Just as comforting.

But also, said a small voice that hadn't quite been lulled to sleep, *just as much a lie.*

THIRTY-ONE
COMMON KNEE INJURIES FOR DANCERS

#2 Periferal meniscul tear

The light was almost blue when I woke up the next morning. It was early—far earlier than I usually woke up, considering my typically late schedule. I would have thought I was still dreaming if I hadn't fallen asleep in Nathan's arms the night before. And this time, he knew it was me he was holding as we both drifted off.

I had never slept better in my life.

Down the hall, I could hear the rumblings of male voices, though whatever they were saying was unintelligible. Probably Nathan and Carrick, who must have returned last night from whatever den he'd found the one before.

I wasn't sure I cared where that was, so long as he stayed out of Nathan's and my business. The man had a special talent for making me feel as shitty as possible, but if he thought he was going to use my life to come between me and his brother, he could think again. After last night, I could handle it. I had to.

My stomach rumbled alongside the conversation happening in another room, so I decided to hell with Carrick's nonexistent sense of propriety as I threw on another of Nathan's shirts and borrowed a pair of his boxer shorts for good measure since my underwear didn't seem to be anywhere in sight. I had to roll the waistband about four times so they would stay put, but they worked. And let's be honest, Carrick had already seen me in a whole lot less.

"I think she'll be curious to hear your thoughts," Nathan was saying as I padded down the hallway after brushing the morning out of my mouth. "I looked up her case. They turned her over to Gifford, who did the original surgery."

"Gifford? He's a hack. Between you and me, he shouldn't even have progressed past his first year of residency."

I turned the corner to find Nathan sitting in the living room. However, it wasn't Carrick on the other side of the room from him. Instead, a man I'd never met before was sitting on one of the armchairs. He looked to be maybe five or ten years older than Nathan.

Nathan's eyes popped open when I entered, flickering over my clothes as his cheeks pinked slightly.

Both men stood immediately.

"Um, hello." I offered a weak wave and suddenly wished I'd done more than shoved my hair into a messy bun. "It's, um, early."

Nathan tipped his head kindly. "It's almost eight o'clock." He turned to the man. "Jayce, this is my girlfriend, Joni. Joni, this is a mentor of mine, Dr. Jayce McAndrew."

"Mentor's probably putting it a bit lightly," replied Dr. McAndrew with a friendly smile.

"Jayce was a fellow during my first general surgery rotation," Nathan explained to me.

"Would have kept you on ortho too if you hadn't been so damn stubborn about burn repair," McAndrew joked.

"You knew that I intended to become a burn specialist," Nathan said, seemingly unaware of the humor.

I smiled. He was so earnest, it was adorable.

Feeling more than a little shy to be standing in front of one of Nathan's colleagues in nothing but his oversized T-shirt and rolled-at-the-waist boxers, I nodded at the men. "Um, nice to meet you, Dr. McAndrew." I waved at my clothes. "Sorry about this."

"It's fine," said McAndrew said. "And, actually, it will make my job easier."

I frowned. "Huh?"

"Jayce is the head of orthopedic surgery at Mount Sinai West," Nathan explained. "He specializes in knee injuries and works extensively with the American Ballet Theatre."

My eyes popped open. "You've fixed dancers' knees?"

McAndrew smiled. "A fair amount of them, yes. I hear you've got one that's bugging you."

Nathan came to stand next to me. "I asked Jayce if he wouldn't mind giving a second opinion as a favor to me."

I looked between them, utterly shocked. "But it—I—"

"I'm going to make her some coffee first," Nathan said before I could stumble. "Jayce, would you like another?"

"Sure, that would be great, man."

Nathan grabbed my hand and towed me into the kitchen before I could say another word.

"Wow," I started to say once the door was shut. "I can't believe you asked another doc—oh!"

Suddenly, I was grabbed by the waist and shoved against the fridge, and Nathan's mouth was on mine before I could say another word. His hands slipped into the boxers to grab my ass and pull my legs up and around his waist with a groan as his tongue met mine.

The kiss didn't last long, though by the time it ended, I was ready for much more. Nathan, however, just let my legs drop to the ground and pressed his forehead to mine.

"Good morning," he said quietly.

"Mmm. Good morning to you too."

"I think we're going to have to have a rule about you not wearing my shirts." Nathan stood up straight and adjusted his glasses.

"Oh no, why?" I whined. "Don't make me do that. They are so much comfier than mine."

"Not in front of company, then," Nathan said gruffly. "Because the next time I see you in one, I'll have to fuck you on the spot. And I might not care who watches."

I gasped. The thing about Nathan was that he meant pretty much every word he said.

"I thought *I* was the one with the exhibitionist streak," I murmured as his hand slipped around my neck again. I arched into his touch.

Nathan leaned down and bit my ear. "Maybe you're a bad influence on me."

"I don't know if *I* think it's bad."

His hand trailed down my side, taking its time to feel my curves. There was an ache in that touch. A need that was pulsing through me as well. "I...Did you sleep well?"

"Y-yes," I managed. "Did you?"

"Very well." Nathan almost seemed to be considering the fact as he readjusted his glasses. His eyes trailed over my mussed hair and the clothes I was wearing. "I like having you in my bed."

Images of us together in said bed, doing all sorts of things, flickered through my mind.

I squeezed my legs together. "Want to go back to it?"

"*Yes*," he said fervently. "But unfortunately, this can't wait."

I pouted.

His brown eyes flared. "Joni."

I pouted some more.

"Please. I need you to move so I can make you a coffee and try to get rid of this embarrassingly large erection."

I edged away from the fridge but didn't hide my admiration for the prominent bulge in his jeans. My mouth watered as more memories of the night came back. And back. And back.

"You need to stop looking at me like that, too," he said as he pulled the milk out of the fridge.

"I thought you weren't good at reading people's expressions."

"That one is pretty obvious."

I chuckled. "Then you need to stop reminding me about your oversized equipment, sir. Don't want a girl to stare at the goods, then don't point them out."

Nathan looked at me for a moment. Then the fridge door was slammed shut, and I was yanked to him for another scorching kiss.

Many more seconds later, I was gasping for breath. Nathan appeared to be having just as much difficulty finding oxygen.

"We have to stop," he said against my lips.

"I know."

He kissed me again. "We have company."

"He could leave."

Another kiss. Then an audible groan. Nathan released me with a quick smack on the butt.

"Go change," he said gruffly. "Before I kick Jayce out and finish what you started."

I grinned but reluctantly followed orders.

A FEW MINUTES LATER, I returned to the living room, where Nathan and Jayce were chatting again over coffee, and a third mug was waiting for me. I had changed into another pair of shorts—ones that fit me properly—and a sweatshirt that didn't make Nathan yank me out of the room again.

I wasn't sure I liked that effect, but it was the polite thing to do.

"So, Joni," McAndrew said, already eyeing the still-dark scar on my knee with interest. "Why don't you tell me a bit about what happened with your knee."

I glanced at Nathan beside me, who nodded.

"Ah, all right. Well, I was a dancer in *Chicago*. And my knee gave out during rehearsal about a week before I was supposed to open."

"That had to be rough," the doctor said sympathetically.

I nodded. Rough didn't even cover it. Having your lifelong dream ripped out of your grasp days before it was supposed to happen was the end of everything for me.

"What were you doing when it happened?"

I told him the story. The basics of the routine which was very jump-intensive. I was one of the few cast members with a solid enough ballet background to handle moves like fouettés and cabrioles—it was one of the reasons why I'd gotten the part, despite not having quite as solid a background in vocal training as some of the auditioners. The choreographer had a lot of new ideas he wanted to implement for the new production. A cross between Fosse and Balanchine.

The combination proved fatal. To my knee, anyway. One twisted landing and I ended up in surgery two weeks later to repair a torn ACL.

McAndrew nodded throughout, asked a few questions here and there, listened carefully, and then had me do a series of evaluative tests to see how strong the joint was. By the end, he had typed out several notes on his tablet, all of which I was dying to read.

"It could be a variety of things," he said after we were finished. "It's possible your recovery is just taking longer than normal, although, in someone with your strength, I'd expect full range of motion by now." He scratched his chin. "I'd like to do an MRI, to be sure."

I wilted on the couch. "Oh. Well. We might have to wait a while then. I can't really afford that now, since I don't have insurance."

"When?" Nathan asked. "She needs to dance, Jayce—this is her livelihood. And it's been almost six months since her operation."

When I turned, his eyes met mine with silent instruction to follow his lead.

I didn't know what that meant, but he knew my situation. How was this going to work?

McAndrew pulled out his phone and made a quick call. "Hey, babe. Quick question—any chance we could get into the MRI twenty minutes earlier this morning?" He listened and smiled. "Thanks, hon." After the call ended, he smiled at me. "My wife's the chief radiologist at Sinai." He winked. "Up for getting some pictures taken?"

TWO HOURS LATER, I sat with Nathan in Dr. McAndrew's office while we waited for him to return with the new MRI images. His wife, Dr. Paola Brunson, was a kind yet brusque woman who had hustled me into a hospital gown and then into the loud, clanging tube that took images of my legs for an hour while Nathan stood with her and Jayce in the control room, and I listened to a true crime podcast about Son of Sam.

It hadn't helped my anxiety.

Now, sitting in the office, I couldn't stop moving. My knees were bobbing up and down, my feet were shaking, and my fingers were tapping out the steps to "All That Jazz" on the chair arms.

One of Nathan's large hands landed on top of mine.

I turned. "Sorry."

"You don't need to apologize for a natural response," he said. "Stimming is an unconscious way of coping with difficult emotional moments like boredom, anxiety, or other stressors. It's particularly evident in neurodivergent people." He looked pointedly at his other hand, which was tapping a pattern on his knee. "I do that one too. It started when I had to take piano lessons as a child."

I bit my lip. "I've never seen you do that."

"I'm not usually very uncomfortable around you."

It was like he knew just what to say. "Have I ever told you how much I like it when you nerd out on me?"

One brow lifted. "Stating simple facts is 'nerding out'?"

I nodded, unable to hide my pleasure. "Oh, yeah."

"And that's a good thing?"

My grin fought its way out. "*Oh*, yeah. You'll be happy to know this girl's got a huge thing for smart guys. Especially when they are also tall, curly-haired doctors with glasses."

Nathan blinked adorably. "I don't know whether that's sarcastic or if you really mean it."

"Come here." I pulled him down for a little kiss with a lot of tongue. When I was finished, his eyes had darkened considerably, and he was squeezing my hand a lot harder than before. "Does that seem like I didn't mean it?"

He swallowed hard. "No."

I considered kissing him again, and he looked like he wanted me to. But I needed to talk about something else first.

"I am nervous," I admitted. "You went through all this trouble, called in favors with these big-shot doctors just for me. And what if nothing comes of it? What if it's the same old response—that my knee just can't dance anymore? Or what if it's something even worse, like a horrible surgery is needed that I absolutely can't afford? What if—"

"All of those are possibilities," Nathan interrupted as he gently took my hand and cradled it between both of his. "With varying levels of potential. But honestly, you won't know until Jayce comes in here to tell you."

For some reason, his frank words made me relax a bit more. Nathan didn't say the things other people would say. If my sisters had been here, they would have been full of platitudes. Lea would have told me to calm down and stop worrying, while Kate and Frankie would have insisted that it would be good news no matter what. Marie would have just said it would be fine, no matter what.

And I would have known that deep down, none of what they were saying was true. I had every right to worry. There was no way of knowing what the news would be. And it wasn't going to be fine no matter what.

"Thank you for just saying the truth," I told him. "Thank you for being here."

Nathan looked up. "I'll always tell you the truth, Joni. I promise."

I squeezed his hand, then leaned in to give him another quick kiss. "Me too."

There was a knock at the door before it opened, and Jayce walked in, followed by his wife.

"Sorry about the delay," McAndrew said as he took a seat behind the desk and logged into his computer. "We wanted to compare the new images to the old ones to see if there were any differences. Took a minute to put them together."

Twin images of my knee popped up on a large flat screen on the other side of the room. We all turned to look at them as Dr. Brunson strode over.

"I spotted it immediately," Brunson said, pointing to the interior of what I assumed was my right knee in the first image. "There."

Nathan's eyes popped open with obvious recognition.

"What?" I asked. "What is it?" They both looked the same to me.

"Meniscal tear?" Nathan guessed.

"Very good," Brunson said. "Better than my former resident could do, and you're in plastics." She looked at me apologetically. "You'll be happy to know he left the program last month. Won't be missing any more stupidly obvious injuries anymore."

"Claflin wasn't that bad," McAndrew said kindly, though it was obviously a joke.

"He was a pain in my ass. I don't have time for that kind of mediocrity," Brunson said as she turned back to the screen. "There." She pointed at the second screen. "Do you see that white line? There's a small one in the first image, but the ACL tear is so obvious that the radiologist missed the one in your meniscus, and apparently, so did your surgeon. And then, while you were rehabilitating the knee, you actually made the meniscal tear worse."

"The pain would have been in a similar spot too," McAndrew added. "So there you have it. Now, do you want the good news?"

Nathan and I both immediately pivoted to him.

"There's good news?" I asked.

Beside me, Nathan was already smiling.

"There is," McAndrew said.

"The good news is, he can fix it," Nathan provided.

"Hey, man, that's my line." But McAndrew was chuckling. "But, yeah, it's a relatively easy fix. The tear is small, and it's in the vascular section—that's the part that blood can get to and help it heal—and I've actually pioneered some recent treatments with stem cell injections I think you'd be perfect for. We'll just trim it off, give you an injection, and you should be good to go."

"Prognosis?" Nathan wondered.

McAndrew shrugged. "Simple meniscectomy. Possible repair if I see any complications, but she should be able to walk out of surgery the same day and start PT. Generally, my patients recover from this sort of injury in six weeks, Joni. It might be a bit longer, given the extra stabilizing needed for the ACL, but I'd say you could be back to regular activity within a few months, barring delayed progress with your ACL. Running, yoga." He looked at me knowingly. "Dancing."

I sank back into my seat, feeling like I'd been punched in the gut. Nathan automatically reached for my hand and squeezed.

"You'll need to be careful, still," McAndrew said. "It's important not to rush things. You don't want to re-tear it."

But I was already shaking my head.

"Oh, no," I said, my eyes brimming with tears. "Six weeks is nothing. Not when you just gave me back the rest of my life." I grinned. "Not when you just gave me hope."

THIRTY-TWO

SISTERS IN ORDER OF MOST TO LEAST ANNOYING (TODAY)

#1 omg still Lea

"Girl, I don't think I've seen you do the most like this since prom."

Rochelle sat beside me in Nathan's living room, getting her nails done with rhinestones while I sat very still as my manicurist painted gold French tips on mine, complete with sculpted gel extensions.

I'd asked for classy, but like a royal. Like Rihanna at a Met gala or Zendaya at her premieres. Someone everyone would look at and want to be, rather than the girl everyone felt sorry for. Someone Nathan would be proud to have on his arm.

Kiara, our girl from back home who owned a salon we'd been going to since we were fourteen, had taken my hard-earned lap dancing money and set aside her entire Saturday to get me ready—and threw in a manicure for Chelle just for kicks. She knew exactly what I wanted, asked for pictures of my dress, and had gone straight to work.

Even Nathan hadn't seen the floor-length gown since it had only arrived from the Bergdorf's alterations department this morning.

Since we were meeting at the gala itself (he had to work until just before), a car was arriving for me at seven on the dot. Which left me four more hours to get ready for what suddenly felt like the most important performance of my life: my debut as Nathan Hunt's *real* girlfriend.

Oh God.

The truth was, while I was admittedly a bit overwhelmed, I'd also been walking on clouds since meeting Nathan's doctor friend earlier this week. Dr. McAndrew said he would be looking to fit me into his surgery schedule as soon as I could come up with the funds. Yes, it would be a while off. Yes, it would mean a few more months of working Kyle's smarmy little game nights to get the money together. But not even getting yelled at by a drunk at last call could dampen my spirits. For the first time in months, I had a plan, a boyfriend, a purpose. I had a life I could almost be proud of.

Or at least I had a vision of one.

"Well, I won't be doing it again for a while," I said. "The rest of my money has to go to pay for surgery."

"I thought your man said he would pay for things like this," Kiara said as she painted a thin stripe of gold at the tip of my nail. "Don't cut my gravy train, babe."

I sighed. "He did, but I don't want to take advantage of him. But don't worry, Ki, I'll find time to get my nails done."

"You better. Because these were trashed. I can't have you messing with my canvas."

Rochelle snickered. "So he's good with you working for Kyle?"

I shifted uneasily on my folding chair. "He's...all right with it."

I didn't know how to answer that question. Nathan had insisted that he had no interest in telling me what to do, so I wasn't sure if the feeling that it wasn't okay was coming from him or just from me.

"That's how you know he's a good one, then," Rochelle said. "Like my Carmine. What did he say about Shawn?" She shook her head. "I swear to God, I wanted to kill him myself when I saw him walk in."

"That asshole showed up?" Kiara's brows lifted. Like any good stylist, she'd heard all of my relationship drama over the years, including bits and pieces about Shawn Vamos.

I cringed and sucked in a breath. "Wellll…"

"Rolling with some gangsters, too," Rochelle added, only to receive a dirty look from me. "What? It's the truth."

"I didn't realize this was 'air Joni's dirty laundry' time," I retorted as Kiara switched to my other hand.

"You're getting your nails done, baby," Kiara said. "What do you think we do?"

All of us chuckled, but Rochelle sobered immediately. "Seriously, though. Don't you think your man would want to know if Shawn comes by?"

I shrugged. "It was a one-time thing. Shawn lost so much money, I doubt he'll show his face there again anyway. You know how much he hates being embarrassed, and I don't think Kyle will want a loser like him poisoning the well."

Before either of them could reply, my phone buzzed on the table.

"Speak of the devil." I leaned over and answered on speaker. "Hey, Kyle."

"Joni, honey, how are ya?"

"Fine, you?"

"Good, honey, real good. Listen, I gotta say, you were a hit with the boys this week. Home run on your first night."

I made a face at Rochelle, who gave a silent laugh. "Thanks."

"So much, you know, that I got a call today from Ares Antoni himself."

"Who?" I mouthed the same word at Rochelle, whose eyes bugged out as she started making hand gestures at the phone. Clearly, someone worth knowing.

"Ah, you don't know him?" Even Kyle seemed confused.

I shook my head when both Kiara and Rochelle seemed to want to know the same thing. "No, I don't. Should I?"

"Maybe. He seemed to know you, kiddo. His dad is Lis Antoni. Older guy at your table last week. Big man, silver hair, don't take shit from no one. His kid was there too. Looks sort of like him, but younger, brown hair, no gut."

I vaguely remembered someone looking that way. Lis must've been the one with the paisley tie that Shawn was fawning all over half the night and Carrick freaked out about. His son must have been the quieter one at the table who never even looked my way.

"Anyway, Lis and his boys are looking to host their own party in a few weeks. It's on his yacht—huge fuckin' thing that's practically a cruise ship. Asked for you and a couple of other girls by name. Good money, kid. All you need is a weekend."

Rochelle was already nodding and mouthing "DO IT" in the loudest silent way she could.

"I don't know..." I said. "I don't mind doing your nights, Kyle, but my ex-boyfriend was at that table, and it got weird. I don't think I should serve his tables anymore, and spending a weekend on a boat sounds sus."

"I get that, kiddo. I really do. But, ah, Lis Antoni isn't really the kind you say no to, if you catch my drift."

Something prickled at the back of my neck. "Um."

"He'll make it worth your while," Kyle went on and rattled off a number that made every mouth in the room drop. "And that's plus tips."

I blinked. That was half the money I needed for the surgery—in one weekend.

"And...it will be safe?" I wondered.

"Oh, for sure it will. The girls get their own suite on the boat, locked doors, plus other security will be there. You'll be locked up tight, honey. Nothing to worry about."

Both my friends continued to look at me, completely aghast. Kiara looked more than a little skeptical, while Rochelle appeared to be waiting for her own personal invitation to the event.

Thousands. For one little weekend.

And yet.

"I need to think about it," I said. "When do I need to let you know?"

"End of the day. We gotta move on this."

I swallowed. Something was holding me back. "Okay, I'll text you later."

By the time we were done, Kiara had finished with my nails, which were safely under her UV light, while she went to work on my hair and makeup.

"You gonna take it?" Rochelle asked. "You'd be crazy not to. Kyle will make you some real money if you let him."

Even as she said it, she looked sympathetic. She knew what it would mean if I went to work with Shawn hanging around.

And even Rochelle didn't know about the video.

No one knew about that.

"I don't know," I said as Kiara started twisting my hair around hot rollers.

But before I could say anything more, my phone buzzed again. This time, with a FaceTime request from someone I definitely didn't want to talk to, but knew I wouldn't be able to put off until later.

"I'm going to take this in my room," I said as I stood up from the chair.

"Don't mess up your nails!" Kiara called. "Or the rollers!"

"I won't." I escaped to my bedroom and answered the FaceTime. "Hea, Lea."

"Joni, what in the *actual* fuck did you do?"

I had to hold the phone away—I honestly thought her voice might have broken the tiny speakers. "Excuse me?"

Lea's face scowled through the screen. She looked even more frustrated and mommish than usual, with her hair tied up on her head and dark circles under her eyes. All my sisters were beauties, but Lea had lost some of her luster over the years. I guessed that's what being married with four kids did to you. At least it did in Belmont.

"You heard me," she snapped. "What the fuck did you?"

I smarted—not at her tone, but at her words. Easily the most church-going of the Zola kids, Lea had cut out the swears a long time ago once she started popping out babies. I hadn't heard her say more than "fudge" in years.

"Well, right now, I just got a kick-ass manicure," I said once I'd composed myself. "But I don't think that's what you mean."

"I'm talking about Monday night. Some seedy bar or club or wherever people like you do these dumb things. What. The fuck. Were you doing with Lis fucking Antoni?"

At that, my mouth fell open. "How do *you* know who Lis Antoni is?"

"How do *I* know who Lis Antoni is? How do *you* know who Lis Antoni is? You're my baby sister! Michael and I have done everything—and I do mean *everything*—to protect this family from that guy. You're out of the house five minutes and already you're bringing trouble to our doorstep?"

I knew she was stressed when she went back to calling people by their formal names. "Michael" meant she was worried about someone she cared about.

Who, at this point, definitely wasn't me.

"Whoa, whoa, whoa," I said. "I literally just heard that name like one week ago, so you need to slow your roll."

"And how did you hear it?" Lea barreled on. "Don't lie to me, Joni. I know where you were at. I know these things because *Michael* got a phone call literally the next day asking him to meet up with those guys. They haven't looked him up in almost twenty years. *That's two decades*, Joni!"

"I know what a decade is," I said as I rolled my eyes. "What do you mean, looked him up? What does Mike have to do with a bunch of gangsters?"

Lea looked like she was about to hyperventilate. I watched as she looked away from the phone, rubbed her face, almost like she was pushing back tears, and then turned back after taking several long breaths.

"It was when you were little," she said. "When Mike and I first met. You wouldn't remember, but he wasn't always the most upstanding guy."

"Everyone in the family knows you married an ex-con, Lea," I informed her just as condescendingly as she had spoken to me. "But no one cares. Mike's always been good to you and us. He's a Zola now."

"Yeah, well, you don't know what it took for him to get to that. To get to this place, with our house, our kids. What he sacrificed to make that good happen."

I frowned. "Sounds like you'd better tell me."

Lea just shook her head. "It was when the Albanians started moving into Belmont. You were so little, but I remember. They bought up a lot of the restaurants in the area, and I guess the mob too. Merged with one of the local families—the one Mike was stealing cars for when he was put in prison."

I calmed down at that. I knew about that part of Mike's record, but not about his connection to organized crime in Belmont. That was no joke.

"They wanted him to come back to work for them when he got out," Lea said. "They only let him out because they respected him, but Antoni always said he would one day call back that favor, and I thought maybe he forgot, but he *didn't*, Joni! He didn't! Because someone in his group saw you at that fucking party, shaking your ass, recognized your last name, and came knocking at our door again. I guess they figured if one Zola was getting back into the life, Mike should come with her. *Fuck*, Joni! How could you do this?"

"Wait. Hold on, I didn't do anything," I protested. "It was a gig, Lea. I was serving drinks at a private party. How was I supposed to know the people there had some weird debt to call in from Mike?"

"You always do this," my sister spat. "You blink your big green eyes and act like you don't know anything so you don't have to take responsibility for what you do. You didn't even think if the 'party' was sketchy, did you? Didn't even wonder if charming random dudes was a good idea."

"It's not like that," I said. "I needed to make some money."

"I'm sure you were doing a lot more than that, baby." Lea sounded so weary. "You act like your bad decisions don't affect the rest of this family. But now you've dragged mine into it. And I don't know what the fuck we're gonna do, because the last time we extricated ourselves from the claws of Lis Antoni, Michael and I both almost got killed. Get it now? Real stakes, Joni! Real lives!"

"Oh my *God*, I am not responsible for bad decisions you and

Mike made twenty years ago!" I practically shrieked. "I'm sorry I served a drink to a bad guy who hates you, but it literally could have been anyone. It's not my fault he came calling!"

"YES, IT IS!" Lea shouted back. Her face was so red that she looked like she was about to boil over. Even tears were starting to form around her eyes. And this sister *never* cried. Lea was tough as nails.

I might have felt bad. I did feel bad. But I also felt angry. Too angry to be nice. Too angry to do anything but bite right back at her.

"NO, IT'S NOT!" I shouted right back. "And honestly, if you can't see that, then fuck you! I don't need this shit, Lea. I'm trying to get my life together, and you accusing me of all sorts of things I am not responsible for isn't helping. So, you know what? You can either start being a *real* supportive sister, or you can legit fuck off." I swiped at my face, aware I was probably ruining Kiara's careful makeup job. "Now, I gotta go. I have another gig tonight that I cannot be late for. With someone who actually cares about me. Bye."

"But, Joni—"

"*Bye*," I said again, then turned my phone off.

I sat on the corner of my bed for a long time, sucking back tears, taking deep breaths, and trying to get myself together. A few minutes later, there was a knock on the door. I looked up to find Kiara and Rochelle poking their heads in.

"Hey, *mami*," Rochelle said as she edged inside, followed by Kiara. "You okay?"

I shook my head. "Lea is *such* a bitch. Apparently, that Antoni guy called her husband for something bad, and she's blaming me. Because I had the bad luck of serving him drinks."

Kiara and Rochelle traded glances, but neither said anything.

"She's just scared," Rochelle said. "No one wants a call like that. Especially since your brother-in-law used to be wrapped up with those dudes too, right?"

I nodded. Like most of our extended family, Rochelle was well-versed in the gossip that had been Lea and Mike's beginning.

"I'm over it," I said as I stood up. "And I know what I need to do."

Without another thought, I swiped my phone off the bed and fired off a text to Kyle letting him know I was on for the boat party. I could go to that, make the money I needed for the surgery, and talk to Lis about leaving my family alone all at once.

"She needs me to take care of it?" I said once I'd set my phone back on the bed. "I'll take care of it. And I'll take care of myself too."

THIRTY-THREE

THINGS NATHAN HUNT'S REAL GIRLFRIEND SHOULD REMEMBER

#5 his freinds names. crap what r they again?

And so, at six p.m., I was waiting in the lobby of Nathan's and my apartment building, ready for the grand finale.

Or so I thought.

Kiara hadn't come to play when she got me ready, finishing my elegant manicure, then rolling my hair into the barrel curls needed for the elegant updo more fitting for a first lady than an out-of-work dancer. The understated makeup was limited to a coy cat eye and nude lips, complemented by tasteful crystal drop earrings and a sedate chain around my neck—the only part of this costume that was mine was the twenty-four-carat gold pendant of Mary Magdalene hanging around my neck.

Because that's what this was, wasn't it? A costume. As beautiful as the Gucci gown was with its pleated, gold lame skirt and the plunging black top, it was hardly something I would ever wear on my own. Beautiful, yes. Glamorous, for sure. But never something I'd ever wear in real life, where I was more at home in thrifted jeans or loungewear.

Still, if it would keep me safe with Nathan's upper-crust world, I'd take every inch of armor he could afford.

I hugged the black mink shrug to my shoulders and pulled out the little red booklet I'd tucked inside my matching clutch, along with my ID, a few extra dollars, and my lip gloss.

It was the final to-do list for this little charade. The one I needed to remember.

Things Nathan Hunt's *Real* Girlfriend Should Remember

1. No interrupting. But also no raising your hand like a little kid.
2. Smile and nod when people talk about things you don't know. It's okay not to stand out.
3. Nathan likes you just the way you are.

"Just to way you are," I repeated to myself as a large, black BMW pulled up to the curb. A driver got out, wearing a black cap that matched his uniform.

I smiled. Nonno used to wear the same thing as a chauffeur before he died, and now sometimes Mike did too, since he and Lea took over the garage and driving business when I was a kid. This uniform wasn't family, but it was a way of having them with me. Even if I was mad at them.

Ten minutes later, the car pulled up to the front entrance of the Natural History Museum on Central Park West. I tipped the driver, a nice man named Miguel, and followed the line of other people toward the entrance.

At the top of the steps, I found Nathan, who had arrived straight from work, though not, however, before changing into an outfit that made him look like James Bond. The classic tuxedo was tailored perfectly to his sculpted body, making his shoulders look even broader while tapering to the trim waist and muscled thighs in ways that put very dirty thoughts into my head. His hair had been tamed with pomade—or as much as it could be since it still misbehaved with a rakish bit sticking up here and there—and he'd foregone his glasses tonight in favor of contacts.

He was casting his sharp gaze over the entire steps, then checking his watch every few seconds, looking like a general surveying his troops. His world.

There was royalty in his blood, I thought as I approached. Royalty to my peasantry.

I couldn't ever really compare. But somehow, he wanted me anyway.

His gaze finally landed on me when I was only a few steps from him, and he startled, forced to jog down to me to prevent himself from falling.

I grinned. Point for the gold dress.

"You look…" He scanned me up and down, his mouth moving like a fish's. "Unbelievable."

I looked down at the pleated skirt, then back up to him. "I'm glad you like it. You don't look so bad yourself, Double-Oh-Seven."

He appeared confused for a moment, but the frown quickly broke. "Oh, James Bond." That produced an adorably shy smile. "Too bad I don't care for martinis."

I grinned back. "No. But you do like your sparkling water with a twist."

He stared at me for a long moment. "I don't know why that makes me want to shove you against the wall over there, but it really does," he said, unable to keep his eyes off my lips. With some obvious effort, he dragged them away and took my hand. "Let's go inside. I'd like to get this evening over with so I can take you home and fuck you in that dress."

I shouldn't have been shocked by his vulgar language—already, I knew that Nathan wasn't one for innuendo. But for him to state his desire so openly and calmly only steps away from some of the richest people in New York, the most proper, I assumed…Yeah, that turned me on more than I could say.

I leaned in and brushed a kiss to his cheek, then murmured into his ear, "Only if you keep the tux on while you do it, babe."

I nipped his ear, enjoying the full body shudder as I pulled away.

Nathan shook his head and mumbled something like "fucking torture" before he tugged me up the stairs and into the museum to show his parents, his brothers, and his entire world that he could be who they wanted him to be.

We followed the trail of people walking through an exhibit on biodiversity, then into the Hall of Ocean Life, where the gala was set up beneath the iconic blue whale suspended from the high, lit ceiling.

I'd been here more than once as a kid. The Museum of Natural History was a common site for field trips, and I'd gone at least once at every school I'd attended through high school. But never at night, like this, with twinkle lights wrapped around the pillars extending to the ceiling, the models of oceanic life haunting us from the corners, and the rest of the room filled with linen-covered tables, a dance floor near the front, and a stage where a band already played big band swing.

"Wow," I murmured as I took in the scene.

On top of the opulent surroundings, the room was filled with what could politely be called the glitterati of New York. They were mostly older. Mostly white. And mostly rich. Very, very rich.

But it wasn't what kids in my neighborhood thought of when they imagined wealth. There weren't gold chains, Birkin bags, or logos on everything. The wealth in this room was quiet, almost uniform. Men in tuxedos, just like Nathan's, with strong handshakes and insincere smiles; women arrayed with subdued diamonds, porcelain skin, and tastefully draped evening gowns. Nothing so flashy as mine. The jewelry they did wear was sedate and tasteful. No one had a hair out of place, too big or too small. They all just blended into one big moneyed tapestry.

And here I was, flashing like a strobe.

Nathan reached down to take my hand, which had been pulling at my skirt, and tucked it into his arm. "You don't need to be nervous."

I turned to him. "How can you say that? I don't fit in here at all."

He glanced back at the room, but his gaze returned to me. "Joni, why would you think I'd ever want you to fit in?" He leaned in to whisper in my ear. "Just the way you are, remember?"

It was like he knew what was written on that list.

He pulled back but cupped my face, drifting a thumb over my mouth, then pressed a gentle kiss there. When he stood up straight, I stood with him, newly energized.

Just the way I was. Now, I just needed to remember my posture and to keep my mouth shut.

It shouldn't be too hard when the whole room rendered me speechless.

Nathan guided me to a table near the front with the name HUNTWELL printed on a placard in the middle next to a vase of pink peonies. We were the first ones sitting here to arrive. I spotted his coworkers at another nearby table; Reagan waved at me and gestured that she loved my dress. I smiled in response.

"I'll have to introduce you to a lot of people in this room," Nathan said as a caterer arrived with a tray of champagne. To my surprise, Nathan took flutes for us both and handed me one.

"Drinking tonight?" I asked.

He took a grim gulp. "Trust me. We'll both need it." He finished off the glass and replaced it with another from a passing server. "The richest people in the tri-state area are in this room. It makes them kind of bloodthirsty."

I frowned. "Aren't they here to *give* money away?"

Nathan shook his head. "Events like these are never really about the charities; they're places for the powerful to convene. Every person here is on the hunt."

We looked around. Suddenly, I was imagining everyone in the room with fangs.

"My sister Marie cooks for a really rich family in Westchester," I said. "That's why she's in Paris. They sent her to some fancy cooking school so she could take over for their chef, who's retiring."

"Who are they?" Nathan wondered.

"I don't remember. Their name sounds like a cat. Tyger. Cheetah. Dammit, I know this."

"Lyons?"

I turned to him with a grin. "That's the one. Marie is obsessed with one of the brothers. His name is Daniel. You know them?"

He didn't look thrilled to be nodding his head. "I'm familiar."

"Of course you are. I bet all you glamor pusses know each other."

Not even a twitch for my efforts. Just a long sigh as he turned back toward the crowd. "Lucas Lyons is on the board of Huntwell, actually. Yes, that's him over there with his mother. They live next door to my parents' house in New Rochelle," Nathan confirmed. "Daniel isn't here, but Lucas and I went to Episcopal together."

I eyed Lucas Lyons, a tall, serious-looking man whom I recognized now from *Page Six*. He looked a lot older than Nathan, if only because of his expression. Ice cold. I resisted the urge to shiver.

"Friend of yours?" I wondered. I hoped he didn't say yes, even though I didn't think Nathan had many friends.

He shook his head. "Acquaintance, mostly. But he seems like a decent person." He turned. "Over there is the de Vries table. Eric is a major stockholder in Huntwell, but Dad is also looking at securing a shipping deal with his company. You might like his wife—she's a designer."

I shoved into his side. "I actually know that. Eric's cousin married my brother. They'd probably be here too, if Nina wasn't eight months preggo. But other than that, I promise I'm a nobody. They're the special ones."

I had just finished speaking when we were interrupted by one of the *somebodies*, as it happened.

"Joni?"

I turned at the sound of a familiar voice—and a British one at that. My eyes widened when I found Xavier Parker, my sister's husband, restaurant mogul, and an honest-to-God duke, breaking away from a conversation to round a table toward me.

I blinked, truly shocked. "Xavier? What are you doing here?"

Frankie, apparently, had the same taste I did in large, steely-eyed men who parted crowds like Moses at the Red Sea. Xavier towered over most people in the room, and if they didn't move, he only had to fix his sharp blue eyes on them, and they flinched like he'd cut them with one of his kitchen knives.

To be honest, none of my family really liked him very much. It was a matter of loyalty. Even if, in the end, Xavier turned out to be kind of nice, seemed to be a good dad, and was stupid in love with my sister, I was supposed to hate him anyway for the years of suffering she'd been through before he came back into her life.

Even if right now, in the middle of this room of circling sharks, he was a life preserver.

"Hey…Xavier," I said again, nervously trying to ignore the curious looks from the people he'd been speaking to.

"Joni, what the fuck are you doing here?" he asked in his typically coarse way, with that not-quite-upper-crust accent Frankie said was from South London. He might have been a duke, but Xavier's origins were just as humble as ours.

"I'm here with my boyfriend." I gestured weakly at Nathan, who stood beside me, taking in Xavier's presence.

Unlike most people, he didn't shrink under that dark blue gaze. Considering Xavier only had him by an inch or so, it was rather like watching two wolves challenge each other. One was bristly, British, and kind of rude. The other was quiet, contemplative, and wouldn't make a move until absolutely pushed.

"The one you just moved in with? Yeah, Ces told me all about that."

Something in my chest hurt at the casual nickname, pronounced "Chess," that my new brother-in-law reserved just for Frankie. For all his brusqueness and intimidation, Xavier wasn't afraid to display the closeness he had with my generally private sister. With him, she was obviously an open book. I got the feeling he was with her too.

I wondered if he understood how special that was.

"So, what're you doing here, then?" Xavier wondered.

"I'm his date," I told him. "Obviously."

"Nathan Hunt." Nathan extended a hand, and I watched as they exchanged a white-knuckle handshake.

Xavier's blue eyes, however, popped open at the name. "Radford Hunt's son?" He turned around as if to search for the evidence.

Nathan nodded. "That's right. My parents should be arriving momentarily."

"Blimey…" Xavier drifted off, rubbing his chin.

"There they are now," Nathan said. He squeezed my hand and let it go. "I'll bring them over here to say hello."

I nodded, and he left me with Xavier, who I had the feeling was ready to launch into the third degree.

I sighed. I didn't need another protective sibling. I already had five.

"What are *you* doing here?" I asked, deciding to go on the offensive. "Don't you live across the ocean? I'd think you have better things to do with your time than bother poor relatives."

Xavier ignored the cutting remarks as he watched Nathan through the crowd. "My CFO sent me over to meet them—he wants me to invest with Huntwell." When he returned to my blank expression, he seemed surprised. "Don't you know who your boyfriend's family is?"

I gritted my teeth. I was getting really tired of people saying that to me. "Nathan's a surgeon. I know his family is rich, good at investing, and they own a lot of horses."

Xavier shook his head. "You Zolas are all the same, you know that? For all your street smarts, you don't question a soul, do you? Even if it would be for the better."

I opened my mouth to protest but found I couldn't. After all, he knew that better than most. Frankie's decision not to look for him cost him the first four years of his daughter's life.

"Radford Hunt is basically a king in his own right on this side of the pond." He tapped his long nose thoughtfully. "And *you* ended up with a prince? How'd that happen, then?"

I grimaced at his disbelieving tone. What was it about me that made people immediately think "no better than trash"?

"He was a customer at my bar," I said through gritted teeth. I caught Nathan watching us as he neared an older couple that I guessed were his parents.

"And he's a surgeon too, I hear?" Xavier nodded at him. "Not for long. Fuck me, that's a lot of pressure."

I shrugged. "Yeah. He seems to like it, but I'd probably freak out if I had to cut people open every day."

BOYFRIEND OF THE HOUR   395

"I don't mean that." Xavier waved the comment away. "I mean, being Radford Hunt's first-born son."

I frowned. "Oh. I guess, yeah. I know they put a lot of pressure on him to act a certain way. I know it's cost him a lot."

Vaguely, I wondered if Nathan's history with Lindsay and her daughter was a secret everyone in this room had known but me.

Xavier just snorted. "Act? Nah. You really don't know who you're shagging, do you?"

I scowled up at him. Not because my brother-in-law was casually discussing my sex life, but because he clearly thought I was stupid. Just like everyone else.

"I know Nathan," I said through my teeth. "Better than you, that's for sure. I know he does what's necessary to keep his life and others' lives intact. Tonight is a formality. Then we'll go back to normal."

But Xavier didn't believe me. "I'm only saying this for your own good. This here posh 'gala' is a sham, arranged only because they knew your boy would come. It's an ambush. I've seen it a thousand times before—experienced it myself with a father just like that. Before you two walked in, the only thing everyone in the room could talk about was the fact that Radford Hunt's about to unofficially nominate your boy as the next CEO of the Huntwell Corporation. And in front of the entire board and half the company's investors, that old man won't be taking no for an answer."

I gaped. "But…they wouldn't do that. Nathan has a job here. He owns his practice—I just met the other doctors a few weeks ago. There's one over there." I pointed to Charlotte Mueller and smiled. She did not smile back. "He's a surgeon, dude, not a CEO."

"Who still serves on the family's board, doesn't he?" Xavier prodded. "As his father's proxy vote along with his own, I'm told."

I couldn't argue with him there. I honestly hadn't even known. Nathan had never mentioned anything like that at all.

"I was a chef until suddenly I had to be duke," Xavier said grimly. "When you're born into a family like this, you don't just inherit money. You inherit a life. Your Nathan might think he has freedom and choice now, but I promise he doesn't. One way or another, they'll get him back."

I gave him a dirty look. "You don't know that."

Xavier held up his hands. "I wish I weren't right. But I am." He nodded in the direction of Nathan, who was leading the older couple toward the table. "Looks like your cue, babe. I'll be at the de Vries table with friends. Find me if you need an escape."

And with that, Xavier disappeared into the crowd, leaving me feeling a bit like a cornered rabbit in a den full of wolves as Nathan returned, his family not far behind.

"The Lyonses, now the de Vrieses, and now the Duke of Kendal?" he murmured.

I smiled, reaching for his hand. "It's just family. We aren't close at all."

"Still. Are there any prominent families you *aren't* connected to?" Nathan shook his head in disbelief. "My parents might enjoy you more than I thought."

God, I hoped that was true.

"Well, I'm in my best Elizabeth Taylor drag, and your parents will take one look at us and think they can't possibly tear us apart," I told him, sounding more optimistic than I really was. "I'll charm the pants off them, no problem."

This time, I had finally earned a small smile. "That's such an odd expression."

I nodded. "It really is. Could you imagine your mother so happy she just ripped her pants off in front of everyone?"

The smile turned into a grin. "I'd really rather not, especially since she's right here."

He turned as the people he was with earlier arrived at the table, followed by two other men, including Carrick, wearing his perennial smarmy scowl.

"Hello, *Gigi*," he sneered.

I shot him a quick glare, making him chuckle before I turned my brightest, most charming smile to the rest of the people with him.

"Joni," said Nathan in a voice that seemed like it would weight him to the bottom of the Hudson. "I'd like you to meet the rest of my family."

THIRTY-FOUR

NATHAN'S FAMILY MEMBERS

#2 Lilian Hunt—mom

"I knew that Ralph Lauren would be perfect on you, Nathaniel. Doesn't he look perfect, Radford?"

The blond woman, petite and elegant in a silver lace dress, looked to be about sixty and spoke with a faint Southern accent as she fawned all over Nathan like she hadn't just seen him moments before.

The tall man beside her, who looked like a silver-haired version of Nathan and Carrick, just grunted and shoved a pair of glasses up his nose while the younger blond man beside him appeared to whisper a snarky remark to Carrick.

"And who's this you've brought with you?" the woman asked as she turned to me. Her brown eyes, so like her son's, were sharp and slightly chilly despite her friendly demeanor. Her tone was sweet, but I couldn't help feeling like a subpar dessert someone had brought for a potluck. It was the same tone Nonna gave her friends when they bought pans of cheap tiramisu from CTown instead of making the real thing at home.

"Mom, this is Giovanna," Nathan said.

"Oh, so it's back to *Giovanna*, now," Carrick snarked, though when he received a daggered expression from Nathan, he quieted.

"This is my mother, Lillian, my father, Radford Hunt, and that's my youngest brother, Spencer. You already know Carrick."

"I do," I said with a short nod his way.

That chilly gaze made my spine prickle. Carrick was the definition of a loose end.

"My, my, my," said Lillian as she openly looked me over. "What a pretty girl. She is a beauty."

I accepted an air kiss in greeting. "Nice to meet you, Mrs. Hunt. You can call me Joni. Everyone else does. Except Nathan sometimes."

I expected her to say something back like "Just call me Lillian, dear," but she stayed silent as she shook my hand. The polite warmth in her smile still didn't reach her eyes.

"Nice," concurred Spencer, who looked nothing like his older brothers, having clearly taken after his mother's blond hair and blue eyes. He flashed a smile that rivaled my own as he looked me over. "Very nice, brother."

I shifted uncomfortably, feeling a bit like livestock being examined for sale while I received nothing more than a curt nod and a quick handshake from Nathan's father, who looked like he wanted to wash his hands afterward.

"That's quite a dress," Lillian said as she looked over my gown. "I don't believe anyone in the room has quite such…pizzazz."

I fought the urge to burrow into Nathan. It sounded like a compliment, but it definitely wasn't.

Nathan, unfortunately, didn't seem to understand.

"She is beautiful," he seemed to agree with his mother as he smiled down at me. "In every way."

Lillian blinked as if her son's agreement wasn't exactly what she was hoping to get out of our particular exchange. I, however, was thrilled.

"Thanks, babe," I murmured, allowing him to pull me into his side.

"I see the de Vrieses over there," Radford said suddenly, as though he couldn't take one more minute of niceties. "Spencer, come with me. They've got a stable on Long Island, so they might be interested in a stud."

With a gleeful eye roll, Spencer followed his father through the crowd.

"I'd best join them," Lillian said. "My husband is very good at business, but he always needs a bit of extra help with the pleasure."

Before I could wonder what she meant by that, she was gone, leaving Nathan and me alone with Carrick, who seemed completely uninterested in leaving.

"They seem...nice," I offered.

Nathan raised one brow.

Carrick snorted. "Our parents are many things, but 'nice' is not one of them."

"Then, what would you call them?"

"Conniving, controlling, and manipulative all come to mind," he replied.

"Sounds like *someone* is projecting," I muttered.

Nathan chuckled, and when he received a dirty look from his brother, he only shrugged. "She's not wrong."

Carrick's eyes flared at me as he grabbed a glass of champagne from a passing server. "Hey, Mac, get me a scotch, will you? The bubbly's not gonna cut it."

The server, a kid who probably wasn't even my age, just bobbed his head and scurried away with his now empty tray.

Carrick turned to me and grinned, looking again like the wolf—or maybe the snake—he claimed he was.

I didn't know what else I'd been expecting, really. Obviously, things were going to be weird. He'd made himself scarce since the gambling night, and I hadn't had a chance to make peace. Or decide if that's even what I wanted with Nathan's jerk of a brother.

"Did you tell him?" Carrick asked as he swirled his drink and raised it in a silent greeting to another guest.

I pretended to smile at someone as well. "Of course I did."

Nathan scowled. "Don't, Carrick."

"Don't what?" Carrick asked. "Don't make sure Little Miss Strip-tease isn't about to take you for a ride?"

"Stop." This time, I was the one to speak.

"Make me, sweetheart," Carrick cut back before finishing the champagne and setting the glass on the nearby table with an audible crack. "I dare you."

I opened my mouth, but nothing came not. Not a sassy come-back, not a flirty retort. Nothing.

I was done for.

Again, Carrick faux-greeted someone else before turning back to us with a face like steel. "Wrong answer," he said before striding away.

Fear sliced through me. What did that mean?

I turned to Nathan. "He's...he's not going to tell anyone, is he?"

Nathan's hands cupped my shoulders and rubbed my arms. "You don't have to worry about that. But even if it did, would it matter?"

I thought about that for a moment. "I don't know...I mean, I didn't come here to keep secrets, but let's be real. I wasn't exactly prepared to be introduced as your stripper girlfriend, you know?"

I flapped a hand at the dress, the jewelry, the whole *costume* I was wearing. It was one thing to be confronted with the realities of my life in my own skin, another completely when I was essentially playing a role to help Nathan out.

Or was I? The dress and jewelry weren't things I planned to get used to. But if this was his life, and our relationship was for real, shouldn't I be preparing myself for more events like this? More polite conversations with his coworkers, meeting with his family, moments where I needed to represent...what, exactly?

Style? Smarts?

Whatever it was, I had the sinking feeling it wasn't me.

I didn't like that feeling. At all.

"Carrick won't say anything," Nathan broke through my thoughts. "For one primary reason: CEO."

I frowned. "What do you mean?"

"Whether or not my brother thinks our relationship is appropri-ate, he would still like this to fail," Nathan said calmly, though his voice walked a razor's edge. "Because Carrick wants the title my parents are hell-bent on giving me: CEO of Huntwell."

My mouth dropped. "He *does*?"

It made sense, as did his obvious resentment toward Nathan. Carrick was the only one of the brothers who actually worked for the company and had for years. And yet his older brother was supposed to be named his father's successor?

Unless he wasn't. Unless Nathan was too happy and settled to move. Unless he was too much of a success in his own life for them to think of dragging him back to Virginia.

Which was where I came in.

"I don't understand," I said. "Why would he torment me, then? Why not just let me continue doing what we're doing?"

"Oh, I think he will," Nathan replied. "But like everyone else in my family, Carrick thrives on control. He definitely wants me safely stowed away in New York. But he doesn't like liabilities. And you seeing him at a place like that is definitely a liability."

"Well, then," I said. "I don't really want to help Carrick, but I guess that's another reason to be the best damn couple in the room, isn't it?"

"Are we back to pretending?" He looked almost worried.

I popped up on my toes and delivered a kiss to his mouth. "Definitely not. Just…on our best behavior."

His lips quirked before he kissed me back. "Well, in that case, what would a good boyfriend do right now?"

I looked around the room, where people were mingling and drinking, and several others had taken to the dance floor before dinner was served.

"He would ask me to dance," I said with a grin. "Right now."

Nathan blinked. Then a slow grin spread across his face. "Would you like to dance?"

His happiness warmed my heart. "I would, thank you."

I let him lead me to the dance floor, where only a handful of couples were currently enjoying the smooth big band sounds blasting through the room. I knew a lot of them—partly because

Nonna loved Dean Martin, but also because a lot of jazz standards doubled as musical numbers.

"I did a solo to this once," I said when the band started playing "Someone to Watch Over Me." "My high school did a Gershwin review. The choir sang the song while I danced."

"Didn't you want to sing too?" Nathan wondered. "You said you could well enough to be on Broadway."

"I'm no soloist, but I have powerful lungs, and I can carry a tune," I said and then began to sing along with the lyrics while he moved me around the floor. "'There's a somebody I'm longing to see…I hope that he…turns out to be…someone to watch over me.'"

Nathan led me through a simple turn, then pulled me back into his arms, almost like he couldn't stand for me to be away from him for more than a second.

"I like your voice," he said, his own suddenly rough. "I think I like everything about you."

I chuckled, even as I lay my head on his chest. "Even my horrible pasta? And my mess in the bathroom?"

The hand at my waist traveled up my back, tracing the groove of my spine with those dexterous fingers. We whirled around again, but this time, he kept me pressed to his chest.

"Everything," Nathan murmured, so low I wasn't sure if he meant for me to hear it.

But I had heard. And it took my breath away.

The song ended, and we broke apart just enough for our eyes to meet. Nathan's hand at my back kept me close while he peered down at me, brown eyes fathomless, immeasurably deep.

"Joni," he said. "I…"

"Yes?" I asked.

This time, I could feel it. A word, deep in my heart. One I'd never said to anyone. Not Shawn. Not any other short-term boyfriend or lover or whatever you'd call them. Not a one.

But I wanted to say it to him. This peculiar man, with his quiet ways and particular rules and shy looks. Four letters. One syllable. Barely a sound at all.

Love.

Nathan opened his mouth to speak again, but suddenly, like he was overcome with whatever he was feeling, he took my face and kissed me.

It was a new kiss. One I'd certainly never experienced. Gentle and rough at the same time, insistent in its pressure yet questioning in its depth. His tongue touched mine, and I opened for him right there on the dance floor, clutching his lapels, uncaring about the people around us.

Would you love me? the kiss seemed to ask. *Would you love me if I loved you?*

Yes, I wanted to cry. *I already do.*

When our mouths finally broke, another song was playing—a rendition of the Charleston that had at least a few people breaking out the familiar moves.

I smiled, stuck in place. My heart was thumping, my hands still in a death grip on Nathan's jacket, my eyes unable to move from his swollen lips and the sight of his pink tongue peeking between them.

More. I wanted more.

And like any addict, I was going to get it.

"You're so beautiful," he murmured as he brushed a strand of hair out of my face, then cupped my cheek. "Christ, Joni, I..." He glanced down to where his own need was somewhat apparent against my leg.

I nearly bit my lip through.

"I don't..." I whispered as I gripped his jacket tighter. "I don't think I can wait until we get home."

At first, he didn't respond, but when the meaning behind my words sunk in, Nathan's eyes popped open. "*Oh.*"

I smiled. "Oh."

He glanced around. "But...where would we..."

"Nathan." I pulled his attention back to me. "Your family is the biggest donor in a room full of very big donors. I assume you can find one private room the museum would be willing to let us use, right?"

He swallowed and tugged at his collar. "I—yes. *Yes.*" Then something appeared to occur to him. "Come with me."

THIRTY-FIVE
MY FAVORITE CONSTELLATIONS

#8 O Ryan becuz he would win a fight.

Nathan Hunt was a man on a mission.

My hand clenched firmly in his, he led me out of the room at a pace that forced me to almost jog behind him. He ignored people calling his name, the appreciative stares of both women *and* men,

"Nathan!" called Charlotte Mueller as she noticed him pass. "Come have a drink with us!"

He didn't say a word.

Instead, he led me out of the hall and up a variety of steps, around corners and down hallways, and then finally down a walkway toward a massive round structure I recognized.

"The planetarium?" I asked. "Can we even get in there?"

Nathan gave me a shy smile. "I might have arranged earlier for it to be open."

I cocked my head. He *planned* this? For what?

"So, you were that sure you were going to get laid, huh?" I joked.

Nathan turned, and though it was too dark to read his expression, tension lifted his shoulders. "No. I only thought we might need a place to take some space." He looked around. "I also thought you might like it."

"Why's that?"

He turned. "Because you grew up in the city. I miss the stars sometimes. I thought maybe you would like to see them too."

He opened the door, then he led me inside the darkened planetarium with reclined seating arranged like a theater in the round circling a platformed stage in the center. Except the reclined seats faced up to a ceiling littered with digitized stars.

I stared up. He was right, of course. The sky was a little darker in Belmont than Manhattan, but the heavens were still mostly hidden by a halo of light that wreathed the city at all hours.

Nathan took a seat at the bottom of the theater.

"Do you mind if I join you?" I asked.

He frowned at the empty seats beside him, but when he realized I was staring at his lap, his expression softened. "Oh. No, of course not."

He opened his arms, allowing me to lie back in his lap so we could both tip back and look up at the faux night sky spinning slowly, constellations glowing in the domed ceiling.

"When I was in high school, some of us would sneak up to Woodlawn Cemetery at night to glimpse a few of these," I said. "But this is much clearer."

"You used to hang out in a cemetery?" Nathan sounded reasonably worried about that.

I chuckled. "Not in a witchy kind of way. We just went because it was quiet. We could smoke weed and look at the stars. Get a little peace from the city."

"I used to do the same thing at my family's house. On clear nights, I'd take a horse and ride out to the center of the property. There's a pond there, and no one around for miles. We'd camp, and I'd pretend I didn't have to go back." His arms wrapped around my waist and squeezed. "Sometimes, I could see the Milky Way."

I sighed, utterly content. The party was forgotten for the moment, as was the constant pressure of needing to perform for so many people, of trying to quiet the chaos in my head, the constant confusion.

Sometimes, it felt like that performance never stopped. I always had to be something more for others. In school, it was torture to stop myself from interrupting, and if I wasn't doing that, I was struggling to pay attention. With my family, it was trying to fit their expectation of what a good Zola should be: responsible, smart, *grown*. And with men…well, I didn't want to think about that right now.

Not when I was in *this* man's arms. I was free to be myself. Free to be only myself.

"There's Leo," Nathan said, pointing to a familiar constellation on the right. "You."

I smiled into his shoulder. "My lion."

A kiss was pressed to the top of my head. "That's right." He gave a long sigh. "I never knew it could be like this."

"What, watching constellations?"

There was a squeeze at my waist. "No. Being with someone." Nathan's nose burrowed into my neck, and he kissed me softly just under the ear. "Being with you."

I hummed in agreement. "Me neither."

Carefully, he turned me in his lap so I was sitting with my feet draped over his knees. His nose touched mine, and he kissed me, soft and true.

Our eyes met, and my heart thumped in response. He looked like he wanted to say something. Like he wanted me to say something.

"Are you honest with me?" he asked.

It was not what I wanted to hear.

"I…"

"Because I know I wasn't at first," Nathan went on as if he hadn't heard me stutter. "I know I kept things from you. Things you had to hear from Carrick."

"You mean about Isla?"

"And her mother," Nathan agreed. "Yes."

I traced a finger around his impossibly sharp jaw. "I understand why you didn't tell me. It's a sensitive thing."

Nathan was quiet for a long moment. "My parents want me to take over the company."

So that's what he was getting at.

"I know," I said. "Carrick told me tonight."

He frowned and muttered something like "fucking Carrick" under his breath. "I'm sorry I didn't tell you first."

"It's okay…" I considered. "But why didn't you?"

"It felt pathetic, I suppose. It's why they are so controlling. My father is obsessed with his first born taking on his mantle, but I've always fought it. I never wanted that."

"But they've used Isla to control you for years. Why set all these other requirements?" It seemed too complicated to make sense.

"Because they always thought I would fail. And maybe then returning home would be my decision, not theirs. And because…" He traced a finger over my knee through the lamé fabric. "Because they aren't bad people. I think they convinced themselves that my personal life, my disorder, allowed them to do things in the name of my best interests. The way many parents think they do."

I nodded. "I understand that one." It was exactly what my siblings had done just last month.

"But I won't fail," Nathan said. Gently, he pulled my face closer to his so our lips hovered over one another. "I won't fail this time because…I have you."

I remained silent, basking in the praise. There was no way he would know how such simple words made me feel.

"*Do* I have you, Joni?" he asked, his deep voice barely more than a whisper.

I sucked in a breath. I wanted to say yes. I wanted to throw my arms around his neck, promise him my heart, swear my love and every other emotion roiling in my head.

Except for the one thing that kept popping into my head.

Love is honest, he once said.

And I still had one more secret.

"What is it?" Nathan asked. "You're not looking at me. I don't know that expression."

Guilt, I wanted to say. That expression is guilt.

"Is there something you need to tell me?" he asked. "Do you not feel the same way? Because if you aren't, I'd rather know—"

"No!" I broke in, twisting around in his lap so intensely that I literally fell off, toppling down to the ground before he could catch me.

I paused there on the floor. On my knees. And looked up at him.

Nathan's eyes sparked with something I hadn't seen before. Something like fear.

"I can't..." He shook his head. "Maybe it's just me. I generally don't read these sorts of cues very well. But I can't help wondering if there was something else you needed to share. Something I need to be aware of." He gripped my hand. "Whatever it is, I can take it."

Tell him, a small voice told me. Tell him now. Tell him everything.

It wouldn't have mattered. I wanted to believe that. I wanted to believe that Nathan was different from literally every person on the planet who would judge me for what I'd done. That he would be exactly what he said he was—

"No," I finally said. "There's nothing you need to know...except that I feel the same."

He stared at me for a long time. "You do?"

I nodded and got up on my knees to lay my head on his stomach. "Yes, you sweet grump. I do. I lo—"

God, I'd almost said it. That was twice now.

But it wasn't right. I had a bad habit of putting the car—or was it cart?—before the donkey or horse or whatever animal.

Nathan wasn't someone to rush.

He was, however, someone worth loving.

And someone worth doing other things to as well.

"I love being with you," I finished as I sat back up on my heels and ran my hands down his powerful thighs. "And I love doing other things to you too. And right now, that includes this."

His mouth fell open as I pulled down his zipper.

"Joni," he mumbled. "I wasn't planning—"

"Don't fight it," I said as I pulled down his briefs, taking out the cock that was as hard as ever. For me. "When a girlfriend offers to give him head, a boyfriend should enjoy it."

That made him smile as I pressed my mouth to the tip, a reverent kiss. Nathan's entire body shuddered.

"I'll have you know," I said, "I've been told I'm very good at this."

His hand landed on the side of my head, urging me forward. "Show me."

So I did. I took his considerable length in my mouth as far as I could, breathing deeply through my nose, willing my body to relax. Nathan watched, seemingly entranced, every so often emitting a groan or a well-placed "Oh, *fuck*" that only spurred me on more.

Then I released him and smiled. "All right?"

He was staring up at the ceiling. "Christ. *Christ.* You weren't joking about your skill."

"I wouldn't joke about something like that." I ran my tongue up his shaft. "Stand up."

He peered down his body at me curiously. "Why?"

"Because now," I said as I pushed up on my knees, "you fuck my face."

His eyes popped open. "You actually want me to do that?" He sounded incredulous.

I tilted my head. "That depends. Would you want to?"

Nathan swallowed. Hard enough to make his bowtie look crooked. "I—yes. But it's not something I'd ever expect you or another partner to do."

I kissed the very tip of him, enjoying the way it made him arch against his seat. "Here's a universal truth about women: The better you treat us outside of our sex life, the filthier we want it to be." I slithered up his body until I covered all of him. "And you treat me very, *very* good, Dr. Hunt."

Too good, I almost said. Better than I deserved.

But instead, I kissed him, and he kissed me back just as thoroughly as ever, grunting as his hand slid over my bare waist, holding me in place so he could grind his hips upward against my waiting thighs.

It was everything I could do not to rotate my hips down and take him bare, just like that.

The idea thrilled and shocked me. Mostly because in all the years I'd been with anyone, I'd never even considered *that*.

"Joni." Nathan's voice was a rumble as his hand traveled up my back.

"Anything you want, babe," I mumbled back before he licked the inside of my mouth. "Just take it."

His tongue tangled with mine more intensely as one hand took solid hold of my hair and pulled just enough to make it bite.

The effect was immediate as I moaned into his mouth.

Nathan slid his other hand down to his waist, where he quickly unzipped his pants, then guided me back down his body until he could stand, and I was back on my knees in front of him, ready to worship at the altar of Nathan Hunt. I watched, mouth watering, as he took his cock in one hand and tapped the tip against my mouth.

"Open," he said quietly.

I obeyed.

Even with fingers threaded through my hair so tightly they pulled, he was careful. Aware of his size. Aware of the way he filled my mouth, inch by inch. Giving me time to taste him, explore him. Waiting patiently for me to open fully to him to enter.

Which I did.

"You look so beautiful like this." He breathed as he pushed into my mouth. "On your knees. My dick in your mouth. Big eyes looking up at me. Fuck."

His words weren't fancy. Just telling me how it was. How he felt. What he was doing. But they were my undoing just the same.

I relaxed my jaw, taking him deeper, enjoying the way he quivered as he started to move, holding the back of my head as he pushed all the way in.

"*Fuck*," Nathan groaned again. "Your throat feels amazing. *You* are amazing."

I blinked, eyes watering as much from my rising emotions as from what we were doing. And yet, I didn't want to fight it. I wanted Nathan to use me precisely because I knew he never would unless I asked. With him, I felt endlessly precious. Appreciated. More than that, I felt free to be his in every way I could. Demeaning ways. Beautiful ways. And every way in between.

He pulled out, and I gasped, unable to think straight as he hauled me up from my knees, back to my feet, back into his arms. Like he knew I needed the help to get my bearings back. Grounding. In him.

Then his mouth was on mine again, a lifeline that banished every thought I had, replacing them only with the energy between us.

"I need to be inside you *now*," Nathan said as he rotated me away from the seats and started walking me backward toward the platform, dragging my skirt up to my hips as we went. "Is that—are you ready?"

My knees buckled against the platform, and I fell backward, taking him with me, slipping my hands under his starched dress shirt to enjoy the ridges of his abdomen, the planes of his chest.

"Babe, you have no *idea* how ready I am for you," I told him honestly. "Like a waterfall down there, seriously."

That broad mouth quirked into another delicious half-smile—the one I was starting to think was reserved just for me. And then his mouth was on mine again as he ground into me, tugging up my dress, pulling aside the yards of fabric until I was finally able to wrap my legs around his waist, hold him close, feel that solid length of him brushing against the very core of me.

"Are you—" He broke away, then pressed his forehead to mine as he took a few deep breaths, clearly trying to get himself together. "Are you using any sort of contraception?"

I sucked in a breath of my own. I could barely think; I wanted him so badly. "Yes, an IUD, but—you don't have a condom?"

The idea seemed totally implausible. Nathan was the most careful, considerate person I'd ever met. It hadn't even occurred to me to prepare when I knew he would—a thought that made me feel guilty.

"No, I do," he said, to my utter relief. "It's only…" Another deep breath. Another deep exhale over my shoulder before he kissed me again.

It wiped every coherent thought from my brain again as he devoured my mouth, and the long length of him rubbed more insistently against my slick entrance.

Fuck. Me.

Literally.

I tilted my hips down. Just a little more. Just a little—wait.

Nathan peered down at me, his dark eyes vast pools of want. I wanted to dive into them and never come up.

"I've never wanted this with a woman," he said as he rocked against me, his cock literally teasing me. "Never wanted to be this... close."

This naked, he meant, stumbling as he was over his words. This bare.

As close as you could get to another person. And he wanted it with me.

I wrapped my arms around his head, wove my fingers into his lush hair, and guided him back for another kiss.

"Do it," I whispered. "Please."

And then he was there. One solid inch at a time, easing his way into me, watching me intently as I adjusted to the sheer size of him.

But this time, I knew what to expect.

"Oh, *God*," I moaned. "Nathan, *please*, baby. Fuck me *hard*."

That seemed to be his undoing. His hips started to move, pistoning in and out of me with the steadiness of a locomotive. He propped one hand over my shoulder so the other could wrap around my neck and squeeze. Just a little.

"Take it," he ordered. "Fuck, Joni, take *me*."

I cried out, though the hand at my throat stifled the sound. Gasping for breath, I flailed under him, under the fullness, the onslaught of his touch.

It was perfect. *He* was perfect. How anyone in their right mind could ever think otherwise was beyond me. Maybe I didn't deserve someone like him in the long run, but I'd be damned if I wouldn't take advantage of every moment just like this. Every second, he undid me completely. Maybe I'd be ruined forever, but I didn't care.

I was his anyway. Maybe I had been from the start.

"Focus," Nathan ordered. The hand at my neck slid down my torso, tugging on the halter of the dress, then falling down, down to find my clit. "Focus on us. Feel my hand on your clit. Feel my cock, deep inside you." He moved faster, sweat beading across his brow as he worked.

I found myself obeying. Because it wasn't exactly hard.

Obsession wasn't a new concept for me. Life had always seemed to work that way. Either things were so overwhelming that I couldn't pay attention at all, or one thing in particular would grab my attention so intensely that I couldn't see anything else.

Few things allowed me to escape the noise in my head and around me. Dance was one. And this…this intense joining of our bodies was another.

I couldn't see, hear, or sense anything else. Not one.

"FUCK!" Nathan shouted as he rammed forward. The thumb at my clit pressed a bit harder, making me jerk under his touch. "Are you close?" he asked. "Please tell me you're close. I can't—fuck, Joni, I can't hold off much longer."

"I'm—oh, *God!*" I moaned as he pummeled forward.

And then I was flying. Pleasure exploded through my entire body as I seized there under the sky. Stars dappled Nathan's face as he roared his climax to the heavens, holding my thighs like a life preserver, the only thing keeping him afloat in a sea of pleasure.

He collapsed forward, catching himself on his forearms, tenting me with his body against the dais.

"Your mouth," he mumbled as his own drifted up my neck. "Give me your mouth."

I did, succumbing to a kiss that was drowsy but no less thorough than ever. It tasted bittersweet with the knowledge that this moment would soon be over. But eager at the thought that there was only more to come.

"Joni, I…" Nathan pushed a few errant locks out of my face, thumb stroking my cheek as he gazed into my eyes. "What I feel… I'm not good at saying it, but…"

"Yes?" I wondered. My heart gave a thump like it wanted to jump out of my chest to meet with his.

I wanted to say it first. But I couldn't. I *couldn't*.

Nathan licked his lips and tried again. "Joni, I think I lo—"

"Nathan?!"

We both started at the sound of a shrill, high-pitched voice that bordered on a shriek.

"Fuck," Nathan muttered into my hair.

I could only gawk. This couldn't be happening.

"Nathan," I whispered. "Did your mother just catch us having sex?"

But before he answered, her voice filled the planetarium again with the worst words possible.

"Get your hands off my son!"

THIRTY-SIX
REGRETS

#1 That fukking video

"Nathan."

Lillian Hunt's imperious Southern voice echoed again around the planetarium's cavernous space. We both scrambled to right our clothes, Nathan tucking me behind him as he zipped up his pants.

We glanced at each other, but quickly broke into identical smiles.

"It's no use," I murmured as I reached up to fix my hair, which had mostly fallen out of its careful arrangement. At least I'd managed to cover my breasts again. "We're a friggin' mess."

Nathan looked as bad as me, his curls a riot atop his head, and my lipstick visible around his mouth, even in the dark.

He grinned back at me. And had never looked more handsome as he quickly tugged me back to him to steal one last kiss.

Apparently, first impressions were out the door. I couldn't have cared less.

"Get your *filthy* hands off my son!" Lillian shouted again as she made her way down to the bottom of the room, followed by, I realized, both of Nathan's brothers, as well as his father.

"Excuse me?" I snapped back before I could hold my tongue. I didn't put up with my fourth-grade teacher calling me stupid, and I wasn't going to take this lady's shit either, even if she was my boyfriend's mother.

"Mom, calm down," Nathan said, despite the fact that absolutely no woman *ever* obeyed those two words. "Joni's my girlfriend. What we were doing isn't exactly out of the ordinary, even if the location is."

Behind Lillian, Spencer snorted. "The Museum of Natural History." He looked up at the stars still circling the ceiling. "Pro move, bro. Didn't think you had it in you."

"None of us did." Carrick appeared beside him, his massive arms crossed over his chest, having removed his jacket at some point during the evening. "Did you really think you wouldn't be missed, you jackass? Dad's giving the keynote in ten minutes. Everyone sat down for dinner but you two."

"We just needed a minute," Nathan said as he hurried to right his clothes.

"Only a minute?" Spencer said. "Nate, I think we need to have a talk about endurance."

He held his hand up for a high-five to Carrick, who ignored him. But when he caught my eye, Nathan's youngest brother winked at me. Under normal circumstances, I might have laughed back. I had a feeling that if things were different, Spencer Hunt and I might have gotten along.

Right now, however, I was stuck on another point. The little speech Nathan's father was about to give. What Xavier had told me it would include. And the fact that his mother was *so* angry he was missing it.

Nathan had stood up for me too many times to count.

Now it was my turn.

"Maybe it's for the best that we miss the speech," I said.

The entire family whirled.

Lillian's expression flared. "And why, exactly, would *you* say something like that, you little trollop?

"Don't talk to her like that." Nathan's voice sliced through the air, causing his mother to reel as if she'd actually been cut.

"Nathan might not know what you were planning, but I do," I put in. "My brother-in-law told me all about it. You might know him —Xavier Parker, the Duke of Kendal. Yeah, he clued me in. Said all people could talk about before we arrived was your little plan to hang Nathan out to dry in front of thousands of people, including his colleagues."

Nathan's head whipped right back to his mother. "What is she talking about?"

She didn't confirm it, but Lillian's guilt played all over her refined features. Along with burning hatred, pointed directly at me.

"How dare you," she gritted. "How dare you interfere in a family affair! First, you wedge into my son's life—a little gold-digging nobody completely undeserving of everything he has to offer. You sashay around in public dressed like a common whore, and then you act like one to a society function? *You* think you have a right to object to *our* family's plans?"

Her harsh words cut like knives, but I wasn't done. More than I hated how she was characterizing me, I hated how she was talking about Nathan. Like at his age, he was nothing but a prize. A ward. Something to *manage* just because he wasn't exactly like her.

The same way people had talked about me my entire life.

"I have the right because, unlike you, I actually care about him," I snapped. "And when you love someone, you're honest with them. You care more about their well-being than your own selfish needs."

Over Lillian's shoulder, Carrick's eyes narrowed. But I was too fired up to notice.

"Did you even tell him you were going to name him the next CEO of your company?" I rattled on. "Or were you planning to threaten a teenage girl's life to force him into that, too?"

Spencer's mouth dropped. "She knows about Isla?"

Lillian covered her mouth. "Oh, Nathan, you *didn't.*"

"She knows everything." Nathan glanced at me and squeezed my hand, his deep brown eyes unexpectedly warm. "She knows me better than anyone."

Carrick looked between us, his shrewd gaze seeing something in the situation I couldn't put my finger on. "Do *you* know *her*, though?"

A chill fell over my entire body. I couldn't have said why. Carrick's eyes were cruel, but knowing as he pulled out his phone. My spine froze. No, he couldn't. There was no way he would know…

Then he punched something into the phone, and a moment later, everyone else's buzzed.

"What the fuck?" Spencer murmured as he opened the message. His eyes met mine with something I should have expected. A little bit of pity, yes. But mostly disgust.

"What is it?" Lillian demanded as she scrambled for her phone. "What did he send?" When she swiped to her messages at last, her vitriol landed on me like a flaming arrow to the heart. "Lord in *heaven*."

"Jesus," Spencer said as his eyes grew wide, unable to tear himself from the screen. "Nathan…you sure know how to pick 'em."

"Stop," I mewed, then turned to Nathan. "Please. Don't."

But he was already watching. And this close, I could see the reflection of the images on his glasses. Could hear the echoes of the familiar sounds.

The sickening slap of flesh on flesh.

The gleeful chuckle of the stranger on top of me.

The haughty comments from Shawn, standing behind the camera.

"You like that, baby?" I could hear him asking. "You like it when he treats you like the slut you are?"

And me. Moaning. Lost in a haze of whatever drug he had fed me that night. Barely conscious of where I was, what I was doing, or who I was doing it with.

Begging to be released. Begging for him to finish. Begging for it all to be over so I could stow it away and forget it had ever happened.

I'd done all right at that.

Until now.

"Joni..." Nathan's voice sounded lost. "Turn it off," he ordered his family. "Turn it all off. Delete it, and *never* look at that garbage again. Do you understand me?"

None of them obeyed.

I wished I were anywhere but here. Any*one* but myself.

"It's not...I didn't..." My head was a howling mess; I didn't know what to say. There were too many things swirling, including the story of how the scene on everyone's phones had happened, which was simultaneously too simple to believe and too complicated to explain.

"H-how?" I finally managed to get out as I turned to Carrick. "W-where did you get that?"

Carrick, at least, shoved his phone back in his pocket and smirked. "You didn't think I'd forget about your little friends at the game, did you? Or did you actually think I wouldn't do due diligence on my brother's supposed new flame?" He flipped his phone into his jacket, and I was grateful to see that Nathan's family had all finally stopped watching the horrible scene. "Your boy Vamos sang like a canary with a little cash. Especially after Nathan beat the shit out of him."

Beside me, Nathan growled. He actually growled at the mention of Shawn's last name.

"You didn't...you don't want to inherit the company at all, did you?" I asked. "You were waiting to sabotage us from the beginning, weren't you? So Nathan would have to come home after all."

"Well, I was hoping you'd fuck it up all by yourself, sweetheart, but you surprised me," Carrick said with a smirk. "Color me shocked that when my big brother finally fell in love, it was with someone like *you*. Even more when it actually seemed like it might work out."

I'd never wanted to punch someone so badly in my life.

"Lucky for me, you left a trail of dirty laundry a mile wide," he continued. "Why would I want that god-awful spotlight when I've already got the perfect place in the shadows?"

He made me sick. The whole situation did.

"Regardless of *my* motives," Carrick went on, "the ends justify

BOYFRIEND OF THE HOUR   421

the means. It's time for Nathan to come home. His judgment is obviously impaired if he's jumping into another relationship with someone like *this*. It's Isla all over again, and we don't want to get saddled with another situation like that."

"No," Lillian said almost gleefully. "We do not."

I turned back to Nathan. "Please. Don't let them do this. It was so long ago, and I didn't know...you have to believe me."

For a second, I thought maybe he would. I thought that maybe, just *maybe*, Nathan would demonstrate the same unconditional tolerance, compassion, and fairness I'd seen from the very beginning. That it wouldn't matter what stupid mistakes I'd made in the past because what we had in the present, what we might have in the future, would matter so much more.

But Nathan wouldn't meet my eye. He wouldn't look at anyone. He swallowed again and again, like he was trying to remember how to do it in the first place. His eyes were glazed, shocked, and his hands were once again opening and closing by his sides. He looked like he was drowning.

Like *I'd* drowned him.

"Nothing to tell me?" Nathan said in a voice shredded by resentment and regret. "Nothing between us?"

I hiccupped as tears started streaming down my face. "I...I tried..." I shook my head. "Please understand. I just...I just couldn't."

"I would have helped you." Those big brown eyes dragged up to meet mine, pools of anger and sadness. "I wouldn't have cared. If you'd just been honest with me. If you'd told me first."

"I didn't," I sobbed. "I didn't mean it. I didn't want to hurt you."

Two fingers slipped under my chin, drawing my eyes up to meet his one more time.

"The only thing that could ever hurt me was a lie." Then he dropped my chin and turned toward his family. "Let's go."

I watched as the four of them filed out of the planetarium, leaving me there, floundering under a sky full of stars that seemed to be laughing as they slowly winked out. I buried my face in my hands and cried until I didn't have anything else to give.

Then I picked myself off the ground and somehow made it out of there, keeping my head down as I passed guests on my way back to the exit.

Leave. I needed to leave. Where I'd go…well, I'd think about that once I was outside.

"Joni?"

I turned at the sound of a familiar voice and found Xavier Parker's tall form striding down the hall.

"Where are you going?" he asked, and his eyes flashed as he took in my condition. "What happened?"

"Nothing." I couldn't stop from crying all over again. "I need to leave."

"What is it?" Xavier asked as he took my arm. He glanced back toward the gala. "What can I do? Where can I take you?"

The blare of the loudspeaker sounded, and vaguely, I heard the sound of a deep man's voice. "I'd like to take this opportunity to announce my retirement from Huntwell Corporation, but that the company will continue in the hands of my capable son, Nathaniel…"

"Marie," I whimpered into my hands. "I just want my sister. I want Marie."

Xavier nodded, though he looked somewhat confused as he punched a message into his phone. "Done. Come with me."

HUNTWELL FARM

Nathan Hunt didn't have a home.

Maybe it was a funny thing to admit, being a thirty-four-year-old doctor who couldn't call anyplace home. But what did "home" even mean, anyway?

He had a place to live, of course. A decently sized two-bedroom apartment on Riverside Drive. It was his first purchase after buying into Manhattan Surgery Associates. But that was just a place to sleep.

Home wasn't the string of apartments he'd rented while attending medical school, doing his residency, completing two fellowships, and becoming the youngest burn specialist in New York City.

Nor was it the dormitory at Duke or the house in Durham he kept his senior year.

Nor did it lie behind the twenty-foot doors he was poised to enter the day before Easter.

His parents loved Huntwell Farm, as had his grandparents, and their parents before them. The estate had been in the Hunt family since General James Hunt had been granted more than fifteen hundred acres for his service to George Washington himself and had built the stone mansion complete with two gatehouses, three servants' quarters, a trout-stocked lake, and the Doric columns framing the front entrance.

Nathan, Carrick, and Spencer had been regaled with outlandish tales of the estate's history since before they could walk. But where Nathan's family saw history, he only saw the people whose backs this wealth was built on. Shadows of enslaved peoples, war criminals, and exploited workers roamed these halls. And, of course, the echoes of the unhappy present.

Those echoes were too loud off the polished oak and black-and-white marble. The rooms were too empty, all of them dressed in damask and curling millwork, like belles waiting for music they'd never hear. And his family was too cold, too forbidding.

No, Huntwell never was and never would be Nathan's true home, whatever that even meant.

He suspected that honor only belonged to her. And now she was gone.

The front door opened a solid five minutes after Nathan rang the bell, and he was met by Holden, the butler/driver/all-around dogsbody who had to be as old as the house itself. The old man pushed back his last surviving tuft of white hair, then offered the same droll expression he might have given the postman.

"Dr. Hunt," he said with the barest hint of familiarity, then stepped aside so that Nathan could drop his suitcase in the foyer.

"Holden." Nathan dropped his suitcase in the foyer. "I'll take that up after I speak to my parents."

"As you wish, sir."

As Holden took his jacket, it occurred to Nathan, for likely the thousandth time, that the butler could reasonably use his given name. Just as it also occurred to him that Holden had no reason to guide him through the halls he'd grown up in or that meetings with his parents might be more comfortable if they were held in the family room or even the rec room rather than one of the formal parlors with stiff antique furniture.

But Nathan said nothing as he followed the butler down the black-and-white-marbled corridor, their footsteps echoing off the high ceilings and portrait-covered walls. Because this was just the way it was here. This was the routine.

Why question it?

They found Lillian and Radford sitting in the second parlor, a fire blazing in one of the house's thirty-four hearths, despite the fact that it was a balmy sixty-four degrees outside. Lillian was always cold, and Radford was always indifferent. Lillian was sipping her customary cup of afternoon coffee—decaf, of course—while Radford puffed at one of his favorite cigars as he paged through the Business section of the *Washington Post*.

"They still haven't made the announcement," he remarked to Lillian. "Damn *Post*. Knew I should have bought it when we had the chance."

"Carrick said they won't until Nathaniel confirms," Lillian replied. "And that stubborn boy refuses to take any of their calls."

"That's because I never accepted it," Nathan said, startling both of them enough that Radford ashed directly onto his cashmere cardigan, and Lillian spilled a bit of coffee onto her linen pants.

"Oh, shoot!" she cried, dabbing at the spot. "Holden!"

"I'll fetch a towel at once, ma'am," the butler said in his droll voice before disappearing into the hall.

"You might have warned us," Lillian said as Nathan entered the room.

She set her coffee on a side table and stood, hand placed on her still-narrow hips. His mother had always been petite, to the point where Nathan wondered if she didn't under-eat. It was common enough in his patients her age. Along with osteoporosis.

"I just arrived," he said.

There were no kisses.

Nathan looked around. "Where are they?"

Lillian and Radford exchanged looks that Nathan couldn't quite interpret. Still, they insisted on sharing these wordless moments together, as if they knew he couldn't participate in them. He never could.

Except with Joni. He knew all of the emotions on her incredibly expressive face and had spent months studying them well before she'd ever visited the clinic. Had a list fifteen pages long in his note-book documenting them. And when, if by some chance, a new expression appeared, she had always told him what it meant. Always.

No one had ever been that transparent. Certainly not these two.

"Nathan, sit down and visit," his mother called. "Don't be rude."

"I didn't come here to visit." He glanced between his parents, daring them to argue. "I've done everything you asked for. I took a sabbatical from my practice, shadowed the interim CEO for the last two months, and learned the business like you wanted. In return, you said you would make things right. So where are they?"

He wasn't exaggerating. He wouldn't have come here at all if it hadn't been for one thing: Joni Zola was nowhere to be found. Until his parents had called last week and said Carrick's contact had finally had some success.

It had been two months since he'd walked away from her in the planetarium; the image of her tear-streaked face burned into his brain. Less than twenty minutes later, right after his father had opened his mouth in front of two thousand wealthy donors to the Mt. Sinai Children's Hospital and announced that he was nomi-nating Nathan to be the next CEO of Huntwell, Nathan had marched back out of the room to find Joni and take her home, only to discover she was already gone.

And he hadn't seen her since.

He'd been angry, yes. But it hadn't taken long before he realized his anger was displaced. It was true that she had withheld damning information and refused to trust him. But obviously, the horrific video that existed of her having sexual relations with another man wasn't consensual.

No, if anything, he was angry at the people who had forced her into that situation and used it to control her, just the same as his parents used Isla to control him. He was angry at Carrick for sharing it with everyone else. And he was angry with himself for how he'd behaved toward her about it. He was angry that he'd left her alone.

And so, Nathan had forced himself to watch it again, if only to verify that, yes, she was clearly under the influence of some kind of drug. Clearly, very young—she couldn't have been older than sixteen. Clearly in a state of distress.

He'd destroyed his phone in a fit of rage he hadn't experienced in well over a decade. Then he had personally gone to every one of his family members to make sure all of them had deleted the incriminating video as well.

It was still floating around out there. But before he could deal with that, he needed to find her first.

The following day, he'd bought a new phone and called her, intending to bring her back from wherever she'd taken shelter for the night.

The call had gone straight to voicemail.

He'd waited another day before calling again. Texting. Another day. Another day.

On the fourth, he'd canceled his surgeries to drive to her sister's auto shop in Belmont. Had seen first-hand the dingy break-room where Joni had been sleeping before she'd come to stay with him.

Lea had called him a bum and threatened to sic her husband on him, but not before telling him that Joni had left New York.

Boston. She had a brother in Boston.

Another dead end, and one that came with more threats of violence.

The Zolas clearly knew where their sister was and weren't worried, and that fact alone gave him some comfort.

So, he continued to leave messages. And waited.

Nothing.

In the end, he'd finally spoken to Carrick again, if only to ask him to get help from his contacts at the FBI and the CIA to find her. Which he would...so long as he made a deal with their parents to get them off Carrick's back. Sabbatical. Huntwell. The two months passed.

Then two days ago, his parents had said Joni was found. And that they would bring her here, along with Isla, to make things right between them all again, if he would come too.

Now, his parents shared that queer look he didn't understand.

"What does that look mean?" he asked. "What are you saying to each other?"

His mother rose to place her hands on his shoulders. Her skin was almost as pale as the white roses planted on the grounds outside but touched with unnatural pink across the cheeks; she pressed it lightly to his. A pantomime of a kiss, scented with Chanel No. 5.

"Now, Nathaniel, don't go getting all upset, sugar," she said. "But things aren't *exactly* like we said."

His hands balled into fists at his side. "What do you mean?"

"Lillian, just tell the boy and get it over with," his father barked, still poring over the fucking newspaper. Smoke wafted across the room toward him, and Nathan wrinkled his nose. He'd always hated the way those things smelled. Not to mention the cancerous effects of secondhand smoke.

"Isla's upstairs in the nursery," Lillian said. "She's eager to see you. So says her companion, anyway."

"That girl is never eager to see anyone," Radford grumbled.

Nathan frowned. "And Joni?"

Another shared glance. This one felt like it dropped a hammer through his chest.

"She's not here," his mother allowed.

"Where. Is. She?" Nathan could barely get the words out through his teeth.

His mother sighed. "Do you really—"

"Where the *fuck* is my girlfriend?" Nathan didn't yell. He almost never yelled—not since he was a child and used to immediately regret the consequences at the expense of his father's backhand.

But he did snap. And at moments like these, he wasn't interested in holding it in.

"Girlfriend? Can you still even call her that?" His mother's tone was playful. Joking. Like the students who used to tease him as a child when he didn't understand knock-knock jokes.

"Where?" Nathan demanded as he smacked his hand on the door loud enough to make both his parents jump.

"She's in Paris," his mother fairly spat out. "With her sister, staying in some little hovel near the river. Though I'm sure I don't know why you're so fixated on the girl. She's nothing but a—"

"Stop right there," Nathan interrupted, already spinning to leave the room. "Especially if you want me to come back."

He marched out without listening for a reply, already tapping in a search for flights to Paris from DC as he took the yawning staircase two steps at a time. At least he had a direction. Now, he had to take care of the other item on his agenda.

He knocked on the door of the nursery, which had barely been touched since he was a child. The walls were still painted sky blue with antique Victorian children's books framed around the room. Two children's beds remained at the far end, perfectly made up as if the ghosts of his and Carrick's childhoods still slept in them every night.

It was an odd room for them to put a seventeen-year-old girl, but it was the only one Isla had ever liked in the big, cold house. So, at least his parents had been considerate enough there.

Isla was sitting on one of the old rocking chairs near the big bay window, looking out onto the back grounds, speaking quickly to the woman sitting next to her, whom Nathan recognized as Mary Brennan, the full-time occupational therapist he had hired when Isla had entered high school.

Mary smiled and stood. "Dr. Hunt, hello. It's wonderful to see you. Isla, Nathan's here. Would you like to say hello?"

Isla stood and turned to Nathan almost immediately, completely unaware of the way the sunlight caught on the ridges of the heavy scarring painting her face. She was dressed in one of the countless pairs of blue ponte pants and shirts she preferred, tailored to be rid of seams. They covered the worst of the scars on her arms and legs, but there were still a few that wrinkled her left hand, permanently curled from the damage.

"Hello, Nathan," Isla said. "Mary said you would be arriving ten minutes ago. You're late. We've been waiting twenty-seven minutes."

He smiled. A greeting. One that included his name. It was quite an improvement from the last time when she hadn't wanted to stop working on a drawing of a horse. She was, however, holding a book with a horse on the front now. Some things hadn't changed at all. He hoped they never would.

"Hello, Isla," he greeted her back. No hugs. She didn't like them, and he couldn't say he blamed her. He only liked them himself from a few people. "What are you reading?"

"*Horse Brain, Human Brain,*" Isla told him. "Spencer recommended it to me when we arrived yesterday. He was out at the stables and said I could see the new stallion, which is black with a white spot on its head like Black Beauty, except Black Beauty wasn't a stallion, he was a gelding, which is unfortunate because he probably would have made lovely foals with a mare. Anyway, your new stallion will probably make a lot of foals." She turned to Mary, who was watching the interaction kindly. "That was technically three sentences, right? Even though the middle was a run-on."

Mary smiled kindly. "Yes, Isla, it was. And they were very good sentence too. Would you like to ask Nathan any questions back?"

Isla seemed to think on that for a moment, then looked up. "Do you know when I'm going back to school, Nathan?"

Nathan nodded. "After the break. Easter's on Sunday, and then the campus is open again."

Isla pinched her cheek lightly as she nodded in the exact same way he just had. "Good. I don't like it when we have to leave."

"I know you don't," Nathan said. "I'm sorry for that. I know it's disruptive. But you seem to be doing well."

"They have a lot of horses there." Which was as close to Isla's agreement as he would get. "My favorite's name is Aurora. She's a gray mare and very gentle. I get to ride her on Tuesdays, so long as I finish my math homework on time. I don't like algebra."

Nathan nodded. The school for autistic children Isla had attended since age twelve included an equine therapy center. It was one of the reasons for the girl's obsession with horses and had been a major motivator in some of her social skills development. Even just a few years ago, holding a full conversation with Isla in this way would have been unthinkable.

He was also glad they had something they could share.

"Are you interested in riding this weekend?" he asked. "I'm sure Spencer would take you out."

That seemed to get Isla's attention. Her gray eyes, so like her mother's, flashed at him before quickly moving away as she reached up to pinch her cheek again. "Why aren't you riding?"

Nathan sighed. "I have to leave tonight. I'm going to Paris."

"To get your girlfriend?"

Nathan peered at Mary, who shrugged, then back at Isla. "How did you know I have a girlfriend?"

"People talk a lot here when I'm around. They act like I don't listen, but I do. Especially when it's about you. They don't like your girlfriend, though. Why don't they like your girlfriend?"

Isla was tapping her fingers on her book now. A clear sign that she was agitated.

"I don't know," Nathan said honestly. "They don't know her very well."

"Do you think I would like her?"

Nathan nodded. "I think you would. She's very nice, talkative, and open with others."

"Why do *you* like her?"

That was easy. Nathan had spent more than one evening cataloging exactly that on too many pages in his little black notebook. The list was very long, but most of the items could be condensed into a few key traits.

"She's honest," he said. "She is who she is, and she doesn't try to be anything different. And she appreciates the same in me and anyone else."

"Is that all?" Isla didn't seem satisfied. "That doesn't seem like very much to like. Does she have any other interests? Does she like horses too? What kind? Has she ever ridden a thoroughbred?"

"I don't know. But there's a lot more," Nathan said. "Too many things to list right now."

Things like the way her green eyes sparkled when she made him smile. Or how she tried extremely hard at everything she did, even if she didn't succeed. Or her abject loyalty to the people she cared about, even when they didn't always return the favor.

Too many things to explain to himself, much less a seventeen-year-old.

"Do you love her?" Isla wanted to know.

Nathan blinked. It wasn't often he was taken off guard by Isla's brutal bluntness, but it did happen. Like it had right now.

Particularly when she was asking something like this. Since when had Isla cared about the concept of love? Or even thought about it?

She really *was* making progress.

"What do you think love *is*?" Isla pressed on. "I read about it in the *Life Lessons from the Heart of Horses*, which was really less about horses than I thought it would be, but the concept is always confusing. Is it a thing or a verb? I know it can be used as both. But how do you know what it is? How do you know which one you are feeling? Or which one someone else is feeling?"

Nathan thought about that for a moment. "I don't know. It's difficult to identify."

Isla nodded. "I mean, I *love* horses. I love learning about them, I love riding them, I love drawing them, and I love everything about them. I'm going to go to college first to get a degree in zoology, and then I'm going to become a big animal vet just so I can continue taking care of them until I'm old. But I don't think that's the same thing as loving a person, is it?" She looked at Mary. "That was four, and then I stopped. But I don't think the first one counted."

Nathan found himself smiling as she spoke. He'd always enjoyed this about Isla—her unabashed dedication to whatever she found interesting. She had the typical fixations of people on the autism spectrum, but there was joy in that kind of attention that a lot of people could learn from.

"I don't think so," he said. "But maybe there are some things in common. Your interest and passion, for instance, might be a feeling you have for a person too."

"What else?" Isla said. "In case I ever feel that way."

"It's hard to define," Nathan said. "I'm learning about it myself. But I think it has to go beyond that. Love is about how you communicate with someone else. More than anything, I think love is honest. It's when you can be completely yourself with another person, and they can be completely themselves with you. And when you care for exactly what each other is, and maybe even care about them as much as you care for yourself…maybe that's love."

Isla looked to Mary. "That was seven sentences. He should have stopped talking."

Mary shrugged. "No one's perfect. I think Nathan may feel as strongly about this topic as you do about horses."

Isla turned back to him. "Is that true? Are you obsessed with love like I am with horses?"

Nathan looked around the room as if searching for an answer. It was then he realized that love wasn't necessarily the same emotion every time, which was probably why it was so unquantifiable. It didn't fit into a rubric, wasn't a clearly described syndrome in the DSM-5, nor could it be diagnosed with a list of symptoms.

But he knew what it was because of the people who inspired it in him.

"No," he answered finally. "But maybe I am a little obsessed with the people I feel love for."

People like the girl in this room, whose blunt manner still charmed him as much when she was seventeen as when she was four.

And people like the woman waiting for him in Paris. The one who still had no idea how he felt.

THIRTY-SEVEN
THINGS I HATE ABOUT PARIS

#10 Marie lives hear but i need her

"It's fine, really. I'm barely here, and it's not like we didn't share a room for most of our lives anyway. I'm used to it."

I blinked my eyes open into the distinct Parisian light. They said the light here was pink, but I wasn't sure I saw a difference. From Marie's apartment, a tiny rooftop studio that was probably a maid's quarters when the building was originally constructed, it looked pretty damn gray to me. Just like my mood for the last two weeks.

My sister's muted voice continued to float in from her balcony, where she was in deep conversation with someone else. Someone I also knew. Sort of.

"It's just weird, you know? She usually bounces back from things like a basketball. When Tommy Lopez dumped her in the tenth grade, she cried for an hour and then found a new boyfriend on the walk home. But she's been in Paris, of all places, for two months, and all she's basically done is sleep, eat, and watch Netflix."

"Ces is worried about her too," came a deeper British voice. "She wouldn't stop pacing the house until I agreed to come and check on her. Again."

I frowned. Xavier was back?

Two months ago, Xavier Parker had been my unsuspecting savior. He'd whisked me out of the hospital benefit so quickly I didn't even remember the steps from the museum to his private car to the apartment, where he'd helped me pack the necessities before bringing me straight to his private jet and taking me to Paris to see Marie as requested.

I'd barely noticed any of it.

I hadn't been able to do anything but wilt once I'd arrived. Had left my phone, battery dead, in my backpack while I spent my days sleeping, allowing Marie to let our family know I was alive. Everyone else could fuck off. I was too busy wallowing in the look on Nathan's face when he saw that video.

Shame, pity, disgust. They were all there. The expressions I'd come to expect from everyone else in my life. But never him.

"Do you think she'd be better off in London?" Xavier was wondering. "Or maybe she should go to Boston or back to New York. Face the music, as they say."

"Matthew's already got his hands full with the new baby, and I doubt London would be any better than here. Plus, with Frankie about to pop any day, you guys deserve some time on your own," Marie replied. "New York isn't any better. Kate's in LA on business, and Lea's just done. She's still mad Joni got wrapped up with those gangsters."

"Yeah. That might not have been Joni's fault, really," Xavier said. "What about Rome, with Sarah?"

"*No.* Nonna doesn't need to get wrapped up in all of this. The only traveling she'll want to do is to visit her great-grandbabies. Don't worry her with Joni's drama."

"Well, I still think Lea's being a bit unreasonable."

"She's right about one thing. Joni shouldn't have been at that sketchy event to begin with. I still don't even know what to think about the video." There was a sigh.

Ah, yes. That. I still couldn't bring myself to say it out loud. My whole family knew about the recording that could not be named. The moment Marie had opened her door, at just past noon her time, I had burst into tears and told her the entire story. About Nathan. About Kyle. About Shawn. About the years of secrets I'd kept even from her.

My brother had been working with his police buddies in New York to track down the original and get it buried. I hadn't seen it uploaded to the internet, but it was only a matter of time. If Shawn knew people were looking for it, he'd also know he had a gold mine.

"Have you had any more luck finding it?" Marie asked. "Or the guy who filmed it?"

I chuffed. Apparently, big, mighty Xavier and his billions had been looped in on the search.

"That wanker's gone missing," Xavier said. "Last seen in Belmont around the Antonis, like your brother said, then disappeared in Newark. He knows we're looking for him."

"I still can't believe I never knew about him."

"Ces feels the same way," Xavier told her. "Says she should have known something was going on."

"Frankie left for school the next year," Marie countered. "Joni and I were still sharing a room until then. *I* should have known something was different. We were still kids."

I cringed at the pity in her voice. Out of all our siblings, Marie was the only one who had never felt sorry for me. Growing up, we'd always been such polar opposites that, as much as I hated to admit it, I'd always enjoyed goading her jealousy. I was the one who was popular, who was pretty, who the boys liked. She never even went to her senior prom. I went to five, starting in the eighth grade. She wasn't even kissed until she was twenty, whereas I'd claimed that honor at nine.

But what had served as badges of honor when I was a teenager now felt like big scarlet stamps that read one thing: Joni Zola. Big fat slut.

The tiny French doors opened with a creak on the other side of the privacy screen separating Marie's "bedroom" from the rest of the apartment. I rolled over into a pillow onto the side Marie had given me and stifled a groan.

"I know you're awake, you bum," she called. "I could see your shadow moving through the window, so stop eavesdropping and get up."

I shoved myself up from the bed with a groan. "Still such a snitch."

Xavier chuckled.

A few minutes later, I joined them in the kitchen, where Xavier was whipping us up some breakfast. I glanced at the clock on the wall. One thirty. Okay, maybe it was lunch.

"You look like you just got dragged through a swamp," Marie said as she took a sip of tea. "Think you might shower today?"

I shot her a dirty look. "You're such a brat, Mimi."

"Pretty sure that's what *you've* always been called. Glad to see a little spark, though."

She seemed to wait for my normal retort, but I had nothing else. Back home, I would have gone for the low-hanging fruit. Teased her about dressing like the Amish or keeping her virginity locked up tighter than a drum.

But all that was gone now. Marie might still have been waiting for the perfect man to deflower her, but the glasses-wearing nun had disappeared during her time in Paris, replaced by a chic, dark-haired nymph that more than resembled a young Audrey Hepburn now that she'd cut her hair last month. And I, usually called the "pretty one" of the family, had morphed back into the ugly duckling in my frumpy bun and faded sweatpants.

Marie sighed. "I'm going to run to the market for the salad stuff. Can you handle her?"

Xavier shot me a quick blue-eyed look, like I was some kind of flight risk. "I think so."

Please. Like I was going anywhere dressed like a homeless puppy.

Marie left, and I flopped at the kitchen table, surprised when Xavier immediately set a steaming cup of stovetop espresso and a biscuit in front of me. It was hard, sometimes, to remember that before he discovered he was a duke, he'd first been a chef and eventually a restaurant mogul.

Apparently, the man hadn't forgotten his way around a kitchen.

"Drink," he ordered. "And then we should talk."

I obeyed while he continued to work at the stove, cooking up something that looked like an omelet.

I honestly couldn't care less. Nothing tasted good anymore anyway.

"We don't know each other very well, do we?" Xavier wondered as he slid the omelet onto a plate and immediately started mixing another like a well-oiled machine.

I looked up from sipping my coffee as he slid the steaming eggs in front of me. "Don't know why we would. You spent maybe five minutes with my family before taking my sister to London with you. And that was after knocking her up and disappearing. But you did marry her in the end, I guess."

It was hard not to sound bitter. In general, I was happy for Frankie. These days, she was living a fairy tale that most people would kill for. Rich husband, baby on the way. She was even planning to go back to school in the fall to study all those stuffy books she loved so much.

She had a purpose. She had everything.

And I had absolutely nothing.

"Yeah, well. That's probably my fault," Xavier said while getting to work on the next omelet. "I've never been good with families."

I crinkled my brow. "How does that work?"

He sighed. "What's Ces told you about my life? How I grew up?"

"That you lived in South London, became a big-shot chef, and then found out you were going to become a duke later." I gave him a pointed look before biting into my biscuit. "And didn't tell her that last part until it was way too late."

The big man had the decency to look ashamed. "Yeah, well. That's more because I didn't quite believe it myself. Not for a long time." He sighed. "I was raised in a two-bedroom flat by a single mum. She died when I was sixteen. After that, my dad shoved me into boarding school just to be done with me. I might have been a duke's son, but everyone said I was a bastard until I was nineteen." He searched my face for recognition. "Bastards can't inherit titles in England. They found my parents' marriage certificate, which made me legitimate, but I could never shake that feeling of being worthless. Just like everyone said."

I scowled at my plate. "If this is a pep talk, it's a terrible one."

Xavier flipped the eggs onto another plate, presumably for Marie, then came to sit next to me at the table. He was a big man. Taller even than Nathan, but not as broad. All sharp angles in his cheekbones and steely blue eyes lacking the warmth and solidness in his body that Nathan had.

God, I missed Nathan. More than once over the past two months, I'd rolled over half asleep to snuggle him, only to find my sister's bony body shoving me away. It made me want to cry every time.

"It wasn't until I met your sister that things really changed for me. For the first time, I found someone who saw me for who I really was. More than a label or a title."

I peered up at him. "And your point is?"

"This bloke of yours. He's been calling."

I perked. "He has?"

Xavier nodded. "Leaves messages with my assistant almost every day. I'm not supposed to say anything, but I wondered...everyone's got their boxes, see? The ones we can't seem to escape until someone else sees us differently. I wondered if maybe he did that for you. Like Francesca does for me."

I looked at him for a long time.

"It wouldn't matter if he did," I said. "I crossed a line. There's no coming back from that now."

"You sure about that?"

I nodded. "If there's one thing this whole disaster has taught me, it's that it's time to grow up. Learn to be realistic and stop wanting to be things I'll just never be."

Xavier worried his jaw a moment, then nodded. "Well, in that case, I think Marie's wrong about you staying here with her. You need to move around, do something. Pull yourself out of your misery."

"Gee, thanks," I spat. "I'll be sure to get on that."

But Xavier wasn't put off by my sour attitude. "I've got six restaurants in London alone and an extra bedroom in our flat. I can get you work, and on your days off, you can help Ces with the babes. You got a better plan?"

I stared at my still-full plate. It was a good offer for someone like me. Someone with no outlook to speak of. No future.

Still, I couldn't bring myself to say yes. Just like I couldn't bring myself to do anything else these days.

"I—I'll have to think about it," I said finally.

Xavier peered at me a bit more, but didn't seem interested in pushing.

"All right," he replied, getting back up to finish lunch. "I'm staying at the George V until Thursday. Let me know by then, and you can fly to London with me." He looked over his shoulder. "But the next time your fella calls, you want me to take it?"

I had to think about that too.

Before I could answer, there was a knock at the door.

Xavier turned. "Marie must have forgotten her key."

But it wasn't Marie. It was someone else entirely.

"Joni?" The familiar voice that had been weaving through my dreams for the last two months sounded deep and tired through the old wood door. "Joni, it's Nathan. Please let me in."

THIRTY-EIGHT
MORNING ROUTINE

Step #4 dont forget to shower

Xavier glanced back at me, a silent question: *Do I let him in or not?*

I was frozen in place, unable to move. Unable to answer. He was here. In Paris. After two months of trying and failing to convince myself that whatever we had was fake from the start, Nathan Hunt stood on my threshold, as real as it got.

In the end, I didn't have to make the decision.

"I'm here, I'm here," Marie called behind him. "I managed to grab the last bundle of parsley, but it's Italian, not curly—who's this?"

She came to a stop next to Nathan while Xavier moved back into the kitchen and leaned against the counter with folded arms, apparently satisfied that Marie could take over, though he'd remain for support.

Neither Nathan nor I answered. We were too busy staring at each other across the doorway while Xavier and Marie looked between us.

"I think it's the doctor," Xavier finally answered Marie's question. "Hunt." He glared at Nathan. "Took you long enough, mate."

Marie mouthed an "Oh" to herself but didn't say anything more as she hovered behind Nathan, who was currently taking up most of the doorframe, hovering on the threshold like a vampire waiting to be let inside.

But he wasn't a vampire, cold and heartless. My Nathan was the definition of warmth, solid flesh, and endless soul.

Well, not *my* Nathan. Not anymore.

Oh, my heart ached.

"Hello, Joni," he said, brown eyes deep and mournful on the other side of his lenses.

"Hi, Nathan." I felt like I was shrinking. My voice, my body, everything.

My body. Otherwise known as the flesh sack that probably smelled like sleep, eggs, and three days without washing.

Gross.

Immediately, I backed away from the door.

"No," Nathan started, reaching out. "Don't—"

"Joni, hold on," Marie started. "Just give him a chance."

"I just, um, gotta j-jump in the showerberightbackbye!" My speech was a blur as I turned and sprinted for the tiny bathroom.

Before anyone could stop me, I locked the door, started the water, and took several deep breaths to calm my tap-dancing heart.

He was here. After months apart and nothing but replays of that horrible night to fill my head, he was here.

And I had no clue what to say to him.

It was the longest shower of my life. Not just because it had been several days since I'd bothered to clean myself at all, but because I was avoiding the fact that Nathan Hunt was sitting in the middle of my sister's apartment, presumably making small talk with my family members, and waiting for me to come out and face whatever he had flown all the way here to tell me.

I was scared to death to hear what that might be.

So, I cleaned. I scrubbed my face and my skin and even my belly button and in between my toes. I washed my hair twice just to make it squeaky clean and actually waited the full five minutes the bottle of conditioner recommended before rinsing it out. I shaved every inch of my body I could reach, brushed my teeth twice over, flossed and gargled, then just stood under the running water for at least ten more minutes until a bang on the door from Marie warned me not to run up her water bill in my misery.

Thirty minutes later, I emerged, hair scrunched into air-dried waves, makeup fully done, wearing my favorite big red hoops, and dressed in one of Marie's ankle-length black skirts with a T-shirt tied above my navel that read "Your Goose is Cooked" across the bust. Not the most stylish outfit in the world, but all my clothes were dirty. It was the best I could do.

I found the apartment suspiciously empty except for Nathan, who was sitting at the kitchen table, drumming his fingers on the worn wood while he waited.

He looked the same as ever. And by the same, I meant fucking delicious in a pair of simple navy trousers that hugged his thick thighs and a white button-down shirt rolled up at the cuffs. Perfect nerd style that only just hinted at the muscle underneath the tailored lines.

My kryptonite. Here to ruin me.

Nathan turned when he heard me approach and stood immediately, reached out, then pulled back his hands as if he wasn't sure what to do with them.

"Hi," I said.

"Hello."

We blinked at each other like owls. Separately, we both could be awkward, but we'd never been awkward together. I couldn't say I cared for it.

"Um, where are Marie and Xavier?" I looked around as if they might jump out from the balcony again. Maybe yell "April Fools!" and rip off Nathan's face like a mask on Scooby Doo.

Okay, admittedly, that was just ridiculous. But my brain was churning. It didn't know where to stop with the catastrophes.

"Xavier went back to his hotel, and your sister said she needed to go for another walk." Nathan's mouth twisted to one side. "I think that was an excuse to leave us alone together."

"I'm sure it was," I agreed. "Honestly, she's probably just excited I finally showered and thinks you're the reason."

"You haven't been showering?" Nathan sounded honestly alarmed.

Shit. So much for playing it cool. I was nervous, and when I was nervous, my mouth had a tendency to run itself, spilling secrets and embarrassing details. Usually, they were about others, which is why none of my friends or family had ever trusted me to keep a secret. But right now, I had nothing to spill but my own mortifying existence.

"I've been...upset," I admitted, suddenly focused on picking lint off the waistband of Marie's skirt.

We stood there for a while longer, but when he didn't reply right away, I forced myself to speak before he could say something that would break me. Something like "Good, you deserve it." Even if it was true.

"Why are you here?" I asked.

Nathan breathed. And took a step toward me. "I found you. And I came."

"What do you mean, you found me?" I asked. "I wasn't hiding."

"You weren't?"

I shook my head, but then wondered if that was kind of a lie. I hadn't purposefully tried to evade everyone I knew. I just hadn't felt like talking to them.

"Your phone hasn't been turned on in two months," Nathan said with another step forward. "And your voice mailbox has been full for the last five weeks."

Okay, no surprise there.

"I tried to contact your family members, but your sisters both slammed their doors in my face, and your brother threatened to have me arrested for harassment if I tried to reach anyone else."

So, that was my problem. I'd trusted that since my siblings knew where I'd gone, they would tell any interested parties that information if and when that was necessary.

Apparently, they'd been holding a grudge against one particular party.

"So...how *did* you find me?" I asked.

One more step. "My brother. Carrick has contacts with the CIA. They tracked your passport to Paris. That's when I remembered you had a sister in school here."

I swallowed and nodded. It all made sense.

"You don't look very good," Nathan said as he ventured to within a foot.

I looked up and up and up with a scowl. "Gee, thanks."

"That's sarcasm."

My scowl deepened. "*Yes.*"

"Just making sure." Nathan frowned down at me. "I don't want to leave any part of this conversation up for interpretation." He looked me over again. "I'll rephrase, you don't look like yourself."

"Because I'm wearing Marie's old Amish castoffs?" I pulled at the skirt. "I think I can make sexy nun work for me."

"You would probably look beautiful in anything," Nathan said without a trace of his own sarcasm.

I hated it when he did that. I hated it because it made my heart quiver. Made me want to throw myself against that broad chest of his and kiss him until we both ran out of breath.

I hated it because I had no right to do those things anymore. If I ever had.

"But you've lost weight, and you were already quite thin," he went on. "There are hollows in your cheeks and under your eyes that weren't there two months ago. Your lips look a bit dry, like you haven't been drinking enough water, and your skin is much paler, despite the fact that it's spring and you should be getting an increased amount of UV exposure as the solstice approaches." Our eyes met. "You're not going outside. You're not taking care of yourself."

By the time he was done speaking, my mouth had dropped. He took that last step so that we were standing toe to toe, close enough that his scent of soap and water and sandalwood washed over me like a rainstorm, making my mouth water and my heart jump at the same time.

"I—" I shook my head. "I—"

"Joni," Nathan said gently. His right hand twitched and hovered just over my wrist. But he didn't take it. Maybe he couldn't.

My heart physically hurt in response.

"I came because—"

"I'm sorry," I interrupted before he could say anything else. The words leaped out of my mouth like they'd been waiting there the entire time. "I'm sorry about that video. I'm sorry your family found out about it. I'm sorry I never told you it was floating around out there and that it ended up embarrassing you in front of them. I'm sorry for everything, and I—"

The words came out in a rush like a spigot had just been broken, to the point where I was only able to stop myself by slapping a hand over my mouth.

"I'm sorry," I said once I wasn't ready to scream into my skin. "That's all."

Nathan shoved a hand into his hair, which I was pleased to see was just as unruly as ever and maybe a little overgrown. He needed a haircut. It made him even more gorgeous.

"Joni, I—"

"I need a walk," I announced suddenly, jumping out of his reach.

Nathan turned in a circle as I danced around him toward the front door. "What?"

I was practically hopping in place like a rabbit, doing anything but look at him. It was too much to handle. The expression that might be on his face. The thing he might be about to say. I'd just laid my deepest regrets on the table, and while I knew eventually, I'd have to hear whether or not he forgave me for any of them, I couldn't do it yet.

"You basically said as much. I'm pale and sickly, right? Better get some exercise, a little sun, and some food. I hear the grub in Paris is great." I shoved my feet into the slip-ons that had been at the door since I'd arrived two months earlier. Marie wasn't exaggerating when she said I hadn't left the apartment. Necessities only had been my motto. And I'd been sticking to it.

But for the first time, her garret actually seemed too small for two people. Maybe it was because of the size of the man standing in here with me. Or maybe it was the size of the emotions. Either way, we needed to be let out.

I grabbed the spare set of keys off the hook next to the door, slung my leather jacket over my shoulders, and then turned to Nathan. "Are you coming?"

He blinked like he'd been stunned. "I—yes. I suppose we can talk at the same time."

THIRTY-NINE

BEST MODERN CHOREOGRAPHERS

#13 Gene Kely

Nathan followed me down the stairs of Marie's little building, out onto her street with its crooked alleys and topsy-turvy buildings, and down the block despite the fact that I had no idea where I was going.

When I'd first arrived in Paris, Marie had let me wallow for exactly a week. Then she tried to use some of her spare time when she wasn't in her cooking classes to take me around the city, but quickly discovered I was only interested in lying in bed. Museums held no appeal. I didn't care about architecture. Music, art, fashion— none were interesting at all.

Since arriving, I'd only left her apartment to buy tampons and chips at the corner store. If I had to find my way back now, I honestly wasn't sure I could.

"Do you know where you're going?" he asked when I'd circled a building that brought us back to a corner that I was pretty sure we'd already passed.

"There's a river somewhere," I grumbled, looking down another identically charming street with white plaster buildings, shuttered windows, and cobbled sidewalks.

Nathan looked around like he thought the river might pop up out of the gutter, then seemed to make a decision. He took my hand and turned to the left. "It's this way."

I snatched my hand right back—not because it burned, but because it felt too good. I'd been yearning for that strong, capable touch for eight solid weeks, and now that he was offering it, I was legitimately afraid I wouldn't let go.

And I had to let go. That was the one thing I *was* sure of.

"How do you know your way around here so well?" I asked, noticing that Nathan seemed comfortable guiding me through the neighborhood.

"My parents took us on several tours of Europe when I was younger. We spent a lot of time in Paris." He looked around. "I always liked St. Germain. It's very clean."

Of course, he'd been here before. Up until two months ago, the fact that Nathan had obviously come from a rich family had been essentially theoretical. I'd always known he had money. The fancy apartment. The luxe wardrobe. The expensive painting.

But having money to spend on things like that didn't compare to an entire lifetime built on that kind of privilege—something I was quickly realizing I'd never really understand about him. Not completely.

"Paris is a notoriously difficult city to navigate because it's not designed on a typical grid, like New York," Nathan said.

He led me down another cobbled street, past several small galleries and a church from which Chopin was floating out to the sidewalk. I only knew that because it was the same song Mrs. Suarez used to play on a rickety piano while my beginner ballet class practiced our pliés.

"The arrondissements are organized kind of like a spiral," he continued. "Your sister lives in the sixth, which is close to the city center. All of the neighborhoods have touchpoints from which the streets extend like asterisks, which can be even more confusing. But if you can find the Seine—that's the river—you can usually reorient yourself pretty quickly." Nathan paused, glancing at me sideways. "I'm going on. Sorry."

I shook my head. "It's interesting. Good to know, I guess."

And it was, I supposed. Especially if I was going to stay here a while longer. Not because I'd listen to that voice read a user manual and be perfectly entranced. Not at all.

Nathan led me down another street lined with apartment buildings similar to the one Marie lived in, with their white plaster exteriors, limestone trims, and the garret roofs with their tiny balconies. The sun was shining, the occasional flower bloomed pink from cracks in the cobblestones, and the city smelled like wine and sunshine.

Under normal circumstances, this might have been the picture of a romantic day—April in Paris with the man I loved. But a cloud of dread hung over me the longer we walked. Mostly because I knew this had to end.

We rounded a corner and found ourselves on a busy street, directly across from which flowed the Seine, twinkling bright blue under the sun. On the stone walkways that ran alongside the water, people rode bikes, walked their dogs, or simply just meandered while smoking their cigarettes. Bridges arched across the water in both directions.

"That's the Jardin," Nathan said, pointing to the long expanse of green across the water. "And beyond that is the Louvre. But I thought we'd go here instead." He pointed to a large building that had massive arched windows and multiple clock towers topped with spires like hats. "It's the D'Orsay."

I stared up at the building. The name meant nothing to me.

"It's where the Degas collection is," Nathan told me. "The artist who painted the ballerinas. I thought you might like to see them in person."

I looked at him, at the hopeful expression on that ridiculously chiseled face.

"What are you doing?" I burst out before I could stop myself.

Nathan reared back, almost like I'd slapped him. "What do you mean?"

I waved my hand around like a flapping bird. It was so small, but I felt like a secret button had been pushed, shoving the adrenaline into my body that had been missing for two solid months. Suddenly, I wasn't stuck in an endless cycle of listlessness. I was energized—mostly out of frustration.

"I mean, what in the mixed signals is going on here? This isn't a date, Nathan. We aren't meeting up for a stroll and a movie. Two months ago, you found out I was in a sex tape and hid it from you. Your family found out, and it ruined your chances of getting independence from them, which means I basically ruined your whole life. And now you're here, acting like nothing happened, and I don't understand. What do you want from me?"

By the time I was done speaking, my voice was cracking on almost every word. Several people glanced at us and murmured in French as they passed, clearly curious about the girl on the verge of a breakdown.

Nathan, to his credit, didn't seem the slightest bit ashamed as he closed the distance between us. His hands hovered over my shoulders, but when I looked at them, they fell to his sides.

"I found out where you were, and it seemed like the right thing to do," he said. "The only thing to do."

"Why?" The question pained. I hated that I didn't know the answer. "To punish me? To sue me? To rub my misery in my face? Or just to show me what I can't have anymore?"

"None of that." His brown eyes were full of something mournful. Something deep. "I came because I had to know you were okay." He shook his head. "What my brother did was deplorable. I don't blame you for leaving at all."

"Blame me," I muttered before I stumbled backward and walked around in a quick circle. Suddenly, I felt trapped in my own body, buzzing with energy that had no way of getting out. "Blame *me* for leaving? What about you? *You* left with them. Walked right out of the planetarium while I was standing there, bawling my eyes out."

It wasn't until I said it that I realized I wasn't just sad. I was also mad. For months, I'd been beating myself up over the whole situation. Depressed that I wasn't enough for him to stand up for. Heartbroken because I'd failed to protect him from my past.

But that was just it. My past. I'd made mistakes. Big ones. But also, I had been so young. That tape was an enormous stain on my life, but it didn't have to define me.

But he had let it. He had looked away from it then, and he was looking away now, seemingly unable to meet my angry gaze while people around us continued to watch and whisper about the odd Americans making a scene on the steps of the famous museum.

"Was I supposed to stay there and punish you?" he demanded right back. "Allow my parents and my brothers to continue talking about you as if you were nothing, hurting you like that? I couldn't bear it, Joni! I couldn't stand the look on your face every time my mother called you a name or someone played that goddamn video. It was fucking torture."

"How do you think it felt for *me*?" I shrieked.

We seethed at each other for a good long minute, letting the sounds of tourists, traffic, and the rest of the city argue for us.

When I tried to turn away, though, Nathan took me by the wrist, forcing me to face him.

"The only thing I could think of was to get them away," he said, his voice back to a normal timbre. "I knew if I stayed with you, they wouldn't go either. So I left. I was always going to come back. Please believe me."

I couldn't answer him then. My throat was too choked with grief, and I was too busy fighting tears to think of anything to say.

"*Pardon?*" We both turned to where a man, maybe a little older than Nathan, was approaching, hand raised to me. "*Mademoiselle, ça va bien?*"

I shook my head. "I don't speak French."

"We're fine," Nathan snapped at him in an unusually rough voice. Then to me, much more gently, "Would you prefer to walk along the water? Maybe a museum wasn't a good idea."

Wordlessly, I nodded. "Sure. The water sounds…fine. I guess."

He could have offered a shipping container for all I cared. I just wanted to get out of this place.

He reached out as if to take my hand again, but then seemed to think otherwise.

Oh, that hurt too.

"This way," he said, gesturing toward a crosswalk.

I followed him across the street, then down a set of stairs that led to the cobbled pathways lining the river. We walked for a while in silence, passing under one bridge, then another.

It was like being on a movie set. I sighed and found myself humming the lilting bars of one of the musical numbers I remembered, just like I used to as a kid. It would get me in trouble at school, but it was one of the few things that would calm my screaming brain when it felt like this, like a caged animal clawing to get out.

"What's that you're singing?"

"'Our Love is Here to Stay,'" I replied, my voice dead. "From *An American in Paris*. Ironic, I know."

When he shook his head blankly, I sighed and went on.

"Gene Kelly sings it to Leslie Caron, and they dance here on the Seine. Nonna and I used to watch that movie when I was little. I memorized all the steps." I did a few of them, just out of habit, then sighed again, dejected. "Leslie Caron wasn't much of a singer either, but she could really dance. I wanted to be just like her."

Nathan watched me carefully through a few more steps but didn't speak, even when I returned to walking next to him.

It took several more steps and then about fifty yards of walking while watching the river before I calmed down again.

"Were we in a relationship?"

I blinked and turned to where Nathan walked; hands shoved into his pockets in a way that made his biceps bulge distractingly. "Huh?"

Nathan's brows were furrowed in concentration. "A relationship. I'm not always very good at figuring those things out, but I thought that's what it was by the end. We lived together. We talked a lot. Had sex. Agreed things were no longer pretending. Wasn't it a relationship?"

I blinked. Usually, it was the girl who had to wheedle these things out of the guy.

"I—yes," I said. "Yes, it was. At least I thought so."

"So, that meant you were my girlfriend, right? My real one."

Past tense, I noticed bitterly. "You would think."

Nathan stopped. "Then shouldn't my girlfriend have told me where she was going instead of just disappearing?"

I scowled. "Shouldn't my boyfriend have stayed in the room when I was clearly in pain?"

"Shouldn't my girlfriend be honest with me about something that was endangering her in the first place?"

"Endangering me? I think you mean endangering *you*—"

"The video of you having sex with another man was never going to do anything to *me* or anyone in my family," Nathan said impatiently. "Despite what my brother and parents might say about it. But the fact that your ex…I don't know what to call Shawn…had a recording of you like that. You couldn't have thought that would end in anything good."

"I *thought* he would forget about it," I said. "And then, when I realized he hadn't, I had hoped not to burden you with it."

"That's a lie. You weren't trying to protect me. You were protecting yourself. You were ashamed and afraid, so you blocked out the possibility instead of dealing with it."

I opened my mouth to argue, but found that I couldn't. He was right, infuriatingly so.

"But if you're in a relationship with someone, you share those burdens, don't you?" Nathan went on.

"Like you shared all your burdens about Isla?"

"Not immediately, no," Nathan admitted. "When I realized what we were…I did share them."

"It was still different," I retorted. "Your burdens make you a hero. Mine just make me an idiot. A sad, stupid…"

He closed the space between us almost instantaneously and grabbed my waist. "Stop talking about yourself like that."

"Why? It's true." I couldn't help the bitterness leaching into my voice. It tasted like poison. I probably deserved it.

We blinked at each other through the afternoon light, seething at each other a bit like cats.

"Whatever," I said in the end. "It's not like I really know the rules. I was the worst person you could have picked to teach you how to be in a relationship, considering I've never really had one before. Not like that."

Nathan stared at me for a long time, some muscle in his jaw ticking before he gave a curt nod and relaxed his shoulders. "Me neither."

I nodded back, not knowing what to say. Why was he even telling me this? Working through his shit so he could be ready for the next person? That Charlotte woman, maybe. Someone on his level. Someone who wasn't such a mess.

Gradually, the cracks in my heart turned to fissures. And when Nathan stepped away, the hand at my waist leaving a print as surely as if it had been dipped in ink, those fissures split completely.

"I didn't like doing it," I blurted out as we continued walking along the water's edge. "The video."

Nathan cast me a wry look. "That seemed obvious. Based on what I know about you…that way."

I could feel myself color at the memories. Yes, he would know what it looked like when I enjoyed myself in bed.

"And I don't like serving drinks topless either. Stripping, whatever you want to call it. And I've been in plenty of risqué shows, even done a burlesque class. Nudity doesn't bother me. Never has."

Nathan nodded. "It makes sense. Bodies are just bodies."

Such a surgeon's clear-eyed assessment.

"I did like yours, though."

Another assessment. He wasn't even looking at me when he said it, but I couldn't help the way my stomach flipped anyway.

Until I remembered he had said "did." In the past.

"Some girls are fine with it, maybe even like it, and that's great for them," I continued. "But I don't like being looked at that way. If someone's going to look at me dancing, I'd rather they see the *dance*. Not the shape of my ass or how well my tits shake in their face. I was only doing it for the money, but I decided I don't need it that much. Not yet anyway."

By the time I was done speaking, Nathan's hands were clenched at his sides, fists opening and closing in that way that meant he was agitated. I took it as a sign to stop talking.

"How old were you?" he asked a few moments later. "In the video."

My face flushed. "I don't want to say."

He stopped and turned. "How old?"

"It doesn't matter."

"Joni. How. Old?"

"Sixteen!" I blurted out. "Sixteen, all right? So, you can't just say I was a child because, by that age, I definitely was not. And yes, the guy behind the camera is Shawn. He said it would be hot. Said it would only be for him, and that it was how I could show him I loved him. You don't know how it is, thinking you're in love with someone like that. Someone who twists your words around all the time, strings you along like a puppy some days, leaves you cold on others. I was desperate, I guess, and stupid, and…"

By this point, tears were streaking down my cheeks. All the emotion that had just been lost in a dead void for two months was rising to the surface, and I didn't know what to do with it.

"I just wanted to be loved," I whispered at the end, then turned to the river as I buried my face in my hands. "That's all anyone really wants."

Several cyclists rode past us, the whir of their bikes filling the silence while I fought and failed to get my emotions under control. As soon as they were gone, I found myself turned back around and wrapped in Nathan's big arms. Wrapped in his warmth. His comfort.

Oh, God, it felt good. It felt like home, though I had no right to think of him that way.

"You are loved," he said as he pressed me into his chest. "You are."

I sniffed into the blue knit of his shirt. "I know I am. I have about a million people in my family who have a new opinion about my life every other second. I know in my heart that if they didn't care, they wouldn't say anything. But back then, I just wanted something different. I don't know how to say it."

"You wanted acceptance."

I looked up, and my heart almost cracked in half as Nathan gently wiped another tear from my cheek and then tucked some of my hair behind one ear. But he didn't speak.

I waited for my own voice to bubble up again, spill out the emotions I generally couldn't keep locked up.

"You have it," he finally said softly. "From me. Joni, I don't care about the video. I don't care if you want to take your shirt off or not while you serve people drinks. I don't care if you want to dance or walk or sit around all day watching television until you figure out what's next. I just want you to be *you* because…I accept you. And I love you."

I hiccupped back a sob. "What?"

Nathan smiled. Just a little. But it was enough to make my heart squeeze in my chest like a sponge wrung out at the sink.

"I love you," he repeated clearly. "And I think you love me too."

We stared at each other for a long time, close enough to take in each other's scents and for the rest of Paris, the rest of the world, to blur around us like there was nothing else.

I waited for him to take it back. I waited for him to tell me that it was all a joke. Or to add an addendum to the whole thing. To tell me that even if he did feel that way, it wasn't enough, because I'd never be the kind of person who would fit into his perfect, ordered life.

But he didn't. Just stood there, as patient as ever, cupping my face and waiting, waiting, waiting for me.

My Nathan. *My* Nathan. Waiting for me to tell him just that.

"I *do* love you," I whispered as one more tear trailed down my cheek. "I love you so much it hurts. I love you so much I want to tear the feeling out of my heart, then shove it back in because I know I couldn't live without it. I don't know what to do with these feelings —they're too much, they're too—"

"Shh." Nathan pulled me back into his chest and gently rocked me side to side as he stroked my hair out of my face. "I know. I know."

"Do you?" I sobbed, not even caring that I was probably streaking eyeliner and makeup across his perfect shirt.

One of those broad hands came up to cradle the back of my head. "I do. Better than you think."

We rocked like that for a moment, back and forth, a quiet, kind repetition that gradually soothed my soul enough that the tear began to ebb, and I was finally about to look up at him again.

Nathan framed my face with his hands, using his thumbs to brush the last of my tears away.

"So beautiful," he murmured.

He didn't look away. Not even a little.

"Can I kiss you?" His voice nearly floated away on the wind.

I popped onto my toes. "Do you really need to ask?"

"I'm just checking. Consent is important. Especially in moments like these." He took a step closer. "Giovanna," he said in that particular way of his, like he was tasting something extraordinarily sweet. "Joni."

I hummed in response. "Nathan," I whispered, but more to myself than to him.

"Can I kiss you now?"

By that point, his gaze was roving. Hungry. Like he couldn't keep it in one place because there was much to take in. Then his brown eyes met mine like he was forcing them to stay. Wide and open.

Chocolate.

"Yes," I whispered. "Please."

We stared at each other for a few more moments. Then Nathan Hunt—my fake boyfriend who had somehow become my true love —slipped his hand around my waist and placed his mouth with the same precision that seemed to direct every action in his life. Maybe even led him to me.

It was a kiss like no other.

Slow but deliberate, it deepened into something that reached to the bottom of my toes and tugged, linking my soul to his like a chain forged from steel. His tongue found mine with a deep caress that seemed to caress my heart.

And he didn't stop. He didn't pull away. He kissed me and

hugged me and loved me until I'd had my fill. Until we'd both gotten everything we needed.

Or at least what we could there on the bank of the Seine.

He pulled away with a gasp, and I whimpered in his response. My hands clutched his hair, unwilling to release the silky locks. He only smiled as he untangled their grip and pressed a kiss to my knuckles.

"I think," he said, "we should go back to my hotel."

"Why there?" I asked.

"Because I don't think your sister will appreciate it if I ruin her apartment. And for the things I want to do to you right now, I'll need some extra space."

FORTY

BEST KINDS OF SEX

#5 Get Back Together Sex

The light was still pink the next morning when I woke up in Nathan's suite in yet another part of Paris I hadn't even thought to explore.

Two months I'd been here.

It suddenly seemed like such a waste.

And yet, it wasn't. My heart wouldn't have been in it, and what would have been the point of trudging through the City of Love with my heart utterly broken.

Now, it had been put back together, and suddenly, I wanted to see it all with him.

The room, while beautiful, was an utter mess. We hadn't lasted more than two seconds yesterday afternoon after the door closed behind us before Nathan had me pinned against a wall and was tearing my clothes off. Marie's skirt was ripped in two places. My underwear was shredded. We'd knocked over two lamps and broken one of them, and to my shock, it hadn't mattered. It was like Nathan could only see me, want me, *need me*.

And I gave as good as I got. First on the minibar, since we

couldn't make it to the bed. Then on the couch after we took a water break. Then on the bed once we'd ordered some room service.

I rolled over to ask Nathan how long he was planning to stay but found him still sleeping, a delectable bit of stubble dusted over that razor-cut jaw as he lay face up. I wedged myself up on my side to watch, but almost as if he could sense me in his sleep, he rolled over, slung a heavy arm over my waist, and dragged me against his body. And his morning erection.

I grinned. Some things never changed.

"Fuck." The word came out as a rumble against my neck as his hand drifted down my still-naked body, taking hold of my ass and using it to pull me toward him.

This time, however, I wasn't interested in just being pulled. If my man wanted morning sex, then that was what he was going to get.

I nuzzled into his neck and licked his pulse, enjoying the warm scent of man that seemed to radiate off him. Nathan grumbled against me and squeezed me harder. Gently, I pushed him onto his back again, but only so I could crawl on top and cover him with my body, dropping kisses along his neck, collarbone, and the swell of his pectorals.

"Mmm." A growl sounded deep in his chest, vibrating against my cheek as his hands drifted up and down my body.

"Good morning," I said before I kissed back up his neck, then pressed a few more along his jawline.

One of his hands drew up my back and to my face, holding me in place so he could find my mouth with his.

After a few moments, we broke apart, though I could feel his long lashes fluttering on my cheekbone. Under my hip, I could feel him ready. I straddled my legs over his waist and rubbed myself up and down him like a cat.

Another groan as those beautiful brown eyes opened. Full of light. And full of love.

I purred.

"Okay?" I asked, poised to sink down on him.

His eyes blinked open as he clearly started to register exactly where we were and what was happening. It was almost like I could read each word as it passed across his face. Room. Morning. Joni. Sex.

Sex.

His eyes opened fully. "*Yes.*"

And then he was thrusting from below, inside me again for the fifth time in the last twenty-four hours.

We hadn't been together long enough for me to realize one key fact: Nathan Hunt was insatiable. And he apparently had the same effect on me.

He paused, noticing me wince. "Should I stop? You're making one of the faces on the pain chart we show children."

I laughed, and it made me relax enough that I was able to take him further. "I'm a little sore, but I don't want you to stop. It feels too good."

He grunted and started moving beneath me, albeit a bit carefully. I laughed again, then pressed a hand flat to his chest, forcing him to stay still so I could work my body atop of his more forcefully.

Nathan made a pained sound as his eyes bulged. "God, Joni. *Fuck.*"

"Does that feel good to you too?" I asked. "Do you like it when I ride you like this?"

His gaze seared as it passed up and down my body. I had never felt more beautiful, and it wasn't because of my clothes or my hair or any kind of performance.

It was because of him.

"Kiss me," Nathan ordered as he slipped a hand between us, finding my clit so he could tease me into a similar state of disarray. "Kiss me while I fuck you. Kiss me while you fuck me. Kiss me while I love you, you beautiful, beautiful woman."

I leaned forward to oblige, enjoying the delicious fullness and the way he sucked at my bottom lip like a piece of candy he wanted to devour.

We moved like that for some time, losing track of the places where one of our bodies ended and the other began. We whispered hushed phrases and unintelligible gasps in between merciless drives, our hands grasping for the other just to keep from floating away in a sea of pleasure.

But it wasn't really Nathan's body or voice or anything else that kept me rooted in this reality.

One word echoed while the others faded. The most important word of all.

Love.

"SO, WHAT SHOULD WE DO TODAY?" I asked as I emerged from the shower in one of the hotel's plush robes. "Marie said Montmartre is fun. Full of artists. Or we could go see those paintings you told me about yesterday—everything all right?"

Nathan was sitting on the bed in a matching robe that barely fit his big body, thumbing through his phone with a frown. He'd put his glasses back on but, otherwise, looked deliciously rumpled, his hair a curly mop from my ministrations.

"Seriously," I said when he didn't answer. "That's quite an expression for a man who's had his mind blown for the past twenty-four hours."

He looked up, and I watched him slowly register the joke before he rearranged his features into a smile and then held out an arm for me to join him.

I went, allowing him to gather me to his side.

"Everything is…well, I don't know if I would call it fine. Do you still want to dance?"

I sat up, taken aback by the abrupt change of subject. "Dance? Like on the Seine?"

"No. Like as a job. Is it still what you want to do?"

"I…" I hadn't even thought about it. That was the one thing two months of misery over Nathan had given me—a reprieve from grieving the loss of my career.

Nathan waited for me to figure it out.

I sat cross-legged and toyed with the wet ends of my hair. "Yes, but—"

"Good," he interrupted. "Because that's the other reason I'm here. I got a message from Jayce—Dr. McAndrew. He has an opening in his schedule this week. He said he could repair your knee on Thursday. I told him you would be there."

My mouth fell open. "You did what?"

Nathan turned, full of urgency. "I can cancel if you want, but it's already paid for. I still owe you six months' rent anyway. You'll have the surgery, stay with me while you recover, and you should be able to go back to Opal within a month. Seems like a fair trade, in my opinion."

My mouth opened and closed like a fish. I was completely and utterly shocked. Was this for real?

"I meant what I said that day in the studio," he said. "Call me a benefactor if you want, or just call me your boyfriend, but either way, Joni, I believe you deserve another chance at your calling. So, I'll ask you again, and this time, I want you to think carefully about it: do you want to dance?"

I didn't have to think about it. I didn't even have to wait.

"Yes," I said, my voice warbling with the intensity of my emotions. "Yes, I want to dance."

I launched myself at him, squeezing him so hard I was sure he couldn't breathe. He didn't push me away, though. He only hugged me back harder and accepted my kisses that said all the words I couldn't find through my emotions.

"Thank you," I finally managed when I pulled back. "It doesn't even cover it, but thank you."

The bashful smile on Nathan's face was a thing of beauty as he straightened his glasses. "We love each other," he said simply. "Doesn't love mean you want the other person to be happy? Shouldn't we try to help each other however we can?"

It was so simple.

And yet, so hard to fathom.

"Yes," I said softly. "I think we should."

He smiled, and it lit up the room. "Good, then it's settled. We'll go back to New York. And then, unfortunately, I'll have to go back to Virginia while you recover."

"Back?" I looked up. "Why were you there at all?"

Nathan nodded his head as he put on his glasses. "I took a sabbatical. An extended leave of absence." He sighed. "I made a deal with my father to focus on Huntwell for a few months. My father *did* end up announcing me as his planned successor at the gala."

That was enough to throw me into a sour mood. "Jerk."

He didn't argue. "I didn't accept. However, I did agree to spend a few months shadowing the interim CEO, fully learning the role. It seemed like a decent compromise. Until now."

"Until you ran off to find me, you mean?" I couldn't help but feel a pang of guilt about it, as happy as I was that he'd come.

Nathan just pulled me closer. "I don't want to compromise anymore."

I wanted to tell him he shouldn't. That what his family was doing to him was horrible, and he should walk away.

But I knew he wouldn't. Because there was something else tethering him to that family besides just basic loyalty and goodness.

I swallowed. "Is it about Isla?" I was starting to become desperately curious about this girl who served as a pawn in Nathan's life.

He nodded. "She doesn't turn eighteen until August, and even then, I'm not sure I'll be able to step in. They haven't said as much, but I think they've already started the process of obtaining a full conservatorship over her care after she turns eighteen."

I pushed back so I could look at him. "Like what they did to Britney Spears?"

He frowned. "I don't know anything about that."

"She was this huge pop star, and then she went a little nuts, so her family used that to lock her down. She couldn't control anything. Not her money, her job, her medical stuff. Not even who she dated."

I shook my head in disbelief. I didn't like much of Britney Spears now, but I used to love her stuff when I was little. "Toxic" was my jam in the fourth grade.

Or maybe it was too easy to see myself in her a little bit. Under different circumstances, my own behavior could have set me up for that kind of control too.

Sadly, Nathan nodded. "It would be like that, yes."

"Does...does she need that kind of oversight?"

Nathan frowned. "It's hard to say. Autism is such a spectrum, and in many ways, Isla has far fewer accommodations than she used to. Her verbal skills have improved enormously over the years, and on good days, she can socialize quite well. She does, however, struggle on others. It's very difficult to engage her on any topics outside of her interests, which often border on obsession. Horses right now, mainly. Transitions are still nearly impossible. And most of her recent evaluations also indicate that her executive function—that's the skills needed to make decisions, set goals, organize one's life, and control impulses—is still highly underdeveloped."

"Sounds familiar," I said dryly.

Nathan turned to me. "ADHD and autism do share some overlapping traits. But it's not the same thing. And Isla's challenges still required substantial accommodation."

I quieted then. He'd mentioned that before, but it wasn't something I'd really considered. ADHD was one of those terms people had thrown at me like a weapon, a nasty name when they were annoyed by my flightiness. Not something that might actually help me.

"I need to observe her more myself," he said as he laid back against the pillow. "But I suspect a limited guardianship would be more appropriate while she continues working with therapists to pursue school and continues learning how to manage her life. And I don't want my parents to have that power."

"To box you under their control too?" I asked.

Nathan didn't say anything, which I took as a confirmation. At this point, having met his parents myself, I had no doubt that his mother at least was capable of that kind of manipulation.

"That's fucked up."

He nodded. "I agree." Then he turned to me again. "I don't want it to continue this way. I *can't*. Not with you. Not anymore. But rather than engage my parents and Isla in a protracted and painful legal battle, I think it might be easier if I play their game."

I didn't like it. I didn't like it at all. But I also couldn't see another way out of it. Nathan cared deeply about Isla. Therefore…I cared deeply too.

"Well, I guess that's that," I said. "How soon after the surgery do we leave?"

He turned to me again. "We? Joni, you don't have to go. It's just the reason I won't be able to stay in New York while you recuperate."

That idea turned me cold. "What?"

"You'll be all right," he said. "Meniscectomies are usually very quick to heal. You'll be walking around the same day. Most patients heal completely in four to six weeks, and then you can work with a PT to get back into dancing shape."

"Yeah, but…but…four to six weeks is more than a month without you!" I almost shouted as I sat up straight.

The bathrobe fell apart, baring a bit more of my chest than was strictly decent. Nathan clearly noticed, but was too much of a gentleman to ogle.

He turned to face me and gently pulled the collar of my robe closed, but didn't release it. Instead, he used it to pull me close, kiss me again, and nuzzle my face, like he knew just what would calm me down.

It worked. But only to calm my tone—not the passion behind it.

"Do I make you happy?" I asked him. "Honestly. If I'm more of a problem, then I don't want to add to what you already have. But would having me around make you happy, even if it's with your parents?"

Nathan's eyes shone bright. "It would. You make me happier than I ever thought possible."

"Then you're not doing this alone," I said, grabbing his collar right back so he couldn't turn away. "I'm coming with you."

"Joni, my family—they won't be kind to you—"

"I don't care about that," I interrupted, though the idea of spending quality time with a woman who had basically called me a whore and a dude who shared my most intimate business with everyone didn't sound amazing.

But there was no way I was letting my kind, sweet Nathan walk into that mess alone. Absolutely not.

"You're not doing this alone," I told him again. "I don't know what I can do to help, but I'll figure out something. Even if it's just being there."

I kissed him again, and this time, he didn't stop me. Didn't argue. Just kissed me back.

"Besides," I told him once we finally managed to break apart. "You're heading back into a lion's den, so you'll need someone with claws on your side. I grew up in a family full of cats, baby. My claws are razor sharp."

FORTY-ONE

SISTERS IN ORDER OF MOST TO LEAST ANNOYING (TODAY)

#2 Lea. Still a nag but i luv her

"All right, Joni. I want you to count down from one hundred, starting now."

The anesthesiologist had a nice voice, but not as nice as Nathan's. I glanced up toward the mirrored windows at the top of the operating room. Nathan was there, watching, he said. He would be there the whole time.

"Okay," I murmured, my voice already slurring. "One hundred, ninety-nine…"

I BLINKED. The room was hazy. The color of eggshells just cracked. Maybe the lace in Nonna's wedding dress. Where was Nonna, anyway?

Oh, Italy. Right.

A moan in my throat. I didn't remember making it.

"Go ahead and sleep a little more, sweetie. We'll be here when you wake up."

I tried to stay awake, but it didn't work. Just a little more rest. Just a little more...

———————

"JONI?"

A warm hand covered mine, the touch slightly electric, even through the haze that still seemed to cover my bones and run through my blood.

I blinked. And blinked again. The recovery room in the surgical wing at Mt. Sinai looked exactly like I remembered it. Which is to say, nothing like Nonna's wedding dress.

I pushed myself up in the hospital bed in my bay but had to stop. I felt dizzy.

Immediately, the hand on mine squeezed. "Take it easy. You're just waking up."

I turned toward the voice and found him. Nathan. Looking stupidly hot in his robin's-egg-blue scrubs, his name on a pass hanging from a lanyard. Was he working?

I frowned. No, he wasn't. That's right, he had used his credentials to be there during the surgery.

"Babe," I murmured, squeezing the hand in response. "Did you watch?"

His eyes crinkled, bright behind his glasses. "The whole thing. It only took an hour, and it went perfectly. Jayce will be in here soon to debrief."

I smiled and tugged him closer. "Come here. I need to snuggle."

"Patients really shouldn't be disturbed—"

"Do it."

There was a loud huff. The next thing I knew, he had wedged himself beside me on the bed, allowing himself to be pulled down so I could rest on his chest.

"These beds really aren't meant to be shared," he said.

"Just don't bump my knee, and we'll be fine." I wasn't sure why I was so concerned. I couldn't feel the incision or anything else except my groggy brain and a sore throat.

Nathan pressed a kiss to my forehead and stroked my hair. "There's someone here waiting to see you."

I turned. "Nathan, you didn't tell Nonna, did you?"

We'd had a whole conversation about it before leaving France. Marie had thought I should ask Nonna to come back from New York to help me for a bit. I had staunchly refused. This was my life. My mess. I was done asking my grandmother or anyone else to help me figure things out. Not when I finally had a real partner.

Nathan shook his head. "No, although I'm sure she knows. Your sisters aren't very discreet."

He gestured toward the door, and I looked across his chest to find Lea edging her way in, looking more than a little suspicious as she regarded the hospital room the same way some people might examine a haunted attic.

On the outside, my oldest sister looked the same as always in the skinny jeans she'd been wearing since 2005, her dark hair pulled back into a messy bun, one of Mike's hoodies tossed over a graphic T-shirt, and a pair of big silver hoops for good measure. A closer look, however, informed me that the dark circles under her eyes were a lot darker than usual, her skin had that sallow look of someone who hadn't been sleeping, and she'd lost a little too much weight since I'd last seen her.

"Hey," I said, pushing myself up fully to sitting.

Nathan stood up and nodded. "Hello, Lea. She's awake."

I glanced between my sister and Nathan when she had nothing snarky to say. No "Thanks, Captain Obvious" or "Glad you cleared that up." Clearly, something had happened between them while I was under the knife. I wasn't sure if it was good or bad.

"Can we have a moment alone?" she asked.

Nathan glanced at me, and I nodded.

"I'll be outside," he said before pressing a kiss to my head and leaving the room.

Lea watched him go. "He was there the whole time."

We both looked over to where Nathan now stood in deep conversation with another doctor. His gaze, however, darted every so often toward me, as if to make sure I was still in one piece.

"He's nice," she said. "And maybe kind of good for you."

"There's no way for you to know that," I argued, even though it was true. "You've barely even met him."

"I just spent the last two hours talking to him. It was a solid introduction. Better than me being a bitch when you moved in."

At that, I finally turned, genuinely surprised. "You were at the surgery too?"

"He called Kate and me yesterday to let us know what was happening." Lea grabbed my hand. "I was worried. He saw me in the waiting room and offered to bring me into the gallery to watch the surgery. It was honestly kind of boring, but he explained what was going on. I'm not going to lie, Jo—he's a bit of a stiff—"

"He is *not*—" I started to protest.

"But he obviously loves you," Lea continued. "And if we're being real, I think you could use a bit of stiffness in your life. And maybe he needs someone like you to loosen him up too."

I didn't reply, but didn't argue either. Because she was right. Nathan and I were polar opposites, but somehow it worked. Not in a condescending sort of way. But more like scales where the weights were finally balanced.

That's how I felt around him. Even. Balanced. At ease.

"Why didn't you tell us about the surgery?"

I sighed. "I don't know. It happened kind of quickly. And things have been…weird."

"Not so weird that I'm not still your sister."

"You don't act like my sister, though, Le. You act like the mom we never had. I understand why—it was shoved on you way too young. But you don't need to be that for me anymore. Not even then."

"Well, if I was, I wasn't doing a very good job." Her green eyes, identical to mine, bore into me. "That tape."

I flushed and looked away. "I don't want to hear it."

"I'm not going to hate on you about it. I just want to say I'm sorry."

I turned back at her. "For what?"

Lea shocked me by wiping a tear from her eye. My sister was tough as nails—I'd maybe seen her cry twice in my entire life.

"For failing you," she said. "I turned it off almost immediately, but not before I...not before I could see *you*, Jo. Your nails were painted in those rainbow colors. Remember? I took you for that manicure myself right before you went to prom with Jimmy Trujillo. You were only sixteen." By the time she was done, another tear had slipped down her cheek. "I failed you, Jo. I was supposed to be protecting you, and I didn't do it. I should have known you were wrapped up with someone like that Shawn character. I should have done a better job at keeping you safe."

By the time she was done, she was almost sobbing. I reached out and pulled her to me, giving her a hug like we hadn't shared in many years.

"It wasn't your job," I said again.

"Then whose was it?" she erupted, practically hopping off me.

"I don't know. No one's. Dad's, except he died when I was one. Or Mom's, except she was still in jail. Not Nonna and Nonno, who barely had enough energy for all of us. Not Matthew's, and definitely not yours." I shrugged. "I guess it was mine, except I was too naive to see what was going on."

I tipped my head. It was a strange sensation, being cooler in the head than Lea. She was the one who always seemed to have things under control or at least know what to do about them.

"Well, it shouldn't have been yours. You were just a kid."

"Maybe not. But that's what we all had to depend on. Ourselves, in the end. At least until we learn to depend on each other like adults instead of children. Like equals."

We both sat with that for a minute; the silence interrupted only by the occasional sniffle from Lea.

"When did you get so smart?" she joked when her eyes had finally dried.

I glanced toward the hall where Nathan stood. He gave me that brief half-smile I knew was reserved just for me. "I think maybe I was smart the whole time, Le. But I had some help figuring that out too."

Lea's own gaze darted between me and Nathan. "I think I can see that." Then she turned back at me. "I also wanted you to know...that

I'm sorry for blaming you for Lis Antoni calling Mike. That wasn't your fault either. I mean"—she tipped her head in that know-it-all way I had a feeling Lea would never really shake—"you *definitely* shouldn't have been working at an illegal gambling club. But...I understand why you were there. And it's not your fault that you're so damn cute a gangster would fall in love with you."

I sighed. "Trust me, I won't be going back. It's just not worth it."

"Good."

But she still looked uneasy. Still looked like something was bothering her.

"Lea," I said. "What is it?"

She swallowed, and her green eyes had a hard time meeting mine. "It's nothing."

"That's obviously not true. Just tell me."

My sister sighed. "It's Mike. He's been acting off. Got really mad when he found out about the video and told off Antoni for even asking about you. He came home one night with bruised knuckles and blood on his shirt and wouldn't tell me what happened. Just said, 'it's been taken care of.' Whatever that means."

As I heard the story, something in me cracked.

"Why would Mike care so much?" I wondered. "It's not like I'm *his* sister. I figured I drove him nuts as much as I did you."

Lea gave me a look. "Of course, you're his sister, Joni. You and all the others. Mike didn't have a family until we got together, remember? And he's about as loyal as it gets. You mess with one of us, you mess with him too."

I blinked. I had never really thought of Mike that way, but it made sense. He'd been my sister's shadow since I was little. Stalwart and patient. Always there.

"Anyway, it's fine," she said as she turned to a mirror on the far side of the room and fluffed her hair. "Now, what's this I hear about Virginia?"

FORTY-TWO
THINGS I LIKE ABOUT HUNTWELL FARM

#8 the colums at the house are really pretty

"That's the duck pond. We have two resident swans who come back every year."

As Nathan pointed out familiar sights, I gazed out the passenger window of the large black Mercedes.

A few days after my surgery, we had flown into Dulles International Airport, about an hour from where Nathan's family lived in the country. Just as Dr. McAndrew had said, I'd been able to walk out of the hospital unassisted and had started basic physical therapy the next day. I didn't want to think about how much all of this had cost Nathan. Frankie had called me as soon as Xavier had arrived home to offer to pay it all back on my behalf, but I'd turned her down. A debt was a debt, whether I owed it to my sister or my roommate-turned-boyfriend.

For whatever reason, I was more comfortable owing it to Nathan. It felt more like mine that way. And maybe, like I knew one day, I'd pay him back.

It wasn't my first time to the DC area. Once I'd been part of a dance troupe that toured through a few theaters in Philadelphia,

Baltimore, and Washington, DC. In between shows, I'd walked around the Washington Mall but mostly saw the inside of the theater and whatever I could glimpse on the bus ride home.

Nathan's family lived about an hour from the city, outside a small town called Warrenton, on a fifteen-hundred-acre property twice the size of Central Park. One of the last surviving land grants from George Washington himself, according to Nathan, who had been drilling me on the estate's American history as a means of courting his mother, who was apparently a nut for it.

It was one of the things that made me very attuned to the differences between us. Nathan's family had been in this country for at least four hundred years, with ancestors whose names were literally on its founding documents. Nonna and Nonno had come over from Italy sometime in the fifties. Any farther back than that, and every ancestor I had was either in Italy or Puerto Rico.

"So, your parents have the house out here, the townhouse in Georgetown, and another house in Westchester?" I asked, trying to remember everything he'd listed so far.

The sheer amount of real estate these people owned was beyond my scope of imagination. In my neighborhood, owning even one crappy little house was considered a big deal.

"On this coast, yeah. Dad bought a house in Del Mar when I was in college. Plus, there's a villa in Tuscany and apartments in Hong Kong, London, and Dubai." Nathan frowned. "It's possible Carrick talked them into a Tokyo residence too, but I'm not sure." He took my hand. "But this is their favorite."

More importantly, Huntwell Farm was the place where Nathan and his brothers had primarily been raised. For that reason alone, I was looking forward to seeing it. Anything that told me more about what made Nathan into Nathan was worth seeing, even if I knew I was driving right into the belly of the beast.

We passed through a set of looming iron gates topped with golden bald eagles, following a neatly paved road through the property. Under early the May sunshine, it was admittedly breathtaking. Rolling green hills were split between acres of forest, meadow, and wildflowers, broken occasionally by things like paddock fences, stables, gatehouses, and staff homes.

It wasn't really an estate. Huntwell Farm was a village in and of itself, eons away from the urban jungle I'd always known.

"Do you miss it?" I found myself wondering as I took everything in. "This is the polar opposite of New York."

Nathan seemed to think about that for a bit. "I miss some things. The space, for one. I've gone riding in Central Park, but it's not the same. Everywhere is still full of people. And sometimes, it would be nice to have space to be alone."

"Why did you come to New York, of all places?" I wondered. "It's a terrible place to be alone."

It had never bothered me. My natural state was one of chaos, growing up in a house full of people. Being alone always felt uncomfortable to me.

Nathan shrugged. "Well, at first, it was because I was matched to a general residency program there. And then accepted to the fellowship at NYU. But in general, I like the city. I like its energy. And since my parents wanted one of us to live in New York to manage Huntwell's financial sector, they didn't fight it either."

He turned to me then and cupped my face with one hand. "I've developed my own methods of finding peace," he said before delivering a quick kiss. "Right now, they involve a lot of this."

He kissed me again and didn't stop. Not when the car rounded a circular driveway and stopped. Not when the driver came around to open our door and waited patiently for us to finish.

He only stopped when I pulled away, feeling a bit drunk from the effort.

"What was that?" I wondered with slightly numbed lips.

"Peace." Nathan smiled. "And something to remember when it's gone in a few moments."

I followed him out of the car, smoothing the green dress I'd worn on the plane. It was another piece from Wardrobe de Nathan, with a strapless silk bodice that gathered at my waist but floated demurely to just past my knees. It paired perfectly with the strappy wedge sandals that wrapped around my ankles. I knew Nathan liked it because of the way it bared my shoulders and matched my eyes; I hoped his family would like the way it mostly covered my legs.

Hand in mine, Nathan led me up the brick walk toward the front door of a mansion that seemed to stretch for miles in either direction. It was white with black shutters and at least three stories built of stone, columns, and windows. A mix of colonial and neoclassical styles, I was told, with eighteenth-century stonework blended with plaster additions and twin columns framing the front door.

"How old is this place?" I asked.

Nathan looked around with me. "The original house was built in 1783. There are a few different additions since then—I think the most recent is a pool house in the back, added in the seventies."

I gawked. There was nothing like this in New York. Maybe a few small houses near Washington Square Park, a couple of old mills and things like that in the Bronx, but most of New York's colonial past had been erased long ago to make room for the townhomes, apartment buildings, and skyscrapers the city was known for today. To a kid learning about things like the Lenape tribe or the Dutch settlers in elementary school, that history was nearly as mythological as the Loch Ness monster.

Nathan, however, had grown up in that history. It was as much a part of him as anything else, a kind of legacy.

Just another difference between us.

The oversized front doors opened, and a short yet imperious blond woman appeared in a navy-blue sweater set and tasteful brown mules that clipped like woodpeckers on the brick stoop.

Lillian Hunt. Otherwise known as the woman who hated my guts.

"Nathan!" she called. "Darling, you're back! And with a guest, I see. So delighted you've finally moved on from—*oh!*"

I summoned my brightest, most charming smile possible. "Mrs. Hunt. It's lovely to see you again."

Lillian's eyes narrowed before she turned to Nathan without even acknowledging me. "*What* is she doing here?"

"You didn't tell them I was coming?" I murmured.

"Of course I did. My mother just likes to be dramatic." Nathan turned to Lillian. "Mom, I was perfectly clear on the phone last week when I said Joni would be joining me after her surgery."

"Yes, but I didn't think you *meant* it." She eyed me up and down. "You have some nerve coming here, missy. I don't know what sort of welcome you expected, but we are not interested in your sort at Huntwell."

I fought the urge to cower into Nathan, but it didn't last long. Only because I reminded myself that I'd never bowed down to a stuck-up bitch before, and I wasn't going to start now. I didn't care if she was my boyfriend's mother.

"Then it's a good thing I'm here as your son's guest, not yours," I said in a sickly sweet tone. I turned to Nathan. "Maybe you're right, and it would be better to get an Airbnb somewhere nearby."

He blinked. We hadn't discussed that at all. The plan was simple: use the time to get back into his parents' good graces enough that they would sign Isla's guardianship over to him without a legal battle. It would be easier, he thought, if we stayed here instead of at an Airbnb, even with the tension between him and his family. And me.

This was the first time I reconsidered coming down with him. My presence would likely delay things, given how much his mother didn't like me.

Nathan, however, had already decided that I was a necessity to him. And if anything, perhaps we could use my presence as a bargaining chip. Particularly if I annoyed Lillian to the point where she would give Nathan almost anything to get rid of me.

That, I could do.

But I recognized something else in Nathan's mother he hadn't yet identified: desperation. As the youngest in a family led by a grand-mother trying to force teenagers and twenty-somethings to Mass and family dinners for years, I knew exactly what that looked like.

And I knew how to manipulate it too.

"What?" Lillian asked. She did a double take toward Nathan. "You would leave so soon?"

Right on cue. Just as I suspected, the woman's backhanded tech-niques of manipulating Nathan's life weren't just about forcing him to lead his father's company. They were ultimately the moves of a mother who wanted her children close. Even when they were a grown-ass, thirty-four-year-old man.

Nathan frowned at me, then at her. "Well, yes. If you won't allow Joni to stay here with me, then we certainly would."

Lillian's pastel-painted mouth opened and closed as she looked between us. "But...but..."

It was everything I could do not to look smug.

"We'll let you think about it." Nathan just looked tired as he guided me around his mother. "In the meantime, I'm going to show Joni around."

The inside of the great house was just as impressive as the exterior. Black-and-white marble floors stretched down an expansive foyer before transitioning to dark wood and delicate wainscoting that had to be at least a hundred years old. Luxe dark curtains dressed windows stretched up toward box-beam ceilings that sheltered antique furniture and paintings of distant ancestors that watched over everything else.

I couldn't help but stare. The foyer alone could have contained Nonna's house—I couldn't even imagine how a single family used all this space.

Still stunned, Lillian followed us inside, along with the driver with our bags.

"Thanks, Carl," Nathan said.

Carl nodded back with the tip of his hat and exited the house, leaving us alone with Nathan's mother. It wasn't until Nathan led me up a grand staircase that spiraled toward a second floor that she finally found her voice again.

"Nathan, stop," Lillian called.

I sighed. I knew round one wasn't going to be a knockout, but part of me had sort of wished it would be.

"You cannot expect us to take this girl, this *hussy*, into our home without a word—"

Nathan whirled around halfway up the stairs and stepped down as if to shield me from his mother's hateful words.

"Stop," he said through gritted teeth that made a muscle in his jaw twitch dangerously. "Stop *right* there."

He released my hand, and I watched as he jogged down the stairs, taking two at a time until he was in front of his mother, towering over her like one of the vast oaks on the property.

"Let me make something very clear," he said in a voice that was quiet but still managed to thunder through the grand entrance. "I've given up my life to play your games. Given up my job, my apartment, my entire routine to heel to your manipulative tactics. But I will not give up her. Not now. Not ever."

"Now, Nathan, be reasonable. The girl is obscene! The definition of vulgar! She humiliated you and the family with that obscene video—"

"Actually, I'm pretty sure I'm the one who is most humiliated by that," I muttered, though I couldn't stop my cheeks from heating up.

"Then you should have thought of that before—"

"Stop," he cut her off again. "And just fucking listen. For the first time in my life, I've met someone I love. Someone who loves me back, just as I am. I don't care what horrible things were done to her almost a decade ago—I care about who she is now. And all *you* should care about is that she makes me happy."

"But Nathan—"

"But nothing," he snapped. "I love this woman. I'm going to be with her. That means I'm going to date her, live with her, and one day, I'm going to marry her if she'll have me."

I sucked in a sharp breath as my stomach flipped. *Marry?* If I'd gone off script earlier, Nathan had just written an entirely new play.

I didn't hate the idea, though.

"So, if you want her to go, she will go," he finished. "But I will be going with her, and you will not see me again. Do. You. Understand?"

It wasn't exactly the slow play of bargaining we'd imagined. Nathan had just laid our entire relationship down like a gauntlet, daring his mother to take it on.

A horrible silence echoed off the hard surfaces of the foyer while Lillian's sharp gaze darted between her son and me. She looked torn between the fact that she'd really like to throw me out with the trash, but also knew her son would probably go with me.

I had only known Nathan a matter of months, but that was long enough to understand that he never said anything unless he meant it completely.

I had a feeling his own mother understood that as well.

Well, good.

"All right," she said, already turning away as if she couldn't bear the sight of her defeat. "I'll just let the cook know we'll have an extra for dinner."

"Thank you!" I called a little too sweetly as Nathan rejoined me on the stairs.

"Marry, huh?" I murmured as he took my hand back in his and kissed the back of it.

"One day," he agreed as we continued up the steps.

I couldn't find it in myself to argue. I didn't want to. Not even a little.

A FEW MINUTES LATER, we entered another set of double doors on the second floor that opened into a suite that was larger than Nathan's entire apartment in New York.

"This was my room," he said as I followed him inside. "Where we'll be staying."

I looked around. The entire space was littered with memorabilia connected to Nathan, an entire life he had lived before coming to New York and striking out on his own. Baseball memorabilia. 4-H ribbons. A tower of CDs in one corner, along with an outdated computer setup. Several bookshelves were built into another corner, filled with well-used books of all genres.

And this was just a living room.

Through another door was a bedroom, plus an en suite bathroom with marbled floors and a mostly empty walk-in closet. The bedroom was neatly made up with more antique furniture and tasteful textiles of blue and white, which matched the rest of the house but were obviously chosen for a boy.

The crown prince, as it were.

"Your mother won't pitch another fit about us staying together?" I wondered.

Nathan shrugged. "Probably, but it will go the same as the last one. I meant every word I said. And I can be very stubborn."

I walked around the entire room, taking in little things like photographs, trophies, and anything else that seemed to belong to him outside of the taste of his mother or an interior designer. Eventually I stopped at the window looking out toward the horse stables I knew Nathan loved so much but never got to see. Nathan came up behind me and wrapped his arms around my waist, tucking his head on my shoulder.

Since we had come back from Paris, he had become that much more affectionate. Even voracious. It was like a dam had been broken, and now he couldn't stop touching me, no matter what.

I wasn't arguing with it. I craved the feel of his skin on mine just as much as he did. For two months, I had been suffering from Nathan withdrawals like any reasonable addict. Or maybe it was just that I had come to need this man as much as I needed things like air, water, and food. Somehow, in the last few months, he had become as essential to my life as anything else.

Maybe I didn't completely understand *why* he loved me so much that he was willing to take on his entire family to keep me around.

But I understood how it felt. I would do the same thing in a heartbeat.

"How's your knee feeling?" Nathan wondered before pressing a kiss to my neck. "The flight didn't bother it, did it? Often, atmospheric pressure can cause joint swelling."

I leaned back into him, half lost again in his touch. "Not at all. It's actually been feeling pretty good. You weren't kidding about the quick recovery." Then I turned around in his arms. "Why? Are you interested in getting a little 'exercise'?"

Nathan frowned. "Exercise?"

I moved my eyebrows up and down a few times like a silly cartoon character.

He stared blankly for a moment before awareness dawned across his face. "*Oh!*"

So cute. Enough that I had to kiss him right there.

A few moments later, he pulled away, though not without lipstick smeared on his cheek.

"Damn," he muttered. "As much as I would like to do that right now, there is somewhere else I'd like to go today before dinner."

"Where's that?" I asked, though I was already starting to unbutton his shirt.

His hands stilled mine. And any idea of getting busy flew out of my mind when I caught his grim expression.

"You look like you're expecting a war," I said.

He ground his teeth. "I suppose I am. But before we start the next battle, you'll want to know what we're fighting for." He squeezed me closer. "I'd like you to meet Isla."

FORTY-THREE

FIRST IMPRESSIONS OF ISLA

#1 Shes so much like Nathan

A nd so, almost as soon as we arrived at the enormous estate, Nathan and I got back into the fancy black Mercedes and drove away. I watched the Virginia countryside gradually grow more and more populated as we closed in on the outskirts of Washington, DC. Eventually, the car moved farther south, and close to an hour later, we parked on a large school campus outside of Alexandria.

The Ferndale Center for Autism and Other Developmental Disorders was one of those places that looked more like a summer camp than an educational facility. Children could live at the center and attend school there beginning at the age of five, which was when Isla began at a similar program in North Carolina before moving to Ferndale when she was twelve, Nathan had informed me on the drive down. Students could remain until they were twenty-five, depending on their individual needs.

The campus was split into several sections for different age groups, along with centers offering different forms of therapy, learning support, and vocational counseling for the students. We passed a culinary institute, a bar, a large gymnasium, a pool, and several other buildings dedicated to the needs of the center's three hundred and forty-seven residents. Including Isla's beloved stables.

We parked near the small administrative buildings at the center of campus. Nathan checked in at the front desk, and we were then escorted down a path and past a locked entrance to the section of the center designated for students between the ages of fourteen and eighteen. Our guide led us to a waiting area in the bottom of the girls' dormitory, where Isla shared a suite with another person like her.

"One of the goals of the center is to help kids like Isla learn how to socialize well enough to function in the communities outside," Nathan told me while we waited. "Right now, she requires an EA—that's an educational assistant—to help her interact with others. But I'm hopeful that one day she'll be able to manage on her own."

"You don't think she could after high school?" I asked.

Nathan shook his head. "Not completely. Cognitively, she can probably handle the course load at one of the local universities with the help of her EA, but she still struggles enough with other independent living, social communication, and executive function skills that it would make it difficult for her to be on her own anywhere."

He explained that today, for example, there was a strong possibility she wouldn't even acknowledge either of our presence. Or if she did, she might not be able to talk about anything outside of her own specific interests.

I knew he was preparing me for potentially uncomfortable moments, but I honestly didn't mind. This girl was important to him, and so she was important to me. It didn't really matter if she was willing to speak to me or not. I just wanted her to know that I cared about Nathan, and therefore, I cared about her.

Impulsively, I grabbed Nathan's hand and kissed his knuckles.

He looked down at me. "Why?"

I smiled up at him. "Isla's lucky to have you in her life. And so am I."

The delight that crossed his face warmed my very soul. But before he could answer, the door to the dormitory opened, and a middle-aged woman carrying a basket of knitting walked in, followed by a girl of about seventeen.

Nathan stood up immediately.

I did with him.

"Good to see you so soon again, Dr. Hunt," said the woman as she reached out to shake Nathan's hand.

"It's good to see you too, Mary," Nathan said. "This is my girl-friend, Joni."

Mary smiled at me with warm gray eyes as she shook my hand as well. "Lovely to meet you. We've heard a lot about you, haven't we, Isla?"

Isla, who had already taken a seat across from us in one of the cozy armchairs, was fixedly drawing something on a sketch pad. We all watched as she worked diligently to finish some shading. And waited. When it appeared she wasn't going to respond, Nathan shrugged at me. I nodded. This was the kind of thing he had prepared me for.

Isla was beautiful. She was tall and blond, with sharp blue eyes the color of a robin's egg that darted around the room, clearly noticing everything. Not unlike her friend Nathan, I thought. Her blond hair was tied back in a very sensible braid, and she wore plain blue clothes without a discernible label, which I later found out were specifically tailored to avoid sensory irritations.

She also had extensive scarring on several parts of her face, also visible on her hands. I had a feeling it extended over other parts of her body too. The horrible remnants of the fire that killed her mother.

"You've been talking about me, huh?" I teased Nathan with a little poke to the side.

He blinked. "Yes. I saw her a few weeks ago and told her I was going to find you and bring you back."

I grinned. Gradually, he grinned back. I fought the urge to kiss him, but made a mental note to do it later as a thank you.

"But I thought your name was Giovanna." Isla surprised us all by putting the pencil down and looking up at me for a second before her gaze darted away almost as quickly.

Beside her, Mary smiled. "What a good observation, Isla. Thank you for joining the conversation."

Beside us, Nathan's entire face lit up. Clearly, he hadn't been expecting much from the interaction.

I smiled at Isla. "It is Giovanna, but everyone calls me Joni."

She worked very hard on shading something on her paper. "Why?"

I shrugged. "I'm not sure, actually. It's kind of short for Giovanna."

"But it's not, really," the girl pointed out. There was no annoyance in her tone. Just blunt observation. "Every time I've seen that name, it's been in books, and the characters are usually called Joan or maybe Joanna or Johanne. Not Giovanna. They don't even start with the same letter of the alphabet."

The more she talked about it, the more stressed she seemed to get. It made me want to reach out and take her hand, but Nathan had warned me that Isla wouldn't appreciate any unsolicited touch. So I kept my hands at my side.

"That's true," I said. "It's probably more because my mom really liked Joni Mitchell, so even though my dad gave me an Italian name, it was close enough that she called me Joni anyway."

"Is that true?" Nathan wondered.

I nodded. "Yeah. Kind of weird, but that's what I've always been told."

Isla seemed satisfied with my answer and went back to working on her drawing, which appeared to be a very realistic sketch of a horse.

"Would you be willing to tell me about your drawing?" I asked.

I wanted to be careful. As a kid, I fucking hated it when people pulled me out of something I was working on without asking first. Nonna did it all the time. If I was singing a song or practicing some dance steps and Nonna told me to sweep the porch, it took me until I was almost in middle school to stop shrieking at her out of frustration. Not because I had to do chores, but because I had to stop something I was *finally* focused on.

It was one of the reasons my siblings all thought I was so spoiled.

And maybe I was. But looking at Isla, I wondered now if we weren't similar in that way too. Maybe it hadn't all been my fault.

"Is it all right if I keep working on it?" she asked with a quick glance at Mary.

"That's a very good question," Mary told her more than us. "Very thoughtful of you."

"I'm fine with it," I said. "I actually like having things to work on when I talk to people too. Otherwise, I fidget too much. I think it's called 'stimming'?"

I glanced at Nathan for confirmation. He was drumming his fingers on his knee again and smiled.

At that, Isla looked up again with another flash of recognition. "I stim too. Most people here do. Actually, most people in the world stim in one way or another. It's the body's way of regulating itself, except some forms of it are more acceptable than others. Do you have autism too, Joni?"

I shook my head, a bit bowled over by the onslaught of facts. Part of me wanted to smile. Isla had a way of speaking that was a bit similar to Nathan's. It was incredibly endearing. "I don't think so. But I think I might be neurodiv-erse?" I glanced at Nathan again for confirmation.

"Neurodivergent," he corrected me quietly. Kindly.

I couldn't have appreciated it more.

I nodded and grinned. "That. Yeah. In other ways. I'm just kind of learning about them."

Isla nodded as she outlined the shape of the horse's ear. "There are a lot of ways to be neurodivergent. ASD, OCD, Down's syndrome, bipolar disorder, ADHD, epilepsy, dyspraxia, dyslexia, dyscalculia, Tourette syndrome…"

Her aide, I noticed, didn't stop her as she went on, and neither did Nathan. It was too easy to imagine the response I would have gotten—the responses I *did* get—went I went on about something obsessively like that as a kid. One of my five siblings would have told me to shut up, another would have made fun of me, and someone else probably would have made fun of me for it later.

Eventually, I'd learned to stop sharing when my interest was piqued. I'd started making lists instead. Sometimes writing them down, but mostly in my head so I wouldn't have to look at my terrible spelling.

Here, Isla could make her lists out loud with people who loved her enough to listen.

I found myself wanting to join her.

"Nathan has social pragmatic communication disorder," Isla finished. "Which is kind of like autism, but missing some of the other traits that I have too."

"Yes, I do," Nathan told her. "Thank you for including me in the conversation. That's really important to me, and I really like knowing that we have that in common."

He was mimicking what Mary was doing, I realized, by praising Isla when she did something that was socially aware. No one was correcting the girl or pointing out her errors—instead, they were working in a system of open communication about her challenges and reinforcing her attempts at working through them.

It was a fucking revelation.

Isla's eyes shone quickly toward Nathan as she continued working on her horse. "We do have that in common. We also have horses in common. We have a new horse that just arrived in the stables this week. His name is Crimson…"

She continued to talk about horses with Nathan, giving me the opportunity to sit back and just listen, observe, and make my own list in my head.

Things I Like About Isla

1. She has no idea how pretty she is. That's always the best kind of pretty because people aren't full of themselves.
2. She was very, very smart. I think she might have a photographic memory. Or at least knows everything on earth about horses.
3. She adores Nathan. I know he thinks she's not very social, but she listens to everything he says, and she responds more to him than anyone. She and I will get along great.

Within about an hour, Isla started to get antsy. Her patience with the conversation began to erode as she tired of drawing and started struggling to control her body. I noticed more than once that she sat on her hands because if she didn't, she would shake them by her ears or start pulling on her chin.

"I would like to go back upstairs," she announced abruptly when Mary was in the middle of telling Nathan about a book Isla was reading for her English class.

Everyone turned to her as she yanked at the knees of her pants.

"Thank you for communicating that," Mary said kindly. "Would you like to say goodbye to Nathan and Joni first?"

She had the option not to, and for a moment, I wouldn't have blamed her if she had just left. It was obviously hard for her to do things like this, and I could tell how uncomfortable she was and how ready she was to leave.

But after she stood up, Isla paused and turned to Nathan and me with a few quick bobs of her head all the way down to her knees. "Goodbye, Nathan and Joni. Thank you for coming."

She turned to leave, but then, almost as quickly, she turned back and gave Nathan a very quick, very awkward embrace, then sprang back almost as though she couldn't handle anything else anymore. Isla grabbed her drawings and exited the room without another word.

Mary watched her go, then turned to us, eyes shining. "First hug, isn't that?"

Nathan swallowed hard and wiped the corner of his eye as if there was something in it. "Yes, it was."

Mary smiled warmly. "She likes it when you come. I hope you can continue to see her more often."

With a polite goodbye to both of us, she followed her ward upstairs, leaving Nathan and me to exit the way we had come.

WE WERE both quiet as we drove back through the campus. As I looked around, I wondered vaguely how much a place like this cost.

Probably more than college. More than most people made in a year. People like the Hunts wouldn't blink at paying that kind of price, but it was completely out of the question for most families struggling with disabilities.

Families like mine. If Nathan was right about me having ADHD, dyslexia, and who knew what else, how might I have benefited from some kind of intervention when I was a little kid? I doubted I would have needed this kind of twenty-four-hour therapy, but even so. What might I have been capable of as a child had I the benefit of therapists, counselors, or better tutors than the honor roll volunteers?

Even now, I made rudimentary spelling errors all the time, had never actually read a full book cover to cover, and couldn't do basic addition without my phone or my fingers. I had also learned little tricks to hide my awkwardness—things like flirting and smiling to cover up the fact that I hadn't been able to follow a conversation, staring a little too hard to demonstrate that I was actually listening, or making myself the butt of a joke when people pointed out how spacey I was. No one was better at making fun of me than me.

Sometimes, my life felt like one big mask.

But as I looked around the school, I couldn't help but wonder what would my life have been like if I'd had this kind of support from the get-go? Would I have been able to finish high school without seducing my teachers? Or actually finished college like some of my smarter siblings?

Would I have even become a dancer at all?

That thought sobered me. Dancing was everything to me. Already, I was eager to get back in the studio, to start practicing the routines that would get me back into shape, to go back to auditioning and performing, to what I'd always thought I'd been made for.

So, not a world without dance. Never that. But maybe a world where I had more options. A world where I might actually be able to choose what I did and when instead of feeling backed into a corner every time I hit a rough patch.

Yeah. That would be nice.

"Thank you for coming," Nathan interrupted my thoughts gently as he turned onto a freeway to head back to the farm. "She liked you. At least she's very interested in you."

I turned to him, suddenly full of more determination than ever to help him out of this horrible situation, but also to help the girl I'd just met.

"She's amazing," I said. "And she deserves to be free from your parents. You both do. And we're going to make it happen, no matter what it takes."

FORTY-FOUR

BEST PARTS OF THE COUNTRY

#6 Sweet conversashuns and kisses by the pond

I'd never been on a horse before. No surprise there, considering I had grown up in a place where the only horses were either ridden by cops or carried tourists around Central Park. Neither of these things had any appeal for the average teenager and certainly weren't things I could ever afford. So horses always seemed like one of those mythical creatures that were only accessible to the very rich or people who lived out in the middle of nowhere.

Nathan's family seemed like both, even though they weren't that far from the city. The vast expanse of their property made it feel like you were miles and miles from any civilization. And I supposed, in a way, we were. Fifteen hundred acres, Nathan told me, roughly converted to two and a half square miles. We could walk all day if we wanted to and never meet another soul.

For the time being, Lillian and Radford seemed content to pretend their son's porn star girlfriend didn't exist. After visiting Isla, we shared a dinner in their fancy dining room, where neither of them even acknowledged my presence. Breakfast of coffee and toast the following morning was equally stunted.

I, for one, found I didn't really care. In an ideal world, would I want my boyfriend's parents to love me?

Sure.

Did I need or even expect that to be the case?

Never.

I was here for Nathan. And if that meant my support existed by doing PT in our bedroom while he tried to negotiate Isla's guardianship, I was just fine with that. What I wasn't all right with was the idea of his mother berating him when I wasn't around. Or being manipulated by other family members. I knew what that felt like all too well. There was just no way I was going to let him go through this by himself.

The following morning, after sharing an awkward breakfast with his parents, Nathan took me out to the stables, about a ten-minute walk from the main house.

The stables matched the traditional architecture of the house but were constructed from a much smaller building that housed livestock when Huntwell was still a working farm. In the early part of the twentieth century, Nathan's great-grandfather had apparently gotten the bug to race horses after the Preakness Stakes started in Baltimore. He was part of the contingent that began the steeplechase races in Fauquier County.

"Supposedly, he didn't think flat races should get all the attention," Nathan said as we walked.

I had no idea what that was, and so I spent the rest of the walk listening to Nathan nerd out about the differences between flat racing and steeple chasing, thoroughbreds versus other kinds of horses, and a bunch of other things I could barely understand because I was too lulled by the music of his deep, sonorous voice.

"I'm actually not much of an expert," Nathan said as we finally got to the stables.

"Could have fooled me," I said with a grin before I popped up to kiss his cheek. "I think I should call you my personal professor instead of doctor. You can teach me anytime."

Nathan smiled, not quite able to hide his blush.

"Well, well, well. If it isn't the prodigal son," called a voice from the other end of the stable.

We turned to find Spencer Hunt emerging from one of the stalls, looking more like a dirty stable boy than the youngest son of some of the wealthiest people in the country. If it weren't for the absurd glow of his golden hair and brilliant white of his teeth, I might have thought he was just another staff member. But he still had that gleam about him that only seemed to come from extreme wealth, I was starting to see.

"I'm only prodigal if I've done terrible things." Nathan stiffly accepted his brother's handshake, but not without obvious suspicion. "You weren't at dinner last night."

Spencer shook his head. "I only got back this morning. Kip ran the Preakness last night, so I stayed over in Baltimore."

As if on cue, the head of an enormous black horse poked over the door of the stall next to me and nosed into my shoulder.

I jumped with a shriek, right into Nathan's arms. My boyfriend, however, wasn't quite able to keep a straight face.

"Kip, that wasn't very nice to the pretty lady," Spencer said as he strode over to the horse and rubbed its large nose.

The horse chuffed like it was laughing and eyed me with more intelligence than I would have imagined.

"Don't race horses have weird names like Sunday Blues or Toothpaste Miracle?" I asked. Even I'd seen *Secretariat*.

"Oh, sure," Spencer replied with a grin. "Technically, this guy's formal name is Christy Climbing, but we call him Kip for luck." He rolled his eyes. "It was Mom's turn to name."

"Rose breed?" Nathan guessed.

"And they say you don't remember where you came from," Spencer joked. "With a name like that, it's no surprise he came in fourth. But he's got a brother coming up next year that I think will make a real run at the Derby. You'll see."

"The Derby?" Nathan asked. "Really?"

"As in Kentucky?" I chimed in.

Spencer nodded with obvious glee. I was starting to see what Nathan meant when he said he wasn't the real expert in the family.

While it was clear that horses were an interest for Nathan, something he missed about his old life, I could tell in all of five minutes that they were a true passion for his youngest brother. Just as I couldn't imagine Nathan doing anything but being a surgeon, it was plain that Spencer Hunt didn't belong anywhere else but the stables.

Which only made it that much sadder that they had parents who couldn't see their sons' real worth. So few people in the world had true callings. The Hunts were fortunate enough to have raised two of them.

"Can we saddle up Gus?" Nathan asked. "I'd like to take Joni out, but she's never ridden. He's mellow and big enough for two, don't you think?"

Kip shook his big head at Spencer, who just wrestled with him a moment.

"Calm down, you big bully. You'll get some exercise today too." Then he turned to us and looked me over. "You go on with Nathan—he'll set you up with boots and a helmet. I'll have one of the grooms put a tandem on Gus and meet you out front."

TWENTY MINUTES LATER, I was kitted out with a black velvet riding helmet and knee-high boots yanked over my knees, sitting atop a truly enormous black horse, and clutching the reins for dear life. I'd needed a boost just to get my foot into the stirrup, and now I felt like I was sitting on top of a skyscraper.

In one easy movement, Nathan swung up behind me, causing me to yelp.

The horse barely seemed to notice, though I was happy when Nathan reached around me to grab the reins. The horse snorted, but didn't seem to care otherwise.

"It would be better if you could refrain from screaming," Nathan's deep voice rumbled into my ear. "Gus is unlikely to throw anyone, but it's a long fall. I like you without broken bones."

I tried to turn to leer at him but was too scared to fall off. "You don't need your own horse?"

"Gus is a Shire Horse," Nathan said. "They can carry almost five hundred pounds."

"Sounds like a necessity in a family full of giant men," I agreed.

He slid one hand securely around my waist and pulled me back against him so I was nestled between his firm thighs. Though my body calmed, my heartbeat sped up a bit as his finger teased the undersides of my breasts.

"Besides," he said. "I'm happy here for now."

Then he gave the horse a gentle kick, and we were off.

IT WAS a beautiful day for riding. Nathan took us through a meadow of wild grass, then through a wooded area to cool off. We passed through a glen dotted with foxgloves and buttercups before reaching the edge of a small pond. There we stopped beneath the broad, low-hanging branches of a massive oak tree.

Nathan dismounted with the ease of a practiced rider, then reached up to catch me by the waist. I was glad for it. On solid ground, perhaps I was relatively graceful, but I had a feeling those stirrups would be the death of me.

Gus seemed content to be tethered to the tree and graze at its base. Nathan fed him an apple from his jacket pocket, then removed a picnic blanket and some food from the panniers attached to the saddle. I walked out to the pond, removed my helmet, and perched on a small boulder to sunbathe for a minute.

"What are you doing over there?" Nathan called. "You look like you're melting."

I grinned at him from my rock. "Oh, I'm definitely melting. It's hot as balls out here, especially in these boots. But it feels damn good after a long, cold winter."

Nathan frowned as he set out some sandwiches. "Testicles are actually about two degrees lower than the rest of the body, you know. Most people carry the most heat in their brains, hearts, and livers. So, really, that saying should be something like 'hot as a liver.' Though I suppose it doesn't have the same appeal."

"Why's that?" I asked as I turned back to the sunlight.

"People seem to enjoy describing various things in terms of genitalia. Especially the weather, for some reason."

I giggled. "True. Like, 'I'm freezing my ass off.'"

I turned to see Nathan nodding as he walked over to me. "Exactly. I honestly don't think that is even physically possible."

"Ooooh, I got another. 'Colder than a witch's tit!' My sister Lea loves to say that one when she's grouchy."

"But why witches?" Nathan wondered, though he was chuckling now.

"Why tits?" I asked right back.

We were both laughing outright now, and it felt *so* good. I thought he couldn't get any sexier. I really did. But turns out that a happy, laughing Nathan was like serious, mysterious Nathan on steroids. About ten times hotter than the sun. Blazing.

There wasn't enough levity in Nathan's life, I realized. And maybe not in mine either. At that moment, I knew I'd make butt and boob jokes every single day if I could hear him laugh like that. I just wanted to make him happy. Like, by some miracle, he wanted for me.

Suddenly, I was swept off the rock like a princess and carried back to the picnic.

"This is so...country," I said as I set my helmet on the ground and took a piece of watermelon from the basket. "I can see why you miss it."

Nathan sank next to me and started fixing himself a sizable but healthy lunch on a paper plate. "If my life could be like this most of the time, I wouldn't have left," he said honestly. "But I'm glad I did." Our eyes met over a bowl of potato salad. "Otherwise, I wouldn't have met you."

I leaned over a plate of cold chicken and pressed a kiss to his lips. Neither of us hurried to stop it. There was no reason to, here on our own.

Until my stomach rumbled, anyway.

I laughed. "Better take care of *that* first."

Nathan agreed and started to dig into his food.

BOYFRIEND OF THE HOUR   501

"Isla would probably like it here," I said. "With the horses and everything. Don't you think?"

Nathan was quiet for a long time. "I've thought that many times." He took a bite of salad, chewed, and swallowed before answering. "Equine therapy has been one of her primary methods for years. It's how she came to love horses so much." His eyes seemed to glow when he thought about it. "She wants to be a veterinarian."

I nodded. "What all would she need to do?"

"College first, of course. She's smart enough, like I said, but it's more a question if she can deal with the discomfort of working through a basic degree in something like zoology before she can study what she wants. She has a few more years to work on that." He looked out toward the pond. "My parents think she should leave next year. Go back to North Carolina, where Lindsay's family lives."

I frowned. "I didn't know she had any existing family."

"She doesn't," Nathan said shortly. "Lindsay's mother ran off when she was maybe fifteen. And her dad is still in prison for larceny. Isla's closest blood relatives are some second cousins who live in an RV somewhere near Charlotte. I'm her only real family."

"So your parents would just…abandon her?" I had a hard time believing it, even for Lillian and Radford.

"No," Nathan said. "They want to have her moved to a state-run facility that teaches people like Isla how to work. They think her idea of being a veterinarian is a pipe dream, and she'd be better off learning how to bag groceries or pack boxes."

"That's terrible," I replied. "And that's just to force you to come home?"

"To my parents, Isla is the reason they lost me in the first place," Nathan said. "I suspect they'll never forgive her for it. They certainly wouldn't take her into their home."

"Then maybe living here isn't the best thing for her," I agreed. "Are there stables maybe closer to New York where she could work? Do you think she could make that kind of transition?"

Nathan stole a quick glance at me with an adorably sweet smile that made my heart glow. "I've actually been looking at properties in

Westchester for some time now," he said. "There's one near New Rochelle that has a small stable on it. I could afford it if I sold some of my Huntwell stock. It's the sort of place where I think she would be happy."

It was too easy to imagine that dream with him. A place where he could continue his own calling and also take care of Isla. And maybe a place where I might fit too.

"Why didn't you become her guardian in the first place?" I wondered.

"I was considered too young," Nathan said. "I tried, but my parents offered, and the state allowed it, likely because my father knows enough judges on the Fourth Circuit to influence any court in North Carolina. At the time, it seemed like the right decision."

I nodded. How could he have known at just twenty-one that his parents were already manipulating him and Isla like chess pieces, putting them into position so that they would be able to maintain control over their eldest son for the rest of his life.

But he didn't need to be a pawn anymore. On top of being a grown man, Nathan was an incredibly accomplished one. He had, in effect, been Isla's guardian for much longer than he realized.

"So, how can we demonstrate that you're the one who should be in charge?" I asked. "Do we get a lawyer? Do we hire a private investigator? Do we need to gather documentation?

Nathan looked up from his chicken, appearing a bit amused. "How do you know about all of those things?"

"I do have a lawyer for a brother. Some of that stuff had to wear off over the years." I tapped my lip. "I remember him talking to Frankie about what might happen if Xavier ever came back into the picture after my niece was born. Frankie got lucky—when Xavier did find out, he wanted to be with Frankie more than he was mad at her for keeping their daughter a secret. But if they went sour, Mattie always told her that she should have lots of documentation of her parenting in case things went south. So that if Xavier suddenly decided he wanted custody, there wouldn't be a case for it."

Nathan looked thoughtful. "I have some documentation. Mostly emails between my parents and me. Things they might write off as suggestions, but were actually directions that I was giving them about Isla's care. I was the one that found Ferndale in the first place. I'm actually the one who pays for it too."

"See," I said eagerly. "That's half the battle."

Nathan leaned back against the trunk of the oak and sighed. "I think the idea of a battle is the problem, Joni. My parents would love to fight because it keeps me involved, and they would bury something like that in court for as long as it takes." He shook his head. "It's better to play their game for a bit. Make them think I'm here to stay for a while. Then maybe they'll give up on using Isla as a pawn, so when she's eighteen, I can quietly transfer guardianship to me."

We finished lunch, then laid back on the blanket together, hand in hand while we stared up at the oak leaves rustling in the wind. It occurred to me just how very much I loved this man.

Here was a person who was always so unabashedly himself but whose sense of justice was so deeply ingrained that he was willing to sacrifice nearly everything to do what he believed was right. The fact that he believed me a part of that quest made me feel better about myself too. It wasn't just Nathan's faith in me that made me love him, though. It was the way that faith turned me into a better person as well. It made me believe that, as a team, we could do anything.

If we only had the guts to try.

I turned over and found his eyes closed, long lashes casting shadows over his cheekbones. Slowly, I crept up and kissed him. He startled, but then returned the kiss almost as quickly.

When he opened his eyes, there was a bit more peace there.

I would have given anything to make it permanent.

"What's that look?" he wondered as he brushed a bit of hair from my face.

I pushed myself up and crawled on top of him so I could straddle his waist. He watched me curiously, then with no little interest as I slowly removed my top, then my bra so that I was now topless.

"Amazement," I told him. "Shock I could ever find myself in a place like this. With someone like you."

No one had ever looked at me like he did. Not just with interest, but with awe. Like I really was the most beautiful thing he had ever seen. Truly a masterpiece in every way possible.

Nathan's hands moved up my thighs, over my stomach and waist, then cupped my breasts so he could brush his thumbs gently over my nipples. He watched reverently as they pebbled under his touch, then sat up in a sudden movement that made every muscle in his torso flex under his shirt, which I quickly removed for him.

We sat there, skin to skin, holding each other for a moment. Then Nathan's head dipped so he could take one nipple into his mouth, pulling it as far in as he possibly could.

I tipped my head back, enjoying the rays of the sun and the feeling of that heated mouth on my breast. He moved to the other, and I quivered under his touch, the rest of me suddenly dying for the same kind of attention.

He released the nipple with a pop, then laid back down to look at his handiwork, where he had left two perfectly shaped hickeys just above each of my nipples.

It should have disgusted me, but it only turned me on.

"Are those out of love too?" I asked with a cheeky grin.

Nathan's hands slipped up around my back so that he could pull me back down to him for another kiss.

"You said you wanted to be marked," he told me before lightly biting my lip. "And I just want to make you happy."

Then, in a sudden movement, he flipped me onto my back, eliciting a shriek from me.

"Hush," he said as he started to remove my pants. "You'll startle Gus, and then we could be stuck out here forever."

It didn't seem to affect the big horse at all, who also didn't notice when Nathan and I were both naked on the blanket, bodies twined together under the sun and the leaves.

"Joni," Nathan murmured as his hands drew up and down my thighs, gaze roving over all of me like he was memorizing every shape I had.

"Show me more about life on the farm, Dr. Hunt," I said as he settled between my legs. "Mark me again."

FORTY-FIVE
WHY I NEED TO QUIT EAVESDROPPING

#2 you keep hering stuff you dont like

My brain was already churning when I decided to go downstairs before dinner. Nathan was still showering off the remnants of our afternoon ride and bliss beside the pond, but after our discussion, I decided I needed to do...something...to improve my relationship with his parents.

I wasn't expecting much. After all, what kind of relationship could I really expect with people who had seen me naked, having sex on the internet (or maybe just their son's phone? A girl could hope)?

That said, I was hoping that, at some point, they would understand I was the victim of that particular crime. That I'd been recorded and put on video without my consent. Nathan had convinced me as much. There was no reason he shouldn't be able to do the same with them.

But what really drove my desire to talk to his parents was the fact that Nathan wanted a relationship with them. I could see that as plain as day. Listening to him talk by the side of the pond, I could hear the yearning in his voice. Nathan didn't want the kind of parents who manipulated him or forced him into decisions he didn't want to make, but he wanted to get along. He wanted a family who supported him as much as he clearly wanted to support them. Otherwise, he wouldn't be here in the first place.

While I personally thought his family could jump off a bridge, I had to admit that maybe their machinations came from a place of love as well, however misplaced. After all, his mother wouldn't want him to be such an integral part of the family if she didn't care, right? I didn't know about his father, who seemed apathetic at best toward his sons, but Lillian Hunt obviously wanted her children around. There was maternal instinct in there somewhere. Perhaps I could appeal to it.

Nathan always said I was good with people. Maybe I could charm his parents into showing their best colors too.

And so, I put on my very best and most conservative dress for the evening—a light blue wrap dress that Lea probably would have loved, but before now, I wouldn't have been caught dead in. I figured it was in my best interest to look more like a socialite than a dancer. To do everything I could to remind Lillian of herself.

I made my way to the dining room, hoping to catch them early. Nathan said his parents enjoyed cocktails before dinner and often took drinks in the library. But just as I reached the doors, I heard voices spilling out into the hall. Including one particularly unwelcome baritone.

"Well, she's got some balls. I'll give her that." Carrick's voice echoed off the tiled floors and molded ceilings of the house. "Nathan too. I honestly didn't think he had it in him."

"He'll tire of her," Lillian replied. "He has to. She's unbelievably inappropriate for a man of his station. A man of his worth."

"Come on, Mom. She's not all bad. If you take away the dirty dancing and the Pornhub entry, she seems all right. Loves the hell out of Nathan, and you know that's not always easy."

I frowned. Carrick was defending me? Wasn't he the one who sabotaged our relationship to begin with?

And easy for who? Nathan was one of the best people I've ever met. One of the easiest. At least for me.

"He could make things easier," Lillian was saying. "Charlotte, for one, is very interested in him. What was the point of arranging for her to work at his silly little practice if it wasn't so he could finally meet his match?"

I sucked in a breath. I knew Charlotte Mueller's presence in Nathan's life wasn't by accident. But a puppet for Lillian? That was legitimately insane.

"I only regret giving him access to his trust that early," Lillian went on. "God knows what will happen if he actually marries this girl like he said. Disaster. Could be billions down the drain."

I covered my mouth in shock. Billions? I knew Nathan's parents were that wealthy, and, yes, I knew he had a trust. But he didn't actually live like I would expect of someone who had billions of dollars.

Xavier, for instance, bought real estate like trading cards, and Frankie often complained about his propensity for showering her with gifts even though she was married to the guy. Their townhouse that was currently being renovated in New York was the size of a hotel.

Nathan's home, while very nice and, yes, containing at least one priceless work of art, was still no more than a two-bedroom, one-bath apartment. It wasn't out of the realm of possibility for most people who had a decent job.

At the same time, I realized quite clearly that I didn't care if he had a secret bank account or if he ever shared it with me. I would have taken him if he had nothing more to sleep in than a cardboard box. And I was pretty sure he felt the same about me.

Just as I was about to walk in and inform Lillian of just that, she spoke again.

"It's clear that something must be done."

"Well, you got him down here," Carrick said. "That was the first step. He still trying to play nice?"

Lillian grumbled, "He is. My good boy."

"Then here's a wild thought. Just give him what he wants. You might be surprised. He might just stick around."

"You can't be serious. If we gave him Isla's guardianship, we'd never see him again. It's like you scooting off to the townhouse. You never come home."

"Don't worry about that," Carrick said. "My leash is plenty tight."

There was something in Carrick's voice I didn't understand. Something dark. Something resigned.

"He might surprise you, though," Carrick went on before I could consider it more. "Nathan's always had a soft spot for family. That's why he's able to be controlled through the girl. He basically adopted her as his own, and now he thinks of her as a daughter. In his own cold fish way."

"No, *you're* the cold fish," I muttered. "A friggin' flounder, you asshole."

"Did you hear something?" Carrick wondered.

Lillian remained quiet, though I could hear the sipping of some kind of drink. A white wine spritzer, I was guessing. She'd had it the last two nights.

"Come on, Mom. Haven't you ever heard the saying if you love something, set it free? Nathan just might come back on his own."

"We did that once with a pair of imported swans. The trainers told us that they were smart enough that they would come back every year and replace the other two. But they didn't. They found a pond on the other side of the county they liked better. It didn't matter that we provided them with everything they'd ever want. They never came back."

"Nathan is not a fucking bird, Mother." Carrick's voice dripped with sarcasm. "He'll come home if you give him a good reason to. One that maybe trades genuine affection for blackmail."

There was the sound of footsteps pacing around the soft carpet inside the library, Lillian taking a few more sips of her drink, and the tinkling of her fingernails on the glass.

"No, I don't think so," she said at last. "Your brother has always been too independent for his own good. The only way to keep him safe is to bring him to heel."

"Nathan's not a dumb twenty-one-year-old kid anymore. And for what it's worth, I don't think Joni is anywhere near the same as Lindsay. I've asked around, and she's actually pretty damn talented. Once her knee's healed up, I wouldn't be surprised if she ends up dancing with a legitimate company again. You want Nathan back in DC? Get his girl a spot on the Washington Ballet."

I tilted my head in surprise. It was the nicest thing Carrick could have said about me. I honestly thought he hated me.

"And in that...video?" Lillian asked. "Was she demonstrating her talent there too?"

My cheeks burned. But honestly, I was just mad. Mad that I'd made such a stupid error, but also that it was apparently going to be held against me forever. It wasn't fair.

"Look, we've all made mistakes. Trust me, you wouldn't want to know half the stuff I did at that age," Carrick joked. "She's a good egg. More importantly, she loves Nathan. I think he deserves to be happy, don't you?"

There was another long silence while Lillian seemed to consider each point. I, for one, was just confused. How could someone who had gone out of his way to sabotage my relationship with his brother suddenly be on the other side of it? Carrick made no sense. What were his motives?

But then Lillian spoke, and I decided I didn't have the time to figure that out. Her next statement was too fucking damning.

"He doesn't know what happiness really is," she said at last. "It's not dating a pretty girl. It's not indulging yourself with only your own interests. And it's not caring for a child who isn't even of your own blood. If we don't guide him now, he's going to wake up one day and realize he's wasted his entire life with trivialities."

I scowled. Our relationship aside, saying Nathan's job or Isla was trivial was beyond insulting. I didn't need to know anything else to know that Lillian Hunt didn't know her son at all. Nor did she really want to.

"It's done," Lillian went on. "Our lawyers are already drawing up the case to present to the judge next week. And it's Edward Carver, so you know it's just a formality."

"You're really going to do it?" Carrick asked. "Force the girl into a conservatorship so she has no say in who cares for her? Nathan says she's pretty smart. Enough to make her own decisions that way, or at least weigh in on them."

"Please. Anyone who's been living in a glorified loony bin for most of her life is in no state to be making decisions on her own behalf."

I felt sick. Had Lillian even met Isla? She was different, to be sure, but hardly incapable. At the very least, she deserved to choose her own guardians. Have a say in the terms of her life.

"We've already been dealing with a caseworker," Lillian went on. "I've been making monthly trips out to the center just to prove my dedication."

"Have you actually seen the girl?"

"Bless your heart. The point is to demonstrate my dedication. Why would I need to see the little urchin for that?"

I listened to Lillian detail the other aspects of her case for guardianship. The bills she had accrued, paying without first talking to Nathan. The backhanded communication she'd established with Isla's school without Nathan's knowledge. Quickly, it became obvious that this wasn't just a last-ditch effort to bring her son back into the family fold. Like a spider, Lillian Hunt had been spinning this web for years with the express purpose of trapping Nathan like a fly, all at the expense of Isla. At the expense of his entire life.

"Now, if we can just figure out how to get rid of his little tramp, everything will be as it should," Lillian said. "Cheers, darling."

I backed away from the door on my tiptoes, feeling sick but not wanting to alert them to my presence. My mind was spinning. What could I do?

Help. I needed help. And not just from Nathan. From someone who had been in a situation like this. Someone who had extricated himself from a devious family. Who knew how to beat them at their own game.

That's when I knew who to call.

And as I turned to go back to my room, I had the inklings of a plan to free the love of my life for good. If only I could play things right.

FORTY-SIX

WAYS TO SAVE NATHAN FROM HIS PARENTS

#4 ~~help him fake his own deth~~ *bad idea*

"You're sure you don't want me to come with you?" Nathan asked.

I shook my head as I shoved a few pieces of clothes into the backpack I was taking with me back to New York. "I won't be long. Just overnight, and then I'll be back here before you know it."

The story Xavier had told me about his family in Paris had been haunting me all night long. Frankie had always called him her shark —he knew how to trap people with their own games, circle them until they were weak, and then attack. He was ruthless and knew this kind of upper crust world better than I ever could.

And, so, the next morning, after I'd put in my second performance of "oblivious girlfriend his parents hate," I'd gone for a long walk on the property in order to call Frankie and Xavier and ask for their advice.

Xavier had listened to the situation. Asked some key questions. And quickly helped me figure out exactly what to do.

It seemed so easy. I wasn't entirely convinced it would work.

People like me weren't supposed to be able to fix things like this with a quick conversation. We were supposed to struggle.

"You have more to offer than you could ever imagine," Frankie had told me quietly once Xavier had gotten off the phone. "People have underestimated you your entire life. Use it to your advantage. Surprise them now. Don't wait for their respect when you can take it for yourself."

Her words buoyed me—maybe because I'd so rarely heard them from one of my siblings. But that, I decided, was exactly what I would do.

I still hadn't told Nathan the plan. Not because I didn't want him to know, but because my man was one of the most truthful people on the planet, and this particular endeavor required a bit of deviousness. He was never going to best his mother in this kind of game. He needed me to play for him.

I'd tell him when I could. But first, I needed to know if my plan would work at all.

I had to be in New York anyway for my first post-operative appointment, which gave me the perfect opportunity to put my plan into motion. But there was another reason for my cloak-and-dagger tactics. I wasn't willing to be the reason Nathan lost his entire relationship with his family. If *he* decided to end things, I'd support him. But mostly, I wanted it to be his decision. Not to be roped into a life with people unless he wanted it. And not to walk away because I'd alienated him beyond belief.

I zipped up my bag, then popped up onto my tiptoes to give him a kiss. "I should probably leave soon to get to the airport on time."

Nathan rewarded me by grabbing my waist and throwing me back on the bed. "We don't have to leave for at least fifteen minutes. And I know exactly what to do with them."

FIVE HOURS LATER, I stood nervously outside an enormous townhouse on Seventy-Seventh Street, a mere block from the Natural History Museum, hesitating in front of the carved front door.

The post-op appointment had gone well. Stitches were dissolving, everything was healing, and I was cleared for increased PT for both the meniscus and the tendon. From Mt. Sinai, I walked directly uptown to the address Xavier had given me without a stitch of pain in my knee.

"I'm not going to make your case for you," he'd told me yesterday. "To start, I don't know all the details, so I'd get torn apart. Eric and Jane are both former lawyers like your brother, so they'll pay attention to every little detail and then ask for them. Good people, but shrewd. They'll give you a listen, but you have to be honest. Don't lie about a thing. And keep your story straight."

I gulped. It's not that I *wanted* to lie.

It was one of those places where only very rich New Yorkers could live, and Frankie and Matthew had assured me these people were some of the richest.

I knew who they were, of course. Anyone who followed *Page Six* knew who the de Vrieses were. A year ago, they'd caused a huge gossip scandal when Eric de Vries had returned to his family fold after ten years away...and quickly got married to a quirky half-Korean lawyer who looked more like a rock star than an attorney.

My connection to them was a bit closer. Xavier had gone to college with Eric once upon a time, but even better, his cousin was married to my brother. I'd actually met them briefly at Nina and Matthew's wedding last fall. At the time, I'd been wallowing in depression over my recent knee surgery, so I had barely remembered their names. Right now, I wished I'd paid a little more attention to the polite conversation we'd shared during the cocktail hour.

I sighed and raised my hand. No going back now. This wasn't for me. This was for Isla. This was for Nathan.

Before my fist hit the wood, the door swung open, and I was greeted by an Asian woman in cat-eyed glasses, whose dark hair was dyed blue and green on one half of her head.

I had to smile. "Jane?" I asked.

She hadn't even said anything, and I was already put at ease. Jane de Vries looked more like my friends who worked in performance spaces like Casper's or frequented my dance classes down-town than a socialite and billionaire's wife.

Immediately, she nodded. "Sorry to scare you by opening the door. I wasn't lurking, I promise. Well, actually I sort of was. The baby's asleep and it's absolute murder trying to get that thing down. I don't know who said that the first few months of a baby's life are bliss because these have been the worst in my life. You must be Matthew's sister, Joni. We met last October at the wedding, didn't we?"

I nodded. "Yeah, but he has a lot of sisters. I—thanks for meeting with me."

"Oh, we'd do just about anything for your family. Your brother saved our lives. Honestly, he feels like *my* brother, too, at this point."

I smiled. I didn't really know anything about that. Matthew had always been tight-lipped about his cases as a DA, and while I knew he'd been involved in the big trial involving the de Vrieses, he had never said much about it.

"Come in." Jane ushered me into the house, then closed the door firmly behind me. "Eric's upstairs making sure the baby's asleep, but he'll be down in a second."

"How old is…the baby?" I'd almost said "it."

Jane grinned. "Three months going on thirteen. I swear, if she's going to scream this loud because she doesn't like her pacifier, I don't know what's going to happen when I tell her she's not allowed to wear shorts that show her ass cheeks."

I giggled, enjoying Jane's candor. "Yeah, that could be a problem."

I followed her into a great room just off the main foyer of the townhouse. It wasn't at all what I expected. Xavier had money like the de Vrieses, inherited from generations of family wealth. But the pictures of his estates in England were so formal, even more so than Huntwell Farm. Jane and Eric's home was modern, full of eclectic art and vintage furniture that was as comfortable as it was interesting.

"How is Nina doing?" Jane asked. "I hear she's on bed rest, poor girl."

"Due any day, I think. I'm pretty sure they're in their own little world up there. Matthew hasn't been to New York since she went on bed rest."

I wished I could have told her more. Between two months of wallowing and the fact that Matthew had been holed up with Nina for months, making sure she didn't get up for anything but the bathroom, I hadn't seen my brother since he helped Nonna move out.

"Poor thing," Jane said. "That last month is murder. Can I get you a drink? I was going to make myself some green tea."

I nodded. "Thanks, that would be great."

"Make yourself comfortable."

She disappeared into a kitchen on the other side of the floor, leaving me to sit on one of the couches and observe the rest of the room. I was up almost immediately, however, when I spotted a small painting on the other side that drew my eye.

I didn't know enough about art to identify the artist, but it was definitely an original made of gold and paint, a curious panting of a couple embracing, one of whom was wearing ballet slippers.

"Like it?"

I startled, then turned to find Jane's husband, Eric de Vries, entering the room.

Like his wife, he didn't exactly look like a billionaire CEO. When I'd met him before, he'd worn a sleek, tailored suit that matched the immaculate grooming of a man of his station. Right now, he was in jeans and a T-shirt, as rumpled as any new father might be.

Then he smiled exactly like my sister-in-law, and I was immediately more comfortable.

"Hi," I said. "It's nice to see you again. Thank you for having me." I gestured toward the painting. "Who painted this?"

"Oh, that's a Gustav Klimt. A gift from my late grandmother to Jane. Glad you like it."

"My boyfriend has one kind of like this. Well, sort of. Just in that, it's a ballerina painting too."

"A Degas?" Eric gave a whistle. "Impressive. Hunt must appreciate art."

I smiled. "I know he likes that one, anyway."

"I've met Dr. Hunt a few times," Eric said as I followed him back to the seating area, where I sat on one large couch around an enormous fireplace, and he sat at another. "It was hard to get a read on him, but he seemed decent."

"Nathan tends to be kind of shy," I admitted. "Well, maybe shy is the wrong word. But he doesn't say much at first."

Eric nodded. "There's something to be said for that, honestly. Especially given the fact that his brother talks too damn much."

I assumed he was talking about Carrick. And honestly, I had to agree.

Jane reentered, carrying a tray with a teapot and some cups. Eric immediately got up to take it from her, but she turned away.

"Jane—"

"I'm not an invalid, Petri. And since I'm no longer pregnant, you can let me carry things again, all right?"

Eric grumbled at his wife's seemingly harsh words, but the sparkle in his eyes told me he kind of liked them. I liked her too. Theirs seemed to be a marriage of opposites—him the staid, solid type, her the brash, outspoken one.

It gave me more hope for my own relationship than I wanted to admit.

"So, give us the goods," Jane said as she poured everyone a cup of the steaming green tea. "When Xavier called to beg an audience— I still can't believe he used that term. He's so British, I can't stand it —my interest was piqued. And, of course, when we found out you were Matthew's little sister, it was a no-brainer."

I accepted the tea and took a sip. Definitely a step up from Lipton's.

"Well, it's like this," I said. "I have a story to tell. And then a favor to ask."

FIFTEEN MINUTES LATER, Eric and Jane had heard my story. Twice.

Xavier wasn't kidding when he said they would pull apart every little detail. My brother, also a lawyer, had the same annoying habit.

"So, they *really* think controlling this poor girl is the secret to controlling their own son?" Eric said.

I nodded. "To them, Isla is just a pawn. And Nathan would do anything for her. He's loyal like that. More integrity than pretty much anyone on the planet."

"That's...fucking unbelievable." Jane's blue and green hair waved around her face as she shook her head.

"Not completely unbelievable," Eric remarked dryly. "Lillian Hunt isn't related to Celeste de Vries, is she? Or a John Carson?"

I shook my head, a bit confused. "I don't think so. I mean, I guess it's not impossible, but I doubt it."

"Former family members with similar conniving traits," Jane explained wryly. "People who would probably give your future mother-in-law some lessons in duplicity."

"Oh, she's not my—"

"Just anticipating the inevitable," Jane said with a wink.

Eric chuckled. "Sorry. She tends to do that."

"Oh, stop. We both saw how Dr. McDreamy was looking at Joni at the Sinai gala, remember? And so did everyone else there. I probably heard ten different socialites moaning about the fact that Nathan Hunt was finally off the market."

Eric rolled his eyes. "She tends to eavesdrop too."

He was rewarded with an elbow to the gut, which he quickly captured with one hand before tugging his wife close to mutter something into her ear that made her blush.

"Got that, pretty girl?" he finished.

Her cheeks looked like apples.

I found myself missing Nathan more than ever.

"Well, we heard the story," Jane said. "And I have to tell you, I don't take kindly to rich, uptight assholes thinking they have the right to run other people's lives. Eric and I have both dealt with enough of that garbage to last five lifetimes. Your man doesn't deserve it either, and neither does your friend Isla."

She turned to Eric, and they shared another meaningful look.

Eric turned to me, gray eyes suddenly like storm clouds. "Jane's right. How can we help?"

HALF AN HOUR LATER, I left the de Vrieses feeling like I was walking on air. Xavier had been understating their potential interest, and in the end, they hadn't just agreed to my proposal but had added some other things to it. I had done the right thing—I knew it. All I had to do was tell Nathan and his parents, and maybe, just maybe, Isla would be under Nathan's care much sooner than we thought. And he could be free to buy that place in Westchester. Or stay in the city. Or do whatever he wanted because it was *his* choice, not anyone else's.

I couldn't fucking wait.

I rounded the corner of Seventy-Seventh just after picking up a slice of pizza, intending to make an early night of it before I flew back to Virginia in the morning.

As I jabbered to Nathan on the phone, it was everything I could do not to tell him, though I knew surprise was essential for all of this to work. His parents had to believe he had nothing to do with it. It was the only way they might forgive him.

"I miss you," I told him openly as I walked toward our building. "I don't know how I'm going to sleep tonight without you."

"Probably well," Nathan said. "It seems like I crowd you a bit in my sleep." Then, a few moments later, "I miss you too."

I sighed. So *this* was what it felt like to be with someone who didn't care what anyone else thought. A man who didn't care about hiding his emotions, who just said what he thought, who loved you well.

I liked it. I *loved* it. A lot.

"You'll pick me up at the airport?" I asked.

"Yes."

"Any chance we could find an empty field someplace?"

There was a bit of a pause. "Why?"

I smirked. "Because I've always had a fantasy of screwing my boyfriend in the driver's seat, and I don't want us to run off the road."

Another long pause. "I'm sure we could find a way to make that happen."

"Then it's a sex date, Dr. Hunt. Right when I get back." Then I grew serious. "I love you, you know. Like so, *so* much. More than maybe anyone."

Nathan waited a long time to answer, but I knew it was because he was processing the information, not because he didn't like what I'd said.

Finally, he responded. "I think that's the first time you've ever said it before I did."

I nodded in agreement, though he couldn't see me. "I feel it, though. All the time."

"You should say it, then," he said.

I smiled. "Rule Number Five applies to me too?"

"Rule Number Five applies to everyone."

"Well, then, I love you like crazy, and I can't wait to see you again and maybe one day get married and have your babies and do all the other things people who love each other do."

The words came out in a rush—words I'd never come close to feeling for anyone else, words that might freak him out, but words I wanted to say.

Because Rule Number Five was the most important of all.

There was one final pause. Then, "I'm sure we could make that happen too."

My entire being glowed.

"Sounds good," I said softly.

"Good night, Joni."

"Good night, babe," I said, then put my phone away.

"Good night, Sunshine."

I stopped at the sound of a voice that erased all the warmth in my body.

I turned to find Shawn Vamos walking down the street, looking tired with dark, shadowed eyes and an unshaven face.

He leered. "Where you been, baby? I've been looking for you."

His voice slithered over me like a snake, making every part of my body recoil.

I backed away, keenly aware of what had happened the last time he cornered me in this exact spot. And this time, I didn't have Nathan on his way down to rescue me. "I don't know what you want, but you need to leave. My boyfriend is on his way down again."

"Your boyfriend is in Virginia," Shawn spat back. "You're a shitty fuckin' liar, Sunshine. Always were."

Fear skittered up my skin, leaving goose bumps everywhere in its wake.

"Go away, Shawn," I said as my back reached the brick of the building. "Just...please. Go."

"Let me think about that...*no*."

I turned to run, but he was too fast. I had almost turned the corner when I was grabbed by the nape of my neck and slammed against the brick while Shawn shoved his body against my back in a sick parody of love.

The hand at my nape slid around until his entire arm was wrapped around my neck.

"Shawn." I could barely speak; his hold was so tight. "What are you doing?"

"You didn't really think I was going to leave you alone after what happened with your boyfriend, did you?" he asked.

Before I could answer, he hauled me across the street toward a white van. The back doors opened up as we approached.

"No," I said. "No, no, no!"

I kicked my legs out wildly as Shawn shoved me toward the van. "Let me go!"

But my voice was dampened by the hand at my throat, my legs so much weaker than normally after recent surgery.

"Shut up and get in."

Shawn hurled me into the van, where two other men grabbed me roughly, blindfolded and gagged me, and secured my hand with zip ties before tossing me into a corner.

Vaguely, I heard the sounds of another person joining us, then the doors to the van slamming shut.

"I got her," Shawn barked. "Let's fucking go."

FORTY-SEVEN
WHY YOU SHOULD NEVER GO ON A BOAT

#4 nothing good in movies ever hapens on a boat!

They didn't remove the blindfold until the van came to a stop, I was yanked back out somewhere I could hear seagulls calling through the air, towed down a distinctly *unstable* walkway, then thrown into a room that smelled like body odor and hot dogs. The door slammed shut over the voices of men barking in an Eastern European language. Then and only then did Shawn rip the blindfold off right before he tossed me onto an old plaid couch in the corner.

The room was small and had no windows in the concrete walls. The couch was the only piece of furniture in it, and it was lit by a single bulb dangling from the ceiling and connected to a pull string.

"What am I doing here?" I demanded. "Where am I?"

My knee throbbed. This was the opposite of treating it gently.

Shawn leered at me like a contractor might assess a wall he was about to demo. I'd seen that look on Matthew and Mike's faces a few times. Some people found something immensely satisfying about destruction. An outlet for their rage. Or in this case, maybe just because Shawn was an asshole who liked to fuck shit up.

"You know, when I first met you, you were a little firefly," Shawn said. "You buzzed around in everybody's faces, and they all thought you were so beautiful. I'll admit, you dazzled me too in the beginning. If I'm being honest, I sort of hated you for it."

"No one told you to keep looking," I said. "No one told you to chase after a fucking child."

The smirk on Shawn's face twisted into something uglier. "You think you were a child at fourteen, sunshine? You were asking for it the second I saw you. You didn't even know, but you were."

"You're disgusting."

His snarl deepened like it was etched with a knife but relaxed as he went on. "After a while, you reminded me of something else, though. You weren't a firefly. Just the fire. A living flame that 'danced.'"

His eyes lit up when he said the last word, almost as if he was making fun of me at the same time as he was lusting over me. I remembered that expression. It always confused me when I was younger.

Sometimes he'd even bring me back to, well, not his apartment. Never that. When I was in high school, it never struck me as odd that Shawn wouldn't take me to where he actually lived. I couldn't do that either.

Instead, he'd take me to a motel—usually one of the ones that rent by the hour. His favorite had mirrors on the ceiling. Sometimes it was a random (and usually seamy) apartment. Often just the back seat of his car.

There, he'd look at me and tell me he wanted me to do…something…for him. And I would perform.

Sometimes it was actually dancing. I'd be so eager to show him the things I was learning because I wanted his approval. I wanted Shawn to look at me like he had the first day we'd met. I wanted him to tell me again that I was talented. That I was extraordinary. Sometimes he would, but not without some undercutting remark.

"You'd be incredible if your ankles weren't so wobbly."

"You'd be as beautiful as a model if you were only a few inches taller."

"You'd be gorgeous if you had bigger tits."

Then he'd tell me what to do to make it up to him. Get on my knees. Give him a kiss. Offer him something else, and eventually, that's what I would do.

I'd been chasing my self-esteem through this man's eyes for a decade. If I hadn't met someone else who gave me the gift of loving me exactly as I was, I might have stayed in this nasty cycle for another ten years or more.

But now Shawn's expression, a clear dare to perform and become something new to please him, held zero appeal.

In fact, it made me sick.

"A flame," he went on. "But you know what the best part of a flame is? That little dancing light on the end of a candle?"

"No, but I'm sure you're going to tell me along with the rest of this boring as fuck lecture," I said.

It was the wrong thing to say.

I was rewarded for my sass with a sharp slap across the face that sent me flying back into the couch.

"What the fuck?" I shouted, even though I was scrambling backward. "Since when do you do *that*?"

"You think you can just run off with another man like that, Sunshine? You think you can make a *fool* of me that way, huh?"

"I didn't do *anything* but move on, Shawn. Please." It was a shaky retort but also a plea to stop. My cheek was burning, probably from his handprint.

It was to no avail.

"The best part of a flame," Shawn went on in a voice shaking with rage, "is snuffing the bitch out."

He loomed over me, a sweaty mass huffing, looking very much like he wanted to continue his assault.

But before he could, the door opened, and a man I didn't recognize poked his head inside.

"Lis wants you," said the man with a brief glance my way.

Shawn nodded and turned back to me. "I look forward to putting out your fire later, Sunshine."

Then he turned out the light, and I was eclipsed by the dark.

I WASN'T EXACTLY sure how much time passed. I knew I slept a lot. I woke up hungry, and someone came in and brought me a bit of bread and a piece of meat I really couldn't identify. Another man dragged me to a mildew-covered bathroom, where, through a tiny window, lights bounced against a horizon, but nothing else was visible in the dark. I still had no idea where I was, though occasionally, it did feel like the room was moving around me. Bobbing, even.

Sometime after my second "nap," I woke to find I had company. The overhead light had been turned on, and I was able to identify the person currently either asleep or, from the looks of him, knocked out at the far end of the couch.

"Mike?" My eyes popped open. "*Michael?*"

The hunched shoulders of my brother-in-law moved with a groan as he pushed himself up to seated, revealing a face full of bruises, an eye almost swollen shut, and a fat lip with a bad cut.

"Joni?" He mumbled, peeking at me through his one good eye. "What are you doing here? Fuck, Lea's gonna kill me."

"Kill *you*? She bit my head off already just because she thought I got you involved with these assholes. What are you doing here?"

Mike shook his head but stopped quickly, as it seemed to cause him pain. "Not now."

"What the hell?" I ignored him completely. "You're wrapped up with the Antonis? Lea already blames all of this on me and is never going speak to me again, so I think I should at least know why."

"If she does that, then she hasn't been fuckin' listening to me for the past two months," Mike said grimly. "The Antonis were always coming back for me. It was just a matter of time. Every so often, they sniff around, and after meeting you, he decided this was it."

"Why?" I asked. "Don't take this the wrong way, Mike, but why *you*?"

He somehow looked even grimmer as his sooty black eyes narrowed at me. "It happened when you were just a kid. When Lea and I first met, and before then. Even before I went away."

I pressed my mouth together. It wasn't a secret that Lea had met

Mike right after he had gotten out of prison. At the time, he was the charity case our grandfather had taken in as a favor to the local priest.

But beyond my conversation with Lea, I didn't know anything else about his connection with the Antoni organization. And I still had no idea why someone like him—a mechanic, sometimes driver, reformed bad boy, and home-centered family man—would earn the attention of a boss like Lis Antoni.

"Because I'm loyal. And because I'm smarter than most of the jackasses who work for him," Mike said. "Before I went to prison, I had a deal with Mancuso, the old head of the organization. Three cars in exchange for them paying my little brother's hospital bills."

"You had a brother?" More information I never knew.

Mike nodded. "He died while I was in prison. Cerebral palsy."

"Jesus." I reached out to pat his shoulder, the only part of him that didn't seem in pain. "I had no idea. I'm so sorry."

"Yeah, well. They didn't pay his bills, which is why he died. So, when I got out and one of the lower soldiers tried to call in the rest of my debt, I told him to fuck off. They brought me to another safe house and threatened your family. I was going to get sucked back in before Lea tracked me down. Reckless woman put herself in danger to protect me. Could have gotten herself killed too."

Mike shook his head like he still couldn't believe it even though it had happened almost twenty years ago. I couldn't either. *Lea* had been involved?

"Lis took a shine to her and to me. Admired her guts, I think. And my integrity. He said a man whose woman would stand up for him that way must be worth having a second shot. It was Ares who did it."

"Ares?" I wondered.

"His son," Mike clarified. "But now Lis wants his due. He wants me. And apparently, he wants you too."

"Me?" I wondered. "What do *I* have to do with it? Why would he want me?"

"Because he fuckin' does, Joni!" Mike burst out, though it looked like it pained him to do so. "Because it sounded like fun. Because he thought you were hot. Because he's trying to control your ex. The fuck if I know, honestly. Guys like these don't do things for the regular reasons everyone else uses. They operate on a different kind of logic. You get me?"

I bit my lip, willing tears—big hopeless ones—not to fall. If what he was saying was true, then we were really fucked.

"Or maybe you just gave him the excuse," Mike said a little more softly now. "But don't beat yourself up over it. He would have found another reason to track me down anyway. Like I said, it was just a matter of time."

He looked tired. He looked angry. But he also looked resigned, and that was probably the scariest part of all.

"Do you know where we are?" I wondered, looking around the dingy little room with its bare walls, cement floor, and the odd couch with its faded tartan that was straight out of the seventies.

"No fuckin' clue. Lis used to have a headquarters in a building in Morrisania. I doubt it's the same place—organizations like these always move around—but could be somewhere similar. I'm guessing it took them maybe fifteen minutes or so to move me here, so we're local. Other than that, I don't know."

"If Lea knows, will she come here?" I hated the idea of my sister getting involved, but she might know where to send the police.

Mike shook his head. "She took the kids up to Boston to see your brother."

I processed that for a moment. It meant we were still in New York. Probably still in the Bronx. But in a city of eight million people, that could be anywhere.

More importantly, there was no one left who cared where either of us were.

Again, I felt that odd bobbing sensation. But a building wouldn't move. Would it?

"Fuck," I muttered.

"You said it," Mike agreed. "Bad news, they won't be back for a week. Good news, once they are, Lea will raise holy hell until she finds us."

"What are we going to do?" I was having a hard time breathing.

"That's easy," Mike replied as he draped a heavy, tattooed arm over his eyes to block out the light. The guy looked like he was in so much pain. I would have gotten up to turn it off, but I wanted to see his face. I wanted to *see* period. "You're gonna do what he says. You're gonna do what he says until they get lazy. And they will get lazy because none of these assholes would be doing what they're doing if they had it in them to make an honest living. So when they do, you're gonna run, Joni. And you'll let me take the blame."

I reared back. "I can't do that. I can't leave you here."

"You can, and you will." Mike moved his arm to peer at me through his one good eye. "Joni, listen to me. You're gonna get the hell out of the city and go straight to your brother's. Matt has friends in the NYPD and in other high places. Those de Vries people. Xavier too—he knows some heavies. They'll know what to do to keep you safe."

Eric de Vries. Xavier Parker.

He didn't have to add Nathan Hunt—or at least his family—but he belonged in that category of the ultra-powerful too.

"But what about you—"

"Don't worry about me. I'll be fine."

"You will not be fine," I argued back. "You're already not fine. I'm not exactly part of 'the life' or anything, but even I know this was probably just an appetizer if they wanted to keep you here. What do they want from you, anyway?"

Mike sighed. "Same thing they want from you. Obedience. This is what happens to people who make deals with the Antonis and don't follow through. I told them they could have me if they left my girl and her family alone—that was twenty years ago, and Lis never forgot. What did you offer?"

"Nothing," I said. "I swear to God, I never promised them anything."

"Not a thing? An extra lap dance at that party, maybe? A wink and a smile? You didn't accidentally agree to something he wanted, even if it was just to get him off your back?"

Mentally, I tried to review that night. Had I done that? Maybe smiled a little too brightly in response to one of his jokes? Given a perfunctory "You betcha, babe!" or maybe a "Can't wait!" to a casual invitation or something equally inane?

I didn't think so. But if I was being honest, I'd been too focused on avoiding my ex's hands and Carrick's disapproving glares to notice anything else.

There was one other thing, though.

"He wanted me to serve drinks at a party on a boat," I said. "My boss—the guy who ran the gaming event—told me about it. But I said no. Or maybe. I don't remember."

"And he was okay with that?" Mike didn't sound convinced.

My silence told him everything he needed to know.

There was another dip again. The feeling of my stomach being in one place while the rest of me was in another.

I didn't think it was only because I was scared.

"It was months ago," I whispered. "Kyle never called me back about it, and I was in Paris, then the surgery and Virginia. There's no way that's what this is about."

Mike's good eye closed, and his grim scowl told me that's *exactly* what this was about. At least for me. Dread pooled in another dip, mixed with the knowledge that we were almost certainly not in the Bronx anymore. And if that was true, then no one was going to find us ever.

"You're going to do what I said," he told me again. "Give him what he wants, and leave when they give you an opening."

"But—"

"Joni. Just do it."

I opened my mouth to argue with him but found I couldn't.

And it was a good thing, too. Because right then, the door opened, and Shawn walked in, followed by Kyle, another man with slicked, dark hair, and lastly, Lis Antoni himself.

FORTY-EIGHT
EASTERN EUROPEAN COUNTRIES

#7 Albania

H e looked a lot different from the jovial Eastern European Rat Pack member I'd served at Kyle's games two and a half months earlier. Right now, Lis Antoni could have been any other old man in the neighborhood in his faded white polo shirt tucked over a thick belly, elastic-banded track pants, a well-worn pair of New Balances, and thinning gray hair combed over a balding top. A thick gold watch and a matching chain kept the outfit from going completely senior citizen, but it was really the hardened eyes and gnarled hands that made him the kind of man you wouldn't ever think to ask for a sucker.

"See, I told you," Shawn said. "Good as new, and ready to go. Give her a quick shower, and she'll be ready to perform in a minute."

"Perform?"

I looked between the four men. Antoni was eyeing me like a buyer at a cattle market. The unnamed man behind him looked bored, Kyle wouldn't meet my eye at all, and Shawn seemed almost gleeful to be presenting me to his—what? Boss? Overlord? The guy he desperately wanted to peg him?

I almost made that joke, but decided I didn't want another back-hand. The first one had hurt badly enough.

"You owe me a party, honey," Antoni said as he wagged a meaty finger in my direction. "My boys liked you. And that's before we find out what you were *really* capable of."

"What's he talking about?" I asked of Kyle, who still wouldn't look at me, then Shawn, who only grinned.

"Oh, I showed him a little precious footage," Shawn said. "We got a nice little business going on Only Fans, see. Only the best girls. Lis here helps me find the right locations, and then we put on a show for our subscribers. The paying ones, naturally." He looked me over. "Though I just might give a piece of you for free, Sunshine. You think you can take it on both ends?"

I wanted to vomit. I almost did. Even a very much *not* genius like me knew what he was getting at. The internet was rife with pornography, too much of it featuring women likely procured against their will and sold into some form of sexual slavery.

Not all sex work was like that. Not all.

But some.

Even a little was too much.

"Don't touch her," Mike growled. "You want her, you'll have to come through me."

"I'm fuckin' quaking in my shoes," Shawn retorted. "Can you even stand up after what Ares did to your knees?"

The look on Mike's face told me he probably couldn't.

Ares. That's what the other man's name was. The younger one who was currently studying Mike like he was one of those frogs we dissected in tenth-grade biology.

"Don't," I said, quickly moving my body between them and Mike. "Don't you hurt him. He doesn't deserve it."

"He stays," Antoni said shortly. "She comes."

Then he walked out, leaving the other three men with Mike and me, menace written across all their faces.

"Ares," croaked Mike. "Come on. You gotta let me out of here. I got kids, man. A family to take care of."

The younger man—Ares, apparently—pushed off the wall and

approached us. He was the other I recognized from my table at the gaming party. His face vaguely resembled Antoni's, but much younger, probably closer to Mike's age. He had a still-lean body, brown eyes so dark they were almost black, and only a few hints of gray feathering the tempers of an otherwise full head of dark russet hair.

He squatted down to look at Mike as if he were looking at a strange new plant growing from the sidewalk. Then he looked from him to me and back again.

"What is it with you Zola women?" he wondered, his deep, Bronx-born voice tinged with something that almost sounded like admiration. Or maybe envy. "First your sister, now you. People say they're ride or die, but you Zola girls actually do it." He looked to Mike. "Is it just for you, Scarrone? I've seen it twice now."

"What is he talking about?" I asked Mike, who only shook his head.

Ares looked between us. "She doesn't know what her sister did for you? How she was in in a room just like this, put her life on the line just like her? For love, she said. She was willing to die for your sorry ass at only seventeen years old."

I gasped. Lea had done *what*?

"Eighteen," Mike corrected him. "And I tried to stop her then too."

"Yeah, I remember." As he rose to standing, Ares shook his head like he still couldn't believe it. "I don't know what you did to earn that kind of loyalty, Scarrone, but I admire you for it. Hope you didn't fuck around on that. She doesn't deserve it."

Mike's voice was steel. "I would *never* do that to my wife."

Behind him, Shawn just rolled his eyes, and Kyle looked less than convinced. Because, of course, they did. These were men who traded in others' sexual proclivities. They depended on marriages being shams and men succumbing to their basest instincts.

But Mike was good on his word. I'd always known that. It had just never occurred to me to ask how, exactly, Mike had come to be so damn devoted to my shrewish older sister. Or her to him.

Well, now I knew. Lea had, apparently, been right there when some of these exact men threatened Mike just like they were doing now. And she'd thrown herself in their way. Nathan wasn't in the room, but I knew without a doubt that if he were, I'd do the same.

I'd do it for anyone I considered my family.

"What is it?" I demanded. "What is it you want? I'll get you anything, I promise. Money? I can get you money. My brother, my sister—they're married to some of the richest people in the world, I swear it—"

Ares turned to me like he was surprised I had a voice, despite the fact that he'd been addressing me earlier.

"You think this is about *cash*?" He made it sound like I'd suggested he accept Monopoly money instead of legitimate tender. "You think my father or I give a good goddamn about your money?" He snorted.

I flapped my hands at my sides. "I—well—isn't it?"

"It's about pride," Ares said gruffly. "It's about principle. It's about promises made and living up to your word."

"*Whose* promise?" I asked.

"The shop," Mike croaked. "He wants the shop. He's always wanted the shop and the cars to help him run shit across state lines."

"My father wants whatever suits him best at the time," Ares said. "That used to be your shop and your cars. Now it's your body. Nothing better then a watery grave to set an example for everyone else."

My jaw dropped. Mike was literally here to be made an example of. He was no better than an man on death row.

"Joni, get out of the way," Mike ordered, his voice rough with pain as he tried to push himself up to standing too.

Tried and utterly failed.

"No." I stuck my chin out at our three jailers. "Lis said he wanted me. Well, I'm here. Let him go." I glanced back at Mike, who was shaking his head, mouthing no. I turned back to our captors. "He's no good to you like this, and he has a family. Three kids, a wife who loves him, a shop to keep. So, just let him go, and I'll—I'll do whatever you want. I'll keep the promises for us both."

The immediate, evil grin that spread across Shawn's face told me

I had no idea the depths of depravity I'd face with that particular proposition. But I stood up tall nonetheless. Chest out. Core in. Ready for the next performance, whatever that had to be.

But Ares just shook his head, almost looking regretful.

"Would that I could," he told me. "But there ain't nowhere for him to go. By now we're miles from New York. In the middle of the Long Island Sound."

"Just got one stop in Atlantic City to pick up the boys, and then it's international waters for us, baby doll," said Shawn as he rubbed his hands together gleefully.

So, we were on a boat. The bobbing wasn't just in my imagination.

Ares sprang around as if loaded in a slingshot, laying a ferocious backhand across Shawn's smug face that sent him flying into the concrete wall.

"And who the *fuck* asked you to run your mouth, Vamos?" he demanded, taking two steps toward Shawn.

That was enough to make the coward flatten himself against the blocks even more. "N-no one," Shawn said. "S-sorry."

I smirked. Now who was the one stuttering?

"Then stay the fuck out of it."

Ares's voice was low but somehow carried more of a threat than any shout I'd ever heard. If Shawn knew what was good for him, he'd listen.

Ares turned to the rest of us. "Kyle, take her down the hall to get ready with the rest of the girls." He turned to Mike. "Scarrone, I'll deal with you later."

"No," I whimpered. "Kyle, please, don't—"

"Best just do what he says, kiddo," Kyle replied, though he didn't seem to be particularly thrilled to be pulling me off the couch.

"Joni," Mike rasped. "Remember what I said."

His eyes met mine with a silent plea.

Shakily, I nodded and allowed myself to be towed away.

Kyle, followed by Shawn and Ares, led me through a corridor that looked a lot nicer than the room I'd been in. I was right—it was a spare utility closet in what otherwise appeared to be an enormous yacht. Outside that miniature dungeon, everything was plush—wood floors, plaster walls, a fully staffed kitchen, and multiple bedrooms dressed in luxe fabrics and custom furniture.

At the end of the hall, Kyle opened a closed door and shoved me inside. There I found a number of other girls in varying states of undress.

"Twenty minutes until we pick up the party," he informed everyone. "Be ready."

He turned and left without looking my way. Shawn, however, gave me one more smile that made my body break out in goosebumps.

"Last show for me, Sunshine," he said as his gold tooth glinted like a star. "Better make it a good one. Otherwise, you don't know who you'll end up with."

The door shut, and we all listened to the sound of a lock turning. I turned around to find six other girls, many eyeing me with similar distrust. Most of them looked like they couldn't have even been fifteen, some even younger than that. Two sat on the bed, doing each other's hair. One was lolling on a pillow, eyes glazed, likely due to some sort of substance. A few others were seated at a table, doing their makeup. All of them were dressed—if you could call it that—in different bits of lingerie obviously designed less for support and more for spectators.

They were all different, too. Different ethnicities, speaking different languages. Some of them looked like they could have been from my neighborhood. It was more the hollowness in their eyes I recognized than any particular ethnic features. The type that came from growing up in a place where you weren't always sure someone would be able to take care of you. Too many kids from certain parts of the Bronx looked that way. Too many people struggling to make ends meet meant that too many children got left behind.

Sometimes I forgot how lucky I was that we Zolas had had a house to come back to. A soft place to land when our own parents screwed up.

Not everyone had that. I was willing to bet some of these girls fell into that category.

"Um, hi," I said, waving to them. "I'm Joni."

Two raised their hands and spoke in an unfamiliar language that sounded a bit like what I'd heard earlier from Antoni and his cronies. Another girl, who looked like she was probably the oldest aside from me, got up from the makeup table.

"You're the seventh?" she asked in Caribbean-accented English

"I guess," I said. "What—what exactly are we doing here?"

A few of the girls shared looks. Others appeared utterly desolate.

"I'm Femi," said the one who had approached. "They're getting us ready to serve up."

"Serve to...who?" I had to know even though I wasn't sure I wanted the answer.

"The big boys," she said dryly. "I hear them talking. A party. They bring us up. The men, they pay for us to use. Some, maybe they watch. Some, maybe they play." She looked me up and down. "You're a bit old for this game, but pretty. If you're smart, you make the big man like you. He don't hurt his girls. He keeps their faces clean, don't want the other men to touch what he wants."

"And who's that?" I asked. "Who's the 'big man'?"

Femi tipped her head. "Lis, of course. But we all want him. So, you better get ready, girl." She dragged a hardened gaze up and down my body again. "Lis likes his girls clean. And you are dirty."

I swallowed back an argument. Part of me wanted to say fuck it. That if I was going to be sold into a prostitution ring, I wasn't going to do it on their terms. They could have me dirty and smelling like basement, after more than a day without a shower, unshaven and unmade up.

But Mike's words repeated in my ear. *You're gonna do what he says. And then you're gonna run.*

Twenty minutes, Kyle had said. The boat was stopping in twenty minutes.

And one way or another, I was getting off.

I straightened and turned to Femi. "Where's the shower?"

FORTY-NINE
WHAT EGOT STANDS FOR

#3 Oscar

I wasn't sure exactly what time it was when the engines of the yacht stopped, but at some point, the yawning of the vessel was even more pronounced. I was already showered, my hair dried and teased into a showgirl-style ponytail, a solid mask of makeup layered on my face, when I put on the bright red teddy that wrapped around my body like it was completely made of ribbons.

Well, I didn't choose it for the aesthetics. It was the potential for camouflage I liked.

"I need to get out of here," I told Femi.

She looked up from the table where she was putting the finishing touches on her own makeup. "It's locked. No way out."

"What if there's an emergency?" I asked. "We're good cargo. They won't want something to happen to us, right?"

Femi just shrugged. "You can knock and bang. But I don't think no one will come, and even if they do, what will you do then?"

I strode up to the door. I could do this. Improv was just a different kind of performance, right? Even if I was scared out of my mind.

I had to knock five times before the door opened.

Not bad.

Even better was the face of the person who opened it.

"There's my sunshine." Shawn's gold tooth made another appearance. "Looking like you *should*. Turn around, baby. Let me see that ass."

I wanted to resist. I wanted to slap him across the face like he had done to me.

But then I saw that look in his eyes—the familiar gleam that meant he wanted me back.

"Best-looking ass in the tri-state area," Shawn commented as I obediently turned in a slow, seductive circle.

I peeked over my shoulder, the perfect coquette.

He practically drooled.

Gross.

But also, I wondered, how could I have been so stupid? Shawn was never going to let me go because I was dating another man. If anything, that was the most interesting thing about me. He had always wanted me more when others seemed to as well. I'd always thought it was connected to my value as a dancer, but now it was obvious it was really about anyone. If someone else found me valuable, Shawn did too.

Well, if Femi was to be believed, there was a whole party of other men who were going to bid to take me to bed in a few hours. Shawn had to know that, and I was going to use it.

And so the real play began.

As I turned back to him, I batted the fake eyelashes Shawn used to love so much. It never occurred to me back then why he liked to dress me up like a sex toy, but now I was wondering if it was because I'd look like one of these girls. One of the ones he wanted for his own.

But something else was different too. For the first time, I didn't feel that confusing twinge of desire for Shawn that I'd always felt, even in his worst moments. Even in mine. For the last decade, he'd had that strange hold on me, as though he'd shaped me into a person who would, if not love him, at least want him in some way.

Even if it was just his approval I wanted. Like his desire for me was somehow the key to my completion.

But no more.

Something in that had broken in the last few months. Maybe it was Nathan. Maybe it was me. But as I looked at Shawn, the only thing I felt was harsh, cold clarity and soul-crushing disgust. He was never my friend. Never my boyfriend. Not even my lover, despite the things we had done. He was only a monster. A captor. A predator in his own right.

And I knew exactly what I had to do.

"Thank God it's you," I whispered, reaching out a coy hand to pet his chest. "I was hoping it would be you."

Shawn looked down at my hand, then back at me. "Don't try that shit with me, Joni. I'm not letting you out."

He didn't, however, move my hand.

"Please, baby," I said as I unbuttoned the collar of his shirt and slipped my hand underneath, rubbing his tattooed skin. "I just needed to see you. You know…to say goodbye."

Shawn frowned. "What the fuck is that supposed to mean?"

"I know what they're doing." I stuck out my lower lip, playing the spoiled baby he always said I was. The one everyone said I was. Except one.

No, I couldn't think about Nathan right now.

"The girls told me all about it," I went on. "And it really made me see the light of what you said."

I undid another button. Then another so I could drag my hand down his torso, lightly scratching over his skin, tracing my nails over his tattoos, just as he liked.

"What's that?" he asked before licking his lip as he watched my hand slip lower and lower.

His body wasn't anywhere close to the trim twenty-two-year-old who had charmed me in the mall. Now he was at least thirty-three, with the face and body of a man who hadn't spent the last decade taking care of himself, but indulging. Softer belly. Graying teeth. Too many wrinkles. Blotchy skin.

How could I have *ever* found this man remotely attractive?

I deserved an Oscar for this performance.

"That I...belong...to...you." Each word was a purr. "You aren't really gonna let these other men take what's yours, are you?"

Shawn's dark eyes squinted. He was suspicious, but he didn't move away.

"Please, baby?" I whispered into his ear before biting his lobe. "You can get us out. It's like you always said. Just you and me."

His familiar odor of menthol cigarettes and Old Spice curled around me. So different from Nathan's clean, simple scent.

I resisted the urge to choke.

"I know what you're doing. And it's not going to work," he said through his teeth, though it was obvious he was tempted. I could feel it against my leg. He grabbed my hand, jerking me back so I couldn't lick his ear anymore. "There's nowhere to go, and even if I wanted to take you off this boat—which I don't—I can't. They're gonna know. And I don't fuck with these guys, Joni. No one does."

Okay. On to Plan B.

I allowed him to keep my wrist in his grip but leaned in and licked his ear again. Shawn was always a sucker for that. Sometimes when I really *was* faking it, all I had to do was stick my tongue in there, and he'd come in seconds.

As always, he shuddered, and I resisted the urge to smirk as his other hand slipped around to take hold of my ass.

Bingo.

"Then take me before they do," I begged, a hot whisper only for him. "Please. So I'll know that when I'm ruined—when I'm sold—you were there first. Because you were *always* there first, weren't you?"

My free hand drifted lower, toying with the waistband of his jeans. Running my nails along his hip bones.

Right on cue, Shawn's entire body shook.

"You nasty little cumslut," he crooned. "Do you want some of this, princess? You want a little bit of what Daddy has to offer?"

What I *wanted* was the vomit all over him. Then escape with Mike, find Nathan, and shower. Preferably in that order.

"You know I do," I hummed right back.

An Oscar and a Tony. Bookend my EGOT right now.

Shawn glanced over my shoulder, where most of the girls were watching curiously, though plenty of them were too drugged up to care what was happening. Then he took my hand, barked over my shoulder, "Stay the fuck here," and dragged me into the corridor.

Step one, complete.

"This way," Shawn said, already undoing his pants as he dragged me past two open bedrooms before opening a third, much smaller one stacked with several duffels full of cash, drugs, and probably other illegal paraphernalia.

I made a mental note. If I did manage to get out of here alive, the cops would want details. And I'd give them everything.

"Come here," Shawn ordered once the door had shut behind him. Stupid man was too blinded by the possibility of sex to even lock it. "On your knees."

"Kiss me first?" I trilled like a chickadee. "Please, Shawn. One last kiss."

He smirked. "Fine. But then I want you to beg."

I let him put his mouth on mine for the last time. Let his hands rove with the familiarity he'd always had, even though now, I felt like a stranger in his arms. Let him grind against my leg like I knew he would and waited for his breath to grow short and shallow until it matched the rocking of the boat.

Then I reached into the ribboned exterior of my bodysuit for the one potential weapon I'd been able to find.

When I was twelve and my brother came back from Iraq, one of the first things he did was teach my sisters and me how to fight. Specifically against men. I'd never stopped to wonder why— Matthew only said he'd seen too much over there, and he was never going to let his sisters be in the same position.

So, for a year, he'd instructed the four of us still living at home in the fine art of self-defense. We'd learned to grapple and feint. How two fingers to the eyes created more opportunity for escape than a knee to the balls. And the correct way to stab someone for maximum impact—left side, up and under the ribs to reach the stomach so the fucker might just bleed out.

I'd carried a switchblade for years, though never had to use it. That blade, of course, was gone, along with the rest of my things after being abducted. But the nail kit provided to the girls did have a cuticle trimmer, one that was just sharp enough to puncture Shawn's soft belly when I jabbed him as hard as I possibly could.

Shawn squealed like a pig as he jumped off me, the trimmer sticking out of his side like an instant thermometer.

"You bitch!" Shawn screamed as he yanked out the tool, then lunged for me again.

Fuck, he was loud. And covered in blood, which was getting all over the bed and carpet. And scary as fuck.

"Get *off*!" I shrieked as I tried to jump over the bed toward the door. "You just got stabbed in the gut! You should be bleeding out, not chasing me!"

"I'll chase you forever, you little whore!"

Shawn grabbed my foot, then dragged me back toward him. He collapsed on top of me, obviously struggling despite his efforts. Then his hand closed around my neck, and all my screams were silenced as I choked, unable to gasp for a single breath.

"You thought you could get away with that?" Shawn's voice warbled too, searching for breath even as he shoved me harder against the mattress. "You thought you could *stab* me and just walk the fuck away? I *own* you, Joni. I fuckin' own you, and now I'm gonna end you—fuck!"

Suddenly, he was yanked away, and I gasped, sucking in several deep, precious lungfuls before I was able to comprehend what was happening. When I finally managed to sit up, I found Shawn on the other side of the room, lifted onto his toes as a large man with slightly disheveled curls pinned him to the wall with a muscled forearm shoved against his neck.

My heart swelled.

Nathan.

I moved to get up but was held back by another hand on my shoulder.

"I wouldn't interrupt him right now," Carrick said behind me. "He's busy."

I gaped between them. How had they even gotten here? How had they even known to come?

"How does it feel?" Nathan was asking Shawn. "Not breathing? Forced to be helpless under someone you can't possibly fight?"

Shawn could only gurgle, though his black eyes shot murder. At me. At Nathan. At Carrick too.

"What did I tell you?" Nathan went on, as calmly as he had ever been except for the muscle ticking furiously in his jaw and the high color on his cheeks. "What did I say I would do if you ever fucking touched her again?"

Again, there was only a half-whimpered response. But Shawn's horrible gaze again landed on me as he reached toward me, then brought his finger up to his throat and drew a clear line across it.

It was a clear promise.

And apparently, the last straw. Nathan shoved his arm even further into Shawn's throat as he took hold of his head with his other hand and wrenched it to the side with a horrifying snap.

Shawn stopped moving completely. His eyes closed, and his entire body slumped. And when Nathan released his neck, Shawn crumpled to the floor, blood staining his shirt from his side wound, head lolling at an impossible angle.

I pushed off the bed, standing on shaky knees, hands to my mouth as the realization of what had just happened washed over me.

"Oh my God," I whispered. "Oh my God, oh my God, oh my *God*."

"Well, that was one way to end it," Carrick said dryly as he got up and walked to Shawn's lifeless body. "Jesus, Nate. I didn't think you had it in you."

"I told you what needed to be done. He was never going to give her up otherwise," Nathan said, though he was already moving back to me. "Joni." He took my shoulders, shaking lightly. "*Joni*."

I couldn't stop staring. "I killed him."

"Actually, I think *I* killed him," Nathan corrected me. "I broke his neck." His tone as dry and unfeeling as I had ever heard it.

I, on the other hand, was a mess. "B-but I stabbed him."

My hands were clammy. My body shaking. I couldn't speak as I took in the scene, the facts of what we had just done coming back to me in shards.

My God. Was he—had he—that snap—it *echoed.*

Carrick crouched next to Shawn's body, then looked up at Nathan. "Well, doc? You want to call it?"

Nathan sighed, squeezed my hand, and then released me so he could join his brother. I watched as he felt for Shawn's pulse in several places.

"He's dead," he said. "It's done." He stood up. "What's that look?"

I blinked. "What?"

"That look. I haven't seen it before. You're upset, but I'm not sure why."

"Upset. Yeah." I was numb. My lips barely worked as I stared at Shawn's body, lifeless on the floor.

"Why?" Nathan demanded, framing my face with his hands, "Don't feel bad for that piece of shit, Joni. He deserved it. He hurt you and who knows how many other people. So, why are you upset about him?"

"Because we just k-killed a man, and I know he wasn't—but we still—" The words stumbled, like water tripping over rocks. I was shaking now. I couldn't seem to stop.

"She's going into shock," Carrick said behind me. "We need to get her out of here."

Nathan yanked me into his chest, wrapping me with his big arms, cocooning me into his warmth like a baby swaddled tight. "I know," he whispered fiercely as he rocked me back and forth. "I know. But it will be okay. Listen to me."

"No," I blubbered. "No, no, no."

"Yes." Nathan took my face again, forcing me to look at him. He wasn't wearing his glasses, but his eyes were deeper, full of that chocolatey warmth that soothed my soul immediately. "Joni. *My Giovanna.* You're okay. You're safe now. I love you, and *I will keep you safe no matter what.*"

His big, capable hands stroked my hair, my face, all of me as if to reassure us both that I was whole.

"Are we done with the therapy session?"

Both of us ignored Carrick. I could only see Nathan. And I was pretty sure he could only see me.

"Okay?" he asked, his voice low enough that only I could hear.

I blinked. And blinked again. And slowly came back to myself.

"Oh—okay," I said. "I'm ready."

"Good, because I'm guessing we have about two more minutes before they come down here looking for us," Carrick said. "We found you, now we're leaving. There's a deck off the back that we can jump off if we're quick. And a team of divers below waiting with oxygen."

"H-how did you know where I was?" I asked as we followed Carrick back into the hall.

Nathan kept my hand locked in his. I wasn't going anywhere without him.

"Carrick was invited," he told me. He shot a look over my head that told me exactly what he thought of the fact that his *brother* was being invited to things like this.

"W-why?" I asked Carrick. "Don't they know who you are?"

"You're not the only one who uses an alias when it fits, *Gigi*," he replied. "I find that blending into...less than reputable spaces is good for business. Gives me leverage when I need it."

I didn't even want to think about what that meant. Or what he would be using that leverage for.

"This way." Carrick gestured toward a door at the end.

But I stopped near the one right before it. The one to the room where Mike still was.

"Stop," I said.

Both brothers faced me like I was crazy.

"Joni, we have to go now," Nathan said.

"It's Mike. He's in there. I can't leave him. We have to bring him with us."

"Oh, for fuck's sake," Carrick mumbled. "Should we rescue every fuckin' person on the boat? The feds are going to take them in about fifteen minutes anyway if they stay within U.S. waters"

"Well, there *are* six other girls about to be sold like cattle, so maybe them too," I snapped. "But we could start with my brother, who is probably going to die if we don't save him." I folded my arms.

Nathan just threw Carrick a look like he should know better, then looked at the door.

Carrick sighed. "On three."

Nathan nodded. "One. Two—"

The flimsy door was no match for the two linebacker-sized bodies hurled at it. The lock gave almost immediately, and we all tumbled into the room where Mike was still curled on the couch, looking even more battered than before.

He startled away, one eye now completely shut. "Lea?"

"No, Mike, it's Joni. And Nathan. And his brother. Come on, we're getting out of here."

"Going where?" Mike said bitterly. "I'm pretty sure we're on a boat. I've been fuckin' seasick for hours."

"Ahoy, there," Carrick snapped. "We're docked outside of Atlantic City for another, oh, five minutes, so we're taking you and Joni to jump off the back, where some very nice people are waiting with very nice oxygen that will allow us all to swim to shore undetected. Think you can handle it?"

Mike coughed. A bit of blood came out.

"Fuck," said Carrick.

I turned to Nathan. "Why is he doing that?"

Nathan shook his head. "It could be a lot of things. Trauma to the throat, nose, chest, punctured lung—"

"Doc!" Carrick snapped. "We need to move. Can he go?"

Nathan looked at me. "I don't know."

"Just go." Mike looked pale, like he wanted to pass out again. "I'll be fine."

We all knew that was a lie.

"Think of Lea and the kids," I told him. "If you stay here, it's a death sentence. They're going to kill you. Ares said so."

At the mention of my sister and their children, one last bit of life gleamed in Mike's eyes.

"All right," he said, shoving off the couch so he could stumble toward us. "Let's go."

He allowed Nathan to sling Mike's arm over his shoulder and tow him toward the entrance. I followed Carrick toward the back door, which we opened quietly, conscious of the sounds of men partying on the deck above.

"All right," Carrick said in a voice that could barely be heard over the party. "Joni, you go first. The divers are waiting just under the surface."

"I don't think so."

We all turned to find Lis Antoni and his son, Ares, standing in the doorway behind us. Lis carried a gun, which was pointed directly at me.

"Going for a little swim?" Lis asked, his accent stronger than ever. "Too bad you can't take Vamos with you. He's bleeding out on my carpet."

None of us denied it. Nor did we move.

"Please," I whimpered. "Just let us go. We won't tell anyone, we won't say a word, but we have families, and—"

"And I don't care," Lis cut me off.

"Is this all really because you want a few more cars stolen?" I couldn't help but ask. "A shop to run? If that's all it is, we'll give you the cars and the shop! Whatever you want, really!"

"Cars?" Lis snickered. "You think this is about few measly cars? This is revenge! For Benjamin Vamos."

Behind him, his son shook his head. "It's your brother," Ares said quietly. "Last year, he and his D.A. cronies put away Benjamin Vamos."

I frowned. Who? As a former D.A., Matthew had put away his fair share of criminals, but what did that have to do with me and Mike?

"You didn't know about that?" Lis taunted. "He was your friend Shawn's father too. Though maybe not your friend no more, eh?" He cackled, a horrible, evil thing that made my gut twist. "I don't care about them. But I do care about my business. No more girls. No more trade." He shoved a fat finger at me. "*You* can take their place.

And your brother"—he gestured toward Mike—"can give his life to teach the rest of them. It's only fair."

My lower lip began to tremble. "But—but—"

"But what?" Lis demanded. He held up his gun. "Come on. Inside, now. All of you!"

I might have done as he ordered. But just as I was about to take a step forward, Ares shook his head ever so slightly. His eyes flickered to the water behind me, his meaning clear as he withdrew a gun from his own belt and tilted it toward his father.

Nathan stood next to me, his arm still holding Mike up, who was close to losing consciousness. On my other side was Carrick.

"All right, boys," I said as I took their hands. "Time to go in."

Mike looked at me as if he knew exactly what I was thinking. "Tell my wife I love her," he croaked.

I nodded and willed myself not to cry.

The gun didn't waver, but Lis's hand did seem to relax as he smiled. "Good girl."

At that, I turned and mustered the biggest, brightest smile I'd ever given in my life. "You have no idea."

And then I yanked on the two Hunt brothers' hands as hard as I could and fell back. Gunshots rang out as we fell into the ocean. I kicked as hard as I could, down and away, praying none of the bullets would reach me through the dark, kelpy water, though just through the wavering green light, I did see something that looked like Ares Antoni turning and shooting his father just as the other gun went off.

Something grabbed my shoulder. A hand. I almost screamed, but didn't before a mask was placed over my face. Oxygen. Just enough to get me by.

I looked through the water just enough to see other bodies receiving similar treatments from people in wetsuits, oxygen tanks strapped to their backs. Nathan and Carrick kicking easily. Mike floating, his eyes closed, being tugged by another man.

They pulled us away from the boat. Down, down.

And then the shadow of the boat was gone.

And so were we.

FIFTY

SISTERS IN ORDER OF MOST TO LEAST...WHATEVER

#1 Lea. 10/10 woud recomend

S everal hours later, I was sitting in the surgical ward of a hospital in Atlantic City along with Lea and her kids, Matthew, Kate, and Nathan. Three of the four mini-Scarrones were splayed on the carpet and chairs of the waiting room, dead to the world while the rest of us waited for news of their dad's surgery. The only one who wasn't asleep was Tommy, the oldest, who sat resolutely next to his mother. He didn't touched her, as if he knew she was like a bomb that might go off. Still, he checked on her every so often nonetheless with a new wisdom in his ten-year-old eyes that had no right to be there.

Mike's injuries were substantial, to the point that it was a miracle he had even made it to shore in the care of the divers and stayed conscious long enough for an EMT to load him into an ambulance. Nathan and I had arrived just behind them only to discover Mike was already being taken into surgery.

I didn't totally understand everything that was wrong with him, but caught some critical words. "Blunt force trauma" was one phrase. "Substantial internal bleeding" was another. "Exploratory laparotomy" was the last, which Nathan said basically meant they were cutting into Mike's stomach to figure out what was wrong and hopefully fix it.

Several hours later, the rest of my family arrived via helicopters from New York and Boston. Nathan and I were both dressed in the hospital's best scrubs (he looked a whole lot more at home in them than I did), and everyone was equally exhausted and terrified as we continued to wait.

I had barely been able to speak to Lea. Or maybe had been too scared. This was my fault, she was going to say. Had I never been involved with these people, her husband would be safe and sound in his bed right now. We'd all be home, right where we belonged, were it not for my stupidity.

"Joni?"

I looked up from where I had unknowingly cowered into Nathan's shoulder. My man glanced between us, then gently unwrapped me from his arms.

"All right?" he murmured as I sat up.

I swallowed, still looking at Lea.

My sister nodded. There was nothing angry in her features. Nothing to be scared of.

And even if there were…I was going to take it. I owed her at least that much.

"It's fine," I told Nathan. "We just need a minute."

"I'll get some more waters, then."

He left, and Lea came to sit down beside me.

"Mattie told me what happened on the boat," she said.

I nodded. As soon as we arrived at the hospital, there had been several police waiting for us to take statements. Gunshot wounds— even ones going straight through a shoulder—required it.

Carrick had made himself scarce as soon as his statement was on record, but I was glad he had stayed if only to provide corroborating evidence. My brother, the former prosecutor, had apparently already gotten access to the statements and given the rest of the family our story so that I didn't have to.

Lea shook her head. "I'm so sorry you had to go through that."

"You're sorry?" I gawked. "Lea, it's my fault. It's just like you said —if I hadn't gotten involved with those guys, they wouldn't have come after Mike, and—"

"Joni, stop," Lea said. "I read the report. I know that's not true. Just like I know this thing goes beyond Mike and a few stolen cars. Or even beyond Mattie's old job. These are bad men, and bad men do bad things. We were just unlucky enough to get caught in the crossfire. And maybe brave enough to stand up to them." She took my hand and squeezed. "We wouldn't be here if it weren't for you either. And by that, I mean that Mike would actually *be* dead, and so would you, and…oh, *God.*"

Suddenly overcome, Lea shoved a hand over her face and sucked in a few pending tears. My sister never cried. Once for each of her children. Maybe a mild sheen at a wedding. But that was it.

"Even if—" She glanced over her shoulder at Tommy, who was now playing a game on her phone, then continued in a lowered voice. "Even if the worst happens, I just want you to know. It's not your fault. I never should have blamed any of this on you. And I love you. You're a good sister, Jo. I'm sorry I didn't tell you that more."

Now it was my tears that were fighting to the surface. I didn't bother to stop them as I pulled Lea to me.

"I love you too," I whispered fiercely. *"Always."*

"Mrs. Scarrone?"

We broke apart, and everyone turned to the doctor who had just entered the room, his surgeon's cap still on. His face looked haggard and drawn, as did the young woman next to him carrying a clipboard.

A pit formed in my stomach. *No.*

Lea stood. "Yes?"

I stood with her, keeping her hand tightly in mine.

The doctor approached. "Mrs. Scarrone, I'm Dr. Mitchell, the surgeon who handled your husband's laparotomy. His injuries proved too extensive, and he unfortunately died during surgery. I'm so sorry for your loss."

Lea let out a wail that filled the entire room, and she immediately fell on my shoulder. I pulled her close, wrapping my sister with whatever strength I could, letting her cry into my hair, my arms, whatever she needed as she succumbed to the loss of her husband.

Her person.

She sobbed.

And I squeezed her as tightly as I could.

It was the only thing I could do. For years, this sister had given me support in the best ways she knew how. All I wanted now was to give it back to her. Especially now that I had any inkling of what she might be feeling.

Over Lea's keening shoulder, I met Nathan's eyes as he rose to speak with the surgeon, presumably to get the other details Lea was too upset to gather. That chocolatey brown gaze was filling with a deep, abiding acknowledgment of the same thing I was thinking: what if this were us?

It had been so close. *So* close. The bullet could have hit Nathan instead of Mike. Those goons could have captured him too and beat him within an inch of his life. It could have been me who had lost the love of my life, only I wouldn't have had four children to care for without him, a whole *life* lived together before he was gone.

I couldn't bring myself to wish Lea and I could trade places, but I could, maybe for the first time, really *feel* my sister's pain. Maybe a bit more of the burdens she had carried so long, so willingly. All for the love of Michael Scarrone. Her first love. Her only love.

One who was gone forever.

Matthew and Kate joined us, both of them wrapping their arms around the nucleus of grief Lea and I formed. Then a few more hands and and arms. Smaller ones, looking for their mother, wriggling their way into the cocoon of our family. The only safe place for them in this world.

We stayed like that for minutes. Hours. I honestly couldn't tell. But I knew I wouldn't move until Lea wanted.

Everything that had ever seemed more important than family faded away in that waiting room.

There were only the people in this room. A few more on the other side ocean who I knew would be right here with us if they could.

This was what mattered in this life. Not dance. Not independence. Not even love, not until it was with someone who could be family too.

Someone like the man behind me.

The Zola family rocked together into the wee hours of the night.

Even after we let go, there were days I thought maybe we would always remain that tight in spirit.

Because bonds like that can't be broken by something flimsy like a few miles.

I just wished it hadn't taken a good man's life for us to figure that out.

FIFTY-ONE
WAYS TO GET HOME AGAIN

Whatever. I don't care anymore

It took days for us to leave Atlantic City. I never even left the hotel room across the street from the hospital. Kate brought the kids back to Lea's house in Belmont so they could have an escape and also so Lea could have some time to figure out how to talk to them more completely about their father's death. Matthew stayed in Atlantic City to deal with the police reports and other legal matters so that Lea wouldn't have to.

Nathan and I stayed mostly for hugs. Well, and to talk to doctors (at least, Nathan did). And to curl up together in our hotel room, murmur into each other's ears about how we loved each other, and try not to think about all the loss and trauma that we'd just endured.

There wasn't much I could really do to help other than be there, but that I would do. And Nathan wasn't about to leave me.

Eventually, though, the paperwork was finished. Too many statements to count were given, especially after the Coast Guard apprehended the yacht just before it crossed into international waters. Mike's body was en route to New York to be buried, followed by Matthew and Lea in a rental car. We'd been through so much in the past few days that I hadn't even thought about where we were going until I followed Nathan to a rental car in the hotel's garage and saw that the plate was from Virginia.

I stopped in front of it and looked up. "Oh—oh no."

Nathan looked up from where he had just opened the driver's side door. "What's wrong?"

I pointed at the plate. "You're going back to…Nathan, I can't go back to Virginia. I'm sorry, but I just can't."

He frowned. "I never said we were going there. I assumed you'd want to follow your family to New York."

"I–yes. But even after that." Sadness wrapped around me. Why did this have to be so hard? "I'm going to have to stay. I don't know what the future is going to look like, but Lea has no one but me and Kate there to help her. And with the kids, and the shop…" I drifted. The whole situation felt hopeless to me. I couldn't imagine what Lea was feeling. "She's been there for me my whole life. I have to be there for her now."

Nathan examined me for a long moment, then rounded the car to take me in his arms and framed my face with his hands so I had to look up at him. "Of course, you're going," he told me. "And so am I."

"But…but…." I sounded like a broken speedboat. "But what about your family? What about Isla?"

For the first time in days, I finally received a smile. The one that warmed me to the core.

"We haven't talked about it yet," Nathan said. He shook his head, as if embarrassed. It was adorable. "I forgot. I never forget things."

I tugged on the pockets of his jacket—the one from the hotel gift shop with Atlantic City splashed in bright pink lettering over a casino table. He made it look like couture. "Tell me."

"You should have told me you were going to meet with the de Vrieses. I would have gone with you." Nathan shook his head. "I'm ashamed I didn't think of the angle myself."

I bit my lip. Holy crap. Had my plan *worked*?

"I'm glad you didn't," I told him. "You're not that manipulative. It's one of my favorite things about you."

One brow rose quizzically. "And you are?"

I swallowed and grinned. "Normally, no. But this was a desperate situation."

"It certainly was." Nathan gathered me close again and pressed a kiss to the top of my head. "I was so scared, Joni. So fucking scared I had lost you. When the doormen said you hadn't come home, I thought I was losing my mind. But Carrick pulled some strings with the FBI. They found you take on a surveillance camera. By Shawn. Carrick had already gotten the invitation for the party, and we put the two together."

A shadow passed over both of us at the mention of my now-dead ex-boyfriend.

My feelings about his death at our hands were...complicated. There was some guilt, yes. A lot of it. And some genuine fear that I might be going to hell for what I'd done.

But there was also remorse. Relief, yes. And grief, even, for the girl who had thought she had loved the man, even if that love was just a manipulation of his.

One day, I'd make sense of it all. Or maybe never.

"I still can't believe Carrick found me," I said. "Or even helped you find me too. I thought he hated me."

"He doesn't like you very much," Nathan admitted. "But he said he respects you. And that we deserved a shot at freedom together even if his sorry carcass had to take the brunt. His words, not mine." He chuffed against the crown of my head. "I don't think I've ever heard Carrick say he respects anything, so that's fairly impressive."

I smiled weakly against Nathan's chest. "So long as he leaves us alone, I'll take it."

He tipped my chin up so he could look at me again. "Your plan worked. At least, I think it was your plan. Apparently, the board received a call from Eric de Vries with a proposal for a major project between his company and Huntwell. It was, however, contingent on a member of the Huntwell board remaining in New York as a permanent liaison." He tipped his head. "Apparently my father found it too lucrative to refuse. Even when I told him I wouldn't sign the paperwork unless they transferred Isla's guardianship to me."

My eyes popped open. "And...did they?"

Nathan's smile was like being enveloped in a hug. "They did. Once she finishes at Ferndale, she'll move up to New York. I'm going to start looking for a house in Westchester when we get back."

"Somewhere with horses," I put in.

He nodded, that smile spreading into a grin. "And a dance studio."

"And an...operating table?"

We both laughed.

"I think we can keep that at the hospital," Nathan said, brown eyes twinkling through his lenses.

We got in the car, and I fiddled with the new phone Nathan had gotten me while he adjusted things like his seat back and the radio.

To my surprise, he didn't immediately put on whatever station he wanted or connect it to *his* phone for whatever he was in the mood for.

It was funny, but in the time we'd spent together, neither of us had really put on much in the way of music.

"What kind of music do you like?" he asked.

I blinked. "What?"

Nathan frowned. "It's a simple question. I realized I don't know, other than your dad's interest in Billy Joel." He tapped on the car's audio interface. "Just picking some driving music. Unless you'd prefer silence, in which case I'll listen to an audiobook on my headphones. I don't want to fall asleep at the wheel."

For some reason, I could barely speak. "I—you want to know what kind of music I like?"

Nathan peered at me curiously. "What's that look?"

I swallowed my shock. "I—it's surprise. A weird, unexpected type of surprise."

"You're surprised I care about your musical taste?" He frowned again. God, he was cute when he did that. "Isn't that something a good boyfriend should do?"

My surprise faded. And eventually, I found myself smiling again. So hard my cheeks hurt, and my chest hurt, and I could barely think, I was so happy. So, instead of speaking, I undid my seatbelt and crawled over the console into his lap, eager to convey with kisses what I couldn't quite put into words.

"Yes," I told him after I finished sucking on his bottom lip hard enough to make him groan. "It's what a *very* good boyfriend should do. I guess I shouldn't be surprised at all, since you are the best."

That dimple appeared again. I licked it, just because I could. And then lost my breath when Nathan kissed me again.

When he was finished, he looked up at me, his question still in his deep brown eyes. "Well? What do you want to hear?"

I bit my lip. "I don't know. What would you pick?"

Was this what it felt like to want to please someone more than yourself?

Nathan shrugged. "Like I said, probably an audiobook for a drive like this. When I'm in surgery, I have a classic rock playlist. I like Fleetwood Mac. Some Steely Dan."

I cringed. I couldn't help it. "I...I mean, those are all right, I guess. It's probably more stuff my dad would have listened to. I would guess, anyway. My brother says he liked some hip hop too, but—"

"Joni," Nathan interrupted as gently as I could.

I stopped babbling, cheeks heated. "Sorry."

He cupped my face and smiled. "It's all right. You can tell me more about your dad if you want, but I want to get on the road. So... music or not?"

I tipped my head. "Everyone likes Adele."

Nathan's chuckle warmed my very soul. "But do *you*?"

Just the way I was. It was in everything he said. Even now.

"Not really," I admitted as I slid off his lap and into my seat. "I'm more of a Rihanna fan, honestly, but I don't really feel like a power ballad right now. How about Drake?"

Nathan shook my head. "Not my favorite. Kendrick Lamar?"

At that, I grinned all over again. Compromise. Of course. "Now we're talking. I have a playlist you're going to love."

He started the car while I connected my phone to the stereo. But before he backed out, Nathan turned to me once again. "Before we leave, I do have another question to ask you. A more serious one."

"What's that?"

"When I buy the new house in Westchester, will you be my room-mate there too? Actually, will you still be my girlfriend who lives with me? For real, this time? Not fake?"

I turned, wondering if he was actually serious.

But the twitch in his mouth told me different.

A joke.

Nathan Hunt was telling me another joke.

And my God, it made me love him even more.

"I'll be whatever you want me to be," I told him as I pressed my lips to his. "Just as long as we can be those things together."

Nathan kissed me back, giving me one of his patented whole-hearted, forceful-yet-gentle, just-like-the-first-time kisses that stole my heart completely. It wasn't a kiss that negated the sadness I knew would hang over me like a shroud for a long time to come. But it told me he was there with me, ready to steal that sadness away for a moment or two anytime I needed.

Like a pirate. Or a surgeon. A roommate. A boyfriend. Maybe even one day a husband.

But none of it mattered now.

He was just Nathan. And with him, I was just Joni. Together, we were perfect.

"What about fiancée?" he murmured against my lips. "Do you think you could be that one day too?"

I couldn't hide my smile. I found I didn't want to. "Maybe one day. When we're ready."

Nathan nodded, though his dimple didn't disappear as he started driving. And didn't for a long time.

"We should start another list," he said sometime later as he turned onto a freeway heading north. He pulled out the little black notebook that was always in his jacket pocket. A new one, I realized. The old one was probably at the bottom of the Atlantic.

He opened to a new page and balanced it on the steering wheel so he could write across the top:

HOW TO BE A GOOD FIANCÉ

I took the book, looked at the title, and thought for a moment before I scribbled down something and handed it back to him.

"That was quick."

"I only had one thing to add."

Nathan looked down at rest the list as I'd written it. It only had one item.

~~HOW TO BE A GOOD FIANCÉ~~ How NATHAN Can Be A Good Fiancé

1. Just be your incredibul self and remember: your one-day wife-to-be loves you just the way you are.

TYPES OF THERAPISTS I HAVE NOW

EPILOGUE

#3 Dr. Clemson—physical therapist

Three months later

"Well, that's the last of it."

Marie Annetta Zola patted the top of her suitcase as she turned toward her phone, where her younger sister's face was shining on the screen.

Joni looked as bright as ever, though with a few small changes. Darker circles under her deep green eyes—she'd struggled with sleep since Mike's murder. A slightly more chiseled face, as she'd returned to full-time dance training once her physical therapist had okayed it last month. And a sweeter smile that wasn't tinged with attitude anymore.

Marie could see the truth: that despite her ongoing struggle with guilt and grief, Joni was happier than she'd been in years. And Marie had a feeling it was mostly because of the quiet, bespectacled doctor who had somehow stolen her sister's heart.

"I can't believe you got that closed," Joni said. "That suitcase is bigger than you. But how are you going to get it down six flights of narrow-ass stairs?"

Marie considered things. "One step at a time, I guess."

It was a lot for six floors. Sometimes, people hired cranes or conveyor belts to lift their things to and from apartments like these, since the old buildings in Paris weren't really designed for moving furniture or transatlantic suitcases. But Marie wasn't going to ask the Lyons family to pay for one more thing. Not when they'd already funded an entire year at the Cordon Bleu and a living stipend while she had spent her time in Paris learning to be their private chef.

"You should ask Daniel to pick you up at the airport instead of me," Joni said with a sneaky grin. "Tell him your flaky sister forgot to show up, and your luggage is too big for a cab."

Marie rolled her eyes at the mention of the youngest Lyons son— the one for whom, yes, she'd nursed a substantial crush all the years she'd worked for the family. Joni might have been happier and more settled these days, but she wasn't beyond a good seduction plot. Marie doubted that would ever change.

"Daniel Lyons has better things to do with his time than play chauffeur to the family cook," she said.

"Yeah, but I bet he'd do it for the newest hottie with a body. I bet he won't even recognize you anymore."

Marie touched the ends of her hair, which now only reached her chin in a chic bob that Louis had modeled after Marion Cotillard. It was only one of the many changes she'd made to her personal appearance since last year. It was hard to live in the most fashionable city in the world without some of it rubbing on of you. Especially when the closest friend you made happened to be a stylist.

The truth was, Paris had been a revelation in too many ways to count. Separated from the noisy Zola clan for the first time in her twenty-five years, Marie had discovered what she was really made of. And to her surprise, that person wasn't the dowdy, slightly bitter, painfully shy wallflower she'd been most of her life.

The external changes were the most obvious. The haircut, of course. Contacts instead of glasses. Clothes that fit instead of the baggy dresses she'd always preferred.

But the internal differences were the most acute. Confidence when she'd had none. A quiet kind of peace. She knew herself now that she'd been on her own, without the voices of her siblings telling her what she was supposed to be. Knew her likes and dislikes, and for once, she wasn't afraid to say them out loud. Knew what she wanted in this life, which was to be the best chef she could, open a restaurant one day, and buy a little apartment where she could practice yoga by herself and just *be*.

She wasn't exactly sure how this girl would survive in the kitchen at the Lyons family's estate in New Rochelle or the spare room in Joni and Nathan's apartment. She'd only seen her family a handful of times in the last year. Everyone had convened for Matthew's wedding last fall and Mike's funeral in the spring—two polar opposites in terms of emotions. She also visited Frankie last month, when she'd given birth to her and Xavier's new baby, and had spent her birthday with Nonna in Rome.

It was a bit strange now to think she wouldn't be returning to the little brown house in Belmont when she returned to New York tomorrow. But at the same time, she wasn't sure she could go back to living with her family either.

Her period of self-discovery was over.

It was time to walk her next path. One step at a time.

"How is therapy going?" Marie asked, mostly to change the subject. Things had changed, but not the fact that she still didn't like undue attention.

"Which one?" Joni, who always liked attention, huffed loudly and rolled her eyes. It was no secret that in addition to the physical therapy following her second knee surgery, she'd also gotten diagnosed with both ADHD and dyslexia and was now working with different specialists to help her manage both—all, Marie gathered, at her boyfriend's insistence.

"That bad, huh?"

"It's fine. Nathan is threatening to stop tutoring me between therapy sessions because I keep trying to seduce him. But that's the best part! What's going to make me focus more than getting off when I get a question right, huh?"

Marie chuckled. "Is Nathan aware he's just one in a long line of conquests? You seduced all your high school tutors too."

"Except Ricky Martinez. He had really bad acne."

Marie found herself grinning. She was pretty sure Ricky Martinez was the only tutor to quit working with Joni *because* she hadn't been interested in him. After that, he'd tried to ask Marie to the prom. She had said no.

"The real problem is that Nathan can't refuse me," Joni said. "But it's not my fault he's so hot. He says I'm terrible for his self-control."

"No, I said *your* self-control is terrible for *me*."

Nathan's deep voice echoed in the background of the video, and Marie considered averting her eyes as her sister reached offscreen, then pulled Nathan, who was apparently sitting next to her on the couch, in for a kiss. He proceeded to devour Joni while Marie tried not to feel awkward. Or jealous.

"How 'bout you control *this*?" Joni murmured after they finally separated.

Both her and Nathan's expressions burned with desire, enough to make Marie's face feel hot too. She might have had plenty of self-growth in Paris, but her romantic life was the one thing that hadn't changed. Even in the city of love.

Nathan leaned toward Joni's ear and grumbled something that Marie couldn't understand, but that turned Joni's face bright red, even through the screen.

Then he adjusted his glasses. "Marie," he said with a nod.

Marie nodded back primly. "Nathan."

"I'll leave you to finish." He looked back to Joni. "Ten minutes. I mean it."

He got up, a massive tree of a man as he briefly took up the entire screen, then disappeared, leaving only Joni in view with a sickeningly dreamy expression while she appeared to watch her boyfriend walk away. And Marie had to admit—in all the years and through all of Joni's conquests, she'd never looked at anyone quite like that.

Marie liked Nathan Hunt. The rest of her family members thought he was kind of weird and standoffish, but she didn't find him off-putting at all. She'd liked the way he stood quietly beside Joni at Mike's funeral, holding her hand while she cried into his shoulder. She'd liked how respectful he was to Nonna and the rest of the family, a solid column of composure in a sea of overly emotive Zolas. Most of all, she liked the way he listened when Joni spoke and seemed to enjoy all parts of a personality others sometimes found "too much."

Joni had said more than once that she and Nathan both loved the other "just the way we are." Marie's heart ached at that idea. No one could ask for more.

"Seems like things are good between the two of you, at least," she said once she was sure Nathan was gone. Probably a vast understatement.

Joni's eyes brightened with something that almost looked like tears. "I didn't know it could be like this. It's…" Her eyes shut for a moment, lashes sweeping across her cheeks, then reopened. "It's a gift. *He's* a gift. Or maybe we're a gift together. I don't know."

"And the rest…you guys are okay?"

Joni didn't have to ask what she meant. In the months following Mike's death, Marie had heard enough to know that both Nathan and Joni had struggled to recover from what had happened that day. The Atlantic City prosecutor had quickly deemed the death of Shawn Vamos a matter of self-defense, but that didn't erase the fact that the two of them were responsible for it or that Joni still carried an immense amount of guilt for Mike's death too. She'd started therapy soon after the funeral, but the shadows under her eyes were still deep. Marie had a feeling they would never fade completely.

"It's a process," was all she said. "I do therapy. Nathan does therapy. Right now we're both just focused on getting back to normal. Or as normal as things can be. Mostly, I'm worried about Lea. She's just…so strong, you know? I wish she'd let herself break sometimes."

Another surprise to come out of all of this had been the way Joni had thrown herself into supporting Lea and her kids over the last few months. Apparently, she and Nathan wanted them to move in with them when they eventually planned to move to Westchester— something to do with providing space for Isla, Nathan's ward.

So far, Lea had refused the idea. But she did let Joni go up to the Bronx three afternoons a week to take care of the kids while Lea managed the shop. Just like she also let Nathan and Joni take the kids for the occasional trip out of town so she could have some time to herself.

It was the best they could do for now. But Marie knew, just like everyone else, that eventually Lea would break. And when she did, it wouldn't be pretty.

"How did the audition go?" Marie asked if only to erase that desolate expression from Joni's face.

Her sister perked. At least she was still easy to distract. "It's not actually until tomorrow. I'm ready. I think. But really, *really* nervous."

"Why? You said your physical therapy has been going great, right?"

Joni nodded. "Oh, for sure. The PT Nathan found is amazing—*so* much better than that crappy guy I had through the union. But it's just…you know…first audition jitters. I'll get over it. Honestly, I can't wait."

"That's got to be costing him a fortune."

"It would be if I hadn't convinced Xavier to lend me the money for it. Nathan keeps saying we should just get married to put me on his insurance, but I don't want to do that."

"Why not?" Normally Marie wouldn't be on board with that kind of scheme, but if anyone could keep the lines between real and fake securely in place, it was her sister's boyfriend.

Maybe not, she thought, recalling the particularly feral expression Nathan had worn just a few minutes earlier.

"For one, because I don't need him to. Xavier is helping, and once I get a real gig, I'll be eligible for union coverage again anyway. Secondly…" Joni drifted off, letting the silence yawn between them.

"Secondly?" Marie pressed.

Joni sighed. And almost looked a little bit shy—the strangest thing to see on her typically outgoing, absurdly confident face. That alone would have told Marie this relationship was special if nothing else.

"Don't laugh, but I don't want to marry him if it's not for real," she mumbled. "Is that corny? That I want to do the whole bride thing with Nathan? Like in a church and everything? It's only been a few months, but when you know, you know. And...I know. I really do."

She looked so unbelievably unsure of herself that Marie almost didn't recognize her.

"I don't think it's corny at all," she said. "Especially since I'd bet money he knows too."

That insecurity shifted a little into hope. "You think so?"

Marie chuckled. "I don't know the guy that well, but I'm pretty sure that man worships the ground you walk on, Jo. And not just because you clearly screw his brains out."

At that, she finally relaxed. "Trust, he's screwing mine out too. And that's good to hear. Especially since I feel the same way."

Again, Marie's heart squeezed. This time with a little bit of envy. Almost everyone in her family had found their person over the years —even the youngest, someone they had all thought was too self-absorbed to love anyone that way.

How wrong they were.

"Listen, I gotta go," Joni said as she checked her watch, a pretty gold thing that was for sure a gift from Nathan. "I need to get uptown to help Lea before the boys get out of camp, and..."

"You also need to get it on with your hot boyfriend before you leave?" Marie supplied.

Joni didn't even look ashamed. "Priorities are priorities."

"Go," Marie said. "I'll see you tomorrow."

"In New York, where you belong! Love you, Mimi."

"Love you too, Jo."

———

Joni

I ended the call and abandoned the iPad in the living room. I was pretty sure Marie hadn't *actually* heard Nathan murmur, "I'm giving you ten minutes to be naked in the bedroom before I carry you in there myself," but even if she had, I wasn't going to be ashamed for wanting to climb my boyfriend like the mountain he was.

Four months into our "real" relationship," Nathan and I were still figuring out ways to please each other. My man was already a quick study, and with the help of the ADHD medication I'd started taking, I was just as eager to study him right back along with everything else I was finally starting to learn.

Things weren't perfect. The noise in my head was still pretty loud, especially in the evenings when the meds wore off. But they were better, and it made it easier to work with the dyslexia specialist I'd also started meeting with twice a week when I wasn't training. Things that had always seemed impossible were far easier now. I could do a load of laundry from start to finish without forgetting it in the washer or leaving it to wrinkle in a hamper for four days. I closed cabinets about half the time now. I could even get through a full chapter of a book if I listened to it on audio at the same time.

These were small changes. But enough to open windows to other possibilities. Other modes of dreaming.

I walked into the bedroom that Nathan and I now properly shared (along with his walk-in closet). Nathan turned from where he was standing at the window that looked out to the Hudson. He wore the same pair of plain navy joggers he'd put on after waking up on this peaceful Sunday morning, but had removed his shirt, putting his bear-like physique on display.

I openly ogled him.

He held up his watch. "You had one more minute."

I had learned over the last four months that when Nathan and I agreed on a particular rule or boundary, he was going to uphold it no matter what.

Like the time he had busted into my PT's office at the hospital when they went over by four minutes, carried me down the hall to one of the residents' nap rooms, locked the door, gagged me with a surgical mask, and proceeded to lick my pussy until I screamed into his hand.

You could say his bedside manner was a bit savage.

I'd fallen even more in love with him than before.

I smiled and sauntered over to the bed. "I'm still on time. No cause for alarm yet."

"Not quite. You're still dressed." His dark eyes burned. Even though his glasses, which he proceeded to remove.

It was a small gesture, but one that made my skin prickle with anticipation.

"Oops," I said, even as I shimmied.

"Time's up." He crossed the room far more quickly than a man of his size any any right to move. "Lift your arms."

"What if I say no?" I asked, sticking my chin out.

Nathan eyed me for a moment. "Are you feeling like a brat?"

Apparently, there was a name for the kind of role-play we occasionally indulged in. The one where I acted like the spoiled child so many accused me of being, and he did what was necessary to assert the control and order he so desperately needed. It wasn't role-playing per se. Or maybe it was—just a kind that didn't force Nathan to read between any lines. He could respond to the situation exactly as he deemed appropriate. I wasn't even sure if we actually knew what we were doing other than the fact that it felt good and worked for us.

I stuck my chin out further. "Maybe."

His expression flared. "I'm giving you ten more seconds to strip, or I'm doing it for you."

It wasn't an empty promise. Rules were rules. And Dr. Hunt never broke them.

I let the seconds pass, biting my lip as they did. Three...two...one...

"Your choice," he growled.

I found myself whirled toward the bed, my T-shirt yanked up and over my hands, which were quickly bound behind my back with the same piece of clothing. With a broad hand at my back, Nathan shoved me to the mattress, tore off my leggings, then pulled my hips back so I was balanced on my chest, ass up for him to examine.

A finger traveled up my inner thigh, then back down the other. Over that exact spot he'd long identified as thrillingly sensitive. Then it moved up, tickling over the center of me.

I shivered, my head turned to the side against our duvet. Unable to see what he was doing, but feeling every delicious touch.

"You have a very beautiful pussy, Giovanna." His breath was warm between my thighs, his face obviously just an inch or so away.

"Oh?" My voice was muffled and shaky against the blanket.

"It's pink. Supple and open. Glistening a little from how wet you are." His lips drifted over one thigh, then the other. "I'm going to taste it."

I considered fighting. Considered continuing our little game from earlier.

But the icy brat was gone, melted in the golden warmth of that voice, speaking those plain words of worship and lust.

"Your inner thighs are shaking, Joni." That breath whispered over my clit. "May I?"

Was he for real?

I'd never stop myself asking.

"P-please," I whispered.

I felt Nathan's smile against my most sensitive flesh. And then I gasped as he went to work.

SOMETIME LATER—OKAY, at least a few hours, multiple orgasms, and a quick nap later—Nathan and I lay together in bed, my head buried in the divot between his pectoral muscles while he played one of those large, capable hands up and down my spine. Neither of us had spoken after reawaking. It was almost noon, and Nathan still hadn't gone to the gym or done any other part of his routine.

It was as if we both knew things were about to change again, and the last few months of peace and healing we'd found together in this apartment were coming to a close, so both of us wanted to bask in the stillness for as long as we could.

Tomorrow, of course, was my first audition in over a year. Maybe I'd get the part. Probably not. But even if I didn't, there would be another audition after that, then another, and another. Now that my medication was stabilized, Tom had also offered to bring me on at the bar five nights a week until one of these auditions *did* land, which meant there would be only a few nights a week where Nathan and I could truly sleep together like we had all summer.

Then there were the other changes coming. Marie returning to New York. Kate traveling more for her own job. Lea finally getting a job as a bookkeeper, which meant she needed more help with the kids. Frankie and Mattie both having babies who needed to be visited.

And then there was the biggest change of all: Isla. After his parents had finally signed over her guardianship to Nathan, he and I had been making bimonthly trips to Ferndale so Nathan could see her more often and gain her trust. Recently, he and Isla had decided together to transfer her to a similar school for autistic people about forty minutes north of New Rochelle, where he had just purchased a house on fifteen acres of land along with a stable including three horses—one for each of us.

Eventually, the goal was that Isla and potentially her educational assistant would live full-time at the house with us, but for now, she felt more comfortable in a residential school like the one she knew. But soon more of our time was going to be spent with her. We were creating a different kind of family than either of us had ever had. I was excited and nervous, yes. But mostly, I wanted both Nathan and Isla to trust that I would be there for both of them no matter what.

So yes, change was afoot, but in the golden light of the afternoon sun streaming through the window, peace still surrounded us. I concentrated on the present, just like my therapist had taught me. Focusing on the now. Observing when my mind wandered, as it still loved to do. But then gently bringing it back to where I wanted it to be, which was happily basking in the love of this man. This wonderful, unique, perfect-for-me man.

Nathan stirred under my cheek, then gently pushed my shoulder back, urging me to sit up and face him.

I did, not even bothering to keep a sheet pressed to my chest. He didn't like it when I hid any part away. Especially since I'd given him to green light to stare as much as he wanted.

His gaze flickered down appreciatively, in a way that told me round two of our Adventures in Bratty Discipline would be coming soon, but soon returned to mine. He had something to say.

"Your birthday is next week," he said as he traced a finger down my cheek and around my jaw.

I smiled. "You remembered."

"It's a date. I put it in my calendar."

"You still remembered to say something to me. That counts."

The dimple on his left cheek appeared along with an adorably bashful smile. "I'd like to help you celebrate. But I realized I don't know what kinds of things you like to do on your birthday."

These were the conversations I loved most. The frank, open questions about who I was and what I wanted. Nathan forced me to check in with myself more than I ever had, but he also made me feel loved through something as simple as basic communication.

I hoped we'd never stop exploring each other this way. I couldn't imagine running out of things to learn.

"Sing to me," I said.

Nathan's brow immediately furrowed. "You want me to sing to you?"

I giggled. He *did* have a terrible voice. Once, I introduced him to my favorite show tunes and talked him into doing karaoke with me at a bar. We sang "Let's Call the Whole Thing Off," at which point I discovered Nathan's first real flaw: he was absolutely tone-deaf.

It only made me want to sing more.

"Yes," I assured him. "Even with your terrible voice." I lay back on my pillow and sighed, imagining my perfect birthday. "When we were kids, our grandparents didn't usually have a lot of money for gifts. Not when there were six of us, right? So, Nonna would make every birthday a big deal in other ways. She'd host a big party with all the neighborhood and cousins. There would be a huge potluck at the house with all our favorite foods—ziti and cantaloupe and antipasti and everything else. And at the end, they'd light candles on her homemade cheesecake, and about fifty people would all sing 'Happy Birthday' to you at the top of their lungs." When I opened my eyes, I almost thought I'd see everyone there. "For me, that was always the best part. Being the center of all that love and attention."

"Should I ask your family to come?" Nathan wondered. "We could have a party here. The house isn't ready yet, but I think we have room for about twenty people in the living room."

I shook my head but stroked his cheek anyway. He was so kind. So much kinder than anyone knew.

"No, everyone has their own things going on. Lea's still in mourning, and Marie's going to have to dive right into work. I think Kate is in LA for another month or two, and Mattie and Frankie won't want to travel with the babies. It's better to keep it small this year. Just us."

Nathan was quiet for a long moment, considering. "All right. But next year, maybe we can have that party again."

"There will be other birthdays," I agreed. "You can have all of them if you want."

We both froze at the throwaway comment. Neither of us had said anything about marriage in the last few months. Not since Nathan had shouted about me being his wife one day to his mother or vaguely mentioned it on the way back from Atlantic City. It was as though both of us, by tacit admission, knew we needed more time to get to know each other before we took that step.

That was still true if I was being totally honest. While I wanted the wedding and the ring and all the things that went with it, just like I'd told Marie, I was also happy to wait. Despite how much we loved each other, there was still so much to learn. And we had all the time in the world.

"Do you promise?" Nathan asked as he lifted my hand to his mouth. He pressed a kiss to my knuckles that made my heart thump a little harder.

I smiled and said without a doubt, "All of them."

His dimple deepened, and his grin lit the room.

"I'll hold you to that," he said, then rolled on top of me so this time he could seal the promise with a kiss.

"It's a deal," I murmured as I opened to him completely. "And this one is one hundred percent real."

THE END

Thank you so much for reading!

There is a lot more of Joni and Nathan's story from his point of view! To read select chapters from Nathan's point of view and some extra scenes (for example, what did he do with his old roommate?), **go to www.nicolefrenchromance.com/bfothextras**

Marie is getting her own story too! Boss of the Year is coming, hopefully this winter, 2024. You can preorder her story, inspired by Sabrina, here: **www.nicolefrenchromance.com/bossoftheyear**

In the meantime, **you may be interested in the love stories already available for the other Zola siblings:**
The Other Man (Matthew and Nina's story)
First Comes Love (Francesca and Xavier's story)
Thief of my Heart (Lea and Michael's story)

Want more from this world of Northeast billionaires and the women who tame them? Consider these:
The Hate Vow (an enemies-to-lovers marriage of convenience)
Legally Yours (a billionaire-student workplace romance)

ACKNOWLEDGMENTS

I couldn't be more grateful for the people who helped me write this incredibly challenging book. There are many, but I'm especially grateful to the following wonderful humans:

To Patricia and Dawn, who read and reread too many early rewrites to count and give me feedback, however brutal. You are gems. I'm also grateful to Kymberly and Lacie, who read some of the early chapters as well.

More thanks to my support team: Danielle Leigh, my assistant with the every-cheery personality; Dani Sanchez and crew at Wildfire Marketing, who never fail to provide flexibility and counsel; Theresa Leigh, who provided excellent editing and delightful comments; and Marla Esposito, whose proofreading is utterly fantastic. You are all essential to this work.

Lastly, to my people. I couldn't have done this without the support and guidance of a few in particular: Lauren, Laura, Lisa, and my husband, Mr. French (and kiddos too). I love you all, Thank you for everything you do.

xo,

Nic

Printed in Great Britain
by Amazon

44183640R00330